The Crosskiller

The Crosskiller

Marcel Montecino

ARBOR HOUSE | **William Morrow**

New York

Library of Congress Cataloging in Publication Data

Montecino, Marcel.
   The crosskiller.

   I. Title.
PS3563.0539C7   1988   813′.54   87-29004
ISBN 0-87795-908-0

Manufactured in the United States of America
Published in Canada by Fitzhenry & Whiteside, Ltd.
10 9 8 7 6 5 4 3 2

This book is a work of fiction. Any resemblance to actual people, events, and organizations is purely coincidental. Although there is, of course, a real Los Angeles Police Department, no character in this book is intended to portray, in whole or in part, any member of that organization.

For T. K.

Special thanks to David Groves, Helen Heller, Allan Mayer, Peter Livingston, and Ann Harris

The Crosskiller

FRIDAY
August 3

$3{:}57$ *AM* "Closing in on the four o'clock hour," said the soft, almost sensual female voice, "is Janna Holmes with All Night Reality Radio. Coming to you with fifty thousand watts of power from Tijuana, Mexico. Broadcasting to the southwestern United States all the news the United States won't let us broadcast. My guest tonight is retired army general Allan X. Wattley, a decorated hero in three wars, a former commander of Green Beret Special Forces in Vietnam, and now the founder and guiding light of Americans in Action. Before we start talking about Americans in Action, General, I wanted to ask you—were things this bad when you were in Vietnam? Is that one of the reasons why we lost that dirty little war so disgracefully?"

The answer came back in the flat nasal tones of west Texas.

"Ha! Disgrace is the perfect word for it, Janna. And, yes, that *is* the reason we lost that war. Why we got our tails beat and got sent home crying. Because this country has lost—"

"Don't forget, General Wattley, that we're broadcasting from across the border. By this country you mean the United States."

"Right, Janna. The United States has lost its Christian resolve. It's lost its will to fight, its hunger to succeed, its appetite for victory."

"And on what do you blame that, General?"

"The mongrelization, Negrification, and Judification of our Aryan Christian culture. Nothing else."

"Do you harbor much hope of our country turning around, General Wattley?"

"Only if we take some drastic steps. Some very drastic steps."

The young man stood alone in the deserted night street, looking up at the blocklike two-story building. His breath came in steady gulps and his face was blank as he traced his eyes slowly over the gray granite surfaces. From the tall, formal entrance, to the upper floor with its row of small institutional windows, to the huge floodlit menorah on the rooftop, and then back again to the door.

A car turned off a side street on to La Cienega Boulevard. Its headlights momentarily panned over him. He spat on the sidewalk, crossed the street in the car's wake, and then turned to watch the building again.

He wasn't tall, but under his sweat-soaked T-shirt his chest and shoulders were wide and well developed, and he looked bigger than he was. His muscled legs jutted white and hairy from his cut-off jeans.

He looked up at the building for several more minutes, until another car passed. Then he retied the kerchief he used as a sweat band and began jogging easily down the boulevard. He ran on for several blocks, turned east on Pico, then crossed the empty late night–early morning street. His deep breathing and the steady slap of his running shoes were the only sounds disturbing the hot silence.

In the yard of Fischer's Foreign Car Service, the Doberman heard those sounds, as she did every night, when the man was still a block away. Noiselessly she rose from her pallet behind the gutted Mercedes sedan and took up a nervous, pacing position at the east corner of the chain-link fence. As the man came abreast of her, she slipped into step with him, her head down, her reptilian eyes locked on his hands.

Halfway down the length of the fence the man reached into the ink-stained carpenter's apron tied around his waist and came up with a tightly rolled newspaper. At the sight of the paper the bitch started to growl. A deep menacing rumble full of hatred and malice.

The man smiled.

And then, without breaking stride, swung the newspaper in a quick back-hand arc flat against the fence. The bitch was there to meet it. Lunging and snarling, she tore at the chain-link, trying to get at the paper, at the man.

He slapped the paper against the fence all the way to the end of the block, driving the dog into a frenzy. At the corner he stopped and, laughing down at the snarling, leaping animal, pushed the paper through the fence. The Doberman tore the paper from the man's grasp and shook it furiously from side to side. With vicious wrenches of her head she proceeded to rip it apart.

The man watched the dog with silent laughter. Then he stepped closer and kicked the fence.

"You black bastard."

The bitch instantly turned from the paper and threw herself at the fence, biting and tearing at the air inches from the man's throat. He laughed aloud. This was a nightly charade he and the dog were playing out, and he enjoyed it very much. The sight of such pure, unbridled hatred—the knowledge that the dog would surely kill him if she could reach him—filled the man with sensual excitement and gave him a peculiar sense of well-being and belonging.

"You black bastard."

"In the sixties you had your left-wing revolutionaries; the seventies were just a winding-down period from the sixties. Now we're at the end of the eighties and you can almost *feel* the pressure building up again. I'm telling you, Janna, the next decade is going to see a helluva lot of change."

"For the worse?"

"Maybe. Maybe. If we continue on like we are. But if *I* have anything to do about it—if me and my Americans in Action have our way, the twenty-first century will belong to the Aryan Christian, as it rightly should, as it was always meant to. As all history has belonged to the white Christian since the birth of our Savior."

"General, do you consider yourself—as you've been labeled—a reactionary?"

"Well, I'll tell you, Janna, that term—*reactionary*—always puzzles me. By definition a reactionary is someone who *reacts,* but against *what?* If a reactionary is someone who reacts against the nonwhite pollution of our American racial heritage, then, yes, I am a reactionary. If a reactionary is someone who *reacts* against this country being bled dry by the Jewish-manipulated Wall Street stock market—someone who *reacts* against seeing this country relinquishing to the slant-eyed, godless Japanese its crown as the industrial giant of the world—then, yes, Janna, I am a reactionary. And damn proud of it."

He left the dog clawing at the wire and concrete and jogged seventeen blocks east, then six blocks south. To a '76 Ford Econoline van parked on a palm tree–lined street of neat front lawns and small Southern California bungalows.

He leaned against the van and took deep breaths for several minutes until he could feel his heart slowing to its normal pace. Then he unlocked the cargo door and slipped it back. The floor of the van was stacked with rolled newspapers; they reached halfway to the roof. Leaning across to the dashboard he turned on the interior lights, then wiped his face with a towel slung across the seat back. Under the driver's seat was a thermos. The man poured a cup of steaming black coffee. Then he slipped behind the wheel, switched off the lights, and sat watching the street. When there was only a swallow of coffee left he felt around under the seat where the thermos had been and came up with a small brown pharmaceutical bottle. There were only two capsules left. He swallowed one and chased it with the rest of the coffee.

He slumped back in the bucket seat and stretched out his legs, watching a cat chase a shadow under a porch. A few blocks away a helicopter hovered over a backyard and circled a spotlight. The man closed his eyes and seemed to sleep.

After ten minutes his eyes opened. He smiled to himself. With a short, decisive grunt he started the van's engine, turned on the parking lights and the interior lights, and then the radio.

"General," said the soft female voice, "tell us what Americans in Action is. We all know what the leftist media and the fellow-traveler bureaucrats call it: a paramilitary armed force, a private army, right-wing revolutionaries. All of those pinko buzz words. *You* tell us what Americans in Actions is."

"Janna, Americans in Action is an organization of loyal, patriotic Americans who are sickened by the direction this country is headed in. To hell in a handbasket my wife calls it. And Americans in Action are not afraid to use any means necessary to return this nation to its God-given place at the head of all nations."

"By 'any means' do you mean armed revolt, General?"

"We like to call it armed *defense,* Janna."

The man filled the apron around his waist with newspapers, cradled several under his arm, then climbed down from the van. He left the lights on, the motor running, and the cargo door open, then trotted down the street, throwing papers at almost every house. At the end of the block he crossed the street and did the same thing on the other side until he was back at the van.

"And who do you accept into Americans in Action?"

"It might sound corny and old-fashioned, Janna, but we take in anybody who's a true blue, red-blooded, white Christian American. Anyone who's not afraid to call a spade a spade. And a Jew a Jew."

The man drove up to the next block and parked. He gathered up another armful of newspapers and repeated the process, on and on into the night.

"Yes, Janna, we have training facilities in Texas, South Carolina, and Idaho."

"And what do you teach at those facilities, General?"

"We have instruction in hand-to-hand combat, automatic weaponry, urban guerrilla warfare, postnuclear survival tactics, karate, judo, and the teachings of Jesus Christ."

Occasionally a paper would smack loudly against a porch or door, and a dog would bark furiously for a few seconds. But otherwise the only sounds were the steady working of the jogger's lungs and running shoes. And whenever he got back to the van, the radio.

"—and I just want to say to everybody out there who can hear me. Not only does Janna *sound* sweet, and say the sweetest things, but, folks, she *looks* sweet, too."

"Thank you, General Wattley. By the way, General, what does the *X* stand for?"

"Why, Janna, *X* marks the spot. Ha, ha, ha!"

* * *

An hour and a half later the sky beyond the eastern mountains was a pale smoggy gray when the man parked the van in an alley behind Pico Boulevard. The street here was lined with small offices, print shops, bakeries, and an occasional kosher butcher. Now the only light on the street glowed from behind a dirty display window. A small sticker in one corner offered to HAVE THE TIMES DELIVERED TO YOUR DOOR. From the other side of the blackened glass Michael Jackson's feathery voice drifted airily upward. The man wiped his newsprint-stained hands across the front of his T-shirt and went in.

The room was long and narrow, with cracked linoleum flooring and smudged stucco walls. Along one wall were low stacks of newspapers, bundled and tied with wire. Two naked 150-watt bulbs hung from the ceiling and bathed the room in harsh light and deep shadows. The place smelled of ink, smoke, and sweat.

"Well, well. Massa Walker."

An enormously fat black man sat behind a scarred desk under one of the hanging light bulbs, reading a morning newspaper. When he spoke, it was from behind clenched teeth that held a stubby cigar in a short, stained holder.

"Hey, chicos. It's the Great White Hope."

A pair of Mexican teenagers sat on a bench at the back of the room, eating doughnuts. Between them on the bench was a large cassette player. One of the kids leafed through a *Penthouse* magazine. They both laughed at what the fat man said and glowered sullenly at Walker.

"C'mon in, dude. Take a load off. You finished throwing your route? Sit it down here and have a cuppa coffee. Or don't you drink coffee with us spicks and spades?"

One of the Mexican kids snickered around a mouthful of jelly doughnut. The other was back into the *Penthouse.* Walker poured a cup from the glass pot on the hot plate and sat down on a metal folding chair across from the fat man.

"You told Fazio? That I wanted to see him?"

"Yeah, dude. I told Fazio. He'll be back soon. Don't bust a gut."

On the wall behind the fat man were taped dozens of nudes. They stretched from floor to ceiling. Impossibly full-breasted blondes; big-eyed Latinas with already thickening waists; slight pubescent redheads dappled with freckles and draped across phallic Harley-Davidsons. Some of the girls from the glossier magazines stood coyly in showers and on balconies, pensively touching themselves. Others, obviously ripped from hard-core publications, lay back on wrinkled bedsheets, their legs spread-eagled, their tongues lolling from the lips in a masquerade of passion. Walker let his eyes linger over the women until they came to rest, as they always did, on the dark-nippled black girl. Her picture was one of the biggest, shiny and professional and prominently displayed. A Playmate of the Month. Her hair was cut in a very short Afro—the photograph was several years old—that was both soft and severe. The skin of her buttocks, partially turned to the viewer, was taut and gleaming. Her heavy breasts hung down ponderously and her aureoles were as big as tea saucers and as dark as chocolate. The nipples in the center were surprisingly small and dimpled.

"Hey, Walker, you like that, huh?" The fat man was watching him over the top of his newspaper. Walker quickly averted his eyes.

"You paddy motherfuckers are all alike. You can't stand niggers but you is *fascinated* with black pussy. That ol' soul snatch. Well, why don'cha go get yo'self some, dude. It ain't like there ain't none around. Just drive down Sunset any fucking night of the week. Any fucking *day,* for chrissake."

Walker took a sip of coffee, moved it around his mouth, then spit it out on a part of the floor where the linoleum was torn and the concrete showed through. The fat man took his cigar from his rubbery lips, then folded the newspaper and laid it before him on the desk.

"You know, Walker, you one strange motherfucker." He paused, then said, "You come in here every fucking night. Don't say boo-diddly-shit to any of us. Not one motherfucking word to a one of us. You pick up your papers. You run around all night like you was in a fucking marathon or something. And then you come back here saying, 'When's Fazio coming back? When's the other white man coming back?' "

The Mexican kids were suddenly very quiet. They watched Walker.

"That's what you mean, ain't it? When's the other *white* man coming back? You just ain't got nothing to say to us, ain't that right, Massa Walker?"

Walker said nothing.

The fat man rose from his chair behind the desk. His stomach swung before him like an honor guard.

"Yeah, that's *mother*fucking right, dude. You fucking hate us, don't you, motherfucker?"

The fat man came closer. He loomed over Walker.

"You know you're the only white man throwing paper from West L.A. to West Covina. The only one. Why do you do it?"

Walker picked his nose. He examined his find.

"It keeps me in shape, Henry," he said with a false smile.

The fat man threw up his hands in disgust and turned to walk away, mimicking Walker. "It keeps me in shape. It keeps me in shape."

Walker's smile disappeared. "Fuck you, Henry."

The fat man stopped and turned around. The room was very still. One of the Mexican kids turned off the cassette.

"Don't mess with me, boy," Henry said softly.

A truck pulled up in the alley outside. Its headlights glared through the dusty window. Walker and Henry stared at each other. Then Walker got up deliberately and walked slowly to the door.

"Lookahere, chicos. Walker running to see his white buddy. His connection."

One of the kids laughed nervously and then stopped short.

Walker went through the door without looking back.

Outside it was dawn. Fazio climbed down from the truck's cab. He was a skinny boy with stringy, shoulder-length brown hair and a face aflame with acne.

"Hey, Sonny," Fazio said.

"Someday I'm gonna kill that black son-of-a-bitch."

"Who?"

Walker nodded back over his shoulder.

"Henry?" Fazio asked. "Henry's all right, man."

"Someday I'm gonna kill him."

"Hey, Sonny. Forget it." Fazio pulled a joint from his shirt pocket. He licked it and lit it.

"You wanted to see me, Sonny? That's why I came back. I came all the way from the printing plant." He offered Walker the burning joint. Walker shook it off.

"I need some more ups. You got any beauties?"

"Well," Fazio said, stretching the word out into several syllables. "I don't have any beauties. But I got these." He dug a squarish bottle from the pocket of his dirty jeans.

"What are they?"

"Dexamyl spansules. Made right here in the old U.S. of A. Good stuff. Clean. Keep you going just like blacks but you don't get as nervous."

"I like beauties better."

"Yeah, but I don't have beauties. And these are cheaper."

"How much?"

"A dollar and a half a copy."

"Jesus."

"Hey." Fazio grinned. "Inflation."

"Okay. How many in there?"

"Fifty."

"Give them to me. I'll pay you next week."

"Hey, Sonny. I can't run a—"

"Give me the fucking pills," Walker said sharply. "I'll pay you the first of the week."

"Okay, Sonny. Okay. Take it easy. I ain't Henry. Here. Take 'em."

Walker got into his van and fired up the motor. Fazio came around to the driver's side.

"Sonny, tell me. How many of them things you taking?"

Walker smiled. "A day?"

"A day."

"Six. Six beauties. Probably more of these."

"A day?"

"A day."

"Jesus, Sonny. You're a good customer, but you got to slow down. You're gonna kill yourself. Your fucking heart's gonna explode."

"What a rush," Walker said, still smiling as he backed the van out of the alley and slipped into the street.

6:05 *AM* Several miles away in the Crenshaw District, Esther Phibbs parked her station wagon in the narrow driveway of her duplex apartment. She killed the motor, snapped off the headlights, and got out. She walked to the rear of the wagon, past the lettering on the door panel that read ESTHER'S CUSTODIAL SERVICE, and lifted out two bags of groceries. Balancing the bags on a fender, she locked the car all around.

The street was gray and empty. And though the sun wasn't even above the rooftops yet, the day was already hot and Esther knew it would be a scorcher.

After closing the front door of the peeling brown building, she paused for a moment at the foot of the stairs and listened for sounds from above. All she heard was the ticking of the clock over the fireplace, so she padded softly down the long hall to the kitchen in the rear of the house. She placed the bags on the table, then filled a kettle with water and turned on the fire under it. After putting the groceries away, she spooned instant coffee into a chipped cup, lit a cigarette, and sat down heavily with a sigh.

She was a tall, tired woman in her mid-thirties, and the worn jeans and frayed plaid shirt seemed only to accentuate her thinness, her weariness. She had long, slender arms and hands, and even her bare feet propped up on a chair seemed elongated and delicate. Her skin was the color of highly polished walnut—a color white people consider dark and black people think light.

"Esther, honey?"

Esther started. "Mama, you scared me. I must've dozed off."

"The water's boiling." The kettle was whistling.

"I'll get it." She started to rise.

"No, honey. I'll fix it. Rest yourself."

The other woman was older and very black. Her eyes were puffy from sleep and she wore a net over her hair. Her blue terry-cloth robe was clean and paper thin. She poured the water in the cup, stirred it, and set it down on the table by Esther's hand. Then she got a cup for herself.

"Why don't you let me fix you a real pot, Es?"

"No, Mama. This is fine. I don't even want this." She stubbed out the cigarette. "If you want, I can drive you home now, before it gets too hot."

"I guess I can wait till you take Little Bobby to school."

"It's gonna be a scorcher."

"I guess I can wait."

Esther rubbed her eyes and the bridge of her nose with her fingertips. The older woman watched her.

"You look real tired, honey."

"I am, Mama."

They both sipped their coffee in silence, and then the older woman said, "You going to see Bobby today?"

"This afternoon."

"You can get some sleep after that?"

"A couple of hours, Mama."

Esther got up. She threw the rest of the coffee into the sink and washed out the cup. She turned around and leaned back against the kitchen cabinets and smiled. "He's coming home Tuesday, Mama."

"I know, honey. Ain't that good news." The older woman smiled, but her eyes were grim.

"Mama, it's gonna be all right this time. I know it."

"I hope so, honey."

"Oh, it is, Mama. It is." Esther sat down and took the old woman's hands in hers. "He means it this time. I know it. I talked to him. He said that if he can quit it in there, he can quit it anywhere. He said there's more dope down in that damn jailhouse than he ever saw out there in the free world. And he said it don't bother him. People can be shooting that stuff right there in the cell with him and it don't even bother him."

"And you believe him?"

"Yes, Mama, I do. Don't you?"

The old woman's gaze was cold and steady.

"Don't you want to, Mama?"

The older woman sighed.

"Of course, I want to, Esther." She paused a moment. "But that boy's broken my heart too many times. He's my only son. He's my flesh and blood, but there's been too many years of lying and stealing. Too many times I've trusted that boy, taken him in, pleaded with him to straighten out, and then he goes and steals from me—steals from his mother. Just to get money so's he can buy some more of that *shit.*" She spat out the last word.

They sat in silence, avoiding each other's eyes.

"That boy put his father in an early grave, grieving over him."

"Mama," Esther said.

"I don't know how it happened. He was such a good boy. All his life he was such a good boy. Not an ounce of trouble from him. When he was a baby, you know. Best baby I ever seen. Didn't cry much. No temper to speak of, hardly. Good little boy, too. Cub Scout. Did you know that?"

Esther shook her head.

"Well, he was. Good, *good* boy. We wanted him to go to college, but he wanted to go to work. Help us out, he said. We said, 'Don't help us out. Go to college,' we said. 'That's what we scrimped and saved for.' But, no, he wanted to go to work. Said he wanted to help out at home, Charles being sick and all. So he went to work at that damn hospital."

The old woman sipped her coffee and pulled her bathrobe tighter around her.

"Esther, I swear, we didn't know a thing. Not a blessed thing, till the police came to our door. For three years—almost four—he'd been stealing that stuff from the hospital, and we never suspicioned a thing."

Esther lit another Salem Light. Outside the kitchen window the world was bright with the new day.

"He promised he was gonna straighten up that time, too. And then he married you. I knew you were a good girl. A little older than Bobby, settled, serious. I thought maybe you could change him. But he still messed around with that stuff. And the day that child upstairs was born, he got down on his knees—*down on his knees, girl*—and swore on that little baby's head that he was gonna quit. And then two weeks later he was in jail for robbing that liquor store. The police told me he was so loaded he couldn't drive away. That's how they caught him. He couldn't figure how to back the car up."

Esther went around the table and held Mama Phibbs in her arms. The old lady was crying.

"Mama, you can't give up on him. We're all he's got."

She wiped away a tear that was tracing down Mama Phibbs's cheek.

"Bobby's my husband, Mama, and I love him. He's the father of my child, and he's your son—your only son—and you love him too. We can't give up on him."

The old lady looked at Esther for a long time.

"You can't give up on yourself either, Esther. Or that little boy upstairs. You owe something to him, too."

"What do you mean, Mama?"

"I mean just what I say." Her face hardened. "Bobby might be my only son. But Little Bobby's my *grand*son. Like you say, my *onliest* grandson. And you're just like the daughter I never had. I won't see you throw your life away—or that little boy's chances—because Bobby can't be a man. I won't see him pull you down with him."

"Mama, he swore to me he was gonna change this time."

The old lady straightened her back. Her eyes burned into Esther's. "And what if he don't?"

Esther took a long time answering. She sat down and took another deep drag on her cigarette, then put it out half smoked. She touched the ashtray gently with her long fingers, as if she were trying to determine its makeup just by its texture. Then she raised her eyes to meet the old lady's.

"This is the last time."

"You got too much going for you, Esther. You work too hard every night, cleaning other people's toilets. And that boy upstairs gifted like the teachers say. He's got a chance to be something. To be some*body*. You can't—"

"This is the last time, Mama."

Esther stood up. She suddenly realized how tired she was.

"This is the last time."

"That boy drove his father to an early grave." The old lady's eyes were seeing something somewhere else. Someplace other than the kitchen.

Esther turned and walked out of the kitchen and into the hallway. As she was climbing the stairs Mama Phibbs called up after her.

"He promised that time too. At his father's funeral."

It was hot in the front bedroom, and the little boy had kicked off the sheets. Esther promised herself once again to get a small airconditioner for this room. She had one in her bedroom because it was the only way she could sleep through the long L.A. summer; but she felt guilty.

She watched him sleep—a private pleasure she treasured. Then she sat on the edge of the bed and kissed his forehead. His eyelids fluttered for a moment, and then he was wide awake. It always amazed her.

"Hey, Mama." He sat up and scratched his armpit. "Who's taking me to school? You or Grandma?"

"I am. I have to stay up and visit your father."

"Good."

"Good what?"

"Huh?" he said, his eyes wide, and she fell in love with her son for the millionth time.

"Good I'm driving you to school? Or good I'm going to visit your father?"

The little boy slid out of the bed and raced out of the room. A moment later, from the hall bathroom, came the sound of an adolescent male urinating in a toilet bowl. Then the boy's raised voice, "Miss Abrams wants—"

"Don't you be talking to your mother until you finish your business." She got up and started to make the bed. "In fact, close the door. You getting too big to—"

He was back in the bedroom, pulling on his pants over his jockey shorts.

"Hey, boy, you got to take a shower."

"I took one last night."

"Well, take another one. It'll wake you up."

"I'm already awake."

Esther laughed. "Ain't *that* the truth." She folded a corner of a bedsheet and tucked it tightly under the mattress. "Go on, boy. Soap and water never hurt no one."

"Okay." He dashed toward the door.

"Little Bobby."

He stopped short. "Yes, ma'am?"

"What does Miss Abrams want?"

"Oh, yeah." His face brightened. "Mama, there's gonna be a field trip. To Catalina. Overnight."

She turned to face him.

"Next month, Mama," he continued excitedly. "Only for the specially advanced class. Mama, we're gonna ride a *boat* over there and—"

Esther had crossed her arms. "Who all's going with you kids?"

"Uh, Miss Abrams and Miss Gutierrez—"

"Uh huh."

"—and Miss Coleman and Miss Silva. Mama, there's gonna be buffaloes and seals and—and—"

"And how much is this trip gonna cost me?"

The boy's smile drooped. "Fifty dollars. But Miss Abrams wants to talk to you about maybe the school paying for me going."

Esther felt her face flush with shame and not a little anger.

"Well, you can tell Miss Abrams that I guess we can pay our own way on some dinky-ass overnight boat ride."

At first the boy didn't understand, and then he yelped with joy.

"I can go, Mama? I can go?"

"Well, 'course, you can. Can't have the whole class go and leave you behind, can we?"

"It's an island—"

"Well, I know *that.*"

"—and there's a town over there, and a National Park—"

"I said yes, didn't I? You don't have to do any more convincing. Now go take your shower or you'll be late for school and they won't let you go anywhere."

The boy ran out of the room and then Esther heard the shower. She finished making the bed and slumped down wearily on the edge of the mattress. She looked around for her cigarettes but they were downstairs.

"Mama."

Little Bobby was standing in the doorway, one foot on top of the other, a quizzical expression on his face.

"What's the matter, baby? I thought you were in the shower."

"Mama," he began, "Darnell and Lloyd and *everybody* at the playground said the only people they know of that go to special classes are kids with something wrong with them."

She was silent.

"So?" she said finally.

Now he was silent.

"Are you blind?"

"No, ma'am."

"Are you deaf?"

"No, ma'am."

"Are you crippled?"

"No, ma'am."

"Then there ain't nothing wrong with you 'cept you're smart as a whip. 'Cept where Darnell and Lloyd and *everybody* is concerned. Now go take your shower. You wasting water."

"Yes, ma'am," he said brightly and was gone.

Esther chuckled softly to herself and shook her head. She patted her shirt, searching for her cigarettes, then remembered again she had left them downstairs. She sighed deeply, then swung her long legs up onto the bed and stretched out. She was instantly asleep.

7:05 AM Walker stepped out of the shower and checked the time. Almost two hours before he had to be at work at his day job. He lay down wet on the single bed and put a towel over his eyes. The amphetamines were coursing through his body, drying his throat and jolting his heart. He felt wonderful.

The apartment was small—one room really—and L-shaped. One end was a tiny kitchen: two-burner stove, ancient refrigerator, stained sink. Set up in the other end was a complete weight-lifting outfit. Barbells and dumbbells, bench and uprights. Clothes and shoes were strewn about the room, and there were yellowing stacks of newspapers everywhere.

Walker got up, still dripping, and went over to the weights. Taking up two fifty-pound dumbbells he started doing curls in front of the mirrored closet door. Inhaling and exhaling sharply, like a steam engine, he watched with fascination as the muscles in his arms and shoulders began to gorge with blood and swell, moving like liquid under his tattooed skin.

He was heavily tattooed: a panther and a skull on his left arm, a cross and a daggered heart on his right, matching birds in flight on his breast and back. And he loved to watch himself working out, the muscles and tendons gliding under the pictures.

After twenty repetitions on each arm he dropped the weights heavily to the floor. It was a garage apartment and there was no one beneath him to disturb. He leaned against a dresser and waited for the light-headedness caused by the exertion and the pills to pass. He raised his eyes again to the mirror and watched himself for a moment, then he began to masturbate. After several minutes he was still only half erect. The amphetamines, he knew. Watching his reflection through slitted eyes, he continued to work at himself. He shivered. Then he closed his eyes completely—thinking, letting his mind fly. Very shortly his penis began to rise. Soon it was hard and red. Walker's legs twitched. A low moan—more like a hum—started deep in his throat.

He was thinking of the girl with the black nipples.

He was thinking of slicing them off.

9:43 AM The dented gray Lincoln glided past again.

"It's going down," Gold said.

"I don't think so," said Honeywell.

"No, it's going down. I can feel it."

The Lincoln sped up and turned the corner.

"That's the third time around. It's a Pasadena," Honeywell said. His black face glistened with a thin sheen of perspiration. The car windows were rolled up and the heat inside was deadening.

"I can always tell about these things. It's gonna go down. I can feel it," Gold said.

"You can *feel* it. What are you—a Jewish voodoo man?"

"So don't listen," Gold said, with a heavy Yiddish inflection. "Watch already."

They were backed into the parking lot of a 7-Eleven across Santa Monica Boulevard from the West Hollywood branch of the Golden State Bank and Trust. Their car was a red Trans-Am, confiscated two weeks before from a Venezuelan coke dealer who had jumped bail and was probably back in Caracas by now. It looked like anything but a police car.

The radio sputtered, and a voice crackled. "They just turned back onto Santa Monica, Lieutenant."

"It's gonna go down," Gold repeated. Honeywell smiled but his eyes were cold and riveted to the street. Across Santa Monica, in the bank's parking lot, a small crowd had gathered to wait for the doors to open.

Honeywell was tall and thin, in his late thirties. He wore a brilliant blue running suit with red piping.

Gold, in the passenger's seat, was older and thicker. He had on a brightly flowered Hawaiian shirt, sneakers, and faded jeans. He wore a golf cap pulled low over his eyes.

The Lincoln passed again. Honeywell and Gold kept perfectly still, trying to will themselves invisible. When the car had gone Gold said, "You know these brothers?"

"I know the little one. Weathers. They call him Dog. I busted him once for taking off a Safeway. He did three years behind that one. The big one's name's Jojo. He's a pussy. I don't even know why he's on this one. But you got to watch Dog. The Dog can kill you."

"They all can kill you."

"Ain't it the truth." Honeywell smiled again. And then: "But I don't know the driver."

"I got the driver," Gold said.

Honeywell looked at him.

"He's the snitch," Gold said.

"He must owe you a lot, to give up the Dog."

"So we have to make it look good."

Just then a heavy-booted gay couple walked by, laughing, their arms around each other's waists. Gold and Honeywell watched them go past. Then the people in the bank's parking lot were crowding in the opened doors.

"It won't be long now," Gold said.

A moment later the gray Lincoln glided to a stop in a no-parking zone a half block from the bank.

"They're stopping, Lieutenant," the voice on the radio said.

"I can see that, Mancuso," Gold said into his handset. Honeywell chuckled nervously.

A tall black man in a black leather coat stepped out of the Lincoln into the murky midmorning sunlight. He was followed by a smaller man in a brown suede jacket and peaked cap.

"It's ninety-five degrees," Honeywell said. "I wonder what the fuck they got under those coats."

The two men stopped at the bank's front door. The smaller man leaned against the building and lit a cigarette, watching the street almost idly from behind mirrored sunglasses. The other man stood very close and was talking to him quickly and excitedly. His right arm gestured furiously as he spoke.

"Looks like your man Jojo got shit down his neck," Gold said.

"Yeah, Jojo's pleading his case. Looks like he's had a change of heart. He doesn't want to move up in the world."

Dog took a last drag from his cigarette and flicked it into the street. Jojo stepped even closer and put his hand on Dog's arm. He was speaking directly into his ear.

"He don't belong here," Honeywell said. "He's a pussy. He should be pushing Sherms behind Compton High. If he pulls out a gun he's liable to blow his dick off. The Dog's the one you have to watch. The Dog can—"

"—kill you," Gold finished with a smile.

Honeywell looked over at him. "Just watch your hymie ass, Jack. That's all."

"I tell you what, Honey. I'll watch my hymie ass. You watch your black ass. And we'll both watch theirs."

Dog said something low and hard to Jojo, and Jojo let go of his arm and almost seemed to hang his head. Then they went into the bank.

"Mancuso," Gold said into the mike, "you and Spicer take out the driver. Don't shoot him—he's ours. Christiansen and Flores, you get behind the retaining wall. But don't show yourself. We take them coming out. Understand?"

"We got it, Lieutenant," another voice said.

"Michaels. You and your partner pull in front and block the driveway. Okay?"

"Okay, Lieutenant."

"All right. Everybody ready?"

The radio was silent. Honeywell reached behind to the back seat and came back with an automatic shotgun.

"Let's go!" Gold said into the handset, already kicking his door open.

Halfway across Santa Monica, almost as if on cue, Gold pulled out his .38 Police Special and Honeywell jacked a shell into the shotgun's chamber. The traffic swerved and jerked around them, blue-haired matrons and bearded construction workers, their mouths gaping and their eyes jolted awake. Prime-time television come to life out here in the midmorning sun. Michaels's car slammed to a stop in the driveway.

"Fucking cowboy!" Gold hissed.

They flattened themselves on either side of the bank's front entrance. The exterior's rough finish dug into their backs. Gold's pulse pounded in his temples. His breath was short and his mouth desert dry. And he knew it wasn't just the quick run across the street.

They waited.

A little boy in the bed of a passing pickup truck waved at them. A woman in a green Seville pulled up to the curb, saw them, and drove away fast.

Honeywell edged his face around to the glass door and looked in.

"I don't see them, Jack."

Gold grunted.

"You wanna go in?"

"No. They'll be coming out," Gold said. "Take it easy."

Honeywell leaned back against the bank's wall and wiped the sweat off his brow with the back of his hand. A sixtyish man in green track shorts leading a dachshund on a leash jogged slowly by. He smiled at them.

"Jesus Christ!" Honeywell said.

This time Gold peered with one eye through the door.

"They're coming out the side."

Honeywell pointed the shotgun to the ground, flat against his leg, and walked casually over to a Pinto station wagon in the first parking space. He made as if to unlock the door, then brought the shotgun up over the Pinto's roof and took a firing stance. Dog and Jojo were halfway across the lot when they noticed Michaels's unmarked car blocking the driveway. They froze. Their eyes darted down the block to the Lincoln, but there was no one at the wheel. Jojo started backing up. Dog's hand went slowly to his coat pocket.

"Okay, motherfuckers!" Honeywell screamed. "Get your hands up away from your sides!"

Jojo kept backing up. Dog seemed to become smaller, his body crouching without any visible effort. His hand was in his pocket now. His eyes were shooting from Honeywell to the unmarked car to the Lincoln and back to Honeywell.

"Give it up, or we'll kill you right here!" Honeywell shouted.

Jojo finally backed against the bank and his hands slowly went in the air. A middle-aged woman in a Chanel jacket came out the bank's side door. She was writing in a checkbook and didn't look up as she strode purposefully toward her Mercedes sedan.

"Watch out, lady!" Honeywell shouted, but Dog already had his arm locked around her neck and the muzzle of his .45 automatic pressed against her temple. She was taller than the Dog, but he wrenched her backward until her legs went out from under her and his hold on her was the only thing that kept her from falling.

"I'll blow her motherfucking brains out!" Dog screamed. The woman's shoes had come off and her stockinged feet were scrambling to get a purchase of the parking lot's concrete.

"I'll blow her motherfucking brains all over the ground!"

Gold slammed through the bank's front door and ran the length of the building shouting, "Nobody goes out this door! There's a robbery in progress! Everybody get on the floor!"

There was a general murmur of surprise and people standing in line to do their morning checking looked at Gold with open curiosity. It was obvious only one teller knew the bank had been robbed.

"Get on the floor!" Gold yelled and pushed a young Asian girl down. He held his gold badge high in his outstretched left hand and turned it so everyone could see.

"I'm the police! Everybody on the goddamn floor! *Now!*"

The crowd realized with a rush what was happening and everyone scurried to flatten themselves on the polished tile. Gold opened the side door slowly.

The woman was kneeling. Dog was crouched behind her, his body close against hers. His hand was twisted in her hair now, and the automatic was still against the woman's head. Jojo was backed against the wall with his arms raised. Gold was so close he could hear him shaking.

"Now we going to this bitch's car!" Dog was shouting.

"Dog, it's no good," Honeywell said. "It's not gonna work."

"*Listen-to-me-motherfucker!* We going to this bitch's ride. Now you get that motherfucking police car out of the driveway and you get it out now."

For a brief moment no one moved, no one spoke. The traffic on Santa Monica buzzed by.

"*I'm gonna kill her!*"

"Okay! Okay!" Honeywell said. "We're moving it!" He gave a sign to Mancuso, who slipped low behind the wheel and carefully backed the unmarked car out of the driveway. Dog yanked the woman to her feet by her hair, taking care to stay close and behind her. The woman was whimpering. Gold braced himself against the doorway and took aim.

"Now we getting in this bitch's ride and driving out of here!"

"We can't let you do that, Dog," Honeywell shouted back. "You know we can't let you do that."

"You fucking *better* let me do that, nigger, or I swear I'll kill this bitch! I'll blow her motherfucking head off! I'll blow her motherfucking head clean *off!* Now you stay the fuck away from us!"

Dog started to inch the woman across the parking lot. Without taking his eyes from Honeywell, he nodded to Jojo.

"Let's go, man."

Gold heard a soft sound from Jojo, only a few feet away, and realized the man was crying.

"C'mon, Jojo," Dog said again.

"Please, Dog," Jojo suddenly sobbed. "Oh, please."

"Let's *go,* Jo," Dog snarled.

"Oh, Jesus," Jojo said, and a dark stain spread out over his crotch. "Oh, please, please, please."

"Get over here, you chickenshit motherfucker, or I'll kill you my own self," Dog said, and took the automatic from the woman's head and pointed it at Jojo. Then he saw Gold in the doorway, saw that Gold had a gun, saw that the gun's muzzle was aimed directly at him. He had decided to shoot Gold when Gold fired. Jojo by the wall screamed and fell to his knees. A tremendous roar came from under his leather coat and Jojo screamed again. Dog was stumbling and blood was pouring out of his side. He started to raise his gun again and Gold shot him twice in quick succession. Dog pitched forward on the woman and went into convulsions. The woman screamed and tried to crawl from under him. Her nails were breaking and her eyes and mouth were opened wide with horror. Gold

walked slowly forward, holding the .38 stiff-armed before him, ready to
shoot Dog again when Dog suddenly went very still. The woman, feeling
the dead weight on her, screamed even louder. Gold grabbed her arm and
pulled her from under Dog's body. He tried to help her to her feet, but her
legs were rubber and she sat back down heavily. She had stopped screaming and was sobbing and gulping for air. The other cops were around them
now, and Mancuso, who was good at that sort of thing, knelt and tried to
calm her. Honeywell and Christiansen were wrapping a belt around the
bloody stump that was Jojo's leg.

"I told you this asshole would blow his Johnson off. Only it was his
fucking foot," Honeywell said. "He had a sawed-off twelve-gauge under
that coat. Shoulda had a dildo, woulda done him as much good."

Jojo moaned.

"Shut up, asshole," Honeywell growled as he worked to staunch the
blood. "You're bleeding all over my best sweats."

Honeywell glanced up at Gold. "Is the Dog dead?"

"If I've ever seen a dead man—and I've seen a lot of 'em—the Dog won't
ever bite again."

Gold steadied himself against the bank's wall.

"You okay, Jack?"

"I think I have to puke, Honey."

Honeywell looked closer.

"Why don't you sit in the car, Jack?"

"I'm all right," Gold said. "Did you call the paramedics for this asshole?"

Honeywell grunted. He was back at Jojo's leg. Flores came up with a
young kid in handcuffs.

"What do you want to do with the driver, Lieutenant?"

The kid was staring at Dog's body. "Jesus Christ," he said softly.

"What do you want, Nolan?" Gold asked him. "I can cut you loose here
and now. Or at the station. Or book you and hold you for a few days, then
let you walk."

The kid couldn't keep his eyes off Dog. "Lordy. He's my sister's ol'
man."

"Put him in the car," Gold said to Flores. "We'll book him and tomorrow I'll talk to the D.A.'s office, and the day after we'll cut him loose for
lack of evidence. It'll look better. I wouldn't think a piece of *dreck* like Dog
had any friends, but you never know. It'll look better."

He turned back to the kid.

"And when I talk to the D.A., Nolan, I'll tell him about what you did
for me, here, this morning. I'll ask him to take care of that thing down in
Downey. This squares it. I'll talk to him and he'll make a phone call."

"Jesus Christ," the kid said. "You blew him away."

"Tomorrow's Saturday," Flores said.

"So he'll stay in until Monday, Tuesday. It'll look better."

"Jesus," the kid breathed. "Lordy."

In the distance an ambulance siren started up like guitar feedback—a thin, dry whine. Spicer was in the street waving away a police helicopter that hovered high in the smoggy sky. A black-and-white had pulled up and the uniformed cops were trying to move the gaping motorists along. Honeywell and Christiansen were still working on Jojo at Gold's feet. Gold watched them for a moment, then crossed the street and went into a small bar. The bar was called the Locker Room and the bartender, who had been out on the sidewalk watching the action with a group of young men, followed Gold back inside and went behind the short leatherette bar.

"Johnnie Walker Black," Gold said and held up his thumb and forefinger two inches apart.

The bartender had a lean, tanned body packed like a sausage into a skintight black undershirt and khaki shorts. His hair was military short, and he wore a golden earring, a red bandanna knotted at the throat, and a huge ring of keys on his left hip. He poured the drink, then stepped back and watched Gold take off half of it in one gulp.

"Are those people dead?"

Gold took another swallow, watching the bartender over the rim of the glass. He put the glass on the bar and pointed to it. The bartender poured another.

"One is. One isn't," Gold said.

Several of the young men had come in from the sidewalk and they gathered at the other end of the bar and watched Gold warily. Somebody put a quarter in the jukebox and played Queen's old hit "Another One Bites the Dust." Someone else giggled.

"I killed a man once," the bartender said.

Gold looked at him.

"Yes," the bartender said. "It took days and days and *days.*"

All the young men laughed. One of them danced forward. He was small and dressed only in baggy canvas pants and an L.A. Dodgers baseball cap.

"Did you *have* to kill that bad man, or is that just the way you get off?"

Gold smiled grimly at the little man. "You better fly away, Tinkerbell, before you get something shoved up your ass you're not gonna enjoy."

"Oooo, listen to Mary!" the little man said and swished provocatively back to his friends amid raucous laughter.

Gold pointed to the glass again. The bartender poured a double, then went to the other end of the bar to be with his friends. Gold took a long, thick cigar from his breast pocket and lit it. He shook out the match and held his hand in front of his face. It was steady. Honeywell appeared in the doorway. His face dripped with sweat. He squinted into the cool darkness, spotted Gold, and came over quickly.

"Jack, what the fuck are you doing?" he asked quietly.

"Honey, have a drink." Gold snapped his finger at the bartender, who started over until Honeywell waved him away.

"You can't do this, Jack. Those assholes from OIS are already here. They want to know where you are and I really can't blame them. It's your operation, your bust, and you're in here juicing. Man, you can't do that."

Gold puffed on his cigar until he was wreathed in gray smoke. Then, sipping his Scotch, peered up at Honeywell.

"OIS is here already?"

"Yeah."

"Didn't take them long."

"Your reputation precedes you."

"Who is it?"

"Kush. And some of his people."

"Sergeant Kush," Gold said slowly and took another drink. "If Kush is here then the cameras can't be far behind."

"There's an independent already setting up. The station's only three blocks away. Up on Sunset."

Gold blew out a cloud of smoke and seemed to be studying the cigar in his hand.

"Jack, for chrissake—"

Gold slowly ground out his cigar in the ashtray before him.

"Jack, please, man."

"All right already," Gold said as he stood up. "Don't be such a *nudzh.*" He took a ten from his pants pocket and held it up to the bartender, who nodded back. Gold drained his glass and put it on the bar over the ten. One of the gays in the crowd said something and all the others laughed again.

Outside was hotter and brighter and smoggier. The Hollywood Hills were a brown smudge against a browner sky. The bank's parking lot had been roped off with yellow police tape, and the coroner's people were just taking Dog's body away. Gold and Honeywell pushed through the crowd that had gathered on the sidewalk by the bank's front entrance. A young man in a three-piece suit and makeup stood by the police barrier talking to a minicam perched on the shoulder of a long-haired Oriental.

"This morning on the smoggy streets of West Hollywood," the reporter intoned, "a violent tragedy took place."

"Do it again, Jeff," the camera man said.

A girl appeared from the crowd and flicked at the reporter's face with a makeup brush. He straightened his tie and stared intently into the camera.

"Rolling?" he asked.

"Rolling. Go ahead, Jeff."

"This is Jeff Bellamy of KZTV in West Hollywood. This morning, on these smoggy streets, a violent tragedy took place. A tragedy that some people think could have been averted."

"One more time, Jeff."

"What the fuck is he saying?" Gold said to Honeywell.

"I don't know, Jack. He—"

"I'll tell you what he's saying," barked a beefy, crewcut man in a plaid sport coat and string tie. "What he is saying is Mrs. Eskaderian is talking about making a complaint against you boys. Maybe even suing the city."

"Hey, Joe Kush. Heard you were around. Who the fuck is Mrs. Eskaderian? Wait a minute. Don't tell me that."

"Right. She's the Beverly Hills bitch who was stupid enough to almost get her ass shot off this morning. The one went dancing with what's his name. Weathers. Seems her husband is a film producer—big famous one—and he just finished working on some documentary about Argentine death squads."

Kush patted his red face with a folded handkerchief.

"So?"

"So she claims that's what you jokers are."

"An Argentine death squad?" Gold asked. Honeywell chuckled.

"No, wise-ass, a Los Angeles death squad. She claims you *executed* that poor underprivileged citizen this morning. Says you were waiting for him—'lying in wait' was the words she chose—lying in wait. And when you found Mr. Weathers in a situation where he could be legally eliminated you killed him dead. Without a single thought as to the many innocent bystanders whose lives you criminally endangered. Of which one was of course Mrs. Eskaderian."

"That's bullshit," Honeywell said. "Jack saved her ass. Dog would've killed her for sure."

"I'm telling you what the lady said. That's all."

"Where is she?" Gold asked. "I'd like to talk to her."

"Too late. She took the same ambulance as the suspect who blew his foot off. What's his name?"

"Jojo."

"Yeah. She was a little hysterical. Understandable from what I hear. Not every day somebody gets blown away and does the Funky Chicken right on top of you. So they gave her a shot and took her in to check out. Wasn't too upset to tell me she wanted your badge though, Lieutenant. And by the time they get to the hospital she and Jojo will probably figure out a way to charge you with murder."

Sergeant Kush gave out a short snorting laugh and showed small, sharp rodent teeth that seemed incongruous in his fleshy face.

"By the way, Lieutenant, just where the hell were you? I looked all over for you when I got here." Kush looked closely at Gold and almost visibly sniffed the air. "You know you're not supposed to leave the scene until OIS has checked you out."

Gold leaned his back against a car and folded his arms across his chest. "I had to peepee, Joe. I didn't know I needed a pass."

"Don't give me a hard time, Lieutenant. All you old-time, hard-ass cops give me a royal pain. And you're the worst of the bunch. You know I've got a job to do. Just like you. So let me do it." Kush's face was boiling red from the heat and aggravation.

"Excuse me, officers," a familiar voice interrupted. Jeff Bellamy, the blond boy reporter, was standing at Kush's elbow, a look of nervous self-importance pinching his face. "Sergeant Kush, can we do that one-on-one now? The other channels are setting up."

"Certainly, Jeff. I'll be right there," Kush said in an oily voice. Then sharply to Gold: "Lieutenant, I'll deal with you later."

"You do that, Joe." Gold laughed. "You do that."

Kush glared at Gold, then hurriedly followed Bellamy, buttoning his collar and tightening his narrow tie.

"Look at that fat bastard," Honeywell said as he sat on the fender beside Gold. "They say he waddles like that 'cause he'll do *anything* for Chief Huntz."

Gold laughed again. He fished another cigar from his pocket. As he was lighting it Honeywell glanced quickly sideways at him.

"What do you think about this Mrs. Eskaderian thing, Jack? Filing a complaint and all. You think there'll be any trouble?"

Gold puffed slowly on his cigar.

"Sergeant Honeywell, I've been on this police force for over twenty-five years, and one thing I've learned: never worry about tomorrow until tomorrow, because tomorrow's gonna get here soon enough." He turned to Honeywell. "Okay?"

Honeywell shrugged his shoulders and held up his palms. "Whatever you say, Jack."

"I say let's watch the Looney Tunes."

Jeff Bellamy was talking earnestly at the camera again.

"We're here with Sergeant Joe Kush of the Officer Involved Shooting

Unit of the LAPD. Sergeant Kush, can you tell us what happened?" Bellamy stuck the mike in front of Kush's red face.

"Well, Jeff, an attempt was made to rob this branch—the West Hollywood branch—of the Golden State Bank and Trust. The attempt was foiled, a hostage was briefly taken, the hostage was subsequently freed, one suspect was killed and another was wounded and has been taken to L.A. Memorial Hospital. After treatment he and the third suspect, a juvenile, will be booked and charged."

"Is there any truth, Sergeant, to the—well—rumor that this bloodshed could have been avoided?"

"Absolutely none, Jeff," Kush said, his eye on the camera. "Preliminary investigation indicates that the officers involved acted quickly and prudently in a very dangerous situation. I think they should be commended for a job well done."

"Go gettum, Sarge," Honeywell whispered.

"What about the reports that the hostage who was freed is considering making a complaint against the department?" Jeff Bellamy asked. "A complaint because of the way this whole thing was handled."

"Well, Jeff, the freed hostage was in a very emotional state and, in fact, had to be hospitalized because of her agitated condition. I feel certain that when she has had time to recover her composure and reconsider this morning's events, and after the ongoing investigation has been completed and all the facts have been examined, it will be obvious to everyone that the officers involved acted in a very, *very* courageous and perfectly responsible manner."

"*Shee-it!*" Honeywell whistled. "That Kush can lay the shit down!"

"That's his gig," Gold grunted.

Two tall men in dark suits and sunglasses crossed the crowded street. They stood before Gold.

"Lieutenant Jack Gold, LAPD?"

"That's me."

One of them held up his I.D. in a leather case.

"I'm Agent Fitzhugh and this is Agent Bremer of the Federal Bureau of Investigation. We'd like to speak with you."

Gold studied the card for a moment, then said out of the side of his mouth to Honeywell, "Some days it don't pay to come to work. You know what I mean?"

Noon   The building was long and low, cubist and modern. The facade was sleek, black, opaque Plexiglas, bordered by dwarf palm trees and bird-of-paradise plants. Behind the building a small parking lot reserved for company executives fronted a warehouse with a loading dock. Behind the warehouse was a larger parking lot for all the other employees.

At precisely twelve o'clock a stream of talking, laughing workers poured out of the warehouse doors and the building's back entrance and gathered in small groups in the executive lot. They leaned on cars and against the black building, smoking and eating and joking.

Walker walked out of the warehouse's gloom and blinked in the brightness. He sat on the edge of the loading dock and dangled his legs over the side. From a creased and greasy grocery bag, he took a ham-and-Swiss sandwich, an orange, and the silver thermos. He carefully refolded the brown bag and slipped it into his jeans' back pocket. Pouring steaming coffee into the thermos cup, he popped two pills and gulped some of the coffee. Then he took a large bite of the sandwich and chewed slowly, squinting up to where the sun hid behind the smog. Most of the people from the warehouse and many of the company's white-collar workers ate at a hot-lunch wagon called Chico's Choo-Choo that was parked a few feet away from the entrance of the parking lot, but Walker didn't like crowding in to order a sandwich or a burrito. He didn't like accidentally bumping into the blacks and Mexicans from the warehouse. And the operators of the hot-wagon were, regardless of the name, Vietnamese, and Walker had heard that the Vietnamese ate dog. Besides, the simple sight of an Asian seemed to make Walker's temper flare, and he was finding it harder and harder to control his anger lately. He wasn't even sure he *wanted* to control his anger.

But the strongest reason he had for brown-bagging his lunch to work was that once a cabdriver at an all-night doughnut shop had told Walker that that very night he had overheard two black ol' mammy maids being sent home in his cab by their employers laughing about how each night when they made their respective bosses a late-night sandwich, before placing the top piece of bread they spit a hawking glob under the lettuce—then watched in secret delight as the paddy bastards ate greedily, smacking their lips and sucking at their fingers. Walker believed the story implicitly, and since he also believed that all nonwhite people were somehow in secret collusion, Walker seldom ate out in the city of Los Angeles.

Walker finished the sandwich, then peeled and ate the orange, wiping his hands on his legs. He stripped off his T-shirt, revealing his muscled, tattooed body, then leaned back against the warehouse wall and pulled a rolled-up newspaper from his other back pocket. He opened the paper carefully and, picking at his chest with one hand, began to read:

THE KALIFORNIA KLARION
VOICE OF THE KALIFORNIA KLAN

So-Called Holocaust a Myth

Desert Vista, California—Dr. Arthur Vogel, a respected educator and chairman of the Society for Historical Accuracy, stated here today that his extensive research has revealed that the "stories" of millions of Jews supposedly killed in World War II have been greatly exaggerated and, in fact, were actually outright lies and distortions.

Speaking before a meeting of the Society for Historical Accuracy here in Desert Vista, Dr. Vogel, who last year was forced from his position as a professor in the state university system by radical Jewish elements, said that the myth of the so-called "Holocaust" was fostered on the world after World War II by Zionist anti-Christian forces in order to gain international sympathy for a national homeland for the Jews.

"We have found isolated instances of Jews killed in the blanket bombings that covered all Europe during the war," Dr. Vogel said, "but you have to understand great numbers of people of all nationalities died in the fire storm that rolled across Europe. The notion, the lie, that Jews were singled out and systematically persecuted by the German people is simply not true. It is a falsehood that was spread, and continues to be spread, by a powerful worldwide network of Zionist terrorists that has contacts and influence in all the cities and nations of the world that Jews had spread to and infected."

Especially Powerful in U.S.

Dr. Vogel said the International Network of Jews is especially powerful right here in the United States. "The Jews," Dr. Vogel charged, speaking before a group that contained State Assembly candidate Jesse Utter, "in their usual insidious way, have used the singular civil liberties of the American courts, the liberal laxness of the American educational system, and the leftist fellow-traveler leanings of the American press to twist the truth and gain uninformed WHITE AMERICA'S sympathy for the Zionist cause. By gaining control of our publishing, of our schools, of our universities, of our films and our television, the International Jewish Network has amplified the lie of the Hebrew Holocaust, has given credence to the myth of the concentration camp, and has generally subverted American institutions and principles to Jewish purposes."

Walker gulped some coffee and read on, moving his lips slightly as his eyes traced over the crude newsprint.

AMERICA COURTS DISASTER IN AMERICA'S COURTS

Desert Vista, California—America's lawyers and judges are destroying the fabric of American society as we know it by turning loose in our streets criminals and killers those very lawyers and judges know should be kept imprisoned or executed, State Assembly Candidate Jesse Utter claimed here today in Desert Vista.

And it is no coincidence that the vast majority of these lawyers and judges are Jews.

And it is also no coincidence that the vast majority of those killers and criminals are blacks.

Kicking off his campaign last week here in his hometown of Desert Vista, Independent

American Candidate Jesse Utter maintained
that Jewish judges and Jewish lawyers are deliberately unleashing on WHITE CHRISTIAN
AMERICA as many black murderers, rapists,
and robbers as possible, in a so far very successful attempt to create havoc and chaos at
America's core.

Speaking at a campaign rally held here at
KALIFORNIA KLAN WORLD HEADQUARTERS,
KLAN KANDIDATE Jesse Utter promised to
combat the International Jewish Conspiracy
in its attempt to destroy America through its
courtrooms.

"These Jews know exactly what they're
doing," KLANDIDATE Jesse Utter charged.
"The American nigger has always been the
dull-witted dupe of the shrewd, conniving Jew,
and today is no exception. Sitting safe and
secure in their privately guarded million-dollar Jew bastions like Beverly Hills and Palm
Springs, the Jew lawyers and judges are acting
in unholy collusion to set upon WHITE CHRIS-
TIAN AMERICA all the DOPE-FIEND, ANIMAL-
ISTIC, NIGGER RAPISTS AND MURDERERS they
can flush down our prison toilets.

"By passing unenforceable laws, by throwing out of court valid cases against black criminals whenever possible, by plea bargaining
away—"

"Hey, Walker. Here comes your old lady, man."

Walker looked up into a wide brown face beaded with sweat under a
knotted blue kerchief. A group of Chicano workers from the loading bay
had clustered twenty feet away, and Gonzales, the man talking, was laughing and cutting slices from a pear with a hunting knife sporting a six-inch
blade.

"She's looking good today, Walker. She got herself together for Mr.
Morrison. What you tink?" Gonzales baited him, and the other Mexicans
laughed.

A tall, heavy-breasted blonde in her late twenties walked quickly across
the parking lot. Several men whistled and someone said, *"Mira, mira,*
Terri," and made a sucking sound with his lips. The blonde ordered two

scrambled egg sandwiches from Ngu Ming, the short-order cook in Chico's Choo-Choo. She had the look of many voluptuous women who constantly battle their weight. Beneath her blue, light summer suit, her body demanded attention from any man around her.

"Hey, Terri!" Gonzales shouted, but she ignored him, busying herself with the selection of a package of cellophane-wrapped doughnuts.

"Hey, Terri! *Mira, mira!* Over here. I want to show you something." The men in the parking lot looked at Terri and smiled. Some of them glanced quickly at Walker.

"Hey, Walker, what you tink?" Gonzales sucked a piece of pear from the point of his knife. "I tink Mr. Morrison he showed it to her already. What you tink?" Gonzales chewed the fruit with his jaw slack and his mouth open.

"Fuck you," Walker said evenly.

Gonzales grinned at Walker a moment, then turned back to the parking lot.

"Hey, Terri. You getting lunch for Mr. Morrison, *corazon?*"

She turned and shaded her eyes with her hand and squinted at whoever was shouting at her. Gonzales waved at her and she waved back hesitantly. A nervous smile played at the edges of her lips until she spotted Walker glaring back at her. The smile quickly faded. She paid for the lunch and hurried back across the parking lot and into the office building.

"Hey, Terri! Ooooh, Terri! Don't leave me!" Gonzales shouted, and even Ngu Ming in the hot truck laughed and watched her buttocks glide along.

"Ay, ay, ay," Gonzales said softly after her, shaking his head. Then he walked away and the others drifted after him. Walker watched them go, then poured another cup of coffee from the thermos. He turned a page of his newspaper and began reading an article under the headline

ARE JEWISH DOCTORS KILLING OUR
CHILDREN?

1:22 PM Sheriff's Deputy Washington watched with bored interest as the tall, slender woman approached his desk. He had been with the Sheriff's Office for over five years now and had been assigned to the L.A. County Jail for the past seven months, so he took pride in the fact that nothing could surprise him. But he was constantly, well, *amused* by the quality of women who visited the assholes under his charge. The finest ass he had ever seen on a white woman had belonged to a nineteen-year-old redhead whose husband had raped and strangled an eighty-six-year-old great-grandmother. And she had visited him twice a week—the allowable limit—until he had been shipped up to Folsom. It—*amused*—Sheriff's Deputy Washington.

"Esther Phibbs. To see Robert Phibbs. Third floor, cell six, B tier."

"I know your name by now, Esther. I mean, how could I forget *your* name, mama?" Sheriff's Deputy Washington smiled and his eyes slipped over her lean, muscular body. He picked up a phone and said, "Phibbs, Robert. Three B-six."

He pushed a list on a clipboard toward Esther and she signed it quickly.

"Thank you," Esther said, not looking at him. She sat on a hard bench a few feet from Sheriff's Deputy Washington's desk. She lit a cigarette and nervously crossed her legs. Beside her on the narrow bench a Mexican girl with silver eyeshadow nursed a baby tucked inside her blouse. From the bowels of the building reverberated a constant muffled cacophony of men shouting, iron doors slamming, toilets flushing—a jailhouse symphony. Sheriff's Deputy Washington watched her through hooded, insolent eyes.

"Ain't you got nothing better to look at, man?"

Sheriff's Deputy Washington smiled broadly, showing large white teeth. "Not a thing, Esther. Not one damn thing."

Esther puffed her cigarette and studied her nails.

Two young white girls with spiked purple hair came down the outside corridor bopping and singing to a techno-punk track blaring from a huge cassette player one girl carried on a strap over her shoulder. The other girl had chains around her ankles that rattled with every step. Sheriff's Deputy Washington's smile faded into a stern black authoritative mask.

"I'm afraid you ladies are gonna have to turn that music off."

"We want to see Johnny Shockwave," said the girl with the ankle chains.

"Shockwave," Sheriff's Deputy Washington mumbled as he flipped through worn Rolodex cards on his desk. "Shockwave. I don't have no Shockwave in here." He looked up. "Are you sure that's his name?"

"He's a musician," said Chains. "A drummer."

"Can we visit him together?" asked the other.

"I'm sorry, ma'am—" Sheriff's Deputy Washington stopped when Esther gave a short ugly laugh at the "ma'am."

"Do you have conjugal visits here?" asked Chains.

"You're gonna have to turn that—"

"We want to visit him together. A conjugal visit. Together. At the same time."

"Yeah, we want to conjugate his fucking socks off."

Another sheriff's deputy swung open the heavy barred door leading to the visiting cubicles.

"Phibbs?" he said, looking around the room.

Sheriff's Deputy Washington shot a glance at Esther's back as she disappeared through the door.

"Turn that goddamn noise off *now,* girl!" he growled at Chains.

When Esther saw Bobby behind the thick glass of the visiting cubicle he smiled at her and she felt her stomach drop and a liquid warmth flow through her body. He put his hand against the glass and picked up the phone. She placed her hand over his on the cool glass and raised the receiver to her ear.

"Hi, baby," he said, and a thrill shot through her at the sound of his voice.

Bobby Phibbs was a very handsome man with a sharply chiseled nose and large, almond-shaped eyes. Had his skin not been dark brown he would have appeared Middle Eastern—even Mediterranean. He had the bulky grace and upper-body development of a natural athlete—a running back or a wide receiver, most probably. His hair was short on top and longish down the back of his neck, and a Fu Manchu moustache curled around a sensual mouth.

"It won't be long now, Bobby," Esther said as she sat down. "Four more days. Just four more days."

"Ain't it the truth." Bobby beamed.

"You know, I read this article in a magazine that said the last few weeks in prison is the hardest. There's more escapes in the last few weeks than any other time."

"That's in prison, honey. That's mens with twenty, twenty-five years. That don't happen here in County."

Esther's eyes searched Bobby's.

"I just hope you're not going through any, you know, *anxiety*. I don't want you going through any pain—"

"I'm not, Es."

"—because there's no reason to be tripping on anything negative, Bobby. Four more days and we put this all behind us. Four—"

"Es, everything's all right. Really. I'm not going through anything. No anxiety. No nothing. I'm just happy as hell to be getting out of here."

Esther took a deep breath and her body relaxed. She put her hand against the glass again.

"Bobby," she said softly. "I love you so much."

"Es—"

"I miss you so much. We all miss you. So much."

"Es, it's gonna be all right. Stop worrying, baby. I'm coming out of here and everything's gonna be all right. Daddy's coming home. To stay."

Esther allowed herself a smile. Her gaze flashed hungrily over his body.

"Bobby, you the only man I ever seen looked *fine* in prison overalls."

"Shee-it, Esther. How many mens you visiting in here?"

They smiled warmly at each other for a long moment, drinking in each other.

"You look fine, too, baby. *Super*fine." Bobby leaned forward as he whispered into the phone. "And I'm gonna tear your sweet ass *up* when I get out of here."

"Hush, Bobby!" Esther flushed, looking around.

"Tear you up!" Bobby said loudly and they both laughed. A guard's face appeared at the glass window in the door behind Bobby and stared sternly for a moment before moving on. Bobby and Esther suppressed giggles. Bobby lit a cigarette and Esther did too.

"You need any more cigarettes, Bobby?"

"No, baby. Any packs I have left when I roll out I only gotta give away to the dudes in the cellblock."

They smoked together in silence. Esther watched the smoke curl out of his flared nostrils and circle his face. She had always loved watching him. Do anything. Smoke. Shave. Eat. Fuck her. *Anything.* He was the most beautiful man she had ever seen and she had been denied him for a year and she ached for him.

"Bobby, I talked to Mr. De Castro at the hospital. He said there's no way you can work there again. Maybe someday, but not now. Not for a long time. But he says he had talked to the woman who runs the hospital cafeteria—I can't remember her name—"

"Mrs. MacArthur."

"Right, Mrs. MacArthur. Well, Mr. De Castro talked to Mrs. MacArthur, and *she* talked to this friend of hers that manages a Piccadilly Cafeteria—you know the one downtown on Grand? *That* one. And Mrs. MacArthur told Mr. De Castro to tell you there's a *job* waiting for you when you get out."

"That's dynamite, Es."

"Isn't it, Bobby? Mrs. MacArthur told her friend how you'd always been such a good worker at the hospital, how the patients always commented on how you made them comfortable and all. And then she told him how, you know, you made some real bad mistakes, some bad decisions, and how you're paying for those mistakes and that's all behind you now."

"That's the truth, baby."

"Mr. De Castro said Mrs. MacArthur said the job wouldn't be anything great. To start, you know. Just bussing tables, cutting vegetables, carrying serving trays out from the kitchen. Cleaning up and stuff. It won't be much, Mrs. MacArthur said, but it's a beginning."

"Baby, that's more than just a beginning. Sugar, that's wonderful. I'd dig ditches. I'd shovel shit. After a year in this hell hole that's gonna be like a *vacation*, Esther."

Bobby's enthusiasm made Esther feel warm and safe inside.

"Oh, Bobby, it's really gonna be good, isn't it?"

Bobby's face grew serious, and his voice was low and tight.

"Esther, I ain't never coming back to this place. Never. I've had a year in here to think about how I fucked up. How I almost lost everything in this world means a damn thing to me. How I almost lost you and Little Bobby. All the pain I caused Mama. And I want to tell you, baby, ain't nothing in this world could make me go back there again. Nothing. *No thing.* Never again. Uh-uh." Bobby shook his head. "Baby, I ain't much, but I'm all yours."

"Bobby—"

"I'm gonna be the best husband, the best father, the best goddamn cafeteria worker you ever *dreamed* of seeing."

"Bobby, I love you so much."

"I love you too, baby."

5:37 PM The late-afternoon smog wrapped around the L.A. basin like a piece of dirty gauze. Walker parked on a quiet side street lined with dusty cars and small run-down frame houses that seemed to crawl up the hillside like mushrooms. He sat in the van and watched two preteen boys coming up the sidewalk from the playground on the corner. One boy carried a baseball bat and wore a Dodgers cap. The other had an outfielder's mitt and was throwing a baseball up and catching it as he walked. One was white and one was black.

When the boys came abreast of the van Walker opened the door suddenly.

"Kevin."

The white boy jumped at Walker's voice. He managed a wan smile.

"Hi, Dad."

"A whole month since I seen you and all the hello I get is 'Hi, Dad'? Come over here and give your old man a hug."

Kevin came forward and put his arms around his father tentatively. Walker leaned over and held the boy tightly. Over Walker's shoulder Kevin rolled his eyes at the black boy. Walker straightened up and looked from Kevin to the black boy.

"So what'cha doing, Kev?"

"Oh, you know, Dad. Nothing. Just a little batting practice. There wasn't enough guys for a real game." Kevin dropped his eyes and picked at the stitching on his glove. The black boy watched Walker with a curious stare for a moment, then began walking away.

"I'll see you later, Kevin," he called over his shoulder. Walker's eyes followed him down the street.

"Who's that, Kevin?"

"Who? Oh, André? That's André. We had homeroom together."

"André?" Walker laughed and shook his head. "He sure as hell don't look French. Is he French?"

"Huh?" Kevin tried to look his father in the eye, but failed miserably and went back to destroying his mitt.

"I said, is he French?"

Kevin was silent. He seemed to shrink.

"Kevin?"

The street was so quiet the hum of traffic on the Hollywood Freeway,

38

half a mile away, could be heard clearly. Walker knelt and looked into his ·
son's downcast eyes.

"Ain't there no white boys in this neighborhood, you got to play with
a nigger?"

Kevin stopped picking at the mitt and was suddenly stone still. Only his
eyelids moved, blinking furiously.

"Answer me, Kevin."

"Dad, he's just a guy." Kevin forced himself to meet his father's glare.
"He's just a guy I play ball with. He's my friend."

"Kevin, I told you before, there's no such thing as a nigger friend. The
minute there's other niggers around he's gonna act like he don't even know
you. Or worse."

"André's not like that, Dad."

"They're all like that, Kevin. And it's not gonna help you hanging out
with them. People judge you by the company you keep, boy, and niggers
are *not* good company. Understand?"

"Dad, I—"

"Understand?"

"Yessir," the boy said weakly.

"Now I don't want to see you going around with that little black chim-
panzee anymore. Or any other damn little pickaninnies, okay? I want you
to make friends with some nice white kids. Some of your own kind. Okay?"

"Okay, Dad." Kevin was picking at his glove again.

Walker stood up. "You going in your mother's house?"

"Uh, no, sir," Kevin said quickly. "I gotta go, uh, I gotta go up to the
Safeway and get some looseleaf paper."

"In August? What for? School's out."

"It's—it's for some book reports we gotta do over vacation."

"You need any money?" Walker reached into his pocket, but Kevin was
already moving down the sidewalk.

"No, thanks, Dad." The boy broke into a trot. "Catch you later."

"Remember what I said," Walker shouted after him.

"Okay, Dad."

Walker watched Kevin run until he reached the corner and disappeared.
Then he turned and walked up the cracked concrete walk to a small white
frame house with a screened-in front porch. The screen door was unlatched
and he crossed the porch and knocked on the wood door. There was a
flurry of movement from inside, then a woman's voice: "Come in—wait
a minute—who is it?"

"It's me."

Cold silence, then: "Sonny? Is that you, Sonny? Wait a minute. Wait a minute. I gotta put something on."

There was another quick frenzy of activity, then the door opened and Terri was standing there in hair curlers, bare feet, cut-off jeans, and a tube top that barely contained her heavy breasts.

"I thought it was Abe," she said, a little out of breath.

"Oh? Do you always answer the door for him naked?"

She frowned. "Very funny."

"Besides, I've seen it all before."

She touched her curlers impatiently.

"What do you want, Sonny? You're not even supposed to be around here. That's one of the stipulations of the divorce. Or did you forget?"

"I have to talk to you."

Her eyes widened with exasperation. "Shit, Sonny! Did you get fired again?"

"No, I just want to talk to you."

She stood in the doorway, one hand resting on her hip. "I don't have time, Sonny. Abe's got passes to a screening and then we're going out to eat. I just got home from work and I still got to get ready. *And* fix dinner for Kevin."

"It'll only take a minute."

She raised her hand to her curlers again, feeling lightly. "You're not even supposed to come around here."

"Look, Terri. I just want to talk to you."

She turned from the doorway and walked quickly into the house.

"All right, but I'm trying to fix Kevin's dinner. And I can't stop."

Walker followed her in. The combination living-dining room was small and cheaply furnished. Nothing matched. Clothes were strewn on the backs of chairs, over doors, and all over a dirty bright blue imitation-velvet sofa. Terri walked into the tiny adjoining kitchen.

"I thought maybe you got fired again. But I guess Abe would've told me about anything like that—him getting you the job and all." Terri started kneading handfuls of ground beef in a blue bowl. Her breasts bounced with every movement.

"So what's on your mind, Sonny?"

Walker leaned on the door frame between the kitchen and the living room and watched her mix the chopped onions and bread crumbs into the meat.

"You always let Kevin fuck around with niggers?"

"You mean André?" Terri said without looking up. "That's his buddy. They're inseparable. He sleeps over there more than he sleeps here."

"That doesn't bother you?"

"No," Terri said as she wiped her hands on a dish towel. "Not a whole helluva lot."

A sneer curled on Walker's lips. "Yeah, well I guess a tramp who sleeps with a Jew wouldn't care if her kid runs around with a nigger."

Terri straightened up and looked at him. "Sonny, don't start up your fucking shit again. I don't want to *ever* have to listen to that shit again, and seven years ago that judge said I *don't* have to listen to it. So if that's what you came here for, just go someplace else and tell it to someone who gives a fuck, okay?"

She yanked a deep loaf pan from a cabinet under the sink and plopped the meat into it angrily.

"I don't want you to marry him, Terri."

Terri smiled to herself and shook her head.

"You are really amazing, Sonny. You are just fucking amazing."

"I don't want my kid brought up to be a Jew, that's all. I don't think that's too much to ask."

Terri was silent as she shaped the meat in the pan, then put the pan in the oven and turned the oven on. She washed her hands under the faucet, poured two mugs of coffee from the Mr. Coffee, and sat down at the plastic dinette table. She pushed one mug toward him across the tabletop and nodded to the chair across from her.

"Sit down, Sonny."

Walker sat down and tasted the coffee. It was stale and bitter.

"Sonny," she said and studied her nails as she spoke. "Sonny, Abe Morrison is a good man, and he's going to be nothing but good for me and Kevin. He's a good father. I know, I've seen him with his kids from his first marriage, and that's something Kevin's needed for a long time. And he's a stable, successful man—a good provider, like they say—and that's something that's been in short supply around here for a long time, too."

She swallowed some coffee and made a face.

"Sonny, men like me. They like to just watch me walk. They—"

"Yeah, that was some show today in the parking—"

She held up her hand. "They like to watch me. It makes them feel good. It makes their whole day. Okay, that's great. But I don't know how long that's gonna last, Sonny. I mean, tits as big as mine, someday they're gonna be bouncing off my knees. It's all I can do to keep my weight at one thirty-five. I had one weekend two weeks ago I didn't watch what I ate and Monday morning I was one forty-two, one forty-three. *One* weekend. Christ, my ass spreads out like manure. I'm twenty-nine this year, Sonny. Sixteen when you knocked me up, seventeen when we got married and Kevin was born. That's twelve years ago. The Big Three-O coming up on my ass fast, and I don't have the first clue where the last ten years went. Sonny, I don't want to be forty and sitting around some fucking honky-tonk listening to Dolly Parton on the fucking jukebox and some asshole is trying to slip his hand up my twat while I'm crying in my beer about all the wasted chances. I'm not wasting any more chances. So, Sonny, I got a shot here to do something for myself and Kevin too, and I'm gonna do it, and nobody's gonna stop me from doing it. *Especially* not you, okay? So don't come around here with any more of your shit, okay?"

Walker watched her as she spoke. Behind the house someone was dribbling and shooting a basketball. It made a metallic *thunk* every time it hit the backboard.

"I don't want Kevin to be a Jew," Walker said.

"Oh, for chrissake, Sonny! Will you stop it! You sound like a broken record. Abe Morrison likes to *fuck* me, man, and he's willing to marry me to keep it coming. He's not trying to win converts, can you dig it?"

"You're still gonna raise Kevin as a Christian?"

Terri threw back her head and laughed.

"Sonny, what the fuck do you know about Christian? I remember one Christmas Eve you broke my fucking arm, you remember? How Christian is *that*? You never been inside a church in your life. Did your old man raise you Christian? My ass! The old bastard worked for the railroad up in Barstow just so he could get drunk and beat the living shit out of you and your mother every night. The only Christian thing he ever did his whole miserable life was getting knocked-out loaded and falling asleep on the tracks in front of that Southern Pacific freight. And then you come along and beat the shit out of Kevin and me. And not even so's you could blame it on that. Just pissed off at the world, I guess. And I'm still waiting for you to do *one* Christian thing. So spare me all that shit, Sonny."

She watched him lean back in the chair, his hands clasped behind his head, his elbows sticking out.

"Sonny, you really have to stop all this crap. I'm trying to talk to you like a friend, not an ex-wife. Sonny, you've *got* to learn to get along with people. You really do. You can't go on like this—hating everybody. That's why you can't keep a job, except for that stupid paper route. Do you know that when I heard it was you at the door I just *knew* it was because you'd been fired. This last job at Techno-Cal is the only one you've been able to keep for longer than a couple of weeks. And Abe got it for you, so why do you want to turn around and bad-mouth the man? All he ever did was do you a favor."

Walker let his chair fall forward. He rested his elbows on the table.

"Hey, he's not doing me a favor. He's doing it for you." He cupped his hands together before him and, using his thumbs like a gun's sight, aimed at a picture of Terri's mother on the wall.

"Besides, I don't need the job. I only took it so we could be together again."

Terri stared into her coffee cup, not wanting to meet Walker's eyes.

"Sonny," she said finally, "that was a long time ago."

"Sure, but—"

"I was sixteen, Sonny. You had muscles. You had tattoos. You had a motorcycle. I thought you were hot shit." She looked at him evenly. "I don't think you're such hot shit anymore."

"Terri—" Walker began and reached across the table to her.

"Stop it!" Terri snapped and snatched her hand back. "Don't do that, Sonny."

"Hey, Terri, don't jump on me like that." He smiled. "Why don't you just relax. Why don't—"

"Look, Sonny," Terri rose and pushed her chair under the table, "I've really got to get going. I've got to do my makeup and fix my hair. I said I only had a few min—"

"You know, we had a good thing one time."

"Hey, that's over, man," she said, raising her hands palms forward. "That's dead."

Terri watched Walker's smile fade and his face grow grim. She felt the old familiar fear flash up from the base of her spine and grip the back of her neck and crawl just beneath the surface of her scalp. She had always been afraid of Sonny. In the beginning that had been part of the excitement; it had added to the pleasure. Now, after all the years, the bruises and pain, it was only fear.

"I think you better leave now, Sonny."

Walker's face was a sullen mask. "It'll never be over, Terri."

"I think you better leave now," she said again.

"I'll kill that fucking kike before I see you marry him."

Terri was silent for almost half a minute, then she spoke in a measured monotone:

"Sonny, you're under a court injunction; if you lay a finger on me, if you even raise your voice, I swear I'll make sure you spend a long, long time in jail. Understand?"

Walker's eyes were hard and cold.

"I want you to leave now," she said, moving slowly to the door, moving the way a man moves in the presence of an unchained, snarling dog. She opened the door and the sun streamed in.

"Please, Sonny."

Walker smiled, hesitated, then rose from his chair. He stretched and scratched his arm. Terri waited. Walker laughed once, then walked to the door. As he neared her, she braced. She knew him. If he was going to hit her it would come now. But he passed her and turned on the screened porch.

"Have a good time tonight," he said, smiling. He looked thoughtful for a moment, then grinned broadly. "It's Friday. You sure he's not taking you to temple?"

She sighed and shook her head slightly. "Leave us alone, Sonny. Please." She shut the door and Walker heard the deadbolt click.

"Thanks for the coffee!" he shouted to the door. He waited but there was no answer.

Halfway down the walk to his van he paused and listened. From behind the house he heard the basketball strike the rim of the backboard. Then a voice. Then another. Then boyish laughter.

He walked quickly across the summer-browned front lawn and around the side of the house, down the short driveway and into the small cemented-over backyard. Kevin was taking a shot and his back was to Walker. Walker was on him with catlike quickness. He cuffed the back of the boy's head, then spun him around and slapped him hard across the face. Kevin's head snapped back and his hand flew to his cheek.

"I told you I didn't wanna see you with that little black bastard!" Walker pointed to André, who was backing away wide-eyed.

The back door of the bungalow burst open and Terri came out screaming, her face contorted with rage.

"Don't touch him! Don't lay another fucking finger on him!"

She had a plastic hair curler in her grasp and she threw it at him. A single strand of hair bounced before her eyes.

"You leave him alone, you prick, or I swear to Jesus I'll have you put in jail!"

Kevin was fighting back the tears. His mouth trembled.

"Get away from here, Sonny! *Get the fuck away from here!*"

Walker looked from Kevin, who was openly crying now, to Terri, who was looking around for something to use as a weapon, then to André and back to Kevin.

"Get away from here! We don't want you here!" Terri picked up the basketball and flung it at his face. It bounced off his chest.

"Kevin—" Walker said, and reached out to the boy, who shrank back.

"Leave him alone!" Terri screamed and wrapped her arms protectively around her son.

Walker started to say something, then turned and walked down the driveway to the street. Terri followed him, shouting invective.

"Leave us alone, you low-life bastard! Just go away and *leave us alone!"*

Walker started his van and screeched out of the parking place. Terri stood in the street, still screaming after him. Neighbors peered from windows. Kevin and André watched from the driveway. Walker roared away. In the rearview mirror he saw Terri growing smaller and smaller.

9:27 PM The motel room was dark and cool. Gold found the wall switch just inside and to the right of the door. It turned on a dim light over a small, circular table. He put a fifth of Scotch and a white paper bag on the table. In the bathroom he found a Sani-Wrapped glass. He kicked off his shoes and unsnapped his holster from his belt. The gun made a familiar reassuring thud on the tabletop. Gold pulled an angular uncomfortable-looking chair up to the table and sat down. He poured a drink, unwrapped a chicken salad sandwich, then reached over and flicked on the TV. As he ate, the screen flickered and warmed, then J. R. Ewing's malevolent smile appeared. The sound was off and Gold made no move to turn it up. Halfway through the sandwich he got up and tried to turn off the air conditioning. He dialed the thermostat to OFF but he could still hear the frigid hum. He left it that way and sat down to finish the sandwich. As he chewed he watched the screen idly. When he finished he felt good enough to take a careful sip of Scotch. He had forgotten to eat this afternoon, as he often did when he was seriously drinking; and when he pulled into the motel on the east end of Hollywood Boulevard, he had been pretty shaky. It had been a hellish day—the stakeout, the shooting, the FBI assholes, the reports to be filled out—and Gold had been drinking through it all.

"I'm getting too old," he said aloud as he carefully swept the crumbs from the table into his cupped hand. He carried them to the wastebasket, then took his gun and his drink to a bedside table. He stretched out on the bed and crossed his legs at the ankles. The bed felt clean and soft and wonderful, and Gold realized how tired he was. Watching Linda Gray and Larry Hagman have a silent argument, he drifted off to sleep.

He slept soundly and dreamlessly for half an hour, until he heard the room door open. His hand moved calmly, reflexively, for his gun.

"Jack Gold. How you doing?"

He relaxed, locked his hands behind his head, and yawned.

"Cookie."

She was a Filipina. Small, dark, and quick. Her hair was straight and reached below her waist. Her tight white pants and tube top contrasted starkly with her glossy skin.

"Jack Gold," she said as she lit a long brown cigarette and sat on the edge of the bed. "You know a fucking asshole cop named Knudsen? Knudsen—like the milk—you know what I mean." She got up quickly and poured herself a drink. "Fucking asshole cop bust me in the Sunset Hyatt bar last week. Had me right, you know what I mean. I solicit him right out. So I say, hey, maybe we can talk about this, you know what I mean."

"I know what you mean," Gold said.

"Yeah, right, okay." Cookie sat on the bed's edge again. She crossed her legs and leaned back. Even in repose, she exuded a nervous energy. "So okay, this Knudsen asshole cop, he say come out to the car, we have a little talk." She swung her leg angrily and clutched her cigarette between long red-lacquered fingernails that looked like nothing so much as bloody talons. "Out in the car he say how much money you got. I say, oh, three, four hundred. He say, give it to me. I think, what the fuck, it's cheaper than a lawyer, you know what I mean. So I give him the gold and I start to get out the car. This Knudsen asshole say wait a minute. I say wait for *what?* And he pulls out his dick. I say, if you're busting me for giving you a bribe that's a funny-looking badge. He say, ha, ha, you real funny, the Comedy Store is right next door—you oughta go over there. Right after you suck this. So he makes me give him head right there in the Sunset Hyatt parking lot."

Her cigarette had gone out and she relit it.

"So you know this Knudsen cop asshole?"

"Cookie, there are seven thousand cops in the LAPD."

"Yeah, but you been around. You know everybody. Everybody knows you."

"Not the young ones, Cookie. And that's all Vice is—smooth-faced babies."

"So what you think I should do?"

"Do? About what?"

Her eyes flashed. "Shit, Jack Gold, this Knudsen asshole. He's one greedy motherfucker, you know what I mean. He should get a blow job *or* he should get the money. But he shouldn't get *both,* greedy motherfucker! You know what I mean?"

"Hey, Cookie, you said he had you cold. And you're the one who suggested the deal. He's the one who makes the terms."

"Aw, Jack Gold, you just saying that 'cause he's a cop. All you—*Ahh, Jack Gold! You on fucking TV!*" Cookie was across the room and turning up the sound. Jeff Bellamy's deep, nonregional voice bounced off the walls.

"—Mrs. Eskaderian issued a statement through her attorney, Mr. Milton Schindler, that she will be filing a formal complaint with the District Attorney's Office against the LAPD in the very near future. Possibly Monday morning. Mr. Schindler said that Detective Lieutenant Jack Gold and Detective Sergeant Alvin Honeywell would be specifically named in the complaint."

"Oh, Jack Gold. What you do?"

"Shhh," Gold said, sitting up in bed.

Joe Kush's red face filled the picture tube.

"The department is very sorry that the hostage, who was freed by the quick thinking of the officers involved, feels the way she does, but the department welcomes any investigation and is confident that any such investigation will prove that the officers involved acted in a prudent and judicious manner, as befitting the circumstances confronted."

"What the fuck he say?"

"He said cops take care of their own."

The camera was panning over the bloodied bank wall where Jojo had blown his foot off. Jeff Bellamy's voice-over was flat and ironic, in his best Mike Wallace imitation.

"Whatever the outcome of any future investigation, the outcome of this morning's five minutes of furious violence will never change: one suspect dead, one suspect hospitalized and forever crippled, one hostage hospitalized and traumatized—possibly forever. This is Jeff Bellamy, reporting from West Hollywood."

"Jesus Christ!" Gold swung out of bed and slapped the television off. "All he needs is a fucking John Williams soundtrack!"

"What you mean, Jack Gold?"

"Aaaah—" Gold flicked his hand at the TV in disdain. He unwrapped a long, slender cigar.

"You in trouble, Jack Gold?"

Gold lit the cigar and squinted around the cloud of smoke. "Nothing I can't handle, Cook."

"Hey, Jack Gold, you one tough, bad-ass motherfucker, you are!" Cookie laughed and her black eyes glinted. She tossed her head, shaking her hair out, and in one quick motion slipped off the tube top. Her breasts were small and her nipples were a shade darker than her skin and stood erect in the air-conditioned chill. Gold sat at the table and watched her.

"That Jeff Bellamy—he's one asshole reporter, you know what I mean. I like the Jap bitch on Channel 2 much better. She could make a lot of money if she wanted to live the life." Cookie pulled her pants off and draped them carefully over a hanger. She stood naked except for white bikini panties, little white "Fuck Me" heels, and lacy anklet socks. She swept off the panties and stuffed them in her handbag. Gold poured a short shot of Scotch. Cookie stood before him and smiled.

"How I look, Jack Gold?"

Gold sipped the Scotch.

"You're a fucking star, Cookie."

"Let's fuck now, Jack Gold."

Gold puffed on the cigar. "Hey, Cook, you know that's not how the game works. Sit down and talk to me. Let me look at you."

Cookie smiled slyly. "Sure, Jack Gold. Sure."

She turned around one of the hard plastic chairs and straddled it, her legs spread and her crotch wide and framed by the open back of the chair. She arched her back and hung her arms loosely over the chair's backrest. Gold poured her a drink and she took it from him and sipped at it, smiling and studying the amber liquid.

"You know, Jack Gold, I had a date last week—seventy-year-old jeweler. From New York. This old man, he can't get it up for years. I took care of this old dude, you know what I mean. He felt like a fucking teenager when he walked out that hotel, you better believe it. He give me a *two-hundred-dollar* fucking tip!"

The light over the table shone down on Cookie's bronze shoulders, making her skin glow. Her pubic hair was trimmed short and the lips of her vulva were thick, dark ridges.

"You look *fine,* Cookie."

She grinned. "You think so?"

"You're a fine motherfucker, Cookie."

"Jack Gold," she said in a voice dropped to a whisper, "let me make you feel good." She caressed her body with her open hand, sliding it over her stomach and down into herself. She inserted the tips of two fingers and began to masturbate. "Jack Gold, I can make you feel *sooooo* good, baby." Gold turned away. He turned back and Cookie was watching him through slitted eyes. She held out a glistening finger.

"Wanna smell?"

Gold stood up abruptly, startling her. He pulled a wad of bills from his pocket and slipped out two hundreds from the middle. He padded on stockinged feet to the bed and tucked the money under her panties in the white patent-leather purse. He came back with her cigarettes. Long, brown Shermans in a flat red box.

"Have a smoke, Cook," he said in a small, strange voice.

Cookie looked at him, then shrugged and took the cigarettes from him. He gave her a light, then relit his cigar. He sat down across the small table from her and topped off their glasses of Scotch. They drank in silence for a while, avoiding each other's eyes. The airconditioner hummed.

"Jack," she said quietly, "pleasing men is my business. Like you a cop. That's your business. Like . . . like being president, that's Reagan's business. You know what I mean." She smiled. "You know what they say. 'Just tell me what you want.' "

Gold made a small, almost Italianate gesture with his hands.

"I just like to look at you, Cookie. Just to look at you. It gives me pleasure."

She eyed him suspiciously.

"Just looking at me gives you pleasure?"

"A great deal of pleasure, baby. Any man could get into looking at you." Gold brushed away some ash from his pants. "Besides, you remind me of someone."

Cookie still stared at him.

"You sure that's all you want?"

"I'm sure, Cookie."

"Just to look at me?"

"That's all."

"And there's nothing else I can do for you?"

"Positive."

"Hey, what the fuck." She stood and threw up her hands in mock exasperation. "You an easy trick, Jack Gold. I don't know why I'm making it so hard."

She walked to her purse with quick, purposeful strides. Her ass was round and hard. From her purse she extracted fingernail polish, a fingernail file, and a small tube of Superglue. She turned her chair around, facing Gold, and sat down. She crossed her legs and began filing a fingernail.

"Thirty-five fucking dollars this Juliette cost me this morning in Beverly Hills." She held out the finger for Gold to inspect, then whipped it back before he could. "I come out of the shop, I unlock my car, and—*powie!*—thirty-five dollars shot to shit."

"Life is hard, Cookie." Gold was grinning. "Especially a whore's life."

"Don't be an asshole." She splayed her hand, palm down, on the tiny table and began repairing the nail with the Superglue.

"So who was she?" Cookie asked without looking up.

"Who was who?"

"The girl I remind you of?"

Gold watched her carefully apply the Superglue in a thin line over the cracked nail. She glanced up at him.

"Was she Filipino?" She turned her concentration back to her fingernail. "You said I remind you of her, so she must be dark. Latin? Was she Mexican? Italian? Hey, was she a Jewish broad?" She looked at Gold again, then looked a little closer.

"Hey, Jack Gold, we don't have to talk about her, you don't want to. We don't have to talk about anything. I was just trying—"

"She was black," Gold said.

"She was black!" Cookie's eyes flashed. "How the fucking shit you say I remind you of some nigger! I don't look like no fucking nigger bitch!

What you trying to say?" Cookie crossed and uncrossed her legs in agitation. Across her belly a single shiver of youthful fat shimmered with health.

"She was very light-skinned, Cookie. She was only one-eighth black. They call that an octoroon. In New Orleans. That's where she was from."

"Call it octo-what?"

"An octoroon. Like an octopus has eight legs. One-eighth black."

Cookie was using an emery board on her repaired nail, sawing at the excess glue with violent slashes.

"So she was beautiful, this octo-macaroon?"

"Very beautiful."

"And that's why I remind you of her."

Gold puffed on the cigar and smiled.

"That's it, Cook."

"And that's why you call me up every three, four months? To come down here and just walk around without no clothes on. 'Cause it makes you think of her?"

"Finally, Cookie, you know my deepest, darkest secret."

"Hey, Jack Gold," Cookie shrugged, "it ain't the kinkiest thing I ever did, by a son-of-a-bitch long shot. But you shoulda kept her. It'd be much cheaper in the long run."

Gold laughed—a single short, mirthless bark. His face emptied of emotion and in the shadows of the motel room light he seemed to grow older.

"She died," he said.

Cookie held her nail up at arm's length and examined her reconstruction job with satisfaction.

"Hey, we all got to go sometime," she said absently. "Am I right, Jack Gold?"

Gold put his stockinged feet up on the table and tilted his chair back.

"As far as I know, that's the way it goes."

"So, shit, have a good time in the meantime, you know what I mean."

Gold tilted farther back in the chair and cradled his whisky glass against his chest.

"Is that what we're doing, Cook? I wasn't aware."

11:52 PM The night was hot and humid. Esther fought her way out of the cruising traffic on Sunset Boulevard and parked in the narrow driveway of a flaking pink stucco apartment house. Several Mexican homeboys lounged across the steps and against the front of the building, passing around a joint and a bottle of Spiñada. One of them made a flapping sound with his tongue as Esther passed through them, and the others laughed. Esther kept her eyes forward and walked to a scarred door at the end of the long entrance hall. Spanish-language television blared from the other side. Esther knocked loudly, then again, louder.

"Lupe. Lupe. It's Esther."

The door opened a crack and a pretty, pony-tailed Latina in a Universal Studios Tour T-shirt stuck her head out.

"Esther, I'm yust putting the little one to bed. She's got a summer cold and she keeps waking up."

"How the hell can she sleep with that TV?"

Lupe smiled. "Aw, she likes it. It keeps her company. It's only the cold that keeps bothering her."

"Well, let's go, girl. We got work to do."

"We'll be right out."

Five minutes later Esther started up the station wagon's motor as Lupe slipped into the front seat next to her. Another, heavier girl followed.

"Hey. Who's this? Where's Maria?" Esther asked.

"La Migra," Lupe said sadly. "She was working in a place downtown. Sewing in pockets. You know, working for you at night, working there in the afternoons, baby-sitting sometimes. Making all the money she can. They came in today, took out twenty-three girls."

"That's terrible. Poor Maria."

"Aw, she'll be back. She loves L.A. All the work in the world, if you *want* to work, that's what she always say."

"She's a hard worker, all right." Esther looked across Lupe at the other girl. "I hope your new friend works half as hard."

"This is my cousin, Florencia. She just got here from Sonora. She'll do real good. I promise."

"Well," Esther said as she negotiated a left turn in the swirling, jerking traffic, "just tell her to do her job and don't steal anything and we'll get along just fine. Tell her that."

Lupe spoke to Florencia in rapid Spanish. Florencia smiled and nodded and answered in a soft voice.

"*Sí. Voy a trabajar muy fuerte.*"

"She says she will work very hard for you, Esther. I have told her you are a very good boss. She appreciates that you give her a chance."

"Tell her this is a growing business. We got new accounts coming in all the time. Tell her if she hustles she can make money with me."

Lupe told her.

"She says she understands, Esther. She will not disappoint you."

"Good. *Bueno.*" Esther smiled over at Florencia. "Let's pick up some doughnuts for later."

Four hours later they sat on the floor of an architect's office in Culver City, eating the doughnuts and drinking tepid Cokes. They had cleaned two dentists' offices in the Wilshire District, a writer's cubbyhole in Brentwood, a suite of law offices, and a commercial artist's studio in Santa Monica.

Esther stuffed half a French cruller into her mouth and wet it with a quick shot of Coke. She chewed for a moment, then spoke with her mouth full.

"After we eat, I'm gonna polish this floor and the one in the hall. We haven't got to them in three weeks, and they look it. You two get at the bathroom and dust the big drafting table, okay?"

"Okay," Lupe said.

Esther watched Florencia eat her doughnut. She ate with an exaggerated fastidiousness that seemed incongruous for such a large girl. She took small bites with big, blocklike teeth. Her massive jaws hardly seemed to move as she chewed. Her face belonged in one of the Aztec murals the Chicano artists painted on the Eastside underpasses.

Florencia saw Esther looking at her and smiled shyly, shielding her mouth with the back of her hand. Esther smiled back. I'd smile a lot more, she thought, if you worked a little harder. Esther's shirt clung to her body, damp with perspiration. So did Lupe's. Florencia's clothes were fresh and dry. Esther was going to miss Maria.

She finished her cruller, wiped her fingers on her faded jeans, and drained the last of her warm Coke. She passed around a pack of Salem Lights. Lupe took one; Florencia declined with a dainty smile. Esther lit her cigarette, then Lupe's, then dropped the burnt match into the empty soft drink can. Stretching out her legs, she leaned back against the wall and exhaled a jet of gray smoke with a tired sigh.

She stared up at the ceiling and said, "You know, Lupe, I really *am* getting more and more clients all the time. Next week I got to go talk to a man about doing a whole building. A whole corporation. Two floors. Fifty offices. Every night." She dropped her eyes to Lupe's. "You think we can handle it, Loop?"

"No problema," Lupe said. "We can do it easy."

"It'll be a lot of work."

"No problema, Esther."

Esther glanced at Florencia and said nothing.

"Don't worry," Lupe said quickly. "She's just new. She work out fine."

"I hope so, Lupe. 'Cause there's gonna be a lot of work."

Florencia saw both of the other women looking at her, then averted her eyes and fidgeted with her shoelaces.

Esther took another deep drag from her cigarette.

"You know, Loop, I can see a time real soon when I'm gonna have to run two crews. There's just gonna be too much work. I'm expecting you to boss that second crew."

Lupe smiled and nodded.

"There's a lot of things involved, though. First, I need to get a second vehicle. Another station wagon. Or maybe a van. Maybe I'll take a van and give you the wagon. I always wanted one of them big-ass vans. Can you drive, Loop?"

"Sí."

"Okay, but do you have a license?"

"No, but I can get one, Esther."

"Okay, okay. But that's just transportation. I get a car and you get a license to drive. I still have to get another floor polisher, another vacuum cleaner." Esther paused for a moment and then smiled. "I guess a new bunch of dust rags'd be cheap enough. But what about girls? I'm gonna need a bunch of new girls."

"I can get them, Esther."

"Good girls," Esther continued. "Girls we can trust. Girls who won't steal. You know, the people in these offices, they know a nigger and a bunch of Mexicans got keys to come in after midnight, they start counting the paper clips. One pencil missing and we're out on our ass. *Finito.* And the word gets around *muy pronto.* These people, they'll go out of their way to bad-mouth you if they catch you pilfering."

"I'll get only good girls. Honest girls."

"And hard workers, Loop," Esther said, glancing again at Florencia, who had cradled her head in her arms on a desktop and was dropping off to sleep from all the English. "I'll expect you to work them as hard as you work yourself. That's what being a boss means. Think you can do it?"

"I'll do a good job, Esther."

"I'm not talking about all this happening tomorrow, you understand."

"I understand."

But someday pretty soon I'm gonna have to run a second crew. You're the only girl ever worked for me I'd *even* begin to trust with the job of running it."

"I won't disappoint you, Esther."

"I know you won't, Lupe."

The two women stared at each other for a moment, then they simultaneously broke into wide grins.

"Hey, Loop," Esther said. "You think this is the way Rockefeller got started?"

Lupe laughed. "Howard Hughes, at least."

Esther threw back her head and laughed with her. "Yeah, I'll be president of Esther Phibbs Enterprises. Incorporated. You can be my vice-president. In charge of . . . personnel development. We'll *clean up!*"

They laughed together.

"Yeah," Lupe giggled. "Pretty soon we'll be in the big bucks. We gonna be fat-cat American capitalists!"

"Yeah, we'll be driving around Beverly Hills in them little bitty Mercedes, buying dresses at Giorgio's, some shoes at Gucci's, getting our hair done by Jo*sey.*"

The girls roared. Florencia, who had been snoring lightly, woke up with a start, frightened by the raucous laughter.

"And when we get tired spending money," Lupe sputtered, tears welling in her eyes, "we'll *take* some *lunch* at Ma Maison!"

Esther slid down the wall holding her stomach. She lay on her back and gulped for breath. Between gulps, she managed to croak, *"Yo' Mama Maison!"* and they were off on a fresh jag.

Lupe elaborately held out an imaginary glass, pinky finger extended.

"Hey, waiter! *Oye, pendejo!* More jampagne, *por favor!*"

Esther curled up in a ball and rocked from side to side. Lupe pounded on the wall with her fist. Florencia, bewildered and confused, managed to chuckle.

"I'm gonna pee on myself!" Lupe shrieked, then jumped up and raced off to the bathroom. That made Esther laugh even harder. She lay on the floor and gave herself up to fits of laughter that convulsed her like sneezes. Lupe returned from the bathroom and, seeing each other, they started again. Finally half a minute passed without either of them laughing. Esther sighed and sat up. She dried her eyes with the tail of her work shirt.

"I guess it's time to go to work."

"Guess so."

That made both of them chuckle. They stood, Florencia quickly following.

"Okay," Esther said. "I'll get the floor polisher out of the wagon. You two clean that bathroom."

"Okay," Lupe said. She nodded to Florencia. *"Vamanos."*

Esther opened the back door leading to the parking lot. She shook her head and muttered to herself. "Yo' Mama Maison," and giggled again.

SATURDAY
August 4

$3{:}47$ *AM* The Doberman tore at the chain-link. Her fangs gleamed in the streetlights and her eyes were clouded with fury and hate.

Walker slapped the fence again and again with the rolled newspaper, and the crazed animal leapt high, twisting and turning with every jump, in a deadly ballet. Finally, Walker stuck the newspaper through the chain-link and the Doberman tore it away and ripped it apart with violent, head-wrenching motions.

Walker stepped back from the fence and laughed. The dog froze over the drifting bits of newsprint, snarling at him. A savage growl rumbled deep in her chest, like an idling engine.

Walker laughed again—a short, boyish giggle—then his face blanked and he started an easy jog eastward down the block. The dog ran ahead of him and stationed herself at the corner where the fence right-angled with a brick wall. As Walker passed, the bitch threw herself at the fence in one final futile attack. Walker seemed not to notice.

He jogged east for several more blocks and turned north up a sleeping street of two-story stucco duplexes. He ran on for three more blocks, then turned down a graveled alley behind a squat, unremarkable building of reinforced concrete. He stepped into a shadowy doorway and waited. His breathing was light and even. Headlights lit up the street and he pressed against the doorway until the car had passed. After a few minutes, he put his hand on the doorknob and slowly turned it. It was locked. He waited. Somewhere far away a siren wailed. Another car passed. Walker reached over his shoulder and dug around in the canvas backpack he was wearing until he found what he was looking for. He waited a few more minutes, then stepped out of the doorway and into the street. The street was empty north and south. He wrote on the building's flat gray side with the aerosol paint can—long, looping, unhurried letters that seemed to paint themselves. When he finished, he stepped back and admired his work. Then quickly, as an afterthought, he slashed a crude two-stroke cross. Then another. Without looking again, he slipped back into the alley. Running smoothly, in five minutes he was almost a mile away.

7:33 *AM* At the first ring, Gold swung his legs over the edge of the bed and sat up, watching the phone. It was an old trick he'd been using for over fifteen years now. He watched it ring and with every ring he willed himself up to a higher level of lucidity. From painful experience he had learned that an abruptly awakened cop should never speak on the phone until he was in full control of himself. Once a skinny little snitch of his that everybody called Charlie Brown had called him at four in the morning and talked to him in urgent, whispered tones. Gold had grunted and gone back to sleep with the receiver still in his hand. An hour later he sat up in bed with a start, waking Evelyn beside him. Three weeks later some Mexican kids playing in a vacant lot in Boyle Heights had found Charlie Brown's rotting, throat-slashed body, wrapped in a tarp and stuffed down a sewage sinkhole.

Usually Gold felt together enough to answer the phone on the fourth or fifth ring. This morning it took seven. As he reached for it, he saw his hand shake a little more than usual. Big night.

"Yeah?" he said thickly.

"Jack. It's Honeywell."

"What's happening, Honey?"

"Jack, we're in deep shit. Tom Forrester from the chief's office called this morning."

"Yeah?"

"They gonna hang us by our balls over this thing yesterday with the Dog. That Beverly Hills bitch made a formal complaint naming both of us, but especially you. The chief wants to see you in his office Monday morning at eight o'clock sharp. I'm next at nine."

Gold sighed and rubbed his eyes with his fingertips.

"Did Tom say what the asshole wanted?"

"Well, he's not completely sure, Jack, but he thinks Chief Huntz is gonna ask for your badge. He's gonna ask you first to take retirement. Then, if you refuse, he's gonna ask for your badge. As for me, Tom said they're just gonna slap my wrist. Maybe a written reprimand. Maybe not. Tom said Huntz was fuming at first. Wanted to suspend me for a month. Then he cooled down. Now all he wants is you."

"What else is new?" Gold said with a Yiddish inflection.

"What do you think we should do, Jack?"

"Nothing. Go see the man Monday morning. That's all we can do."

"That's how I see it too."

"All we did was our job. If they can't see that, then that's their problem."

"They can make it our problem, Jack. That's *their* job."

"Fuck 'em."

There was a short silence. Then Gold said, "Honey?"

"Yeah, Jack?"

"I'm sorry if I got you caught up in this thing. It's just Huntz. He's always had a hard-on for me."

"Hey, partner, like you said. All we did was our job. Fuck 'em if they can't take a joke."

"All right, Honey."

"All right, Jack."

"See you down there Monday morning."

"Right," Honeywell said and laughed nervously.

Gold sat for a moment after hanging up, trying to collect his thoughts. The alarm clock on the cluttered bedside table went off, making him jump a little. Nerves are shot, he thought as he turned off the alarm. The digital clock read 7:45. Gold tried to sweep the cobwebs from his mind and remember why he had to get up at 7:45 on a Saturday morning. Then he remembered. Today was the day of his son's bar mitzvah. Or *her* son's bar mitzvah. His shoulders slumped and he wondered, with a grim smile, if it was too early for a drink.

Gold stood and walked to the bathroom. The efficiency apartment was small and crammed with cheap furniture that looked as though it had all been rented. Which it had—years ago. On a plastic-topped, overflowing desk were several framed photographs of a chubby-cheeked blonde in various stages of growing up—baby, child, teenager, young woman. Over the desk was taped a final snapshot of the same blonde, holding a laughing baby. Also in the picture was a bearded dark man in his late twenties. In the bathroom, Gold leaned over the toilet and urinated. He suddenly became aware his head was throbbing. He shook down the last few drops, then walked naked to the kitchen and the refrigerator. Ripping the tab off a can of Coors, he drank it down in slow, regular swallows, then opened another and sat heavily at the plastic dinette table. Standing sentinel with the salt and pepper shakers was an economy-size bottle of Bayer's aspirin. Gold shook out four and washed them down with the frigid beer. He belched loudly, beginning to feel better. He finished the beer and crushed the can, then threw the two empties into the trash bag next to the stove.

When is the day of your's son's bar mitzvah a day to be dreaded? When you're ol' Jack Gold, he thought.

When is your son not your son?

"Riddles," Gold said aloud. "Fuck it."

He scrambled two eggs and toasted some stale English muffins he found in the back of the refrigerator. He started to make some instant coffee, then turned off the fire under the kettle and opened another Coors. Why be awake today? He put the beer and the food on the dinette table. He opened the front door a crack and the sunlight leaked in. Across the courtyard two fat old ladies in floppy straw hats were already pruning their rose bushes. Gold found a musty bathrobe on the floor of his closet and tied it around himself. Squinting against the sunshine, he stepped barefoot out onto the slate tiles of the courtyard. Instantly a fluffy little dog that had been hiding behind one of the old women's legs raced to the middle of the courtyard and barked wildly with little stiff-legged jolts. The old ladies looked up and smiled.

"Ah, it's Mr. Gold. Good morning, Mr. Gold. Look, Celia, it's Mr. Gold. *Hush,* Genghis!"

"*Lieutenant* Gold, Toby. He's a police officer. A *lieutenant* yet. Shut up that dog, Toby!"

"Good morning, Mrs. Ackermann, Mrs. Shearer. How are you ladies today?" Gold searched with quiet desperation along the steps and under the hedge. The little dog was flying about the courtyard, snarling and snapping at Gold's ankles.

"Genghis! Be a good boy!" Mrs. Ackermann admonished.

"Did you lose something, Lieutenant Gold?" asked Mrs. Shearer.

Gold searched in rude silence for a moment, then realized the ladies were watching him.

"Uh—I can't seem to find my newspaper."

"Oh, it's that damn paper boy. He comes running hell-bent through here every morning. Such a racket! Scares my little Genghis to *death.* Poor thing barks for an hour after that. I can't get him back to sleep. Maybe you could speak to him. Maybe if a po—"

"Ah! Here it is!" He pulled the paper out of the hedge and retreated inside, saying, "Good-bye, ladies."

Mrs. Ackermann was still talking, but Gold quickly closed the door. At the table the food was cold, the beer warm. As he ate, he read the headlines on the top half of the page. The city was going through another budgetary crisis. The continuing smog was said to be responsible for two deaths so far. In Riverside County a hilltop fire had destroyed half a dozen million-dollar homes. A CHP officer was killed in a shootout in Bakersfield. Gold didn't recognize him from the picture. Gold flipped the paper over. In the lower right-hand corner was a photograph of a gutted, smoldering building. Over the front entrance a shattered Star of David was barely recognizable. SYNAGOGUE FIRE-BOMBED IN GENEVA. Of all places, Gold thought. Geneva. Under the photo the legend read: WAVE OF ANTI-SEMITISM SWEEPS EUROPE. SEE STORY PAGE 3. Gold turned to page 3. Another photograph showed a Jewish restaurant in Paris that had been raked by machine-gun fire. The accompanying story said that in the past seventy-two hours Western European cities had weathered a frenzy of attacks against Jewish and Israeli institutions. In Rome the Israeli ambassador had been ambushed, barely escaping with his life. His limousine had been riddled with bullets. In London the secretary of an eminent Jewish publisher who had espoused strong support of the Israeli government had had her hands blown off by a letter bomb meant for her employer. Credit for most of the atrocities had been claimed by the radical arm of the PLO or the Red Brigade, but a few of the later acts were being attributed to a new group of European ultraconservatives. They seemed to have their own reasons for hating the Jews. The report went on to say that it appeared almost certain that the majority of the attacks had been initiated and orchestrated by a central cadre of international terrorists, with the active support and assistance of several Arab states. The right-wing incidents seemed to be of the copycat variety. Getting in on a good thing. No arrests had been made.

Gold finished his breakfast and beer. He washed the fork and plate perfunctorily and put them in the rack to dry. On the way to the bathroom he flicked on the stereo that dominated a small bookcase against one wall. The room was instantly flooded with a tenor saxophone's plaintive wail. Coleman Hawkins, he registered unconsciously. He listened a little more closely, trying to recognize the rhythm section. Ray Brant on piano, Kenny Clark on drums, and it could be George Duvivier or Al McKibbon on bass. Recorded '58 or '59. Gold didn't remember the label.

In the bathroom he turned on the shower and waited for the water to get hot. He had acquired his taste for jazz back when he was with Narcotics. A million years ago. At that time there had been many jazz clubs around town—a lot more than now—and several of them had become dealers' havens. Most of them were up on Sunset, a few down Western, some on Washington at the edge of the black ghetto. Gold had spent countless nights in those dark, smoky clubs. Looking for dope dealers, spying on dope fiends, waiting for dope deals. And night after night he found himself enjoying and understanding the music played in those clubs more than any music he had ever heard before. The arabesque and abstract solos that at first seemed like so much bleating became, to his ear, both lyrical and logical. The swing, the beat of it all—which Gold at first had felt was no more than something animalistic for a junked-out drummer to nod along with—he saw finally was really the pulse of life, the throb of a heartbeat. Once given breath it seemed to move inexorably forward on its own energy. After that revelation, whenever he found himself busting one of these musicians, as he often did, he treated them with kindness and respect. The musicians understood him and returned that respect. He became a kind of legend among them. They swapped war stories about Detective Gold. They said that he could listen to you stretch out on a couple of choruses and tell you whether you were high or not, how much shit you had done up, how long ago, and who you bought the shit from. Just by the way you played. Gold was honored. He felt pity as well as respect for the players he arrested. The pushers he took in the alley behind the club and broke their jaws or their ribs. The Good Old Days. The ancient days. Before the Beatles, before LSD, before revolution. The pre-historic era, when the truly *hip* people still wore pinstripes, shot heroin, and listened to jazz. Twenty-five, thirty years ago. Gold hadn't been with the force long then. He had been a comer. A young lion. He made detective in record time and had been assigned to Narcotics. He stayed with Narcotics fifteen years—until the day Angelique died. He had met Angelique in one of those clubs. Slim, sleek Angelique, with long, straight hair and *café au lait* skin. Sweet, beautiful Angelique, with her brains all over the blue bedspread.

Gold stepped into the shower. The hot water drummed against his back and shoulders, clearing out the last dusty corners of his mind.

The Day the Music Died. That was from a song. That's what the kids called the day some rock 'n' roller died. That's what he called the day Angelique died. The Day the Music Died. The day everything died. He could see Huntz's smooth, sneering face. In that little apartment off Vermont. Huntz wasn't chief then. He was with Internal Affairs. I'm going to cover your ass because you're a cop, Huntz had said. But you'll never get another promotion. I'll see to that. You killed that girl. Gold had been a lieutenant then. He was still a lieutenant. One of the oldest on the force. Huntz had kept his promise.

The Day the Music Died. The day his career died. The day his marriage died. He could see Evelyn's face now, twisted, contorted, tear-streaked. Evelyn banging on the car's windshield with her fists, screaming, *"You bastard! You bastard!"* His clothes were scattered all over the rain-wet front lawn of that little house in Culver City, all torn and ripped and shredded. *"You bastard!"* She had beat at the car's windows. She had *kicked* at the car's windows. He had never thought Evelyn capable of such passion.

The Day the Music Died.

Wendy had seen Evelyn beating on the car. She had been—what?—

seven then. A chubby little blond girl with frightened eyes hiding behind the front door. And Gold had thought, Oh, God, does Wendy know about Angelique too?

And two months after that, after he had found an apartment—this apartment—the phone had rung in the middle of the night. It was Evelyn's voice, dripping with venom. "I'm pregnant, you bastard. And you'll never see it. I'm praying to God it's the son you always wanted. Because you'll never see it. I promise."

And she had kept her promise, too.

Oh, he had seen pictures. Snapshots of a slim, blond boy with Gold's blue eyes. He had seen the photographs at his mother's before she died. She and Evelyn had stayed good friends. Evelyn was at his mother's side when she died. It was *him* his mother couldn't stand, after That Day.

"How could you, Jack?"

"You threw everything away, Jack."

"He doesn't even know who his real father is, Jack."

"You had it all, Jack. And you threw it away."

"For a *shvartzeh*, Jack?"

It was all connected. Interconnected. Huntz and Angelique and Evelyn and Wendy and everything. Images ran through his mind like a film slightly out of focus. With a Coleman Hawkins soundtrack. Only it wasn't the Hawk. It was Mint Julep Jackson, who played tenor with the biggest, warmest sound in his horn and the biggest, warmest load in his arm.

"Take care of her," Julep had said, his big black face dripping with anxious junkie sweat, his eyes heavy-lidded. "She fragile, man," Julep had said in his thick Delta patois, "she fragile. Take care of her."

He had busted Mint Julep in the tiny dressing room of the Falconeer Lounge. Gold had found the heroin in the bell of the saxophone, right where the snitch had said it would be.

"Lordy, Lordy, Lordy. That's all she roll for me," Mint Julep had said. "That last judge say I take one more fall and I go away for life. That's all she roll."

"I don't make the rules, 'Lip. If you want to play you got to pay."

"I know it, Mr. Gold. I know it."

Mint Julep was a big man, almost three hundred pounds, and now he was crying, his tears mingling with his sweat in the hot dirty little dressing room. His fat arms were handcuffed behind his back and he was sitting on his hands in a rickety red plastic chair.

"Lookahere, Mr. Gold. You always been real straight with me, so I got to ask you for a favor." He looked up at Gold. "There this girl, she been staying with me. Angelique St. Germaine, you know the girl? Real pretty thing. High-yeller gal. She could pass, you know the one I mean? Angelique St. Germaine? Fancies herself a singer. Well, she been staying with me, you know, and I really care about her. I love that little girl. Lordy, *Lordy,* how I love that little girl. Well, Mr. Gold, you got to help me. You got to go over my place, get that girl, and put her on a bus back to Loosiana. 'Cause if you don't, them pimps around here be all over her like flies on honey, and it would really pain me to be up in the joint and hear 'bout that happening. I seen how they be looking at her when I bring her around, and, Mr. Gold, she too sweet and innocent to help herself. She ain't strong, you know? She fragile, Mr. Gold. Please, Mr. Gold. You got to take care of her."

I took care of her all right.

Fragile Angelique. Sweet Angelique. With long, slender fingers that played like feathers up and down your spine while you fucked her. Beautiful Angelique, who would lock her legs around you when she came and came, screaming and sobbing, until the neighbors banged on the wall.

"What are you people—animals?"

And they had barked and mooed and crowed and howled until they fell into each other's sweaty arms, laughing until they cried.

"Oh, Jack. I need you so much. I need you more than *it.*"

More than shit?

"Take care of her, man. She fragile."

"I love you so much, Jack."

More than it?

Gold stepped out of the shower and toweled dry. In the other room Miles was playing with his Harmon mute. Red Garland, piano. Philly Jo Jones, drums. Paul Chambers, bass. Nineteen fifty-seven? Before Miles's downfall. Before he became afraid to be tender. Before we all became afraid to be tender.

He thought of Cookie last night. Poor Cookie. A whore who isn't allowed to fuck is like an artist not allowed to paint. But how could he tell her it had been almost fourteen years since he'd had a woman?

Since the Day the Music Died.

How could he tell her that he only saw her because she made a woman dead for fourteen years seem a little bit alive? How could he tell her that she was a stand-in for a ghost?

Gold checked the time. It was just after nine. As good a time as any. He poured himself a double Scotch and sat at the dinette.

He didn't have to go today. He could just sit here and drink until it didn't hurt anymore. Who would miss him? Oh, sure, Evelyn had sent him an invitation. But she was just trying to open an old wound. She just wanted to parade before him the son she had denied him. Maybe flaunt her new husband. New? They had been married twelve years now. That was almost as long as she and Gold had been together. Evelyn Markowitz. Dr. and Mrs. Stanley Markowitz. And their son, Peter. Peter Markowitz. Well, at least Wendy had kept his name. Until she got married. Now she was Mrs. Howie Gettelman. And their son, Joshua. He looked at the photograph over the desk. Wendy had called and asked him to come today. Chubby, blond Wendy, who, when he finally won visitation rights, had been waiting at the curb with an overnight case. "Daddy, do you still love me? Are you divorcing *me,* too?"

What a fucking weekend. Chief Huntz Monday morning and this bar mitzvah today. Too many memories. Sounds like a song, Gold thought. Too Many Memories. And So Little Hope.

Wendy knew he would come if she asked him. He had never refused her anything. Hot dogs at Disneyland. Summers in Spain. All these years Wendy had been the only one who wanted to be with him. The only one who had loved him, forgiven him. And Gold knew Evelyn had not made it easy for her. Through his mother, Evelyn would learn what Gold would be giving Wendy for Hannukah or on her birthday, and then would give her the same present, only a much more expensive version. She had the money now to play those kind of games. The good doctor's money. Dr. Markowitz, who was famous in Beverly Hills, Bel-Air, and Encino among women who were slipping into the dark side of forty. Nip and tuck. Lift and tighten. With a lucrative sideline of reconstructing deviated septums for those same women's little cokehead sons and daughters.

Gold carried his drink back into the bathroom. He inspected himself in the mirror. He was deteriorating. Like a car when one thing goes wrong, then another, then one morning it just won't start. His face wasn't so much lined as filigreed. Tiny rivers of wrinkles coursed down from the corners of his eyes, the edges of his mouth. His complexion was pale and translucent. I look like a corpse, he thought. Except for his nose. The whisky was breaking down the capillaries and his nose shone with a rosy gloss. An Irishman's nose. A corned-beef-and-cabbage paint job on this lox-and-bagel beak.

Gold sipped his Scotch and looked down at his body's reflection. All his life he had been on the thin side, but that definitely wasn't the case anymore. Hard, muscled legs were crowned by a bulging, egg-shaped trunk. And he wasn't sure but he could swear his arms were getting smaller, frailer, thinner. He was shrinking like his ninety-year-old Uncle Manny. But only in the places where he wasn't expanding. His shoulders and chest were covered with heavily matted, white-tipped hair that turned dark again as it grew down his belly and into his crotch. Angelique had said he was an ape. A *Great* Ape. She had loved to run her fingers over his chest, twisting and curling the hair into little whorls with her graceful fingers.

Gold grimaced at himself. Dead fourteen years and every time he looked into a mirror he thought of her.

He shaved and combed his hair. His hair was silver streaked with black now, instead of the other way around, and he wore it trimmed fashionably short, only he had worn it that way since long before it came into fashion. At least he wasn't going bald the way his old man had before he died.

Gold started to dress in his best suit, a dark blue wool mix, then remembered the day would be a scorcher and reached for his lightweight summer brown. He had pulled both legs of the trousers on when he stopped, yanked them off again, and dressed quickly in the blue.

For a man never overly concerned about his appearance, he thought, you sure are antsy this morning.

"I need another drink," he said aloud, without realizing that he had.

As Gold poured the drink, he checked the time. It was almost ten.

He slumped into a small, uncomfortable armchair in front of the TV and lit his first cigar of the day. Digging under the cushion he found the remote control and punched it on. The stereo still played. Some piece of fusion crap that Gold hated. He flew around the television channels, past the cartoon shows, the black awareness committees, the brown awareness panels, until he found an early baseball game from the East Coast. The Angels at New York. He watched a boring half inning. Nothing went out of the infield. Wally Joyner struck out. When the commercials came on he spun through the channels again. He stopped when he spotted "Talk to the Reporter." Gold liked that show. The anchor was a beautiful light-complexioned black woman named Audra Kingsley. She reminded him of Angelique.

"With us in the studio this morning," Audra was saying from between peach-glossed lips, "is a very special guest, City Councilman Harvey L. Orenzstein, from the West Los Angeles City Council District. Councilman Orenzstein, who many people expect to make a strong bid to be elected Los Angeles's first Jewish mayor in the upcoming election, was not scheduled to 'Talk to the Reporter' this morning, but we asked the councilman to come down to the studio at this time to discuss with us the ugly wave of anti-Semitism that has burned across Europe in the past week. And we understand that there may now be events of much more immediate concern to our viewers. After this brief message, we will go into these and other matters with City Councilman Harvey L. Orenzstein. When he will 'Talk to the Reporter.'"

Audra Kingsley was beautiful, but not the way Angelique was, had been. The skin color and the hair were the same, but Angelique's eyes had been light, hazel, almost green sometimes. Angelique would have hated Audra

Kingsley because she hated television. She hated movies, too. She couldn't sit through one. She hated rock 'n' roll, the Motown Sound, and fucking with the lights on. She was a woman of passionate tastes.

She fragile, man.

She used to say that everything she loved started with a *J.* Jazz, junk, and Jack Gold.

And jiving. That's what she called sex—jiving.

"Welcome, Councilman Orenzstein. And thank you for coming to 'Talk to the Reporter.' "

"Thank you for inviting me, Audra."

Harvey Orenzstein was a floppy bear of a man in a wrinkled suit and a white shirt with a wilted collar. He had come to politics from the campus revolts of the sixties, and although his hair was no longer shoulder-length and the faded blue jeans had been forsaken, he still made a five-hundred-dollar, custom-made, English-tailored three-piece look cheap and ill fitting. The first time he ran for office his aides had discovered that he didn't own a pair of socks. Of *any* color. He had worn only sneakers and sandals for years. He was a campaign manager's nightmare; but the Jewish liberal Westside reelected him with stubborn regularity. Even Gold voted for him.

"Councilman Orenzstein. Where have you come from this morning to visit our studios?"

"Audra, I am sorry to say I have come here from the site of the sickening desecration of a synagogue."

"And where was this desecration, Councilman? In Paris? In Geneva? In any of the European cities we've been reading about lately?"

"No, Audra, I am even sorrier to say, it was right here in Los Angeles."

"Will you tell us about it?"

"Well, Audra, I received a phone call early this morning. It was from my good friend Rabbi Martin Rosen at Temple Beth Achim. He was in a terribly, terribly agitated state, as you can well imagine. He gave me the shocking news that his synagogue had been defaced. Sometime between midnight last night and six this morning, when the maintenance man arrived to get the temple ready for Shabbes services, someone had spray-painted scurrilous and obscene anti-Semitic *filth* over the outer walls and across the entrance door of his synagogue. I calmed Rabbi Rosen down and told him I would get over there a.s.a.p. Right away. As soon as I hung up the phone rang again."

Gold's phone rang.

"—was a member of the congregation, one of my constituents, telling me about the desecration, and asking me—no, *demanding* that I do something about it. In fact the telephone never stopped ringing for the ten or fifteen minutes it took me to leave the house. Not all members of the congregation, not all even Jewish, but all of them citizens of this city disgusted and infuriated by this kind—"

Gold rose from the armchair and answered his phone. He listened intently, grunting occasionally, still watching the TV screen.

"We immediately sent a film crew there and we have some tape we're about to roll. Councilman Orenzstein, will you tell us what we're seeing?"

Audra Kingsley's face dissolved into blackness, then the image of a gray concrete wall jumped onto the screen. Across the wall, in looping red letters, was spray-painted:

KILL THE JEWS

KIKES DIE

And then the two crosses:

A small gray man in a pearl-gray suit was pointing excitedly to the wall and speaking to two uniformed policeman.

"That's Rabbi Rosen. You can see the state he was in."

Gold barked a few short questions into the phone. His face was grim and his jaw set.

"Councilman Orenzstein, viewing this tape in the light of recent events, one obvious question *must* be asked. Do you think that the recent attack on Temple Beth Achim was part of a concerted international effort? Could the perpetrators of this act, here in Los Angeles, be in any way linked to the terrorist atrocities in Europe?"

"Well, Audra, at this point I think it's too early to discount anything."

Gold hung up the phone. He tossed down the rest of his drink and clamped his cigar firmly in the corner of his mouth. He pushed off the TV but left the stereo on. Halfway out the door he hesitated, then came back in and got his gun and holster from their place in the bedside drawer. This time he made it out, but not before noticing they were playing Mint Julep Jackson's recording of "Blue Angel." Julep had written that tune for Angelique.

What a *verkakhte* day, he thought.

$11:23$ *AM* Beth Shalom Reform Temple stood over the San Diego Freeway like a castle above a moat, shining white in the hot and smoggy glare. Gold had taken off his coat and was leaning against the fender of his battered green Ford, sweating profusely and wishing he was anywhere else. Any*one* else. He had parked at the far end of the temple's lot, a lot filled with Sevilles, Mercedes sedans, and an occasional Rolls, and had watched, chewing on his cigar, as latecomers arrived and hustled inside. The last one had been twenty minutes ago. It was now or never.

Gold flung away the stub of wet cigar and strode quickly across the parking lot and up the front steps. Stopping at the entrance, he pulled on his coat and withdrew from the inside pocket a blue, gold-trimmed yarmulke. He placed the yarmulke carefully on the crown of his head, opened the door, and entered.

Inside it was cool and dim. Sunlight filtered through blue-stained glass windows. Gold stood in the rear and watched a boy with straight blond hair standing at the dais and reading from the scroll. The cantor stood behind him and to his left, the rabbi to his right, smiling and nodding approval.

Where had the blond hair come from? Wendy's, too? Some long-dead Ukrainian soldier with a gun and a hard-on? A German storekeeper resettled in Russia who had held out to some pretty young thing venturing out from the ghetto the promise of a good meal or a good job in return for a good fuck?

"Today I am a man," the boy said nervously. *"Hayom ani mekabel et hamizvot."*

"Thank you all for coming to my *simcha*. And a special thanks to my mother and father. And also to the rabbi and the cantor. For today is the most important day of my life."

Gold stepped outside and was lighting another cigar when someone slipped an arm suggestively around his waist and started gently massaging his ass.

"Hi, Jack," a voice breathed in his ear. "It's good to see you." Gold was hit by the heavy scent of expensive perfume. He turned to face a busty blond woman in her early fifties, well dressed and well tended. She wore one of those deliberately tattered outfits that was all the rage that summer, and she was a little too old for it. Around her neck a thick rope of gold and diamonds screamed for attention. She seemed to have a ring on every finger.

"Jack, I don't think you've met my husband. This is Arim. Arim, this is my *best* ex-brother-in-law, Jack Gold." Carol laughed lightly.

Gold had heard of Arim. He was Carol's fourth husband. Or was it fifth? He told everyone he was Persian, but he was really an Iranian Jew who had gotten out before the Ayatollah madness. And *with* his money. None of Carol's husbands had been poor, but Arim was rumored to be the wealthiest of the lot. He was a short, slight, insignificant man with dark hair and dark eyes that darted everywhere suspiciously. If I were married to Carol, Gold thought, I'd be suspicious too. Arim was also dressed expensively. A light blue shirt with an off-white collar that reeked of Rodeo Drive. A darker blue silk tie that Gold guessed would set you back at least fifty. He didn't even want to speculate on the suit.

The two men shook hands perfunctorily as Carol laughed. "At least I think he's the best." She leered at Gold. "He never let me find out, did you, Jack?"

Carol was Evelyn's younger sister. She had been rubbing her leg against his under dinner tables and leaning against him as they passed in halls for almost thirty years now. Ever since he had first started dating Evelyn, fresh out of the navy and full of self-righteous zeal. Every time Gold picked Evelyn up for a dinner date to Chinatown or a movie on Hollywood Boulevard, Carol would be there. Even if she had a date of her own—a law student from USC, a dentist from Pasadena—she would sit them down and make them wait while she fawned over Gold. Doting on him. *Leaning* over him. Always in something low-cut. *Leaning* over to put a cocktail napkin under a highball. *Leaning* over to offer a tray of cashews. Carol had always been proud of her tits, and they had done well by her. Four husbands—or was it five? But she had always wanted Gold, and he had always eluded her. Even after he and Evelyn were married it hadn't stopped. Whenever Evelyn left the room Carol would be on him—whispering, groping, moistening her lips with her tongue. It always amazed Gold that Evelyn never suspected what her horny little sister was up to. And then one day after the divorce became final, he had stopped by his mother's apartment with some groceries and Carol had been there. "Just visiting. Just stopping by for a cup of tea," she said, smiling. And when Mama Gold excused herself to go to the bathroom, Carol had arched across the room like a cat, rubbing her open palm against his crotch.

"You're not Evelyn's anymore," she whispered. "She's not between us now."

Gold had backed against a wall.

"Carol, for God's sake. My mother."

She slipped her hand behind his belt and down his pants, clutched his cock and caressed it lightly with her fingertips.

"I'll show you things Evelyn can't even imagine."

"My mother's in the next room, Carol."

She was jerking him off and grinding herself against his hip. "I'll give it to you like you've never had it before. *Never!* Not even from your black bitch!"

Before Gold understood what was happening, he had wrapped the fingers of his left hand tightly around Carol's throat and slammed her against the kitchen wall, sending a spice rack crashing to the floor. He pulled his clenched fist back and held it there, poised and trembling.

"Shut your filthy mouth!" he hissed from between gritted teeth.

Carol tore at his fingers around her throat, trying to pry them loose. Her eyes were aflame with fear and lust and excitement. She glared at him defiantly, triumphantly.

"You *did* kill her!" she whispered. "You *did* kill her!"

Gold wanted to smash her face then. He wanted to put his fist right through the back of her head. Instead, he threw a short, straight punch that plunged through the drywall, six inches to the right of Carol's cheek. Carol made a small, squeaky sound like a mouse panicking in a trap.

"My God, Jack!" Gold's mother gasped from the doorway. "What on earth are you doing?"

He had turned and stalked out of the house. An hour later, doing ninety miles an hour on the San Bernardino Freeway, he realized he had broken a knuckle.

Now, Carol stood before him, her makeup starting to run in the August heat, her arm linked with her toylike husband's.

"Wasn't it a beautiful service, Jack?" she oozed.

"Yes, it was, Carol."

"It was very, uh, nice of you to come." She tried to affect a piercing stare, but the melting mascara made her eyes water. Her tiny husband was showing definite signs of boredom. His attention had been diverted to a young redhead in a white sundress who was bouncing down the temple steps.

"Such a beautiful boy, Jack," Carol said. She fished a wadded Kleenex out of her purse and dabbed at the corners of her eyes. Gold said nothing. People were beginning to stream out of the temple and down the stairs. A few of them eyed Gold with interest. Arim was crowded against Gold, and Gold was assailed by a strong human musk emanating from under the Rodeo Drive suit.

"It was a beautiful gesture, your coming today," Carol said.

Gold sighed. It was really going to be a long afternoon. Maybe he had made a mistake in coming.

"It was a beautiful gesture. It was a beautiful service and he's a beautiful boy. And even though it's smoggy as shit and hot as a bastard, it's a beautiful day. Everything is beautiful, Carol. Fucking beautiful."

At the harsh tone of Gold's words, Arim's attention snapped back to Gold. Carol merely shook her head sadly.

"Jack, Jack, Jack. So impetuous. So much anger. Such a macho. Even now at your age. Won't you ever change?"

"I guess not, Carol." Gold puffed on his cigar. "I'm not a bottle of wine. I don't mellow with time."

"Oh, Jack, things could have been so different," Carol said wistfully. Her husband's eyes darted between Carol and Gold. His ferret ears perked up. Carol took Gold's hand and gave it a squeeze.

"Things never work out the way we want them to, do they?" Carol clung to Gold's hand. Gold could *smell* Arim's heat rising.

"Things work out the way they work out, Carol. That's the way life is."

"But it's all so sad."

"For God's sake, Carol."

Carol, in the act of composing herself, seemed to shake herself like a parakeet smoothing its feathers. She gave a final dab to her face with the Kleenex and jammed it into a pocket.

"Have you talked to Evelyn yet?"

"No."

"Well, you *are,* aren't you?"

"I don't know."

"You're going to the reception?"

"I'm afraid I have to."

"You have to?"

"I want to see Wendy and Howie."

"Oh, Jack, I saw them inside. They have the baby with them. Such a beautiful little baby." Suddenly Carol started crying. Her mascara ran in rivulets down her cheek. She left her husband's side and threw her arms around Gold's neck and sobbed openly. The people coming out of the temple stopped and stared.

"My God, Carol. Please."

"Oh, Jack. Oh, Jack. *Another* beautiful little boy!"

Gold stood helpless, his arms pinned to his sides. He looked over Carol's head to Arim, but the little man only glared back. Gold couldn't believe the day had gone so badly, so quickly. He had made a major mistake in coming.

Just then a white-haired man in a pink leisure suit laid his hand gently on Carol's shoulder.

"Carol, they're taking pictures of the close family in the rabbi's office. Stan and Evelyn want you back there."

"Oh, shit! I must look like a witch!" Carol said and pulled away from Gold. "Come on, Arim. I have to find the ladies' lounge and fix my face." She was already halfway through the door. "We'll see you at the reception, Jack? Hurry *up*, Arim!"

The little man hurried after her, then turned to say something, thought better of it, and disappeared through the door.

"I was going to say, 'It was good talking to you,' but I don't think he said anything," Gold said to the white-haired man.

"It's hard to get a word in edgewise when one of my sisters is around. With a phonograph needle they were vaccinated. Besides, the only English that little camel jockey knows is what Carol's taught him: 'I'll take it' and 'Charge it.' "

Gold laughed and stuck out his hand.

"How've you been, Charlie?"

"Eh! I can't complain. You going to the reception? Good. It's around the other side of the building. Together we'll walk."

"Don't you have to be in the pictures? With the *close* family?"

"I already did that. Enough already. Besides, Stan's family I can do without."

"The good Dr. Markowitz? Of the Bel-Air Markowitzes?"

They were strolling along the pathway that curled around the side of the synagogue. Cars were lining up to leave the parking lot.

"Yeah, well, Stan's all right, I guess. He's good to my sister and all that, but I don't fit in too well with the rest of those people. You know, I went to a party at Stan and Evelyn's last year. October, I think. Up in Bel-Air. You ever see the house? No? What a house, Jack. A house? Ha! A mansion. A house like that I'll never get cutting flowers, believe me. Four stories. *Four stories* this house has! So anyway, I'm at this party. Sitting on the sofa having a few drinks with some friends of Stanley's. One of the people there is Stanley's brother. Orey. You know Orey? No? Well, he's got an English accent. Like an Englishman he talks. So, I said, I didn't know Orey was English. Why don't the rest of the family talk like that? So this Orey says he went to school in England. At Oxford. I said, So when? Can you believe 1959! One year! Almost thirty years ago and he's got an *accent*. A phony Englishman I'm talking to. So I'm talking to these people. Nice people. Or so I thought. Anyway, they're talking about this and that, about what's wrong with the world, what's wrong with the country. Reagan stinks. Deukmejian stinks. Everything stinks. So, I got an opinion too, right? Just like everybody else, right? So when there's a lull in the conversation, I speak up. What ruined this country, I said, is the *shvartzers* and the unions."

Charlie stopped and held Gold's arm.

"Jack, you shoulda been there. It was like I brought a ham sandwich to a kosher wedding. They all acted like I'd farted or something and they were all too well mannered to notice it and embarrass me."

They walked again.

"Well, then, after a minute they started talking again. Like I wasn't there or something. All right, a hint I can take. I keep my mouth shut and drink my whisky. They don't wanna talk to me, I don't wanna talk to them. Who needs 'em, right? But pretty soon this one little putz, I forget his name, but this one little *faygeleh* starts saying how Israel going into Lebanon was just like Germany invading Poland. Can you believe that? Then this same little *shmuck* says the way Israel treats its Arabs is no better than the way Hitler treated the Jews, and Begin was worse than Hitler because he pretended to be a righteous man. Israel was a corrupt joke foisted on the indigenous people of Palestine after World War II by the guilt-ridden Western world. Jack, let me tell you, I couldn't believe my ears. And all these other *shmucks* are agreeing with him. 'That's right.' 'How true.' Jack, I think I'm at a PLO meeting. The Arab-American League. Arafat is a goddamn *hero* to these people, for God's sake. *Khadaffi!* And, Jack, I look around me, I couldn't believe it. *These are all Jews!* I couldn't believe it!"

They had come to the end of a long line that had formed leading to the doors of the banquet room. Other people queued up behind them, wiping their brows and fanning their faces and complaining about the heat. The line moved slowly.

"So me being me, I gotta call a spade a spade. I can't keep my big mouth shut, *especially* when some asshole's saying these kinds of things. So, I tell this jerkoff he don't know a thing he's talking about. I tell him he better pull down his pants and look at his *putz* and see who he *really* is, because if it ever comes to that, and you never know, you never know, that's the first thing the bully boys and the brownshirts are gonna do, just like they did before. I said that him and every other Jew in the world better thank God every day that now there's a place in the world they can go to if things ever get bad wherever they are. Even this country, God forbid. You see the news this morning? You listen to the radio?"

"The synagogue? Beth Achim? On Beverly? I saw it."

"You see what I mean? Anywhere it can happen. Anywhere. So, I tell this little *gonif*—he's one of Howie's lawyer friends so I figure he's got to be a *gonif*—I tell him better he should shut his mouth and thank God in heaven there's an Israel, strong and proud, after two thousand years. So this little bastard, Jack, he laughs at me. *Laughs* at me. Says who am *I* to be giving him a political science lecture. So I say, who am I? Who am I? Why, I'll tell you who I am, I tell him. I'm the sixty-year-old fart who's gonna kick your kosher ass all the way down Benedict Canyon. Jack, Jack, you're laughing, but you shoulda seen this little worm, he jumped across the room like a rabbit or something. And he's screaming. *Screaming!* At the top of his lungs. 'You better stay away from me! You better stay away from me!' Now, Jack, this kid can't be a day over thirty. He can't *be* thirty. *May*be he's twenty-eight. What kind of people are the law schools turning out, anyway? *This* is what education does for you?"

Gold was still laughing as they moved up in line.

"Charlie, I didn't know if I should have come today, but seeing you and hearing you talk has made me feel a lot better."

"Wait a minute, Jack. Let me finish. So Evelyn and Stanley take me into the bedroom. Evelyn says she's never been so humiliated in her whole life. She's crying, for chrissake. She says there are very important people at the party, and her own brother has mortified her. *Mortified,* she says. And Stanley says, 'Charlie, perhaps you'd better leave now.' So I says, 'Don't worry. Don't worry. I'm going. I don't wanna stay in a house with a buncha anti-Semitic Jews.' So I storm out of there and Evelyn calls me the next day to apologize, and then Stanley the next, and I tell 'em both to go to hell. Finally they got Wendy to call me. Now you know I've always had a soft spot in my heart for your little girl. Ever since she was four years old and used to ride on my shoulders and hold onto my ears and call me 'Unka Chaddie.' So then Wendy talks to me and smooths things over and we're one big happy family again. But you know, Jack, I've never been invited to Stan and Evelyn's house since then. And I think they know if I did get invited I wouldn't go."

"I'm sorry to hear that, Charlie. You and Evelyn were always so close."

"Yeah, but things change. *She* changed. She and Stanley, they run with a different bunch now. Bel-Air. Palm Springs. Switzerland they go skiing. *Switzerland.* I didn't know Jews could ski." Charlie shook his head. "No, Jack, it's not like the old days. Remember? Me and Dot, God rest her soul. You and Ev. Carol and whoever. Remember we used to go down to San Pedro and watch the fishing boats parade in the harbor every year? And we used to drive to Vegas in that old Olds wagon of mine? When drinks were a quarter and you could see Sinatra for twelve, fifteen dollars. Dinner and all. And when they found out you were a cop we'd get comped half the time anyway. Those were the days, eh, Jack?"

They had reached the entrance and a shapely brunette in a starched nurse's uniform stopped them with a gentle but firm hand.

"Could I have your names, gentlemen?" She smiled sweetly.

"I'm Gold and this is Wiegand."

She studied a stainless-steel clipboard for a moment.

"Let's see. You're Jack and you're Charlie."

"Bingo," Charlie said.

She reached behind herself to a small table and picked out two clear plastic wristbands. She took a small punch from a pocket and snapped one of the bands around Charlie's wrist.

"What the hell is this?" Charlie said.

"This, gentlemen, is a hospital I.D. And *this*"—she moved out of the doorway and waved her hand at the crowded reception hall—"is a theme bar mitzvah. The theme is, of course, doctors."

The hall was decorated to look like a hospital. Everything was white—tables, chairs, paper decorations. Medical charts were pinned to walls. High-intensity O.R. lights were stationed among the tables. I.V.'s hung from metal stands and filled with Hawaiian Punch, were wheeled around the room by waiters and waitresses dressed as nurses, orderlies, and doctors. They squeezed the ends of the I.V. tubes and red jets of juice squirted into the children's glasses. They squealed with delight. Other I.V.'s contained strawberry margaritas, pink champagne, and rosé for the adults. Hors d'oeuvres were being served from wheeled metal hospital tables. Two of the more comedic actors from the NBC series "St. Elsewhere" were set up by a photographer's booth, having their picture snapped with the kids. Thermometers imprinted with the name Peter Markowitz and the day's date were being passed out to use as swizzle sticks. The smaller children were all pretending to listen to each other's hearts with toy plastic stethoscopes they had been given. The teenagers were checking their pulses against the chrome watches they had found gift-wrapped by their name cards. These, too, were engraved with each recipient's name and the date.

"Doctors, eh?" Charlie grunted. "Why doctors?"

"Why, the boy's father is a doctor," the nurse said as she snapped the other I.D. bracelet around Gold's wrist. "You must know that."

"Stanley?" Charlie snorted. "Stanley's not a doctor. Doctors heal people. Cure sickness. Stanley's a beautician. He's a makeup artist."

The nurse frowned at them darkly.

"We'll just go get a drink, if you'll excuse us," Gold said, taking Charlie's arm.

"One minute, gentlemen," the nurse said and snapped her fingers briskly. Two young men who looked like part of the USC defensive line in hospital drag pushed up a gurney and a wheelchair.

"These orderlies will take you to your seats."

Gold and Charlie looked at the gurney and then back to the nurse.

"You got to be kidding," Charlie said.

The nurse sighed and leaned over closer to them. "Look, assholes," she said in a low, hard whisper. "I've got my SAG card, my AFTRA card, and my Equity card, I can act fucking rings around Meryl Streep, and I've had three weeks of work this whole year. This is a way to pay the bills and it's usually a pretty easy way. Except when I run into a couple of old farts who want to give me a hard time because they can't give *any*body a hard time anymore. So do me this one small favor and be good little boys and let me do my job."

Gold and Charlie glanced at each other, then Gold said, "Well, since you asked so nice," and lay down on the gurney.

"Right." Charlie sat in the wheelchair.

The nurse smiled. "What a happy coincidence. Both of you gentlemen will be sitting at table twenty-seven."

"Hey, we've been well behaved," Gold complained. "At least take us to the bar."

"Right away! Boys," she said to the thick-necked young athletes, "take these patients to the bar. They need medication. Good-bye, gentlemen. Enjoy."

As they were wheeled through the partying crowd Charlie leaned over. "That was one cold *shiksa* bitch, if you ask me. Take her home one night, give her a *shtup,* you'll wake up with a frostbit prick. Take my word."

As they crossed the noisy ballroom Gold could see people recognizing him, nudging their neighbors and whispering behind their hands. The Big Secret didn't seem so secret. At the bar on the other side of the ballroom Gold slipped off the gurney—feeling not a little foolish—and turned his back to the crowd. He ordered two double Scotches from the bartender.

"Thanks," Charlie said.

"*L'chayim.*"

"*L'chayim.*"

Charlie leaned his back against the bar and surveyed the room. Gold kept his elbows on the bar and his eyes to the wall.

"So, Charlie. Been to Hollywood Park lately?"

"Last week."

"So how'd you do?"

"Not bad. I made expenses."

Both men chuckled and sipped at their drinks.

"Think the Dodgers are gonna do it this year?"

"I'll tell you honestly, Jack, I don't go to games anymore. Won't even watch them on the TV. It's all the same. You see a *shvartzer* pitching, a *shvartzer* catching, a *shvartzer* at bat, and another *shvartzer* in the outfield goes after the ball. It's all *shvartzers* now. They even got *shvartzer* umpires. And most of 'em are *shvartzers* can't even speak English. This is the Great American Pastime? Ah, they ruined the game!"

A band was setting up in a corner near the bar. The keyboardist was stacking speakers against the wall. The drummer was tuning his heads, striking them and then tightening them with a silver drum key.

"Uh oh," Charlie said. "Here comes a headache. These kids today, they don't care about music except one thing: is it loud? That's all they want to know. Is it loud?"

"Speaking of kids, Charlie, how's Lester?"

Charlie stirred his drink with a thermometer and shook his head slowly. He looked around and leaned closer to Gold and spoke in softer tones.

"I tell you, Jack, don't get me wrong, but you ask me you're better off without a son, the way things turn out sometimes. You might've had a son like Lester."

"What do you mean, Charlie?"

"I mean—when's the last time you saw Lester?"

Gold thought for a moment. "At Dot's funeral. What was that—two, three years ago?"

"Three years, three months, and sixteen days ago. You bury the best part of your life and you never forget a date. Pray to God it doesn't happen to you."

Angelique's ghost ran its hand up Gold's spine and he shivered.

"So anyway, Lester comes to me three days—*three days*—after the funeral and guess what he tells me?"

Gold scratched his nose. "That he was gay?"

"You knew?"

"I suspected."

"Yeah, well, I guess Rambo you would never mistake Lester for. Ever. So, anyway, he comes to me right after Dot's funeral and tells me he's coming out of the closet. Says he waited until after Dot died to declare himself because he didn't want to hurt her. 'So why didn't you wait until *I* die?' I ask him. 'Me you *want* to hurt?' He says he's thirty-seven and he can't live a lie any longer. I say, 'Why not?' Everybody I know is living a lie of one kind or another. What makes him so special? But he wouldn't listen. His mind's made up. So now he has a beach house out in Venice with some seventeen-year-old Mexican kid. *Mexican,* Jack. His mother must be turning over in her grave. Couldn't he find a nice Jewish boy?"

A shout went up from some kids playing the video games that had been trucked in and set up in an anteroom. The bartender brought two more doubles. Charlie and Gold both dropped twenties on the bar but the bartender held his hands up.

"It's an open bar, fellas. Compliments of Dr. and Mrs. Markowitz."

Gold was relighting his cigar. "Are you sure there isn't an eighty-six list? The last time I talked to Evelyn she didn't act like she wanted to buy me a drink."

"Aw, forget about it, Jack. My sister's rich now. She's got other concerns. She doesn't dwell on ancient history."

"You know, Charlie, I don't even know why I came today. I've got to talk to Howie, but I could've done that later tonight. Maybe that's what I should've done."

Across the crowded ballroom a plump blonde in her early twenties caught Gold's eye and waved. She lifted a baby from a baby carriage and began to weave her way through the tables toward him.

"Hey, Jack, Lester tells me this joke last week. I think you're gonna like it. You know why San Francisco got all the gays and L.A. got all the lawyers?"

Gold watched the smiling young woman approaching.

"Why?"

" 'Cause San Francisco got to choose first. Tell that one to Howie when you see him. Or better yet, let's have Lester tell him."

"Hi, Daddy."

Wendy was short, pretty, and twenty-five pounds overweight. She wore a khaki-colored jumpsuit with zippers and buckles everywhere, and wide pleated legs that tapered down to tight-fitting calves. The outfit would have been stunning on a Vogue model. On her chubby body it was pretty ridiculous. But her whole appearance was saved by her face. Her complexion was porcelain—clear and smooth and glazed with pale good health. Her eyes were her most striking feature. They were bright sky blue and twinkled with energy, optimism, and an innocent intelligence.

"Hi, baby," Gold said as he enfolded her in his arms tenderly, taking care not to hurt the baby.

"Thank you for coming, Daddy," she whispered in his ear. "I'm so glad you came." Gold held her to him a long time. Until Charlie stepped forward and tapped him on the shoulder.

"Say, can anyone break in on this dance?"

Gold released his daughter, but she held his hand tightly. Her eyes glistened with pride and love.

"Wendy," Charlie said. "How about a kiss for your old 'Unka Chaddie.' And let me see that little boy. I haven't seen him since the *bris.*"

Wendy let Gold's hand go reluctantly, threw her free arm around Charlie's neck, and squeezed tightly. "Uncle Charlie, how are you? How's my favorite uncle?"

"I'll tell you, Wen. I'm about as good as a sixty-year-old widower can be. It don't get up as much anymore, but that's just as well, because there's no place to put it."

"Uncle Charlie!"

"Now, let me see that little boy. He's the closest I'll ever come to having a grandson."

"Oh, Uncle Charlie. You just have to give Lester time."

"Wendy, Lester doesn't need time. Testicles, he needs."

"Uncle Charlie!" Wendy said, and they all laughed.

"Now, damn it, let me have my little grandnephew. Let me see little Joshua." Charlie took the baby from Wendy's arms and stood him up on the bar. The baby gripped Charlie's index fingers in his tiny hands and tottered back and forth on his fat legs. When he realized he wasn't going to fall, the questioning frown on his chubby face dissolved and he looked around the room and laughed uproariously.

"Would you look at this little *tummler,*" Charlie said. "He's the image of my father. Looks just like him."

"That's funny," Gold said. "I was going to say the same thing. He looks just like my old man."

"You're crazy," Charlie said. "Your side of the family never learned how to laugh. He looks like my father, God rest."

"Actually, Uncle Charlie," Wendy broke in, "Howie says he's a carbon copy of *his* grandfather who came over from Minsk."

"Aw, that's ridiculous. Who ever heard of a face this beautiful coming from anywhere as miserable as Minsk?" Charlie put his face to the baby's tummy and pretended to bite through the thin blue flannel. Joshua giggled and clutched at his belly and almost lost his balance. Charlie laid him down on the bar and hovered over him, making goo-goo sounds and funny faces. The baby laughed and kicked his legs and played with Charlie's chin.

"Would you look at that face!"

The band started playing. Rather than something loud, they played a soft, sensual bossa nova. Some Jobim melody that Gold recognized from a decade and a half ago. The jazz players had liked this tune and they had all included it in their wee-hours sets. Angelique had loved it.

"Daddy, dance with me," Wendy said, already leading him onto the dance floor. "Uncle Charlie will watch over Joshua, won't you, Uncle Charlie?"

"I'd pay *you* to let me watch over this baby."

They were the only couple on the dance floor. Wendy clung to him and rested her head on his chest. Gold could see all the other people were staring at them. Evelyn's cousins the Watermans, the Jasons up from La Jolla, her mother's best friend's son Joe Marshall and his *shiksa* wife from

Toronto. Gold even thought he saw one of Carol's ex-husbands, but he wasn't sure.

"I'm very glad you came, Daddy," Wendy said up to him. "Thank you. I know it wasn't easy."

"Ahhh—" Gold said, in an effort to pretend it was nothing.

"Daddy," she admonished gently, "I know how hard it is to be here."

He held her close as they danced. "I came to see *you,* baby."

They danced without speaking for half a minute. Gold unconsciously noted that the bass player sounded pretty good.

"Have you talked to Mother?"

"Not yet." So far, I've been spared that pleasure, he thought.

"Have you seen Peter yet?"

He hesitated a heartbeat and then replied, "Only in the temple."

"He's really a great kid, Dad." And then: "You would have been very proud of him."

Gold said nothing.

"Actually, Daddy, he's just like you." Wendy looked up at him and whispered conspiratorially. "From the day Mother brought him home from the hospital I could see you in everything he did. The way he held his spoon, the foods he likes. *Every*thing. And the older he gets, the stronger the resemblance. He's just like you, Daddy!"

"Now, Pieface. There's no use talking about this again. There's absolutely no percentage in opening this door."

"I know, I know." Wendy ran her fingers absently across his shoulder. "You know, he's asked me about you."

"Oh?"

"Several times. Once, years ago, when he was just a little boy, I caught him looking at that picture of you on my bedroom bureau. He wanted to know all about you."

"Really? And what did you tell him?"

"Oh, you know, you're my father; you and Mother used to be married. All that stuff. But I think he suspects more."

Gold held her away from him. "What makes you say that?"

"Just the way he gets quiet and listens real close whenever Aunt Carol and Mother start to talk about you. I think he knows Stanley isn't his father."

"Did your mother tell him that?"

Wendy laughed lightly. "What Mother said to him was, 'Your father and I weren't married when you were born, Peter. Aren't I terrible?' "

Gold smiled grimly. No, Evelyn, you weren't terrible. You just weren't Angelique.

"Anyway, Daddy, I was determined that you should be here today. I mean, Stanley's a very nice man and he was always good to me and he adores Peter—just adores him. But you're his *real* father."

"Pieface, your real father is the man who raises you, and just like you said, Stanley has raised Peter, and he's obviously done a very good job."

"But, Daddy, aren't you curious? Don't you—"

"Not in the least, sweetheart."

"Then why did you come today?"

Gold kissed her straw-colored hair. It smelled of shampoo. "I came to see *you,* Wendy. *You* asked me. *You* called three times to remind me. I knew it meant so much to *you,* Wendy. No one else. And don't ever forget it."

Several more couples had joined them on the dance floor. Solly Simon, Evelyn's stockbroker high school sweetheart, danced by with his young wife.

"Hi, Jack, good to see you. Caught that thing on the news last night. Good work. Oughta shoot all that scum. Wendy, how's the baby?"

The Chartoffs, who used to live down the street from Evelyn and Gold when they had their first little house in Culver City, were dancing. They nodded to him and smiled knowingly. Gold hated them. More couples made their way to the floor. It was becoming crowded. The band segued seamlessly into another bossa nova.

"Are you coming to dinner tomorrow? I'll make that chicken enchilada casserole, the one you like so much. You can watch 'Sixty Minutes' and play with the baby."

"I'll see, Pieface."

"Please try, Daddy. Howie said he might have to see a client, and Joshua and I will be all alone."

Gold's police instincts automatically clicked on. It was very disconcerting. He had never used them around his family before. Angelique, yes, but never his family.

"Howie has a business meeting on a Sunday? That doesn't sound like our Mr. John McEnroe. Mr. Six-Sets-on-Sunday. Who on earth would he be seeing?"

"Oh, I don't know. Some other lawyers. He said he had to take a meeting with some other lawyers."

"What about?"

"What?" Wendy's eyes were just a tiny bit startled.

"What's the meeting about, honey?"

"Gee, Daddy, I haven't the foggiest."

"Where *is* Howie? I haven't seen him yet."

"After *shul* he said he had to make some phone calls. I'm sure he'll be here soon. He's looking forward to seeing you."

"Oh?"

"Yes, this morning he asked me *three* times if you were going to be here. He really likes you, Daddy."

Right, Gold thought.

"Do you know what he wants to see me about?"

"Oh, nothing in particular I guess, Daddy." She had a thought and laughed at it. "Maybe he wants to teach you how to play tennis?"

Gold forced a laugh, but his eyes were cold.

"I'm so glad you came today, Daddy," Wendy said and snuggled closer to Gold as they swayed to the music. Several photographers were roaming the jammed noisy room, posing "candid" shots of old men and little girls, fathers and daughters, mothers and son. Waiters at one end of the room uncovered a long buffet to a chorus of "ooh's" and "aah's." The photographers snapped pictures of the molded chopped liver and the pickled herring. Guests lined up and heaped their plates with seven different kinds of salad, fresh fruit, shrimp cocktail, teriyaki chicken breasts on wooden skewers, rice and lobster Newburg. A sweating chef carved thick, bleeding slices off a prime rib roast and slathered them with *jus* and horseradish.

The band ended the medley with a ritard, a drum fill, and a tenor sax flourish. A few couples applauded. Gold locked arms with Wendy and led her back toward the bar. Charlie Wiegand welcomed them with a wide grin and a booming voice. "Think we got an emergency here, Wen."

Wendy took the baby from his arms and felt its behind.

"Definitely a major emergency, Uncle Charlie."

"Think we better call the Fire Department?"

Wendy laughed at Charlie's hoary joke, which she remembered from her childhood. "No, Uncle Charlie, I think I can handle it."

She laid the baby over her shoulder, her eyes darting back across the ballroom to where she had left the Aprika and its supply of Snuggies. "Daddy, I want at least another dozen dances, but I'm afraid Joshua is the most important man in my life at this minute."

"Hey, what about me?" Charlie lamented. "Don't I even get one turn on the dance floor?"

"As soon as I get back. As soon as I get back." She was making her way around the edge of the dancers. "Daddy, tell Howie where I went," she called back.

Charlie and Gold watched her hurry through the crowd.

"That's one great girl you got there," Charlie said.

Gold nodded agreement. "Yeah, Charlie, I did one thing right in my life."

Charlie threw him a sideways glance, then put his drink down on the bar.

"Y'know, that Joshua had the right idea. I gotta find a bathroom." He pointed to his drink. "If anybody tries to touch that, arrest him."

When Charlie had gone, Gold turned his back to the crowd and rested his elbows on the bar. The bartender came over.

"Freshen that up for you, sir?"

"Sure. Why not?"

The bartender was tall, broad, and dark-skinned. His hair was a jungle of loose curls. His nose was wide and had once been broken.

"Funny, you don't look Jewish," Gold said to him.

The bartender cracked a grin, revealing bright white teeth.

"Hawaiian?" Gold asked.

"Samoan." The bartender wiped the short bar with a cloth.

"You guys make good football players."

The bartender crossed his arms across his massive chest. "And you guys make good lawyers."

Gold sipped his drink. "Wash your mouth out with soap, son."

The bartender chuckled, then moved his gaze to a point just to the left of Gold's right shoulder. Gold turned and looked up into his ex-wife's malevolent smile.

"Jack. How good of you to come. It's so nice to see you."

Gold felt as if he were a small boy caught masturbating. He had an urge to check his fly. He suddenly realized that Evelyn was the only person in the world he feared.

"Evelyn, you're looking wonderful."

She wasn't. She looked like a death's head mask. The good Dr. Markowitz had practiced on his wife once too often. The skin around her eyes and mouth was stretched tight. Under the deep Palm Springs tan her cheeks were shiny, like glazed pottery. She looks like a burn scar, Gold thought. The day they broke up, the day after Angelique's death, Evelyn had been thirty pounds overweight. After Peter's birth, he heard she had gone on a crash diet and had lost those thirty pounds and another fifteen. The skin had sagged; the flesh had quivered. She had asked around for a good plastic surgeon. That's how she met Stanley. And now he had made her over. Presumably into the woman *he* wanted. Didn't anybody want her the way she was? The way she had been? Gold couldn't see but he knew, he had heard: there had been breast implants, a tummy tuck, an ass lift. She was a walking advertisement for cosmetic surgery—Dr. Stanley Markowitz variety. Gold thought, and not for the first time, that Evelyn Wiegand Gold Markowitz had been ill served by both of her husbands.

"Thank you, Jack." Evelyn's eyes glinted with pride. My God, Gold thought, if I saw you on the street I wouldn't recognize you. I wouldn't recognize you as something *human*.

"It's been a long time, Evelyn."

"Too long, Jack. Let's see, just how long? At Wendy's wedding you ran out of the temple as soon as the ceremony was over. I didn't even get to say hello. And then somehow we missed each other at Dot's funeral—what a sad affair that was. Why, it must have been Uncle Max's funeral."

Deaths, he thought. Too many deaths between us, Ev. Starting with Angelique's.

"That must be what," she continued, "six years ago. How have we managed to avoid each other for so long? *Why* have we?"

She was wearing a simple white raw silk dress that Gold knew was an original. He estimated seven, eight hundred dollars. Instead of her sister Carol's ostentatious diamonds, Evelyn had on a single strand of perfect pearls Gold recognized to be much dearer. As she held out her hand for Gold to take, he noticed the huge pearl on her middle finger. It looked like a small glossy egg.

"You know how it is, Evelyn. Time has a way of slipping away from us."

"From some of us, Jack," Evelyn said archly, sipping her pink champagne and looking at Gold over the crystal rim with hate-filled eyes set in that frozen face. "I, myself, have never felt younger. I can't wait to get up every morning. Isn't it that way for you?"

Gold took a quick hit of his Scotch. He was going to need it. His eyes never left Evelyn's.

"I'll tell you the truth, Ev. When I get up in the morning I feel every year. And then some."

Evelyn smiled. It was awful. She looked like an opened wallet. A slashed seatcover. People *pay* for this? Gold thought.

"It's your guilty conscience," Evelyn said. "Too many sins on your mind. You probably can't sleep well either. Bad dreams?"

Gold shivered, and he didn't know if it was because Evelyn was too close to the truth, or because she was still smiling that twisted grimace. Who are you? Gold thought. You're not Evelyn. You're not even human. You're an alien. *What have you done with Evelyn?*

"I saw you dancing with Wendy a moment ago. That was a touching sight. A father and his child. By the way, have you met my son, Peter? I don't think so. No, I don't believe you've ever met Peter." Evelyn placed her empty champagne glass on the bar and scooped up another. She had never been able to drink more than one margarita. With dinner. Gold looked out across the ballroom. It seemed to him that every pair of eyes in the place was trained on them, he and Evelyn.

"You haven't met Peter? You haven't met the bar mitzvah boy?" Evelyn asked again.

"Not yet."

"Such a boy, Jack. Such a boy. He's the kind of son that would make any parent proud."

Gold returned her chilly smile.

"Valedictorian of his class, you know," she continued. "And he's ranked seventh in his age group in California Junior Tennis. Bet you didn't know that."

"No, I didn't, Evelyn."

"No, I didn't think you did." She sipped her champagne. "Handsome. Graceful. Intelligent. He's going to be a doctor, you know." She looked hard at Gold. "Just like his father."

Gold, refusing to be baited, waved his hand at the decorated ballroom. "So I noticed. Don't you think that's a little premature?"

Evelyn laughed around her champagne.

"Premature? Oh, no, Jack. It's never too early to start planning for a successful career. But, then, you wouldn't know about that, would you?"

That's one for your side, cunt, Gold thought.

"No, Evelyn, I guess I wouldn't."

"I mean, how many fifty-six-year-old lieutenants does the depart—"

"Jack! How are you!" A tall, thin, white-bearded man in a powder-blue safari jacket stuck out his hand and shook Gold's firmly. "It's really good to see you." Dr. Stanley Markowitz was one of those earnest men of unrelenting good cheer who drives everyone around them crazy. Gold figured he was so happy because he felt that everything wrong with the world could be fixed with a few tightening stitches, a little well-placed *plastique.* If Reagan had that turkey gobbler neck pulled up, he would look at the world with a much freer perspective. Arafat, with a good nose bob, would be a lot less belligerent. Get rid of Gorbachev's livery birthmark, the man could go up for Alex Karras roles.

"It's been way too long, Jack. We have to see more of each other." He sported a collection of heavy gold chains around his neck. They twinkled in a bed of fine white chest hair. He wore tinted sunglasses, and his upturned shirt cuffs revealed a precision gold watch the size and thickness of an after-dinner mint. Every hair on his face and head had been carefully trimmed so as to look *un*trimmed. Dr. Stanley Markowitz had definitely gone Hollywood.

Gold was very glad to see him. "Stanley. How the hell are you?"

"Couldn't be better. Listen, how about dinner some night? How about—"

"I know," Evelyn chimed in. "I just heard of a great new place in Brentwood. It's Ethiopian."

She smiled sweetly. There was an embarrassed pause.

"Or there's another place on La Cienega. West African, I believe."

The men were silent.

"Well, you *do* like to go native, don't you, Jack?"

"Ev, *please,*" Markowitz began.

She swilled some more champagne. A trickle ran down her chin. Her eyes were hot and bright.

"I read an article in *Psychology Digest* just last week that dealt with the reasons some men prefer women of the darker races. It's got something to do with low self-image or something."

"Ev, don't do this."

"Don't do what?" Evelyn snapped. "I'm only talking to my ex-husband." She turned back to Gold. "Do you have a low self-image, Jack? I shouldn't wonder. And what *do* you do with your nights now? Still running around all the seamier parts of town? Still have a taste for the *dark* side of life?"

Her voice was rising, becoming shriller.

"Wait a minute. I know what you like to do. I saw it on the news last night. You like to kill things, don't you, Jack?" She emptied her glass in one furious gulp. "You always have. Loved to kill things. Marriages. Careers. Men." Her eyes lasered into his. "Young girls."

The two men stood in stunned silence while Evelyn glowed with a kind of bright, drunken righteousness. People seated at the tables around them were openly staring. The band was playing "Satin Doll." Badly. Gold set his drink on the bar.

"I think I'd better leave," he said.

"Not *now,* Jack," Evelyn snarled. "The fun's just beginning."

"That's quite enough, Evelyn," Dr. Stanley Markowitz said sternly. "You're making a scene, and I won't have that. This kind of uncivilized behavior may be suitable for some fish market on Fairfax Avenue, but it's totally unacceptable at my son's bar mitzvah."

At the words "my son's bar mitzvah" Evelyn looked at her husband a long time.

"That's right. He's *my* son, too. I seem to be the forgotten party at this party. Remember me? I'm the one who'll sign the checks that will pay for all this. And I will not have this ballroom turned into a surgical amphitheater where you and Jack can slash open old scars. So, Evelyn, please try to control yourself. And if you can't bring yourself to do it for me, then do it for Peter. It is his party, or have you forgotten that, too?"

Evelyn's eyes widened with fury and surprise. Then they began to tear. She snatched another champagne from the dozens lined up on the bar and rushed off in the direction of the ladies' room.

The two men stood there in the awkward silence.

"A regrettable incident," Stanley Markowitz said finally.

"I have to go."

The doctor sighed. "Nonsense, Jack. Have you had something to eat?"

"After that? I don't really feel hungry, Stanley. I think I'll be going."

"That's ridiculous, Jack. Don't let Evelyn spoil this day. It's Peter's day. Besides, even if you're not hungry you've got to try this new caterer. Anton's of Beverly Hills. One of my clients—I won't mention her name, professional integrity, you understand, but you'd recognize her face in a minute—she gave me his unlisted number. It's the only way you can get it. You *must* try the glazed chicken."

He put his arm around Gold's shoulders and steered him toward one of the few empty tables.

"Sit here, Jack, and I'll break into the buffet line. It's the father's prerogative."

"Stanley, I shouldn't even be here. I don't belong here."

"That's crazy, Jack. Wendy wanted you here, and I want you here."

"But I just seem to upset Evelyn so much."

"She'll get over it, Jack. She's supposed to be somewhat mature at her age."

"Stanley, I—"

"Stop *kvetching.*" Markowitz pushed Gold gently down into a padded chair. "Besides, *I'm* the one who should be upset."

"Why is that?" Gold looked up at him.

"In twelve years of marriage, I've never seen Evelyn as passionate about anything as she was just a few minutes ago with you."

Gold studied his napkin for a moment, then said, "That's hatred, Stanley. That's not passion."

"It's passion, Jack, believe me."

Gold looked up at the doctor. "It only started with the hatred. It was never there before that. Maybe that was part of the problem."

"Enough, Jack." Markowitz held up a hand. "I'm a plastic surgeon, not a psychiatrist." He smiled. "Right now I'll be your waiter."

He started moving away, toward the buffet line at the other end of the room. "A little taste of everything okay, Jack?"

"That's fine."

"You *must* try the chicken," he called back over his shoulder. Then a man was shaking his hand and a woman with an eternally surprised look stretched over her face was whispering in his ear. Markowitz laughed, smoothed his white beard away from his mouth, and kissed the woman lightly on her cheek. Then the crowd closed behind them.

Gold stripped the cellophane from a new cigar and lit it. He looked around. He caught a few people with curious expressions on their faces looking at him. He stared them down. He looked for Charlie in the direction of the front entrance, but the pink leisure suit had disappeared. Gold thought about getting up to get a drink, but he drank the ice water on the table instead. He puffed on his cigar and tried to convince himself to stay. He wondered where Wendy was. The noise level in the ballroom had risen dramatically. Small children were running through the tables like one of those miniature trains in city parks. The room was beginning to feel a little drunk. The band was playing light rock now, and the keyboardist was singing something that sounded vaguely familiar to Gold. The dance floor was packed. A mixed group of fourteen- and fifteen-year-olds sitting at the next table was whispering and giggling conspiratorially. Three of them got up and walked across the ballroom and out of the front door. If I follow them and throw them against a car, Gold thought, six to five they're holding. Grass at the very least. In one corner of the ballroom a man in clown makeup and a doctor's frock with a headlamp banded across his painted forehead had set up a make-believe X-ray machine and was performing for twenty or thirty children. He made a little girl stand behind the machine and flicked on an oversized switch on the side. The screen brightened and there was a creepy crawler—a big hairy spider—inching through the girl's stomach. It was some kind of video recorder. The children watching squealed and gagged and laughed. The next little boy had swallowed a white mouse. A little girl with raven-black hair ran away holding her hands to her mouth. The clown held his stomach and pantomimed hearty laughter. His red nose lit up.

Gold looked around again for Charlie or Markowitz, but they were nowhere to be seen. He stood up and went to the bar. The bartender poured a Scotch and pushed it across without being asked. Gold gulped it down.

"Fuck this. This grief I don't need," he said aloud. The bartender just looked at him with a studied lack of expression. Gold turned on his heel and walked across the ballroom and toward the exit. Just to the right of the doorway was a short hall. He went down the hall, looking for a bathroom. He found it up a half flight of carpeted stairs.

The men's room was empty. Gold closeted himself in a stall, pulled down his pants, sat down quickly and, puffing on his cigar, emptied his bowels. The bathroom wasn't air-conditioned, and a line of perspiration broke out on his forehead. His intestines rumbled. Suddenly he didn't feel very well.

After flushing, Gold stood before the wide mirror and examined himself for the second time that day. A little green around the gills, he thought. He filled the basin with cold water, leaned over and splashed his face, letting some of the water run down the back of his neck. He was patting himself dry with paper towels when the lounge door opened.

"Jack. I thought I'd missed you."

"Howie," Gold said coldly, watching his son-in-law in the mirror.

"Wendy said she thought she saw you heading this way."

Howie Gettelman was a small, muscular man with a close-cropped black beard and thinning hair on the crown of his head. His dark, pin-striped suit was Savile Row–tailored and fit him impeccably. Howie looked like a lawyer even on his day off.

"Jack." Howie gripped Gold's arm and shook his hand tightly. "I've got to talk to you about something."

"No shit."

Howie inspected Gold more closely. "You know?"

Gold tightened his tie, still looking at Howie in the mirror's reflection. "I know."

"How the hell—"

"Sammy Pearlman called me this morning just before I left for *shul.*"

"That fucking *gonif!*"

"Look, Howie, you call a bail-bondsman—a man I've known for thirty years, a guy owes me a lot of favors—and you use my name, you say you're my son-in-law, you're in jail, you need his services but you don't want me to know a thing about it. And you really expect him not to call me to check it out?"

"He *swore* to me it was all in strictest confidence."

Gold sat on the sink's edge facing Howie. "People break oaths. That's how lawyers like you eat. Besides, why didn't you call me direct?"

"I didn't think you'd understand."

Gold shrugged his shoulders. "What's to understand? My daughter is married to a dope fiend."

"Jack—"

"Worse. A pusher, yet. A dope peddler."

"Jack, it's not like that."

"Oh? How is it?"

"It's just a misunderstanding. A small problem."

Gold took his cigar from his mouth and twirled it between two fingers. "A small problem? A half pound of high-grade cocaine—a small problem?"

"Jack—"

"That's worth what? Ten thousand on the street minimum. Twenty if you step on it *once.* By the time the narcs and the D.A.'s office inflate the value for the arraignment it'll be closer to fifty, sixty thousand. We're talking major criminal activity here."

"Jack, don't get emotional on me. This whole business can be contained if—"

"*Contained? Contained?* Do you know the statute you're charged with? Do you know how it reads? 'Possession of a controlled substance with the intent to sell, distribute, or otherwise disseminate.' That's possession for sales, Howie, and that's a big bad felony. 'First offense punishable by not more than three years in the state penal system.' You know what that means, son-in-law? Do you? Disbarment. End of career. Shame for my daughter. Shame on my grandson's name."

"For chrissake, Jack. Listen to me."

"No, Howie, you listen to me. What the *fuck* are you doing with a half pound of coke? I know all you young, hip lawyers smoke a little weed, drop an upper or two before you go into the courtroom in the morning, then a Quaalude to get your dick hard at night. But eight ounces of blow is *not* 'intended for personal use,' *bubeleh.* Eight ounces of blow is a heavy-duty bust. You're lucky you didn't make the 'Eyewitness News.' Now, what the fuck were you doing with that much coke?"

Howie dropped his eyes to the floor. He was a neat, fastidious man with polished fingernails. He had always looked soft to Gold.

Howie raised his eyes to Gold's. "I was doing a favor for some friends."

Gold snickered and shook his head. "Then you've got no problem. You go into court and tell everybody who your friends are and they'll let you go."

Howie's dark good looks darkened further. "I can't do that. I'm not that kind of guy."

"Oh? What kind of guy are you?"

"Look, I'm not one of your street snitches, you know. I'm not a goddamn informer. I can't do that to these people. I *won't* do that."

"Who the fuck do you think you are? Bugsy Siegel? Meyer Lansky?" Gold pointed at Howie with the wet end of his cigar. "You stand in front of me and tell me you're a right guy, a stand-up guy, a man; and I'm telling you you don't know first thing about what you're talking about. Stand-up guys do *time,* asshole. Good people go to *jail.*" Gold clamped the cigar between his teeth. "And make no mistake about it, the joint is no picnic for a Jew, son-in-law. There's no Jewish gang you can club up with for protection. Ain't no Jewish mafia. The Aryan Brotherhood will make your life a living hell, and the Black Muslims, they have a couple hundred reasons to put a pipe upside your head or a shiv in your back. So—"

"Stop it, Jack! I don't want to hear this cop sermon! Are you going to help me or do I just walk away now?"

The two men glared at each other. A fat man in a lime green suit and a burgundy yarmulke came into the men's room. He smiled and nodded at both of them, but they ignored him. He stood before a urinal, unzipped and pulled his penis out, glancing back over his shoulder. Gold ground his cigar between his teeth. Howie's eyes smoldered with anger. The tension was palpable. The fat man's urine wouldn't come.

"Nice party, huh?" the fat man said in embarrassment. He was answered by stony silence. He almost grunted as he strained, tried to will himself to piss. Nothing happened. He glanced once more over his thick shoulder, then zippered quickly, almost catching the fleshy head of his penis in the tracking mechanism. He exited without looking back.

"Why should I help you?" Gold asked quietly. "There's never been any love lost between us."

"You know why."

"Don't be coy with me, counselor."

Howie turned to the mirror and examined himself. With satisfaction. He straightened his silk tie and brushed a piece of imaginary lint from his lapel.

"For Wendy, Jack. For Wendy's sake. This kind of thing would break her heart. You couldn't let that happen to your little golden girl, could you?"

Gold felt the old familiar anger rising in him, ice cold and white hot. He had suppressed it for so long that he almost welcomed it back. He almost enjoyed it.

"You know how much our little nuclear family means to her," Howie was saying. "Maybe because of what happened with you and Evelyn when she was still so young and impressionable. But if anything happened to me, if anything threw a wrench into our perfect little world—well, *I* wouldn't want to be held responsible." Howie leaned forward and inspected his beard in the mirror.

In his mind's eye, Gold gripped the back of Howie's head and slammed his face into the glass. He imagined smashed bone, slashed flesh, shattered teeth. He fought to control the rising tide that welled up in his blood.

"You've done well for yourself, haven't you, Howie? Marrying the renowned Dr. Stanley Markowitz's stepdaughter."

Howie turned and faced Gold.

"Don't act as if I don't love Wendy, Jack, because I do. Very much. From the first time I saw her. She's the most wonderful, good-hearted human being I've ever met. And I live for the baby. But I will admit that I wasn't disappointed by the fact that Wendy's father—excuse me, *step*father—was plastic surgeon to the stars, to the very people I need to know to further my career in this town. I intend to be a major power in entertainment law someday, and you've got to be competitive in the Business. You've got to use whatever connections you've got. You've got to do whatever you have to do to get to the people who can help you. That's something you can't understand, Jack. You've never reached for anything like that. You've never had the ambition to *be* somebody. All you've ever wanted to be is a fucking cop, for chrissake."

"Don't push me too far. I'll squash you like the little conniving, self-serving New York cockroach that you are."

Howie's eyes were black and hard. "Hey, we all can't be as pure as the driven snow. Like you."

The two men hated each other across the narrow bathroom. Gold stood very still, until the blood-red surge behind his eyes cooled at last. He looked at Howie but made himself see Wendy, think of Wendy. It worked. After a while he leaned loosely against the tiled wall, crossed his arms over his chest, and stuck his hands under his armpits. Finally he said, "So—in the interest of furthering your career you've taken to selling flake."

Howie relaxed a little and sat on the edge of a sink.

"You really don't understand. This business *runs* on coke, on Quaaludes, on a little heroin. It doesn't hurt these people. They know how to handle themselves. They're not going to mug someone to get money for drugs. They're not criminals."

"They're using drugs," Gold broke in. "That's a crime. That makes them criminals."

Howie smiled condescendingly. "Jack, you still don't get the picture. One of Bockman, Fleischer and Bernhart's clients, a film director, grossed over three hundred million dollars last year. *Three hundred million.* That's more than most countries. You can't tell this man what he can or cannot stick up his nose. You can't do it. Cocaine is like coffee to people like this. You hang around with these people, you forget it's illegal. It's everywhere. It's everyone. This is *royalty,* Jack. They do what they like."

Gold leaned against the wall and watched his son-in-law talk.

"If I'm going to deal with these kinds of people, if I'm going to relate to them, make them trust me, make them believe in me, *need* me, I've got to be able to communicate on their terms, on their level." Howie paused for a moment, thoughtful. "Let me give you an example. I'm taking a meeting last week. In the firm's conference room. Our client, a major rock band, is resigning with the biggest record company in the world. A *platinum*-selling rock band. We're hammering out the last details. I'm the third junior partner in attendance. That's like being a gofer. I'm one step above the secretary who's making the coffee. Well, before we're fifteen minutes into the meeting, the lead singer says, 'I can't negotiate without a cool head.' So he opens his briefcase on the boardroom table and he's got a kilo of coke in there. *A fucking key!* My boss, Ted Bockman, is in the room. He sits on the board of six major companies. He's chairman of two. The president of the biggest record company in the world, who flew out from New York just for the signing—*he's* in the room. Well, I'm horrified. I'm thinking these guys are going to storm out of the room. Call for the police. Something. These men have lifelong reputations to protect. Right? Wrong. In two minutes they're leaning over the table and holding their ties so they don't drag them through the blow. Passing around a solid gold straw and going after it like pigs I've seen in France sniffing after truffles. And the lead singer looks over at me and winks. He's laughing at them. At me. A guy with purple hair and his belly button showing. So what am I supposed to do? Yell rape and run for my honor? Call the FBI? C'mon, Jack. This is the way it *is*. People like this don't go to jail."

"No, they get *shmucks* like you to do that for them."

"Look, the bust was a freak accident. It was never supposed to happen."

"You know, you sound more and more like the scum I've been sending to prison all these years."

Howie shook his head. "Is this the way it's going to be? We're just going to score points off each other?"

Gold puffed on his cigar. "So, tell me how it happened."

"Well," Howie began, examining his glossy fingernails, "there's about ten of us—all lawyers, one guy's a public defender. Mostly we do what we do just enough to do a little business, and to have a little snow for ourselves. I want you to understand that, Jack."

Gold kept silent.

"We all chip in a few thousand apiece and buy a healthy chunk of blow. We cut it up, step on it with some Italian baby laxative, and sell it to our friends. Other guys in our offices. Sometimes we use it to entice a famous client into signing with the firm, in which case we write up a phony expense voucher and the company reimburses us."

"No questions asked?"

"None. They write it up like a travel expense or something. Entertainment. Sometimes it's a tax deduction. I was going to use this last pickup to romance this certain TV actress into letting us represent her. I almost had her firmed up. God knows what's going to happen now."

Gold stared at him in disbelief. "Howie, do you have any idea how many laws you're breaking? Conspiracy? Possession? Trafficking? Tax evasion?"

"Aw, give me a break, Jack. I thought I explained it to you. That's the way the Business *is*."

"Then you're in the wrong goddamn business."

"Do you want to hear this or do you want to keep playing policeman?"

"Go ahead."

"So, it was my turn to make the buy. I met with the connection in the parking lot behind the Sunset Theatre, you know where I mean? There's that little shopping center off to the left? So I make the buy in the dealer's car, I get back in my car and I'm about to start the motor when all of a sudden there're cops all around the car. Guns drawn and everything. One guy tells me to put my hands on the wheel where he can see them or he's going to *shoot* me. He's *screaming* at me! I couldn't believe it was happening, and I almost didn't react quickly enough. I think I almost got *shot,* Jack. I still can't really believe it all."

"Believe it," Gold said flatly. "What about the dealer?"

"He had already driven away."

"So? They didn't give pursuit?"

"Uh—no, I guess not."

"What the fuck is that?"

"I'm not sure I know what you mean."

"You were set up."

"That's ridiculous, Jack. I told you. I know all of the people involved. They're all my friends. My associates."

"What about the dealer?"

"It's out of the question. He's got a reputation a mile long. A lot of the best people, the really *important* people in this town, buy from him. The last thing he wants said about him is that he gives up his *customers,* for chrissake. Besides, I told you, it was a fluke, just a piece of shitty luck. The cops were there on an auto theft stakeout. Someone has been stealing cars out of that parking lot and they were watching it. I just happened to come along and they saw what looked like a controlled substance when they stopped me. They thought I was stealing my own car."

"They told you that?"

"They happened to let it slip."

"And you believe them?"

"Of course. And that might be the angle I need to beat this case."

"That they thought you were stealing your own car and just happened to find the coke?"

"Exactly. I'll move to have the evidence suppressed. The judge'll throw the whole thing out of court."

"You're such an asshole, Howie."

Howie looked at Gold and blinked rapidly.

"You are *such* an asshole. What a *shlemiel!* If you were a criminal lawyer you'd starve. Or get your fucking head blown off by a dissatisfied customer. Because you are *such* an—"

"All right!" Howie shouted.

"They were narcs!" Gold shouted back. "Fucking narcs! Sammy the bondsman knows the names on the arrest report, and they're all fucking narcs! And they were waiting for *you,* Howie boy. No car thieves. No parking lot stakeout. They were watching you, *shmuck!* You were set up!"

Howie's face drained of blood. He steadied himself against the wall, then sat down heavily on the edge of the washbasin.

"That's impossible. The police told me . . ." he stammered.

"It's an old trick, Howie. They're just trying to protect their snitch."

"Snitch? Snitch? My God, I can't believe it. Only my friends knew."

"Who do you think snitches are? Strangers?"

"Why—why would anyone do that to me?"

"Oh, fucking grow *up,* asshole! They did it for the same reason snitches always do it—to pay off a debt, to get their own asses out of a sling. You were a tradeoff, Howie boy."

"My God," Howie said again. "My God."

The lounge door burst open and three small boys ran in, breathless and laughing.

"Get out of here!" Gold growled.

"We gotta pee!" piped the biggest boy, a fat-cheeked redhead of about nine. He was already unzipping his fly.

"There's another bathroom downstairs. Or use the ladies' room. This one's out of order."

The two other boys stopped and watched Gold with wide eyes. The redhead was skeptical. He strode forward and flushed the urinal. It gushed with swirling water.

"It's not broke," the redhead said.

Gold leaned over close to the little boy's face. "I'm a policeman, and if you don't get out of here right this minute, kid, I'm going to arrest you for failing to heed an official police order, and you'll be old and gray before you ever see sunshine on the playground again. Have I made myself clear?"

The redhead was fearless. "If you're a cop, where's your badge?"

Gold pulled his wallet from his back pocket and flipped it open before the boy's eyes. The redhead studied the gold shield closely, then looked up at Gold with a cunning leer.

"How do I know you didn't steal it?"

"Get out!" Gold shouted. *"Now!* Before I stick my foot up your little *tuchis. Move!"*

The little boys scrambled out of the door, but not before the redhead turned and flipped Gold the bird while making an oily farting sound with his mouth.

"You dirty little bastard!" Gold said and made as if to lunge at him. The kid was gone in a flash.

Gold turned back to his son-in-law. Howie still looked as if he were going to throw up. His eyes were liquid and unfocused. His hands weren't steady. Gold chewed on his cigar and studied him. After a while Howie looked up at him.

"I—I'm in big trouble." Howie's voice was soft and slack.

"I think that's probably a pretty fair assessment."

"I guess—I guess I'll have to see it all through to the end. Go to trial, I mean."

"Yeah. Or cop a plea. Maybe get it reduced to simple possession."

"You think so?"

"It's a possibility. But you'll have to talk to them. Be cooperative. You're gonna have to give them some names."

Howie shook his head slowly. "I can't do that."

Gold watched him. Howie looked up again.

"You don't think I can get the evidence suppressed?"

Gold shrugged. "You're the lawyer, Howie. But from what you've told me, the way you described it, the way it went down—they got you dead bang. It was a righteous bust. Clean and mean."

Howie shook his head again. "My God."

Gold braced one foot on the lid of the trash receptacle and began buffing his shoe with a paper towel. Howie said something inaudible. Gold went on shining his shoe. Then he straightened up and looked at him.

"What?"

Howie swallowed hard. "Can you help me?"

Gold, moving slowly, leaned over and started polishing his other shoe.

"That's funny, Howie. You asking for *my* help. That's really funny." Gold worked at the shoe. "Not surprising, though. Just funny. But I'll bet you never thought you'd be asking *me* for help. Did you, Howie?"

Howie was silent.

"No, I don't think so. Why, I can remember *offering* you my help, and you almost laughed at me. Can you remember that?"

Howie wouldn't look at Gold.

"Let's see. It was the morning of the wedding, wasn't it? I went up to you and said—what did I say? Oh, yeah. 'If there's anything I can do for you, if there's anything you need to start your married life together, just ask me.' Remember that? And you said, how did you put it? Oh, yes. 'Well, Jack, between Stanley and my father, I really think everything's taken care of, but have a good time at the reception, okay?' You did everything but pat me on the head, didn't you, Howie?"

"I'm asking you now, Jack." Howie's voice was almost a whisper.

"You said, 'My father's taken care of the honeymoon.' Europe, wasn't it? 'And Stanley has given us the down payment on the town house, so I really can't think of anything *you* could help me with.' Isn't that about what you said?"

Gold examined his shoe, then spit on the paper towel and started buffing again.

"Jack—" Howie began.

"Well, why don't you get them to help you *now,* son-in-law? Why don't you go to them now?" Gold straightened his back and glared at Howie. "Let me guess. You don't want all the *nice* relatives to know what you've done. Is that it, dope peddler? You don't want them to know who you really are. So you come to *me* to clean up your mess."

"Please, Jack. This isn't easy."

"You're damn right it isn't going to be easy. It's going to cost a lot of money—"

"I'll get the money somehow."

"And it's going to take the right connections."

"I appreciate that."

"Even then it's iffy."

"I understand."

"But it *can* be done, if you know the right people."

"That's why I'm asking you, Jack."

Gold was silent. He washed his hands again, then dried them on a clean paper towel. He threw the paper towel in the metal receptacle. He faced Howie.

"All right. It's over. Forget about it. I'll take care of it. Go enjoy the party."

Howie was incredulous. "Just like that? Is it that simple?"

"For me it is. This is something only *I* can do."

"How much money do you need? When do you need it?"

"I said I'll take care of it."

"Jack, I know this is going to be expensive."

"You, son-in-law, know nothing. This is my wedding gift to my daughter. The one you wouldn't accept three years ago. This is the one even the famous Dr. Markowitz and his wife can't match. Or spoil. So go. I'll take care of it."

"Jack, I don't know how to thank you." Howie reached for Gold's arm. Gold shook the hand off.

"Understand something, counselor. I'm doing this for Wendy. As far as I'm concerned you're a piece of *dreck.* A phony little condescending New York prick. I wouldn't piss down your throat if you were dying of thirst, if it wasn't for Wendy and the baby. Understand?"

Howie stood there grim-faced, his mouth a tight, white line above his beard.

"And another thing. This cocaine shit is over *now*. And from now on. You've made your one mistake, *bubeleh,* and that's one more than most people are allowed with me."

"That's over."

"I don't want to hear one word about you and drugs. And from now on I'm gonna be listening. And I have a lot of ears out there."

"It's finished, Jack. Never again. *Emmes.*"

"It better be."

"I swear it. On my son's life. My right hand to God."

Gold studied him closely. Then he took the cigar from his mouth and jabbed the end lightly into Howie's chest. "You take care of my daughter," he spat out. "And my grandson."

"Jack, Jack, Jack—" Howie said, smiling and shaking his head.

Gold held his hands up, palms out. "That's all I'm going to say." He turned as if to leave. Howie reached for his sleeve again.

"Thank you, Jack." He held out his hand. Gold looked down at it.

"C'mon, Jack. Aren't you going to shake my hand?"

Gold hesitated for a moment, then shook Howie's hand firmly.

"Let's get out of here," he said. "We spent the whole party in the can."

"I've got to use the toilet," Howie said. "I'll be down in a minute."

Gold looked at him. "We've been in here an hour. All of a sudden you get the urge?"

Howie smiled with embarrassment. "I need privacy. Can't go when anyone's around."

Gold pushed on the door. "Well, then, you better not go to jail."

"Right," Howie laughed.

"All right. I'll see you downstairs." Gold pushed out into the hallway. He stopped and stood there. The hallway was empty. Downstairs the band was now playing rock 'n' roll. A middle-aged woman in a short leather skirt came out of the ladies' room opposite. She smiled warmly at Gold, but when he didn't respond, hurried down the stairs. Gold turned around and slipped quietly back into the men's room. Howie wasn't visible. He had gone into one of the stalls. Gold stood stock still. He immediately heard the sound of someone inhaling sharply from behind the second stall's door. It was rapidly repeated. Gold leaned back against the low lavatory for support and kicked out at the door with both feet. The light metal crumpled, but the bolt held. Gold lashed out again. This time the frame collapsed and the twisted door exploded inward. Howie was crouched in the back of the stall, an almost comic book expression of horror on his face.

"My God, Jack, what are—"

Gold yanked Howie by his tie, dragged him from the stall.

"Jack, for chrissake!"

"*Where is it?*" Gold shouted.

"What are you talking about?"

Howie's left hand was bunched into a tight fist. Gold grabbed his wrist and pried at the clenched fingers.

"Give it to me!"

"Jack, stop it!"

Gold slapped Howie hard across the face. The sound reverberated hollowly off the walls. Howie tried to pull away and Gold slapped him again. He twisted Howie's arm behind his back and pushed upward. Howie's fingers opened and a small glass vial with an attached gold chain and tiny gold spoon fell to the floor and rolled across the tile.

"*You stupid little punk!*" Gold shouted. He jammed his arm under Howie's throat and crowded him against the wall, almost lifting the shorter man off the floor. "I told you not to lie to me!"

"Jack, you're choking me!"

"*I'll kill you, you little* putz! *I'll kill you!*"

Gold pushed up against Howie's throat and the smaller man was lifted in the air, his legs and feet working. Howie tore at Gold's arm. His face reddened and he began to choke. His words became garbled and unintelligible.

"Puh-puh-puleeze!" he rasped.

Finally Gold stepped back and let him sink to his knees, coughing and sputtering, tearing at his shirt collar.

"*Don't forget this!*" Gold shouted down at him. Then he dropped his heel on the coke vial and after the vial disintegrated with a tiny *pop!* ground the glass and the cocaine into a sparkling, dusty smear on the dark blue tile. The delicate golden spoon was twisted and flattened.

"Don't forget this!" Gold shouted again. "You don't do this while you're married to my daughter! Ever again! I'll kill you! *I'll fucking kill you!*"

Howie was still on his knees, coughing and spitting, gulping to catch his breath. Gold spun on his heels to leave and walked right into the belly of a fat man with a curly, black beard. The fat man took in the scene with a face that registered his incredulity. Gold paused for only a second, then made his way around the fat man.

"Excuse me, rebbe," Gold said and then was out the door.

He walked quickly down the short flight of stairs and was on his way out to the parking lot when he changed his mind and went back into the ballroom.

The ballroom was very loud and very drunk. The dance floor was jammed with bouncing, sweating bodies. An overweight girl with Bo Derek beads was screaming the latest Pointer Sisters hit into a microphone in front of the now coatless band. The line of giggling preschoolers was still snake-dancing through the crowded tables.

"I thought you'd left," the bartender said and poured a double Scotch over ice.

"I needed one more of your specialties. For the road." Gold saluted the bartender with his glass and emptied it. The bartender immediately refilled it.

"You ever run for president, you got my vote," Gold said and dropped a sawbuck into the bartender's tip jar. The bartender laughed and thanked him, then moved to fill another order.

The girl stopped singing and the guitarist took a solo. Lots of distortion and feedback. The noise level in the room shot up ten decibels.

"Where'd you go?" Charlie Wiegand was shouting into Gold's ear. "For three minutes I visit with one of Dot's nieces. I come back to the table and everybody's gone. Poof! Disappeared!" Charlie belched loudly. It could be heard even over the rock 'n' roll.

"Good food!" he shouted. "And caterers I know! I must have worked with a zillion of them! That's good food! Did you get any?"

"I'm not hungry!" Gold shouted back.

"Wendy was looking!"

"What?" Gold leaned closer and cupped his hand over his ear.

"Wendy was looking for you!"

"Where is she?"

"The rabbi's office!"

"Where's that?"

"You know the stairway up to the bathroom?"

"Yeah!"

"Don't go up the stairs! Go past the stairs! You'll see it!"

"Thanks, Charlie! I'll see you later!"

"You're coming back?"

"I don't think so!"

"You're going home?"

"I think so!"

"Give me a call!"

"I will, Charlie!"

"No, I mean it!"

"I mean it!"

"You mean it?"

"I mean it!"

"All right! I'll see you later!"

Gold finished his drink and then fought his way back across the crowded room. The hallway was a cool, quiet haven. Gold found the door marked OFFICE and was about to knock when a voice from behind stopped him.

"Jack. I wanted you to meet someone."

The short hairs on the back of Gold's neck tingled. He turned to face Evelyn and Peter Markowitz.

"This is the bar mitzvah boy," Evelyn said and pushed Peter forward. Her eyes were still red from crying, but now they glinted with triumph. "Isn't he a picture?"

Gold and the blond boy examined each other. Gold searched for something familiar, a fragment of himself, a piece of a broken mirror. Then he stuck out his hand.

"*Mazel tov,* Peter."

Peter shook his hand and smiled widely.

"Thank you, sir."

They dropped their hands and stood there in embarrassed silence. Then Peter said, "I know who you are."

Gold's neck hairs tingled again; his testicles shriveled. He shot a glance at Evelyn. Her face was turbulent with fear and confusion. Behind the leathery suntan, it was visibly drained of color.

Gold turned back to the boy. "Oh? Who am I, Peter?"

"You're my mother's first husband."

Evelyn caught her breath with a sharp intake.

"That's right, son," Gold said.

The boy's smile grew even wider. "You're Wendy's father. You're a policeman. She told me about you. Can I see your gun?"

Evelyn began to cry softly with relief. Gold himself felt a mixture of release and regret.

"I didn't bring it," Gold lied. "Besides, it's not good policy to bring handguns to a public place, Peter. It's too dangerous. An accident could easily happen."

"Oh," the boy said.

"Firearms are not toys," Gold said, and felt very stupid saying it.

Suddenly Dr. Stanley Markowitz was there, his arms encircling Evelyn and Peter, turning them away from Gold.

"What *are* we doing here?" he asked with a hard look at Evelyn. "The photographers want a shot of you two boogieing down together. They're about to go home."

He shepherded them quickly down the hall, turning to speak to Gold over his shoulder.

"Sorry you have to leave so soon, Jack. We *must* have that dinner. Call me at my office."

Gold stood there for a moment after they had gone, then sighed to himself.

He knocked softly on the rabbi's office door. There was no response. He knocked again and opened the door. Wendy was sitting in a big leather chair behind the rabbi's desk. The khaki jumpsuit was opened to her navel and she was nursing little Joshua. She looked up and smiled.

"Daddy. Come in."

Gold hesitated, embarrassed.

"Oh, come in and shut the door." She laughed and, as well as she could, pulled the front of her clothes together.

Gold entered the room and closed the door behind him. He stood before the desk.

"Come here," she said, holding out her free hand to him.

Gold came around the desk and took her hand. He caught a glimpse of the baby nuzzling Wendy's swollen nipple. Then he made a concentrated effort to avert his eyes. On the wall across from the desk was a painting pleated like a fan. Looked at from the right it was Golda Meir; from the left, David Ben Gurion. Gold studied the effect closely.

The baby coughed. Wendy looked down at him. The office door opened slightly and Howie peered in. He had combed his hair and adjusted his clothes, but he carried his tie in his hand, his collar was open, and a red mark was visible on his throat just below his beard line. He was startled to see Gold. Gold glared at him and willed him to go away. Howie looked from Gold to Wendy—her head bent over the baby—and then back to Gold. Soundlessly Gold raised his right hand and pointed at him. Howie stared at him for a moment, then quietly faded back and closed the door.

The baby was nursing easily again. Wendy looked up at Gold happily.

"Tell me the truth, Daddy. Aren't you glad you came? Didn't you have a good time?"

Gold smiled down at her.

"The best, Pieface."

10:17 PM The black hooker stood on the corner of Sunset and Sierra Bonita, waving and shouting at the cars that sped by when the light changed. Everything about her was oversized: her breasts, her ass, her lips, her eyes. She looked like a cartoon, a Disney character gone berserk. Minnie Mouse on PCP. She wore bright orange shorts, a T-shirt cut off just below her breasts, and black leg warmers. Whenever a shout would go up from a passing car filled with males she would execute a stripper's bump and grind, ending with an obscene snap of her hips in the direction of the shout, her pelvis thrust out suggestively and her tongue darting around her lips.

"Puss-*sayyy,*" she hollered, slapped her ample ass and cackled with evil laughter. "Good puss-*sayyy.*"

After a while another whore strolled over, a thin white girl in a dirty white satin dress. She offered the cartoon hooker a cigarette. They smoked and talked until the cigarettes were gone, then the white girl drifted listlessly away.

A few minutes later a low-slung black '67 Porsche pulled up. The cartoon hooker leaned over and talked through the passenger window. Then she opened the door and got in. The Porsche peeled rubber as it roared away.

Across Sunset and down about a quarter of a block Walker started his van, snapped on the headlights, and jerked into the bumper-to-bumper traffic. Four blocks east the van got caught behind a Chevy low-rider packed with homeboys and the Porsche disappeared through a red light. Walker spun the wheel and whipped into a side street. He drove the back streets, heading eastward and jolting to a sudden stop at every intersection, until he got on the Hollywood Freeway. He took the van up to sixty-five and cruised north, toward the desert. He rolled down all the windows and the hot night air rushed through the van. After passing the northern rim of the San Fernando Valley he was in the desert.

"—trying to establish, Janna, what we're attempting to alert the American public to, is that we are being flooded, inundated with foreign-born immigrants. Southern California, especially, is simply drowning in undocumented workers. The INS threw up a roadblock, a roadcheck, if you will, last week on the 405 freeway forty miles north of San Diego, and they discovered an illegal alien in *every fifth car.* The traffic got so backed up they finally had to wave the rest of the cars through. They weren't equipped to handle the sheer numbers."

"I saw a news report about that, Doctor."

"That's only one incident, Janna. The tip of the iceberg. Every night, all along the two-thousand-mile border—you can practically see them from this radio station—thousands of Mexican nationals are crossing over and slipping into the mainstream of the United States, like a virus injected into the bloodstream of a healthy human being."

"Uh, I think, Dr. Tichner, that we have to remember that we're here, now, broadcasting this show, because of the hospitality of the Mexican government, of the Mexican people."

"Oh, I don't blame the Mexicans, Janna. It's not their problem. It's ours. I love Mexico. For Mexicans. And I love America. For Americans. And it's not just *Mexican* nationals I'm talking about. We are being swamped by illegal aliens from all over the world. Nicaragua. Guatemala. Vietnam. Cambodia. The Philippines. Iran. My God, we're being swamped by *legal* aliens. You can walk for blocks in Los Angeles and hear every language spoken *but* English."

The traffic on the freeway thinned out about an hour outside of L.A. The desert wind sluiced through the van and made the hairs on Walker's arms tingle.

"—talking tonight, on Reality Radio, with Dr. Phillip Tichner, who heads the organization Close Our Borders, which, of course, is dedicated to doing just that. Tell us, Dr. Tichner. What is the primary danger of continued unchecked immigration?"

"Janna, I'll tell you. There are so many dangers. But the immediate one, the one that disturbs me the most, is simply the negative impact it has on our society, on our culture."

"Can you elaborate?"

"Well, Janna, forget about the jobs taken away from American workers. Forget about the millions of dollars being pirated to other countries by undocumented *braceros*. Forget about the millions of dollars in tax monies uncollected from these same people. Forget about the drain and strain on our schools, our charities, our social services put there by these very same people. Instead let us zero in on the attitudes and opinions, the morals these people are bringing to our land. We are being crushed by people who have no interest in our way of life, our Christian ethics, our democratic form of government, our language, our life-styles. These people don't want to become *Americans*. This is no misty-eyed exodus of poor and huddled masses floating in under the shadow of the Statue of Liberty. These people are simply merchants seeking a bigger and richer marketplace."

Walker slipped down an off-ramp and took a left under the freeway onto a two-lane state road. He was looking for a way to get back on the freeway heading in the other direction, back to L.A., but he saw movement and bright eyes caught in his headlights half a mile up the road. He drove straight toward the shape, pressing down on the accelerator. The coyote was awash in the headlights now, loping easily along the edge of the cement. It looked back once at the approaching vehicle, then trotted down the soft shoulder and into the desert where it knew no vehicle would follow. Only this time a vehicle did. Walker left the highway doing seventy-five, gripping the wheel tightly in both hands and laughing out loud. The coyote realized he was being hunted and feinted to the right, then lunged to the left. But the blue van bore down on him. In one final effort the coyote turned back on itself, almost a hundred and eighty degrees. The van spun in the loose sand, momentarily tottering on two wheels. Then Walker stomped the pedal to the floorboard and the Ford leaped after the coyote. The animal veered to the right again, back onto the highway, and then the van was upon him. The coyote screamed once and went under the wheels. Walker felt a soft furry bump. He braked hard and the van fishtailed to a screeching stop on the rough concrete. He backed the van to the coyote. The animal was down, snapping at itself, smelling its own blood. It struggled to get up but its hind legs were crushed. Its tongue lolled out of its muzzle. It swung its gray head and its eyes, shocked and unseeing, rested on Walker. Walker laughed.

The coyote lurched forward inch by inch, dragging itself along by its front claws. Then it stopped, threw back its bloody head and gave one quick, short howl at the moon. It lay down on the highway and was dead. The wind off the desert ruffled its dirty gray fur.

Walker gunned the engine and the van burned rubber for fifty yards. He screamed out across the empty wasteland.

"These people don't have any idea, Janna, of what this country stands for, of what it means to be an American. They don't understand the principles of democracy, the responsibilities of freedom, or anything but the basest, most fundamental tenets of our economic system. The vast majority of these people have come here from the equivalent of the seventeeth or eighteenth century. They were little better than peasants, feudal serfs in their Third World homelands. They're primitives—unschooled and unprincipled, unwashed and unhealthy. What kind of impact can we *expect* them to make on this country?"

"Language is what bonds a people, Janna. Holds them together. Cements them and gives them a national purpose. These people have absolutely no interest in learning English. And that is fragmenting our society. For the first time in our country's history we're becoming a *nation of factions,* as I like to call it. Some very intelligent, very concerned people—whom I respect a great deal—have expressed to me the fear that Southern California may someday become a separate, *Spanish*-speaking state. Maybe even a *Mexican* state. And this may all come about a lot sooner than you may think. Maybe even before the turn of the century."

Walker roared back to the city.

"Dr. Tichner, are you suggesting, then, that we beef up our border patrols, strengthen our visa approval program, et cetera, et cetera, in an attempt to halt the numbers of illegal aliens coming into this country?"

"I am suggesting much more than that, Janna. I am suggesting—no, de*mand*ing—that we halt, stop, cease, and resist *all* immigration into this country. Legal or illegal. For now and evermore. This nation isn't a frontier anymore. We don't need settlers as we once did. We need to preserve and protect what we already have. COB means to do just that: Close Our Borders. America for Americans, if you will. The world today is a very different one from the one envisioned by the writers of our antiquated, asinine immigration laws."

Walker got back to Hollywood after two o'clock. He cruised Sunset and Hollywood Boulevard. The hookers had disappeared; the traffic had dwindled. It was still too early to pick up his papers.

He thought about eating. Taking the speed, he sometimes forgot about food for whole days. Now he was hungry. He passed hot dog stands, hamburger huts, single slice pizza spots, all-night chicken franchises. They were all crowded with blacks, Mexicans, and assorted white street people jostling to give their orders and pick up their greasy food. In all of them blacks, Mexicans, and Asians were cooking and serving. Walker finally pulled into the parking lot of a 7-Eleven on Selma, just off Hollywood Boulevard. Here, too, there were several black males drinking and killing time, but Walker was convinced that the food here was machine-wrapped, prepackaged in heavy, heat-sealed plastic. It was clean, untouched by nonwhite hands. He selected chicken and tuna salad sandwiches and a carton of milk from the cold cabinet. He had carried his thermos into the store and now he filled it from the pot of the coffee maker. The cashier was a Pakistani, and Walker held the sandwiches up so the cashier could read the prices without touching them. He bagged them himself.

Out in the parking lot on the way to the van one of the young blacks separated himself from the others and stepped in Walker's path.

"Say, man. You got a cigarette? Gimme five dollers." He was shirtless and shoeless, and his pants were soiled. Walker tried to step around, but the other man crowded in.

"Hey, motherfucker. Didn't you hear me? I said gimme five dollers." He pushed lightly on Walker's chest. Walker slapped the black's hand away.

"Don't touch me, nigger."

Instantly the other bloods were alert and moving toward them.

"What you say, motherfucker?" the man in front of him said.

Walker pushed around him and walked toward the van.

"Hey, where you going, motherfucker?" The shirtless man trailed after Walker, pointing and gesturing. "Who you calling nigger, punk? Mother-fucking white punk. Where you going in such a big-ass hurry? Come over here, call me nigger again."

The others were around the shirtless man now, glaring angrily at Walker. One of them threw an empty half-pint bottle wrapped in a paper sack. It shattered on the van's door as Walker climbed in. An angry shout went up from the crowd.

"You don't like niggers, motherfucker? Ask yo' mama 'bout niggers. *She* sure as shit like niggers. She like them *big* niggers."

The others laughed.

"She sure like *this* big nigger."

"Honky motherfucker."

"Paddy punk. Where the fuck you think you going?"

The men crowded around the front of the van. Some of them pounded on the sides. One of them dragged a house key up and down, scratching the paint.

"C'mon out, cocksucker."

Walker keyed the motor, popped the clutch, and floored the accelerator. The van lurched forward, scattering the crowd left and right. One of the men wasn't fast enough. The van's tire rolled over his toes and he screamed in pain and rage, "I'll kill you. I'll kill you, motherfucker!"

Another threw an empty Thunderbird bottle after the van. It landed in the street and rolled unbroken into the gutter.

"We *know* you, motherfucker! We got you, motherfucker!"

"Believe *that,* whitey. Believe *that.*"

Walker laughed as he sped down Yucca. He ran a few red lights on the deserted street, then slowed, turned, and headed south, away from Holly-wood. In a few minutes he was in a wealthy residential neighborhood. The streets were lined with oaks and willows. The homes were brick and flagstone, fenced with wrought iron and protected by electronic security systems. The gutters were swept clean. Walker parked away from the street lights, at the edge of a small, darkened public park. He unwrapped his sandwiches and ate in the van. The streets were silent, empty. He drank some of the milk. An LAPD black-and-white turned into the street, cruis-ing very slowly and flashing its mounted searchlight into the trees of the park. Walker stayed still. The patrol car passed him and drove slowly away. He emptied the carton of milk down his throat and crushed it flat, then slipped out of the van and locked it.

He walked nonchalantly into the park, his hands thrust into the pockets of his cut-off jeans. Past the trees that lined the perimeter of the park was a baseball field encircled by a jogging track. Walker broke into an easy trot on the track. The cinders crunched beneath the soles of his running shoes. He went around the track twice and was halfway around again when he right-angled from the track and cut straight across the closely cropped lawn that ended in a seven-foot brick wall at the rear of the park. He didn't even slow his pace, but hit the wall running, leapt high, and vaulted gracefully over. He was in an empty parking lot. Walker crouched down, frozen and tentative, like a cat. After a few minutes of silence he straightened and went over to the rear of the building. The building was red brick, like the parking lot wall, and white marble steps led up to the building's back entrance. Walker stood before the wall and examined it in the moonlight, looked up at it like an artist before an empty canvas. He chuckled. He rubbed his hands over the front of his T-shirt, then reached into the waistband of his cut-offs and pulled out the aerosol cannister. After a few minutes he was done. He jumped back over the wall and the parking lot was empty again.

SUNDAY
August 5

10:15 AM Esther's eyes fluttered open. She peeked around the pillow she was hugging, spied the clock, then groaned, pulled the covers back over her head and pushed herself deeper into the mattress.

She lay like that, sleepless, for a full five minutes. Then she threw off the covers and reached for a cigarette. She got up, went to the window, and peered around a shade. The Hollywood Hills looked like gray ghosts behind a shroud of smog. On a *Sunday,* Esther thought. She turned off the airconditioner, and as the fan wound down she could hear the television blaring downstairs. She walked downstairs barefoot, still wearing the over-sized black L.A. Raiders jersey she had slept in and carrying her cigarettes.

Little Bobby was in his jockey shorts, spread-eagled on the floor before the TV. Surrounding him was a crazy quilt of Sunday comics, textbooks, novels, and a world atlas opened to the state of California.

Don't this boy *ever* get tired of reading, Esther thought.

"How can you think with that noise box so loud?" Esther said from the foot of the stairs.

"Hi, Mama." Little Bobby jumped up and ran to her, giving her a hug. She put a hand on either side of his face and kissed him.

"Clean your glasses, baby."

Little Bobby whipped off his glasses and wiped them on the cloth of his underwear.

"You eat any breakfast, baby?" Esther went into the kitchen.

"No, ma'am." Little Bobby followed her. "I had a banana."

"How come you ain't out there soaking up all that beautiful smog with all the other kids?"

"I just got up a little while ago. Grandma and I watched the late, late show last night."

Esther had started making coffee. She stopped and looked at him.

"Grandma and *I?*"

Little Bobby sounded peevish. "Well, that's correct."

"Correct?" Esther laughed. "My, my, my. Ain't that something. Correcting your own mama."

"Mama!"

"Okay, okay. Lookahere. I'll make you a deal. Go turn that damn TV off and I'll make us a big old fashioned Sunday morning breakfast."

"Mama, I'm *watching* that program."

"Then at least turn it down, why don't you."

"Okay." Little Bobby ran out of the kitchen. Esther put on the coffee. She whacked open a cylinder of buttermilk biscuits, snuggled them together on a baking sheet, and slid the sheet into the oven. Next she boiled some water and simmered a pot of instant grits. Then she brought out two heavy black frying pans, cut thick slices of Canadian bacon from a tube and fried them up, along with four eggs. She arranged the two plates of food on a serving tray, added the basket of biscuits along with some butter, jam, and maple syrup. She made room for a tall glass of milk and her coffee cup, then carried the heavy tray into the living room. Little Bobby was again flat on his stomach in front of the television, his bare heels waving in the air. Esther edged the tray onto the coffee table, pushing aside some magazines and the Sunday paper.

"You gonna eat in your underwear?"

"Uh huh."

"No, you ain't."

"Mama, *you* didn't change."

"That's me. That ain't you."

"Aw, Mama."

"Let's go! Biscuits getting cold!"

Little Bobby leaped up and took the stairs three at a stride.

"You be careful!"

While Little Bobby was gone Esther turned the TV down several notches, pulled the armchair up to the coffee table, and opened the *L.A. Times.* She broke her egg yolks over her grits and mixed them together with a pat of butter and some black pepper. Little Bobby came bounding down the stairs. He sat cross-legged on the floor by the coffee table and pounced on a biscuit.

"You washed your hands this morning, boy?"

Little Bobby paused, the biscuit halfway to his mouth. He thought for a moment, and then said, "Yeah."

"Say what?"

Little Bobby looked at the biscuit and then at his mother.

"What are you supposed to say?" Esther asked.

"Yes."

"Yes *what?*"

"Yes, ma'am."

"That's more like it. Now eat your breakfast."

Little Bobby took a big bite of steaming biscuit.

"Mama, nobody else in school says 'yes, ma'am' and 'no, ma'am.' "

"Well, I'm not concerned with 'nobody else.' I'm only concerned with you."

The boy gulped at his milk to cool the hot biscuit. The milk left a perfect white moustache over his lip.

"Miss Abrams says 'yes, ma'am' and 'no, ma'am' and 'yes, sir' and 'no, sir'—talking like that—was just a way the white slaveholders had of keeping black people in their place. She called it"—Little Bobby chewed thoughtfully—"she called it the language of inferiority."

Esther swallowed a sliver of Canadian bacon and took a sip of coffee. She looked at her son.

"Well, baby, Miss Abrams got all kind of college diplomas, so she must be pretty smart and all, but she sounds to me like one of those white people who's got, you know, a problem with being white. Guilty about it and all. Now you tell your Miss Abrams that my great-aunt Miss Rosalie Gibbons taught me my manners, and she sure as *hell* wasn't no white slaveholder. Woman was so black she was purple, Aunt Rosalie. And didn't feel inferior to no-bo-dy either. Aunt Rosalie used to say good manners are the cheapest thing in the world. Don't cost you a nickel. And at the same time they're the most precious thing in the world. Next to Jesus, of course. Aunt Rosalie was real big on Jesus."

Esther lifted a forkful of grits and egg.

"Aunt Rosalie would've had a heart attack, the way these California kids talk to grown-ups. 'Yeah' and 'nah' and 'uh huh.' So you tell Miss Abrams that as long as you're my son you're going to address your elders with the proper respect. If for nothing else, in honor of the memory of my Great-aunt Rosalie."

"But, Mama, I don't even *know* Aunt Rosalie."

"Of course not, baby. She died before you were even born."

"Then how come—"

"Look, baby, I'll make you another deal. When you get as old as me you don't have to say 'ma'am' and 'sir' anymore. Deal?"

Little Bobby looked askance at his mother. "You're trying to trick me."

"Say what?" Esther smiled.

"When I'm as old as you are, you'll be older than you are now."

"You're the smart one, Little Bobby. You can figure out a way. Now eat your breakfast."

They ate in silence, Esther reading the paper, Little Bobby watching the tube. Little Bobby poured syrup on his emptied plate and flattened his biscuit in it. Esther finished her food and lit a cigarette. She curled up in the armchair, tucked her long, slender feet under herself, and leafed through the *Times,* searching for the classifieds. She had to start looking for a secondhand van.

"Mama?"

"Uh huh?" she answered absently.

"What's a synagogue?"

"What's a what?"

"What's a synagogue?"

Esther peeked at Little Bobby over the top of her newspaper.

"Well, baby," she started slowly, "it's kinda like a church. It's like a church for Jewish people."

"Don't people like synagogues?"

Esther took a long drag on her cigarette. "Why do you ask, baby?"

" 'Cause on 'L.A. at Large' they said people were de- de- de*facing* synagogues." Little Bobby pointed a syrupy finger at the television screen. Esther glanced at it. Two white men were seated in ultramodern leather chairs around a free-form table, arguing earnestly. One of them wore a yarmulke.

Esther's smile radiated real pride and pretended exasperation.

"Why can't you watch the cartoons like everyone else's child?"

Little Bobby smiled back. "Mama, everybody knows the cartoons come on *Saturday* morning."

"Smartypants," Esther laughed. She took a chance and went back to reading her newspaper, but when Little Bobby got started he was not to be denied.

"*C'mon*, Mama."

"Okay, okay, okay." Esther folded the paper neatly and laid it on her legs. She lit another cigarette off of the butt of the burning one.

"Why are they defacing the synagogues?" he asked again.

Esther looked at her son. "Do you know what *deface* means, baby?"

Little Bobby blinked at her, momentarily unsure of himself. "I—I think so," he stammered.

At that moment Esther Phibbs thrilled with love and pride at the life she had made. She had never encountered such curiosity, such a hunger to know. She marveled at it. And that it had dropped from *her* body.

"Deface means to like scar, or tear up. To ruin something. To vandalize—"

"I know what vandalize means. Our school was vandalized last year."

"Well, it's the same thing."

"Why are they doing it?"

Esther sighed again, heavily. She pointed to her empty coffee cup. "Go get me a refill, baby. Put about a spoon of sugar in it."

Little Bobby grabbed the cup and was up and running to the kitchen. Esther unfolded her long legs and leaned forward in the chair, poking out the flame on her cigarette. She tried to collect her thoughts, to arrange what she was going to say to her boy. He was so damn insatiable. And her with a ninth-grade education. In a black-ass rural Georgia school, for God's sake. She knew that someday—someday soon—he was going to look at his mother and realize how mule-dumb she was. How uneducated. How unsophisticated. How *country*. She was trying to postpone that day as long as she could.

But right now, for the very first time, she had to attempt to explain prejudice to her scarily gifted son.

Little Bobby hurried back with the coffee. He resumed his position on the floor, looking up at her. Esther took one of the last biscuits from the wicker basket. She buttered it, then spread it thickly with strawberry jam. She took a bite and chewed slowly.

"What did they say on TV?"

"They said somebody was spray-painting mean things on the outsides of the synagogues. Graffiti, like the guys in the gangs. The Crips and the Brims. Only mean things. *Scurrilous* things."

Now what the hell does *that* mean? Esther thought.

"Well, baby, I think what's happening is this." She took another bite of biscuit and swallowed some more coffee. "Remember the first day we enrolled you in the Exceptional Class? We were walking up the school steps and we heard that white woman say to her little girl"—Esther mimicked a haughty sneer—" 'I wonder how they managed to let *him* in.' And you asked me why she said that? Remember that?"

"Uh huh."

"Well, I didn't explain it to you then, because you were just a little kid. But now I can tell you. That lady was prejudiced. She don't like black people. She *prejudges* them. Understand?"

"Yes. Yes, ma'am."

"It don't matter if the black person is good or bad, nice or mean, man, woman, or child. She just don't like us. Wants no part of us. She's *prejudiced* against us."

"But why?"

"For no reason, and for a thousand reasons. Fear is one. Ignorance is another. Usually they go hand in hand. People are a lot of times scared of what they don't understand, what they're not used to. And then again, some white people are just ornery. They do everything they can to keep the black man down, then hate him because he *is* down. A lot of them kind of people back home in Georgia, let me tell you. Some of them crackers down there think God *told* them to lord it over the black man. I overheard these two old white women talking one day. My Aunt Rosalie kept house for them and she brought me along this one time. I wasn't but nine or ten. And this one white biddy says to the other that her preacher told her why black people are black. Seems like when Cain killed Abel, God got real mad at Cain and sent him off into the wilderness. Well, there wasn't any women in the wilderness, seeing as how Cain was Adam and Eve's only surviving child, and they was the only couple producing at the time, and so Cain, in his loneliness, mated with a she-ape, and their offspring was the beginning of the Negro race. So that black skin was the sign, the curse the Bible speaks of, that God put on all the children of Cain. And therefore all black people are half ape and half murderer."

Little Bobby thought a moment about what Esther had said, then he looked at his mother.

"That's stupid," he said.

"You're right, Little Bobby. It's stupid and ignorant and mean and ugly and horrible and all those things. But it doesn't change the fact that those old ladies *believed* it. Believed it like religion. Those old ladies had a prejudice against all black people because of that belief. Understand what I'm saying?"

Little Bobby nodded.

"Well, a lot of people are prejudiced against Jewish people the same way."

"But *they* don't have black skins."

"No, they don't. People have a whole bunch of different reasons for being prejudiced against the Jews."

"Like what?"

"Some people blame the Jews for Jesus being crucified. You know, nailed to the cross."

"But that was so long ago."

Esther shrugged. "Some people got long memories. They been mad at the Jews for two thousand years over what happened to Jesus. They been persecuting them—you understand that word?—they been persecuting them all that time. And they still doing it. And that's why they're vandalizing those synagogues. It's people still mad at the Jews doing it."

"But that doesn't seem right."

"It ain't."

"Then why doesn't someone talk to them? Explain to them that they're wrong?"

Esther gave out a short, bitter laugh. "You can't talk to these people, baby. They're all mean-spirited and full of hatred."

Little Bobby wrinkled his nose and blinked his lashes behind his thick lenses. "I think hatred sounds stupid."

"It *is,* sweet baby."

"Then we should stop it."

"Well, I'll tell you what, little man. You keep studying hard in school, you get smart enough, maybe someday you can invent a pill people can take that'll stop all the hatred in the world."

Little Bobby frowned. "Mama, I'm not going to be a scientist anymore."

"Oh?"

"I'm going to be an anchorman like Dan Rather."

"Do tell? What happened to winning the Nobel Prize, like you was gonna do last week?"

"Miss Abrams says communications will be the most important field in the twenty-first century."

"Field?" Esther feigned a shocked face. "That white woman g'wan have my boy working out in da field, in dem ol' cotton fields back home?"

"Mama!"

Esther laughed. "Come over here, baby." She patted the cushion of the armchair. Little Bobby came over and sat beside her in the crook of her arm.

"Listen, little man. This conversation's much too heavy for a Sunday morning. What's your calendar look like today?"

"What do you mean?" he asked with a suspicious air.

"I mean, do you think you could find time for a date with a tall, dark, sexy lady?"

Little Bobby frowned. "I don't want to go to Grandma Phibbs's, 'cause on Sundays she always has those church ladies over there, and they pinch me and give me big wet kisses and—"

"I'm not talking about going over to Grandma Phibbs's."

"—and Dwayne's coming over later to play baseball—"

"Well, hey, I'm not asking you to run off to Timbuktu or something. Just a little afternoon drive with your mama. Can you handle that?"

Little Bobby was thoughtful for a moment, then smiled and kissed Esther's cheek. "Sure, Mama."

"Well, let's go, boy. I don't want to keep you from your really important appointments." She gave him a hug, holding him close and whispering in his ear, "Last one ready to go washes the dishes when we come back." Little Bobby ripped away from her and Esther was running right behind him, laughing and pulling at the tail of his T-shirt as they pounded up the stairs.

Twenty minutes later they were cruising southward in medium traffic on the Santa Ana Freeway. The smog had thickened, unusual for a Sunday. The palm trees that lined the freeway seemed to droop in the sulfurous ozone. Esther rolled up all the windows and turned on the station wagon's airconditioner. Little Bobby twisted the radio's knob, sliding past all the music channels.

"Hey!" Esther complained. "That was Whitney Houston!"

Little Bobby didn't even acknowledge her, but kept turning the dial until he found a broadcast of a Dodgers game. He turned to his mother and smiled.

"Dwayne says it's gonna be the Dodgers and the Angels in the World Series."

"Oh? Do tell?"

"Dwayne says it's going to be the first time; it never happened before."

"Really?"

"Dwayne says that in our school nobody from the Exceptional Class ever made the baseball team."

"Well," Esther began slowly, "there's always a first time for everything. Dwayne's mouth ain't no prayer book. Everything he says ain't gospel."

"You think so, Mama?"

"I think if you want to make the baseball team bad enough, ain't nothing or nobody *I* know of can stop you."

They rode for a while without talking, the traffic whooshing around them. On the radio, Vin Scully expounded on the Dodger infield's woeful fielding this whole season. Esther glanced over at her son.

"Baby?"

"Uh huh?" Little Bobby answered absently. Esther lowered the radio's volume.

"You know your father's coming home on Tuesday."

Little Bobby looked over at her. The sunlight glinted off his glasses.

"Yes, ma'am."

"Well"—Esther fidgeted uncomfortably—"I mean, how do you feel about that? Aren't you happy about it?"

"Sure, Mama. I guess so."

"You *guess* so?"

"Well, you know, sure I'm happy about it."

"You miss your daddy, don't you?"

"Sure, Mama. Only . . ."

"Only what?"

"Only I hope there won't be any more fights and screaming like there always is when Daddy comes home. It's hard to do my homework when there's fighting and screaming."

Esther felt her soul shrivel like a scrap of paper brushed by a flame.

"And, Mama." Little Bobby turned to face her profile. "Mama, you said that Daddy went away because he was *sick.* But Dwayne said only *bad* people go to jail. He said they put sick people in the hospital."

Esther made a mental note to include rat poison in the cookie dough the next time Dwayne came over for chocolate chips and milk.

"That's usually true, Little Bobby. But sometimes they make mistakes. Sometimes they put sick people in jail, and sometimes they put bad people in the hospital."

Little Bobby watched her without volunteering anything further.

"Your daddy was sick," Esther said finally.

"Is he okay now?"

Esther kept her eyes on the road. "We all hope so, baby. We all hope so."

" 'Cause I can't do my homework when there's fighting and hollering."

"Don't you worry, baby." She reached over and patted her son's thigh. "Ain't nothing gonna get in the way of your studying. *Nothing.* I promise. Hey! We're missing the exit!"

Esther pulled sharply to the right. The car behind them braked and blew its horn. Esther and Little Bobby giggled as they curled down the off-ramp.

"Where are we going, Mama? I've never been here before."

"This is the City of Industry, baby."

"Well? Where are we going?"

"I told you."

"What?"

"It's a surprise."

"Well, when are we going to get there?"

"Rigggght now!" Esther rolled into a gravel driveway that led back to a low, brick building. Behind the building was a long row of sheds that fronted a high fence. An official-looking sign on the side of the building announced: SOUTH CENTRAL ANIMAL SHELTER. Esther turned off the station wagon's motor and the air was filled with the sound of baying, barking dogs. Little Bobby looked over at his mother with a puzzled expression.

"Ta-*dah!*" Esther trumpeted. "Surprise!"

Little Bobby looked at the building, then back at his mother. "I don't get it, Mama."

"Well, you remember Miss Regina—the lady used to work for me?"

"Uh huh."

"Well, she works here now. For the Animal Control Board."

"Oh." Little Bobby looked back at the building.

"She's been on the lookout for something. Something for you."

Little Bobby's face was a mask of confusion.

"Lookahere." Esther feigned exasperation. "What do you want more than anything in the world?"

Little Bobby thought for a moment. "To pitch for the school team."

Esther shook her head. "What *thing* do you want more than anything else in the world."

Bobby chewed at his bottom lip. "A home computer."

"No, no, boy. After that."

Little Bobby stared at his mother.

Esther decided to help. "A Buuurrrmmmeeessseee—"

"Kitten!"

"You got it!" Esther squealed. "Let's go!"

Little Bobby was out of the car and bounding up the three steps to the entrance before Esther even got her door opened.

"C'mon, Mama! C'mon!" Little Bobby danced around like he had to pee. "Hurry *up*, Mama!"

"I'm coming! I'm coming!"

Inside, the building was all worn tile and shredded newspaper. In the air hung the pungent odor of animals and animal excrement, overlaid with the acrid bite of a heavy disinfectant. Behind a Formica counter that ran down the middle of the room stood a dark brown woman of indeterminate age in a tailored brown Department of Animal Regulation uniform. She and the uniform were the same color. Behind her were floor-to-ceiling racks of cages that held cats, kittens, small dogs and puppies, even a clutch of spitting raccoons. One cage contained a pair of green parrots.

"Esther!" the uniformed woman shouted. "How you doing, girl? How you be's?"

"Regina. Look at you in your uniform," Esther laughed. "Ain't you looking go-o-o-o-d!"

Regina was a meticulously attired and accessorized woman of luxurious proportions. Her breasts were large and cushiony, her hips wide, and her ass comfortable. The white shirt under the Eisenhower jacket was stiffly starched. Her gold bracelets glittered and jangled.

"Come here, Es," Regina said, rounding the counter and taking Esther into her arms. "I swear, girl, you've gotten skinnier, if that's possible. You ain't nothing but skin and bones, is all."

"Well, you know me, Ree. Nothing I eat ever seems to stick to me. Always been that way."

"That ain't it, I expect." Regina released her from her soft embrace. "You been working too hard. And too long. And *that's* what always been that way."

"Well, you know what them football players say, Ree. No pain, no gain."

"I heard that. And who's this looking like he's about to bust?"

Little Bobby was in obvious torment. He jumped from one sneakered foot to another. His eyes danced.

"Where is it, Miss Regina?"

The two women laughed.

"Mind your manners, Little Bobby," Esther said. "Say hello to Miss Regina. We haven't seen her in six months."

"Hello, Miss Regina. Where is he?"

Regina laughed again, looking down at Little Bobby. "Hello to you, too, Robert. You don't look like you've grown an inch since I seen you last. I suspect you gonna sprout up all at once. You gonna be big and strong like your daddy?"

"Yes, ma'am," Little Bobby said, having visible difficulty controlling himself.

"What'cha gonna be? A football player or a basketball player? All of mine's wants to be either a football player or a basketball player. A Raider or a Laker."

Little Bobby looked up at the two women in desperation.

"He told me this morning he was going to be an anchorman," Esther said proudly. "He likes that baseball, but he's gonna be an anchorman."

"An anchorman? Well, how do you like that? I don't think I ever—"

"Please, Miss Regina!" Little Bobby shouted loudly enough to quiet all the caged animals for a millisecond.

"Little Bobby!" Esther tried to scowl but she couldn't help but smile.

"I'm sorry, Mama, but *please.*"

"That's all right, Es." Regina moved back behind the counter. "Let me just get this little package before this boy busts a gut." She went into a back room and came back with a fluffy, cocoa-colored kitten with dark paws and golden eyes. It looked around at the humans with mild curiosity.

"Here you go, Mr. Phibbs." Regina put the kitten into Little Bobby's outstretched hands. "Now hold him like this when you carry him. Not tight, but plenty of support. Makes him feel all safe and secure. Like a kitten without a care in the world."

Little Bobby carried the kitten to a corner of the green tile and sat down.

"Baby, that floor's filthy," Esther complained, but he didn't hear her. The kitten had climbed up his sleeve and was perched on his narrow shoulders.

"Say, you. What do you think you're doing?" Little Bobby said softly. He gently plucked the kitten from its perch and cuddled it to his chest. The kitten immediately ran up his arm again. This time he balanced precariously on Little Bobby's head.

"Say, who do you think you are?" the boy whispered.

"Would you look at that?" Esther said wonderingly.

"Two little babies," Regina said. "Wish we had a camera."

They watched the little boy and the kitten play. Then Esther shook her head. "A Burmese kitten. Most little boys want a dog—a German shepherd or a Doberman or something like that. Something big and mean. This one wants a kitten."

"He's something special all right, Es."

"And not just any old kitten. Got to be a *Burmese* kitten. Whoever heard of a Burmese kitten? *I* sure never heard of no Burmese kitten."

"They real rare, all right. That's the first one I ever seen the whole time I been working here."

"It must have been real hard to get him, Ree. I really appreciate you finding him."

"Well, I been looking for one ever since you asked me to. How long I been working here—six months? And last Thursday this man comes in here with that kitten and I swear to God, girl, that man had tears in his eyes. Said he bought that cat for his little girl's birthday, and turns out she's allergic to felines. Every time she touches the kitten she takes into coughing and sneezing and choking. And every time he takes it away from her she starts screaming and crying and carrying on."

"That's a shame."

"Ain't it, though. Man said that there kitten almost broke up his marriage. Said his wife threatened to divorce him if he didn't get it out of the house and come back with a puppy. The cat breeder wouldn't take the kitten back, so he finally brought him here. That cat cost him four hundred dollars, too."

"Four hundred!"

"White people are *crazy,* girl. Anyways, when I saw it was the kind of cat Little Bobby wanted I made an immediate trade with the man. Sent him home with one of the cutest little cockapoos you ever seen. Supervisor was saving it for some relative, but I told him the dog died during the night."

"Ree. You shouldn't have done that."

"Happens around here all the time, Esther. That's what this place is *for,* Es. Killing animals."

A man and his two sons came into the building. He asked about adopting a dog and Regina took them back to the kennels. Esther lit a cigarette. Little Bobby was on his back in the corner and the kitten was stalking the finger he kept hiding under his T-shirt.

"That floor's filthy, baby," Esther said again, lovingly.

Little Bobby looked up at her. "Is he really mine, Mama?"

"He's really yours, baby. But don't you leave here without thanking Miss Regina. A real *good* thank you. She's the one really got it for you."

"Yes, ma'am. I will." Little Bobby went back to playing with the kitten.

"What you gonna call him, baby?"

Little Bobby smiled. "Bagheera."

"Ba-*who?*"

"Bagheera. It's the name of this black panther in this book Miss Abrams read to us. *The Jungle Book.* About this little boy who lives with the wolves. And his best friend is this big old black panther named Bagheera."

"Well, that little thing ain't no black panther, but if that's what you want to call him."

Regina came back in, twirling a heavy ring of keys.

"Ree, I want you meet Bagheera. King of the Jungle."

Regina laughed. "Bagheera, huh? Well, how'dja do, ol' Mr. Bagheera. That sounds African. Is that African? Sounds real exotic."

Little Bobby scrambled to his feet and stood solemnly before Regina, clutching the kitten to his breast. "Miss Regina, I want to thank you very much for Bagheera. He's the best cat in the world. And someday when I'm a famous network anchorman I'll come back here with a news crew and a minicam and a sound truck and do a story about you and your animal shelter and make you famous."

Regina smiled down at him. "Little man, in my own small circle of male acquaintances I'm already pretty famous." She shot a mischievous wink at Esther. "But I will take a kiss, if you've got an extra one or two hanging around." Regina bent down and smacked Little Bobby's cheek, leaving a perfect lip print with her rich red lipstick. Little Bobby walked away whispering in Bagheera's ear and wiping the kiss off with the back of his hand.

"He really is special, that one, Esther. He really is something."

"Yes, he is," Esther said with pride.

Little Bobby sat back down on the floor. Bagheera walked around him, strutting like a gangster.

Regina leaned her elbows on the counter. "So? How the hell you been, girl? Won't Bobby be getting out soon?"

"Tuesday morning."

"Well, I'll bet you're happy about that."

"I am, Ree. I am."

Esther lit another cigarette. Regina watched her.

"You are, but what?"

Esther squinted at her through the smoke. "Huh?"

"C'mon, you can tell your ol' buddy Regina. She always knows when something's wrong."

Esther smoked her cigarette and sighed. "I'm scared to death, Ree."

"I'll bet you are, honey."

"I promised Mama Phibbs, if Bobby messes up again, that's it. I shut him out of my life. And you know, Ree, I think I mean it this time."

"I heard that."

"It's just I'm so damn in love with the man, Ree."

"He's a fine-looking man, all right."

Esther dragged on her cigarette. When she spoke again there was a quiver in her voice. "I'm so scared, Ree. *So* goddamn scared. I can't even imagine a life without Bobby."

"Take it easy, girl." Regina stroked Esther's hand.

"I mean, seems like for the past five years Bobby's been in jail more than he's been home. But I always knew he would be there at the end of his time. Three months, six months. This time a year. He was always, you know, in my dreams. Part of my future."

"Yes."

"But I know it can't go on that way forever. I don't want that little boy growing up with a father always in prison. What kind of life is that? It's just not *good* enough. Not him with the mind he's got, Little Bobby. He needs, you know, a stable home environment."

Esther paused, watching Little Bobby play with Bagheera.

"The counselors at school talk to all the parents of kids in the Exceptional Class, and they say these really bright children are very sensitive. They attuned to everything, you understand what I'm saying?"

"Uh huh."

"Things affect these babies. More than regular children. A parent got to be doubly careful with a gifted child, the counselors say. I mean, when he was just a baby it didn't matter. He didn't know what was going on. I'd leave the baby with Bobby and go to work, come back and Big Bobby'd be knocked out stoned in the middle of the floor and this one saying, 'Daddy fell asleep, Daddy fell asleep.' "

Regina shook her head in commiseration.

"A coupla times I'd come home and Bobby'd be gone. Just left the baby completely alone, gone out to score some dope. God only knows how long he been gone. Thank Jesus this one's smart enough on his own not to go outside, or play with matches or whatever. Jesus, Ree, one day I come in, Bobby's gone out and he left a loaded gun on the kitchen table. *Laying right there on the kitchen table.* This one had his head stuck in the television, but, my God! Regina, how much luck does one family have?"

Regina shook her head again. "That heroin's the devil's handsoap, all right."

"But Little Bobby's getting big, you understand? He realizes stuff, understands things. One day soon he's gonna look at his father—the father he hardly knows—and see what? A goddamn junkie, that's what. A criminal. And what does that make me? A junkie's wife. And that ain't how my son's gonna think of me, Regina. I swear to Jesus, that's not how my son is going to think of me."

Esther was whispering hoarsely now. Her eyes were moist. Regina came around the counter and enfolded her gently into her arms.

"Now, now," she crooned, patting Esther's shoulder. Little Bobby looked up from playing with Bagheera and watched the two women embrace, then his attention went back to the kitten.

"But, Ree," Esther whispered into the other woman's collar, "when I go visit him. When I see him, and him looking so clean and clear-eyed, like the man I married, my heart just wants to burst with love. I want to touch him so bad my hands *itch,* girl, you understand what I'm saying?"

Regina didn't say anything, just held her.

"I can't even begin to think of life without Bobby. But I know it can't go on like this, either. Oh, Ree, I'm so damn scared."

"Hey, now"—Regina patted—"maybe this time Bobby'll do right. Maybe he'll square up and do right."

The two women separated. Esther wiped at her eyes with the back of her hand.

"That's what I'm hoping for, Ree. That's what I pray for every night."

"Well, then, there you are." Regina smiled, exposing bright, perfect teeth. Just then the man and his sons came in being pulled by a half-grown part-Airedale puppy. The dog spotted Bagheera and lunged forward. The man yanked back on the plastic leash and the dog sat down clumsily, barking at the kitten. Frowning, Little Bobby scooped up Bagheera and held him protectively in his arms.

"Go away, old dog," Little Bobby said and kicked out in the direction of the puppy. "Shut up!"

While Regina handled the Airedale's paperwork Esther came over and squatted on the floor beside her son.

"That ugly old dog is scaring Bagheera," Little Bobby pouted.

Esther ground out her cigarette under her heel. Little Bobby turned and inspected her.

"Are you okay, Mama?"

Esther smiled and nodded. "Sure, baby, I'm fine."

"I saw you crying."

Esther laughed lightly. "That don't mean especially much. Ladies cry sometimes. It makes them feel better. It's something you'll understand when you grow up."

Little Bobby watched the dog watch Bagheera.

"Are you crying because of Daddy?"

Esther brushed her fingertips across her blue-jeaned thighs.

"I'm crying because of *life,* baby. That's all." She smiled again. "Sometimes ladies do that, too."

The Airedale had lost interest in Bagheera and was now lustily sniffing his new owner's crotch. One of the boys looked at Bobby and Bagheera, then wrapped his arms around the dog's neck. The puppy licked the boy's face and wagged his tail with excitement.

"I like Bagheera much better than that ugly old dog," Little Bobby whispered to his mother.

"So do I," Esther whispered back.

Little Bobby was silent for a moment, then he said, "I hope Daddy likes him."

Esther studied her son's face carefully.

"Don't you worry, baby. Your daddy will like Bagheera just fine, don't you worry."

8:15 PM Walker padded silently down the paved path that ran between the two rows of apartment blocks. All the windows had been opened to the cool twilight and from behind the Levelors the spicy odors of cooking food drifted out. Televisions glowed and spoke and, where the windows were shut, airconditioners hummed. The path ended at a steep embankment that rose up fifteen feet and was overgrown with weeds and grasses. Walker looked behind him to see if anyone was watching, then took a fistful of weeds in each hand and scrambled up the embankment. At the top was a narrow dirt strip maybe seven feet wide; then the earth plunged down the equivalent of three stories into the gaping canyon of a freshly paved parking lot. Beyond the parking lot was bustling Pico Boulevard, and across Pico was a new, ultramodern building constructed of steel and rough-hewn stone, with a futuristic metallic sculpture of a tortured Star of David in front of it. Beside the building's entrance sleek brushed-steel lettering spelled out WEST COAST CENTER OF HOLOCAUST STUDIES.

Walker lay down on his stomach in the tall grass that edged the drop-off and watched the building. Limousines, Rolls-Royces, and Mercedes-Benzes pulled up to the red carpet rolled out on the sidewalk and disgorged tuxedoed men and glittering women, then double-parked down the block, their emergency lights flashing. Quick-moving parking attendants in short green jackets helped equally elegant people out of the other luxury cars, then jumped behind the wheels and with much screeching of brakes and flooring of accelerators, U-turned across Pico and crowded the cars into the parking lot directly below Walker. Through the tinted floor-to-ceiling glass panels that fronted the newly constructed building, Walker could see the people laughing and drinking, nibbling at hors d'oeuvres passed around among them by young Latin-looking women in black-and-white uniforms.

Walker lay watching for over an hour, until the expensive cars stopped arriving. The two parking attendants lounged against the building, joking and laughing. When no cars were passing on Pico, Walker could catch snatches of the Spanish-language Dodger game the Mexicans were listening to on the ghetto-blaster they had set up on the center's steps. The night had closed in and the parking lot below, its safety lights not yet installed, was cloaked in darkness and shadows. Walker stood up. He walked along the narrow crest of the embankment until he found a spot where the grade was a little less steep, then sat down, slipped his feet over the rim, and lay on his back, his head raised to watch the attendants. A few minutes later someone on the Dodgers drove in a run and the two Mexicans laughed and exchanged high-fives. Walker pushed off and slipped down the slope, sometimes braking with his heels, sometimes propelling himself with his hands. Through his thin T-shirt he could feel the freshly dug dirt sliding past under his back. He landed at the bottom of the slope running, a tiny avalanche of soil and pebbles tumbling around him, and quickly knelt behind the front end of a polished gray Corniche. He could hear the attendants chuckling and congratulating themselves and the Dodgers.

Walker peeked over the glossy hood of a 450SL. As he watched, one of the serving girls dashed down the steps with two paper plates of hors d'oeuvres for the parking attendants. They thanked her and flirted. One of them made as if to slap her rump, but she jumped away and shook her finger at him, smiling. The young men laughed and she ran back into the center. The attendants sat on folding chairs at the curbside and ate with their fingers. Taking the paint can from his waistband, Walker shook it vigorously and spray-painted JEW on the side of the big gray Corniche. He duck-walked over to a black Biarritz and wrote KIKES across the driver's side in foot-high scarlet letters. He moved over to a nondescript brown Mercedes and painted NIGGER LOVER on one fender, then JEW LIAR on another. He went on like that for almost ten minutes, painting effortlessly, almost instinctively, in the dark lot, moving crouched up and down the rows of cars. He was elated. His blood seemed to be surging in his body, boiling through his arms and legs. After the twentieth car he leaned back against a chrome bumper and swallowed deeply. His breaths were short, his heart pounded against his rib cage, and he was surprised to find he had an erection. He touched himself and it felt good. He turned to the car he had been leaning on—a burgundy Jaguar sedan—and was painting KILL THE JEWS over the hood when someone across the street shouted, "Hey, you! What the hell are you doing over there?"

On the steps of the center a tall, thin man with longish silver hair was pointing at him.

"I saw him from the second floor! You're supposed to be watching those cars!" he shouted at the attendants. "Go get him!"

The two attendants ran across Pico and came for him. Only instead of separating they came together down the row of automobiles, so Walker loped easily into the shadows at the rear of the lot, drawing them after him; then cut back quickly, zigzagging through the cars until he got to the street.

"There he is! You're letting him get away!" the thin man yelled. He had been joined on the steps by several other men from the party, and they took off after Walker.

Walker jumped the low chain strung around the parking lot and turned right, down Pico, to the first cross street and then cut right again. The land rose into gently hilly residential lawns. He ran easily, unhurriedly, uphill, glancing back from time to time. The two young Mexicans were keeping pace about a half block behind him. The men from the center in their tuxedoes and patent leather pumps were a half block behind the attendants and losing ground rapidly. Walker ran straight for several more blocks, then turned left across a neatly trimmed lawn and then right at the next side street. The hills leveled out here, and he took the time to stop and look back. The younger men were gaining on him. Walker made a series of right-angle turns, then ducked down an almost invisible hedge-lined alley that ran between the backyard fences of two dark streets. Halfway through the unlighted alley he turned and dropped to his belly on the packed ground and watched the alley's entrance. A few seconds later the Mexicans ran by, their heads down and their legs pumping. When they had passed, Walker leaped to his feet, turned and trotted down the rest of the alley. His blue van was parked a few feet from the exit. He unlocked it and slipped behind the wheel. While he ripped off the T-shirt with the soiled back, he keyed the van's motor and shot out of the parking place. He tossed the T-shirt under his seat, then threw the spray can after it. As he gunned the van down the rounded hills he pulled on a bright red windbreaker and covered his sweaty hair with a yellow Michelin Tires baseball cap. At the foot of the hills he turned east on Pico Boulevard and braked down to the speed limit. Six blocks down, in front of the newly dedicated West Coast Center of Holocaust Studies, several police cars were parked in the street, their lights flashing and turning, turning and flashing. A uniformed cop was waving the gawking traffic through. On the sidewalk and on the steps of the center people stood with grim, shocked faces. Women in evening gowns were crying. Across the street in the parking lot men with flashlights were moving among the vandalized cars, pointing and cursing.

Walker pulled down the bill of his cap and drove by, smiling.

MONDAY
August 6

4:02 AM The rolled-up newspaper smacked against the front door. In the apartment directly opposite little Genghis started barking. Gold poured himself another cup of coffee, pulled the plug on the percolator, and carried the cup out with him. He was wearing a lightweight tan suit and a white shirt unbuttoned at the collar. Outside it was still dark; Genghis was still barking. Gold quickly examined the headlines under the bug light. Another synagogue vandalized on the Westside. In Compton a man had shotgunned his wife, his mother, and both of his daughters, then had turned the weapon on himself. Why the hell not? Gold thought. The eighties' answer to a Sunday drive. Gold stuck the paper under his arm, locked his apartment, then walked across the courtyard and down the curving path to the complex's garage. The Ford's door opened with a metallic screech. He threw in the newspaper, straightened up, looked around for a split second, and then went to one of the supporting wooden beams at the rear of the garage. Reaching up under the eaves where the beam disappeared into the ceiling, he felt around in the darkness and brought down a small silver key and put it in his pocket. He backed the car out of the garage, drove slowly over the speed bumps, then turned onto the street.

It was a hot night by L.A. standards, only about ten or twelve degrees cooler than the daytime's broiling highs. Gold rolled up the windows and turned on the old Ford's airconditioner to low. It was the only thing in the car that still worked right, and it blasted cold air at his crotch. He drove leisurely on surface streets all the way to the Santa Monica Freeway, took that east to the Santa Ana, then the Santa Ana south. These few hours between deep night and early dawn were the only time the freeways weren't a demolition derby. He lit a cigar, relaxed back into his seat, and turned on the radio. As always, it was tuned to KKGO, the jazz station. The disc jockey was spinning an old Cannonball Adderly side. Gold puffed on his cigar and thought about the day ahead, the day behind. He hadn't left the apartment yesterday. Actually, not since Saturday night. He had come home from the bar mitzvah, sat at the dinette table with a bottle of good Scotch, and had drunk until he couldn't fucking see. He woke up early Sunday afternoon, brushed the fur from his teeth, and poured himself another drink. He drank like that all day. The phone rang seven or eight different times, but he didn't answer. He knew it was Wendy, wanting him to come over. He felt guilty, but not guilty enough to pick up the phone.

Around six he phoned out for a pizza delivery, then rang up a series of people, calling in some old favors, until he got the number he wanted. He punched the digits on the Touch-Tone and waited. An adolescent male's voice answered.

"Is your father there?" Gold asked.

"Uh, yeah. Who is this?"

"Just get your father, *bubeleh.* "

"Uh, okay."

There was a clatter as the phone was laid down. Gold heard the boy shout, "Somebody tell Dad he's got a call."

A full three minutes later a gruff, deep voice came on the line.

"Who is it?"

"McGriffey?" Gold asked.

"Yeah. Who is it?"

"This is Jack Gold."

There was a beat of silence. Then Gold said, "You know who I am?"

Another short moment of silence, then: "Yeah, I know who you are."

"I'd like to buy you lunch tomorrow."

"Why?"

"Why don't we talk about it then?"

The voice on the other end seemed to be thinking. "Yeah. Okay. Where?"

"There's a Cuban restaurant on Pico just east of Vermont. Called the Cuba Libre. I'll meet you there at eleven-thirty."

"Why there?"

"Because I've been going there for over ten years and I've never seen another cop in the place."

There was another long pause at the other end. "All right. Eleven-thirty."

"Eleven-thirty."

Gold eased the old Ford around a huge RV with Montana plates that was obviously driving the early morning hours in an effort to beat the fabled L.A. traffic. Probably getting off at Anaheim, Gold thought. For Disneyland. Anaheim was where he was headed, too. Gold scratched his stomach with his free hand and thought about the day before yesterday. The day of the bar mitzvah. My God, what a fiasco! What a *verkakhte* mess! Well, it wasn't as if it was a surprise. He *knew* he should have stayed home. Even still, he certainly had done his best to fuck up his life even further. Oh, the argument with Evelyn was unavoidable. No way around it. But did he really have to try and kill his own son-in-law, for chrissake? Not the way to cement family ties, all right. Suppose Howie forbade him from seeing Wendy and the baby? They were the only things left in his life now. Would Howie do that? Was he asshole enough? Definitely, Gold thought. The little *putz* was asshole enough to do almost anything. Didn't he have any idea the trouble he was courting, fucking around with coke and coke dealers? No, it was obvious he didn't. Well, maybe he had scared him Saturday. Put the fear of God into him, like the Bible thumpers say. Maybe that will be the good thing to come out of the whole *megillah.*

Just past the Orange County line they were doing some night work on the freeway, and all the lanes but one were coned off. Gold braked down to fifty and whooshed along behind a CHP vehicle.

It had been a strange sensation, seeing his son for the first time. His son who wasn't his son. Peter Markowitz might be his blood, but he definitely wasn't his son. He was Dr. Stanley Markowitz's son. Gold thought about his Uncle Max, who had been like a father to him after Gold's real father died when he was nine. It had been his uncle who had taken him to the Coliseum to see the Rams play for the first time back in the late forties. It had been his Uncle Max who had paid for *his* bar mitzvah, small affair that it was—cold cuts, potato salad, and his Uncle Max and Aunt Minnie's front parlor. It was to his Uncle Max he had looked for support when he told his mother he was shipping out with the navy and not going on to college. Even before he joined the force he had talked to Uncle Max about it. When he thought of a face, a figure, to go with the concept "father" it was always his mother's robust, life-loving brother Max who came to mind, not the dim memory of a timid, nearsighted little Russian tailor coughing his consumptive life away into his handkerchief.

The man who leaves a mark on you, on your soul, on your psyche— *that's* your father, Gold thought. And that meant he was *not* Peter Markowitz's father. He hoped it meant he was Wendy's.

Gold slipped off the freeway just before the exits for Disneyland. The streets were totally deserted, lined on either side by unimpressive tract homes that Gold knew were selling for a quarter of a million and up. Evelyn had always talked of living down here in Orange County. "It would be like being a pioneer," she used to joke. "The first Jews south of Long Beach. The next best thing to joining a kibbutz."

Gold smiled in the dark at the memory of Evelyn's laughter. She hadn't always been the spiteful stretch mark that she was now. No, Gold blamed himself for that. When he met her in '58 she had been a slim, pretty girl of twenty, two years out of Fairfax High, going to Cal State L.A. during the day, helping out along with everyone else—her father, her mother, Charlie, and Carol, sixteen months younger—at the family fish market at night and on Sundays. Gold's mother had shopped there for years.

"Have I got a girl for you," she had said and then laughed at the cliché. "Such a girl!"

They had dated for six months. She said she found him fascinating. He had been to Japan, Korea, Okinawa, New Zealand. She had never met a navy man before, she used to whisper breathlessly, then giggle. She had pressed books on him: Camus's *The Stranger, The Catcher in the Rye,* poems by a faggot named Ginsberg. Gold had never cared much for books, and he liked the ones she gave him even less. They all seemed to Gold to be peopled by selfish, immoral characters who shit on everyone around them. Still, she urged him to study, to enroll in college. To better himself. They were married on a hard, bright day in July and drove down to Rosarita in Uncle Max's Cadillac. The next week Gold went into training at the academy. His Aunt Minnie had a friend who worked as a secretary to a judge, so Gold had taken every Civil Service exam in the county. The LAPD had been the first to reply. It was a means to an end, the newlyweds told everyone. Police work during the day, college at night, law school to follow.

A stepping stone. A smart move. Credit union. Complete hospitalization. Dental care. For the whole family. Including children.

"From your lips to God's ear," Gold's mother said.

And then the second week out of the academy—his *second week* on the fucking streets—he was involved in a shootout. On Main Street, for chrissake. They had responded to a robbery call at a liquor store. As they got out of the black-and-white three Latins ran from the store, shooting. Gold's partner, a twenty-year veteran named Cutler, had gone down immediately. Gold had stepped away from the patrol car, taken a protective firing stance over his fallen sergeant, and emptied his revolver at the perpetrators. Then, though he could never remember it, witnesses later said he calmly flipped open the .38, releasing the spent cartridges, and snapped in six new ones. He did remember thinking that bullets actually do *whiz* by, because he could hear them zinging all around him. He resumed his position and recommenced firing. The Mexicans stood their ground and shot back. Witnesses looking down from an upstairs poolroom later gave statements to the effect that it was like watching an episode of "Gunsmoke," only for fucking *real,* man. When it was all over Gold had reloaded two more times, two of the perpetrators lay dead in the street— one with a much discussed bullet hole between his eyes that even rookie Gold couldn't explain away without a smile. The third suspect stayed in I.C. for three weeks. He later avowed that the shoot-out was the turning point in his life. While in prison he renounced crime and Catholicism—not necessarily in that order—became a born-again Christian, and was ordained a minister in his new religion. Upon his release, he founded a mission in National City, California. The Reverend Ortega always swore, right up to his untimely death in an automobile accident in 1981, that he owed his soul's salvation to two extraordinary Jews: Jesus Christ and Jack Gold.

Investigating the shoot-out, Officer Involved Shootings found sixteen bullet holes in the patrol car that had been only a few feet from Gold. There were even holes where bullets had ripped through the loose fabric of Gold's sleeves and trouser legs. The wounded sergeant said it was the bravest act he'd ever witnessed, including his four years in the Pacific. He said he owed his life to the rookie. By the time Gold got back to the stationhouse he was a celebrity. Cops crowded around, clapped him on his back, and reached to shake his hand.

"Good going, kid."

"That was all right, rook."

"Lemme buy you a couple tonight, Jack."

Gold smiled sheepishly and mumbled thanks. He overheard things. Things like "That hymie kid's got the balls of a brass monkey." And "That young Gold is one tough fucking Jew."

And then some cop noticed that the store the robbers had been ripping off was called O.K. Liquors. Someone else noted that the shoot-out had taken place at approximately twelve noon. Instantly the incident was dubbed the Gunfight at the O.K. Corral. On Main Street. At high noon. Rookie Jack Gold became an overnight legend on the LAPD. He was christened Wyatt Earpstein. And Marshall Earpbloom. And behind his back, Billy the Yid. For six months he couldn't buy himself a drink in any bar frequented by policemen. The *Times* did a Metro story on the young rookie sensation. And his family. There was a photograph of Evelyn looking up at her young husband. She was smiling proudly. The Jewish weekly *Heritage* ran a whole front page about the "homegrown hero." The Fairfax Avenue Businessmen's Committee gave a banquet for him. At first he resisted, but Evelyn wouldn't hear of it. It was held at a local temple. Three hundred people attended. The mayor sent a gofer with a silver plaque. The councilman from the Fifth District came. Evelyn's parents came. Uncle Max and Aunt Minnie came. His mother. Carol. Charlie. Sergeant Cutler hobbled in on crutches and gave an impassioned speech, his voice soaked with tears at the climax. The three hundred stood and cheered.

After that, though it took years to finally admit it to Evelyn, Gold knew he could never be anything but a cop. The role of "tough Jew cop" fit him like nothing he had ever tried on before. Overnight the differentness he had always felt became specialness. When he left the house each day to go to work, he honestly felt as if he were going off to do battle with the forces of evil. He had always liked interacting with different kinds of people; that was the major reason he had signed up with the navy. Now it was his *job*. That he was the only Jew working Central Division, and one of only a handful on the whole force, didn't bother him. In fact, he rather liked it. He had spent two years at sea on the carrier *Yorktown,* and out of 1,900 sailors aboard there had been only two other Jews. He got along well with his Gentile shipmates. Oh, there had been a few ugly incidents, but Gold had proved himself to be quick and vicious with his fists, and if any further remarks were made, they were never said to his face. Anyway, Gold had never been very observant of his Jewishness. All religion seemed somehow pointless to him, to his world. His mother used to send him out on the Shabbes to go to *shul,* and he would spend the night at Uncle Max's house, drinking beer, eating pretzels, and farting while watching the Friday Night Fights. He asked Uncle Max about the Orthodox men he saw on Fairfax, men with flowing beards, long black coats, and heavy fur hats. In *July.*

"Ach! Those people," Uncle Max used to say. "They think they're closer to God than you and me, Jackie."

"Are they, Uncle Max?"

"Jackie, if I believed that, then *I* would wear a long black coat."

"But why do they dress like that?"

"Why do accountants in Texas wear cowboy boots and ten-gallon hats?"

"I don't know."

Uncle Max shrugged his shoulders and smiled. "For the same reason, Jackie. For the same reason."

Gold parked the Ford before a long electric gate on wheels. A sign on the gate said LOCK AND LEAVE in big, bold letters and then below that: PRIVATE SECURITY MINI-WAREHOUSES. Gold got out of the car and pressed the twenty-four-hour buzzer. He relit his cigar. It was almost dawn now. The sky to the east was glowing. The air down here was almost clean. Gold pressed the buzzer again, then leaned back against a fender, smoking and waiting.

And remembering.

No, after that banquet there had never been any question in his mind. He was a cop. For better or worse, that's what he was. A cop. And Howie Gettelman, his coke-dealing *shmuck* of a son-in-law, was right: that's all he ever wanted to be. He struggled through two more years of night school, making C's and D's. Once his professors learned he was a cop they were reluctant to flunk him, so he sleepwalked through his classes. Finally he told Evelyn he needed a semester off. He was overworked, he told her. Afraid of burning out. She argued heatedly with him. She relented, at last, when he promised to enroll again in six months. When he reneged on that promise she gave him a whole year of hell.

"A *cop!* What kind of profession is that?" she demanded. "I thought you wanted more from life, Jack."

She was still going to Cal State L.A. full time, and she needled him with that.

"What are we going to talk to our friends about? Marksmanship? The care and cleaning of handguns? The best way to bust a head? My God, what kind of friends will we have? Nothing but other cops! Foul-mouthed fascists! Drunks and bullies!"

She got her degree and went on to UCLA graduate school. She was no longer Sam Wiegand the fishmonger's daughter. She joined study groups. She read books Gold considered subversive. She went to poetry readings at Venice coffeehouses and art shows in West Hollywood. She became part of the awakening social consciousness of the early sixties. She gave parties at the small house in Culver City they had just managed the down payment on. She called her little get-togethers "talk tanks," and invited pallid young Jewish leftists and soft-spoken Negro activists. Gold would stay a few minutes, dribbling coffee cake crumbs and smelling up the house with cigar smoke, until, at a prearranged time, his partner would phone. He was working Narcotics by then and could be called away at any time. Gold would excuse himself quickly—Evelyn would look relieved—and as he walked away from the little white frame house he would hear Evelyn's laughter as someone told her a joke.

They drifted farther and farther apart. Gold took up drinking as a serious pastime. After one of Evelyn's parties he discovered the butt of a marijuana joint in an ashtray. They fought for hours after that. Evelyn joined various civil rights organizations. She talked of going to the South on a Freedom Ride. Gold went to a cop's bar every night after work and juiced with other cops. Evelyn got a job with the Sunshine Coalition, a statewide group devoted to almost every liberal cause imaginable. She worked nights for a Ban the Bomb initiative years before such movements became fashionable. Gold started banging some of the "stationhouse girls" who hung around the cop bars. He wondered if Evelyn was doing the same with some members of the Sunshine Coalition. Not that sex had ever been a problem with them. Evelyn was not the old joke: *How do you stop a Jewish girl from fucking? Marry her.* Even after one of their many lung-searing, glass-smashing arguments, they still called a truce at the bedroom door and made hot, angry love, only to turn their backs on each other in the dark afterward.

After six years of marriage they were at an impasse. A dead end. They weren't friends; they weren't companions. They were lovers only in the most clinical sense. Gold wondered who was going to suggest divorce first.

And then two things happened. Two things that ultimately didn't save their marriage, but at least prolonged it.

The first was that Carol got married.

Evelyn's younger sister had grown into a voluptuous young woman with rinsed blond hair and iron-hard brassieres that resembled Roman breast-plates. A critic reviewing one of her many high school productions called her a young Lana Turner, and she affected that look, wearing tight cash-mere sweaters and a scarf knotted at the throat. She even took to slowly sipping cherry cokes at the soda fountain in Schwab's Drugstore on Sunset Boulevard, smiling at every expensively dressed older man who walked by. One of them actually *was* a producer. He got her a few bit parts in television shows, usually no more than a walkon. Maybe a few lines. She would be the shapely foil for the comedy star, or the moll on a gangster's arm. In one episode of "Perry Mason" she was the beautiful bikinied corpse, sprawled across a tiger-skin rug. She graduated to small films—"B" westerns, private-eye shoot-'em-ups, and toga epics. In the sex-and-sword-play potboilers she would always be cast as a lady-in-waiting to the queen, one of a score of busty women arranged behind the heroine's throne, their hair teased high and their necklines plunged low. A studio press agent dubbed her a blond Sophia Loren, and she began studying her profile in every mirror and asking people if she should get a nose job. She called herself Carol Wanderly. She was seen around town on the arms of many up-and-coming male starlets. She was even almost offered a long-term contract with Warner Brothers, the last studio still signing up talent.

And then it all stopped.

When Carol reached twenty-five it all suddenly stopped. There was a whole new generation of fresh young faces and firm young bodies. And since acting was never Carol's strong suit—she had never wanted to be an actress, only a star—she couldn't move on to roles that called for more than an ingenue.

So the phone stopped ringing.

The parts stopped coming.

It only took a few months for Carol to realize what was happening, what *had* happened. Then she did the only thing a girl in her position could do. She married the first rich man she could get to ask her.

Eric Kaplan was a sixty-five-year-old ex-movie producer who told every-one he was forty-nine. He had once been one of the busiest filmmakers in town, scoring hit after hit with his string of Flint Steele private detective thrillers in the late forties and early fifties. Every penny he earned he immediately reinvested in Southern California real estate, making him in short order a very rich man. When he wed Carol he hadn't produced a

movie in over ten years, and his two major interests in life were beating
his four grown sons at tennis and marrying young, beautiful women.

The Golds received an expensively embossed card inviting them to a
party to celebrate the recent "nuptials in Nevada." It was the first time
either of them had ever been to Bel-Air. The driveway to the house was
a half block long and ended at a six-car garage. Evelyn stumbled around
the house with a stunned look on her face. The expression reminded Gold
of the way a suspect looked after having been body-beaten and questioned
for twelve hours. Carol led them through the mansion, proudly pointing
out the indoor swimming pool, the library, the private screening room, the
atrium, the leaded glass, the inlaid marble. the Picassos, the Cézannes, the
de Koonings. Evelyn's jaw sagged.

On the drive home she kept shaking her head and whispering, "It's like
a palace. A sultan's palace."

A few minutes later she muttered, "I can't believe people really live like
that."

Gold glanced over at her. She looked like a patient in shock treatment.
Her world had been rocked. For years she had railed against the wealthy
and privileged as one would criticize a distant country. Then she had
visited that foreign land for the first time and found herself both charmed
by the natives and awed by the scenery. Wealth had always seemed to her
an evil, unreal fantasy. Suddenly it seemed close, attainable—not foreign
at all. My God, *Carol* lived in that house. Hadn't she always been better
than Carol at everything, tits excluded? Wasn't *she* working on her master's? Hadn't *she* married tall, virile Jack Gold, whom she knew Carol
had always lusted after? No, if her sister could live in a palace like that,
so could she.

The next day, a Monday, Evelyn quit graduate school and enrolled in
a real estate course. For months Gold would come in after a late-night
stakeout to find her poring over books and charts at her tiny bedroom desk,
or asleep on the living room couch, pencils and pamphlets strewn about
her. She let her membership in the Sunshine Coalition lapse. She stopped
going to Urban League luncheons, CORE dinners. She canceled her sub-
scription to The *New Masses.*

Evelyn got her realtor's license with the highest rating anyone could
remember. The following week she had a job with Jon Gerber and Associates, the largest mid-range office in the county. Within three months she
was the top-selling saleswoman in the company. Her photo was printed in
the *Times* real estate section. She joined B'nai Brith, the Jaycees, the
California Real Estate Council. She read *Fortune,* the *Wall Street Journal,*

Architectural Digest, Better Homes and Gardens. She registered as a Republican.

And then one Sunday morning over bagels and lox she told Gold to turn off the Lakers game, she wanted to talk to him. Gold's pulse quickened. He had been waiting for this. She was going to ask for a divorce.

Evelyn sipped her coffee, looked over her cup at him, and smiled.

"Jack, I guess you've noticed I've been making a lot of changes in my life lately."

Here it comes, Gold thought. I'm the next change.

"Well, I think we have to make some changes in our marriage, too." I knew it.

"If we're going to save it."

What? What? Gold leaned forward and listened more closely.

"We've been practically strangers for a long, long time now. Strangers living in the same house, under the same roof. Now, I'm not blaming that on you. It's been both our faults. Mine as much as yours. Fully mine as much as yours. But I think we may still have a chance to save this marriage. *If* we discuss our problems openly. *If* we tell each other, right out, what we expect from each other, what we need from each other, what we want from each other."

Gold stared at her and nodded numbly.

"I'll go first, Jack. Okay?"

"Okay," Gold muttered.

She sighed. "Well, first I want to apologize deeply to you." She looked at him. "I think I've really treated you shabbily. I guess I've been acting like a bitch for a very long time. When you decided to stay on the force I have to admit I was very disappointed in you. I hated you for it. I'm sorry, but that's how I felt. But what I didn't realize at the time was it was *my* shortcoming, not yours. I couldn't see the long-range advantages of the job. Now I do. Do you have any idea how strong the Peace Officer's Credit Union is?"

Gold blinked. "Well—we bought this house."

"This place is a given, Jack. Any day laborer with a part-time job could have financed this place. I'm talking about investment properties. An apartment house, a parking lot, maybe even a small shopping center."

"My God, Evelyn, we can't afford that."

She smiled slyly. "Don't be so sure. I see unbelievable deals cross my desk every day. We just need to act on them. With the right bookkeeping a good Civil Service profession can finance anything. And the police force is probably the best Civil Service profession."

Gold listened to her drone on, becoming more and more excited with the sound of her own voice.

"But, Jack, if you're going to make it your career, then let's do that. Let's make it your *career.*"

"I don't understand, Evelyn."

"Jack, you've already made detective. You told me yourself that a lot of good cops never get out of uniform, and you made it without even trying." Evelyn's eyes flashed. "That's what I want you to do, Jack. Try. That's all. You just stumble through life. Nothing interests you. Nothing impassions you. You could be the best policeman in the department if you only tried."

Gold smiled weakly. "A lot of people think I *am* the best cop in the department."

Evelyn tossed the suggestion off with a shake of her head. "The bravest, maybe. The craziest, no doubt. But I'm talking about being the *best,* Jack. The top. I'm talking about the chief's office."

Gold stared at her incredulously.

"That's crazy, Ev," he stammered. "And even if it wasn't, who the fuck wants—"

"A lot of people!" Evelyn shouted. She stood and paced their small, yellow kitchen. "A lot of people want to be at the top of their respective occupations, no matter what that might be. Does that come as some sort of *shock* to you? My God, Jack, don't you want more? This is enough?" She waved her hand around the tiny room. "Your whole life is one big showing-off-for-the-boys. Slapping asses in the showers. You've never grown up, Jack. You're still killing things and bringing them around for your friends to see, only now those things are people!"

Evelyn glared down at him. Gold dropped his eyes after a moment. She paused in her tirade, then turned to the stove and put on the kettle to boil. The silence was icy. She made a cup of tea for herself, then sat down again, across from him.

"Jack," she began softly. "You're a goddamn hero. You're young. You're Jewish. There are no limits to what you could achieve in the department."

"If you think for one minute that there aren't a lot of anti-Semitic cops—"

"Look, Jack, America is entering the age of the minority. I can see the day when people are going to get on the force, get promoted, just because they *are* Mexican, or Negro, or women. Or even homosexual."

"That'll be the day!"

"And being Jewish is like being the perfect American minority. You're white. You speak English. You're native born. So why shouldn't we get some of the gravy?"

"Ev, I've never heard you talk like this before."

She reached across the table and took his hand. "My eyes have been opened to a lot of things lately, Jack. And I just want to open yours. A lot of men have used the department as a springboard to bigger and better things, *much* better things."

"What are you talking about?"

"I'm talking about politics, Jack. I'm talking about city councilman. I'm talking about City Hall. Maybe the D.A.'s office, if I can get you to go back to night school."

"Ev, you're the one who's crazy."

"No, visionary. I have a vision of us, both of us, together, successful, important." She stroked his hand and leaned closer. "The Golden Golds. That's what they're going to call us, Jack. We can have it all. If only we try. *Try!* Please try for me, Jack."

And try he did. He went back to night school for a year. He moonlighted as a security guard at Dodger games, Rams games, demolition derbies, whatever. He made money any way he could. He got his lieutenant's shield in a few years. Some of his fellow officers who years before had congratulated him for the Gunfight at the O.K. Corral now gossiped behind his back that he got his second promotion so quickly because he was a Jew. Gold heard the rumors. He didn't care. The way he had it figured, they denied you things because you were a Jew, then accused you of getting them for the same reason.

He brought his paycheck home to Evelyn. Sometimes he brought cash to her, more cash than he should have earned. Sometimes much more. She didn't seem to notice. At least, she didn't say anything. Under her direction they invested in a couple of duplexes, a triplex in Santa Monica, a grocery store in South Central—all bought with very little down and big monthly payments. Gold brought more unexplained money home. Evelyn never asked a question. In their seventh year of marriage she became pregnant with Wendy—the second reason they stayed together—and had to quit work at the real estate office. Now all the payments fell on Gold, and he met them without a falter. After Wendy was born Evelyn said she wasn't going back to work, she was going to stay home and manage their properties. It went on like that for another seven years, until the day Angelique died.

Then it all fell in like a house of cards.

"Sorry, Cap. I heard the bell, but I was right in the middle of a good shit, and you know you can't interrupt a good shit."

The burly watchman with the florid complexion startled Gold out of his memories.

"No problem," Gold said, holding the numbered silver key up for the watchman's inspection. The watchman waved the key away.

"I never check a white man," he said with a smile. He unlocked the gate and wheeled it open. Gold got back in the Ford and the watchman waved him through.

"Just honk when you're ready to get out. I'll be in the office."

"Okay," Gold said. "Thanks."

Gold drove slowly down the long fluorescent-lit rows of garagelike sliding doors until he came to the one that had the same number stenciled on it as his silver key. Yanking up the metal door he smelled the stale air rush out. He hadn't been down here in three or four years. He paid his bill for the whole year on the first of January, burned the receipt, and hid the key in his garage back up in L.A.

Gold pulled the chain on the naked 150-watt light bulb and the twelve-by-fourteen cement-floored cubicle was flooded with harsh electric light. It was the same bulb he had screwed in sixteen years ago, when he first rented this storage space. That's how often he came here.

He pulled down the door behind him.

There was a mattress leaning drunkenly against a wall, a splayed sofa bed with dirty cushions, a few old kitchenette chairs of a style that isn't seen anymore, an empty bookcase with only dust on its shelves. Gold had bought all this shit from a garage sale in Santa Ana sixteen years ago. He had paid a Mexican twenty dollars to cart it over here in his pickup, and here it had lain all these years.

Gold dug under a rolled-up fake-Persian rug that had been thrown behind the sofa and came up with a cheap, lightweight red suitcase. He laid the suitcase across the back of the sofa and, with a glance toward the closed garage door, snapped the clasps and pulled open the lid.

In the suitcase, under a torn blue bath towel that Gold had lifted off carefully, was money. Stacks and stacks of fives, tens, twenties, and even some packs of fifties and hundreds, fastened together with rubber bands and arranged neatly. At a glance, Gold knew the money hadn't been tampered with since he'd been here last. He counted out ten thousand dollars in fifties and hundreds, ten thousand in twenties, and another ten thousand in fives and tens. It took him the better part of an hour. He put the thirty thousand in a large manila envelope, then rearranged the rest of the money in the red suitcase, took a mental picture of how it looked, and spread the blue bath towel over the money and closed the suitcase. He replaced it behind the sofa bed and pulled the fake-Persian rug over it.

On the way out the red-faced watchman waved at him as he drove through the gate.

"See ya next time."

Gold got back on the freeway and edged the speedometer up to seventy. It was dawn now, and soon the freeway heading north would freeze up with traffic like a drainpipe clogged with hair. He had to get to L.A. before that happened. He had to make his eight o'clock appointment with Chief Huntz.

Gold cruised north and thought about the stacks of money in the red suitcase. There was $220,000 still in there. The thirty thousand in the manila envelope making a helluva bulge in his coat pocket was the first time he had added to or dipped into the quarter million since the day Angelique died, almost fourteen years ago. The red suitcase had stayed behind the sofa bed, virtually untouched except for a few quick checks, all those years.

"Jackie! The interest! The *interest!*" Gold could imagine his Uncle Max admonishing him, and smiled at his reflection in the rearview mirror.

The story of the money in the red suitcase all started a long, long time ago. He had been assigned to Narcotics, and his partner and boss was a squat little half-Greek named Joe Corliss. Corliss was an old-line cop—gruff and brutal—who seemed to belong to an earlier era. He was marking time until his retirement, and so categorically refused to take any part of any shit off anybody. For some reason known only to Corliss, he took an instant liking to Gold. Took it upon himself to show the young detective the ropes, the ins and outs of catching dopesters, to hip him to the ways of the streets. He showed him how to work a snitch, taking just enough without burning the informer down. He explained to Gold the basic personality differences between hypes and speedsters, downer-freaks and cokeheads. Showed him how to spot a junkie in desperate need of a fix from a block away; how to tell who was dangerous, who was lethal, and who was simply befuddled.

And then one day, after they had been working together for some six months, Corliss came over early one Sunday morning with a couple of six-packs. Evelyn greeted Corliss with what Gold recognized as condescending graciousness. Joe just smiled back at her and scratched his crotch. Evelyn said she had errands to run and excused herself quickly. Gold and Corliss watched a Rams game for a while, drinking the beer, then Corliss said, "You wanna take a ride? You got time?"

Gold looked at him and said, "Sure, Joe."

As they were walking out Corliss said, "You got your piece?"

"With me?"

"Yeah."

"No."

"Why don'cha get it."

Gold didn't hesitate. Corliss was his partner, his mentor, his leader. Gold trusted him like no one else in the world.

They drove to a low-income neighborhood in Eagle Rock and parked in an alley behind a rambling white frame house. Corliss jimmied the back door with a tire iron. He put his finger to his lips and motioned for Gold to follow. They padded silently through a dirty kitchen and down a urine-scented corridor to an entrance hall closet. Corliss slipped into the closet and Gold quickly followed. They stood motionless behind some musty overcoats, wishing they had taken the time to piss out the morning's beer. Time passed. Somewhere women chattered in Spanish. A baby cried. At the end of the second hour they heard the sounds of several men entering the house. A little while later the first men let some others in. Gold and Corliss heard them walk past the hall closet and into a room farther back in the house. A door closed. Their voices were muffled murmurs. Corliss drew his pistol, an oversized Colt .45, and Gold followed suit. They tiptoed out of the closet, across the scarred wood floor of an unfurnished living room, and took positions on either side of a blue-painted door. The voices were coming from the other side. Corliss nodded to Gold, stepped back, and kicked the door in with one savage thrust of his thick, short leg. Gold followed him into the room with his gun held out stiffly before him.

"Freeze, motherfuckers!" Corliss shouted. "Police!"

"Police!" Gold echoed. "Don't fucking move!"

There were seven men standing around an old-fashioned porcelain-topped table. Five of them were black; two were dark Latin types—Sicilian or South American. On the table were a postal scale, a small chemical-testing set, and an opened leather briefcase. Visible inside the briefcase were several taped and bulging glassine packages of a white powder.

"Okay, assholes!" Corliss shouted again. "Everybody get on the fucking floor! Now! *Now!* Everybody on the floor!"

The seven men lay down on the floor.

"Okay!" Corliss continued shouting. "Everybody lock their hands behind their heads. Move real slow or my partner there'll blow your fucking asses off."

Corliss went from man to man, leaning over them and patting them down. All but one of the Latin types had a gun. Corliss stuck the guns under his belt all around his waist and laughed. Then he quickly inspected the tabletop, the contents of the briefcase.

"All right, where's the money?"

Gold, standing tense-armed in a firing position, glanced at him but said nothing.

Corliss kicked one of the Latin types in his ass. "Where's the money, asshole?"

The Latin type's voice had a blurred Spanish accent. "You yumped de gun, cop. De money ain't here."

"Say what?" Corliss said and kicked him again, harder.

"Dis was yust de taste test. De money come later. Ju missed de money, greedy cop motherfucker."

Corliss kicked the guy in the head, then did it again. "Watch your mouth, el spicko, or I'll put another fucking hole in your ass."

Corliss closed the briefcase and snapped the locks. Then, as an afterthought, he said, "Every one of you assholes turn your pockets inside out. Move real slow now. That's it. Real slow. Let's go, spicko."

Both the Latin types had thick rolls of hundred-dollar bills ringed with rubber bands. The blacks all had heavy bankrolls. Not as big as the Latin types, but seriously hefty. Corliss scooped all the bills up and stuffed them into his pants.

"All right," he said, standing by the door. "You ready, partner?" Gold nodded to him. Confusion was running riot in Gold's mind, but he kept his face a mask of icy resolve.

"Okay, assholes," Corliss smiled. "You can count yourself lucky you ain't going to jail today. In a way, this is your real lucky day."

"Fuck ju mother," the Latin type said.

"Think of the bail money I'm saving you. The lawyer's fees. The judge's bribes."

"Jive motherfucking pig," one of the blacks said.

"*Adios,* assholes." Corliss motioned to Gold and they ran through the house and across the small weed-choked backyard. Corliss gunned the car's engine and fishtailed down the alley in a shower of gravel, Gold keeping his gun drawn and looking back through the rear window.

An hour later they were eating cold chicken sandwiches in the paneled den of Corliss's Van Nuys ranch-style. Upstairs Corliss's teenage daughters were squealing over some rock singer on the local affiliate's imitation of "American Bandstand." Corliss poured an icy beer into a chilled long-stem glass and set it before Gold. The unopened briefcase was beside them on the poker table. Arrayed around the briefcase were the six pistols that Corliss had stuck in his belt. Corliss took a huge bite of the sandwich and started counting out money from the seven wads of bills. When he finished he leaned back in his chair and grinned.

"Over thirteen thousand. In their fucking *pockets!* And the real money wasn't even there yet. We missed that, goddamn it."

Corliss divided the bills into two even stacks and pushed one across the green felt to Gold. Gold looked at the money, wiped a dab of mayonnaise from his mouth with a paper napkin, then looked at Corliss.

"Joe. What the fuck is happening?"

Corliss laughed and took a swig of beer. "What's happening, Jack, is I'm about to hip you to the ways of the world. I'm taking you under my wing, like they say. I'm gonna be your rabbi. You ever had a Greek Orthodox rabbi, Jack?" Corliss laughed again, a hoarse, sandpapery sound. He looked at Gold warmly, then leaned forward over the table and spoke earnestly.

"Jack, in my twenty-five years out on the streets you're the best fucking partner I ever had. You got the biggest balls I ever seen. I'd walk through a shit-storm with you, no problem. You and me together, I'd go down to hell and bust the fucking devil, not even think twice about it."

Gold said nothing.

"But you're a fucking baby, Jack, and there's a few things you gotta learn."

Corliss lit one of the sixty-odd unfiltered cigarettes he smoked every day.

"First thing you gotta learn," he continued, "is that there are all kinds of cops. Good cops. Bad cops. Smart cops. And stupid cops. And you can be both at the same time. But you don't *have* to be." He dragged deeply on the cigarette. "Right now, you're a damn good cop, Jack. When we finish talking today, I hope you're gonna be a smart one too."

Gold still said nothing.

"Jack," Corliss said, "I see you brown-bagging it in every day with them fake baloney sandwiches your wife fixes for you. Half the fucking restaurants in L.A. will give a cop a break on the bill but you can't even afford that."

Gold felt his face redden.

"She's got you stretched so tight you gonna break, Jack. What you making payments on now, two duplexes? And you told me she's looking at a triplex. And that's all besides the house you're living in. Who can afford that? On a cop's salary?"

Gold shrugged. "We get by."

"You get deeper in debt every fucking day, is what you get. And who you trying to fool with this night school shit? That ain't you, Jack. That ain't who you are at all. You're just like me. You don't like reading anything more complicated than the newspaper, and even then you know everything but the sports page is bullshit. You're never gonna be a lawyer, Jack, and thank God for *that*. One thing this world don't need is another Jew lawyer. You're a street cop. A damn good one. That's what you was born to do. And that's another thing. She's telling you you're gonna be chief someday, and that's all a lot of bullshit. The U.S.'ll have a nigger president before a Jew is chief of the LAPD. Believe you me."

Gold's lips were tight, white lines.

"I'm telling you how it *is,* Jack. Not how it should be. You made detective real fast, and you'll probably make lieutenant just as quick, just because of what a good cop you are, but they'll freeze your ass there. For a long time. Maybe forever. Nobody wants a Jew captain in this department, Jack. It just ain't gonna happen."

They sat silently a moment, wreathed in Corliss's thick, poisonous cigarette smoke.

"So what are you telling me, Joe? That I should quit the force?"

"No! No! No!" Corliss's voice rose. "You're not fucking listening to me. Didn't I just say you were first, last, and always a great street cop? Didn't I? I'm just saying don't expect to be having lunch with the mayor in twenty years or so. Besides, you don't have the temperament for it. You couldn't brown-nose a superior officer to save your fucking soul. I'm saying, don't let your wife try to make a silk purse out of a sow's ear, if you'll pardon the expression."

Corliss put out his cigarette and immediately stuck another in his mouth. He let it dangle from his lip, unlit.

"I'm saying, you got to look out for yourself in the real world." He pointed to the briefcase. "There's probably a hundred and fifty thousand in heroin in there, Jack. Split four ways, that's still a healthy chunk of money. Put it with the cash we took from those scumbags' pockets, and that's more than we make in years."

"That's dope in there, Joe. That puts us in the dope business."

"Hey, Jack, fucking wise up! Who *ain't* in the dope business? You ever met a retired judge without a cabin cruiser parked in the marina? Or an ex-politician who had to work? The lawyers, the prosecutors, the bail-bondsmen—everybody gets rich off of dope. *Everybody.* Everybody but the poor slob cop who's out there trying to stop it all. They don't want it stopped, Jack. They just want it maneuvered in their direction. They laugh at us, Jack. We're like a goon squad. We're animals. We're fucking German shepherd-ass watchdogs. They throw us out there like a piece of meat to a pack of wolves. What did that guy call us? The thin blue line? We ain't supposed to stop it at all, Jack. I don't think we're even supposed to slow it down. We're just supposed to make a bust every now and then so the fucking judges and lawyers can keep paying their law school alumni dues, you get my drift? If we break up one out of twenty—fuck!—one out of *fifty* of the big dope deals in town, then the lawyers get to make their taste, and they can charge the fucking bad guys whatever they want because the fucking bad guys *know* how much they made on the other forty-nine deals that went down, and they can't fucking afford to do no time, so they pay through the fucking nose to the fucking shysters and whore judges to get 'em off the hook.

"Can't you see it, Jack? It's all a game. A big phony fucking game. And we're the juice that keeps the whole thing rolling. Make a bust. Grab a few headlines. Show the TV assholes a bagful of dope and a couple sawed-off shotguns, and John Q. Public sitting at home with the family feels safe and secure. His tax dollars at work. His government is out there protecting him, keeping the dope peddlers at bay. When all we're really doing is running a cheap little squeeze play, a fucking protection racket. Capone couldn't've done it better."

The door leading out of the den opened and Corliss's small, dark, Athens-born wife stuck her smiling face in.

"Can I get you men another beer?" she chimed.

"Not now, Katrina. In a little while. We're talking."

"Okay." She left the room, still smiling.

Corliss lit the cigarette hanging from his lip.

"Jack," he said, leaning forward, "it's 1966. Before the sixties are over dope is gonna be as easy to buy as beer. They gonna be selling it on every street corner, like the afternoon newspapers. It's the coming thing. It's gonna explode. If I could do it legal I'd take all my money out of stocks and bonds and put it on dope. It's the wave of the future."

"You really think so, Joe? That's terrible."

"Aw, kid, it makes me sick to think about it. But you can bet on it. I seen it coming for years. Ever since the war. And then when they integrated the services over in Korea, all those nice white kids living asshole-to-elbow with them big, black, buck niggers. They all came home smoking muggles and eating pussy. That was the beginning of the end, believe you me. And then the kids started listening to that fucking noise they call music"—Corliss pointed to the ceiling where the bass from his daughter's hi-fi was rattling the light fixture and shook his head—"can't get 'em to stop, no matter how hard you try. But at least they don't wanna be beatniks. All *those* assholes do is lay in bed all day smoking weed and taking pills. God help this country if *they* take over, believe you me."

Corliss drained the last of his beer, wrapped the remains of his sandwich tightly in a napkin, and threw it across the room into a wastebasket stamped with tiny Ivy League college pennants. He suddenly looked weary.

"Did I tell you Janet's getting married in June? Some Pasadena blue blood she met up at Stanford. Old money and all that shit. At least he agreed to get married in the church. Don't know how we got lucky like that. Anyway, we're giving her one helluva wedding. At the Huntington. Right in her fiancé's stomping grounds. We ain't gonna scrimp on a thing. First class all the way. Katrina said why don't we make up a dozen pans of dolmathes, bring some spanakopeta, but I said no, let's pay through our noses for bad beef like real Americans."

Corliss chuckled, choked on a lungful of smoke, and coughed viciously into his fist. When he had himself under control he continued.

"Patrice is going into her second year of graduate school at USC. Good thing she's got a brain. Poor thing's the homeliest female been in my family for five generations, and I've got all the pictures from the old country to prove it. She'll never get a husband. I'll probably have to keep her in college the rest of her life. But that's all right. She can have whatever I've got. Anything I can afford and then some, you get my drift? And then this one upstairs—" Corliss rolled his eyes heavenward. "When she was seven she had what the doctors called a 'light bout' with polio. Somehow it left her with her spine a little off center. Four operations before she was twelve. Physical therapy three times a week ever since. The department pays for maybe this much." Corliss held his thumb and index finger an inch apart. "I won't use the doctors they recommend, so I've got to foot the bill." Corliss scratched at his crotch. "You and Evelyn planning to have children? Of course you are. You have any idea how much it costs to bring up a kid today? I mean first class. Anybody can dress their kids at Zody's. At Fedco. But what about first fucking class, so's your daughters don't cry themselves to sleep because they can't have that dress they wanted for their fucking prom? And that's just *that.* What about schools and doctors and medicine and orthodontists and therapists and summer camps and shoes and books and party dresses and yadida yadida? Do you have any idea? And I'm talking first fucking class all the way. Or do you want your kids to wear cheap-shit junk and out-of-style shoes? You want to feel like a fucking stupid asshole like every other slob out there trying to put two pennies together to buy a loaf of bread while the fucking Wasps are eating steak and lobster and sticking it up the little guy's asshole?"

Without losing a beat Corliss turned and shouted at the door. "Trina, you can bring us them beers now."

"Jack, you think I bought this house on what the department pays me? No way, José. You think you gonna raise kids *and* buy up half the Westside on a fucking detective's salary? Wrong-O, Charlie. You can bet your ass the bubble's gonna bust someday. It's just a question of when. *Then* where you gonna be?"

Katrina came in with two sweating bottles of beer. She smiled at each of them in turn, glanced at the guns and the money arranged on the poker table, smiled again, and left. Corliss drank some beer and belched loudly. He lit another Camel, striking the match with his thumbnail.

"You make a decision one day, Jack. You're out there every day busting your hump, hanging your ass out there for every bad character in the world to shoot up, or cut up, or bust up. And one day you make a decision. One day you ask yourself, who comes first? Them? Or me? Me and mine? And you start looking out for yourself. Picking your spots. Taking your shots. I mean, this ain't New York. This ain't that cesspool. There ain't no fucking bagmen collecting for the whole fucking division. This ain't fucking *Manhattan,* for chrissake. This is L.A. We got the cleanest police force in the whole fucking world." Corliss grinned. "But you pick your spots. You take your shots. Like this thing today." He waved his hand over the poker table. "This little transaction. Somebody working on another investigation, maybe even in another department—you don't need to know that, right?—somebody's got a wiretap on a bad boy, and these somebodies hear something over the wiretap. Something interesting, something where a little money can be made easy, no sweat, only these somebodies don't wanna handle this thing themselves. They're too close to it, if you get my drift. So they call someone away from it all. Somebody they can trust, you follow me? That somebody is me. And now it's you, too. That's why we're splitting what we got here in the briefcase four ways. I wanted you to understand."

Corliss stopped talking, and the room seemed very quiet. He reached for his beer and Gold could hear him swallow. Corliss dragged on his cigarette. He leaned back in his chair and hooked his thumbs in his belt.

"I'm telling you right, Jack. You're my partner and I ain't never told you anything but right. And I'm telling you right now. You gotta look out for yourself. Nobody else will. And nobody expects any different. You pick your spots and take your shots. Make a few good people your friends. Your *clients,* kinda. And you work with them people. One on one, kinda. Independent contractor, kinda, if you get my drift. You make a few steady customers. Good people. A coupla Italians, maybe. A coupla Jew lawyers. Maybe some cops in another department. No niggers. No spicks. No riffraff. Just good people. I know these kinda people, Jack, and I'll be retiring soon. I wanna introduce you around, if you get my drift."

Corliss paused and took a deep breath.

"You look out for yourself, Jack. That's what you got to do in this world. You got to look out for yourself."

That day was the beginning of the money in the suitcase.

It was after seven and full daylight when Gold pulled into the underground parking lot at Parker Center. Cops in three-piece suits bustled through the lobby, looking more like ambitious junior executives than policemen to Gold's eye. He walked three short blocks down Temple Street to the Criminal Courts Building. The courthouse cafeteria was filled with cops more to his liking—street cops killing time before they had to testify on one of their cases. Against one wall the legendary perpetual poker game was in session. Several cops waved at him.

Gold bought a late-edition newspaper and an apricot danish and sat in a corner nursing a coffee, wishing it were whisky. There was a liquor store a half block away that depended on juicer cops for its survival, and Gold was tempted to make a run over there before his eight o'clock meeting with Huntz. Pick up a pint and open his eyes. But he knew he wouldn't. A man had to say no to himself sometime. Guys who can't say no to themselves wind up weighing three hundred pounds, or knocking up fourteen-year-olds, or like Timmy Starnes, walking his beat on Broadway dead drunk at ten in the morning and stumbling right into the middle of a jewelry store heist and laying on his back with tubes in his arms for three months.

At 7:40 Gold finished his coffee, threw the Styrofoam cup into a trash container, and crossed the cafeteria, stopping at several tables to shake hands and kibitz with old friends. At 7:58 he entered the cool, well-appointed waiting room of Chief of Police Alan Huntz's sixth-floor Parker Center office.

"May I help you?" asked Cherry Pye.

Cherry Pye was Sergeant Shari Pye, Huntz's personal secretary and, according to departmental scuttlebutt, his secret girl friend. A man with a wife and three children and his eye on the mayor's job can't afford to be too open with his liaisons.

"Jack Gold. I have an eight o'clock with Huntz."

Cherry Pye grimaced at the disrespectful use of her boss's name.

"Take a seat, please. *Chief* Huntz will see you in a moment."

Cherry Pye had been a legend in the department ever since her first day at the academy, when she stopped in the middle of calisthenics to adjust her 38DD full-figure uplift. The whole class stopped with her to watch. So did the instructor. By the middle of her second week at the academy half the force was dropping by to jog a few laps and try to catch a peek of her jiggling bod. That's where Huntz saw her. She'd been his private secretary ever since.

Gold plopped down on the plush leather couch.

"So. How they hanging, Cherry?"

Cherry Pye peered peevishly over her designer frames.

"I beg your pardon."

Gold picked up a copy of *Law Enforcement in America* and thumbed absently through the glossy pages.

"You know, how's it going?" He nodded toward Huntz's door. "Your lover boy cheat some poor cop out of his pension yet this morning?"

Cherry Pye's stare went from cold to frozen. She ripped the letter she had been typing from the carriage and crumpled it into a ball. She held the ball over her wastebasket, glaring at Gold, and dropped it in.

"I'll tell Chief Huntz that you're waiting." She strode from the room and left Gold alone.

Gold peeled the cellophane wrapper from a fresh cigar and lit it. Chief Huntz hated smokers, everyone in the department knew that, and cigar smokers most of all. Fuck him, Gold thought. If he's gonna take my badge anyway, I might as well funk up his fucking office.

Gold searched for an ashtray on the walnut end tables, then looked for one on Cherry Pye's desk. Finally he dropped the snuffed-out match into the ceramic pot of a Boston fern. On the wall behind Cherry Pye's desk were dozens of framed and carefully mounted photographs of Huntz shaking hands with various celebrities. In each photo the pose was practically identical—Huntz always on the right, wearing a wide politician's smile— only the celebrities changed. There were the usual Hollywood bigwigs: Hope, Heston, Peck, Sinatra. There were several of Sinatra. There were six different shots of Ronald Reagan—as an actor, as a California governor, as a president. There were pictures of other less recognizable people, too. These were captioned, in the event the observer couldn't quite place the important personage taking time out from his busy schedule to shake hands with his old friend Alan Huntz. One caption read GEORGE P. SCHULTZ, SECRETARY OF STATE. Huntz was still a deputy chief in that one. The next said TIP O'NEILL, SPEAKER OF THE HOUSE. Another actually read ROSS HUNTER, IMPORTANT HOLLYWOOD PRODUCER. Gold chuckled at that one. The first photograph of Huntz as chief showed him shaking hands with one of his predecessors, Daryl Gates. Gold was trying to figure how the fuck a picture of Huntz with his arm around the shoulders of François Mitterand had gotten on the wall, and if Huntz even knew who the hell he was, when he heard a door open behind him.

"The chief will see you—my God!" Cherry Pye gasped. "You're smoking!"

"Very perceptive, Cherry. You shoulda been a cop." Gold brushed past her and into the inner office of Chief of Police Alan J. Huntz. Cherry Pye followed him in, sputtering.

"You can't bring that—that *thing* in here! You can't—"

Huntz was seated behind his highly polished, spartan desk, speaking into a leather-encased phone receiver. The desk and Huntz's slick leather chair were elevated on a riser a foot higher than the rest of the office. That was also a legend in the LAPD. The way Huntz could talk *down* to everyone who came before him. The chief, still whispering softly, inaudibly into the receiver, stared at Gold's cigar a long time. Gold smiled at him and stuck the smoking stogie into the corner of his mouth.

"Alan! How's by you?"

Huntz looked through him as if he weren't there. Cherry Pye jiggled around between them and got in Gold's face.

"You're going to *have* to put that stinking thing out now. *Now!* The chief won't allow it!"

"Don't sweat it, Cherry. If Alan doesn't like it let him tell me."

Cherry fumed. She thought of snatching the cigar from Gold's mouth. Gold saw the idea flicker across her face like a shadow.

"I wouldn't do that, Cherry," he said in a small, tight voice.

"Sergeant Pye," Huntz said, momentarily putting his hand over the phone's mouthpiece, "that'll be all, thank you. Everything's all right."

"But Alan—" she sputtered.

"That'll be enough for now, Sergeant."

Cherry Pye hesitated, her anger confusing her. Then she walked out, closing the door soundly behind her well-rounded ass.

"I'll be with you in a moment, Lieutenant," Huntz said, looking at Gold directly for the first time, then started whispering into the phone again. That was also a tactic much discussed in bars frequented by L.A. cops. The fucking chief would keep you standing and waiting for a half hour, sweating in your socks while he whispered into that goddamn phone. And *no*body believed there was ever anyone on the other end.

"No problem, Alan." Huntz winced at the use of his first name. Gold dragged a low armchair away from the wall and flopped down in it. He crossed his outstretched legs at the ankles, puffed on his cigar, and winked at Huntz. Huntz did his best to ignore him. Gold cleared his throat, sucked at his teeth, polished his shoes on the back of his legs. When Huntz still didn't respond, Gold brought out a nail-clipper and began trimming his fingernails and dropping the cuttings onto the carpet. Huntz muttered something that sounded like good-bye and hung up the phone.

He fixed Gold with a hard glare and held it without speaking. That was another of his specialties. Hit you with the evil eye and make you break first.

"Alan, I thought you had something to say to me. If all you want to do is flirt with me, we could've met at the Café Swish."

Gold started to rise.

"Sit *down*, Lieutenant," Huntz growled. He was a narrow man in his middle fifties, with a Marine Corps haircut softened only a little for the television cameras. Everything about him gave the impression of too-early toilet training.

Gold sat down. "What's on your mind, Alan?"

Huntz refused to be rushed. He crossed his arms over his chest and swung his swivel chair around to the view from his window of the smog-encased skyscrapers of downtown L.A. He shook his head and gave out with a dry hollow laugh.

"This used to be a very good police force. This—"

"Aw, for chrissake, Alan—"

"—used to be the best police force in the world. In the *world*. Now I've got cops who commit burglaries, cops who fornicate with Girl Scouts—"

"I didn't come up here to listen to this shit."

"Cops who smuggle drugs."

Both men's voices were rising.

"Cops who contract to commit murder."

"So what the fuck's that got to do with me?"

"It all started with people like you!" Huntz swung back to face Gold. They were both shouting now. "It all started with people like you!" Huntz shook his finger at Gold.

"Go fuck yourself, Alan. What do you want, my badge? Ask for it then. You're the big man. Ask for it. I'm not gonna just walk in and hand it to you."

Huntz quieted himself. He touched his fingertips together and studied Gold over them.

"There's nothing I would like better," he said softly. "You've been a thorn in my side for twenty years. And a black mark on this department's reputation even longer. Do you know that the late Mr."—he consulted a page of paper on his desk—"Mr. Weathers you *terminated* at that ridiculous bank robbery Friday morning was the *eighth* man you've killed in your less-than-illustrious career with this department? Or don't you keep count?"

"I have paper pushers like you who do that for me."

"And that's just the ones on the record. God knows how many others this department has had to cover up."

Gold was silent.

"I know of one girl myself," Huntz said.

The room was very quiet.

"There's always room for one more, Alan," Gold said finally.

Huntz barked a short, astonished laugh. "Are you threatening me, Lieutenant?" His voice was full of bravado, but he couldn't meet Gold's eyes. "You're going to push me too far one day."

Gold felt old and tired. "What do you want, Alan?" he asked wearily.

"Do you know how much trouble you caused me this weekend?" Huntz snapped, happy to be back in a posture of reprimand. "How many phone calls I've answered because of you? The head of the local FBI office is furious. He wants to know why the bureau wasn't notified about an ongoing investigation involving a possible bank robbery. I really don't know what to tell him. Banks *are* their concern, you know."

"There was no ongoing investigation. I got a tip from a snitch about a heist. We followed the car. They could have been heading for a flower shop, for all I knew."

"That scenario doesn't clear with my information. I was informed you had a stakeout in place two full hours before the attempt. Is that true?"

Gold shrugged and showed his palms in a Fairfax Avenue gesture.

"Two full hours," Huntz continued, "and you couldn't notify the federals of the possibility that maybe one of their banks was being taken off?"

"Aw, those fucks come down and push their weight around. They treat everybody like shit and then take all the credit. It was *my* snitch, *my* bust, *my* bad guys. Fuck those assholes."

Huntz gaped at him. "You're unbelievable!"

"Hey, everything turned out all right, didn't it?"

"Everything turned out all right!" Are you *completely* crazy? When the FBI wasn't screaming in one ear, I had Mrs. Eskaderian's lawyers in the other. She wanted to sue the city, the department, me, you—everybody. She still might. All over that trigger-happy cowboy stunt you pulled in the bank's parking lot. She maintains you unduly endangered her life with your 'reckless and blood-thirsty manner.' She claims she sustained 'deep emotional trauma' as a result of your reacting 'with inappropriate haste' to a delicate situation that could have been negotiated. But I think I've talked her out of her hysteria. I think I've worked out a compromise." Huntz gave Gold a thin-lipped sneer. "And it centers around *you.* "

Here it comes, thought Gold. He's going to ask for my badge.

"I had to assure Mrs. Eskaderian and her solicitors that I would remove you from any situation where you might react a little too—overzealously. That's how I got her to drop any future suits against the department. So, Lieutenant, I'm taking you off the street. Off Robbery. Off Felonies. Out of any situation where you might exercise that penchant you have for shooting this city's citizens."

Gold was relieved and confused. He was keeping his badge, but for what?

"What are you talking about?"

Huntz leaned back in his swivel chair and smiled down at Gold. He looked like a cat. "I'm reassigning you. I'm making you the leader of a brand new, very important task force."

Gold felt a strong sense of foreboding.

"From now on the bad-ass Jack Gold is going to be apprehending bad-ass graffiti artists." Huntz laughed.

"What the fuck does that mean?" Gold demanded.

"It means you are the new leader of the just created—just this second—Anti-Defamation/Anti-Defacement Task Force."

"What—what's that?"

"Surely, Lieutenant, you've heard about those very bad perpetrators who've been running around painting mean, ugly things all over *your people's* places of worship?"

Gold said nothing.

"Well, all Saturday and Sunday when I wasn't on the horn trying to placate Mrs. Eskaderian or Ed Fortier over at the Federal Building, my phone lines were being burned up by your coreligionists. This morning too. The switchboard's been jammed since six o'clock. I guess you could say that one way or another the House of David really screwed up my weekend."

Huntz smiled coldly at him.

"Spit it out, Alan."

"I am. I am." Huntz was enjoying himself. "Why, just before you barged in here with that stinking weed, I was talking to Councilman Orenzstein—not one of my favorite of your fellow Hebrews—and he was *demanding* that I do something about those terrible things that have been happening. Especially after last night. I guess you know about last night?"

Gold blinked. "No."

"Oh? I thought you people all talked to each other." Cold smile again. "Seems that last night some desperate character spray-painted a whole lotful of Jew canoes. Rollses, Mercedes, Sevilles. Caused over a quarter of a million in estimated damages." Huntz laughed out loud. "I guess that's really hitting you people where it hurts, eh?"

Gold wondered for a split second if he could shoot Huntz, here and now, and get away with it. Dan White had done something similar in San Francisco. Gold decided against it. For now.

"So Councilman Orenzstein was demanding—on behalf of his 'Westside constituents,' but we all know who that really means—demanding that I take action on these *atrocities.*" Huntz saturated the word with irony. "So I have. I've created the crime-solving, racket-busting, headline-grabbing Anti-Defacement/Anti-Defamation Task Force. That slob Orenzstein was very happy about that. He was even happier when I informed him I was making one of his coreligionists the head of the task force. He'd even heard of you."

I don't need this shit, Gold thought. I could hand in my badge right now. Pull the pin right here and now. And then what? Be left alone with nothing to do but sift through my memories all day? Go fishing? Take up calligraphy? Ceramics? Suicide?

"That's a bullshit job. The whole thing's bullshit. You know as well as I do that it's probably just a coupla punk kids with overactive thyroids. They're bored. They drink a few too many beers and they draw some swastikas on a men's room wall. It's all bullshit."

Huntz held up his hands in a supplicatory gesture.

"Is it my fault your race sees Hitlers under every rock?"

"Twenty-nine years on the force and you're putting me out to chase schoolboys, bullshit misdemeanors?"

"Oh, don't worry about that. Orenzstein is introducing a bill to the council today. Makes it a felony to deface a place of worship. Something about civil rights. Now we all know that 'place of worship' really means a synagogue. When's the last time someone painted on a Lutheran church?"

"It's still bullshit."

"Well, bullshit or not, that's the way it is. They're cleaning out a broom closet on the eighth floor right now. That'll be your office. The office of the Anti-Defacement Task Force."

The two men glared at each other across the glossy sheen of Huntz's desk.

"I won't do it."

Huntz lunged forward across his desk, sputtering with anger.

"You'll do it if I tell you to do it! Who the *hell* do you think you are, Lieutenant? I'm your boss and don't forget it. If you don't want to follow a direct order from your chief, then you can damn well leave your shield on this desk right now. I've wanted to get rid of you for a long time. I'd have fired you after that fiasco Friday morning, but I didn't want to face your old cronies on the Protective Association. You may have a lot of admirers in this department, Gold, but I'm not one of them!"

"And thank God for that!" Gold shouted back.

"I'm sick and tired of having to stand up in public and defend murderers like you every time they empty their guns into a kid or a pregnant woman!"

"What do you know about murderers? You've never faced anything more dangerous than a stapler your whole fucking career. You haven't been out on the street in fifteen years. And then you were the last chief's fucking chauffeur, for chrissake!"

"I knew you were a bad apple a long time ago, when you killed that black tramp you were sleeping with. It's immoral, dishonorable men like you that have made this depart—"

"Every rookie out there riding around on his first day in a black-and-white knows more about being a cop than—"

"—should I expect from someone of your kind!"

"—and more balls, too! You chickenshit motherfucker, you think every cop in this department doesn't know that you couldn't keep a partner? That's why you kept getting office jobs. Nobody would ride with you, you spineless piece of *dreck!* You tried to walk behind every partner you ever had. You ain't got nut one!"

"Get out!" Huntz screamed, standing and pointing to the door.

"I'm getting out, all right! This place stinks, but it's not from my cigar."

"Get out! *Get out!*"

When Gold reached the door Huntz yelled at him, "Lieutenant Gold, you be at your new assignment at one o'clock this afternoon or I'll have your shield and your weapon!"

Gold turned from the opened door. "Go fuck yourself, Alan," he said as he walked out.

Behind her typewriter Cherry Pye's mouth was agape and her face drained of color. Huntz, in the inner office, was still shouting something.

"You better go in and give your superior officer a superior suck job and cool him out. He's about to have a stroke." Cherry Pye rushed from behind her desk and into Huntz's office, slamming the door behind her and cutting off Huntz's screaming.

Gold turned to Honeywell, who was seated on the short leather couch, waiting for his appointment. He too looked shocked at what he had overheard, and his face was somehow pale.

"Jack, what the hell—"

"Don't worry about a thing, Honey." Gold made an okay sign with his thumb and forefinger. "I talked to him for you. Just mention my name."

Then he walked out.

9:35 AM "My job, Mrs. Phibbs, is to save this company money. I'm very good at my job. I'm counting on you to help me do an even better one."

Abe Morrison was seated behind a hand-carved nineteenth-century table he used as a desk. The whole office was filled with antiques: a brass hat stand, a massive rocker, even an ancient water cooler topped with an oddly shaped glass bottle. Esther hadn't seen so many old things in one room since she'd left Georgia.

"I'll do a great job for you, Mr. Morrison. You can count on that."

"You see, Mrs. Phibbs," Mr. Morrison continued his memorized speech, hardly hearing Esther, "you see, the semiconductor industry is very volatile, as you probably well know."

What's *volatile?* she thought. What's a *semiconductor?*

"As with all microchip computer-hardware manufacturers, Techno-Cal experiences a lot of highs and lows, ups and downs. I was brought on board three years ago to lessen those vacillations, to soften up our variables."

Esther nodded.

"I have to say, I've been quite successful in the rather unorthodox experiments I've made in cost cutting. We've restructured our pension programs, reworked our health plan, just cut dead weight all around. Would you believe, Mrs. Phibbs, that this company used to maintain a cafeteria? A cafeteria for a hundred employees! It lost money every fiscal year, and no one ever thought to close it. Now everyone eats at the hot truck, Chico's Choo-Choo, which is what they all did anyway. Which is why the cafeteria lost money."

Abe Morrison threw back his head and guffawed. The skin around his eyes creased with laugh lines, and he exuded a pleasant confidence. Esther laughed with him.

"And now we're terminating our janitorial staff. It's simply not cost-effective to keep a three-man crew on the payroll, what with Social Security, the IRS, and all that. Using an independently contracted service like yours should benefit everyone in the long run. Besides, there's been a good deal of unexplained pilferage lately, and I'm pretty confident I've traced it to the former janitors. Working alone, at night, in an unsupervised situation can be very tempting for some people."

"Oh, Mr. Morrison, you don't have to worry about—"

Abe held up his hand to stop her.

"I didn't mean *that,* Mrs. Phibbs. Your work and your character come highly recommended. I wouldn't be talking to you if I didn't trust you."

Esther smiled. "Thank you, Mr. Morrison."

"Well, I guess that's all for now, Mrs. Phibbs." Morrison rose from his Victorian swivel chair. He was a short, thick man with a balding head and a salt-and-pepper beard. He wore a pale yellow short-sleeved shirt and rubber-soled shoes. Leading her to the door, he said, "My secretary will show you the plant and give you a set of keys. You understand your responsibilities? Good. You're to start next Sunday night. That's the twelfth."

Esther nodded quickly.

"Good. A check in an envelope with your name on it will be left on the receptionist's desk every other Friday. Unless there are some unforeseen difficulties we won't be seeing much of each other. I *hate* working over-time." Morrison again threw back his head and laughed at his own joke. He opened the door and spoke to the chesty blonde who was filing a letter in an antique walnut file cabinet.

"Terri, would you get Mrs. Phibbs straightened out? The right forms and all that. Then show her around."

He stuck out his hand and smiled warmly.

"Welcome aboard, Mrs. Phibbs."

"Thank you, Mr. Morrison," Esther managed before Abe Morrison disappeared back into his office.

"Here you go, honey," the blonde said as she handed Esther a sheaf of papers and a pen. "Fill these out and your whole life flashes before your eyes. In triplicate. Sit down over there and I'll get you a cup of coffee. How do you take it?"

"Thank you. Cream and sugar."

The blonde came back with the coffee and a tin of English biscuits.

"My name's Terri Walker. Care for a cookie?"

"No, thanks. I'm Esther Phibbs." The two women shook hands lightly and smiled at each other. Then Esther went back to filling in the employment contracts. Terri sat behind her desk. Several minutes passed. Esther was laboring over a question that asked, "Have you or any of your immediate family or those of any of your coagents ever been convicted of a felony?" Absently she felt for her purse and dug around for her Salem Lights. "Is it all right if I smoke?" she asked without raising her eyes.

"That's a dirty filthy habit."

"What?" Esther looked up and Terri was laughing and waving a freshly lit cigarette. Terri tossed a fluffy purple cigarette case over to Esther. A tiny gold lighter hung from the case by a thin gold chain. Esther lit up, then leaned forward and slipped the case onto Terri's desk. "Thanks."

"Abe keeps on me to quit. Mr. Morrison. On my case morning, noon, and night. I did quit once. Years ago, when I was carrying my baby. Started right back up again, though. And he's the only male I'd quit for."

The women nodded knowingly at each other. Then Terri said, almost shyly, "We're getting married, Abe and me."

"Congratulations. When's the date?"

"Next month. It's no big thing. We're just gonna drive to Vegas for a weekend. I might even bring my son."

"How old's your boy?"

"Twelve. I got married real young. Too young."

"Mine's ten."

"You got a boy, too? Ten?"

"Going on a hundred and ten."

"Smart, huh?"

"As a whip. I got him enrolled in a class for high I.Q. kids. He's so smart he scares me sometimes."

"My Kevin's not brainy like that, but he's got the best heart I ever seen. A good heart's a real important thing. In a boy or a man. You learn to appreciate a good heart when you been kicked around like I been."

"Amen. Say it again."

"You know what I'm talking about?"

"I do. I do."

The two women assessed each other as they smoked. Esther examined Terri more closely. The voluptuous blonde was attired primly in a blue cotton shift, but Esther had no problem visualizing her in leather and jeans, even biker colors. The girl was stone street. Her mouth gave her away every time she opened it.

"Abe, he's got a good heart, too. The biggest. That's why I'm marrying him."

"He seemed real nice."

"Aw, he's the best. You're gonna love working for him. He leaves you alone, can you dig it? Do your job, and he leaves you alone. How many bosses can you say that for?"

"Really."

"You finished that application form yet?"

"Uh—almost." Esther took a chance. "This question fifteen is giving me trouble."

Terri looked at her. She puffed on her cigarette and tapped a pencil against her neck.

"The one about felonies?"

Esther met her eyes. "Yeah."

Terri drummed the pencil against her throat. It made a hollow sound. "Are you a felon, Esther?"

"No. It's my husband. He gets out of County tonight. Finishing up a year and a day."

"What for?"

"Possession," Esther said quickly.

"A year and a day for simple possession. He had a bad lawyer."

Esther hesitated for a heartbeat, then said, "And armed robbery. They reduced it to carrying a concealed weapon."

Terri tapped the pencil and looked at Esther for several long moments. "Is he gonna work here with you? Will he be on your crew?"

"No. No way, Terri. I keep that separate."

"You sure?"

"That's for real, Terri. He's my husband and I love him, but Esther's Custodial Service is *mine*. All mine."

Terri smiled. "Yeah, I can dig it. I know the feeling. *Men!* Can't live with 'em, can't live without 'em. If they didn't have dicks they oughta shoot 'em."

Both women laughed.

"Look," Terri said, "I like you, Esther. And I always go with my first impression. My first impression of you is I like you and I trust you." Then, in a softer, conspiratorial tone: "Besides, if your old man ain't gonna work here, what the hell does the company need to know about your private life, right? It's *you* they're hiring, right? Not your husband. Anyways, I've always thought that question fifteen was illegal. It's a fucking invasion of privacy or something like that. Just write in no and fuck 'em if they can't take a joke. If there's ever any problem later on down the line we'll just say you didn't understand the question."

"Thanks." Esther finished the questionnaire, signed it, and handed it over.

"Come on," Terri said and took a big ring of keys from her desk. "I'll give you a guided tour of the dump. Show you which locks all of these go to."

Esther followed Terri down the building's central hall. Terri's dress clung to her hips and swayed with every moment. Male office workers stopped in mid-stride to appraise her as she passed.

This girl is built! Esther thought. No wonder she's marrying her boss. No way she was going to work for any man and he wasn't going to try and get some.

"There's only two floors, but some of the offices are cut up into these little bitty cubes, or whatever you call them. You're responsible for cleaning everywhere inside the building except Research and Development. They clean up after themselves. Secret shit and all that." Terri giggled.

"Are there bathrooms on both floors?" Esther asked.

"Yeah, and another one in the president's office at the back of the second floor. He's a real freak about being clean, too. He fired a janitor once because he found a pubic hair on his toilet seat he claimed wasn't his own. Said the janitors had been shitting in *his* toilet. He couldn't handle that."

"Thanks for the warning. If nature calls I'll be sure it's not at second floor rear. How do you get to the dumpsters?"

"They're in the back by the loading dock. There's a ramp leads right down to them, and hand trucks in the old janitor's closet. Here, I'll show you."

Terri led Esther through the big metal doors. The sun's heat and glare hit their faces like a slap. On the loading dock across the executive parking lot men worked stripped to the waist, the crotches of their pants soaked with sweat. Some of them stopped their work and admired Terri, wiping their faces dry with knotted handkerchiefs tugged from their pockets. One man who had been stacking crates by himself in a corner of the dock stood and gawked. He was heavily muscled and had tattoos all over his chest and arms. He cupped his hands and shouted something. Esther couldn't make it out.

"Uh—" Terri seemed to be stammering. "Uh—we used to have a rat problem back here, but Abe had it cleaned up. So—"

The man shouted again. The other workers were all nudging each other, stopping work to watch.

"—so be careful when you unload your trash you don't drop any on the ground. Abe says sloppiness is what brings rats."

"What's he saying?" Esther shaded her eyes and peered across the parking lot at the tattooed man.

"Who?"

"That man. Over there."

"Who knows." Terri was flustered, embarrassed. She took Esther's arm. "C'mon. I'll show you the employees' lounge. It used to be the cafeteria. There's coffee makers, candy machines, microwave—"

Finally Esther could make out the man's voice through the shimmering heat of the parking lot.

"First it's Jews and now it's niggers!" he was shouting. "You got a nigger buddy just like Kevin? Does *she* sleep over too?"

Esther stopped short. "Did you hear what he said?"

"First the Jews and then the niggers, that's how it always starts!"

Terri, her hand on Esther's arm, guided her through the door and back into the building.

"Aw, he's crazy. Nobody around here pays any mind to him."

"But—but who's he talking to?"

"Who knows? Himself probably. I told you he was crazy."

"But who is he?"

Terri looked at her. "I honestly don't know, Esther. Abe hired him. I think I'll tell him to get rid of him. He's going to be big trouble someday." Terri's eyes burned as she strode down the hall. "Someday someone on that loading dock is gonna drop a crate on his goddamn head. And the sooner the better."

Terri's face was set, her expression grim. Then she smiled brightly. She turned to Esther. "Did you know we have shower facilities? Men's and women's. You get all sweaty cleaning up the place you can wash up right here. C'mon, I'll show you."

11:32 AM When McGriffey walked in the front door of the Cuba Libre, Gold thought to himself, A Martian would know this Irisher was a cop!

McGriffey looked around the restaurant packed with the lunch-hour rush of small dark men. Gold, seated at the counter, held up a finger and McGriffey spotted him. He was a big man just beginning to go to fat. His face was scarred with deep pockmarks. He sported the de rigueur thick moustache and his mousy brown hair hung just over his collar. His eyes were a washed-out blue.

"Jack Gold?"

"There's a room in the back they only use for dinner," Gold said as he stood up. "Let's go back there." He led the way.

The second dining room was long and narrow, a row of oilcloth-covered tables along each wall. In the rear hung a huge painting of Cuba, with all the province names lettered in red. This room was cool and quiet after the other.

"You hungry?" Gold asked as they sat down.

"You asked me to lunch, didn't you?" McGriffey shot back.

Gold sized him up over the table. "That's right, I did."

"What kinda restaurant you say this was?" McGriffey asked dubiously as he looked around.

"Cuban," Gold said flatly. "That's why they call it the Cuba Libre."

"A hundred thousand Mexican hash houses in L.A., you got to pick someplace Cuban."

"Stop bitching, you're not paying. Besides, maybe you'll learn something. You look like a man who enjoys a good meal."

McGriffey looked up at him quickly. Then he said, "So what the fuck's Cuban?"

Gold shrugged. "Rice and beans. Beefsteak. Pork chops. They eat a lot of pork."

Angelique had loved this place. She said the food reminded her of New Orleans. That's why he kept coming back all these years.

"Pork, huh?" McGriffey smiled. "That's surprising."

Gold smiled back, a thin-lipped, wolfish snarl.

Of all the cops on Narcotics, he thought, I had to draw this asshole. Oh, well, you play the hand that's dealt you.

Just then the waitress came into the back room to take their order. She weighed three hundred pounds, with dyed blond hair and a wart on her cheek. She recognized Gold as a regular customer and nodded.

"Can I help you, sir," she said, with a rapid-fire Caribbean-Spanish accent.

"I'll have the breaded steak, rice and beans, and some fried bananas." She turned to McGriffey. "And you, sir?"

McGriffey studied the thin paper menu, then looked up at her. "Do you have burritos?"

"No-o-o-o-o-o," she said, drawing the word out.

"Tacos?"

She looked at Gold and rolled her eyes. "Ess a *Coo*-ban restaurant, sir."

McGriffey slapped the paper menu with the back of his hand. "Yeah, but I don't know what any of this shit is."

"Let me order for you," Gold said. "I think I know what you'd like." And then to the waitress: "Bring him the breaded steak, too. Rice and beans, just like mine."

The waitress scribbled it on her little green pad.

"Anything to drink?"

"What kind of beer you got?" McGriffey asked.

The waitress smiled widely, revealing several gold-capped teeth. "We have many Mexican beers, señor."

"Dos Equis?"

"*Sí.*" The waitress wrote it down. "And you, sir?"

It was after twelve and Gold figured he wouldn't be breathing in Alan Huntz's face for the rest of the day.

"I'll have a Corona. *Muy fria, por favor.*"

"*Sí.*"

After she was gone McGriffey lit a cigarette. He leaned back in his chair and stroked his moustache. "So, the great Jack Gold is going to be chasing fence writers, street artists?"

Gold managed a wry smile. "Bad news travels fast."

"There aren't too many cops who can make Huntz explode like that. The way I hear it, you're about the only one."

"It's a dubious distinction. Look where it's got me. Running down kids with paint cans."

The waitress came back with their beers. "*Dos mas,*" Gold said and pointed at the beers. She nodded and left.

They drank and talked. Cop talk. Feeling each other out. McGriffey asked about some people Gold had been working with on Robbery. Gold in turn inquired after some old friends with Narcotics. They talked about the smog, the Dodgers, who would replace the mayor if he got elected governor, who would replace Chief Huntz if he got elected mayor.

After the food was served they ate in silence. McGriffey covered everything with ketchup and sucked it up with relish. The rice and beans made Gold remember Angelique with fresh sharpness. She used to say that rice and beans were the soul of New Orleans. Gold had often thought of visiting the town, but never got around to it.

They finished eating and the waitress brought American coffee. McGriffey lit another cigarette. Gold unwrapped a cigar. They smoked for a while, belching and picking their teeth with matchbook covers.

"I asked around about you, Mac," Gold began finally. "I talked to some people I respect and they told me you were good people. They told me you could be trusted."

McGriffey said nothing, just stared at Gold with those washed-out blue eyes. The way he was supposed to.

"They told me you were the kind of man somebody could talk to. They told me you could be reasoned with."

McGriffey still said nothing.

"Is that true?" Gold prodded, wanting some response.

McGriffey held his hands up, palms out. "Hey. I'll always listen to what someone's got to say."

Gold knocked the ash from his cigar into a greasy spot on his plate.

"You busted a lawyer Friday night. For coke. About half an L.B."

McGriffey smiled broadly.

"What's so funny?" Gold asked.

"I love to collar lawyers. Love it. I hate the slimy bastards. I arrested a prick from the ACLU once. It was the best feeling I ever had. I'd rather bust a lawyer than a dope fiend child molester."

Inwardly, Gold groaned. This was going to be harder than he had thought.

"Back to the case on the docket," he said. "You busted this particular lawyer Friday night. In the parking lot of the Sunset Plaza."

"What was his name again?"

"Howard Gettelman."

"Oh, yeah. That's right. I remember him. Little dark-haired prick. With a beard."

"That's him."

"What about him?"

"He's my son-in-law."

"Ooooh. That's too bad. But then he should have known better. A half pound of coke is pretty heavy duty."

"So I've told him."

"These fucking lawyers, they think they're above it all. They think they can get away with anything."

Gold kept quiet, letting McGriffey rant on. He knew how McGriffey felt. He felt the same way. All cops did.

"Do you know, those fucking lawyers your son-in-law is mixed up with are running a fucking distribution ring? They're acting like big-time dope dealers."

"Hey," Gold said, "from what I can understand they kept everything amongst themselves. Just a little in-house trading."

"Yeah, well, that's bullshit. You been getting bad information. These fucking assholes are selling coke to all their big-shot show-biz clients. They're *dealing* to these people."

McGriffey lit a fresh cigarette. He leaned forward. "Look, Narcotics has been getting a lot of heat from upstairs. The whole fucking country knows Hollywood is the cocaine consumption capital of America. Every other week little Junior's favorite TV star checks himself into a rehab hotel to dry out his nose. Guys on the Dodgers are copping to it, for chrissake. And all that action makes us L.A. Narcotics detectives look like a whole flock of assholes. Everyone thinks we can bust some niggers pushing crack down in South Central, but we sure as hell can't control Big Money Hollywood. Or everyone thinks we *won't,* which is worse. So if your boy got caught in bed with these assholes, don't come around here screaming he was a virgin. He knew damn well what he was getting into."

The waitress came around with more coffee. Gold ordered another Corona instead. When she had brought it Gold said, "Look, my son-in-law is not nearly smart enough to be the big criminal mastermind you're making him out to be. You and I both know somebody—probably one of his lawyer friends—paid off some kinda debt by snitching on Gettelman. And it was probably a debt owed to *you,* since it was your operation."

McGriffey didn't reply to that. He threw his arm over the back of his chair and watched Gold through his limpid, dishwater eyes.

"So?" he asked finally, quietly. "What do you want?"

"I need a little help for my son-in-law."

"No big deal." McGriffey picked up his coffee and sipped at it. "Tell him to give me some names—maybe just one if it's the right one—and I'll take care of everything."

"He can't do that."

McGriffey sipped at his coffee and stared at Gold over the rim of his cup.

"He's got to work with these people the rest of his life. He can't go around informing on them. It'll ruin his career."

"Tell him I'll protect him. I don't go around putting my people's business in the street."

Gold shook his head. "It's not you I'm worried about. It's him. He's a fuck-up. Look at this mess he's gotten into. He snitches on somebody, he's liable to get himself killed." He shook his head again, more emphatically. "No, that's definitely not the way to handle it."

McGriffey put his cup down with a clatter. He shrugged. "So what can I do?"

"You can tell me what it would cost to end this business right here at this table."

McGriffey stared at him a long time. "I don't think I under—"

"I'm asking you what it would cost me to squash this thing right here, right now."

McGriffey tittered—a short, nervous little laugh.

"You *are* crazy. Just like everybody says. Man, you can't do that kinda shit out here. Maybe in New York or Miami, but not in L.A."

Gold held up his hand to silence him. "Hey, McGriffey. Save that shit for the Review Board. I worked Narcotics for nine years, remember?"

McGriffey watched Gold thoughtfully, slowly stroking his moustache.

"I want to know," Gold patiently began again, "how much it would cost to clear up this—"

"How do I know you're not wired?"

"I'm not."

"But how do I know?"

"I just told you."

"But how do I know?"

McGriffey suddenly leaned across the table and reached to pat Gold's chest and waist, but before his hand got there Gold had grabbed him and held his wrist in a tight, viselike grip. McGriffey, not a weak man, tried to pull away, but Gold's grip just grew tighter. Now McGriffey's eyes were hot and piggish.

"Look," Gold said, his voice a whispered rasp, "we could go into the men's room and I could strip, and you could see that I was clean. But then I'd have to use your face to mop up the pissy floor. That way my son-in-law would lose out on the help I came in here looking for, and you would lose a bunch of teeth and a whole helluva lot of money. So why don't you just take my word when I tell you I'm not wired? You know my reputation. You know I'm a right guy. Why the fuck would I turn over now, after all these years?"

Gold released his grip and McGriffey jerked his arm back. He settled back and rubbed his wrist. After a while he looked up at Gold. He was not a pretty man.

"For ten K I could guarantee probation. Maybe a wobbler, reducible to a misdemeanor after the probationary period."

Gold shook his head. "It's his first offense. He'd get probation anyway, if we just walked into the courtroom cold and pleaded guilty. That's not good enough."

"Well, what the fuck do you want?"

"I told you. I want it squashed. Over. Kaput. Finito. I don't want my son-in-law ever to have to worry about this matter again. I don't even want this to go to arraignment."

It was McGriffey's turn to shake his head. "You don't want much, do you? How long you been a cop? Thirty years? Then you know how many people are involved in something like this. The D.A.'s office, the other guys on the bust, the judge, the fucking clerk-of-court, for chrissake. That's a lot of people have to be, uh, stroked before a felony can just fucking *disappear*."

"Give me a figure."

"Look, even with enough money I'm not sure it can be done. This isn't a parking ticket we're fixing here. There are a lot of elements to be—"

"You're jerking me off now," Gold interrupted. "You're trying to jack up the price with this bullshit. I talked to a lot of people about you. They all said you were a man who can get things done. If I didn't know you could handle this I wouldn't be talking to you now. I would have gone another way. So stop fucking around and tell me how much."

McGriffey studied Gold's face. He lit another cigarette. He drained his coffee cup. In the other dining room the juke was blaring salsa—all percussion and repetitive piano figures.

"Thirty thousand."

Gold snorted. "He's not charged with mass murder, for chrissake. A simple possession charge, thirty thousand?"

"There's nothing simple about a half pound of blow. And a lawyer to boot. Judges hate lawyers who get caught. It makes the whole profession look bad."

"Twenty."

McGriffey shook his head. "No, that's impossible. There are too many individuals who have to be considered." He paused for a brief moment, stroking his moustache again. "I could probably do it for twenty-five."

"Twenty-two," Gold said quickly.

"Hey, what the fuck is this!" McGriffey was angry. "You're trying to Jew me down, for chrissake! This ain't South Broadway and I ain't no greaser buying a pair of fake alligator shoes. *You* asked *me* to this party, remember? Now pay the check."

Gold held up his hand in apology. "Okay. I'm sorry. It's a deal." He stood up. "Wait here."

McGriffey was instantly suspicious. "Wait here? For what?"

"I'll be right back," Gold said. "Relax."

Gold went down the short hall to the men's room. He could feel McGriffey's eyes burning into his back.

Once inside the men's room he bolted the door and withdrew the thick yellow Manila envelope from his coat pocket. He counted out twenty-five thousand dollars, slipped a rubber band around the remaining five thousand and shoved the roll into his left pants pocket. Then he put the twenty-five thousand back in the envelope and resealed it, took a quick piss, and came back into the dining room. McGriffey was waiting for him, still nervous and fidgety.

"Funny time for nature to call," he growled.

Gold sat down and slid the envelope across the tabletop. McGriffey pocketed it quickly, his eyes darting around the empty dining room.

"You carry around money like that?"

Gold shrugged. "Who's gonna take it from me?"

McGriffey smiled and shook his head again. "You really *are* everything they say about you."

"And more, Detective McGriffey. Much, much more."

The waitress came into the back room with the check. Gold gave her a ten and a twenty and told her to keep the change. She flashed him her glittering smile, gathered up the dirty dishes, and left. Gold rose to go. McGriffey, casual and loose now, looked up at him and yawned. "If you ever need another favor—" He chuckled.

Gold put his hands on the tabletop and leaned across until his face was only a few inches from McGriffey's.

"Listen, you fat asshole," he spat out in a low voice, "twenty-five thousand dollars is no fucking favor. Twenty-five thousand dollars is stone cold business, and don't ever forget that, because if anything at all goes wrong with this business deal, if my son-in-law even *hears* about this matter again, I'm gonna hold you completely responsible, and twenty-five thousand dollars is a helluva fucking lot of responsibility."

"Hey, take it easy. Don't worry." McGriffey grinned sheepishly. "It was just a figure of speech. I know how the game works."

Gold straightened up. "So long as we understand each other."

"We do." McGriffey nodded. "Man, you really are something else. You know they still talk about you up in Narcotics."

"Oh?"

"Yeah, whenever a narc does something particularly mean and nasty. To a dealer, you know, or just anybody, well, they say that cop is as 'cold as Gold.' At first I thought they meant like *gold,* you know, but then somebody told me how they meant you."

"I'll see you around, Detective," Gold said and started to leave.

"Yeah, okay." McGriffey called after him: "Listen, don't be too hard on them graffiti guys. Some people think they're real *artistes.*"

McGriffey's laughter echoed hollowly in the empty room.

Gold drove back to Parker Center through the choking afternoon smog. The radio reported second-stage alerts for most of the L.A. basin, all of the valley, and for many of the communities east of downtown. The air was "unhealthful to breathe," according to the Air Quality Management Board.

Gold wandered the green hallways of the center's eighth floor for a half hour, until he got a custodian to show him Room 8112B, the office of the brand new Anti-Defacement Task Force. Located in a corner the farthest possible distance from the elevators, the office actually *was* a converted closet—a storeroom really, about twelve by twelve—that had been used to stack Xerox equipment: cartons of paper, toner, and boxes of ink. Now the tiny room contained two small, scarred desks set up facing each other, a pair of straight-backed chairs, and a dented file cabinet. There was no window. On one of the desks lay a single thin folder. Gold shucked off his coat, sat down, and put up his feet. He lit a fresh cigar and opened the folder. It contained the penciled reports of the three cases of defacement that had occurred that weekend, the report on Sunday night's orgy of vandalized cars on top. Gold started with that one, then read back to Saturday night's incident, and finally on to the account of Friday's occurrence. It was all as he had expected: simple cases of what he had once heard a police psychologist refer to as "contemporary American angst manifesting itself in antisocial behavioral aberrations." Young punks painting walls. One item contained in Sunday night's report bothered him, though. Several witnesses stated they had caught a fleeting glimpse of the alleged perpetrator and he was described as a lone white man in his middle thirties. That didn't gibe with Gold's theory. But the descriptions were very spotty, and he had always found eyewitnesses to be extremely unreliable, even under the best conditions, and these were definitely not the best conditions. Gold drew on his cigar and reread Sunday night's report. He was halfway through when the office door opened. Gold looked up. A young cop was standing in the doorway, his I.D. hanging from his shirt pocket.

"Can I help you?" Gold asked.

"Is this the Anti-Defacement Task Force?" The young cop looked around and smiled incredulously.

"It ain't the men's room. That's bigger. If you got business here, state it. If you've come merely to gawk at the opulence of my office, then tell your story walking."

The young cop came in and closed the door. "I've just been assigned to your staff. It looks like I *am* your staff. Are you Jack Gold? I'm Sean Zamora." He held out his hand. Gold took it slowly.

"Sean Zamora? How the hell'd you get a name like that?"

The young cop's grin grew wider. He was good-looking, of medium height, with thick, blondish hair. His features appeared to have been sketched with a fine point pencil, then slightly smudged by the artist's thumb.

"That's a long story. When we have a dull moment I'll run it down for you."

"We should have a lot of those around here," Gold said. "Well, don't just stand there, staff. Sit down."

Zamora sat.

"So, tell me. What did you do to piss Huntz off?" Gold asked.

Zamora laughed. "How'd you know?"

"Why else would you be here, assigned to me and this chickenshit job? So what did you do?"

Zamora was reticent. "It's no biggie."

"Hey, you're making me interested. Now I have to know."

"Well," Zamora began sheepishly, "you know the magazine *Playgirl?*"

"The one the faggots buy?"

"It's a *woman's* magazine."

Gold gave a short laugh. "What about it?"

"I did a layout for it."

"A what?"

"A layout. A spread."

"Speak English," Gold barked.

Zamora sighed. "They took some pictures of me and published them."

"What kind of pictures?"

"Well, you know."

"Naked pictures?"

"Well—yeah."

"Completely naked?"

"Well. Not completely naked."

"Oh?"

"No. In a couple of shots I wore my shoulder holster."

Gold marveled. "No shit. That's not quite the image Huntz has in mind for his boys in blue."

"Not quite."

"How much did they pay you to—to—to layout?"

"Fifteen hundred."

"Fifteen hundred? That's not much money for a whole career."

Zamora was puzzled. "I don't get you."

"Cops who piss Huntz off never get promoted. Don't you know that, Detective Zamora? That's the basic axiom of the LAPD. And I'm living, breathing proof that it's true."

"Aw, Huntz can go fuck himself. I'm not gonna be a cop much longer."

"Really?"

"No, I'm an actor. Just got my SAG card, too. In June I did *Sweet Smell of Decay* at the Callboard. The *Times* gave me rave reviews. Maybe you saw them?"

"I don't read play reviews," Gold said dryly.

"Anyway, I'm gonna take a month off in December and do this low-budget that's gonna film down in Mexico. Twenty-one-day shooting schedule. That's gonna be brutal. And I'll probably hafta *shlep* the lights around, but I'm gonna get third billing."

"Whatever," Gold said.

"My agent got me the spread in *Playgirl*. They're hyping me as a cross between Erik Estrada and Don Johnson. And I'm a for real cop, too."

"So—when do you expect this stardom to strike? Today, maybe?"

Zamora chuckled. "Well, probably not today."

"Then you got time to do a little police work with me?"

Zamora grinned. "I think I can squeeze you in."

Gold got up and threw his coat over his shoulder. Zamora stood with him.

"Do you always go the suit-and-tie route, Lieutenant?" Zamora asked as they walked down the hall.

"If we're gonna work together you might as well call me Jack. And no, I don't. I'm usually partial to loud, polyester shirts. The kind all of us old men wear."

Zamora glanced over at Gold. "You know, Jack, it's really an honor to work with you. I've heard a lot about you."

Gold made a deprecating gesture with his hand as they reached the elevators. "The honor's all mine." He pressed the button. "Anyone so young who's already made an enemy of Alan Huntz is all right in my book. By the way, how did Huntz hear about the *Playgirl* pictures? I don't think he's a subscriber."

The elevator doors roboted open.

"No, but maybe Cherry Pye is."

Gold threw a questioning look at Zamora as they got in. Zamora winked. "As I was leaving the chief's office she asked me for a date."

Gold laughed all the way to his car.

2:26 PM Councilman Orenzstein was just finishing up a news conference on the steps of the West Coast Center of Holocaust Studies when Gold and Zamora parked across the street.

"And so," he was saying as they approached the outer fringes of the small crowd of reporters and cameramen, "hopefully, with the positive action that I have initiated, with the newly created Police Anti-Defacement Task Force, with the concerted efforts of the entire Westside citizenry, we can prevent this kind of horror, this kind of outrage, from recurring in our city. Thank you."

There was a light smattering of applause, and then the technicians began coiling up power lines and repacking cameras.

"Hey," Zamora whispered. "What about you? You're the task force. Isn't he going to introduce you?"

Gold shook his head. "I've been on the news a little too much lately."

Zamora nodded in comprehension. Orenzstein, shaking hands with a few supporters, caught sight of Gold in the crowd. He made a small gesture, nodding toward the steel doors of the center. Then he excused himself from his audience and went up the steps and inside.

"C'mon," Gold said. "Let's go in."

The entrance chamber of the center was high and dark and cool. The walls were steel and rough-hewn rock, and a central fountain splashed water over a coppery sculpture. A semiabstract mural that covered the area behind the receptionist's desk depicted faces and forms twisted in agony. The figures wore striped camp uniforms.

Orenzstein was beneath the mural, surrounded by his entourage. He broke away and took Gold's arm, leading him away from Zamora and the others to a quiet corner.

"You're Jack Gold. I'm Harvey Orenzstein." The two men shook hands. "Congratulations on being named head of the task force. I pushed for a ranking Jewish officer. You certainly fill the bill."

"Actually, Councilman, I don't think this assignment calls for congratulations."

Councilman Orenzstein was puzzled. "I don't believe I understand what you mean."

Gold shrugged. "This is all bullshit, Councilman. You're making much too much of this thing."

"Oh, am I?" Councilman Orenzstein said stiffly.

"The way I see it, what we got here are a couple of isolated little cases of vandalism."

"Over a quarter of a million dollars' damage to those automobiles—that's a little case, Lieutenant?" Orenzstein sniffed.

"Okay. An expensive little case. But all this shit—TV crews, press conferences, task force—you're just going to perpetuate this kind of thing. The assholes that do this kind of thing want nothing better than a whole lot of media *megillah*. It's why they do it in the first place. The best way to handle this is just to let it die quietly on the vine."

"Then I take it you think the people who did this aren't particularly dangerous."

"Probably not."

"And you feel we should downplay the whole incident?"

"Exactly. Don't give in to a lot of paranoia."

Councilman Orenzstein's mouth had a grim set. "I can't believe I'm hearing this from a senior police officer. A *Jewish* police officer yet."

Gold sighed. "Look, Councilman. When I catch these assholes I'll break their fucking kneecaps. But the way you're going about this is only gonna bring more weirdos out of the woodwork."

"Lieutenant, I want to draw more weirdos out of the woodwork. I want to draw out all of the weirdos. My life has been dedicated to exposing bigotry and inequality of every stripe, exposing it whenever and wherever I find it. And if anti-Semitism is raising its hideous countenance in my district, in my city, you can be assured I won't rest until it's sought out and destroyed."

Gold examined Councilman Orenzstein closely. "Tell me, Harvey. This holy quest. It couldn't have anything to do with this being an election year?"

"Don't be impertinent!" Orenzstein snapped back, keeping his voice compressed into an angry whisper. "From what I can glean, you need every friend you can muster just to keep your pension. It was my influence that salvaged your job this morning, so I damn well expect you to at least be civil to me during our weekly progress reports."

"Our what?"

"Weekly progress reports, Lieutenant." Councilman Orenzstein raised his voice so his entourage could overhear. "My office will be in daily liaison with the task force. I want to be kept abreast of every facet of the investigation. I don't intend to just let this issue be forgotten."

"I'll bet you don't," Gold mumbled.

One of Orenzstein's aides rushed up. "We really have to get going, Councilman. Those old ladies protesting that condo conversion are passing out in the heat. I don't know how long we can maintain a viable gathering."

"Right, right." Orenzstein extended his hand to Gold and smiled broadly. "I'm glad we're working together on this, Lieutenant." Several cameras clicked. Flashbulbs popped. "United we'll lick the bastards!" he boomed. That was Orenzstein's decades-old campaign slogan, all the way from the sixties. He said it again, louder: "United we'll lick the bastards!" There was another small flutter of applause, then Orenzstein and his people swept out of the center, followed closely by the remaining media, and then the general gawkers. In less than thirty seconds the place was emptied.

Zamora strolled over. "What did he say? When you were alone?"

"He said he knows which side his bagel is buttered on."

Zamora looked at Gold quizzically. "Well, what do we do now?"

"Who knows?"

"Well, we're the cops," Zamora laughed. "What's your general procedure?"

"Usually, if I'm looking for bank robbers, I start rousting all the bank robbers I know. Eventually somebody will give up the asshole I'm looking for." Gold was lighting his cigar. "The same thing if I'm looking for dope pushers or peeping toms or forgers or pornographers. You shake the tree until your man falls out." He had it going. "Only problem is I don't know any graffiti artists. Do you?"

"Gang members. The Crips. The Bloods. The White Fence Homeboys. You want to throw some of them against a wall? Shake 'em up, see what rattles out?"

"Naw, not really. Not unless you got one that's overtly anti-Semitic. No, our perpetrators aren't normal graffitists. They don't even paint in that gang member scroll."

"Why do you keep saying 'they' and 'them'? Our eyewitnesses say they only saw a single Cauc male."

They had walked outside. The air was hot and still and noxious. The sun was a fiery ball behind a glaze of smog.

"A lone male Cauc in his mid-thirties screws up my drunken teenagers theory," Gold said, looking across the street to the parking lot. "A lone male Cauc in his mid-thirties could be a lot more dangerous than a bunch of drunken teenagers."

"You think so?"

Gold chewed his cigar. "Who the fuck knows?" He grinned at Zamora. "You feel like looking for clues? Let's go across the street to that parking lot and look for clues like good little detectives."

Zamora smiled back. "Sure. Why not?"

They were halfway down the steps when two white vans screeched to the curb and ten armed young men bolted out onto the sidewalk.

"What the fuck!" Zamora was already reaching for his weapon.

"Take it easy. It's the JAR."

"The *what?*"

"Jewish Armed Resistance. I was half-assed expecting them."

The young men took up military stances at various intervals along the front of the center and up the marble steps. They were dressed alike in blue berets, blue jeans, and blue T-shirts stenciled across the front with a Star of David, crossed fists breaking loose from vicious barbed-wire bonds, and the letters *JAR*. They carried M-1's, M-16's, and two of them fingered submachine guns.

"*¡Jesus y María!*" Zamora gasped. "Those are Uzis!"

Gold threw his cigar to the pavement. "C'mon. Let's put a stop to this."

A gray-bearded man in his fifties climbed out of one of the vans. He had a large paunch and electric eyes. He barked orders to the others and they snapped to attention.

"Who the fuck's in charge here?" Gold demanded of the gray-bearded man.

"I am," he barked back. "I'm Jerry Kahn, Western Forces Commander of the Jewish Armed Resistance. Who the hell are you?"

"I'm Captain Fantastic of the Klingon Empire. Now get these children out of here before one of them shoots himself."

Kahn sneered. "Believe me, if one of my troops shoots something, it won't be an accident. Now get out of our way."

Gold was grim. "Get these people out of here *now.* You can't carry automatic weapons on the city streets, for chrissake. Get those weapons back into those vehicles immediately and get the fuck out of here or I'll confiscate every one of your little toys, and you'll be spending the rest of the day trying to make bail."

Kahn was unimpressed. "Say, you really *do* think you're Captain Fantastic."

One of the young men standing stiffly at attention a few feet from Kahn turned his head and said, "He's Jack Gold, Commander. He's the token Jew we heard about on the radio. In charge of that bullshit task force."

"Oh, yes." Kahn's malevolent smile broadened. "The turncoat. The ghetto policeman, getting his own people ready for a short train ride to a 'relocation center.'"

"Shut up, asshole," Gold hissed.

"*You* shut up, Uncle Ike. You know what an Uncle Ike is, don't you, Gold. That's what we call you Jewish Uncle Toms."

"Kahn, stop shooting your stupid mouth off and get these kids outta here before I have to start making arrests."

"Us he's going to arrest!" Kahn turned and shouted to his followers. "They desecrate our temples, they terrify our women, they defile the memory of our sacred deceased, they call us kikes and threaten us with death—and then they send this Judas goat Jew to arrest us for protecting ourselves. Typical apologist bullshit!" Kahn turned back to Gold, his face a mask of hatred. "You would have been right at home in the camps, Gold, licking the Nazis' boots. You make me sick!" He spat on the sidewalk at Gold's feet.

Gold was fighting bravely to control his temper. Zamora watched the whole scene in astonishment, his mouth agape.

"Kahn," Gold said slowly, "I'm asking you for the last time. Get in your vehicles and—"

"We're not going anywhere, Ike. We're staying right here, on patrol, twenty-four hours a day, to protect Jewish lives and property. We're staying right here to do the job *you* should be doing. From what I hear, the job you *could* be doing if you didn't spend your life chasing *shvartzeh* puss—"

Gold moved with incredible speed for a man his size and age. He wrenched Kahn's right arm behind his back, grabbed a handful of his gray hair, yanked him a few feet to a parked car, and slammed him down across the hood. Kahn's people lunged forward, but Zamora had his gun out and was jerking, stiff-armed, in every direction, trying to cover everyone.

"Nobody move another muscle!" he shouted. "Just stay put!"

The troops froze, their trembling hands flexing around their weapons. Late-leaving reporters who had been getting into their cars across the street cursed as they fumbled to get out their cameras.

Gold jerked Kahn's head up. Blood was streaming from Kahn's nose. It ran into his mouth and dripped from his chin. The nose looked broken.

"Now," Gold whispered in Kahn's ear, "do you want the arm busted too, loudmouth?" Gold pushed up on Kahn's arm and Kahn grunted involuntarily from the pain.

"Asshole," Gold spit into Kahn's ear and applied more pressure.

"Please don't," Kahn sputtered.

Gold leaned even closer. "Say uncle."

"Uncle," Kahn managed.

"Now say Uncle Ike."

Even through his pain Kahn's fury surfaced. "Fuck you."

Gold jerked up hard on Kahn's arm, lifting him off the street for a second. Kahn screamed.

"When an arm pops," Gold whispered into Kahn's ear, "sometimes you can hear it a half a block away."

Kahn was crying.

"Say it," Gold demanded. "Say Uncle Ike."

"Uncle Ike!" Kahn rasped, in too much pain now to care.

Gold released Kahn's arm and Kahn slumped to the street, cradling his arm and trying to stanch the flow of blood from his nose. Several of his Resisters rushed to his side.

"Now you people get the hell out of here," Gold shouted. "You take these weapons home and put them away in your closet. This is not the way to handle this thing. This isn't the Middle East. You go back to helping old ladies home from *shul.* And don't ever try to do police work again."

They were helping Kahn into one of the vans. "Anti-Jewish pig!" one of the girl Resisters pointed at Gold accusingly. "Nazi lover!"

"Move it!" Gold barked.

They got Kahn into the van and climbed in after. They pulled away from the curb shouting and brandishing their rifles.

"We'll be back!"

"Never again! Never again!" Someone started the chant and they all took it up.

"Never again! Never again! Never again!"

Their voices drifted away as the vans disappeared down Pico. Zamora slumped against a car and wiped his sweaty face with the back of his left hand, his Police Special still clutched in his right.

"Jesus, Mary, and Joseph." He looked up at Gold. "Is every day with you like this?"

Gold was lighting a new cigar. "Stick with me, kid."

10:42 PM The minipickup turned off of Sunset onto Gardner and then took the first left. It went down two blocks and then slammed to a stop at the curbside of the darkened street. The cartoon hooker lunged out, yelling back into the truck.

"Jive motherfucker!" She slammed the door viciously. "Cheap motherfucking wetback motherfucker! Go see if yo' Mexican mama will fuck you for ten motherfucking dollahs, motherfucker!"

The minipickup jerked away and fishtailed down the street.

"Motherfucker!" the cartoon hooker shouted after it.

Walker's blue van eased up to the curb. The hooker peered in suspiciously.

"Now what *you* want?"

Walker leaned across the seat and rolled down the passenger window. He tried to smile warmly. "Hi."

"Hi, yourself," the hooker said. "What's your story, sugar?"

"Well, you know. Just looking for a little company."

"Oh, yeah?" She softened a little and leaned into the van. "I hope you don't want it for free, like that other motherfucker."

"No, I got money. Whatever you need."

The hooker smiled. "Whatever *I* need? No, sugar, it's whatever *you* need." She opened the door and climbed in.

"You gonna have the time of yo' *life* tonight, sugar. You gonna tell your grandchildren 'bout the pussy Honey Dew laid on you." Walker drove away from the curb. "Just go down to La Brea and turn right, sugar. There's a nice clean motel there I do bidness with. Real reasonable."

"Uh—" Walker tried to look nervous, innocent. "Well, you know, I'd really like to stay in the van."

"Say what?"

"Well, you know, do it in the back of the van. I'd like that."

She turned in her seat and inspected him. "A little van perversion. You into that, sugar? Is it clean back there?" She looked over her shoulder into the back of the van.

"Oh, yeah, I vacuumed it today."

She looked back at him. "You understand, that's gonna hafta cost you a little more."

"That's okay."

188

"Where you gonna park this thing? You can't just stop and fuck in the middle of Sunset." He was driving up Laurel Canyon now.

"I know a place up off of Mulholland. Nobody knows about it."

"Up off of Mulholland?" She looked at him with suspicion again. "You ain't no weirdo, are you, sugar? You ain't into no violent shit? 'Cause I been known to knock a motherfucker clean out. And I got something in here"— she patted her cheap, beaded disco bag—"will stop an unruly motherfucker for *good,* you understand what I'm saying here, sugar?"

"I'll give you a hundred dollars," Walker said quickly.

"A hundred?" the hooker said back, even more quickly. "Why, sugar, you taking me a half hour off the Strip. I'm gonna lose me two or three dates going off with you. Baby, when you wanna party with a star like Honey Dew up on Lovers' Lane Mulholland Drive, then, sugar, you gots to pay."

"How much do you want?"

"Two hundred."

"Okay."

"Well? Where is it, sugar?"

"Now?"

"Oh, yeah, baby, now. Let's get the bidness over with so's we can get down to *pleasure.*" She drew out the last syllable into three others.

Walker dug a wad of bills out of the pocket of his cut-off jeans and counted out two hundred dollars by the headlights of the car behind. He gave the money to the hooker.

"All right, sugar," she said, snapping the money into her silver beaded bag. "Let's get to where we going so we can get to it!" She laughed lasciviously and leaned closer to him. She put her hand on the back of his neck and he shivered violently.

"Aw, now," she cooed as she massaged his neck. "You all wound up, ain't cha, sugar? I'm gonna take care of you good, don't you worry."

She ran her hand up and down his muscled arm. "You white dudes sure love them tattoos, don'cha, sugar?" she said idly. Her hands on him felt like a snake crawling over his skin, exciting and repugnant at the same time. She ducked her head down and licked at the skull-and-dagger tattooed on his forearm. She traced it with her tongue. Then she looked up at Walker and smiled.

"You taste real good, sugar."

Walker glanced at her. His throat was dry and his heart was pounding. His face was blank now, unsmiling. The van was filled with electric sensuality and the odor of passion.

She settled her hand on his knee and trailed it slowly up to his crotch.

She worked her hand down the front of his cut-offs and cupped him gently, rolling his testicles around with two fingers.

"Don't you want Honey Dew to suck that big mean white thang right now, while you driving, sugar? While you driving yo' big old van around?"

"We're almost there. Wait till we get there." His voice sounded strange to him—distant, faraway. He wondered whose it was.

"Mmmmm," she moaned, nibbling on his shoulder through the thin fabric of his T-shirt.

He turned the van off of Mulholland, drove up a dark driveway, and parked behind a row of cedars. The lights of the city twinkled below behind a lacework of branches. After he turned off the ignition and killed the lights it was still and shadowy.

"You want to come in Honey Dew's sweet black mouth?" she breathed. "Turn yo'self around here and give me that big beautiful white cock." She knelt between his legs and tugged his cut-offs down. His cock was limp and shriveled. She cupped it in one hand and stroked it with the other.

"C'mon, sugar," she whispered. "I want your big white cock so *ba-a-a-a-aad.*"

She took his flaccid penis between her lips. He felt her tongue darting around his glans, pulling and tugging, like a fish nibbling at a line. She looked up at him and gave him her best hungry whore look. He shivered again. He was having trouble breathing, as if his chest were constricting. He felt like a man watching rats nibble his toes.

"Hey, c'mon, sugar, you got to try with me. You ain't had nobody else tonight, have you?"

He shook his head. He couldn't speak.

"Well, then, sugar. Let's get it on."

"Take your clothes off." He had found his voice again, only it still sounded like someone else's.

She looked up at him for a moment, then nodded almost imperceptibly. With one hand she yanked down her tank top and her pendulous breasts popped out and quivered in the moonlight. Walker gasped. She went back to work on him. She took all of his limp cock and as much of his balls as she could get into her mouth. He felt her tongue laving him, pulling at him, sucking on him. Leering up at him, she took one of her fat breasts in her left hand and squeezed and kneaded it, putting on a show for him. She pinched her nipple until it was hard, then rolled it between her fingertips. Walker watched, mesmerized. It was as if a sleek, dark animal were devouring him, ingesting him from his center outward.

She opened her mouth and he plopped out, slick and wet and soft.

"Say, sugar, I ain't got all fucking night. You sure you ain't—"

He hit her hard with a short brutal blow, and her head snapped back and bounced off the dashboard with a sickening crack. She stiffened, her eyes danced and began to roll under her eyelids, and instinctively tried to pull away. He punched her in the face again and she lost consciousness. He caught her by her hair as she began to slip down and he pounded the back of her head again and again against the dashboard. The metal dented and buckled. Her skull shattered like an egg. When Walker finally stopped beating her, the front seat of the van was soggy with dark cranial blood. Walker's T-shirt clung wetly to his body with the stuff. He jerked the van's door open and fell out, vomiting. When he straightened up, his cut-offs still bunched around his ankles, a puff of cool night breeze brushed across his turgid flesh. *Now* he was hard. He touched himself and immediately ejaculated.

11:59 PM Esther lit a fresh cigarette off the last one. She dropped the dead butt to the cement floor and ground it nervously into an ashy tobacco smear. All the while her eyes never left the big rusted clock bolted high on the yellowing wall.

The minute hand jerked forward with a tiny metallic jolt.

Esther walked instantly to the cage.

"It's midnight. It's the seventh."

The deputy was a woman—fat, black, with bored eyes and short, mannish hair.

"Take it easy, honey," she said with a thick Alabama drawl, "it takes 'em a few minutes to roll 'em out. There's paperwork needs doing, you know."

Esther paced the empty waiting room, puffing furiously on a fresh cigarette and glancing continually up at the clock. When it read 12:04 she stopped pacing and watched it intently. When the minute hand went to five after she exploded.

"What the hell is this?" she demanded of the deputy. "The judge said a year and a day, and he did a year and a day. You got no right to keep him any longer. It's the seventh now, damn it. It's the—"

The iron door clanged open and Bobby Phibbs walked through, wearing the dark blue suit she had brought to jail for his court appearances. He had gained a little weight on the inside, and the suit pulled across his broad chest and shoulders. He smiled at her and folded her in his arms and she started to cry. She had promised herself she wouldn't, but she did anyway.

"Oh, Bobby. Oh, Bobby," was all she could say as the tears kept coming.

"Let's go home," Bobby said softly as he put his arm around her waist and guided her out.

He told her to drive the freeways home. He wanted to feel the freedom of the open sky. He kept his hand on her knee all the way home, and whenever she could she covered his hand with hers.

As they were walking arm in arm up to the house on Crenshaw he sniffed at the air and grinned.

"What is *that*?" he laughed as she put the key in the lock.

The parlor was decorated with paper streamers and colored balloons. There was a big, yellow bow over the fireplace, and tinsel letters strung on a thin string of wire spelled out WELCOME HOME. Mama Phibbs smiled and dabbed at the corners of her eyes. Little Bobby, his eyes behind his glasses puffy with sleepiness, blew on a party horn and said, "Hey, Daddy, welcome home!" and pointed to the sign.

"Thank you, son," Bobby said solemnly, taking the boy's hand. "I missed you a whole lot." He knelt and swept Little Bobby up and held him close.

"Are—are you home to stay this time, Daddy?" Little Bobby asked, obviously uncomfortable in his father's embrace.

"You damn right! They done stole too much of your childhood from me. I ain't gonna let them have no more."

Esther shot a worried look toward Mama Phibbs. The old lady was staring back at her and her face was grim.

"Mama made your favorites, Bobby," Esther said quickly. "Fried chicken and spaghetti and meatballs."

"Don't I know that? Didn't I smell that chicken a block away?" Bobby stood up and turned to his mother. "Hello, Mama."

"Hello, Bobby." She took him to her breast and held him tightly with clenched fists wrapped around his neck. A tear coursed down her cheek and she whispered fiercely, "We're counting on you, son."

"Don't you worry, Mama." He patted her back gently. "Don't you worry."

They sat around the dining table and watched him as he ate. Esther rattled on about the new contracts she was acquiring, about how she had started last night's work at five in the afternoon so she could be there to take him home, about how she was getting ready to start a second crew, about the job at the cafeteria Bobby had waiting for him.

"Well, baby," Bobby said, his mouth full of bread and spaghetti sauce, "if you doing so damn good and you need help and all, why don't I just come to work for you?"

There was an awkward silence, and then Mama Phibbs said, "Bobby, I don't think they'll allow that."

Bobby tore a wing apart. "Why not?" He sucked the meat from his fingers.

"I don't think they'll allow you to be in a situation where you're being supervised by your own wife."

"Oh." Bobby looked around the table. "Well, maybe later, huh?"

"Sure," Esther said confidently as she stroked his arm. "Sure. One day at a time."

Halfway through the meal Mama Phibbs scooped up Little Bobby, who had fallen asleep on the couch, and carried him upstairs to bed. Esther sat by Bobby, her hand on his arm, while he ate. Mama Phibbs came downstairs with her coat on. She was always cold, even in August.

"That was dynamite, Mama," Bobby said as he pushed his plate away. "Ain't nothing like that in County. Ain't *nothing* like that in County." He belched and smacked his lips.

"I'm glad you enjoyed it, son. It gave me a lot of pleasure cooking it for you." She smiled. "I guess I'll be getting home now."

"Mama," Esther said, standing, "you don't have to go so soon," and rejoicing that she was.

"Yes, I do," Mama Phibbs said resolutely. "Give me a hug and a kiss, Bobby."

Bobby stood quickly and his mother held him tightly.

"I'm really glad to see you home, son." She held him at arm's length away. "I hope you never go away again."

"I said don't worry, Mama, and I mean *don't worry.*"

Mama Phibbs buttoned the top button on her coat and opened the front door.

"Now, I'll be staying away for a few days, give you two young people a chance to be alone. Call me if you want me to mind the baby. I'd be glad to."

"Thank you, Mama," Esther said and shut the door behind her. She locked it and then turned and leaned against it. Bobby smiled devilishly at her. Esther laughed.

"What?" she demanded coquettishly. "What *you* thinking about?"

Bobby sat on the couch and patted his leg. "Come here, girl."

"I gotta clear the table."

"Uh-uh. Not now."

Esther came over and he pulled her down into his arms and kissed her roughly. She began to pull back and then he softened his kiss and she responded hungrily, her arms going around him. He broke away and she covered his face in tiny kisses, murmuring, "Oh, Bobby. Oh, Bobby." He dug at the buttons of her shirt and she said, "Let's go upstairs. Let's go to bed."

She took his hand and led him up the stairs. When they reached the top he lifted her and carried her to the bed. They helped each other undress in the dark room. She ran her hands over his chest and his shoulders.

"Oh, Bobby, it's been so long."

He laid her back on the bed and raised her legs up over his shoulders.

"There's been no one, you know that, don't you, Bobby? Nobody, baby. I waited for you, I waited for *you!*" she cried as he plunged into her. She clutched his back and arched up to get him.

"Fuck me, Bobby, just *fuck* me!" she groaned in his ear. "I've missed it so much!"

He came then with a grunt and she felt him shudder and relax. He buried his face in her neck and after a long moment he said, "I'm sorry, Es."

"Just stay in me, Bobby. You feel so good, just stay in me."

She ran her hands down to the cheeks of his ass and raked her fingernails gently across his skin. She did it again. And then again. She felt him harden inside her and he began to rock rhythmically on his knees. She climaxed twice before he shouted something angry and unintelligible and spurted again. She held him close and felt him crying softly.

"It's all right, baby," she cooed. "Everything's all right."

TUESDAY
August 7

7:32 AM Gold came to work early. He bought a cup of coffee and a bagel and cream cheese from the machines on the mezzanine and brought his breakfast up to his new office. As he ate at his desk he read the morning paper he had brought from home. On the third page was a photo of him throwing Jerry Kahn across the hood of a Toyota. The caption read HEAD OF JAR RESTRAINED BY POLICE—NO ARRESTS. The short accompanying story stated that the incident was symptomatic of the increasing tension between the LAPD and the Orthodox Jewish community, exacerbated by the recent spate of anti-Semitic vandalism. Gold was thankful his name wasn't mentioned in the story.

Gold was thankful too, as he leafed through the paper, that there seemed to have been no new incidents overnight. He had checked at Control when he came in, and there had been nothing for the Anti-Defacement Task Force. Now, over his coffee and newspaper, he lit his first cigar of the day, noting that his entire staff—one Sean Zamora—was ten minutes late for work.

At seventeen after eight Zamora called.

"Jack, I'm going to be late."

"You already are."

"Uh—then I'm going to be later."

"Well, there isn't a whole helluva lot happening around here. If it's important, do what you have to do. But get in here as soon as you can. I'm lonely in this big, cavernous office."

"It's very important, and I'll be in as soon as possible."

As soon as Gold hung up the phone, it rang again.

"Lieutenant Gold?" Cherry Pye's officious voice asked. "Please hold on for the chief."

A moment later Huntz was barking into Gold's ear. "Gold? For chrissake, man. What the hell is wrong with you?"

"Whatever do you mean, Alan?"

"I put you in the least confrontational post in the city; I *create* it, for chrissake, just to keep you out of trouble; and the first day on the job you make the *Times* by manhandling a respected community spokesman. Dealing with you is like trying to put out a fire with gasoline."

"Look, Alan, I didn't ask for this chickenshit job, so if you don't like the way I'm doing it, just put me back on Robbery."

"Oh, no"—Huntz's smirk came over the line—"you're not going to handle me like that. You can *kill* as many of your goddamn coreligionists as you want, I don't give a damn. I'm giving you all the rope you want, Lieutenant, and I'm quite confident—"

Gold hung up on him. The phone rang.

"Don't you dare hang up on me! I'm the ch—"

Gold hung up again. This time Huntz didn't call back.

At 10:30 Zamora burst in, patting down his wet hair and buttoning his shirt.

"So it was important," Gold said, stretching back in his chair. "How was she?"

"No, no, Jack, you've got it all wrong. It was an interview. For a job."

"For a job?"

"Yeah, a commercial. For Sparkle Scented Soap. I get out of a shower with water beaded on my shoulders and wrap a towel around me"— Zamora acted it out for Gold—"and I tell the camera, 'All the girls at the office ask me what kind of cologne I wear. I tell them I don't wear cologne, it's just my Sparkle Scented Soap they smell. None of them believe me. So I invite them home to take a shower with me. That always convinces them.' Then I flash the camera my best Redford smile"—Zamora flashed Gold his best Redford smile—"and then I walk off camera."

"Dear God," Gold said.

"Whaddya think, Jack?"

"Well, it doesn't make me want to shower with you, but then I'm kinda old fashioned."

"I think I got the gig. They made me and another guy strip and step in and out of the shower seven times."

"You sure them Hollywood fags didn't just want to ogle your wet bod?"

"I'm pretty sure I got it. The other actor just didn't have *presence,* you know what I mean?"

"I think I do. Gifts you have to bring these people."

"You're ribbing me, Jack, but this is serious shit. If I get a callback I'm this far away from twenty or thirty thou a year. For one day's work. And then there's the national exposure."

"Seems to me you already exposed yourself in that fag magazine."

Zamora slumped into his chair.

"Pearls before swine," he said, grinning.

"Watch that swine shit, *goy.* "

"C'mon, I'll buy you lunch. I'm starved. My agent called me for this interview at six this morning, and I didn't have time for breakfast."

Gold shook his head. "Come in to work three hours late, and ten minutes later you want to stop and eat. You know, if you don't watch out you're gonna make a very good cop."

They drove to a place Zamora suggested on Western Avenue. His cousin worked there. It was a hot, unair-conditioned grill called the Blue Dot. Its exterior was painted a shocking blue. Inside the walls were covered with hand-lettered signs advertising food: BURRITOS—CHICKEN, BEEF, OR PORK; BISCUITS, GRITS, AND COUNTRY GRAVY; PASTRAMI DIP; HAM & EGGS; KOREAN BAR-B-Q; TERIYAKI STEAK SANDWICH; TERIYAKI TACOS.

"Christ," Gold said, surveying the signs, "it's a regular United Nations in here."

SPAGHETTI & MEAT SAUCE; BEEF & RICE BOWL; RICE & BEANS PLATE; CARNE ASADA; KOSHER HOT DOGS; HAMHOCKS & CORNBREAD; CHICKEN CURRY.

"That's L.A.," Zamora said. "Haven't you heard? We're the world's new melting pot."

The chubby Mexican cook sweating profusely over the grill spotted Zamora and shouted a greeting, waving his spatula.

"¡Aurela, vato! What's happening?"

Zamora and the cook gave each other a soul handshake and kibitzed in street Spanish. Gold took a small table near the door where the café's heat was occasionally stirred by a smoggy breeze. Zamora broke away from the cook and came over.

"Know what you want yet?"

"Polish sausage and cheese sandwich."

Zamora shouted the order to the cook in Spanglish and sat down opposite Gold.

"So that's your cousin? You really are Mexican then?"

Zamora nodded. "Except when I go visiting my mother's people in Dublin. Then I'm as Irish as a potato from the auld sod," Zamora said, slipping easily into a thick brogue. "Let me run it down for you, Jack. My father's older brother immigrated here to L.A. from some podunk village down in Chihuahua back in the thirties. The war broke out and my uncle enlisted in the U.S. Army. They shipped him off to England to wait for the Allied invasion of Europe. He got a weekend pass to London, found himself hung over in Piccadilly one rainy Sunday morning and decided it was time to go to mass, there being a war on and everything, and you never know when your number was coming up. On the church steps after mass he struck up a conversation with the parish priest, who took a liking to him and invited him back to a nice little keep-up-the-morale-of-our-brave-boys-in-uniform get-together later that afternoon. Sugar cakes and tea, maybe spiked with a little Irish whiskey, that sort of thing. Well, my uncle went to the church social and met this little Irish girl there. She had come over to work in the English war industries where the salaries were a lot better than back home, her having three younger sisters to help raise and all. One thing led to another, and my uncle married that little Irish girl and after the war they came back to L.A. You want me to finish this?"

"Go ahead."

"Well, about ten years after the war my uncle took my aunt back to Dublin for a visit, and he brought his younger brother with them. Oh, I forgot to tell you, all the rest of my uncle's family came up from Chihuahua, after my Uncle Luis—that's my uncle's name—after my Uncle Luis got his citizenship papers for serving in the army. But that was right after the war. Ten or twelve years after that my Uncle Luis took my Aunt Maureen back to Dublin for a visit, and they took my father with them. I think my dad was eighteen or nineteen at the time. He was the baby in the family. Anyway, my dad took up with one of my Aunt Mo's younger sisters, brought her back to L.A., and married her. That was my mother."

"Wait a minute. Two brothers married two sisters?"

"It happens."

"Obviously."

"Makes my cousins cousins on both sides of the family."

"Everybody still together?"

"All within a few blocks' radius in East L.A. Zamoras coming up the ying-yang. A couple of my cousins are cops, that's why I joined the force in the first place. But I always wanted to be an actor. I did a few plays in junior college and I guess I'm definitely what you'd call bitten by the bug."

The food was ready. Zamora went to the counter and brought back the sandwiches—Polish sausage and a chiliburger wrapped in white wax paper.

"They sell beer here?" Gold asked, and Zamora shook his head, his mouth full. They ate in silence, sweating in the stifling heat. The cook brought over a couple of Cokes and they washed down their food with them.

"What's going to happen with these graffiti artists we're supposed to be chasing?"

Gold swallowed a mouthful of sandwich and sucked at his teeth. "Whaddya mean?"

Zamora, poised over his greasy burger, shrugged. "I don't know. Are we going to catch them?"

Gold bit into his Polish sausage and cheese and spoke with his mouth full.

"We might, we might not. Best thing we can hope for now is they just crawl away and disappear. Then we can go back to being cops."

"You really think it's just kids fucking around?"

Gold pointed a finger at Zamora. "Don't get me wrong. I don't think we're dealing with Halloween pranksters here. These Boy Scouts write some deeply disturbing things on those walls."

"Could they be part of the neo-Nazi right-wing movement?"

"You mean like the Silent Brotherhood, the Aryan Nation, the Kalifornia Klan? One of them?"

"Yeah?"

"It's possible, I guess. I'm getting so fucking old I figure I've seen everything and so maybe something outside my own experience throws me for a loop. It's possible."

Zamora finished his chiliburger and wiped his mouth with a paper napkin. "You know, I've never understood those weird hate groups, what makes 'em tick."

Gold shrugged as he chewed. "What's to understand? They don't like people."

"But I mean, to hate like that, certain groups, other kinds of people, you know what I mean, it seems so—so—so un-American."

Gold shook his head. "Don't be naive, Sean. Bigotry is as American as the Fourth of July. A hundred thirty years ago in this country you could *own* a person if they belonged to the wrong group. And anti-Semitism, forget about it. Some of America's finest citizens have been rabid Jew-baiters. Henry Ford. Charles Lindbergh. Ernest Hemingway. Those are the kind of people wish we hadn't won the war until Hitler had finished the job."

"Why does everyone hate the Jews? I got an aunt, every other word out of her mouth is *pinchi Judío.* Why the Jews?"

Gold made a supplicatory gesture with his hands. "You're the Gentile. You tell me."

Zamora was helpless. "I don't know, Jack."

"Then neither do I." Gold relit a cigar he had laid in a tiny plastic ashtray. He puffed on it. "Look, besides the obvious reason—we're supposed to have killed your Christ and all that shit—the real reason I think for the whole history of bullshit is that Jews refuse to be stupid, they refuse to fail. People hate them—us—for that. If in every country the Jews went to they had resigned themselves to being janitors or shop clerks or cesspool cleaners, they would have a lot less shit heaped on them. But Jews refuse to be flunkies. They didn't go for the okey-doke two thousand years ago, and they won't go for it today. A Jew works in a business, he always thinks he can run it better. He always wants to own it."

Zamora smiled. "They why didn't you become chief instead of Huntz?"

"That was somebody else's dream. Not mine." Gold got up. "Let's go back to the office. At least it's cool there. How much do we owe your cousin?"

Zamora stood with him. "It's been taken care of. I'm bribing you for letting me come in late today."

Gold gave him a grim little smile. "I can be bought, but not for a Polish sausage sandwich."

They laughed and walked out into the smog.

12:15 PM The clerk behind the counter of Gun City looked up from his copy of *Soldier of Fortune* magazine as Walker walked in, breaking the electric eye and sounding a loud beep. The clerk was a narrow-chested stringbean of a man got up in a camouflage jumpsuit, heavy-duty hiking boots, and a flak jacket. He had a Rambo knife with a fourteen-inch blade strapped to his leg and a green baseball cap with a skull-and-cross-bones stitched in gold thread over the visor. His cheek was a chipmunk's pouch packed with three sticks of Double-Mint.

"What can I do for you, Cap?"

Walker smiled nervously, then his face went serious, sincere.

"I've got to buy a gun."

"Well, you come to the right place." The clerk popped his gum and closed his *Soldier of Fortune.* "If you was looking for baby rattles this would definitely be the wrong place. But seeing as how it's a gun you're shopping for, I'm pretty sure we can do business. What kinda weapon you in the market for?"

Walker shrugged and smiled again. "I don't know."

The clerk leaned across the counter. "Why don'cha tell me what you need the piece for, and maybe we can figure out what kinda iron would be best for you."

"I—I have a paper route," Walker started haltingly. "Sometimes, late at night when I'm throwing my route, I get hassled by—by—you know."

"Niggers?"

"Yeah."

"They rob you?"

"Once they did. Mostly they just kinda push me around."

The clerk eyed Walker's shoulders, his arms. "You don't look like a dude gets pushed around too easy."

"Sometimes they gang up. Three or four of them."

"And you need a little equalizer? A little rocket in your pocket?"

"Right."

"For protection."

"Right." Walker's smile widened and warmed.

The clerk ducked behind the counter. "Got just what you need." He came up with a silver-plated revolver. "Forty-five-caliber Smith and Wesson. Best frigging handgun ever made." The clerk handed the gun butt-first to Walker. "That'll stop a boogie's clock right at the midnight hour. Just show a shine that son-of-a-bitch and he be breakdancing all the way back to Nigeria, black bastards, I hate 'em all. Here, press that button right there."

Walker pushed the button and the cylinder popped open. He snapped it back in. He brought the gun up to eye level, took a firing stance, and dropped the hammer. It made a sharp, mechanical snap.

"You been around firearms, I can see."

"A little." A memory flashed back through Walker's mind like an old movie on a makeshift screen: his father, staggering drunk, and him shooting cans out in the desert. Every time he missed, the old man would slap him hard across the back of his head. Every time a bullet *pinged!* off a can, the old man laughed and took another swig of Ten High.

"Then you know how good that weapon is," the clerk was saying. "And right now I can give you a real good deal on it, too."

"How much?"

"A hundred ninety-five. And I'll throw in a holster for another twenty."

Walker dug into his jeans and came up with a wad of worn, stained bills. The clerk slipped a pink index card over the counter.

"Just fill this out while I write out the receipts."

"What's that?"

"That's your eligibility card, Cap. Fill it out, pay me, and in two weeks this baby will be yours."

"Two weeks?"

"What is there, an echo in here? That's the law, Cap. State of California don't want handguns falling into the wrong hands, and ain't that a yuck? Ain't seen a nigger yet fill out one of these cards. They all get their guns breaking into white people's houses."

"But I need this gun now."

"No can do, Cap. It's really out of my hands. Why don't you buy a shotgun instead? Ain't no wait on them." The clerk nodded at a rack of shotguns against the far wall. Walker looked at the rack a long time, then turned back.

"I want one of them, too. But I need something I can hold in my hand."

The clerk laughed. "Try your dick, Cap." Then, when Walker didn't laugh, he said, "We all need something, Cap."

Walker looked down at the revolver like a small boy gazing at a longed-for toy. The clerk watched him closely. Walker's eyes rose to meet his.

"I really want this now."

The clerk snapped his gum and scratched his crotch.

"Was you in Nam, Cap?"

Walker hesitated only a second. "Sure was."

The clerk brought his fist down into his open palm. "I *knew* it! I can always spot a fellow vet from gookland. I pulled two tours of duty, myself. Sixty-nine through seventy-one. When was you there?"

"Sixty-six."

"In the beginning, huh? You don't look that old. Was you marines? You look marines."

Walker nodded.

"Figured it. I can always spot an ex-jarhead. Was you in the First?"

"Uh—they moved me around a lot. Now, can I have the gun?"

The clerk popped his gum again and smiled. "Well, I can't let you have this one. This one has papers. But I don't want to see a fellow vet running around without a little backup. Why don't you wait here a minute?" The clerk disappeared behind the camouflage flap that covered the door to the stockroom. Several minutes later he came back with a large, black, wicked-looking piece with an elongated barrel. The clerk spoke in conspiratorial tones.

"Three fifty-seven Magnum. I personally don't think it's as good a weapon as Mr. Smith and Mr. Wesson, but it'll stop an elephant dead in his tracks. Or a gorilla." The clerk smiled. Walker smiled back. The clerk handed the gun tenderly, turning it this way and that. "Friend of mine brought this piece in from Texas. Said it had seen some action down Nicaragua way. Blowing up Communists. Nothing in the world better than blowing up frigging Communists."

He gave the gun to Walker.

"Little did we know, eh, Cap, that those were the best years of our lives. Nam, I mean. At least we had a purpose in life, huh? At least we knew what we was fucking *about.*"

"How much?" Walker aimed at a mannequin in a hunting jacket and pulled the trigger. It made a louder click than the other gun.

"Well, I'll tell you, Cap. I could really get my ass in a sling doing this. Lose my job, big-ass fine. They can even give you time for this kind of thing."

Walker aimed at an NRA poster of a busty blonde with a rifle and pulled the trigger.

"I mean, it ain't like I do this every day."

"How much?"

"Three fifty, couldn't go a penny under."

Walker laid the Magnum on the counter and counted out three hundred and fifty dollars from his wad of stained bills.

The clerk smiled and popped his gum.

"Now, lemme show you them shotguns, Cap."

1:37 PM Clarke Johnson made a tent of his fingers, tapped the end of his nose, and peered over his fingertips at Bobby and Esther Phibbs seated on the other side of his desk.

"Mr. Phibbs, in this office we consider parole and probation a privilege, not a right."

"Yes, sir," Bobby answered earnestly. Esther held Bobby's arm and nodded in agreement.

Clarke Johnson looked at Bobby more closely and he seemed a little peeved.

"You don't have to call me 'sir,' Mr. Phibbs. That kind of thing doesn't mean much around here. Now, as I said, probation is a privilege, not a right. A lot of my clients don't realize that. I hope that you do."

"Of course, we do," Esther said softly. Johnson glanced at her, then continued.

"You're very lucky, Mr. Phibbs. The offense you were convicted of, the conditions under which you committed that offense—being in a drugged state, possessing a firearm, your prior convictions—all these factors prescribe a lengthy sentence in the state penal system, not just a year and a day in the County Jail, followed by three years' probation. You were extremely lucky. Reading over the paperwork"—he shuffled some paper—"I think the mitigating circumstance in your sentencing was the impassioned speech given by Mrs. Phibbs"—he again glanced at Esther, and his eyes lingered a moment—"at the time of your trial. I see no other reason for such a light sentence. As I said, you were lucky."

"Yes, sir," Bobby mumbled. Johnson looked at him sharply, and then went on.

"Now you come to me, your probation officer. You and I will have a very close relationship for the next three years. That's if everything goes well. If everything goes badly, then I'll be forced to violate you, and you shall go to prison and serve the full three-year sentence you probably should have received at the inception of this case."

When he had stopped talking the small office was completely silent. Outside in the reception area a baby was crying.

"I'm sorry if I seem harsh, but those are the realities, and I want you to understand we only deal in reality here. No maybe's, or what should have been's, or what's going to be. Just what is. Do we understand each other, Mr. Phibbs?"

Bobby nodded.

"And the reality of the next three years is that your future will be entirely in your own hands. Probably more so than the vast majority of other Americans. You and only you can decide your fate. No one else." Clarke Johnson glanced at Esther for a third time.

"We can give you support. We can be there for you to talk to. But we cannot make choices for you. If you decide to use drugs again, then that will be your decision. If you choose not to use drugs, that also will be your decision." He stared at Bobby. Esther fidgeted and coughed.

"Mr. Johnson, is it all right if I smoke?" she asked softly.

"Of course," he said, smiling at Esther, then looking quickly away. Esther fumbled in her purse for a cigarette.

"You realize your civil rights have been suspended," Johnson said to Bobby, "and will remain suspended for the term of your probation. Your home is subject to search at any time, no warrant necessary. You must report any change of address to me in writing within twenty-four hours. Also any change in place of employment. I understand a job is waiting?"

Bobby and Esther nodded simultaneously.

"That's very good. But any problems arising on the job I want you to report to me immediately. Any problems of any nature, you are to contact me at once. Don't wait until you've already used drugs before you ask for my help. Am I making myself clear?"

Johnson leaned back in his chair and tented his fingers again. He was a compact, well-built black man in his late thirties, clean-shaven and close-cropped. His round, rimless glasses gave him an owlish appearance.

"But the most important facet of your probation will be random urinalysis. You will be given a phone number to call every night, and a code number. If your code number is included on the taped message that will answer, you must report here, to me, before seven o'clock the next morning. At that time I will ask you to give me a sample of urine, under my observation, and that sample will be tested for any traces of controlled substances. If any trace of controlled substances is detected, or if you fail to appear in this office when your code number is called, or if, on appearing in this office, you refuse to furnish a sample of your urine—if any of these conditions occur—you will be in violation of your probation and you will have to appear before the magistrate who sentenced you and give just cause why you should not be sent to prison for the duration of your sentence. Do you understand all this?"

"Yes," Esther answered, and both men looked at her briefly.

"Mr. Phibbs." Clarke Johnson tapped his chin with his thumb as he spoke. "A lot of probation officers in this department pride themselves on being understanding with their probationers. A lot of parole officers in this department tell their clients that it's okay to come in here and test dirty once in a while, that they'll overlook an occasional dirty test as long as the probationer doesn't lie to them." He aligned Bobby's file with the edge of his desk. "I'm not like that. I don't want to be understanding where drugs are concerned. I refuse to understand dope. I don't think it's my job to be understanding after you've started using. That's not what I'm employed to do. If you resume your use of narcotics and I catch you with a dirty test you're going back to jail. No if's, and's, or but's. Do we still understand each other?"

Bobby's face had hardened.

"Mr. Phibbs, do we still understand each other?"

Esther glanced nervously at Bobby, then said, "Of course we do, Mr. Johnson. We understand everything, don't we, Bobby?"

"Sure do," Bobby said curtly.

Clarke Johnson leaned forward and rested his elbows on his small desk.

"Mr. Phibbs, I am here to help you however I can. You can call me any time of the day or night. If you have a problem, I want to know about it. I'm here to help you. But, as I said before, your future is entirely up to you. You might say you're at the crossroads of your life. You can take one path, do the right thing, and put the unfortunate past behind you. Or you can take the wrong road and inevitably wind up in a prison cell again. It's all up to you."

The room fell silent again, everyone waiting for someone else to speak. Finally Esther shifted in her chair and said, "Don't you worry, Mr. Johnson. Bobby's finished with that business. He don't want to go back to jail."

He sat back and surveyed Bobby closely.

"Is that correct, Mr. Phibbs?"

Bobby's mouth smiled, but his eyes were case-hardened steel.

"I'll never go back to jail again."

After a long moment the probation officer said, "Good." He tore a piece of paper from a pad and scribbled down some numbers. "Here's the phone number you are to call every night, and your code numbers." He held the slip of paper out to Bobby, who looked at Johnson's hand with the beginning of a sneer playing around his lips. Esther stood up quickly and took the piece of paper.

"Thank you for everything, Mr. Johnson. We won't let you down."

"I hope not, Mrs. Phibbs. Mr. Phibbs."

Clarke Johnson stood and shook Esther's hand. Bobby stalked sullenly out of the office. Esther looked after him, stricken. She turned back.

"Don't worry about a thing, Mr. Johnson," she breathed.

She hurried after Bobby.

3:52 PM "Just my motherfucking luck to get a nigger with something to prove," Bobby Phibbs said around a mouthful of Big Mac. "A signifying motherfucker. Out to impress his white bosses. Mother*fucker.*"

Esther glanced over at Little Bobby, who was staring wide-eyed at his father. They were in the McDonald's at Crenshaw and Olympic. They had come here after picking Little Bobby up from school.

"That nigger's gonna be on my ass like white on rice. Motherfucker say 'you'll be doing the three years you *should* have done' and 'probation is a privilege' and shit like that. Motherfucker. Nigger talk like that liable to get his motherfucking *head* blown off, he don't watch who the fuck he talking to."

Esther fished a five-dollar bill from her purse.

"Baby," she said to Little Bobby, "go get me some McNuggets."

"You don't like McNuggets, Mama."

"Today I do. Now go get me some."

Little Bobby climbed down from his seat and ran to take his place in line.

"Bobby, don't talk like that in front of the child. He don't need to hear such gutter language."

Bobby put down his Big Mac. "Say what?"

"Talking about hurting people and violence and using curse words and all that. He don't need to hear trash like that. I spend my life trying to keep him away from trash like that. And I never use the word *nigger* around Little Bobby. He don't think of himself that way, and I don't want him to start."

Bobby Phibbs pointed a finger at Esther.

"You ain't doing that boy no favor coddling him that way you do. You think some white man ain't gonna call him 'nigger' someday? You think that ain't ever gonna happen?"

"If it does, then Little Bobby'll be strong enough and confident enough to know it's the man calling the name who's the real nigger."

Bobby frowned. "You fill that boy's head with foolishness, talking 'bout Harvard and UCLA. How we gonna afford to send him to college?"

"When the time comes that child's going to any school he wants to. Miss Abrams says he's smart enough to be accepted anywhere he applies, and I'll wash floors and clean toilets twenty-four hours a day to make sure he can go to any school he wants to."

Bobby wiped his mouth with a paper napkin. "What for? If he goes to every motherfucking college in the whole motherfucking country he's still gonna be black. You can't change that. He's still gonna be a nigger, and don't you think for a minute the white man gonna let him forget that."

Esther's hands trembled slightly as she set down her Fishwich.

"Bobby, good Lord. What's gotten into you? Just listen to the way—"

Little Bobby returned with the Chicken McNuggets. He slipped into the seat beside Esther.

"Baby," Esther said, "you got me sweet and sour. You know I like barbecue sauce."

Little Bobby rolled his eyes in exasperation. "Mama! How am I supposed to know that? And besides, my Big Mac is getting cold!"

"Do as your mother says," Bobby Phibbs said harshly, "and do it quick if you don't want to get backhanded across your face."

Little Bobby dropped his eyes and got up from the table. "Yes, sir," he mumbled softly and walked away toward the counter.

Esther lit a cigarette. Her hands were shaking now. "Bobby, don't ever talk to my son like that again."

Bobby grew still and glared at her. "Maybe you'd like it better if I slapped the shit out of *you*. Right here and now."

Esther avoided her husband's eyes.

Bobby smiled. "That's better." He opened the carton of his second Big Mac. "It's plain to see things have been going real slack around here since I been away. That shit is gonna change." He bit off a massive mouthful of burger. "If I don't watch out that boy there is gonna grow up to be a real honky-imitating nigger—just like that Mr. Clarke Johnson. A real motherfucking white-ass-kissing nigger."

Esther spoke slowly, choosing her words carefully and still not looking directly at her husband. "Bobby, that man's just doing his job. All he told you was if you start using again, you gonna get in trouble. Well, you said you don't want to ever do that again. Right? Then we don't have anything to worry about, right"

Bobby shook his head. "It ain't got nothing to do with that. It's all about that white-hearted nigger telling me I was motherfucking *lucky* to do a year in County. He acts like a year in a motherfucking cage is like a walk in the motherfucking park. Well, it *ain't.*" Bobby sucked some Coke up through a straw. "I want this shit over with *now*. Enough is enough." He dropped a handful of French fries into his mouth and chewed thoughtfully. "I had a cellmate rolled out a coupla months back. He gave me the name of this Jew lawyer in Beverly Hills. You see, you can go to court and have your probation changed so that you don't have to call in every night and all that shit. You don't have to test or nothing, just go by once a month and sign in. But you need a good lawyer, not no public defender dump truck. A good Jew lawyer. I got his name."

"Those Beverly Hills lawyers cost a fortune, Bobby. How we gonna afford—"

"That cellmate I was talking about, he said to look him up when I got out. Said he might have something we could do together and make us a little something."

Esther fought to hold herself together. "Bobby, those kind of people are just gonna get you in trouble again. They just gonna drag you down to their level. You only been out less than a day. Please don't talk about stuff like that. You got a good job waiting for you at the cafeteria. Starting tomorrow morn—"

Bobby waved his hand. "That shit. That's like being a motherfucking kitchen nigger. That's like being a slave. Everything but the motherfucking chains. I'm talking about better than that."

Esther began to cry softly. "Oh, please don't talk like this. Please don't talk like this."

Bobby's face softened. "Don't cry, Es. Don't cry, woman." He reached out for her hand but she snapped hers back.

Little Bobby was suddenly standing there, his eyes downcast.

"Mama, they're out of barbecue sauce," he said. "I asked everybody, but they're out. I'm sorry."

"Oh, baby." Esther took her son in her arms and rocked him gently.

9:06 PM Gold stood in the doorway of Montenegro's and peered into the dim coolness. The restaurant was plushly appointed and thickly carpeted. The walls were covered with quality fake impressionist paintings and the several intimate dining rooms were partitioned by etched sheets of smoked glass. In an alcove just off the bar a pianist was playing a languid rendition of "Summertime in Venice." The music drifted lazily over the hum of conversation and clink of silverware.

Just as the maître d' made for Gold, Howie Gettelman waved from across the room.

As he crossed the restaurant Gold's cop sense automatically checked out the other patrons. The place was jammed with foreigners—dark, swarthy men in European-cut clothes and rattling thick gold jewelry. On his way across the room Gold heard Spanish, Italian, Arabic, Hebrew, and what he took to be Greek. The women were almost all Americans—blond, blasé, and stylishly dressed.

"Jack, I'm so glad you came." Howie had on a sharply tailored blue double-breasted and a pastel yellow shirt. He seemed to belong to this crowd.

"How long have you been doing your drinking on Rodeo Drive?" Gold asked as he slipped into the booth beside Howie.

Howie smiled and winked. "More business is done here than at the Polo Lounge."

"What kind of business?" Gold said, looking around the restaurant. At the table directly across from theirs a famous TV actor, obviously well lubricated, was alternately nibbling at his crabmeat salad and at the ear of a young starlet type whose face was vaguely familiar to Gold.

"Jack, thank you for coming," Howie said. "First I want to apologize for that incident Saturday. I want you to know I understand your anger completely. I don't think you overreacted in the least."

"Neither do I."

"Right. Right. I understand where you were coming from. I can appreciate your motivations. You don't understand drugs. You don't understand why anyone would ever use drugs."

"That's where you're wrong, Howie. I've been dealing with dope and dopesters for a long, long time, and I understand perfectly why people use drugs. That's why I see red when I find out my daughter's husband is using."

"Jack, Jack." Howie grinned and straightened his tie. "A little recreational cocaine can hardly be called 'using.'"

Gold took a sip of water. There was a sliver of lemon in the glass. He fished it out with his fork.

"Don't try to bullshit me, Howie. Save it for your dingy clients."

"Well, anyway," Howie said quickly, "that's all over." He took hold of Gold's hand across the rich tablecloth. "You hear me, Jack? All over. *Emmes.* He gave Gold a deep, soulful stare. "My right hand to God, Jack." He raised his right hand. "That business is finished."

Gold stared at his son-in-law a long time. Then he reached into the bread basket and withdrew a small, crusty roll. He split it and buttered it.

"Don't lie to me, Howie. I get real pissed off when I'm lied to. I think you know that."

"Jack, did I just raise my hand to God? Just this minute? Do you want me to swear on my son's life? Look, I'm swearing on my son's life. I swear on Joshua's life—"

"All right already. Enough already. And I'm glad to hear it."

The waiter came around and gave them menus. They ordered double Scotches. The waiter went away. Gold peered at his menu in the dim candlelight.

"Am I going blind in my old age, or are these prices for real?"

Howie waved a hand. "Don't worry about it. This is mine."

"Seven seventy-five for a dinner salad?"

"You pay for the name, the ambience. For the chance to be seen here."

"But seven seventy-five?"

"Jack! Don't worry about it! Listen, order the veal. The veal here is the best in the city."

"It better be. For these prices they should bring you the whole fatted calf. No wonder you were selling dope. You need that kind of money just to pay these prices."

"Jack," Howie laughed, "just order."

"And why isn't my daughter having dinner with us? She isn't good enough for this place? She's home alone eating a TV dinner so you can afford to play Mr. Beverly Hills big shot?"

"For God's sake, Jack, take it easy. I bring Wendy here all the time. I needed to talk to you alone. You know that. Now order the veal marsala or the veal parmigiana. You can't go wrong with the veal."

The waiter came with their Scotches. They ordered and he went away with an unctuous smile.

"Jack." Howie sipped at his drink. "I got a call from the assistant D.A. this morning."

"Oh?"

"All charges have been dropped. He even apologized to me for any inconvenience I might have suffered."

"That was nice of him," Gold said with a chuckle.

"Jack." Howie shook his head. "How'd you do it? How in hell'd you do it?"

Gold touched at the ice cubes in his Johnnie Walker with a fingertip. "You put in almost thirty years, you begin to learn how to get things done."

"Well, Jack, I'm incredulous. I'm blown away. I had no idea you could get such results so quickly."

"I told you not to worry, didn't I? Didn't I tell you I'd take care of it?"

Howie smiled. "Yes, you did."

"You didn't believe me."

"I didn't believe you. I'm sorry."

Gold shrugged. Howie reached into his inside breast pocket and withdrew an alligator skin checkbook. He clicked the top of a gold ballpoint pen.

"What are you doing?" Gold asked.

Howie laid the opened checkbook on the tablecloth. "Jack—" he began.

"What are you doing?"

"Jack—"

"Howie, put that away. Don't insult me like that."

"Jack, I know this must have been very expensive. It's priceless to me. Let me at least take care of the expenses."

Gold shook his head. "I told you I would take care of it, and I did. That's it. It's finished."

"Jack, please."

"Howie, please."

Howie sighed, closed the checkbook, and slipped it back into his jacket. "If there's ever *any*thing I can do."

Gold swallowed some Scotch. "I told you what I wanted, Howie. I told you what I expected."

Howie held up his hands. "That's over. Finished. My right hand to God. Never again."

Gold smiled. "Then that's it."

The waiter served their salads. A leaf of lettuce laid on a small plate, topped by a couple of slices of cucumber and a dollop of dressing.

"Seven seventy-five for this?" Gold said, staring down at the salad. "These people are thieves. They should be arrested."

Howie laughed.

11:23 PM "It's twenty-three minutes after the hour, and this is still your hostess Janna Holmes, talking tonight with Jesse Utter, candidate for the California State Assembly from Desert Vista, California. Also Grand Exalted Wizard of the Kalifornia Klan. Obviously, Mr. Utter, you don't think the two things are exclusive of each other. Is that true?"

"Call me, Jesse, Janna. And if you mean belonging to the Klan and concurrently running for election to the State Assembly, no, I don't. I don't think they're exclusive of each other at all. In fact, I think being a leader of the Kalifornia Klan is probably the best possible preparation for being a state assemblyman."

"Why is that, Jesse?"

"Well, Janna, let me explain. Being a member of the Kalifornia Klan is not an easy thing. It's a very hard road to hoe. You are constantly being attacked—verbally, physically, mentally, abusively—by the liberal fellow-traveler press, by the Communist-sympathizer government, by the so-called Christian clergy, by the powerful and clandestine Jewish-Zionist lobby. Being a Klan member is a very lonely job. Sometimes you feel you are—just as our Lord was—a voice crying out in the wilderness. A single, solitary voice of reason and truth, being drowned out by a cacophonous wail of screaming insanity. It can be very depressing. But it toughens you, hardens you for the task ahead. Klan members are fire-tempered. We can't be budged on our beliefs, on our principles. They can tell us something is true that we know to be a lie—they can tell us it's true a million times, and a million and one times we will spit it back in their face and tell them it's a lie. And I don't think there's a single member of our State Assembly possessing anything near that kind of resolve."

Walker parked the blue van in the service alley that paralleled Pico Boulevard. He left the motor running, the lights on, and the radio blaring, and trotted a few feet along the chain-link fence that surrounded Fischer's Foreign Car Service.

"Jesse, what do you make of these recent incidents involving vandalized synagogues and other Jewish buildings?"

"Well, it certainly doesn't surprise me, Janna. For years I have been telling anyone who cared to listen that there is a huge, throbbing hidden heart of anti-Jewish disgust in this country. I think these recent acts of heroism bear me out."

The Doberman bitch heard the familiar footsteps, left her blanket under

217

the Mercedes' front end, and took up her station at the fence. She bared her teeth in a lethal grin. Walker giggled.

"You can't be a race of manipulators, a race of usurers, of cheaters and liars, of deceit and dishonor and treason and trickery—you can't be a race of people who indulge in these kinds of despicable practices and not expect a great deal of hatred vented your way. Eventually the man on the ground is going to throw off the foot on his throat."

Walker kicked at the chain-link and the bitch jumped at him, tearing at the fence, clawing and snarling.

"Look, Janna, these attacks are symptomatic of the frustration felt by the white Christian American today. Who speaks for him? Who looks out for him? Absolutely no one. The Negro has the NAACP and the Urban League; the Jew has all the press and television networks; the Latins have their Roman church. Even the Indians have a government bureau to look out for them. But who speaks for the white Christian American?"

Walker laid the barrel of the .357 on the fence wire and pushed it through. The bitch lunged at it and clamped down her jaws. There was a muffled roar and the night air was filled with flying chunks of flesh and gristle. The right side of the Doberman's head was gone, the left side a shattered remnant holding a flat, lifeless eye, like a stuffed animal's. Blood spurted all over the grease-slick concrete. The bitch's body danced sideways a dozen feet, tottered, and tumbled over. The delicate black legs quivered and jerked—claws clicking together—then were still.

"Are you aware, Jesse, that many people—people like Jerry Kahn of the JAR—are convinced it's members of your Kalifornia Klan who are vandalizing these temples?"

"Excuse me for laughing, Janna, but that amuses me. Jerry-the-Jew Kahn and his little band of Yeshiva boys try to blame me and my brothers for half the crimes committed in Southern California. No, I'm sorry to say, whoever is doing these patriotic acts, they're not members of the Kalifornia Klan. But I would be proud to recruit them. Very proud. They're just the kind of people we need to turn this country around."

Walker slammed the van into gear and roared away.

WEDNESDAY
August 8

12:47 AM Esther was crying. She was scrubbing the washbasin in the restroom of the photographic studio and the tears were rolling down her cheeks and dripping off the tip of her nose. She straightened up and wiped at her face with the back of her hand. She caught her tear-streaked reflection in the mirror and groaned.

"My Lord. Look at that."

She left the bathroom and went through the photographer's waiting room, unlocked the front door, and stepped out onto Robertson Boulevard. She dabbed at her face with a torn shirttail and leaned back against the building, resting one foot on the wall. A moment later the door opened and Lupe stepped out carrying two steaming mugs of coffee. Wordlessly she offered one of them and Esther took it the same way. Lupe squatted Indian style on the sidewalk and sipped at her coffee. A private security patrol car glided past and the guard inside nodded at them.

"*¿Qué pasa, hermana?*" Lupe said finally. She was looking up at Esther. Esther shook her head.

Lupe looked back at the deserted boulevard. On the other side of the street was a shop that sold huge, elaborate dollhouses. The shop called them "miniature estates."

"It's my old man," Esther said eventually. "It's Bobby." She took a swallow of coffee. Lupe watched the street, waiting.

"I'm afraid he's gonna start using again."

Lupe scratched her shoulder. "Esther, he's only been out two days. Not even. You got to give him a chance, *chica.*"

Esther shook her head again. "I know him, Loop. I can feel it. It's like there's a spring inside of him getting wound tighter and tighter, until he's about to bust, and nothing ever softens him until he shoots up some heroin."

"You got to give him a little time, *hermana.* He's been in jail for a year, *esse.* It takes a little time."

Esther started to cry again. Her eyes filled momentarily, and a single teardrop came out. Then she shivered and cleared her throat.

"I think he lied to me, Loop. I think he's been using all the time he's been in jail. I think that's why he's so wound up now. He's fucking with*drawing*, girl."

Lupe looked up at her. "You think so?"

Esther nodded. "I'm sure of it."

Lupe stood up and rubbed the back of her legs. "What's gonna happen?"

Esther poured the dregs of her coffee into the gutter and flicked the last few drops from her cup. She arched her back wearily and massaged her neck.

"I don't know, Lupe. But I do know I ain't going through *that* hell again. *Uh uh!* No way, José." She shook her head at the smoggy night sky. "That shit is dead."

3:24 AM Gold's battered Ford wheezed off Mulholland and bumped along beside a row of cedars. At the end of the cedars the paved road stopped at a wide, flat clearing that dropped off over the side of the mountain. Sean Zamora's red Corvette was parked there. Beyond the Corvette were several police vehicles, their red lights flashing, and a coroner's van. The Ford's headlights caught Zamora sitting on his Corvette's fender, his jacket thrown across his shoulder. He was eating yogurt from a paper cup. Gold cut the engine and got out. The ground was dry and hard beneath his shoes. The faint night wind ran across the summer-dried grass like a knife ripping through satin. A police helicopter was circling a quarter of a mile down the mountainside. Its searchlight bathed the area with a ghostly white brightness.

Zamora came over, throwing the empty yogurt carton into the tall grass. "I waited here like you said. What's happening down there? What's going on?"

"I don't know. I got a call. Let's go see," Gold grunted, and stuck an unlit cigar into the corner of his mouth.

"I wouldn't light that. The whole hill is liable to go up."

Gold grunted again and led the way through the police cars and around the coroner's van. A yellow police tape had been strung up where the mountain plunged down a slope. A uniformed cop stepped into Gold's way. Gold flicked his I.D. at him and the uniform moved aside, saying, "Sorry, Lieutenant."

"Where's Ligget and Lytel?"

"In the house, right down this path. It goes right down to the swimming pool."

Gold lifted the police tape and slipped under. Zamora followed him. The path curled around and down the hillside for fifty yards and came up right at a large kidney-shaped pool. On the other side of the pool was a low, rambling, California-style house perched on thick concrete pilings embedded in the side of the mountain. All the lights in the house were on. Gold and Zamora walked around the pool and knocked lightly on the back door. A large, fleshy, dark-complexioned man came to the screen.

"Jack. Wait a minute." The large man turned to say something to the room, then opened the screen door and stepped out on to the patio.

"Did we wake you up? I think we got something you'll be interested in."

"Sam. This is my new partner, Sean Zamora. Sean, this is Homicide Detective Sam Lytel."

The two men shook hands. Lytel glanced back toward the house and spoke in a dry whisper.

"Goddamndest house you ever seen, Jack. Got a fucking waterfall in the fucking living room. Paintings on the wall, must be worth a fortune. Guy's got two live-in broads. *Two*. Either one make a dead man come. Some limey movie director. Ridley—Ridley—"

"Ridley Weems? This is Ridley Weems's house?" Zamora stepped back and surveyed the house with interest.

Lytel peered at Zamora in the dim light and then looked quizzically at Gold.

Gold shrugged. "He's an actor. But he's okay. What went down?"

"Well, this limey Weems been away for a couple weeks down in Mexico. Puerto Vallarta. With the two babes. They flew back late tonight. On the way home from the airport they pick up Weems's two Rottweilers where he's been boarding them while they was away. You ever hear of a kennel with a twenty-four-hour pick-up service? I guess if you're rich enough you can buy anything. So they come home and Weems lets the dogs out the back door. Says he always gives 'em the run of the mountain at night. Especially after they been cooped up for a couple weeks in a kennel run. So they start to unpack, or fix coffee, or lick each other's assholes, or whatever these kind of people do. Drag out the coke stash, if you ask me. And right in the middle of whatever they was doing the two dogs run back into the living room, and they're fighting over something. You know, growling and pulling in different directions. Like cute little puppies. Well, one of the babes goes over and says, 'Bad doggies, now stop that,' and gives them each a little love tap on their noseys. The Rotts drop their toy and go running back outside, and the Babe gets a paper towel to clean up the messy-poo. Only when she picks it up she realizes it's a motherfucking *tit!* She goes into hysterics and loses her Mexicana Airlines dinner all over the pretty shag carpet. She's still in the bathroom. The other tramp is in there with her now. Trying to console her. And would I love a Polaroid of *that*."

"Did you find the body?" Gold was lighting his cigar.

"Did we ever! All over the fucking place. Motherfucker did a *number* on her, you hear me? Cut off her tits. Looks like he *ripped* her fucking head off. Beat her face in like a mashed potato. I ain't never seen nothing like it. He musta took a bath in her blood."

"Who was she?"

"Street whore. Trick name Honey Dew Mellon. Real name Thalia Mae Robinson. Negro. Twenty-seven years old. Would've been twenty-eight in September."

"Could it have been her pimp?"

Lytel shook his head. "Nah. If you'd have seen the body you wouldn't ask that. Pimp wouldn't have done that, even if he wanted to kill her. They got too much respect for the merchandise. No, this was definitely a freako scene. Some whacked-out trick did this. And he sure got his money's worth."

Gold shifted his weight on his feet. "How long's she been dead?"

"Some time last night, M.E.'s flunkie said. He'll know more when he makes some tests."

The screen door banged open and a short, thick, balding man in a Mexican *guayabera* shirt stepped out onto the patio.

"Jack."

"Lou. How've you been? Sean, this is Louie Ligget. These two have been partners for what—?"

"Fifteen years."

"—fifteen years. Ask anybody downtown about Ligget and Lytel. Sounds like a soap company, don't it?"

Everyone chuckled. Then Ligget said to Lytel, "You show it to him?"

"Not yet."

Ligget turned back to Gold. "Follow me. We got something I think you'll want to see."

Lytel led the way back up the hill, shining a high-intensity flashlight on the ground before them. Halfway up to the road and the clearing Ligget turned down another path descending in the other direction. They followed him down and around the mountain. Below, in the distance, the San Diego Freeway was a thin string of bright lights, with the occasional car's headlights slipping through the string like bubbles through a syringe. The helicopter that earlier had been hovering over the hill suddenly whomp-whomped down on them, filling the air with dirt and noise and whipping the grass in every direction.

"Fucking *asshole!*" Ligget shouted up at the chopper and windmilled his arms frantically. "Get away from here!" He turned around to Gold, who was behind him. "I hate them fucking things!" he shouted in Gold's face. The chopper hit them with its spotlight and they were illuminated in a phosphorescent white glare. Their clothes flapped in the wind; their collars slapped at their faces. "Up there, asshole!" Ligget gestured to the chopper. "Not here!"

The helicopter swooped away and hovered over a spot on the hillside fifty feet farther down. Its searchlight shone down on something.

"Christ!" Zamora said. "It's just like Vietnam."

Ligget twisted his neck and peered over Gold's shoulder at him. "You were in Nam?"

"No," Zamora said, "but I saw *Platoon* seven times, and this reminds me of it."

Ligget looked at Gold, who shook his head and smiled in the dark.

The last twenty feet were a steep incline down to an outcropping of huge boulders pinpointed by the chopper's searchlight. The four men slipped and slid down in a flurry of dirt and curses.

"I'm too old for all this," Gold growled, out of breath. "I'm a city cop."

"Here it is," Ligget said, and beamed his flashlight at the partially lit rock. There were two crosses crudely spray-painted in red. They stared at the rock in silence.

"Is that blood?" Zamora asked at last.

"No," Gold answered slowly.

"He's moving up in the world," Ligget said. "He's ambitious."

"At least he's an equal opportunity murderer," Lytel said.

Gold looked at him. "He hasn't offed any Jews yet."

"Yet."

The four policeman stood around staring at the rock.

"Could be some kind of copycat thing," Ligget offered.

"Could be," Gold said.

"But you don't think so?"

Gold shook his head, eyes fixed on the crosses.

Ligget scratched at his crotch. "Huntz is gonna *love* this."

They all laughed nervously.

Back at their cars, Gold opened the Ford's door and rested his elbow on the roof. "We might as well go on in to Parker. Try and figure this thing out before all hell breaks loose."

Zamora seemed preoccupied, excited. "Jack, wait a minute." He opened the trunk of his Corvette and took something out. Something in a flat postal envelope. "I'll be right back." He trotted back through the police cars and disappeared down the mountainside path. He was back in three minutes, grinning with embarrassment.

"What the hell was that all about?"

Zamora was a little breathless. "For chrissake, Jack. That's Ridley Weems lives down there."

"So? What was that you brought him?"

Zamora grinned. "Jack, I had to! It was my picture and resumé."

4:07 AM Anna Steiner slid the shallots, thyme, and tomatoes from her chopping board into the big battered iron pot and, stooping to see better, set the flame to very low. From the big commercial oven she took the shallow pan of preboiled cabbage leaves warming in an inch of water and set the pan on her work counter next to the big bowl of stuffing—ground beef and rice, chopped onions and parsley. She plucked out a tender leaf and working with swift, deft fingers set about wrapping the cabbage leaves around little oblongs of stuffing, tucking in the corners with rapid twists of her small, gnarled hands. She was a short, gray woman in her early sixties, with a sharp mind and kindly blue eyes and, on the inside of her left arm, the unfaded blue numbers B27372. They had been tattooed there at Dachau when she was thirteen. She hardly ever thought of that time anymore, but lately she had started having the nightmares again. Not nightmares, really. Just memories. For what could be more nightmarish than simply remembering. She had had a—a memory—last night. She had shouted in her sleep and awakened herself. She had reached for Samuel, but he hadn't been there. She had sat up in bed then, and after a moment remembered that Samuel was in Cedars-Sinai, waiting for the results of the latest tests. Waiting to see if they would have to cut off his leg. "My God!" she could see Samuel saying as he held his domed head. "How much misery in one lifetime!"

Anna Steiner arranged the stuffed cabbage leaves in four wide, low pans, three rows abreast, then covered the rows liberally with sauce from the big iron pot. She put the pans in the oven, adjusted the temperature, straightened, and wiped her hands on a stained terry-cloth rag. She poured herself a cup of tea and rested, leaning against the work counter, as she looked out through the big front window with the backward lettering that spelled out, from the street, STEINER'S WEST-PIC CAFÉ. The night's blackness was lightening, and for a moment Anna Steiner thought she saw a movement outside. She walked through the small, six-table café and peered through the dark glass. There was nothing. The sidewalks and street were empty. Still, Anna Steiner felt a sense of forboding fall over her like a shadow. It was the feeling she had had in her nightmare last night. She had been back at Dachau. It had been raining—a gray, freezing morning—and she and all the other girls from her barracks had been lined up in the main yard. The icy rain had turned the ground into muddy slush a foot deep. A strikingly handsome young German officer in a fur-collared overcoat was walking before the ranks, pointing with his riding crop at random girls. Girls who were to be taken away—taken away to work in the town, taken away to service the soldiers in the brothel, taken away to die in the showers. Each time the German officer took a step his boots made an obscene sucking sound as he pulled them out of the mud. The raindrops were beading on his beautiful fur collar. The officer was coming closer and closer to where he would pass before her. A siren was screaming—or was it really a scream?—and it was growing louder and louder. The German officer was directly in front of Anna Steiner. He turned and looked at her. He smiled. He was as handsome as a cinema star. He was raising his riding crop. He was going to point it at her.

That's when she had made herself wake up. Anna Steiner shuddered. It was unlike her to have such thoughts. She was an optimistic woman. A glass was always half filled for Anna Steiner. She even found positive things to say about those years. When customers noticed her tattoo and commented, as they always did, she would say that the German people had been good people, but it had been the government that had gone berserk. She would recount instances of kindness that truly were much clearer in her memory than all the horrors. A German doctor touching her face with kindness during an examination. A Gestapo soldier throwing her a thin, lice-ridden blanket because she shivered so violently in an open boxcar. The citizens of her native Budapest lined along the streets, their faces grim and teary, as she and the other Jews were herded to the rail station.

"Ach!" Samuel would cry. "You are a madwoman! You lose your parents, grandparents, and three brothers to those animals, and all you can talk about is one soldier who gave you a filthy rag to cover yourself with. Such kindness must not go unheralded!" Samuel would shake his head in wonder, but she knew he loved her fierce optimism; it nourished him. For Samuel himself had been broken by the camps. He had lived long enough to be saved by the Americans, but the best parts of him had not survived. She had met him there, at Dachau, after the liberation. He had been a walking corpse, hollow-cheeked, sunken-chested, dead-eyed. Not that she had looked much better, but she had had such a strong will, such an iron determination to survive. And she had dragged him behind her—dragged him out of the grave and into the world of the living. While he was still too weak to feed himself she had held his head and spooned in the food from the G.I. mess trays. When she had put some weight on her teenaged frame and the American boys started to take notice of her, she flirted with them and laughed at their broken German, and then ran back to Samuel with the chocolate and cigarettes they gave her.

"Ach!" Samuel would say, lighting a Chesterfield. "You are no better than a whore! But what can you expect from a Hungarian, a Gypsy?"

"Shut up, old man," she would laugh, because he *was* like an old man, even though he was only two years older than she.

They were married in the camp, then she brought him back to Budapest with her—he had been a Berliner—because she still harbored hopes that some of her family might have survived the camps, and she knew that if they were alive they would return to Budapest. None ever did.

They opened a small café—an alley with a ceiling, really—and Anna Steiner saved the little money they made with the same fierce determination she had used to live through the camps. She hated the Communist government bitterly and remembered with fondness the laughter and generosity of the American soldiers. She dreamed of emigrating to America. The decision came with the revolt of '56. Anna Steiner tied up all the hoarded money in a kerchief, stuck the wad between her breasts, pulled on her heavy coat, and kicked open the door of their tiny apartment.

"Let's go, old man," she said to Samuel, and he followed her, as he always did, bitching and complaining, as he always did. They walked across the border into Austria; from there they were shipped to Zurich, then London, New York, and finally Los Angeles. Because she was both a Jew and a Hungarian she was able to appeal to several different relief groups, parlaying the charity into a tiny hamburger stand on Vermont Avenue.

"It's smaller than the place in Budapest!" Samuel cried. "For this we risked our lives to come halfway around the world? To make greasy sandwiches for *shvartzers* sixteen hours a day, seven days a week?"

"You expected to be a king?" Anna Steiner shouted. "There are no kings in America, old man. Only middle class. We will become middle class."

And they did. They bought a Buick, a television, a hi-fi. They went to Las Vegas two weekends a year and played the nickel slots. The hamburger stand became a corner grocery in Venice, but the junkies robbed them monthly, and Anna Steiner was afraid Samuel would get killed because he cursed the hypes in German all the while they held the gun on him.

"Scum, bastards, degenerates. If you didn't have a gun I'd kill you."

"Shut *up*, old man!" Anna Steiner would growl from the side of her mouth as she gave the thieves the fives and tens from the cash drawer. The twenties and fifties she kept stashed in the cracked cup to the right of the register.

They sold the grocery twelve years ago and bought this place, the West-Pic Café. Now lawyers and accountants came all the way from Century City to lunch on Anna Steiner's beef stew, her eggs and onions, her stuffed peppers and cabbages.

Anna Steiner brought out the huge, dented soup kettle and banged it down on the stovetop. She peeled the skins from a dozen Irish potatoes, three bunches of carrots, and several onions, then sliced them directly into the kettle. They made a hollow ring when they hit the bottom of the stainless steel pot. Next she added celery stalks, zucchini strips, bits of cauliflower and cabbage, tomatoes—then poured in several quarts of water. Stirring the simmering kettle with a big wooden spoon grasped in her left hand, with her right she added salt, black pepper, garlic powder, one tablespoon of sugar, and, of course, Hungarian paprika. Anna Steiner's vegetable soup was said to be the best in town, and she went to the downtown produce market every morning to handpick her own ingredients. The food she served in her restaurant was the same food she served guests in her home, Anna Steiner would proudly tell customers who complimented her on their meals.

But it was getting harder and harder to maintain that quality, now that Samuel was sick. She had to do all the work herself, not that Samuel was ever much help. So here she was, preparing food before dawn. She had even lately considered selling the place and retiring. They had enough put away if they didn't live too long. If Samuel lost his leg they would have to sell. Poor Samuel, she thought, poor old man. On top of everything else, now bone cancer. Anna Steiner shook her head. She wished it was she who had caught the cancer; she could have handled it better.

Anna Steiner heard something in the alley behind the kitchen. The sound of someone kicking a discarded bottle. She set down the big wooden spoon, went to the heavily screened back door, and peeked out. The night sky was a deep blue now, and Anna Steiner could see shapes and outlines against the approaching dawn. Something moved in the corner of her eye and she gave a start. A fat white cat froze in the middle of the alley and glared at her. Anna Steiner chuckled and held out her hand.

"Here, kitty, kitty," she said in Hungarian.

The cat hissed and darted away. Anna Steiner came back into the kitchen and picked up the wooden spoon. She tasted her soup broth. It needed something. She was reaching for her salt shaker when she heard someone try the locked front door. The deep sense of dread she had been experiencing enveloped her again and she turned slowly to look. There was a figure silhouetted against the glass in the predawn light. Someone in the street. As she watched, the dawn slipped over the horizon and she could see it was the handsome German officer. He was pointing his riding crop at her. It was her time. Only it wasn't the German officer. It was someone else. And it wasn't a riding crop. It was a gun.

And then Anna Steiner's world exploded.

4:42 AM Freshly showered, powdered, and perfumed, Esther slipped into bed beside Bobby and wrapped her arms and legs around his body. He moaned in his sleep and turned over on his side, away from her. She snuggled her lean, long body against his and ground her pelvis rhythmically into his buttocks. She reached around him and took his penis in her hand and stroked it gently. He stirred.

"Bobby," she whispered. "Bobby."

He turned over on top of her, then pushed her legs up to her shoulders, and slammed into her.

"Bobby," she whimpered, "Bobby," but he lunged into her again and again and again, until he climaxed with a garbled shout. He rolled off of her and turned his back. A moment later he was snoring.

Esther lay still for several minutes, then reached for a cigarette from the pack on the bedside table. She lit it and wiped at the tears coursing down her cheeks.

11:30 AM Gold closed his eyes, pressed his fingertips into his eyelids, and willed the scene he had been witnessing to go away. He opened his eyes and Police Chief Alan Huntz was still there, leaning over Gold's desk, flanked by several of his flunkies—Cherry Pye; Captain Madison, the chief's heir apparent; and Sergeant Orm, the chief's chauffeur. For some reason Gold had never been able to fathom, in Los Angeles chauffeurs of police chiefs eventually became police chiefs. It had happened with Huntz, and Chief Gates before him. Maybe it had something to do with their safe driving record.

"Lieutenant, there's no way in the world you should head this investigation. No possible way. I would feel safer having a crook in that position than an incompetent like you."

Huntz wasn't shouting but his face was blood-red. The six of them—Gold, Huntz, Cherry Pye, Madison, Orm, and Zamora—were crowded into the tiny office of the Anti-Defacement Task Force, Gold and Zamora behind their desks, the others standing.

"Lieutenant," Huntz was saying, "do you have any idea the amount of media we have downstairs? Reporters from *Time, Newsweek,* all the networks, including CNN. The *New York Times.* The London *Times.* There's a correspondent down there from goddamn *Pravda,* for chrissake!"

Gold made a gesture with his hands. "Look, I didn't ask for any of this."

Huntz ignored him. "Do you think you're equipped to deliver a news report to a crowd like that?"

"There's nothing to report."

"'Sixty Minutes' called me an hour ago. They want to do a feature on the 'new anti-Semitism' that's being born right here in L.A." Huntz was shouting now.

"I didn't ask for any of this," Gold repeated.

"The whole world is going to be watching this police department, and all eyes are going to be trained on you. My God!" Huntz turned to pace the room, but banged into Cherry Pye's tits, which were situated just at his right elbow. "My God!" He turned back to Gold. "I'd rather give them my—my—dog!"

"How about your chauffeur there?" Gold nodded toward Sergeant Orm. "Or are they one and the same?"

Huntz slammed across the desktop, shaking his finger under Gold's nose.

"Don't you *dare* get cute with me, Lieutenant. Don't you—"

Gold slapped Huntz's hand away and stood up, sending his chair crashing to the floor behind him. "Fuck you, asshole!" Gold shouted into Huntz's face. Zamora, at his desk, actually covered his eyes so he wouldn't see.

"*Fire me!* I didn't ask for this shitfucking job, and I don't want it now. I never wanted it. If you're fucking hot under the collar because you think I'm gonna get all the glory and not your sweetheart ass-kisser Madison there, then give him the job. Or better yet, you take it. I don't fucking want it!"

"I'd love to!" Huntz's eyes were bulging with fury. "I'd love to have *any*one else in this department take this job. But your coreligionists on the council have informed me that they want one of their own kind to pursue this case. They demand that you continue on as head of this investigation."

"Since when did you ever listen to the City Council?"

"In this particular instance I have no choice. My hands are tied." Huntz, fuming, held his hands out in front of him, locked at the wrists, to illustrate his point.

"Wait a minute," Gold said thoughtfully. "I'm beginning to get the picture. See how this plays. You want to be mayor. And there's four Jews on the council who want to be mayor, too. And the only thing they hate more than you is each other. So you're afraid to alienate any of them, because at one point in the future you're gonna need some of them to get elected. You're making a deal with all of them now so that some of them can stab each other in the back at a later date."

Huntz just glowered.

"And I'm the recipient of this little power play. Only I don't give a rat's fuck, understand? So if you want to replace me, that's fine with me. And if you're not gonna replace me, then get the fuck out of my office and let me get on with my job."

The room was still for a full minute. Gold and Huntz glared at each other across the desk. The others watched them. When Huntz finally spoke his voice was brittle.

"Have you inspected the crime scene yet?"

"An hour after the victim was discovered. Mrs. Steiner."

"Find anything?"

"A lot of neighbors who wanted to lynch somebody. Seems Mrs. Steiner was very popular. And the red crosses across the front windows. Our boy's calling card. And his message. What was it, Sean?"

Zamora stirred. "Uh—'All Jews must die.' "

"And what about the other victim? The prostitute?"

"Looks like the same guy."

"Any connection between the two?"

"Hardly. Except they both were the kind of people that piss our guy off."

"Huh?"

"Jews and blacks."

Huntz thought for a moment. "You suspect it's just one perpetrator?"

Gold shrugged. "Who knows?" He righted his chair and sat down. "I was wrong to think it was the work of young punks. We obviously have a major loony on our hands here. A serious bad guy. With an ideological loop in his circuitry."

"If it is just one bad character, maybe he's got a support system. Maybe we're dealing with an ultraright-wing SLA type thing."

Gold made a brushing motion across his desktop. "It's possible. I'm not ruling anything out at this point. I underestimated this asshole a couple of times already; I'm not going to do it again."

"Then you'll be checking out those types of groups, I suppose? Detaining people and questioning them?"

Gold smiled up at Huntz. "That's very good, Alan. You do understand police work."

Huntz didn't smile back. "I'm assigning twenty Homicide detectives to work full time with you on this."

"Alan, I don't need twenty—"

"If this thing gets any worse I'll put more men on it."

"They'll be tripping over each other's dicks. They'll—"

Huntz held up his hand for silence. "I want results on this, and I want them quickly. Now, you'll be in nominal charge of this investigation, but I don't want you to *sneeze* without first checking it out with Captain Madison here. Officially, he'll be my liaison officer for your task force, but in reality he'll be running the whole damned show. I'm not about to let a trigger-happy drunk like you foul up a case like this, with international attention and political ramifications. You run everything you plan to do in front of Captain Madison. *Beforehand.*" Now Huntz smiled. "Do you understand the rules, Lieutenant?"

"Madison's a desk jockey. He needs a road map to find his fucking car."

Huntz's thin smile tightened. "Do we understand each other, Lieutenant?"

Gold leaned back in his chair. It squeaked. "Oh, we understand each other all right, Alan."

"Good. Then I'll leave you to your work." He turned to leave and Cherry Pye stepped back quickly. Huntz seemed to see Sean Zamora for the first time. He frowned. "Detective Zamora will be reassigned to another division. Something more fitting his outside interests. Like Pornography."

Zamora reddened and looked down.

"Detective Zamora stays with me." Gold said.

Huntz glanced at Gold and stared distastefully at Zamora. "Whatever. You two deserve each other."

As Huntz swept out of the office, he stopped before Madison and shook his hand solemnly.

"Good hunting, Captain."

"Thank you, sir," Madison shot back, just as solemn. Then the chief walked out, followed closely by Cherry Pye and the chauffeur.

Gold pounded his desk and laughed. "Good hunting!" He threw back his head and guffawed. "Good hunting!" Zamora sneaked a look at him and started laughing, too.

Madison walked over and stood before Gold's desk. Gold was still laughing, holding his stomach.

"Jack, I hope any bad blood between you and the old man won't affect our relationship. We have to work very closely on this thing, and I want to be friends." He stuck out his hand. He was an unremarkable man of medium height, medium build, medium complexion. Everything about him seemed to be a compromise.

Gold stopped laughing and, rubbing his eyes, looked up at Madison's hand. He took the hand and Madison pumped it vigorously.

"What about an analysis of the paint?" Madison asked cheerfully.

"What?"

"What about an analysis of the spray paint? On all those crosses. At the different scenes of crimes. The synagogues, the Holocaust Center, Steiner's West-Pic Café. And that rock off Mulholland. I'm going to order an analysis of the paint chips."

"To what end?"

"To ascertain whether it was the same paint. Ergo the same suspect."

"I could look at it and see it was the same paint."

"That's true, it is the same exact shade, but"—Madison held up a finger, he was warming to his subject—"but maybe we could pinpoint the manufacturer, ergo the distributor, ergo the suspect. I think it's worth a try."

Gold threw a glance at Zamora and shrugged. "It can't hurt. If it'll make you feel any better, Dolly, go ahead." Madison winced at the use of his departmental nickname, but it slowed him for only a second.

"Also, I'm going to order a fingerprint check of all the doorways and lampposts on the same block of Pico as the West-Pic Café."

Gold gestured to Zamora and started to rise. Madison, a tiny glint of panic in his eyes, talked faster.

"I know there were no prints at the Mulholland location, but—"

Gold, standing, held up his hand. "Dolly, before you do that, there are a few things I want you to do for me first."

"Yes?"

"First, get an APB to the whole department to put pressure on all the macho-type Caucasians they can find—bikers, rednecks, truckers, whatever. I want them rousted, searched, busted. Legal or not, haul 'em in. Charge 'em and book 'em, then tell them they can walk if they know something about this—this cross dude. After you do that run up to Terrorists and Subversives and get a printout of all the right-wing radicals in Southern California. You know, the Ku Klux Klan, the Silent Brotherhood, the Aryan Nation. What's that bunch out in San Bernardino County? In Desert Vista?"

"The Kalifornia Klan," Zamora said. They were walking quickly down the corridor now, Madison pumping to keep up and writing furiously in a little black notebook that had magically appeared in his hands.

"Right, the Kalifornia Klan. All those types of hate groups. Terrorists and Subversives has all their names in a computer somewhere. I don't know how current their information is—they'd rather be surveillancing liberals up there—but get it anyway. Then run a check against all the upcoming L.A. County felony trials, from assault up to kidnapping and murder. See if any of the same names pop up—and they will—and then bring those people in and see if they know anything about our boy, and see if they want to make a trade. Also check that list of right-wingers against all purchases of three fifty-seven Magnums in the last, say, six months. Our boy just might have bought his piece retail, with papers and everything."

They were at the elevator. Zamora pushed the button.

"Then call the wardens at San Quentin, Folsom, and Chino. Tell them you're working with me. Tell them to put the word out to the Aryan Brotherhood and the rest of the white gangs in their joints that a dude could get some time lopped off his sentence if he knew something about our boy and wanted to discreetly pass it along."

"You think they might know something up there?" Zamora asked. "In the joint?"

"It's possible. Sometimes they find out shit on the inside faster than you can out here on the street. Half those hate clubs started in the slammer."

The elevator doors slo-mo'ed open. Gold and Zamora stepped into the empty elevator.

"If none of this works," Gold said to Madison, "we'll just start at letter A and bring in everybody on the list. If that don't get it, then we'll run through the frigging phone book. *Some*body will know who this asshole is and give him up."

The doors started to close. Madison held one back and they jerked open again.

"What about the press?" he asked.

"You handle them, Dolly. Just tell them we're working our asses off and that an arrest is imminent. The usual snow job."

Madison wouldn't let go of the door. He looked around and then whispered, "Where are you guys going? Can I come?"

"We're working on some lunch," Gold whispered back, "and, no, you can't come."

"Why not?"

"You've got to go talk to the press, remember?"

"Oh, right."

Gold touched Madison's hand with a finger and Madison pulled it back as if he had been burned. The doors were almost closed when he stuck his hand in and they pulled apart again.

"Dolly—" Gold growled.

"I'm still going to order an analysis of that spray paint. You never know what may turn up."

"You never do," Gold said as he pushed the DOOR CLOSE button.

"Listen, where will you be having lunch? In case I need to reach you."

"We'll call you." The doors finally made it together.

Madison was still shouting, and it echoed down the shaft. "They got Son of Sam because of a parking ticket. Don't forget to leave a number . . ." His voice trailed off.

Gold and Zamora rode down silently for a few floors, then turned to each other and said simultaneously, "Ergo fuck yourself."

12:16 PM Fairfax Avenue was simmering—literally and figuratively. The air was foul; exhaust fumes cooked by the 98 degree heat crept along the street like a poisonous steam bath. There wasn't even a threat of a breeze. Old people, some of them leaning on aluminum walkers, stood around in groups on the sidewalks in front of the kosher meat markets and European pastry shops, arguing and gesturing. There was an electric charge, a sense of impending disaster in the neighborhood, like a town bracing for a natural disaster—a hurricane or a flood or a forest fire. The inhabitants had come out to reassure each other. On several street corners kids from the Jewish Armed Resistance stood stern sentinel in their uniform of light blue T-shirt and dark blue beret. One of them recognized Gold and shook his fist as they drove by.

Herschel's Delicatessen was a cool, clean sanctuary after the putrid heat of outside. The glass-fronted deli case near the entrance exuded the sharp, honest odors of freshly sliced pastrami, corned beef, smoked tongue, imported cheeses, and the acrid bite of dill pickle. The bakery section filled the restaurant with the dark, heavy musk of rye and pumpernickel, the snap of onion roll. From the kitchen in the rear came whiffs of melting butter, frying eggs, toasting bagels. The place was large and worn and crowded, and saturated with the smells of sixty years of good food. The walls above the unintentionally fifties-chic booths were lined with the signed photographs of famous show business stars from the thirties, forties, and fifties. Eddie Cantor was there, and Al Jolson, Burns and Allen, Pickford and Fairbanks, Arnaz and Ball. Milton Berle in drag. Jackie Gleason. Bob Hope. They had all worked at the television and motion picture studios that were only a few blocks away, in Hollywood, and they had all been regulars at the twenty-four-hour deli. Beside them on the walls were eight-by-ten glossies of rock stars from the sixties, seventies, and eighties—Herschel's more recent clientele.

"Jack," Herschel said over the deli case as he wiped his hands on a towel, "how are you?" Herschel leaned down from his perch on the elevated wooden runners and they shook hands over the turkey bologna. "Listen, I heard it on the radio. When you gonna catch this *putz*, this killer?"

"Soon, Herschel. Real soon. Herschel, this is my new partner. Sean Zamora."

"Hello, Mr. Guzman."

"Herschel. Everybody calls me Herschel. So, Jack, this is your new partner? So young! Listen, kid, you do what Jack Gold tells you, you stay alive. You listen to him, you learn a lot. But don't learn how to drink that Scotch like him."

They all laughed.

"I worked here when I was a kid," Gold said. "For Big Herschel, Herschel's father. Bussing tables and washing dishes. I went to Fairfax High, right across the street, and worked here after school. Twenty-five cents an hour."

"And all the liverwurst you could steal."

"You remember that?"

"Of course. I used to eat it with you."

They all laughed again.

"What can I get for you? I'll make it myself." Three people besides Herschel were working behind the counter, rapidly filling orders for the lunchtime crush crowded before the deli case.

"Two pastramis, the very leanest—"

"Of course."

"—on rye. The good rye."

"Of course."

"Mustard only."

"Naturally. And to drink?"

"Two Dr. Brown's cream sodas."

As Herschel made the sandwiches, he talked.

"The woman who was killed. The little place on Pico. I didn't know her but a lot of my customers did. She was a good woman. She ran a tab on those young lawyers like my father used to on out-of-work actors. A lot of people liked her."

"I know."

"She'd been in the camps, you know. She was a survivor."

"So I heard."

"You really gonna get this guy soon?"

"As soon as I can, Herschel."

"The sooner the better, is what I say. Then maybe they'll give him the electric chair, like they should. You know, I voted Democrat for forty, forty-five years. Never again. The Republicans brought back the electric chair, and I believe in the electric chair. An eye for an eye, that's the only way. Maybe if they do more of that then maybe honest people will be safer when they walk the streets. I had a customer—a good customer—come in here last week to buy a dozen bagels. Right outside the door a colored guy runs up and grabs the gold necklace around her neck and rips it off.

Knocked her down. She took eighteen stitches at the hospital around the corner—you know the one? Bring back the electric chair is what I say. Here's your pastramis."

"Thanks, Herschel. How much is that?" Gold made a halfhearted move toward his wallet.

"For the kid, nothing. For you, double."

Laughter all around.

"Thanks, Herschel."

Herschel waved them away. "Just catch that son-of-a-bitch that killed that woman. The electric chair is too good, is what I say. *Next!*" He was already taking another order.

Gold and Zamora picked a table in the back, in a slow station. They ate for a while, then Gold said, "It's good, huh?"

Zamora nodded, his mouth full.

"New York Jews," Gold continued over his sandwich, "they come out here saying you can't get good pastrami on the West Coast, saying, 'Oh, you should taste the pastrami at the Stage, at Zabar's,' wherever. Well, they're full of shit. I went to New York when I was in the navy and they're full of shit. The best pastrami in the world is right here at Herschel's. Is it good?"

"It's good. It's good," Zamora agreed.

Gold crunched on a pickle contentedly.

"I been here before," Zamora said.

"Oh?"

"Yeah, my acting class comes here some nights. After an improv."

"What's an improv?"

"Well, it's like a bunch of actors get together, on a stage, and you set up a premise—"

"A what?"

"A premise. A location, a time, a couple of characters, and you make up a scene."

"Right there? On the spot?"

Zamora nodded as he took another bite.

"That sounds more like writing," Gold said. "More writing than acting."

"It's kind of both." Zamora wiped his lips with a paper napkin. "But, yeah, I guess you could call it writing. I'm into that, too. I've written a couple of screenplays with this friend of mine. He's had a few things optioned. One script we wrote together I got to Joe Wambaugh, you know, the ex-cop who writes?"

Gold shook his head.

"Anyway, Wambaugh liked it. Said it had possibilities. Said it sounded real." Zamora took a sip of Dr. Brown's. "Speaking of screenplays, I hope you don't mind, Jack, but I've started a notebook on this case."

"For what?"

"Well, you know, this case looks like it's going to be really important. So when it's over I'm going to work up a treatment, pitch it, and see if I can get it into development."

Gold's eyes had a mischievous twinkle. "Sean, you're the strangest fucking cop I ever met. And I've met some pretty strange cops."

Zamora grinned. "Well, you ain't no straight-arrow Joe Friday type yourself."

It was Gold's turn to laugh. "Maybe Huntz was right. Maybe we do deserve each other."

Gold finished his sandwich and unwrapped a cigar. Zamora drained his soda and leaned back in his chair. "Jack," he asked, "you think bringing in all those right-wingers and grilling them is going to get us anywhere?"

Gold was picking his teeth with a matchbook cover in preparation of lighting his cigar. He shrugged.

"It's gonna get us a lot farther than Dolly Madison and his paint chips. That kind of Dick Tracy shit only works in the movies." He pointed to Zamora when he said *movies*. "I'd trade all that lab shit in the world for a good snitch or a good wiretap. Throw the right punk against a wall and jam a knee up under his balls and he'll be giving up people even *he* didn't know he had."

"You think somebody will give him up?"

"If we stumble over somebody who knows him."

"Maybe this particular asshole doesn't have any friends."

"Everybody's got friends, for chrissake. Hitler had friends. The Ayatollah Khomeini's got friends. Even Alan Huntz has friends." Gold pushed his chair back and stood up. "C'mon, let's go talk to some red-blooded all-American anti-Semites. Maybe we can find one who hates Mexicans, too. Irish-Mexicans especially."

5:07 PM Bobby jerked open the door of the station wagon and got in, slamming it hard behind him.

"Bobby!" Esther said. "What's the matter?"

"Aw, let's just get the motherfuck away from this sorry-ass motherfucking place."

"Bobby, for God's sake, tell me what happened. On your first day!"

"Look, Esther, either drive the motherfucking car, or move over and let *me* drive it. One or the other, woman."

Esther started the engine and slowly pulled away from the Piccadilly Cafeteria on Grand Avenue in downtown L.A. The traffic was heavy, stop-and-go, and Bobby simmered through three red lights before he exploded, punching the padding in the wagon's roof.

"That greaser bitch!"

"Bobby, what on earth happened?"

"Aw, that spick bitch, Mrs. Villanova, she on my ass the whole fucking day, saying pick up this, mop up that, empty that over there. All goddamn day. Treat me like some goddamn kitchen nigger, some kinda galley slave."

"But Bobby—"

"And then, 'bout an hour ago, I was using the telephone, and she comes by and give me some shit. Say, 'You been on the phone way too long, Mr. Phibbs, you ain't even suppose to use the phone when you suppose to be working,' and shit like that. And just now, when I was leaving, she call me over and say, 'Mr. Phibbs, if you don't want this job there are a lot of people who do.' Yeah, her fucking greaser relatives, I bet. And the bitch *know* I'm on probation. She *know* that. She holding it over my head."

In the middle of all the downtown rush-hour congestion, a traffic signal was malfunctioning. A traffic cop was trying to redirect cars down a side street. Mostly nobody moved.

"Bobby," Esther began tentatively, "you need that job."

"I don't need shit!"

"Bobby, Mr. Johnson said it was important for you to 'find and maintain employment.' He—"

"*That* nigger! Let *him* clean up after them dirty old white women. Let *him* scrub up the toilets where they take their shits. *I* ain't gonna do it!"

She took a hand from the wheel and reached over to touch his arm. "Baby, it's just a beginning. It's just a place to start."

He shook her hand off. "It ain't no damn beginning. It's the end, the bottom, the finish. It's the ass-end of everything."

They sat in silence for a moment. Then Bobby said softly, "I'd rather be back in motherfucking jail."

Esther lit a cigarette. She rolled down a window and blew the smoke outside. She glanced over at Bobby. His face was tense and sweaty. His eyes were dancing.

"Who you talking to on the phone, Bobby?"

His head snapped around. "Who you, my probation officer?"

"No," she said slowly. "I'm your wife."

"Then act like it!" he spat out.

The car ahead inched up a few feet. Esther automatically followed.

"It was that man you met in County, wasn't it? That one you was in the cell with?"

Bobby said nothing. He kept his eyes forward.

"Baby, people like that are only gonna cause you grief. Can't nothing good—"

"I'll be going out tonight."

She started to cry. "Bobby, oh, please don't. Please don't start that stuff again."

"I got something to do. Something make me some money."

"Bobby—" she sobbed, gripping the steering wheel.

He turned in his seat to face her. "Esther, you got to understand." His voice was pleading. "I can't do this kinda job. I just can't—"

"*You lied to me!*" she shouted, suddenly angry. "You were using in jail, weren't you, you low-life bastard? You need a fix right now. I can look at you and see it. You going out robbing and shooting dope again, ain't you? You don't care about me, or Little Bobby, or anything but that goddamn dope. Then go 'head, *go!*"

Bobby was already out of the station wagon.

"*Fuck you, too!*" he screamed, then slammed the door viciously, cracking the Safety-glass. He walked away into the crowd on the sidewalks.

Esther sat behind the wheel, crying softly, trying to ignore the stares of the drivers around her.

9:31 PM As always after a particularly smoggy day in L.A., the sunset had been spectacular. The whole western horizon had been aflame with crimson and orange, vermilion and gold. Now the sky was a murky blue sludge, no stars or clouds visible overhead. The smog had not blown away with the coming of night.

Walker placed two capsules on the tip of his tongue and let them rest there, dissolving in his saliva. The bitter taste of the speed spilled down his throat and he shivered slightly. He eased the van into first gear and let up on the clutch gently as the light changed. He drove the streets slowly, gliding past the clumps of people who had come out onto their stoops and sidewalks to escape the heat of their apartments. The city dwellers had set up folding chairs on the sidewalks and argued and laughed in their native languages. Every language imaginable. Spanish and Korean. Cantonese and Tagalog. Vietnamese, Japanese, the universal broken English. And snatches of Yiddish.

Walker bought a coffee and a doughnut at a Winchell's. He ate half the doughnut and threw it away. He wasn't hungry. He got back in the van and cruised the streets, up and down, up and down.

10:10 PM Gold let himself into his apartment and locked the door behind him with a sigh of relief. It had not been a good day. After returning from lunch at Herschel's, he and Zamora had gotten down to the tedious, disheartening chore of questioning the belligerent, bellicose social misfits that the street cops were pulling in. Dolly Madison kept running into the interrogation room with off-the-wall ideas until finally Gold told him to write them all down so he could study them more completely at a later time. At about three o'clock twelve members of the American Nazi Party, having been summoned by a phone call to their San Fernando Valley headquarters, showed up at Parker in full brownshirt regalia, complete with gleaming hip boots and swastika sleeve patches. They marched in locked goose-step formation down Los Angeles Street, across the Parker Center lawn, and into the lobby, coming to a loud, heel-stamping *heil* before the astonished cop at the information desk. The squad leader demanded to see "the Jew in charge." Gold came downstairs and argued with the squad leader for fifteen minutes, trying to convince the ugly little man that there was no way he, Lieutenant Jack Gold, or any of his men, was going to "interview" the squad leader's people while they were in a Nazi uniform, so they had the choice of either going home to change or spending the night in jail. After a lot of shouts and insults the squad leader sneeringly relented and ordered his troops about-face and out the building. Halfway across the center's lawn the Nazis were jumped by twenty-five baseball-bat-wielding members of the Revolutionary Communist Party. A riot ensued. Cops poured out of Parker with wide grins on their faces, each one more than eager to break the heads of devotees of either side. For them it was a "no-lose" situation. Eleven people were eventually hospitalized, including two policemen. Several cannisters of tear gas fired into the melee finally broke the party up. Gold went upstairs dabbing at his eyes with his shirttail and calling down God's wrath on anybody and everybody.

A little before six Dolly Madison called a news conference in Chief Huntz's private press room. He had hardly begun his carefully prepared statement when the reporters, quick at detecting the rich aroma of bullshit, shouted him down, yelling out questions and demanding to see Jack Gold. Madison, dripping sweat and smelling of terror, quickly sent someone running for Gold, who had chosen to sit out the news conference in his broom-closet office. Gold refused to come out. A few minutes later Chief

Huntz burst into the office and ordered Gold down to the second floor to face the media. Gold told Huntz to kiss his kosher ass. The shouting match lasted fully twenty minutes, after which Gold and Zamora went down to the news conference and Gold told the reporters that, yes, the investigation was making definite progress and, no, they hadn't arrested anyone as yet but, yes, an arrest was imminent, as soon as enough evidence was gathered. Zamora stood at Gold's elbow, trying to smile at all the cameras at once. The reporters were insatiable, shouting and jostling and demanding. Finally Gold said, "Look, my job is to catch the asshole who's doing this shit, not to supply the fucking six o'clock report with a fucking lead-off story," and stalked off the podium.

In the stunned silence that followed, Zamora looked as if he was going to continue the press conference, then reluctantly trailed Gold out of the room. The reporters immediately fell to arguing as to how they could edit Gold's last statement so that it could be broadcast.

At about seven-thirty a six-foot-six-inch biker who was being questioned by some of Gold's team spit in an officer's face. The cop went berserk and tried to stomp the biker's balls back up into his belly. The biker threw the cop through a wall. It took eight members of the task force to subdue the biker. The cop had a broken arm.

At nine, just as Gold was getting ready to leave, word came in that both the Revolutionary Communist Party and the local chapter of the American Nazis had filed police brutality charges against the department. The Nazis' complaint named Gold specifically. And at the close of business, after "interviewing" 157 extremely dislikable characters, he and his team were no closer to the killer than they had been sixteen hours earlier.

No, it had not been a very good day.

Gold took off his clothes and threw them into a heap on the floor of his closet. They reeked of tear gas and sweat. He padded naked across the room and stood before the stereo, selecting a record. He needed something soothing, something unhurried, something to cool out his troubled psyche. He selected an old Ahmad Jamal—'62 or '63. Chuck Israels on bass. Sam Jones on drums. Commercial, yes. But spare, uncluttered, unpretentious. Simple and beatific, just what he needed tonight. As the first shimmering piano chords filled the room, Gold sat in his armchair, broke the seal on the fifth he had brought home, and poured out a triple.

Angelique had liked Ahmad Jamal.

Gold drank and listened to the music, stopping only to get up and flip the record over. At eleven he turned on the news but kept the sound off, choosing instead to listen to a Bill Evans side. Cerebral, yes, but in his own way just as accessible as Ahmad.

He sat and drank and watched the parade of silently talking heads fill his TV screen. Chief Huntz and Dolly Madison. Councilman Orenzstein. The mayor. Jerry Kahn of the JAR. The little rat-faced Nazi. His own. He knew what they were all saying. He poured another drink. An unfamiliar black face came on. The graphics read JOHN PRIMUS—URBAN LEAGUE. Gold couldn't figure out what the man was so angry about, so he turned the sound up slightly.

"—we are forgetting is that a member of the black community has been murdered. Probably by the same racist hate-mongers who killed that white woman. But you don't hear—"

Gold turned the sound back off. He had another drink. The sports came on and he drifted off to sleep. Evans was playing "Emily." Gold started to snore lightly.

The phone jangled him awake.

He thought about letting it ring. It could only be bad news. On the fifth ring he picked it up.

"Daddy," his daughter Wendy sobbed, "Daddy, oh, my God, Daddy. Please help me!"

11:42 PM Gold's Ford screeched to a halt before a row of elegant Brentwood town houses. He jumped from the car and ran up the flagstone walk. The door was locked. He banged on it.

"Wendy! Wendy!"

Something moved inside. Gold listened intently, then banged again.

"Wendy, are you all right?"

Someone was unlocking the door from the inside. Gold stepped back and, reaching inside his shirt, lightly ran his fingertips over the butt of his .38. The door burst open and Wendy rushed through and into his arms. She clung to him and sobbed incoherently.

"Daddyohdaddyohdaddy—" he made out. He held her close and patted her shoulder.

"It's all right, Pieface. Daddy's here. He'll take care of you. Now, what's wrong, baby?"

She clung to him desperately. He gently pushed her away so he could see her, but she turned her face away. He held her chin lightly and turned her face back to him. She had a black eye, and her cheek was badly bruised and swollen. Her lip was bleeding.

"I'll kill him," Gold said softly and rushed past her into the town house.

"Daddy! No!" she cried after him, but he didn't hear her.

Howie was sitting at the dining room table, his head in his hands. He looked up, saw Gold, and started to rise.

"Jack, I—"

Gold caught him flush on the side of the face with a right and Howie went over backward in his chair. The chair splintered with a loud crack. Wendy was in the doorway screaming. In the adjacent nursery, the baby woke up frightened and started crying. Gold kicked Howie in the ribs and he grunted. Gold kicked him again. The baby was shrieking. Howie was crawling along the blue plush carpet and Gold was kicking him. Wendy got between them. She clutched at Gold's arms and shouted.

"Daddy! Stop it! What are you doing?"

Howie was using an armchair to pull himself up. Gold brushed past Wendy and grabbed Howie by the front of his shirt. He ran him backward across the living room and crashed him into a glass-fronted china closet. The beveled glass shattered and glass and china rained down on them. Gold pulled Howie out of the cabinet and threw him back in. More dishes and crystal smashed. Wendy leaped across the room and threw herself on Gold's back and wrapped her arms around his neck.

"*Stop it! Stop it! Stopitstopitstopit! He didn't do it, Daddy! He didn't do it!*"

Gold paused, his fist drawn back. Howie had his hands up, shielding his face. Joshua was bawling in the next room.

"*Stop it! Stop it! Stop it!*" Wendy sobbed as she slipped down Gold's back to her knees. She shook her head and pounded the floor with her fists, shrieking, "*I can't take any more! Oh, Daddy, why are you doing this?* Please, Daddy. Oh, please, *please, please, please—*" She was out of control now, her body racked with huge, sobbing convulsions.

"Dear God," she choked out, "what's happening? What's happening?"

Gold knelt beside her and put his arms around her. She jerked back in shock and looked at him with wide, terrified eyes. Gold took her in his arms again and held her close. She wailed; her face collapsed into a mask of grief and fear.

"Daddeee, Daddeeeee," she keened—an eerie, primordial sound. "Dad-ddeeeeeeee—"

Gold sat on the floor and held her tightly. "Are you all right, baby?" he whispered consolingly. "Do you need a doctor?"

She clung to his chest and cried and cried. Howie, holding his left arm against his rib cage, picked himself up gingerly from amidst the shards, limped over to the sofa, and fell back onto it. The baby was still yelling.

After several minutes Wendy had cried herself out. She seemed to hear Joshua's screams for the first time, pulled away from her father's embrace, and went to her baby screaming in the nursery. She reappeared with Joshua over her shoulder, sat in an armchair, and opened her shirt. The baby immediately began to nurse. She cooed to him while wiping at her own teary face with the back of her hand. She winced when she touched the bruises and the baby laughed. She began to cry again, softly.

For a long time no one spoke. The only sounds in the room were Joshua's sucking and Wendy's sniffles.

Gold went into the bathroom and got a hand towel. He crossed the dining room and went into the kitchen. He filled a corner of the hand towel with ice cubes and came back into the living room and gave it to Wendy. She stared at it stupidly and he took her hand and guided it against her eye. As he was pulling his own hand away she clutched it and kissed it. She seemed suddenly embarrassed and couldn't meet his eyes.

Gold sat on the edge of the coffee table and studied the tops of his shoes. Finally he stared at Howie and asked, "What happened?"

"It wasn't Howie," Wendy said quickly. "Howie wouldn't hurt me."

"Oh?" Gold still stared at Howie.

"We were robbed, Daddy. We were robbed." Wendy was sobbing again. The tears coursed down her battered face. "We were watching television, and they came in the kitchen door. Two horrible, horrible . . . *men.* " She shot out the word like a bullet. "They came in with guns and—and—and they robbed us and—and Howie won't tell me what they were after and, and"—she couldn't stop herself—"and, and they put the gun to my Joshua's head and said, 'Where is it?'—or they were going to kill my baby, my beautiful, beautiful baby!" She was choking on her own tears. "And then, oh, Daddy, they took me in the bedroom, oh, my God, and then, oh, Daddy, ohdaddyohdaddyohdaddy, they raped me!" she wailed. "Oh, my God, they *raped* me! And then one of them told me to—you know—do these things to him, these horrible things and I said no and, and, oh, Daddy, he beat me, Daddy, he beat me, oh, look at me, Daddy, *why did they do that, why did they do that?*"

Little Joshua was crying again, too. He had been frightened by Wendy's heaving breasts.

"Oh, Daddy. Oh, Daddy. They raped me, Daddy! I took a shower but I feel so dirty, oh, Daddy, why did they do that? Why did they do that, those—*animals!*" She threw the hand towel viciously to the floor and the ice cubes skittered across the broken glass. "Why did they do that? Why did they do that? What did they want? *Howie, what did they want?*"

Wendy and the baby were both crying uncontrollably now, clinging to each other and wailing. Wendy got up with him to run into the bedroom, then stopped abruptly. She stared at the bedroom door and gasped. There was a look of horrible accusation across her face.

"I can't ever go in there!" she shouted. "I can't ever go in there again!"

She ran into the bathroom and slammed the door. Her sobs and Joshua's could be heard in the living room.

Gold was still staring at Howie, who was leaning forward on the sofa, holding his head in his hands again.

Gold's knuckles were white, gripping the edge of the coffee table.

"What did they want, Howie?" he said softly.

Howie wouldn't look at him.

"What did they want, Howie?"

Howie slowly raised his head and met Gold's eyes. His face wore a dazed, uncomprehending glaze. He was crying now, too.

"Oh, dear God, Jack," he whispered hoarsely. "Dear sweet G—"

"Shut up." Gold held up a hand. "Don't—say—a—word."

Gold got up and walked quickly outside. He stood in the middle of the empty street and looked up at the night sky. The rage coursed through Gold's blood like a white-hot liquid, like heroin through a junkie.

He thought of Angelique, nodding out into her morning coffee.

He thought of Willie Davis, a cop he had known years ago. An under-cover narc who had gotten himself strung out on heroin. He thought of what Willie had turned into. He thought of how he, Gold, was always so afraid of heroin because he feared, he dreaded, it might make the rage go away. And that would be the end of him, if it made the rage go away.

He glanced back up at the moon. Funny, how the moon seemed so close. Close enough to touch. Or hit with a .38 Police Special steel-jacket.

Gold sat down on the curb of the street and ran his hand over the manicured grass.

A middle-aged man in slippers and a terry-cloth robe was turning off the sprinklers on the next lawn. He watched Gold for a moment, then came closer.

"Say," he said, "what the hell's happening in there? All the yelling and screaming. And breaking things. I was about to call the cops a couple of times."

"I am a cop," Gold said softly. "Go away."

"Well, what the hell's happening? This isn't that kind of neighborhood, you know."

Gold looked up at the man. "Go away."

The neighbor was about to say more, but saw something in Gold's face that warned him not to persist. He huffed back into his town house, muttering to himself. "This isn't Watts, you know. This isn't Compton."

Gold plucked a few blades of grass from the edge of the lawn and smelled them. He tasted the severed tips with the end of his tongue. They were bitter. Bitter herbs. Gold remembered a fight he had in the navy, aboard his ship. Thirty years ago. A big-ass Mississippi boy had called him a fucking kike, and they had fought in one of the ship's storerooms. Just the two of them. Grunting and sweating, kicking and punching, until Gold had managed to drive his elbow into the redneck's windpipe and the sailor went down choking. Gold had found a piece of wooden crating and had stood over the cracker, pounding on him for God knows how long. He would have killed him if some shipmates hadn't chanced by. And it took four of them to pull him off the battered, unconscious redneck. He was put in the brig and almost kicked out of the navy for that one.

The rage.

Gold got up, brushed off the seat of his trousers, and walked back up the flagstone and into the house.

Howie was still where Gold had left him, seated leaning forward on the sofa, his elbows on his knees and his head in his hands. Wendy was running water in the bathroom. Gold dragged a dining room chair over the shards of glass and sat down a few feet from Howie. The crystal pieces crunched under his shoes.

"Howie," he began evenly, "what did they look like?"

Howie raised his head from his hands and stared at Gold.

"I could hear them," he said hoarsely. "In the bedroom. I could hear them. One of them would stay here and laugh at me while the other one took Wendy in the bedroom. They took turns. And I could hear them."

Howie's tears glistened in his black beard.

Gold looked at Howie a long time before he spoke.

"Howie, you're barking up the wrong tree if you're looking for sympathy from me. I never wanted anything in life the way I want to kill you right now. Step on you like the bug that you are. And it's still a very distinct possibility. So just tell me what I want to know, and save the rest for your analyst. All right? So what did they look like? Give me a description."

Howie swallowed and said, "They were black. Niggers. They were both big. Over six feet—oh, my God, Jack, I never wanted—"

"Stop it!" Gold snapped. "Pull yourself together and answer my fucking questions, asshole. Now, they were both big. Over six feet. Black. Dark black or what?"

Howie stared at him, blinking, trying to comprehend. "Uh—one was kind of medium. Dark but medium. The other one was light, real light-complexioned. He had a bald head."

"Which one, the light one?" Gold was writing it all down in his little black notebook. Later he would have to tear those pages out.

"Uh, yes. The light one. The light one had a bald head."

"Okay, let's stay with him. What else about him? Did he have any hair at all?"

"No, no. I told you, he was bald."

"If he had no hair at all, then he probably shaves it. Did he have any hair at all?"

"No, you're right. It *was* shaved. Like Marvin Hagler."

"What else?"

"He was really tall. Taller than the other one."

"How tall?"

"Six six. Six seven."

"Build?"

"What?" Howie's attention was drifting.

"Heavyset? Thin? What?"

"Oh. Medium. But real tall."

"Okay." Gold wrote it down. "What else?"

"He had funny eyes for a black guy. Bluish. Blue-green."

"Then he was really light-skinned?"

"I guess so."

"Could he have been something other than black? Spanish? Puerto Rican?"

"No, he was black. Just light-skinned with those funny blue-green eyes. And he had an earring. On his left ear. It was a feather and it dangled down."

"Any scars or anything?"

"No. At least none that I noticed."

"What was he wearing?"

"One of those shiny track suits. Maroon. With white stripes down the leg."

"Sneakers?"

"I don't remember."

"Okay. Let's go to the other one. How tall was he?"

Howie ran his fingers through his thinning hair. He winced with pain at the movement and brought his arm down.

"The other one?" Gold prompted coldly.

"The other one was about six, six one. Real muscular. Big chest, big arms. Like a football player. Like he worked out with weights."

"Uh huh," Gold said, writing quickly. "Go on," he said automatically. Victims often need encouragement.

"He had styled hair. Little ring curls I think they call that style. He looked like an actor. Handsome. And he had a Pancho Villa moustache. Came down around his mouth."

"Complexion?"

"Just black. He wasn't dark or light. Just black."

"Medium?"

"Medium."

Gold wrote it down.

"No noticeable scars?"

"Uh-uh." Howie started to rise, grunted with pain, and sat back down holding his arm to his side.

"What do you want?" Gold asked.

"A drink."

Gold poured out two tumblers of Scotch at the bar in the corner and set one on the table before Howie.

"Did they use any names? Did they address each other by name?"

"Just once," Howie said grimly. He took a long swallow of whisky and grimaced. "When the one with the moustache was in the bedroom with Wendy and, and I could hear what was happening, the other one—the bald one with the funny eyes—laughed at me and said, 'Bobby be tearing your bitch's pussy up.'" He gulped some more Scotch. "Black fucking apes!"

Gold let a few minutes drag by. He lit a cigar and sipped some of his drink. Wendy could be heard cooing to Joshua in the bathroom.

"How much coke was there?"

Howie wouldn't look at him. He fidgeted with his coaster and swirled the ice in his glass.

"How much, Howie?"

"Jack," Howie pleaded, "I never thought this would happen. I never—"

"Save it!" Gold growled. "I've heard that song before. Just tell me how much cocaine you were holding."

Howie tilted his head back and shootered the rest of his Scotch. He shivered and rubbed his temples with his fingertips.

"Howie—"

"Ten kilos."

Gold stared at him. "How's that?"

"Ten kilos," Howie repeated, still avoiding Gold's angry eyes.

"Ten kilos of coke." Gold enunciated each word carefully. "Well, you really *have* made the big time. A quarter of a million worth of blow. Wholesale." Gold shook his head and said sarcastically, "A Hollywood success story. Little worm makes good. Only this movie doesn't have a happy ending, does it?"

"Jack, don't do this, please."

"Ten keys of snow and I'll bet you don't even have a water pistol in the house. Not that a shyster like you would know what to do with a piece, anyway. Ten keys of snow and they waltz in through your dollar-and-a-quarter deadbolt and put a gun to your son's head and then knock off a coupla rough-stuff quickies with your white bitch wife, because after all, a woman's fair game in a heist like this—all you gangsters know that, because who you gonna call? The police? I think not."

"Jack—"

"Howie, you fucking *putz,* I told you these people ain't choirboys." Gold's voice was low and compressed and ominous. "You start fucking around with these people, these quantities of dope, a little *shmuck* like you has got to get burned. These are serious people, Howie. They eat assholes like you for breakfast. I warned you. I told you to stay away from this kinda shit. But you're a smart boy. You're going places, right? Howie, I want you to know one thing. If it wasn't for my daughter, if it wasn't for Wendy, I'd beat you to death right here, right now. I want you to understand that. Do you understand that?"

Howie nodded slowly.

Gold chewed his cigar, letting his anger subside.

"Why did you have that much flake in your home, and who knew you were holding it?"

Howie made a helpless little gesture with his hands. "It was just like always. A bunch of guys all chipped in on a buy—"

"All lawyers?"

"—yes, all lawyers. Only this time the buy was bigger. A lot bigger. And—my God!" Howie gasped suddenly. "I'm responsible for that coke. I'm going to have to make good on everybody's money."

Gold stared at Howie incredulously.

"Howie, you really are a piece of shit. Wendy's been gang-raped and beaten like a dog and you're worrying about replacing dope money. What more can these bastards do to you? Kill you? The world should be so lucky."

Howie rubbed his brow with his fingertips and kept his mouth shut.

"Now," Gold continued, "why were *you* holding the coke?"

"It was my turn. It was only for tonight."

"Even so, don't you think it's strange to have you hold the goods, after you just got popped less than a week ago?"

Howie stammered, "I—uh—I guess I kind of bragged about how easy I had that first bust squashed. I guess I volunteered to make the purchase and hold the package until tomorrow, at the office, when we could cut it up."

"You *offered* to hold it?"

"Uh—yes, I guess so."

"Why?"

"Well, you know—"

Gold nodded slowly. "Yeah, I think I do know. So you could dig into the stash and take a little extra for yourself. Replace it with a little baking soda, maybe?"

Howie stared into his empty tumbler.

"You fucking *gonif*. You never cease to amaze me."

"My God, Jack. I never dreamed anything like this would happen."

The bathroom door opened and Wendy came out with a sleepy-eyed Joshua cradled over her shoulder. Gold was instantly on his feet.

"Wen, let me call a doctor. I know some guys I can get to come over here right away."

Her eyes on him seemed vacant and expressionless. She shook her head, then went into Joshua's room and shut the door. Gold gazed at the closed door a long time, then tore a page out of the little black notebook and laid it and his pen on the table in front of Howie.

"I'm going to make a phone call," Gold said. "I want you to write down the names of all the people who knew about the buy, who knew you would have the coke here tonight." He rose from his chair.

"Jack—"

"Do it!" Gold snapped. He went through the swinging door and into the kitchen. The lock on the back door leading into the small backyard had been popped. It could have been done with a heavy screwdriver. Anyone who wants to get in, can. Gold punched out a number on the yellow wall phone. A man answered, laughing.

"Honey?" Gold asked.

"Yeah?" Honeywell answered. There were other voices in the background.

"Honey, this is Jack Gold."

"Jack! How you doing? Sure do miss your gray ass. Hollywood Division ain't the same without you. You catch that crazy bigot motherfucker yet?"

"No, not yet. Working on it. Listen, I hope I didn't wake you."

"Nah. Not at all. We're just breaking up the party. Weekly Wednesday meeting of the Black Peace Officers' Association. A little poker, a lot of beer. I won thirty dollars tonight. First time in a year. Say, Jack, you know that porn star we had in County last year? Johnny Jism?"

"Uh—yeah."

"Well, we ran some confiscated stag films tonight—just for laughs, you understand—and that motherfucker turned up. Man, let me tell you, *this* is the actor you whities oughta run for president. Dude had a johnson on him a foot and a half long. Never knew anything white could *be* so big. In this one scene he's slipping it to this fine little brown sister, and let me tell you, Jack, the smile on that girl's face had every brother in the room pissed off. Talk about threatened! What goes around comes around, eh, Jack?" Honeywell's voice broke into laughter again.

Gold tried to be polite and chuckle, but it stuck in his throat. Honeywell seemed to sense his ex-partner's mood.

"You all right, Jack?"

"No, Honey, I'm terrible."

"What can I do, man?"

"I need to find two bad guys. Both black male adults. One medium complexion, muscular build, six foot to six foot one, Pancho Villa–type moustache, first name Bobby. The other one is six six or seven, light skin, blue-green eyes, shaved head, and wears a feather earring."

Honeywell thought for a moment. "Let me ask the guys."

Gold could hear Honeywell say to the room, "Gentlemen, gentlemen. I need aid in identifying a pair of criminal types. First one's six foot seven bald-headed, blue-eyed nigger with a feather in his ear—"

Gold heard the room break up with loud laughter, then the buzz of conversation, and then more laughter. Then Honeywell came back on the line.

"The tall one could only be one dude: Alonzo Firp. Alias the Black

Kojak, for obvious reasons; alias Sky-Eyes, for other obvious reasons. He's a hype and a shooter. Just got out of County a few months back behind some little strongarm thing. The Bobby somebody I don't have pegged yet. You want me to locate these brothers?"

"I would really appreciate that, Honey. I'm up to my ass in this cross asshole. Can you call me at Parker tomorrow?"

"Tomorrow? You want these dudes *bad.*"

"Yeah, Honey, I do."

"Consider it done, man."

"And Honey—"

"Yeah?"

"This is personal business. Off the record."

"What record you talking 'bout, boss? One o' dem hairy ol' jazz records you always be playing?"

"Thanks, Honey."

"I'll get back to you as soon as I can."

Back in the living room Gold picked up the slip of paper.

"There must be a dozen names here."

"Thirteen," Howie said.

"You lawyers are unbelievable." He scanned down the column of names. There was no one he knew.

"You picked up the keys tonight?"

Howie nodded. "I went to the dealer's house and made the buy. I brought it back here."

"Is the dealer's name on this list?"

"No."

"Who *is* the connection?"

"Jack," Howie whined. "I can't give you the dealer. You're a cop, for chrissake."

Gold sighed deeply. "Howie, you still don't understand, do you? They beat and raped my daughter. Somebody's gonna have to pay for that. Now, I'd like nothing better than for that somebody to be you, but I don't think it would be good family relations to make my daughter a widow and my grandson an orphan. Not yet, at least. So I'm gonna have to know everyone who was involved in this thing, because one or all of them are responsible for what happened here tonight. And believe me when I tell you I am not asking as a cop." Gold was keeping his voice low, but the anger and threat of violence was still very audible. "If you don't give me the name of the dealer right now, I'm gonna slap it out of you. So who's the dealer?"

Howie traced his fingertip around the edges of his coaster.

"It's another lawyer."

"So? What am I supposed to be, shocked?"

Howie looked full at him. "It's Natty Saperstein."

Gold whistled and sat down slowly on the edge of the coffee table.

"Natty Saperstein?" he said, dumfounded. "Natty Saperstein is in this thing?"

"You know Natty?"

Gold nodded. "Yeah, I know Natty. But then cops are *supposed* to work in sewers. What excuse do you have?"

Howie seemed miffed. "Natty Saperstein is the best criminal defense attorney in California. He's a celebrity. He's a best-selling author. He's a nationally known figure. He's—"

"—a crook and a fixer. A shyster and a whore. He'd've defended Hitler if the price had been right. He's also a corrupter of young boys."

Howie bristled. He was becoming his own self again. "Who are you, Jerry Falwell? Champion of the Moral Majority?"

Gold smiled a thin-lipped snarl. "Don't talk back to me, Howie. Not tonight."

Howie seemed to shrink back into himself. When he spoke it was softly and without sarcasm. "The whole L.A. legal community respects and admires Natty Saperstein. His Christmas parties are legend. You have to be on the 'A' list to get invited."

"That's how you met him?" Gold said with venom. "Because you're on the 'A' list?"

"He's the best there is."

"He's the worst there is."

Howie chose not to continue the argument any further. Gold picked up his dead cigar and relit it.

"So? Natty's not satisfied defending pushers and smugglers anymore. He's dealing now. I guess he decided to cash in on all his Colombian acquaintances."

Howie nodded. "He supplies a lot of people in the industry. A *lot* of people."

"And he was the dealer on last week's buy? When you got popped in the parking lot? Natty Saperstein was the seller in that one, too?"

"Yes."

Both men were silent for a while. Gold picked a piece of tobacco from the tip of his tongue. Then Howie said, "I can't believe this night happened. It's like a nightmare. I just can't believe it."

Gold rounded his ash in a crystal ashtray. Howie looked up at him. "What's going to happen now?"

"Well," Gold began, "we can file an official complaint on this, you and Wendy can go to the station with me, and Wendy can tell them she was assaulted and raped, and with the descriptions you gave me I'm pretty sure we can catch these assholes. Of course, the police are gonna try to figure why the suspects picked your particular house to break into. And when they arrest them, those two assholes aren't gonna be particularly careful about what they tell the cops. The ten keys are going to come up, probably sooner than later. And then somebody's going to remember you got busted last week for possession, and when they try to look up that little matter they're going to wonder why that case was dismissed so quickly, why it didn't even come to arraignment, why there isn't any paperwork on it. No," Gold said slowly, "I don't think that's a viable course of action."

"God, no," Howie said, shaking his head, "that's out of the question."

"That's what the people who planned this little party figured on. In situations like this revenge is usually the only alternative. And I'm pretty sure they weren't too fearful of that where you were concerned." Gold crushed out his cigar. "Too bad they didn't figure on me."

"What are you going to do?" Howie demanded.

Gold stared at him. "Maybe it's best if you don't know, counselor."

"Look, Jack," Howie sputtered, "you can't go around throwing people through their furniture the way you did me. There are some very important attorneys on that list. You can't use your Gestapo tactics on them. They'll know I gave you their names, they'll know I told you everything, they'll—"

"What the fuck kind of man are you?" Gold broke in angrily. "What kind of weak fucking shit are you made of? They raped your wife, man! They put the muzzle of a gun to your son's head! And it was all planned by somebody you know, somebody you have coffee with at the office, someone you buy dinner for at one of those fancy-ass restaurants. Someone who pretends to be your friend. Someone who's going to smile at you the next time he sees you. Doesn't that make you want to *hurt* a motherfucker, Howie? Doesn't that—"

"You *knew* those people?" Wendy said from the nursery door. She no longer held Joshua. Her gaze was fixed on Howie.

"Wendy—" he began.

"You know those animals?" Wendy walked slowly into the room. Toward him.

Howie dropped his head and started massaging his temples with his fingertips again, shielding his eyes from Wendy's accusatory stare.

"Someone you *knew* sent those people to our home?"

"It was a mistake, baby. A business transaction," Howie said softly. "Only everything got screwed up."

"A business transaction?" Wendy echoed with astonishment. "A mistake?" She looked from Howie to Gold and back again. Howie couldn't face her.

"A mistake?" She glared at Howie. "How could you know someone who could send those beasts to our home?"

Howie wouldn't look up at her.

"Answer me."

She loomed over him. All five two of her.

"What were they looking for, Howie? When they pointed that gun at my Joshua? What did they want?"

"Wendy—" Howie couldn't look at her.

"I have a right to know," she said. Howie kept massaging his brow, seemingly trying to drive his fingers through flesh and bone and into his brain. She turned in confusion to her father.

"Daddy?"

Gold came over to her and moved to put his arm around her.

"Wen, honey, everything's all right now. Everything—"

"Stop it!" she snapped and pushed him away. "Stop treating me like that! I'm the one who was raped! I want to know why this happened tonight. I want to know why it happened to me. I have a right to know."

Gold searched her eyes. "Tell her, Howie. She does have a right to know."

Howie sniffled. He was crying. Gold shot him a quick, disgusted glance.

"You tell me, Daddy," Wendy demanded.

"It's not my place—"

"Goddamn it! Isn't either of you man enough to talk to me?"

Gold studied her face a long time. He had never before seen this side of his daughter. It reminded him of himself.

"Howie has a drug problem. He's been using and selling cocaine. To-night he had a lot of it in the house. Somebody who knew that sent those two black guys over here to rob him. What happened to you was just—just icing on the cake, because they knew Howie couldn't call the police. And that's about everything."

"Cocaine?" Wendy said incredulously, turning back to Howie. "Co-caine? Is that true, Howie?"

Howie's shoulders were shaking; he would not look at her.

"How can you keep something like that a secret? What kind of marriage do we have if you can keep something like that from me?"

He raised his head. His eyes were wet.

"I'm so sorry, Wendy," he whispered.

"How could you do *anything* that could ever bring people like that to our home?" Her voice was rising, trembling.

"I know how you feel, Wen. I'll make it up to you, I swear."

"How could you know how I feel? They didn't rape you. They didn't twist their hands in your hair and shove your face *down there.* They didn't make you do those things. How could you ever make that up to me?"

"Wendy—"

She slapped him hard across his face. His eyes registered his shock.

"How could you ever make something like that up to me? How, Howie? *How?*" She was shouting now. She bunched her fist and punched him with a stiff roundhouse haymaker. Howie's head snapped back.

"You bastard!" she shouted. "How could you ever do anything that could bring those *things* into our home?"

Gold stepped closer and put his hand on her shoulder. "Wendy, baby, c'mon."

She didn't hear him. She made her hand a claw and raked Howie's cheek with her nails. His hands flew up and came away bloody. He gasped. There were three red gashes down the side of his face.

Gold took hold of her from behind, a hand just above each of her elbows. She struggled to free herself.

"Get out!" she screamed at Howie.

"Wendy, please!" Howie sobbed. "Oh, baby, please."

"Get out!"

"I'm so sorry, baby. Oh, please, please."

"Get out! Get out! Get out!" She kicked out at him viciously. "Let me go! Let me go!" She fought against Gold's hands.

Howie stood up. Where it wasn't bleeding his face was ashen, gray. He looked very sick.

"My God, Wendy, please, I love you so—"

"Get out, you bastard!"

He moved slowly toward the door.

"What good are you anyway?" she shouted after him. "Go find your rapist friends. Go find your cocaine! We're better off without you, Joshua and me."

Howie was at the door.

"I'm so sorry, Wen. Please don't—"

"Get out!" she shrieked.

Howie was gone. The town house was filled with a strange quiet. Gold loosened his grip on her arms and Wendy ripped away from him. She walked slowly around the room, her flats crunching the broken crystal. She refused to look at her father. She went into the kitchen and returned with a dust pan and, kneeling, began picking up the pieces of glass. She pricked her finger on a jagged edge and stopped. She squeezed her flesh and a dewdrop of crimson blossomed on her fingertip. She studied it with detachment, then put her finger in her mouth and sucked on it. She sat on the couch and opened a drawer in an end table, withdrew a pack of cigarettes, took one from the pack and looked up at her father, who was still standing in the center of the room.

"The housekeeper left these," she said. "I haven't smoked since I learned I was pregnant with Joshua."

"Why start now?" Gold said quietly.

She shrugged. "Why not?" She held the cigarette up. "Do you have a light?" Her hands were shaking.

He lit her cigarette. She took a tiny drag and exhaled. She grimaced. "That tastes terrible," she said, but made no move to put it out.

Gold sat down on the coffee table across from her.

"Are you all right, Pieface? Let me call you a doctor."

She blew out a plume of smoke. "I'm fine," she said, but she was crying softly again. She looked around the living room. She looked at the bedroom door.

"I can't stay here tonight."

"Do you want to spend the night at my place? I can sleep in a chair, no problem."

She managed a wan smile. "No, but could you drive me to Mother's? There's so much room there. I think I want to go to Mother's."

"Of course, baby. That's a good idea. She and Stanley can look after you."

She looked around again. "I don't think I can ever spend another night here."

Gold reached over and patted her hand. "You're gonna be all right, Pieface. You're gonna be okay."

"Sure," she said. "I'm fine." Her gaze drifted back to her bedroom door. She fixed on it.

"I guess I should pack a few things. For Josh, too."

"Do you want me to go in there with you? While you pack?"

She was embarrassed. "No, Daddy, I'll just be a minute." She stood with a sigh and walked toward the bedroom.

"Wendy?"

She turned around.

"I just want you to know," he began haltingly. "Those people who did that to you. I—I'll make sure they can never do that to you again."

After a long while she nodded slightly. "Good." She turned and went into the bedroom to pack.

THURSDAY
August 9

1:00 AM On the twentieth ring Esther hung up. She was in the office of the photographer's studio, making the call from the receptionist's desk. She tapped out the number again. On the twelfth ring she slammed the phone down.

"Lupe," she called. "Lupe!"

Lupe came out of the shooting studio with a broom in her hand.

"¿Qué pasa, Es?"

Esther tossed her a thick ring of keys. "There's something wrong at my house. No one's answering. Mama Phibbs was at a church function and I had to leave Little Bobby alone and now no one's answering."

"Maybe's he's asleep. It's one o'clock."

"Maybe. Those are the keys to this place. I'm gonna have to leave you and Florencia here for an hour or so. I have to go home."

"No problema, Esther."

"If you finish before I get back just grab some z's on the couch over there."

"You got it. Florencia, I think she's asleep already."

"I heard that," Esther said as she dashed out the door.

"Be careful," Lupe shouted after her. *"¡Con cuidado!"*

Esther screeched the station wagon out of the photographer's parking lot and sped up Wilshire, watching closely for traffic cops.

Bobby hadn't come home. She had waited until after ten, but he hadn't come home. Why had she pushed him like that? Why hadn't she talked to him in a more loving manner? No man's going to like cleaning toilets, slopping garbage, washing dishes. Why hadn't she tried to understand him better, helped him more to readjust to the outside? Why did she have to get in his face like that? Leave him no exit, no alternative but to storm away the way he did? Any man would have.

But he hadn't come home. What was he doing? Oh, sweet Jesus, what was he doing?

It took twenty minutes of hard eastbound driving to get to the Crenshaw District. She slammed the car to a stop in the driveway and jumped out. She was halfway up the dark walk when she froze, her blood chilled.

Little Bobby's still form was sprawled across the front stoop of her apartment.

For a microsecond she didn't know whether to run to him or tiptoe. She ran.

"Baby, baby," she said and touched him. His flesh was warm and supple. He stirred. Esther felt her heart start beating again, pushing blood throughout her body.

"Mama," Little Bobby muttered sleepily and sat up on the steps. He was holding his kitten in his arms.

"Why you out here, baby?" Esther asked.

Little Bobby rubbed his eyes with the back of his hand. "They said they were gonna let me back in. They left the door open and Bagheera ran out. I went out to find him. They said they were gonna leave the door unlocked, but they must've forgot."

"Who's *they,* baby?"

"Daddy's friends." Little Bobby automatically began stroking Bagheera's fur.

"Daddy's home?" Esther said, looking up at her bedroom window. There was a dim light on behind the shade.

"Uh huh."

"How long you been out here?"

Little Bobby's face turned quizzical in the glow of the street lamp. "A long time I guess. Daddy came home with his friends and they made a lot of noise, laughing and all, and they woke me up. When I came downstairs Bagheera ran outside and the white lady promised she'd let me back in and—"

"The white lady?" Esther was unlocking the door.

"Uh huh. And I knocked and knocked and knocked but nobody ever came. I pushed the doorbell, too."

Esther let the door swing open. There was no one in the parlor or the hall, but she felt the presence of strangers in her home. There were unfamiliar scents in the air—cheap perfume and the faintly sulfurous odor of burnt matches.

"Baby, why don't you go into the kitchen and get yourself some milk and cookies."

"I really should be getting to sleep in my own bed," Little Bobby said testily, mimicking his grandmother. "I have a grammar quiz tomorrow."

"Just for a little while, baby. Please."

"Oh, all right. C'mon, Bagheera, you want a dish of milk?"

The boy carried the kitten into the kitchen and the door closed behind him.

Esther looked up the stairs. There were no sounds from up there. She started up. Just as she reached the top she thought she heard a moan. She stopped. She listened. Nothing. Then a woman's languorous laughter.

Esther straightened her back, stalked purposefully to her bedroom door, and flung it open.

For a few seconds she had the unnerving sensation that she was in the wrong room, the wrong house. Her bedroom wasn't blue. Then she realized. Someone had draped a blue towel around her bedside lamp, bathing the room in an azure haze.

Her eyes adjusted, and she saw—

A thin-hipped, small-breasted white girl was in her bed, naked. Bobby was lying beside her, also naked. Sitting on the floor by the bedside a light-skinned man with a shaven head and wearing only white jockey shorts was shooting up, the needle still in his vein, the belt twisted tight around his upper arm. He looked at Esther and smiled. His eyes were a cloudy sky-blue.

Bobby slowly swung his legs off the bed and got up shakily.

"Es, you should be at work," he said stupidly. His voice was thick and dreamy. He came toward her and when he was close she reached up and slapped him. She swung again and he caught her hand and held it.

"What's a matter, baby?" he slurred. "Everything all right." His eyes were heavy-lidded; his pupils were pinpoints. He was loaded.

"How dare you bring that junkie whore to my bedroom," she hissed between clenched teeth. "How dare you bring that shit into my home, where my son sleeps. How dare you lock my son out of his—"

"Aw, baby, don't be tripping like that. This girl's Alonzo's ol' lady. We just be kicking back, that's all. Ain't nothing to it."

"Get out of this house and never come back," Esther said evenly.

"Aw, c'mon, baby. Everything gonna be all right, now. Every*thang* gon' be all *right.*" He was having trouble keeping his balance.

"You low-life bastard," Esther said, almost whispering.

"Who's that bitch, Bobby?" the white girl said from Esther's bed. "Tell her to go away and come on back here."

Esther exploded. "You get out of my bed, you dope-fiend slut, and *you* go away!" she screamed. "All of you get out of my house now—*now*—or I swear to Jesus I'll call the police down on all of you." She turned to leave, but Bobby grabbed her arm and held it tightly.

"Don't be talking 'bout no police, Esther," Bobby slurred. "Don't be doing that."

"You threatening me now, Bobby? You threatening me, you miserable motherfucker? Get out of this house and don't ever let me see your face around here again." She ripped her arm away and stalked out of the room. In the tiny hall she whipped around. "All of you get out of my home *right now,* or I'll call the police! *You hear me?* Get out *now!*"

One of Little Bobby's schoolbooks lay on a table in the hall. Esther threw it through the door at the bed and it struck the window beyond, breaking the glass behind the shade.

She ran down the stairs, fighting back the tears. She lost the battle in the hallway to the kitchen, and the sobs hit her like a blow to the stomach, almost buckling her knees. Blindly she stumbled into the kitchen, jerked open her cutlery drawer, and pulled out a wicked-bladed butcher knife. She gripped the knife by its haft and turned around. Little Bobby was seated at the table watching her with wide, frightened eyes, a cookie poised on its way to his gaping mouth.

"No! No! *No!*" Esther shouted and threw the knife clattering across the floor. Bagheera bolted from Little Bobby's lap and disappeared behind the refrigerator.

"Oh, Jesus, sweet Jesus!" she cried and tore from the kitchen. She stood alone in the living room, crying, unable to focus her mind. The world seemed to be tilting, and for a moment she wondered if she was experiencing an earthquake. She looked up and Bobby was at the top of the stairs. He had pulled on his pants and a shirt unbuttoned down the front. He was carrying his shoes. He started down the stairs.

Esther ran up to meet him.

"Es, baby," he said thickly, "just chill out, baby. Just chill—"

She flung herself at him, scratching at his face, tearing at his eyes, pulling at his hair. He tried to push her off, away, but she attacked him with renewed strength and malice, biting and scratching and trying to ram her knee into his groin. He shoved her away and she lost her footing and tumbled down the stairs, turning end over end. She lay in a heap on the landing, stunned and shaken.

"Crazy motherfucking bitch!" Bobby yelled down at her. "Crazy motherfucking bitch!"

Little Bobby was suddenly at Esther's side, standing over her, brandishing his fist up at his father.

"You leave my mama alone! You leave her alone!"

"That's *just* what I'm gonna do!" Bobby turned and shouted back in the direction of the bedroom. "Let's get out of this bughouse!" He came down the stairs and the white girl and the shaven-headed man, now dressed, appeared and followed him.

Bobby stepped over Esther and hesitated at the door. He turned and looked down at her.

"Couldn't have been no other way," he said down at her, and then the three of them left, slamming the door.

Esther sat up with her back against the wall and cradled her knees against her breasts. She hid her face and let the hurt wash over her.

"Don't cry, Mama. Don't cry. I'm still here."

She took her son in her arms and held him tightly. She rocked back and forth while she cried.

2:22 *AM* Queenie had to go outside.

Irving Rosewall was trying to decide how to murder Georgina. A fall
from one of the manor house's many balconies was the obvious method,
but so bloody and messy, so unimaginative. Poisoning was another option,
but that seemed so mundane. No, he was definitely leaning toward strangu-
lation. Committed with the belt of a silken dressing gown, preferably. Nice,
dramatic, horrible. Perfect for a bitch like Georgina. But where would he
leave her body? In her bedroom? Boring. In the library? It's been done.
Stripped naked and discarded on the compost heap behind the servants'
quarters? Irving Rosewall toyed with that idea for a long while, but finally
rejected it as too graphic and direct. He eventually convinced himself that
floating face down in the reflecting pool was the only correct answer. Clad
only in a sheer, clinging nightgown. Discovered by moonlight. Sexy—but
not freakish. Frightening yet glamorous. Exactly! Just like Georgina herself. And the constabulary would pay the devil trying to ascertain whether
she had been killed before she was thrown into the pool, or if drowning
had been the true cause of her demise.

But Queenie had to go outside. *Now!*

"All right already," Irving Rosewall said as he rose from his tiny desk
in the small alcove off the living-dining combo. The little Jack Russell
terrier spun in tight, excited circles. Her eyes were bright and dancing.

"Okay. Okay. Hold your horses." He took a sweater from the closet. He
was always cold now, even in August, even in L.A. One of the many little
perks of being seventy.

He unclipped Queenie's leash from the hook behind the water heater and
the small dog ran frenzied through the apartment, round and round the
furniture, then jerked to an abrupt halt at the front door, her head low,
her haunches high, her tail wagging furiously.

"Got to go, huh?" Rosewell muttered as he slipped the leash into the
catch on her collar. The dog barked happily.

"Shhhh! It's late, you know." He opened the door and she darted out,
dragging him behind her.

He marveled at it. After a lifetime of rising at six o'clock every morning,
to discover in the last few years that you were really a night person. He
did everything at night now—marketing, washing, cooking. He had even
found a twenty-four-hour cleaners. But he especially loved writing at night.
It seemed fitting. Almost, well, artistic. All the lights in the apartment off,

except for the one over his desk in the alcove; a cup of steaming tea by his hand; the whirr of the electric typewriter; chamber music playing softly in the background. He loved it. Sometimes he would write until dawn; always until the paper bounced against his apartment door.

He had been writing now for almost five years. Since just after his retirement. Since Rachel passed away, a year later. He had always been a voracious reader. He would read anything, Rachel always claimed. The first week of their marriage she had forbade him ever again to bring a book or a magazine to the table. Five minutes later she caught him reading the label on the pickle jar. She had been too astounded to be angry. She surrendered him to the English language for the rest of their life together. He had even been reading when she died. He had glanced up from the latest Ludlum and he knew she was gone. He had summoned a nurse, and the nurse had asked how long did he think she'd been, well, dead? He'd been filled with shame. He hadn't any idea. When he was reading he lost all track of time, of place, of people, of his entire environment—of everything but the world contained in the printed letters on the page before him.

And now he was creating his own worlds. He was a writer! After thirty-seven years of selling men's clothing at Francovich's Big & Tall Wear, Wilshire location, he was now a writer. After thirty-seven years of shoehorning the gargantuan rumps of thyroidal misfits into pants that looked like collapsed pup tents, he was actually an artist, a novelist.

Oh, he hadn't published anything yet, but all his classmates in his extension course at UCLA said it was only a matter of time. He was the star of the class. Imagine—him. Even the professor—not a man to bandy compliments about—declared him to be "eminently publishable." Irving Rosewall savored those words. *Eminently publishable.* The very sound of them excited him, made his step a little lighter.

Once outside, Queenie didn't seem in such a big hurry anymore. Nature's call had become a gentle whisper. The little black-and-white bitch ambled along, sniffing idly at the sun-dried remains of earlier passings-this-way. Rosewall slipped the leash around his wrist and followed absently behind her—pausing where she paused, moving on when she moved on. Lost in his thoughts.

The ironic thing was, since he had begun his writing, he seldom had time to read anymore. The Book-of-the-Month Club and Literary Guild selections—which came whether ordered or otherwise—sat, still in their shipping wrap, stacked waist high by the door, waiting to be added to the floor-to-ceiling bookcases that lined every wall in his rent-controlled apartment. Three weeks' worth of yellowing newspapers, the string still tied around their middles, lay unread on the cluttered dining room table. Magazines from several months back were strewn across the floor by his bed. Current events didn't interest him anymore. Nothing interested him anymore, but his writing. And why shouldn't it be that way? That world of his own creation was so much more vivid and alive than anything in his gray, repetitive life had ever been. The people! My God, the people! Georgina, now recently deceased, but when she was alive—good Lord, what a woman! Voracious in her appetites, ruthless in her ambitions, treacherous in her methods. During one twenty-four-hour period she had consecutively bedded the lord of the manor, both of his handsome sons, and the stallion of a groundskeeper, professing total love for each one and goading each one into murderous jealousy of all the others. What a woman! Equally as willing on a bed of hay as on satin sheets. But finally caught up and destroyed in a web of her own making.

Then there was Gilbert. Lord Ashcroft, really. A stock player. A weak, doddering old widower—prisoner of his heritage, slave to his passion for Georgina's body.

And then the sons: Phillip and Hawley. Yin and yang. Good and bad. Cain and Abel. But was Phillip so completely virtuous? And Hawley so totally evil? And who was Malcolm the mysterious groundskeeper? Where did he come from? What did he want?

And which one of them had strangled Georgina and left her body in the fountain?

Irving Rosewall smiled to himself in the dark. He loved Gothic mysteries, no less his own.

Queenie had finally sniffed out a place worthy of her droppings. She made three quick turns around the base of a streetlight, then hunched her back and with a dull, preoccupied cast in her eyes, relieved herself.

"That's a good girl," Rosewall said, absently.

A blue van came slowly down the otherwise empty street, passed Rosewall, and turned the corner.

"Let's go, girl." Rosewall was suddenly anxious to get back to his apartment, back to his writing. He had decided to go back and write the passage containing the discovery of Georgina's body. The description should be voluptuous. It needed water dripping from her heavy breasts as her corpse was pulled from the fountain. Her nightgown should be sheer, clinging—maybe she *should* be naked. You can't get too graphic and sexual for today's readers.

"Let's go, girl," Rosewall said again. The little dog daintily tore up some grass with a few quick backward slashes of her paws, then pranced down the sidewalk on her way home. Rosewall walked beside her.

"Hey, Jew!"

Irving Rosewall was so deep in his thoughts that he didn't hear the man shout at him. He walked on a few more steps until the taut leash told him

Queenie had stopped. He looked down at her. She had taken up an alert, stiff-legged stance and was growling at something behind him.

"Hey, Jew!"

Rosewall turned to face the man who belonged to the voice. The man shot him.

When Irving Rosewall became aware of things again, he realized he was on his back, looking up at the night sky through a spider's web of overhead telephone wires. Queenie was whining and licking his face; he could feel her tail wagging against his shoulder. He tried to lift an arm and couldn't. He was horribly cold.

Queenie was barking at something.

A snake! There was a snake somewhere near. He could hear its hissing. Rosewall began to shiver. He let himself realize that he was dying.

No, no, no! his mind screamed. I haven't finished yet. No one will know who strangled Georgina and slipped her body into the reflecting pool.

Queenie came back and licked his face. She whined and pawed at him. Then she pointed her muzzle to the sky and gave out a mournful howl.

Irving Rosewall never heard her.

$4{:}00\ AM$ "The time is four A.M. This is radio station XXERA, Reality Radio, broadcasting from Tijuana, Mexico."

"The following is a rebroadcast of the 'Janna Holmes Show,' taped earlier this evening."

Mozart came on. A few seconds of a string quartet, light and airy and precise.

"Good evening, Southern California and all the Great Southwest. This is the 'Janna Holmes Show,' and I'm Janna Holmes. With me tonight is a guest who was with me earlier this week, California State Assembly candidate and grand exalted imperial wizard of the Kalifornia Klan, Jesse Utter. I asked Mr. Utter back so we could talk about the recent developments in Los Angeles, and the, well, riot, I guess we would have to call it, on the lawn of the Los Angeles Police Headquarters. A riot between troops of the American Nazi Party and members of the Revolutionary Communist Party. First, Jesse, if I may call you that?"

"Of course, Janna."

"We're old friends by now."

"New friends. Even better, Janna."

"Thank you, Jesse. As I said, first I want to clarify the situation as regards your organization, the Kalifornia Klan, and any relation it might have to the American Nazi Party. There seems to be some confusion in the minds of some of our listeners. Is there any connection between the two groups?"

"None whatsoever, Janna. None whatsoever."

In the darkness of his unlighted garage apartment, Walker was naked on the floor doing rapid situps, his hands locked behind his head, the soles of his feet pressed flat against the wall. Each time he pulled himself up he grunted and spat out his breath from between clenched teeth. His pace was regular, rhythmic, and very fast.

"National socialism is a foreign-born, foreign-bred concept that fails miserably to address the contemporary problems facing the Americans in general, and Californians in particular. The American Nazi Party is a joke, completely unable to pursue an effective course of action. I think—no, I know—that the majority of their membership are young, undisciplined, badly motivated misfits who join the party primarily to drink beer and wear those cute uniforms. They like to dress up in leather and swastikas and parade around in front of their girl friends. They're a farce."

273

Without breaking rhythm Walker unlocked his hands from behind his head and stretched his arms out straight. He touched first one foot and then the other with each situp. His naked body was covered with a sheen of perspiration that gleamed in the dim moonlight. He had picked up his pace.

"Jesse, tell me how your Kalifornia Klan differs from the Nazis."

"The Kalifornia Klan, as I have stated before, is an elite cadre of committed white Christian revolutionaries who have dedicated their lives to the holy task of wresting control of this country back from the Jewish-Negro-atheistic-Communist syndicate that is poisoning this once great nation. And to complete that task by whatever means necessary."

"Including violence?"

"Janna, the Kalifornia Klan is ready, willing, and able to take whatever steps are required to save this country from Jewish mongol anti-Christian domination. We are taking a page from the leftist urban guerrillas of Europe and South America. We have learned our lessons in ruthlessness and sacrifice. And with the knowledge that God is on our side, we are prepared to do whatever is necessary to reach our goals and objectives."

"So you condone the recent killings in Los Angeles?"

"Killing is always regrettable, Janna, but sometimes unavoidable. Sometimes it's the only way to spotlight a problem, to bring attention to an injustice. The Jews of America have to realize they cannot subvert and demoralize and pollute this great nation with impunity. Not forever. Someone has got to pay the piper. They have brought these things upon themselves."

"Then you consider the killer a hero? You would welcome him into your Klan?"

"Yes, I guess you could call him a hero. In the ancient Greek sense of the word. He has single-handedly taken it upon himself to do battle with the International Jewish Conspiracy. I would call that a hero, wouldn't you? As to his joining our Klan, I have said before, he is precisely the kind of clear-thinking individual our Klan attracts. We welcome all such recruits."

"Then you are actually seeking new members?"

"We are always looking for a few good men, Janna. Just like the marines. Ha, ha, ha!"

Walker's hands were clapsed behind his head again. The sweat poured from his face, down his body, into his crotch. The muscles in his stomach were knotting. With each situp he was gasping now, but his tempo hadn't slackened. He pushed himself on and on.

6:53 AM Los Angeles was in for a bad day. The night before, the Air Quality Management Board had predicted an inversion layer over the entire basin, and it had been correct. The temperatures near the ground had fallen a few degrees during the night, but because of the extreme heat of the preceding few days, the upper atmosphere had remained constant. These conditions had resulted in a severe inversion layer trapping all of yesterday's smog and not allowing it to dissipate into the outer atmosphere overnight. The millions of morning commuters on the gridlocked freeways were adding to that poisonous haze, their exhausts spewing out nitrogen oxides, sulfur oxide, carbon monoxide, and lead. The intense August sun cooked the mess into a brown stifling stew that made eyes water, throats itch, nostrils burn. Second-stage alerts were forecast all over the place—Alhambra, Pasadena, the whole valley, and all the way out to San Bernardino and Riverside. Children in school were not to be allowed to play in their schoolyards. Companies with more than fifty employees had to implement car pools. Some industries had to shut down completely. Invalids and consumptives were advised to stay indoors. Surgical masks began to appear over faces in the downtown area. L.A. was in for a very bad day.

Gold sat at his desk drinking coffee and eating doughnuts, surrounded by the medical examiner's photographs of Irving Rosewall's corpse. Several of the photos also pictured Rosewall's little Jack Russell terrier. The little bitch had stood, fangs bared, daring anyone to come near her master's body. The cops who had responded to the call, black-and-whites and detectives from the task force, were to a man unmoved by the sight of one more dead body, but they were all touched by the bravery of the big-hearted little dog. Especially after a neighbor said she thought Irving Rosewall had been a widower with no living relatives. And even more especially after the dog had bitten three Emergency Medical Unit personnel who had been attempting to ascertain Rosewall's status, which was obvious: almost immediate death due to a close-range gunshot wound to the chest. Several of the officers had volunteered to take the terrier home with them, but Dolly Madison shot that idea down immediately. Running around in a trench coat over his pajamas—for chrissake!—he had called for Animal Control, who were none too happy about a 4:30 A.M. call. They finally arrived, threw a net over the canine, and stuck her into one of the plastic compartments on the side of their vehicle. The cops had booed.

Gold took a bite from a jelly doughnut, and red goo plopped down the front of his shirt. He swore and dabbed at the stains with a Kleenex.

He inspected a picture of the defiant little dog standing death guard over her fallen master. Gold knew the media had the identical shot and that by late afternoon it would be on the front pages of newspapers all over the world. The reporters had swarmed like ants. The television networks had already been setting up their lights when Gold arrived on the scene. A print guy from *Paris-Match* had told him that since the terrorist attacks in Europe had abated, this was now the biggest story in the world.

Gold sipped at his cold coffee and pulled another photograph to the top of the stack. It was a closeup of the three red crosses spray-painted on the sidewalk a few feet from Rosewall's body. In the upper right-hand corner of the photograph the body-bagged corpse was visible.

"One a night now, eh, Lieutenant?" a reporter had shouted across the police barrier. "He's on a roll."

Gold grimaced at the thought and reached to his pocket for a cigar. Now they were calling it the "Cross Killings," and the perpetrator the "Cross-killer." It made good copy.

As Gold lit his cigar, Zamora started snoring lightly. He was at his desk across the tiny office, his feet propped up and his head resting on his wadded-up jacket. Gold, too, was sleepy. After leaving Wendy and the baby at Evelyn's house last night he had gone home and studied the ceiling above his bed for a couple of hours. Then he got the call on this Rosewall thing. It was confusing him. It was beginning to get all jumbled up in his mind. If he stared at the photos of Rosewall's corpse for too long, he would begin to see Wendy's battered, teary face, and the fear and rage would start up again. He forced himself to concentrate on the business at hand.

He was stymied, and he knew it. He was no investigator. He didn't put his faith in clues and leads, paint scrapings and microscopic pieces of thread, personality composites and computer printouts. His stock-in-trade was intimidation. You turned up the heat and the rats began scurrying in the walls. You leaned on some snitches. You flushed a few toilets. You kicked a few asses. Sooner or later your man turned up. Only he was afraid it was going to be more later than sooner. And he didn't have the luxury of time. A lot of people expected him to come up with some results fast. And he knew they were only going to increase the pressure.

He didn't have long to wait.

At precisely 7:30 City Councilman Harvey Orenzstein and three of his aides came through his door looking grim and serious.

"Didn't your mother teach you to knock?" Gold growled.

Zamora jerked awake, almost falling over backward in his chair, and stared, blinking, around the room.

"Aw, you woke the baby," Gold said sweetly to Orenzstein.

"Lieutenant," Orenzstein began, "I'm holding a press conference in my office at twelve o'clock. I want you to be there."

"People in hell want ice water. That don't mean they're going to get it."

"Then I want a statement from you on how this investigation is progressing."

"Councilman, if I had any statements to make—which I don't—about any new developments in this case—which there ain't—I would release them through the normal channels—which is to say the P.R. apparatus of the Los Angeles Police Department. Not through your office."

Orenzstein glowed with indignation. "Then what the hell am I going to tell the press?"

Gold smiled. "Sounds like a personal problem to me, Councilman."

Zamora snickered.

"Look," Orenzstein sputtered, "the people want to know what the hell their police department is doing about these killings."

Gold smiled again. "You can tell the *people* that throughout the day we will be continuing to question possible suspects."

Orenzstein waited, then asked, "That's it?"

"That's it."

"You mean you don't even have a good description of the killer?"

"I wish I could get this little dog to talk," Gold sighed and tapped one of the photographs on his desk. "Nobody else's even seen the perp, except from behind, a block away. He's like a phantom. He disappears into the night. In fact, we don't even know for sure if it's just one suspect. Could be a hundred. I have a gut feeling it's one guy, though."

Orenzstein shook his head. "That won't do, Lieutenant."

Gold smiled a third time. "Kiss my keister, Councilman."

Orenzstein was embarrassed. He glanced furtively at his aides behind him, then pulled up a chair, sat down, and leaned over Gold's desk. When he spoke his voice was slick as Vaseline.

"Lieutenant, why are we at each other's throats like this? We should be working together on this thing. After all, we both want the same thing, right?"

"I'm not sure. What is it you want?"

"Why, I want this murderer apprehended, of course," Orenzstein sniffed.

"That's funny. I thought you wanted to be mayor."

Orenzstein ignored that one. "Jack—may I call you Jack?"

"You just did."

"Jack, a lot of people think Chief Huntz is dragging his feet on this case." Gold started to say something and Orenzstein waved him down.

"Chief Huntz's relations with minorities are deplorable. Everyone knows that. He's insulted his own Hispanic officers; his record with the black community is *abysmal;* he's alienated women and gays with his crude remarks. The man's a bigot. Plain and simple. And now he's pursuing this case with less than total vigor. And why? Because the victims are Jewish and he's an anti-Semite. It's as simple as that." Orenzstein sat up straight, as if to punctuate his statement. "This whole thing wasn't even treated seriously until the streets became littered with Jewish bodies, and the international press zoomed in on it. And we both know there was plenty of warning. And how many men are assigned to this case? Twenty? For a case of this importance? That's ridiculous. That's criminal." Orenzstein leaned forward again. "Jack, I want you to help me to expose Huntz for what he is. A man like that in the office of chief of police in a city with the Jewish population that Los Angeles has. It's shameful. It's unconscionable. I want you to join with me in turning this man out of office. We can hang him out to dry on this one. We owe it to ourselves." He leaned even closer. "We owe it to our people."

Gold was a long time in answering. He arranged the coroner's photographs into a neat stack, tapping the edges into a straight line. He brushed some powdered doughnut sugar from the top of his desk and threw the empty Styrofoam coffee cup into the wastebasket between his knees. Then he held up his left hand, the fingers splayed wide, and pointed to his thumb with the index finger of his right hand.

"Number one," he said. "If anyone underestimated the dangerousness of the situation, of the suspect, it was me, not Huntz."

He moved to the next finger.

"Number two. At six this morning Huntz assigned another forty detectives to this investigation. Over my objections, I might add. That's sixty-odd all told.

"Number three. No one hates Alan Huntz more than me and, yes, he is a bigot. But I don't think there's a single cop on the force—including the black ones—who couldn't be classified as at least prejudiced. Where do you think they find us—Sunday school? The academy gets very few applicants who are also Nobel candidates, you know.

"Number four. As distasteful as Huntz is, I find you much more so. You come in here wrapped in the flag of Israel and talk about *our people* and all that shit, and all you want out of this is political mileage. You couldn't care less about Anna Steiner or Irving Rosewall or especially Honey Dew Mellon. You're using these people's corpses as stepping stones to your fucking career goals. You're a piece of political *dreck*. You insult me as a man, a police officer, and a Jew. You make me want to puke.

"Number five." Gold pointed to his little finger. "Get the fuck out of my office and never come back."

The office was sepulchrally quiet. A computer could be heard spewing out information down the hall. The aides' eyes flashed from Gold to the councilman.

Orenzstein stood slowly and pulled his wrinkled suit around his belly. His voice was low and threatening.

"A man with a reputation like yours doesn't need new enemies."

"A man with a reputation like mine doesn't have a helluva lot to lose," Gold snapped back. "Close the door behind you on your way out."

Orenzstein grimly ushered his aides out into the hall. Then he turned back to Gold and pointed his finger. "I'll remember this, Gold. I'll never forget this."

"You do that, Harvey," Gold laughed. "You do that."

Then Orenzstein was gone, slamming the door behind him. Zamora was shaking his head and scribbling furiously into his little notebook.

"In-fucking-credible," he muttered.

"What?" Gold asked.

"The movie this is all gonna make. In-fucking-credible!" He looked up at Gold. "Do you think I'm too young for your role?"

"Too faggy. Why don't you just play yourself?"

"Nah. Part's too small. My agent would scream."

Gold stood up and reached for his coat. "Well, some of us have to go through life with smaller parts than the rest of us. That's the way of the world. Comb your hair, we're going out."

"Where to?"

"A funeral. I figured we needed cheering up."

Before the war Boyle Heights had been the center of Jewish life and population in Los Angeles. A hilly community of modest frame houses a few miles east of downtown, it had supported a synagogue on almost every corner. Now there was only one congregation left, and the *Times* ran a story on how often there weren't enough men available for a *minyan*. As quickly as they had climbed the economic ladder, the Jews had departed for better places—addresses that didn't remind them of the inner-city sweatshops and discount clothing stores where their grandparents had toiled twelve and fourteen hours a day. They fled to Encino in the Valley. West L.A., Beverly Hills, Brentwood, and Pacific Palisades, Malibu and Santa Monica. There were only a few old Jews left in Boyle Heights, too tired or too stubborn or too poor to move out. Now the Heights was hard-core Mexican, and the walls and fences bore the graffitied names

Sleepy and Dopey, Loco and Negro, Chuey and White Boy, Chindo and
Chaco. Legends that read like a Latin fairy tale: China White and the Seven
Homeboys.

There were several Jewish cemeteries in Boyle Heights, and on the
deceased's birthdays and anniversaries people came all the way across town
to bring flowers and pay respects. One of the cemeteries was Cedars of
Zion. Anna Steiner was to be buried there this morning.

Gold parked on a side street and he and Zamora sat in the car and
watched as the funeral procession drove slowly onto the cemetery grounds.
The crowd had been swelled by the news reports of Anna Steiner's murder,
and the media and the paparazzi, stopped by the police at the gate, were
tripping over themselves in their attempts to get a bankable shot. There
were also many onlookers and curiosity freaks, leaders of the Jewish community, several politicians—the mayor was there, two gentile city council-
men and all the other Jewish members of the council, Wachs, Pickus,
Yaroslavsky, Galanter, Bernson, and Braude, but not, for some reason,
Harvey Orenzstein—and many of Anna Steiner's former customers who
had come to say their last, sorrowful good-byes.

As Gold and Zamora watched, two white vans screeched up and a dozen
blue T-shirted members of the JAR spilled out and took up military stances
up and down the block on either side of the cemetery entrance. Some of
them carried sticks and baseball bats, but more than a few held weapons—
semiautomatic rifles and machine pistols. The photographers clicked away,
yelling encouragement to the stern-faced youths, who pretended not to
notice.

"Oh, no. Not again," Zamora groaned and glanced out of the corner of
his eye at Gold.

Gold sighed and shook his head. "No, this time they get a pass. I can't
handle any more complaints against me. The paperwork is a killer. C'mon,
I know a back way in."

They got out of the car and Zamora followed Gold around the block to
a narrow iron gate set in a small alcove in the back wall of the cemetery.
Gold reached his hand through the rusted bars and threw the latch. The
gate creaked open.

"You know your way around here," Zamora said.

Gold smiled. "This used to be my turf. Before you spicks moved in.
Before my mother and I moved to Fairfax. I used to steal hubcaps and
fence them to a thief used to live right across the street. Here, put this on."
He handed Zamora a plain black yarmulke, then put one on himself.

They walked quickly through the rows of cement markers—cracked and
weathered Stars of David on blocklike pedestals with raised Hebraic lettering. Anna Steiner's coffin waited next to a freshly dug grave. Gold and

Zamora stood on the fringe of the crowd and listened as the mayor read a prepared statement. Then a city councilman spoke for a few minutes about the hatred in men's hearts that must be rooted out. The rabbi read the eulogy and said Kaddish in Hebrew. They lowered Anna Steiner's coffin into the grave with a forklift. Silently the crowd began to make its way toward the exit. Gold slipped through them to the side of a frail-looking old man limping along with a cane, flanked by the mayor and the rabbi.

"Mr. Steiner."

The old man shaded his eyes with his hand and looked up at Gold. He appeared confused, startled.

"Mr. Steiner, I'm Lieutenant Jack Gold. I want to tell you how sorry I am."

The old man stared at him. Then he looked around and sat down painfully on the edge of a well-kept crypt. He massaged the knee of his bad leg with a knobby, arthritic hand. The mayor glanced at his watch, hesitated a moment, then walked away briskly, followed by his aides. The rabbi moved a few yards out and hovered. The old man looked up at Gold, squinting.

"Do you know my Anna? I don't recognize you. Are you one of our customers?"

"No. I'm a policeman. I'm going to catch the people who killed Mrs. Steiner."

The old man studied the crowd milling its way out of the cemetery.

"Who are all these people?" he asked. "Did they all know my Anna?"

"I don't know, sir."

The old man shook his eggshell head. He looked gray and sick. He kept rubbing his bad leg.

"What am I going to do without Anna?" he asked Gold. He seemed to be waiting for an answer. Gold sat down beside him and put his hand on the old man's bony shoulder.

"What am I going to do without my Anna?" he repeated. He had a thick German accent.

"Everything's going to be all right," Gold said. "You're going to be fine."

The old man shook his head again. "No, I'm not."

They sat together in silence for a while, then the rabbi approached. "I have to be getting Mr. Steiner back to the hospital."

Gold nodded and stood up. He and the rabbi helped the old man to his feet. "The car's just outside the gate," the rabbi said to Mr. Steiner. Then to Gold: "He refused the wheelchair. He wanted to walk."

The rabbi put his hand under the old man's arm and led him away. Gold watched them leave. He never asked *why,* Gold thought. When you've been through Dachau you never have to ask why.

Zamora came over and stood next to Gold. "That's really rough. When we catch this asshole I hope he gets a thousand years."

Gold fished a pair of sunglasses from his suit pocket. He put them on. "This one will never see the inside of a jail cell."

"Oh? Why's that?"

"Because I'm gonna kill him."

Zamora nodded slowly. "Okay."

They were driving back to Parker when Gold swerved the car across three lanes of traffic and whipped down the wrong exit.

"Hey, what's happening? Where we going?"

"It's cemetery day," Gold said tightly. "The Day of the Dead."

"Nah, that's November second."

Gold kept his eyes forward. "Okay, it's *my* Day of the Dead, okay?"

In just these few days Zamora had learned enough about Jack Gold not to press him.

"Whatever you say, boss."

Gold parked outside a small Catholic church named St. Maria Goretti. Adjacent to the church grounds was an ill-kept, hilly cemetery. The surrounding neighborhood was a litter-strewn, burned-out ghetto. Gold took a long time lighting a fresh cigar. Zamora pulled out his notebook and leafed through it, feigning intense interest.

"Wait here for me. I'll just be a minute."

"Huh?" Zamora said, looking up. "I'm sorry. I didn't hear you. I was studying my notes. Why don't you go do what you have to do? I'll just stay here and tighten up my script."

Gold smiled behind his cigar. "You're all right, kid."

"I really have a lot of work to do here, Jack. Do me a favor and give me a few minutes."

Gold grunted. He got out of the car and puffed up the slight hill into the cemetery. He walked slowly down the rows of crosses, the cement virgins with their outstretched, supplicant arms, the frozen agonies of tortured Christs. He hadn't been here in several years, and it took him a few passes before he found the marker he was looking for.

ANGELIQUE ST. GERMAINE

Gold sat on a concrete bench directly across from the grave and crossed his legs. He wasn't a pious man; he never had been. Prayer didn't rest easy on his lips. But he came here every so often—more often then than now—

to, well, to simply pay his respects. To remember. To remember her. He came because he knew no one else did. There had been a grandmother back in Louisiana—Algiers, Louisiana—but on the phone fourteen years ago she seemed befuddled, ashamed. She told Gold she didn't have the money to ship the body back. He had suggested that she be buried here; he'd take care of the expenses. She had hesitated only briefly before acquiescing.

"She was a good girl," the old lady had said.

"I know," Gold had commiserated.

"Before she got mixed up with them drugs. She was a good girl."

"I know."

"You give her a pretty funeral, now, you hear?"

"I will."

He hadn't dealt with the reason why he didn't want to ship her body back South. Later—much later—he admitted to himself that he couldn't give her up, even in death. He had claimed the body from the morgue, telling them he had the next of kin's verbal permission. Then he had called churches all over the city. None of them would bury her. Finally the priest at this poor black parish had agreed to see him. He was a stubby, silver-haired Irishman with the lilting cadences of Dublin in his speech. Skelly was his name.

"Scotch is it?" he had asked as Gold sat in his rectory, and poured two healthy portions.

"You see," Father Skelly began, "in our Roman religion we can't bury a suicide in consecrated ground. It can't be done."

"She would have wanted a Catholic burial. I know that."

Skelly shook his head. "I can't even speak at a suicide's graveside. It's strictly forbidden. Some of the archdioceses take a more liberal view of this subject, but I'm afraid my cardinal is a bit of a reactionary."

They sat and drank. Gold waited. Skelly could have told him this on the phone. There would be more.

"But it's come to my attention from some of my countrymen on the force that there is some controversy as to whether the poor lass took her own life. Oh, that's the official line, all right, that's what's on the death certificate, but officialdom and the Church don't always agree on these things. At least not in this country." Skelly wet his lips with Scotch. "So if you could give me some kind of assurance that the girl died by other means. By other hands, so to speak."

He and Gold looked into each other's souls.

"I can assure you any such information would be kept in the strictest confidence. We priests are very good at that."

"Are you asking to hear my confession, Father?"

Skelly smiled. "Aren't we a bit long in the tooth to be converting,

Lieutenant? I just need some sign that a poor Catholic soul is in danger of being denied her church's last rites because of some human error, as you might say. I just need to be told by someone who was with her during her last moments that the girl's death was somehow—*accidental.* You might say."

Now it was Skelly's turn to wait.

When Gold spoke he used a phrase he was to hear used a great deal a few years later in the Watergate investigations.

"I have no problem with that."

Skelly put his arm through Gold's as he showed him to the door.

"Perhaps you noticed the basketball court we're building next to the school. My parishioners dearly love their basketball. At least it keeps them busy when they're not out being turned down for jobs. It's a bitter shame we may have to halt construction. Paucity of funds, y'know."

Gold acknowledged him with a nod.

"Business is business, eh, Father?"

"Everywhere in the world, Lieutenant. And isn't that the bitch of it."

They buried Angelique here the next afternoon in a cold drizzle. Just Gold, Skelly, and the two gravediggers. Skelly read from his missal, then the gravediggers lowered Angelique into the damp ground. They were still doing it by hand and rope then. Skelly read some more, then closed the book and said some things about a life cut down in its prime, a promise unfilled, and then about the greater plans of gods. The drizzle turned into a steady downpour. Skelly crossed himself and turned up his collar. Then he and Gold walked across the street to a quiet Mexican bar and killed the rest of the rainy afternoon drinking tequila shooters chased with *cervezas.* The next day Gold left a plain white envelope with Skelly's housekeeper. It contained thirty hundred-dollar bills. He had taken the money from the red suitcase.

Gold, sitting in the graveyard, was startled out of his memories. He looked up into a young, unblemished, all-American face above a starched clerical collar.

"What?"

"I asked if you wanted to talk. You looked so troubled."

Gold stared at him. "Is this still Skelly's parish?"

"I'm sorry. I'm afraid Father Skelly passed on last year. Is there any way I can help you?"

Gold shook his head.

The young priest persisted. "Are you sure you don't want to discuss whatever's bothering you? Sometimes all we need is to talk a thing through."

"I'm a Jew," Gold said flatly.

The young man gave him his best seminarian smile. "We're all the children of God, my son."

Gold stood up. "Fuck off, Father."

He walked quickly out of the cemetery.

Back at his desk, Gold looked up Stanley and Evelyn Markowitz's number and dialed it. Evelyn answered. She sounded flustered and embarrassed when she recognized Gold's voice.

"How's Wendy doing?"

"As well as can be expected, I guess, Jack. She had a nightmare early this morning and woke up hysterical. Stanley gave her a heavy sedative, and she's still sleeping. Howie's been calling all morning, but I won't wake her. I'm not even sure she wants to talk to him."

"She was pretty upset last night. The best thing for her is to be over there, with you and Stanley. Right now she needs to feel safe and secure. Protected. With people who love her."

"I can't believe what happened. I just can't bring myself to face it. It's horrible. I've never seen Stanley so angry. He thinks of her as his own child, you know. Just like Pet—" She let the sentence trail off, then quickly rushed to say, "I am so shocked by all of this. We thought the world of Howie. How could he let this happen? *Cocaine!* For God's sake! A lot of people we know use coke. Nothing like this ever happens."

"You open the door to let in the cat, and sometimes a tiger comes in after. Howie let things get out of hand. He tried to use cocaine to hurry along his career. This town is full of people who do the same thing. And a lot of them get burned, just like Howie."

"But our poor Wendy is the one who has to suffer. And to think we can't even prosecute those creeps. They're getting away scot free."

"Not if I have anything to say about it."

There was a beat of silence, then Evelyn said, "I saw you on the news this morning. They killed another one last night. That lonely old man with that little dog. My God, what's the world coming to?"

Gold waited for the inevitable question.

"When are you going to catch that creep, that Crosskiller?"

"Soon. Real soon."

"Stanley and I were talking this morning over breakfast. We're thinking of moving to Palm Springs. Stanley's practice and everything. This town is getting more like New York every day. You can't feel safe here anymore."

Gold searched for something to say. "That sounds like a good idea."

Evelyn stammered breathily, then said, "Jack—Jack, I want to apologize for my outburst at Peter's bar mitzvah Saturday. I don't know what got into me."

"Hey, don't worry about it."

"No. No. I was completely out of line. I know that. I guess I've been overly tired lately. But even so, that's no excuse for my abominable behavior. I had no right to act that way."

"Ev, really, I understand."

"Even so, I'm very sorry. And I'm very glad you came. By the way, Peter was quite taken with you. Fascinated, I guess you could say. Isn't it interesting—Stanley has brought home movie stars, rock 'n' roll idols, once the governor—and Peter was completely unfazed. But he meets a real live legendary police lieutenant—his sister's father, no less—and he's totally bowled over. Proves you can't second-guess children, doesn't it?"

What the hell does that mean? Gold thought.

"What I'm getting at, Jack, is Stanley and I had a long talk, and we want you to be a part of Peter's life. We want you to share the experience of Peter's growing up with us. What do you think of that?"

Gold didn't know what to say.

"I don't know what to say."

"Whenever you want to spend some time with Peter—a ball game maybe, or a movie, something like that—just give us a call a week or so in advance and we'll be delighted to have you over to pick him up."

Rent-a-Son, Gold thought.

"Of course, we'd expect you not to attempt to change the status quo. You will always be my ex-husband, Wendy's father, and only that. We don't want to confuse the boy. We don't want him to think we lied to him."

Definitely Rent-a-Son.

"And Stanley insists we pick up the tab on any such nights on the town."

No, it's the Father-and-Son Escort Service. The Unknown Dad. Maybe I should wear a bag over my head, Gold thought.

"To show our good faith. To prove our eagerness to have you join in Peter's life."

Gold's mind wandered. He stared at the top photograph of Irving Rosewall's corpse and the defiant little dog. He thought of a small dog he had when he was a boy of six or seven. In Boyle Heights. A Manchester terrier mix. He couldn't remember the dog's name.

"Jack, Jack—are you still there?"

Suddenly Gold felt tired, empty. Old.

"Jack?"

"Why don't we leave things the way they are, Ev? Why change things now, after all this time?"

"Well—"

"What possible difference could it make now?" Gold felt himself getting angry—he didn't know why or at what—and he fought to control himself.

"Let's just leave things the way they are. I think that's best for everyone. Okay?"

"Well, of course, Jack, if that's what—"

"Tell Wendy I'll call her later. Or have her call me."

"I will, Jack, the minute she—"

"Good-bye, Ev."

Gold hung up. He sat at his desk for several minutes, staring at the opposite wall. He wanted a drink very badly. The telephone rang. Instead of answering it he got up, left the office, and went down the hall to watch an interrogation.

11:22 *AM* Esther turned the flame on under the water kettle and slipped a paper coffee filter into the plastic cone. Then she spooned in six tablespoons of coffee.

"Well, better now than later," Mama Phibbs said, seated at the kitchen table. She was in a black-and-white polka dot dress with a long skirt. Her hair was done up.

Esther took two cups down from the china cabinet and set them on the table. She sat across from Mama Phibbs. She sniffled and blew her nose on a wadded Kleenex. She had been crying again.

"Better now than later," Mama Phibbs repeated resolutely.

"Oh, Mama! How can you be so cold about it!" Esther blurted out.

The old woman was intense and unsmiling. "How can I be? It's easy. You know why? 'Cause that boy ain't never gonna change. He always gonna be a dope fiend and a thief and a criminal. He ain't never gonna be nothing better. He done set what they call a pattern to his life. He done turned his face from God. It pains me and breaks my heart to say that, but it's true. And that's that. Now I got to worry about the living—my daughter and my grandson. That's what concerns me now."

Esther reached over and Mama Phibbs took her hand. The old woman held it tightly, caressing it.

"Can we write him off that easy, Mama?"

"Easy?" Mama Phibbs snorted. "What's been easy about it? He put my Charles into an early grave, grieving and worrying, and left me a lonely old widow woman who's got to sleep in an empty bed every night. You think that's easy? And you, pining away every time he goes to jail. Letting your juices dry up and go to waste. Working your fingers to the bone to pay for lawyers and such. You call that easy? No. I'm telling you, girl, that boy is dead. And that's the way you got to look at it. He's dead, and you got to worry about the living. Yourself and Little Bobby. That's all they is to it."

"You don't think we'll ever see him again?" A tear rolled down Esther's cheek.

"Oh, sure, he'll be around. Next time he needs a fix and ain't got no money. He'll be knocking on the door, begging like a dog. And if they ain't nobody home he'll break in and steal the TV. That's what he *is*, Esther."

Esther dropped her head and dabbed at her eyes with the balled-up tissue.

"You got a responsibility to that little boy. And to yourself, Esther. You're still a young woman. You always dragging yourself around here like an eighty-year-old hag. Bobby done that to you. Well, it's time to stop all that. Don't be throwing any more good years after bad."

The doorbell buzzed. Esther stood up.

"Now who the hell can that be?" She walked through the apartment to the front door. On the other side of the screen door stood Clarke Johnson.

"Mrs. Phibbs. I'd like to see Bobby."

"He ain't here."

"Mrs. Phibbs, I'd like to come inside."

"I told you, he ain't here."

"It's my job, Mrs. Phibbs. I have to come inside."

Esther stared at him through the screen.

"Mrs. Phibbs, you have to let me in. It's the law."

Esther unlatched the door and pushed it open. "All right, but Bobby ain't here. He's gone."

Johnson stepped inside. "Bobby didn't appear for testing this morning. Do you know where he is?"

"I told you, he's gone."

"You mean for good?"

"Forever, Mr. Johnson. Forever."

"And you don't know where he is, where we went?"

"Have no idea."

"When did he leave?"

"Last night."

He studied Esther from behind his delicate, gold-rimmed glasses. "What happened?"

Esther shrugged. "He left. He's gone. That's what happened."

"Did you argue?"

"You might say that."

"Over what?"

"That's personal, Mr. Johnson."

"Over drugs?"

"No."

"Was he using again?"

"I really wouldn't know about that."

Johnson sighed. He looked at Esther's swollen red eyes. "Are you all right?"

"I'm fine."

"Do you feel your husband poses any immediate danger to yourself or"—he consulted his clipboard—"your son?"

"No."

"Mrs. Phibbs, it's obvious your husband has violated the terms of his probation. I'm afraid he's become a fugitive. I'm going to have to ask you some questions; fill out a form. Is it all right if I sit down?"

"Of course, Mr. Johnson. I didn't mean to be so rude. I'm still a little upset. Can I get you some coffee?"

"I'd like that very much." Clarke Johnson smiled for the first time that Esther could remember. He sat in the armchair and looked around the living room.

"This is a very nice room. You and your son live here alone? Now that Bobby's left?"

"Uh huh."

He smiled again. "It's a very nice room."

"Uh, I'll get you that coffee."

"Thank you, Mrs. Phibbs."

In the kitchen, Mama Phibbs was standing behind the door, eavesdropping and peeking out.

"Who's that, Es?" she whispered.

"That's Mr. Clarke Johnson, Bobby's P.O. He's looking for Bobby."

Esther took another cup from the cupboard. She turned to the kettle. "Hey, the fire's off."

"I turned it off," Mama Phibbs said absently, still peeking out the door. "Didn't know how long you'd be."

Esther turned on the flame and leaned back against the counter. Mama Phibbs glanced her way, then did a double-take.

"What you doin', Es?"

"Mama, I'm waiting for this water to boil so I can make that man a cup of coffee."

"But he's all alone out there." Mama Phibbs's face wore a strange expression.

"I think he'll live through it."

The old lady came over to her. "Es, I don't think you should leave company alone."

"Mama—"

"I'll fetch you when the water boils. A watched pot never boils, you know."

"Mama—"

"Better yet, just let me make it. You go out there and talk with Mr. Johnson." Mama Phibbs fairly pushed Esther back out into the living room. Esther stood in the doorway, confused and a little embarrassed.

"The coffee'll take a few minutes."

"That's fine with me, Esther. May I call you Esther?"

For the first time Esther looked at him the way a woman looks at a man. He was short and solid, well built but certainly not beautiful. Certainly not Bobby.

"May I call you Esther?" he asked again.

"You can call me anything but late for supper," Esther said offhandedly in an attempt to disguise her sudden nervousness.

Johnson threw back his head and laughed raucously. A pirate's laugh, and totally unexpected from such an owlish man.

"That's very funny. What is that?"

"What is what?"

"What you just said. That expression."

"Oh, that's just something my Aunt Rosalie used to say. Back down South."

"Is that where your family's from? The South?"

"Just like everybody's."

"Not everybody's. My family's lived in the Seattle area for almost a hundred and fifty years. For as long as anyone can remember."

Well, whoop-dee-doo for you, Esther thought.

She sat down in the other armchair.

"What happens to Bobby now? I mean, when you catch him?"

He clicked his ballpoint and laid it on his clipboard.

"Well, I'm afraid he'll most assuredly go back to jail whenever he's caught." He studied Esther closely. "Does that upset you?"

"Well—" Esther pulled out her cigarettes and stuck one in her mouth, but before she could light it, Johnson leaned over, took the book of matches from her hand, and struck one. He held it out for her. She felt herself blush as she touched the cigarette's tip to the flame. "Well, he's still the father of my son. We been married over ten years. I will always bear some concern for him, Mr. Johnson. I hate to think of him winding up back in prison."

"Uh, just how deep is your concern, Mrs. Ph— Esther? Will you still be seeing Bobby from time to time?"

Esther's eyes flashed with anger. "If you mean is Bobby gonna be coming by for some overnight visits every once in a while, no, that's not gonna happen."

"Esther—"

"But if you think I'm some kind of snitch who's gonna call you up if and when Bobby ever does try and come back, you're very wrong. Bobby's out of my life now, but I'm not gonna be the one to help you to put him back in a jail cell."

"No, I—"

"So don't be asking me for no information, 'cause I don't have any."

"Esther, please. You completely misunderstand me."

Mama Phibbs came quickly out of the kitchen, saying, "The water's boiling, Esther." She smiled at Johnson. "Hello."

He stood up.

"Mr. Johnson, this is my mother-in-law, Mrs. Wanda Phibbs. Mama, this is Mr. Clarke Johnson."

"Please, please, call me Clarke," he said to Esther. "Mrs. Phibbs, I'm very pleased to meet you. I'm sorry it has to be under these circumstances."

"So am I. Es, that water's gonna boil away if you don't make that coffee."

"Excuse me." Esther followed her mother-in-law back into the kitchen. When the door was closed Mama Phibbs turned on her.

"What the hell's wrong with you, girl?" she hissed.

"What are you talking about?"

"That man's *interested* in you. Can't you see that?"

"Oh, Mama." Esther scoffed as she poured the bubbling water over the coffee.

"Don't 'Oh, Mama' me. I'm still woman enough to recognize that look in a man's eye, even if you ain't."

"Mama, you're crazy."

"Crazy like a fox. Now you go out there and at least be civil to that poor man. It wouldn't hurt you none to smile occasionally either. Something good might come out of all this yet. Maybe at least one of us won't wind up singing the Empty Bed Blues."

"Mama! Don't talk that way! I'm still married to Bobby."

The old woman's face grew cold and stern. "Bobby's married to that damn heroin. And it's gonna be the death of him, just like an old black widow spider. You got to look out for yourself, girl. Starting right here and now."

The two women stared at each other for a long moment.

Esther suddenly gave out a youthful giggle. "You really think so, Mama? You really think he's interested in me?"

Mama Phibbs smiled back. "I sure enough do."

"But, Mama. He's so damn *square!*" Esther moaned.

"Square is something we could use more of around this house."

For the first time Esther became aware she was still wearing the Raiders football jersey she had slept in, and the patched blue jeans she had slipped into. She hadn't even brushed her hair.

"My, God, I must look like a witch." She ran her fingers over her head.

"Well, it's pretty plain Mr. Clarke Johnson don't think so. Just go out there and treat that man like a human being, Es."

Carrying two cups of coffee, Esther stopped before the door and composed herself, blanking her face. Mama Phibbs winked at her. Esther pushed through the door.

Johnson jumped up from his chair. Esther set a cup on the table in front of him. She sat down on the sofa, pulled her legs up under her, and sipped at her coffee.

"Mrs. Phibbs. Esther," he began as he sat back down, "I'm afraid you have completely misunderstood my intentions. I'm afraid we've gotten off on the wrong foot."

"Oh?" Esther said, peering over the rim of her cup.

"Yes, you see," he said haltingly, "you see, I was asking those questions more from a personal standpoint."

Esther said nothing. She looked at him and waited.

"Uh, you see, I, uh, I've been thinking about you. Since you came into the office with your husband."

"Really? Do you make a practice of thinking 'bout married women?"

"No, no, of course not," he stammered. "Never. It's just that I was very impressed with you. At my office. I thought to myself, Now there goes a strong woman, an independent woman, smart, ambitious. And very attractive, too. A good woman for any man. I thought your husband an extremely fortunate man, in spite of his difficulties."

"Well, I guess he didn't think so."

Johnson smiled. "I wish I could say I'm sorry."

Esther felt a smile start to play around her lips, but she steeled her face and kept it straight, noncommittal.

"What I'm, uh, I'm trying to say, Esther, is I, uh, I have some tickets for tomorrow night. Pasadena City College. I thought possibly—"

"Mr. Johnson, what the hell kind of game you running?"

He blinked rapidly. "I'm sorry, I don't un—"

"You run this scam on all your parolees' wives?"

"Please, I—"

"Am I supposed to come across with sexual favors in exchange for preferential treatment for my husband? Is that the way it's supposed to work?"

From the kitchen came the sound of a cup, dropped to the floor, shattering.

"No, no, no, Mrs. Ph— Esther. It's not like that at all."

"'Cause I don't care how many other women went along with your little scheme, I sure as hell ain't. Anyways, Bobby's gone, there ain't nothing to hold over my head. And I'll bet you could lose your job for trying to coerce women like this."

"Esther! Please stop!" Johnson was aghast. "You've got it all wrong. I'm not coercing you by any means. I'm not that kind of man. I only asked you for a date after I was convinced your husband had deserted you. That your marriage was in complete disarray. And I have never, never asked any other probationer's wife out. *Never.*"

Why me? Esther thought.

"Why me?" she asked.

"What?"

"Why me?" she repeated. "Why am *I* the lucky one?"

He selected his words carefully. "I'm not a flighty man. In fact, I'm quite serious. Probably too damn serious for my own good. Old fashioned, I guess, but I can't help that. That's the way I am. Most of the women I meet are put off by such a serious man. Everybody wants to party down and all that. I'm not a boogie down kind of man."

You sure as hell ain't, Esther thought, and then giggled—a quick shoolgirlish titter. Johnson, heartened, pressed on.

"The other day, in my office, when we met, I felt you were a kindred spirit. Immediately. It was almost as if we had known each other before. Have you ever had that feeling, Esther? I felt as if I'd known you all of my life. And that you—like me—were a serious person, too. I was instantly attracted to you. And now, learning that your relationship with your husband had ended, I would be a fool not to try and know you better. I want to spend some time with you. I want to know everything about you. I want you to get to know me."

Esther ran her fingers slowly through the hair on the back of her neck and studied him through suspicious eyes.

"When did you say you had tickets for what?"

"Tomorrow night," he said eagerly. "Pasadena City College. A modern dance program."

Sweet Jesus, Esther thought. This man is not to be believed.

"The Alvin Ailey Dance Theater. Eight o'clock. And afterward I thought we might have a late dinner and maybe go dancing."

Esther smiled at him.

"Boogie down?"

He laughed again—that surprising hearty laugh that caressed Esther's backbone.

"Right. Boogie down."

Esther thought for a moment. "Tomorrow night? What's that—Friday?"

Johnson nodded.

"Can't make it Saturday?" she asked.

"They're only giving the one performance," he said sorrowfully.

"I'm sorry, Mr. Johnson—"

"Clarke, please."

"I'm sorry, but I have to work Friday nights."

The kitchen door swung open and Mama Phibbs burst out.

"Excuse me for barging in, but I couldn't help overhearing. Es, why don't you double up tonight and pick up the rest of the slack on Saturday. I'm sure your employers won't mind. It's summertime and you told me just last week ain't nobody going to work on Saturdays anyways. Take the night off. I'm sure Lupe and the other girl will be happy to have a Friday night off. 'Sides, you starting that big new account Sunday night anyways. This way you at least got one night off this week."

Johnson smiled at Mama Phibbs, then turned back to Esther.

"I'm afraid you're outnumbered."

Esther laughed. "Looks like it, don't it?"

"Well, then. I'll call for you at seven?"

Esther hesitated, looking from him to her mother-in-law. Mama Phibbs gave her a hard glare and nodded.

"Okay, Mr. John—"

"Clarke."

"Okay, Clarke, you may call for me at seven. Sevenish." She laughed again.

"That's wonderful." He beamed. "That's grand."

Just then the beeper on his belt went off. He clicked it dead.

"I have to be getting back to the office." His face went stern. "Esther, there's just one more piece of business. If Bobby phones or comes by, I don't expect you to call me, but please urge him to come in himself. We may still be able to keep him out of prison—if he turns himself in in time."

Esther nodded. "If he calls, I'll tell him what you said. But I don't think he will."

He stood up. He offered his hand to Mama Phibbs. "It was a pleasure to meet you, madam."

Mama Phibbs smiled at him. "And you too, Mr. Johnson."

Esther walked him to the door.

"Tomorrow then?" he said with a smile. "Sevenish?"

Esther nodded. "Sevenish."

"Good-bye." He let himself out the screen. Esther shut the front door behind him. She turned to Mama Phibbs, and when the two women caught each other's eye they both burst into laughter.

2:03 PM The coroner's assistant pulled the heavy body drawer out of the bank of vaults.

"There's your man," Honeywell said. "That's Alonzo Firp."

"That *was* Alonzo Firp," the coroner's assistant said with a nervous giggle. He was a thin, effeminate black with a pink splotch down the side of his throat.

"Is this the dude you were looking for?" Honeywell said to Gold.

"I think so. Does he have blue eyes?"

The coroner's assistant reached over and lifted the corpse's eyelid. He smiled.

"Blue as the Pacific," he lisped with regret in his voice. "Too bad. He must have been a beautiful man."

"How did he get dead?" Gold asked Honeywell over the body.

"Girl friend. Seems like Alonzo here woke up in an ugly mood. Found his bitch in the bathroom shooting up his wakeup. So he proceeded to beat the living shit out of her. Did a pretty good job, too. I talked to her about an hour ago, and her face is a mess. Anyway, when Alonzo finished pounding on her, he went back to bed. Guess he needed a nap after his morning exercise. He'll never need another. Soon as he dozed off the girl stood over him and emptied his own piece into him."

"Some broad."

"White bitch, too. Scrawny little thing. You wouldn't believe it of her."

"I'm too old to be surprised, Honey."

The coroner's assistant coughed. "You gentlemen finished with Mr. Cadaver? I haven't had lunch yet."

Out in the corridor, Gold lit a cigar to burn the stench of chemicals and death out of his nostrils.

"What about the other one?"

Honeywell flipped open his notebook. "The girl friend gave me his full name. Robert Rupert Phibbs. I'll have a picture of him later this afternoon. He was in the other bedroom when the shit went down. When he saw what she had done he lit out like a firecracker. Long gone, like a turkey through the corn. Pissed the miss off, too. Tells me they were doing a three-way freak scene, and she was falling in love with Phibbs. That's why she was so quick to off old Alonzo. Broke her heart when Phibbs ran out like he did."

Two attendants wheeled a body-laden gurney past them into the morgue. Gold sat down on a hard-backed wooden bench. Honeywell continued.

"Phibbs just got out of County on Tuesday. He was scheduled to appear for drug testing this morning, but he didn't show. His P.O. listed him in violation. Here's the address he was staying at." He handed Gold a scrap of paper. "His wife's place, but my contact down at Probation says he ain't welcome there anymore."

Gold studied the address. "That doesn't mean he won't show up."

"That's true. And he fits the description you gave me. Muscular, handsome, moustache. I think he's got to be your man."

"Anything else?"

"Yeah. The girl friend said Phibbs and Firp made a helluva score last night. Went out around nine and came back at eleven, eleven-thirty with some money and some dope—heroin *and* cocaine. They went to Phibbs's place so he could get some clean clothes, and proceeded to shoot up some speedballs. Phibbs's wife came home unexpectedly and threw them out. This morning when Phibbs rabbited on the little murderess, he grabbed all the money and took it with him. The bitch said if the gun hadn't been empty she'd've killed Phibbs, too."

Gold whistled. "Hell of a woman."

"Man, I'm telling you."

Gold looked up at Honeywell. "What else?"

"That's it, Jack."

Gold stood up. "Thanks a lot, Honey. I owe you a big one."

"Nah. It was easy. After Firp obliged us by getting his ass blown away, everything else just followed. I don't think I made five phone calls."

"I still owe you. Call me whenever you need anything."

Honeywell grinned. "Why don'cha come back to work with me in Hollywood? I miss your hymie ass."

"I'd like nothing better. This fucking gig I got is killing me."

"When you gonna catch that—"

"Gimme a break, would you, Honey? As soon as I can."

"Uh huh." Honeywell nodded. "Well, when you do, pump one in the motherfucker for me, too."

Now Gold grinned. "You know me too well, Honey."

"Uh huh."

$2{:}57\,PM$ Desert Vista was a sun-baked bedroom community carved out of the rock and sand of the Southern California scrubland and strung out along both sides of the Pearblossom Highway like litter thrown from passing cars. Once Desert Vista's Main Street had been the primary artery for Angelenos on their way to and from the lurid pleasures of Las Vegas, but then the interstate went through, and now the curio shops and gas stations and "home-style" luncheonettes were mostly closed up and boarded over. The blue-collar workers and retirees who had moved here to escape the urban nightmare, and who made up the majority of the town's population, did their shopping at the big shopping centers in Victorville or up in Barstow. The town's only notable attraction was a museum dedicated to an aging cowboy movie star, and that was on the verge of bankruptcy. The daytime temperatures in the summer seldom dipped below 95 degrees and often shimmered for weeks around 110. Airconditioner repairmen had status well above their usual station, and indeed, the last three successive mayors of Desert Vista had been airconditioner dealers or mechanics.

The first service station attendant Walker spoke to grinned and gave him directions to the Kalifornia Klan World Headquarters: up a steep road freshly knifed out of the baking hills, along the railroad tracks that ran out of town, and up again to the sagebrush-studded hills that looked out over the empty desert.

The headquarters was a rambling, unfinished brick structure built just under the crest of one of the brown hills. The rear of the house abutted the side of the mountain, and the naked red earth still bore the teeth marks of the earth-mover parked to one side. The front yard was a bare, grassless expanse that ran for a hundred feet, then dropped off over the jagged edge of the mountains. A flagpole, anchored in a tractor tire filled with cement and half buried in the sandy soil, flew two flags fluttering in the hot breeze—a Stars and Stripes and the Klan banner, two red K's superimposed over a yellow silhouette of the state of California on a field of white silk. The banner had a homemade look about it.

Walker parked the van beside the other vehicles—three Harley-Davidsons, a pickup, three passenger cars—where the dirt driveway simply ended in a flat clearing just below the house, and got out. Two men came out of the house and watched from the wide front patio as he made his way up the slope. One of them was slight and blond. The other weighed over three hundred pounds, had a fiery red beard that reached halfway down his T-shirt and a sloppy gut that hung over the belt straining to hold up his jeans. When Walker got closer he could see both men wore sidearms.

The redhead held up his hand, indicating that Walker should stop.

"What y'all want?" His voice was hoarse and his accent southern.

Walker squinted in the blistering sunshine. "I want to meet Mr. Jesse Utter," he said. "I want to talk to Jesse Utter."

"What for?"

"I want to join up. The Klan."

The two men on the patio looked at each other and smiled. The smallish blond stepped forward a few feet. He sported a leather vest and a wispy goatee.

"What makes you think the Klan wants *you?*"

The two Klansmen laughed. Walker chuckled along with them.

"Where you from?" the blond called.

"L.A."

The blond shook his head. "Third World Wonderland. They got a nigger mayor, a spick population, and the Jews pull the fucking strings. How can you stand that place?"

"That's why I want to join the Klan. That's why I want to talk to Jesse Utter."

"Wait here," the blond said, and went into the house. Redbeard leaned back against the brick wall, watching Walker, his hand resting on the butt of his pistol.

Walker ran his hand through his hair and looked at the sweat on his palm. "Fucking hot, ain't it?" he asked.

Redbeard said nothing, just eyed the intruder insolently. The blond came back out and motioned to Walker. He came up the hard-beaten path and when he got to the patio Redbeard stopped him roughly with a hand on his chest.

"You carrying, boy?" he asked, as he watched the blond pat down Walker's body, run his hand up and down his legs and over his waist area.

"He's clean," the blond said.

Redbeard held the door open and Walker went in.

Inside was dimly lit and frigidly air-conditioned. When Walker's eyes adjusted he made out six or seven men sitting and lounging around a large room with walls painted a flat, dull black. The floor was carpeted a cheap gold color, and there were a variety of couches and chairs positioned about the place. Two young women—one red-faced and overweight, the other pretty and shapely—were trying to control three small children who were running pell-mell around the floor. One of the children was crying. Hung high along all the walls were large, spotlighted, black-and-white blowups of photographs, posters, and postcards. On the wall to Walker's right was a picture of three starving Ethiopian children, their bodies shrunken and misshapened by hunger, eating small, undigested kernels of corn from a steaming cow pattie. Under the poster a strip of white cardboard bore the legend, in bold, beautifully executed script: SOUL FOOD. The next blowup showed a single gaunt African child so tormented by his hunger that he had thrust his whole face into a dairy cow's anus. FRESH SOUL FOOD was written beneath this blowup. The next scene was a shot of a Nazi concentration camp. Several Allied soldiers stood looking grimly at a field covered with charred skulls and skeletons: BERLIN BARBECUE. Then there was a thirties snapshot of Hitler looking fit and thoughtful as he gazed from his balcony at Berchtesgaden: THE RIGHT MAN FOR THE JOB. A grainy twenties photo of a southern lynching. Several of the mob wore the white robes and hoods of the KKK: ONE GOOD NIGGER. Begin, Sadat, and Carter at Camp David, smiling and shaking hands: A KIKE, A COON, AND A CLOWN. Jesse Jackson preaching from a pulpit. This picture had a circular target superimposed over Jackson's image. The bull's-eye was right in the middle of Jackson's forehead: PRESIDENT-ELECT.

"You look like you're in church."

Walker's attention snapped to the wide, bare desk directly before him. A thin man in a white shirt and tie sat behind it. He had fine black hair combed straight back, black thick-framed glasses, and a pale, pasty complexion.

"You look like one of those papists the first time they go to the Vatican. 'Oh, Holy Father,' " he mimicked in a high, mincing whine. " 'Can I kiss your Roman ass? Can I lick your dago dick?' "

The men in the room chortled with good humor. The two women laughed loudly. The children paused in their play, looked around, then started running again.

"Or Polack prick, as the case may be."

More chuckles.

"Are—are you Jesse Utter?" Walker stammered.

"In the flesh." Utter smiled and took a sip from the sweating can of diet Dr. Pepper at his right hand. "Now, what do you want with me?"

Walker glanced nervously behind him, at the men and women staring at his back.

"I—I heard you on the radio. On the 'Janna Holmes Show.' " Walker stopped.

"Yes," Utter said slowly, squeezing the aluminum can lightly with his fingertips and letting it pop back out.

"You said you was looking for new people. For recruits."

Utter smiled. "So?"

"Well, I would like—I want to join you guys. I want to be a Klan member."

Utter's smile broadened. "Oh, you do, do you?"

"Yes, sir." Walker gulped, and looked around at the people giggling behind him.

"Tiny. Get our eager young novitiate a seat."

Redbeard pushed over a modern leather-and-chrome chair, and Walker sat down slowly.

"And something to drink, Tiny."

Tiny popped the tab on a can of Coors and handed it to Walker. Walker mumbled a nervous thanks.

"Comfortable?" Utter asked.

"Yes, sir," Walker said humbly, as he grabbed a quick draught of beer.

Utter leaned back in his swivel chair. "You like our world headquarters?" he asked slyly.

"Oh, yes," Walker said, glancing around the room. On the walls, between the posters, were gun racks holding rifles and shotguns, MAC-10 submachine guns and Armalite automatic M-16's. Several swords were mounted around the room. Behind Utter, used as a backdrop, was an oversized replica of the Klan banner flying outside. There were file cabinets, a photocopier, a large printer, and along one wall a low shelf holding a row of personal computers.

"This is just the beginning," Utter said with a smug smile. "The time is ripe for the truth. America is waking up to its enemies within."

Walker didn't know if Utter expected him to reply. Finally he said, "Right. That's exactly right."

"Do you agree with what the Klan stands for?"

"Definitely," Walker said emphatically. "Right down the line."

"And you want to be a member? A brother-in-arms in the Final Struggle?"

"Yes, sir. More than anything in the world."

"More than anything in the world? That *is* serious."

One of the women snickered.

"You know," Utter said, dropping his cynical manner, "it isn't easy to become a Klansman. It isn't easy being a Klansman. We make a lot of demands on our brother Klansmen around here. Klandacy requires dedication, devotion, self-denial. It takes a very unique individual to meet our standards. Tell me, why do you want to be a Kalifornia Klansman? Tell me in your own words."

Walker fidgeted uncomfortably. "Well, you know, I read the *Klarion*, and I go along with all the things you say. You guys are the only people telling the truth. I believe in the things you stand for."

Utter took another quick taste of his diet Dr. Pepper, again squeezing the can gently, making the metal pop.

"Tell us in your own words, in your own experiences, why you want to be a Klansman. Make us understand."

Walker dropped his eyes and studied the picture printed on his beer can. A Colorado mountain spring.

"I—I—don't—I'm not really good with words. Not like you are. In the *Klarion.* You say all the things I want to say."

"What things?" Utter prompted. "Tell us those things."

Walker grimaced. His eyes darted around the room, looking for aid.

"I—I—" he started, then stopped.

"Go ahead," Utter urged. "Take your time."

Walker stared down at his beer can. Finally he looked up and met Utter's eyes.

"You know. The Jews. The niggers."

"Yes? What about the Jews and the niggers?"

Walker shrugged. "You know. How the Jews are taking over the country. Giving it to the niggers."

"Go on. Tell us about it."

Walker started slowly, stabbing at each word. "Well, that's not the way America was supposed to be. That's not how it was supposed to be in the beginning. When they wrote the Constitution and all. When they wrote the Constitution they didn't mean for the niggers to be free. And equal. Equal to white men. Niggers was slaves. They was all slaves. All those guys who wrote the Constitution and the Declaration of Independence. They all had slaves. All of them. Niggers was never meant to be as good as a white man."

Walker abruptly halted his flow of words, seemingly embarrassed by the quantity.

"That's all true," Jesse Utter said. "What else?"

Walker made a nervous gesture with his head. A tight little duck. He wished he had taken another amphetamine. He wished he could pop one now.

"Well, you know. About how the way they teach history today, they don't tell you the truth about the olden days. They don't teach you about the way it was. The way it really was."

"Yes, yes," Utter urged. "And why is that?"

Walker shrugged. He tilted his head back and poured some beer down his throat. He wiped his mouth with the back of his hand.

"The Jews, they lie. In all the history books. And all the history books are written by Jews. You can look at all the names and tell that. And they don't tell the truth. They twist the facts all around. Make them say what they want them to say. Like with the niggers. Like I was just saying about the niggers, how they was never meant to be equal to the white man. The Jews made that whole thing up. To cause trouble. They're always causing trouble."

Utter was leaning forward on his elbows. "Continue."

Walker was warming to his subject. He so seldom had someone who would listen.

"The Jews are always trying to make trouble. So's to weaken America. Make the white man look like fools. Make us look like monsters. They do that in the books, in the newspapers, on TV, in all the movies. You check out all the names on the list at the end of a movie. It's all Jews—the writers, the actors, the others. All of them. Newspaper writers. TV reporters. They're all kikes. They control all them things, what do they call them things, the media? Jews own all of that shit. They make sure they do, that way they control all the information." Walker nodded at Utter. "You said that in the *Klarion.*"

Utter squeezed his soda can. "I've said all these things in the *Klarion,* that's true. But I like the way you express them. Go on."

"That way the Jews, they only show their side. They tell their lies, and there ain't no way to fight it, 'cause they own everything. There ain't no way to get the real truth heard. So the Jew tells his lies, makes himself look good, like a hero or something, makes the nigger look good, makes the Mexican and the Chinaman look good, 'cause they ain't nothing but off-shoots of the nigger anyway. Makes everybody look good but the Christian white man. Makes the Christian white man look mean and stupid. All the time."

"And why do they do that?"

"To weaken America," Walker said quickly. He could feel a glow of approval emanating from the men and women in the room. Someone kept grunting affirmation whenever he made a point. Walker had found his home.

"To make America soft and rotten. At the core."

"Why?"

"So the Communists can take over. Just walk in and take over. That's been the Jew's plan all along. The Jews invented communism—"

"Karl Marx," Utter said, nodding approvingly.

"—and then right after that they came over here in droves, like rats, to spread communism, foment trouble, poison America. 'Cause America is the *real* Promised Land, and the Jews had to try and destroy it. So they started the unions, they agitated the niggers, they sold the bomb to the Russians—they did all that. It's all there. You can look it up."

Walker took another swig of beer. He went on without being asked.

"They're getting America ready for the big takeover. Making the white man soft and scared. Scared of his own shadow. Making the white man unsure of himself. That's the Jew's plan. That's why the Jew got us into that war in Vietnam, then made sure we'd lose it, so we'd feel weak and afraid. So when the Commies come over they'll just walk right in and take over. No problem. No fight. That's the Jew's scheme. And it's working real good."

"And why does the Jew want international communism to triumph?"

"So they can kill Christianity, for once and for all. Then the Jew will have beaten Jesus. They'll spit on Christ's body, the slimy bastards. Then they'll turn all the white men into slaves to work in their factories; they'll make all the niggers our bosses and overlords. They'll give our women to the niggers to mate with, and in one generation there won't be any more white people left, except for the Jew, and he ain't really white, but he's smart and cunning, and all the half niggers will be stupid, and the Jew'll just run the whole world without any trouble at all, just getting richer and richer."

Walker paused, a little out of breath. The room behind him had grown quiet. Jesse Utter stood and moved around the desk. He sat on the edge of the desk and crossed his arms over his chest. "It's all true. Everything you say is true. It's just a shame there aren't more people like you who can see the truth."

Walker beamed.

"So now you want to join our organization?" Utter asked, grinning down at him.

"More than any—"

"—thing in the world." Utter finished the phrase for him, prompting good-intentioned laughter from the audience. Walker was suffused with the warmth and support being channeled his way.

"We aren't simply a debating team," Jesse Utter was saying. "We don't sit around contemplating our navels, like a lot of well-meaning pro-American groups we know of." More laughter. "Hanging around the clubhouse, drinking beer and telling each other how tough they are. That kind of talk isn't going to save our civilization. We need action. Positive action."

"That's true. That's true," Walker said eagerly.

"That's why I'm a candidate for the State Assembly," Utter said, pacing the gold carpet. "We have to get the information out there. We must make the truth be heard. We must be willing to make a total commitment to the redemption of our national race. A brother member of the Kalifornia Klan is a foot soldier on the front line of Aryan-Christian survival." Utter stood before Walker's chair, staring down at him. "Are you ready to make that kind of commitment?"

"Yes, sir."

"Are you sure? We don't want any sunshine patriots among us. Are you sure you can make that kind of commitment?"

Walker swallowed hard. "I already have."

Utter surveyed Walker's face quizzically. "What do you mean?"

Walker glanced nervously around the room.

"Speak up, son. We're all secure here."

Walker swallowed again. "You know them Jews down in L.A.? The ones getting blown away?"

Silence.

"I'm the one's been doing it. I'm the Crosskiller."

Utter stared down at Walker for a long time. The smile on his lips faded into a grim, hard-set line. Walker, confused, felt the mood of the room behind him become ugly, threatening. His back went cold. He maintained his smile.

"You're the hero?" Utter asked him softly.

Walker nodded. "Yes. Yes, I am."

Utter moved quickly away from the desk and stood before the poster of the concentration camp scene, his back to Walker and the rest of the room. He stood there, studying it. Walker watched Utter's back and tried to figure out what was happening. The warmth and well-being he had been full of only moments before had drained away like liquid through a sieve.

The room was deadly silent. Even the children were watching, waiting. Finally Utter spoke.

"You didn't fool me for a minute," he said, his back still turned.

"What?" Walker asked, his smile still fixed in concrete.

Utter whirled around. "I said, you didn't fool me for a second."

Walker shook his head as if to clear it. "I don't under—"

"But I'll bet the rest of you were taken in, weren't you?" Utter shouted to the other people in the room. "I'll bet the rest of you went for this Judas's story hook, line, and sinker."

Walker's mind ran riot. He couldn't piece any of it together.

"Please, I—"

"Who are you?" Utter shouted at him, his face twisted with hate. "Who sent you? FBI? Justice Department? Are you one of Jerry Kahn's hired spies?"

"Mr. Utter, something's all wrong."

"Never mind. You don't have to tell me. I *know* you're FBI. I just wanted to see if you'd continue your fabrication. I knew you were FBI when you entered the door. I knew you were coming three days ago, when you were first assigned to infiltrate our core group."

Walker was lost. He was so confused his mouth worked but nothing came out.

"You people are sadly mistaken if you think Jesse Utter doesn't have friends in high places. A lot of people approve of what I'm doing. A lot of very important people. And these people send me messages!" Utter was screaming. "Messages that warn me when government informants are being sent to try and glean enough information to prosecute Jesse Utter, to stop him from his holy mission. Throw this Jew-loving Judas out of here! Get him out of my sight!"

Strong hands gripped Walker's arms and lifted him from his chair.

"What did I do?" Walker wailed. "What did I do?"

"Don't play the innocent with me!" Utter sputtered. "What was your assignment? What kind of case were you sent to make against me? Conspiracy? Treason? Murder?"

"Please tell me what I've done!" Walker screamed.

Utter stepped closer. "I'll tell you what you've done," he hissed softly. "You've underestimated Jesse Utter. Again. That's your big mistake. I've known who the hero down in L.A. is from the very first day. From *before* the first day. From the planning stages. I am in constant contact with the Crosskiller. I give him his orders, turncoat, I give him his fucking orders!"

"That's not true!" Walker lunged at Utter, and Tiny gave him a quick, vicious blow to the kidneys. Walker grunted and went to his knees. The pretty young woman kicked him in his crotch and he pitched forward to the floor, writhing and twisting.

Utter stood over him. "You think someone like the Crosskiller could operate in Southern California without my having intimate knowledge of his every move? When you walked in here I was just telling my troops about the last communiqué I received from him. You made a big mistake, informer. Throw this abomination out of here!"

Tiny and another huge biker type half carried, half bounced Walker across the floor and toward the door. Several men took swings at him as he was dragged by. One of the children spat in his face. Outside in the harsh glare of the sun, the two bikers flung Walker from the patio into the sandy soil.

"You git your sorry ass outta here, boy," Tiny said, and the biker went inside.

Walker rolled over in the dust. The pain in his back and groin pulsed through his body with his every heartbeat. He stood up shakily and wobbled back toward the brick house.

"It's not true! It's not true!" he shouted. Tears streamed down his cheeks.

Tiny and the other biker came back out on the patio. Tiny carried an M-16.

"If you know what's good for you, you'll git outta here, son," Tiny said.

"It's not true!" Walker shouted. *"It's not true!"*

He took a shaky step closer and Tiny squeezed off a burst from the M-16. The dust across Walker's path puffed up, then drifted listlessly away.

"I told you to git outta here," Tiny drawled. "Now git!"

Walker stood his ground. He was sobbing now, gulping back the tears. Faces crowded into the headquarters' two small windows, peering out.

"It's not true," he cried softly to Tiny.

Tiny came down from the raised patio and stood before Walker. With a flash of movement from his fleshy arms he slammed the flat side of his rifle butt across Walker's unprotected stomach. Walker thudded to his knees in the dirt, clutching his belly. His chin bounced off his chest as he struggled for each breath.

He raised his head and looked up at Tiny.

"It's not true," he choked, almost a moan.

Tiny rested the muzzle of the M-16 on Walker's cheek, just below his right eye.

"Do you want to die, son?" Tiny asked him.

Walker swallowed a sob. He looked up at Tiny and nodded.

"Yes," he whispered.

For several seconds the desert seemed to hold its breath, motionless. Then a large, ugly raven squawked clumsily down into the yard. Tiny jerked the rifle up, away from Walker's face.

"Git your nigger-loving ass outta here, son," he said, almost gently. "Let somebody else put you outta your misery."

Tiny stepped back and pointed out to where the cars were parked.

"Go on, *git!*"

Walker sobbed. He buried his face in his hands and rocked back and forth on his knees while he cried.

Tiny gestured to the other biker. They took hold of Walker under each arm and dragged him to the edge of the naked, sun-baked yard and rolled him down the incline to the makeshift parking lot. Walker lay where he fell, crying into the dust.

"You git in your van and git outta here, son, while you still can," Tiny shouted down at him.

The two bikers walked back up to the house.

After a while Walker got up, climbed into his van, and drove away through the brown hills.

8:15 PM It was still light out.

Nathan "Natty" Saperstein screeched the white Corniche off the west end of the Sunset Strip, swooped down into the sunken parking lot of Le Parc, braked to a jolting halt, and tossed the keys to Gregorio, the red-jacketed parking valet.

"Good evening, Mr. Saperstein. Will you be staying long?"

Saperstein smiled at Gregorio, and Gregorio returned the smile even more warmly. Too bad his taste ran to fair, Saperstein thought.

"I think we'll be staying through dinner, Gregorio. So I won't need the car for a few hours. Take good care of it."

"Of course, Mr. Saperstein," the boy said, licking his lips lightly as he jumped into the driver's seat.

Cheeky little bitch, Natty thought with amusement.

Just before opening the restaurant's high-tech polished-chrome doors, Natty checked out his appearance, as he did every night, in the panel of blue-tinted glass just to the right of the entrance. And, like every night, he was deeply pleased by what he saw: a small, gnomish, but distinguished-looking man, impeccably dressed. Nathan Saperstein had long ago come to terms with his five-foot-two-inch height, or lack of it. He learned that a man's power, a man's dangerousness, a man's status, had little to do with his physical stature. Today, when Natty Saperstein walked into a court-room, assistant district attorneys who had played in the offensive line for the USC football team swallowed their saliva and avoided his eyes. He had ended more than one budding legal career by tearing to shreds an unpre-pared opponent's seemingly airtight case. Freshman prosecutors drew straws to see who would argue against him. He was a man always described in personal profiles as a martinet, and Saperstein loved the sobriquet. It bespoke a ferocity, an inexhaustibility, that rich clients would pay dearly to have at their table in a courtroom. And many did. Natty Saperstein was a legend in L.A., a place peopled with legends. He was, simply, the best criminal defense lawyer in town. Period. If you had killed your wife or stabbed your lover, if you had gotten nabbed at LAX with a couple of keys stuffed into a false-bottomed suitcase, if you had embezzled from your company to finance base habits—if you had done any of these things, and were very rich, then Natty Saperstein's name had probably crossed your tongue. Mafiosi, movie stars, corporate executives, drug dealers—they had all used Natty Saperstein's expensive services. John De Lorean was rumored to have inquired at Saperstein's office initially, but felt he couldn't afford Natty's retainer. There had even been a story making the rounds a few years ago that an aging superstar, upon learning that her young, virile Italian "protégé" was also boffing the superstar's teenage son, had called to retain Natty's services, and only *then* had gone into the other room and shot the stud dead. She wanted to be sure Saperstein would defend her before she made her move. Natty, of course, neither confirmed nor denied the rumor.

Natty perused himself in the blue panel and smiled. There were those who said Natty had copied the sartorial style of the writer Tom Wolfe, and others who said just the opposite. Natty never commented on that story, either. Today he was wearing a lightweight three-piece vanilla-colored suit, a dark blue shirt with a white collar, a light blue tie, and a slouching fedora that perfectly matched the color of his suit. Every suit Natty owned had a similarly color-coordinated hat. It was his trademark. Natty had found decades ago that when practicing law in Hollywood, a little theater reassured the clients.

Below the hat Natty's shoulder-length silver hair spilled out perfectly over his tiny shoulders. The fashion of the eighties dictated a return to shorter hair, but Natty's career had skyrocketed in the late sixties when he had made the then much-deliberated decision to let his hair grow long, and now he refused, either through vanity or superstition, to cut it. Besides, the young boys adored it. Natty leaned closer into his reflection and twirled the waxed ends of his handlebar moustache, aligning them with symmetrical perfection. The moustache was also his trademark, and young men loved it, too.

Satisfied that his appearance was perfect, Natty opened the restaurant's doors and entered.

Henri, the maître d', rushed forward wearing an oily smile.

"Monsieur Saperstein, your party is already here. I put them at your table."

"Yes, I know, thank you. What's fresh tonight, Henri?"

"The sea bass looks very good, Monsieur Saperstein."

Natty's table—the booth in the farthest corner, against the back wall—was reserved for him every night except Sunday. Sundays Le Parc was closed. Even on the few occasions when Natty supped elsewhere, no one would be seated at his table. Crossing the room, several former clients—some with nationally recognizable faces—waved and said hello. Natty acknowledged them with a dry smile, but didn't stop to chat. He slipped into his booth next to an achingly beautiful young blond man with eyes so blue they looked painted in. Natty pressed the side of his body against the boy's and under the table slipped his hand up between the boy's legs and gently cupped his goodies. The boy smiled and squeezed his legs together.

"Natty, I haf zo much to tell you," the boy said in a thick Berlin accent. Once Natty had considered consulting a shrink to delve into the dark, Freudian passion he had for ass-fucking young Teutonic Apollos, but he quickly had shunted that thought aside, recognizing that if he ever opened the mental floodgates of his behavioral aberrations, he would likely be washed away in the deluge.

"So tell me," Natty smiled, accepting the martini the waiter had delivered automatically.

"Helen read my cards today." The boy beamed and nodded to the frumpy young woman seated across the table from them. "They were *wunderbar!*"

Natty didn't hate women. He simply had no use for them, except as clients. Then he could be as charming as a cobra. This poor thing was Eric's psychic—a usually harmless fantasy—and she kept him amused during the daylight hours.

"What did the *wunderbar* cards say, Helen?" he asked her.

Helen was a pale, overweight woman dressed in loose-fitting black garments. She wore an excess of black eyeshadow. When she really wanted to impress friends, she admitted that she was a witch.

Helen smiled mysteriously. "Good things are in store for our Eric," she breathed softly from between purple lips.

"It's zat part, Natty. Ze movie I vent up for," the boy said excitedly. "I told you I give a gud reading."

Natty sipped his martini. "That *is* wonderful."

"I'm going to get zat part. I know it. Ze cards were very positive. Right, Helen?"

"Very."

Natty smiled at her.

"Ze Queen of Cups came up," Eric said. "Helen zaid ze Queen of Cups never comes up. Isn't zat right, Helen?"

"Never."

"Helen zaid clients vould pay her to haf ze cards come out like zey did for me."

"The cards foretold a great future," Helen said. "Success in business. Fame. Fortune. Harmony. Happiness."

"That sounds delicious." Natty opened a black onyx cigarette case and withdrew a long gray cigarette. He lit it with a gold lighter.

"And luff," Eric said, smiling at Natty. "Ze cards predicted passionate, romantic luff."

Natty gave Eric's testicles another small squeeze under the table.

"We already have that," Natty said. Eric sighed and laid his head on Natty's shoulder.

Across the restaurant, at the bar hidden behind an ivy-covered trellis, Gold bought another double Scotch. He watched Natty and his party order their meal, saw the appetizers arrive, watched them eat the appetizers, saw the waiter take the plates away and bring the salads. Gold caught the bartender's eye and the bartender brought him another. Two young men in business suits whom Gold took to be lawyers stopped by Natty's table. Kibitzing. Paying court to the king. Natty said something and the two young lawyers laughed. Then they went away. Gold took his drink with him to the public phone booth by the cigarette machine.

Evelyn's voice answered.

"It's Jack. How's Wendy?"

"Jack. Wait a sec. Stanley wants to talk to you."

A few moments later Dr. Stanley Markowitz came on the line.

"Jack? It's Stanley."

"Stanley, how is she?"

"She's sleeping. I gave her a pretty heavy sedative again. We hired a nurse for Joshua. I don't want her thinking too much about what happened. Dwelling on it. She was pretty badly banged up, you know."

"I know."

"She was raped anally, too. Did you know that?"

Gold turned in the phone booth to watch Saperstein's table. The young blond boy was proposing a toast and Natty and the ugly woman had their wine glasses raised. They were all laughing.

"Jack, are you there?"

"Yes, I'm here. No, Stanley, I didn't know that."

"Still, I guess we're lucky. She could have been killed. She was certainly frightened enough."

"She didn't seem so—so disturbed last night when I took her to your place. She was furious at Howie, but otherwise she was pretty much in control of herself."

"Jack, have you handled many rape cases?"

"No."

"There's an aftershock syndrome. It can be pretty harrowing for some women. Wendy fits that profile to the letter. That's what I wanted to talk to you about."

"Yes?"

"Evelyn and I discussed it, and we want to take Wendy and the baby down to Cabo for a few weeks. Get her away. We've got a condo down there and I think a change of scene would be very beneficial right now, very recuperative. She doesn't even want to *see* Howie, and there's nothing else in town to hold her. What do you think, Jack?"

"I think that's a very good idea."

"Do you? Excellent. Evelyn's going to fly down with them tomorrow morning, and I'll follow as quickly as I can get away. I really think Wendy needs to put some distance between herself and last night's experiences."

"I couldn't agree more, Stanley. Thank you."

"What a horrible thing to happen to our little girl. And we don't even have any recourse."

The waiter was preparing a pasta dish on a hot cart at Natty's table. The flames leaped three feet high. The young man applauded.

"You never know, Stanley," Gold said.

After hanging up, Gold tapped out the number of his office. Zamora answered.

"You're working late," Gold said. "Anything turn up?"

"Not a thing. Say, Jack. Why don't we patrol the Westside together tonight? Our boy's bound to try again."

"That's a good idea, Sean, but let's do it single-O. We can cover twice the area in separate cars."

"Whatever you say, Jack." Zamora sounded disappointed. "I just want to be with you when you nail this dude."

"Don't worry, Sean. I promise you'll be there."

"Okay."

Gold went back to the bar and got a fresh drink. He watched Natty Saperstein through the ivied latticework.

"Zere vas only one bad card in ze whole reading," Eric said, popping a chunk of lobster onto his tongue.

"What was that?" Natty asked idly, twirling his linguini around his fork.

"Ze Skeleton. Ze death card."

Natty slipped the linguini into his mouth. A single strand dangled from his lips and he sucked it in.

"Zomeone very close to me is going to die," Eric said. "And very soon. Isn't zat true, Helen?"

Helen was buttering a piece of bread. "Very close. And very soon."

"It *must* be my grandmother. In Berlin. She's been very ill."

Natty took a sip of his Cabernet Sauvignon. "How old is she?"

"Ninety-one."

"What's her name?"

"Bertha."

Natty raised his wine glass in salute. "To Bertha. From Berlin. You can't live forever, but Bertha has surely done her best."

"Oh, Natty." Eric laughed and slapped his arm.

The bartender turned on a small television beside his cash register. The tube brightened and Audra Kingsley was at her anchor desk.

"—management and staff of this station wish to apologize to anyone who was offended by our erroneously referring to the perpetrator in the recent Westside killings as the *Christ*killer. We understand that that particular term is deeply resented by some segments of our viewing audience and we have had many phone calls pointing out our mistake. And that's exactly what it was—a mistake. An oversight. A slip of the tongue. And one for which we are gravely sorry. Now, here's Jeff Bellamy with our continuing coverage of the *Cross*killer investigation."

Jeff Bellamy's talking head filled the screen for a few seconds and then they went to filmed footage: the mayor at a press conference, Chief Huntz at a press conference, live cutins of increased police protection on the Westside, film of Jerry Kahn's JARs walking patrol in the Fairfax District, film of Jack Gold avoiding reporters' microphones outside Parker Center.

"Say," the guy to Gold's left said. "That's you."

Gold drained his glass, threw a twenty on the bar and left quickly, glancing back at Natty Saperstein's table. The waiter was offering them the dessert cart.

"When you gonna get that Crosskiller creep?" the guy at the bar called after him.

Gold crossed Sunset and got behind the wheel of his old Ford. It was well after dark now, and Gold switched on his headlights before U-turning across all five lanes. He headed east for a while on Sunset, turned south on Western, then came back over to Crenshaw. He found the address Honeywell had scribbled on the scrap of paper and parked down the block on the other side of the street. It was a duplex and in need of a paint job. Graffiti covered the fence.

When he was growing up, this neighborhood had been all white, or at least 90 percent. Gold could remember a few coloreds, a few Mexicans, but Crenshaw had been largely European immigrants—Armenians, Greeks, Poles, Italians—some Okies. There were even a few Jews. Then in the fifties and sixties it became almost all black. Now the Koreans were moving in and taking over.

There were lights on in the house.

Gold left his police radio on low. He felt around under the seat and came up with a silver flask. He unscrewed the cap and took a healthy swig. He scrunched down in his seat and watched the house.

Half an hour later the front door opened and light spilled out over the straggling brown lawn. A small black woman in her sixties came out, followed by a boy of nine or ten. On his shoulder the boy carried a knapsack bulging with what looked like books. They got into a late-model Buick parked at the curb and drove away. A few minutes later a slender, brown-skinned woman came out of the house.

She reminded Gold of Angelique. Angelique had been much prettier, of course, but there was some resemblance.

That would be Phibbs's wife. Gold checked the piece of paper for her name. Esther.

Esther Phibbs carried two new cellophane-wrapped mops and a plastic pail. She threw the stuff into the back of the station wagon in the driveway, went back and locked the house, came back out to the wagon, got in and drove away, heading north.

Gold considered following her. She might be going to meet Bobby Phibbs. She might be lying to the probation officer. She might be on her way to him right now.

On a hunch, Gold decided to stay put. He took another slug from the flask and kept his eye on the house. No one moved inside the duplex apartment. No shadows across the windows; no silhouettes on the shades.

Gold chewed his cigar and watched, listening closely to his radio.

He waited over an hour. Nothing happened. Nothing over the radio. Nothing in the house. Nothing on the street, if you didn't count a couple of high school kids in football jackets passing a joint as they bounced a basketball on their way down the sidewalk.

Gold started his car and pulled away from the curb. He checked his wristwatch as he passed under a streetlight. Ten fifteen. Gold clamped his teeth down on his cigar and drove back to Le Parc.

Natty Saperstein's Corniche with the DEFENSE license plates was not in the parking lot. Gold drove around the lot three times to be sure. Then he dropped the Ford into low gear and stomped it up the steep incline into the Hollywood Hills. His all-American gas guzzler wheezed and smoked its way up to the summit of the street, and Gold pulled over and parked to let it cool down. From up here, even through the smog that wouldn't blow away, L.A. was beautiful—a wide expanse of twinkling night lights that stretched out forever, looking like a Christmas display on PCP.

When the Ford stopped smoking, Gold started it up again.

Natty Saperstein's house was not hard to find. It had been famous in Los

Angeles for over sixty years, since its construction in the early twenties by a silent screen siren. It was not particularly large or lavish, but its Egyptian temple motif and garish pink-and-green stucco walls made it a favorite of guided bus tours through the hills.

Gold parked the sputtering Ford around the curve of a hill and walked back. Natty's Rolls was in the driveway. Gold looked around and, seeing no one on the street, walked quickly across the tiled patio and around the house to the arched doors that led out onto the balcony, overlooking the city, which ringed the outer walls of the house. There was music playing inside. Prince. Gold stepped carefully, silently, watching not to trigger the old house's security system. He carefully pushed aside a leafy branch and looked in a beveled glass window.

The young German boy lounged across a cushiony sofa, flipping through a magazine, naked except for black bikini underwear. His supple young body was oiled and glistening. Natty Saperstein stood at a polished mahogany bar, wearing a long, black silk kimono cinched at the waist with a matching sash, spooning cocaine into a tiny glass vial. He was hatless, and his silver gray hair was pulled back into a pony tail. After adding baking soda and a little water, he heated the vial over a delicate golden Bunsen burner, swirling the contents of the vial from time to time to separate the impurities from the coke. When the water in the vial was bubbling, Natty put it aside to cool. He lit a long dark cigarette and smiled over at the boy. When the coke had cooled sufficiently, Natty strained the contents of the vial through a square of silky cloth. The small chunks remaining were pure cocaine. He picked up one of the chunks gingerly and placed it on a tiny screen over the bowl of a tiny pipe. He flicked a gold lighter and touched the flame to the pure coke, inhaling sharply. He held his breath for almost a full minute, then exhaled slowly. The German boy, watching from the sofa, giggled. Natty turned to him and smiled.

"Come here," the little man said thickly. The boy rose languidly from the sofa and padded like a cat toward Saperstein. Natty held an arm out to him and the boy slipped into his embrace, rubbing his body against Saperstein's. The two men kissed passionately, Natty sliding his free hand over the boy's bikini-encased buttocks. The boy broke away with another coquettish giggle.

"Is zat mine?"

Natty smiled and placed some more cocaine onto the pipe's screened bowl. The German boy slid the stem between his lips, still giggling, and Natty put the lighter to the bowl. The boy sucked up the smoke through clenched teeth, his eyes tightly closed. When he had enough he turned his head away slowly. Natty put the bowl on the bar. The boy exhaled in another burst of giggles.

"You wasted it," Natty scolded softly.

"I am sorry," the boy said, and circled his arms around Natty's tiny neck. Natty pinched the boy's nipples and licked his throat. He stuck his hand down the front of the boy's bikini and pulled out his uncircumcised cock. He stroked it to an erection.

Gold made his way back to the car. The Ford took the way down the hill much more easily.

10:30 PM Hyman "Herschel" Guzman pushed his 260 pounds up laboriously from his E-Z Lounger in the den of his Encino split-level and snapped off the TV, immediately waking his tiny wife, Ruth, who had been dozing for an hour in the next chair.

"Herschel," she said sleepily, eyeing the ring of keys in his hand, "you're going to the store? At this hour?"

Herschel couldn't remember the last time anyone had called him by his given name, Hyman. Everyone, including his wife, called him Herschel. After his father. After the deli. Even when he was a kid and his old man was still alive, customers called him Little Herschel. Then, thirty years ago, his father died and he became *the* Herschel. Now, even he thought of himself as Herschel.

"Yeah," he grumbled, "I gotta go in."

"What for?" Ruth asked, already falling back to sleep.

"Jackie Max is coming in tonight. Probably bring in a big party. I gotta be there."

In reply, Ruth started snoring.

Herschel let himself out the back door, setting the lock quietly. He eased the big Eldorado all the way down the driveway before flipping on the headlights. On the way over the hill into Laurel Canyon Herschel made a mental check list of things he wanted to look into when he got to the deli: the chopped liver—Jackie Max lived on chopped liver on onion roll. The soda—Jackie hated ice in his soda, but he hated a warm Dr. Brown's even more. The bread—had they baked enough this morning? Jackie Max would be very disappointed if they ran out of onion rolls. He would make a scene in front of his whole party. Going for laughs, of course, but still putting Herschel down. That was his style, his *shtik*. He was a put-down comedian.

Herschel Guzman and Jackie Max had been—what? friends, you could call it that—for almost thirty years. Since right after Big Herschel died and he took over the store. Jackie Max had been a young, unemployed comedy writer then, scuffling around for gigs; emceeing strip shows on the eastern end of Sunset; hanging around CBS Television City, just down Fairfax from Herschel's Deli; looking to meet anyone who would give him his shot, his big chance.

Herschel had taken pity on the skinny, wolfish New York street punk. One night, unasked, he made Jackie Max a glorious chopped liver on onion roll, the chopped liver piled three fingers high, the dills crisp and glistening, the roll warm and sweet-sour smelling. He dropped it at Jackie Max's table, where the hungry-looking kid was nursing a cold cup of coffee and poring over a week-old issue of *Variety*. The kid looked at the sandwich, then up at Herschel.

"I didn't order that."

"I know."

"But—but, I don't have any money. I can't pay for it."

"That's all right. Pay me when you become a big star. Like everybody else around here."

Jackie Max's face grew serious. "I *am* gonna be a star. But I'm not like everybody else around here. I wanna work for this sandwich."

"Eat, kid," Herschel laughed. "Don't worry. It's only a sandwich."

"No, Herschel, I wanna work for it. Do you have any pots to clean, any dishes to wash?"

"Hey, kid, I got *shvartzers* to do that kinda thing. Do me a favor, just eat the sandwich."

"Wait a minute," Jackie Max said, looking around the deli. "All your signs are old. You need new signs. I can make 'em for you. My old man was a sign painter. He taught me how. In the morning I'll come back, I'll make all new signs. They'll make the place look great. Save you a fortune, too."

With that Jackie Max attacked the sandwich lustily, smiling up at Herschel and chewing with his mouth full. And in the morning, sure enough, he came back with his pens and brushes and made all new signs, bumping all the prices 20 percent without even asking. When Herschel complained, Jackie Max said, "How long those signs been up there?"

"Two years."

"It's time," Jackie Max said with finality.

"But the prices on the menus will be all wrong."

"The menus I'll fix."

After that Jackie Max came by every night after midnight. He would kibitz with the other young comics, trying out new routines, then he would order a chopped liver sandwich and a Dr. Brown's, and when the sandwich came he would say to the waitress, loudly and grandly, "Put this on my tab."

And he changed the signs regularly. And the menus. Then he painted the inside of the place, then the outside. The exterior of the building hadn't been redone in twenty years. Jackie Max made the old place gleam. And Herschel liked and respected him more than all the other show biz people who frequented his place. Actually, Herschel himself had little use for entertainment types. His father had been the one dazzled by the glitter, not him. He found the movie and television people who were his restaurant's mainstay a loud, lazy lot—cruel to each other, unfaithful to their women, untrustworthy in business dealings. He had no patience for actors who refused honest labor, but sat around his deli all night complaining about being out of work. Actors, shmactors! And their agents and managers— even worse! He had a drawerful of bad checks, dating back twenty-five years, written by big-mouthed young *gonifs* who told everybody they were the next Sam Goldwyn, then disappeared when the bank statements were mailed.

No, to Herschel Guzman, a man to whom sixteen-hour workdays had been the norm his entire life, show business people were highly overrated.

That's why he had taken a liking to the scrawny young Jackie Max thirty years ago. He was an exception to the rule.

Herschel still enjoyed telling customers about the day Jackie Max came to him and said, "Herschel. I can't make your signs anymore."

"Oh? You're going home? Good. Hollywood, shmollywood! This place is not for you."

"That's not it, Herschel," Jackie Max said with a face-splitting grin. "I got a series."

And *oy!* What a series! By its second month on the air "So This Is Love" was television's number-one-rated show. The joke-mined half hour series about a Brooklyn garbage man newly married to a Manhattan socialite seemed to reach down and touch 1950s America's heart and funny bone. The next-door neighbor's shrewish "Mr. Max, do us all a favor. *Take a bath!*" became the nation's newest catchphrase. The show was an un-qualified hit. And Jackie Max owned the whole damn *megillah.* He was the writer, director, and star. By the third season he was the producer, too. That was the year it was called "Jackie Max and So This Is Love?" The next year it became simply "The Jackie Max Show."

Altogether the series ran eight seasons, making Jackie Max a millionaire many times over. After the show's cancellation in 1964 Jackie Max starred in two self-financed movies that went straight into the dumper. The Holly-wood smart money, always eager to disseminate bad news, pronounced Jackie Max a small-screen star, said he couldn't make the transition to films. They said he was washed up, a period piece, a has-been. Jackie Max quietly retired to a farm in upstate New York and stayed there for over ten years. It was the decade of revolution, of change, of drugs. Jackie Max's gentle, sad-sack type of humor just didn't fit in an era when the word *Quaalude* always got the biggest laugh.

Then, in '78, Jackie Max started making limited appearances again. In nightclubs, in concerts, but most important, on various TV talk shows— Merv and Dinah, David and Dick. And, of course, Johnny. And he was so different! Fifty pounds heavier, his hair gone salt-and-pepper, clothed in English-tailored double-breasteds, he came on with a new kind of humor—sharp, acerbic, and hilarious. He had become an insult comic, a put-down artist, in the Don Rickles genre. But where Rickles was sweaty and manic, Jackie Max was cool and contained. Mr. Control. His barbed comebacks were like little diamonds of intelligent precision. They cut you and you bled mirth. Carson sprawled across his desk with uncontrollable laughter. The audience howled. The panel guest who was the recipient of Jackie Max's poisoned dart forced a smile and blushed with the effort.

Jackie Max was back!

Las Vegas, Atlantic City, Lake Tahoe. At first, to open for people like Sinatra, Martin, Davis. Then as a headliner. By the early eighties he was doing Nevada thirty weeks a year, sold-out concerts the rest of the time, pulling in five or six million per annum.

Then came the call from Neil Simon. A new play on Broadway. One of the principals written with Jackie Max in mind. Much less money than he was presently making, but what prestige, what respect!

Herschel Guzman made his first visit to New York—a cesspool!—to see his old friend in his new triumph. Herschel didn't think the play was so funny, but the audience obviously did, and that's what was important, right?

The show ran for two years, and now the New York company was coming out to L.A. Tonight's party at Herschel's Delicatessen was in celebration of the first day of rehearsal. Jackie Max insisted on its being held at the old place. And the party had to begin after eleven, Jackie Max's old prowling hours at Herschel's Famous Deli on Fairfax Avenue.

Herschel smiled to himself as he braked the Eldorado down Laurel Canyon Boulevard. He stopped at Sunset, watching the traffic go by.

Through all these years, Jackie Max had been a loyal—what?—friend, you had to say. Every time Jackie Max played the Tropicana or the Desert Inn, or Caesar's, Herschel got a call from Vegas, inviting him and Ruth over, everything taken care of. Everything on Jackie Max's tab. They went often, too. Ruth loved Vegas. Herschel, too, for that matter.

In fact, Herschel Guzman's strongest image of Jackie Max was of him in a luxury Vegas hotel suite, lying on a freshly made bed, naked except for a diamond-encrusted Star of David twinkling in his chest hair, being fellated by a *shiksa* hooker.

Herschel had knocked on the door of Jackie Max's hotel suite.

"Who is it?" Jackie Max called out through the door.

"Herschel."

"Where's Ruth?"

"Downstairs. At the slots."

"Come in. It's not locked."

Herschel opened the door and there was Jackie Max, superstar, stark naked, cracking jokes to a beautiful, fully dressed, Las Vegas Strip hooker, crouched over him on the bed, polishing his knob.

"Herschel," Jackie Max said, "I'm auditioning a new secretary. Right now she's taking shorthand, you might say."

The hooker giggled around Jackie Max's glistening cock, never breaking stroke.

"Or maybe you could call it *dick*tation."

The whore giggled again and mumbled something unintelligible.

"That's a mouthful, honey." Then to Herschel, "What a head for business!"

Another giggle.

"And I want you to know, Miss Fletcher, if you get this position, I'll never ask you to make coffee."

That did it. The hooker burst out laughing and Jackie Max's red, spit-shined *putz* plopped out of her mouth and bounced on his belly.

"I guess you realize, Miss Fletcher, this means you don't get the job."

The hooker doubled over with laughter, her arms wrapped around her stomach.

Herschel, turning down Fairfax Avenue, chuckled at the memory.

Jackie Max was something special, all right. That's why everything had to be perfect tonight. So stop worrying, he told himself. What could go wrong? What could go wrong! With the night crew? *Oy!* Everything!

He once had a night-shift waitress who turned tricks in the ladies room. Coffee, tea, or me? Me? Second stall on the left. I'll be there in five minutes.

Another late-shift waitress, an innocent-looking young thing, he caught pushing marijuana to customers who looked like they might be interested.

Once, years before, a busboy, barely sixteen, had cut the throat of a dishwasher back in the kitchen in the middle of the after-theater rush.

What can happen? With the night shift, anything. Anything and everything.

Herschel parked the Eldorado in his own parking lot, which, he noted with satisfaction, was almost full. He walked the half block to the deli. It was 11:15.

11:40 PM Walker slowly cruised the streets of the Westside of Los Angeles, trying to figure out what God was attempting to tell him.

He knew God was trying to give him a message, but he just couldn't make it out. It seemed always to be just out of vision, just out of reach, out of hearing. But always around. So close and all around.

God works that way. Walker knew that.

Walker popped another upper.

Like today. With Jesse Utter and his henchmen. That had been a test. He knew that now. Like Jesus was tested in the wilderness, in the desert. An obstacle sent by God to test his mettle, to examine his resolve.

Those people were all Jews. Sonny realized that now. Jews and dupes. Devils and witches. Anti-Christs. He would scourge them with flame and pain. He would make them pay for what they had done. The blood was on their hands. The blood of the baby Jesus. They had brought Jesus' revenge down upon their heads.

The Jews must be punished for what they had done. Then all mankind would finally be free.

God help the Christkillers.

11:41 PM Gold, sitting in his car parked on Crenshaw Boulevard, watched the well-built man walk to the end of the block, turn, come back, and walk past. It was his third time by. This time he passed under the ghostly glow of the street lamp. He was the man in the photograph Honeywell had messengered over to him this afternoon. He was Bobby Phibbs.

Phibbs walked in front of the house again. This time he paused, looked up and down the street, then moved quickly up the walk. He took a key from his pants pocket and inserted it in the lock. It wouldn't turn. He examined it closely under the porch light. Then he tried it again. It still wouldn't turn.

"Bitch!" Phibbs spat angrily, shaking the doorknob. "Motherfucking bitch!"

Phibbs left the front door and went around to the rear of the house. Shadows darkened the small, hedged-in backyard. He went to a window and clawed at a screen. It was eye-hooked from the inside. He dug in his pocket and came up with a three-inch switchblade. He popped the blade, pushed it through the screen, and ripped up along the edge of the wooden frame.

"Don't move, asshole," Gold said, touching the back of Phibbs's head with the muzzle of his gun barrel. "Don't turn around."

"Motherfucker!" Phibbs cursed softly. "Mother*fucker!*"

"Just keep it relaxed," Gold said from behind, carefully plucking the blade from Phibbs's hand.

"Hey, man." Phibbs laughed. "You think I was breaking in my own damn house? This is my own house, man. I lost my key. No shit, brother, I live here. Lemme show you my I.D."

Phibbs started to turn around, and Gold slammed him against the house.

"You try that again, I'll blow the top of your fucking skull off, hear me?"

"Okay. Okay, man. Whatever you say. I'm just trying to tell you, man, that you making a mistake here, man. I fucking *live* here, man. You can't burglarize your *own* motherfucking house."

Gold pulled Phibbs's arms back and handcuffed his wrists behind his back. He patted him down quickly.

"Man, would you please listen to me!" Phibbs said in exasperation. "This is my own motherfucking house!"

"Shut up, Bobby."

"Hey, man, you know my name. Then you know I live here. Me and the ol' lady had a little thing last night. I came back to get my clothes, and the crazy bitch done changed the motherfucking locks. I'm going to see 'bout a job in the morning and I need some clean—"

Gold rammed his elbow into the small of Bobby Phibbs's back. Bobby grunted and leaned against the house.

"I said shut the fuck up!" Gold rasped.

Gold yanked a folded pillowcase from his pocket and whipped it open. He pulled it over Bobby's head.

"Hey, man, what the—"

Gold slammed the barrel of his .38 against the back of Bobby's head. Bobby's knees buckled and he crumbled against the clapboard, sinking down to the hard ground.

Gold ran down the driveway and checked the street. It was empty both ways. He ran back to where Bobby was lying in the dirt, moaning. He pulled the handcuffed, blindfolded Bobby Phibbs to his feet.

"Walk where I tell you to walk and don't say a motherfucking word."

Gold quick-stepped Bobby down to the Ford and opened the door on the passenger side. He pushed Bobby Phibbs's considerable bulk down on the floorboard into a praying position, his pillowcased face against the car seat. Gold ran around to the other side of the car and got behind the wheel. Steering away from the curb with his left hand, he pulled his .38 from his belt and pushed it hard into the pillowcase fabric.

"Just relax," he growled. "Don't move. Don't talk. Nothing."

He drove for only about five minutes. To a place just north of downtown where five freeways intersected, twisting back and cloverleafing over each other like an engineer's absently doodled curlicues. Gold parked the Ford on an empty street of industrial warehouses that dead-ended in a wire fence looking down onto the swirling traffic of the converging freeways. Gold dragged Phibbs from the car, pushed him over to the fence where the wire had been snipped and the chain-link folded back. Gold went through the opening and pulled Phibbs behind him. There was a steep, litter-strewn dropoff down to a row of massive, reinforced-concrete pillars—part of the freeway. Gold stepped behind Phibbs and pushed him hard with the tip of the baseball bat he had taken from the Ford's trunk. Phibbs crashed end over end until he thudded heavily against one of the pillars. Gold slid down after him. Phibbs was trying to get to his feet. He was breathing heavily behind the pillowcase. Gold pulled him up by the handcuffs.

"Hey, man!" Bobby's voice was shaky, fearful, muffled. "Who the fuck are you? Who the fuck are you, man?"

Gold didn't answer. He prodded Bobby through a narrow corridor between several of the freeway pillars. On the other side of the crevice was a perfect man-made cave formed by the converging overhead freeways. The

walls, the ceiling, the littered floor—all were graffitied cement. U.S. OUT
OF EL SALVADOR. DOMINIC AND ROSA. FOR A GOOD BLOW JOB CALL
REUBEN. Something scuttled away through the discarded cigarette butts.
This place had been a popular shooting gallery years ago, until a slasher
started offing blissed-out winos and junkies in here. Now the street people
never came around. They said the rathole was haunted.

Gold pushed Bobby Phibbs into the center of the cave and then stepped
away from him. Both men were sweating heavily.

"Are you a cop, man?" Bobby shouted through the pillowcase over the
roar of the traffic echoing above them, all around them. "If you a cop, then
motherfucking arrest me, man! Take me back to motherfucking jail! But
don't do this shit, man!"

Gold leaned back against a dirty pillar and pulled a cigar from his
pocket. He lit it. He blew the smoke in Bobby's direction.

"What you want, man?" Bobby yelled.

Gold blew another puff of smoke.

"What you—"

"Did you have a good time last night, Bobby?"

Bobby was silent.

"Did it make your dick harder, beating up on that white bitch?"

Bobby turned his head slightly, as if to see Gold better through the
pillowcase.

"Which did you enjoy more, beating her or fucking her?"

"Hey, man, I don't fucking know what you talking about."

"Getting high, hurting, and raping. Life don't get much better than that,
does it, Bobby?"

"You crazy, man! You motherfucking crazy!"

"You and Alonzo had a real party last night, didn't you, Bobby? Well,
we're gonna have another party. Tonight. Right here. Just you and me.
And when the party's over you're gonna tell me everything I want to know.
Who set up the takedown. Who gave you the mark's address. Who you
took the keys to. But before then we gonna have fun, baby. Fun-n-n-n!"

"Man, you outta your motherfuck—"

Gold swung the bat viciously, low and hard. Bobby Phibbs's kneecap
exploded with a hollow *pop!* like a light bulb dropped from a second story.
Bobby screamed and writhed crablike on the shitty cement, kicking out his
good leg in an effort to escape the pain.

"It wasn't me, man! It was Alonzo!" he screamed. "It was all Alonzo!
He come to me with the score! His lawyer give to him! Jew lawyer! Natty
Saperstein! He set it up! Natty Saperstein! *Natty Saperstein!*"

Gold stepped over Bobby and raised the bat again.

"It's not gonna be that easy, Bobby," he said. "Not nearly that easy."

FRIDAY
August 10

2:37 *AM* Herschel Guzman was extremely pleased. Everything had gone well. Beautifully, in fact.

Jackie Max and his party of forty-one—*forty-one!*—had arrived at 12:15, laughing and joking as only show people can. They had taken over the whole front dining room. They ordered lox and bagels, eggs and sausage, blintzes, pastrami, ham and Swiss—everything. Herschel constructed an enormous chopped liver on onion roll and presented it to Jackie Max with an exaggerated flourish that prompted a big round of applause. Jackie Max laughed and stuck his tongue down the throat of one of the chorus line dancers seated at his table. More applause. In the crowd were also writers, musicians, techies, actresses, groupies, and a couple of the money people—basking in the glow of their rented celebrity. Herschel also recognized several theater critics, that fag reviewer from TV, and a few old Las Vegas lounge comics from Jackie Max's early days.

The party was loud and raucous. Soon even the other customers became part of the celebration. Someone pulled a gallon of whisky from a paper bag—Herschel's had a license for beer and wine only—and for the first time in his life, Herschel pretended he didn't see. Jokes were told, old stories embellished, outright lies concocted. Jackie Max got staggering drunk and kept threatening to pull out his *putz.* Herschel told him he'd slice it off and display it in the deli case. Jackie Max boasted it would feed thousands. Everyone laughed loudly.

Around two o'clock the crowd had started to trickle out. Jackie Max was one of the last to leave, supported by two busty chorines. At the door on his way out he threw his arms around Herschel's neck and kissed him on both cheeks.

"Hey, *bubeleh,* you need any signs painted?"

The chorus girls carried him to the waiting limousine. The rest of the party staggered after.

Now Herschel and his waitresses were clearing the tables, clattering the dirty plates and glasses back to the kitchen, moving chairs around so the busboys could mop the floors. Herschel was cleaning and polishing the big stainless-steel meat slicer behind the deli case. It never got done right unless he did it himself.

There were only a few late-night customers left—rock 'n' roll types sitting around sipping coffee and telling each other their rock 'n' roll dreams.

The biggest party was a table of six: three members of a thrash-bang, recently signed postpunk garage group called the Scuzz and the lead singer's old lady, seated across the table from the drummer and bassist of the all-girl band the Lollipops. For the past fifteen minutes the bassist from the Lollipops, who called herself Qwikie, had been playing footsie under the table with Scar, the Scuzz's lead singer, and Scar's old lady, an ex-Hell's Angels possession and not a bitch to be fucked with, was deciding whether to slash Qwikie's face now or stomp the shit out of her in the parking lot.

Along the wall, under the autographed caricatures of the famous, were three tables of deuces: two young New York actors telling each other why they hated L.A. so much, a fortyish gay couple trying to talk themselves out of breaking up, and two female screenwriters hashing out the climax of their third unsold screenplay.

Birdie, a fat old blond waitress of sixty, was the first to see him.

"Get out of here!" she shouted and started lumbering clumsily toward the kitchen, scattering tables and chairs in her wake.

Qwikie, facing the door, saw him next and let out a high-pitched scream that survivors later testified made the hairs on the back of their necks jump as if electrified.

Scar stood up and turned around. A sneer curled on his lips. A nihilistic punker to the end, he laughed, picked up a beer bottle by its long neck, and started toward the man in the doorway.

Herschel, just that moment kneeling behind the deli counter to retrieve a fallen butcher knife, heard Birdie shout, heard Qwikie's frightful scream, and then Scar's strange chuckle. These goddamn musicians, he thought to himself, then straightened up and looked over the deli case.

Just in time to observe the man with the shotgun in the doorway pump two quick shells into Scar's belly. Scar's midsection exploded like a ripe watermelon, squirting flesh and blood out of the front, back, and sides of his black *X* T-shirt. The blasts knocked his already dead body back onto the table where he had just been sitting. Qwikie's scream, which had never really stopped, jumped to a new hysterical pitch. Then it was cut short by another shotgun blast, and Qwikie's head became a gooey, bloody mess. She toppled over in her chair, her black-stockinged legs twitching grimly.

By now everyone else in the deli, a second ago frozen in horror, was throwing themselves under tables and booths, trying to claw through the tile flooring.

Big Birdie, still lumbering toward the kitchen, was the obvious target.

The broad back of her white uniform erupted into a geyser of crimson and she went down like a felled elephant.

From behind the counter, Herschel flung the butcher knife at the gunman. The blade clattered to the floor ineffectively, ten feet short.

The man in the doorway turned toward Herschel and pumped a shell at him. Herschel, ducking, felt a white searing heat in his left shoulder as he threw himself to the work boards that ran behind the counter. The man in the doorway fired six times rapidly into the deli case, raining flying glass and bits of meat down on Herschel's back.

Then he stepped a few feet into the deli, calmly reloaded the 12-gauge, and randomly emptied the weapon around the room. Someone hiding under a table screamed *"Stop it! Stop it!"* over and over.

The man held the shotgun with one hand, turned, and with the other spray-painted a huge dripping red cross over the big front window of the delicatessen.

Then, unbelievably, he was gone.

The lady screenwriter, cringing behind an overturned table, still howled, *"Stop it! Stop it! Stopitstopitstopitstopit!"*

2:59 AM Fairfax Avenue was empty.

Walker ran to the corner and headed west, leaving the bright lights behind. He ran for several blocks before he realized he was still carrying the empty shotgun. He slipped down a dark, narrow alley between two apartment houses. At the end of the alley he kicked out the cover of a basement crawl space, tossed the shotgun deep under the house, then pulled the cover back into place.

Back in the street he turned again toward the west. And froze.

An LAPD patrol car, red and blue lights flashing, was blocking the intersection.

Walker raced across the street and down another alley. At the end of the alley he clambered over a crumbling concrete wall, sprinted across the roof of a garage, and dropped down into a shadowy driveway. He ran down the driveway and into the next street.

The patrol car screeched around the corner, coming after him.

He ran across the street and down another driveway. He jumped onto the hood of a car, pounded over the roof, and leaped over a weed-choked wire fence. He found himself in a long, gravel garbage-collection alley. He managed a full tilt half block before another police car, siren screaming, roared into the end of the alley. Someone behind him was shouting something. He heard little faraway pops, then something whistle past his ear. They were shooting at him.

Walker threw himself down alley after alley. Hedges and rose bush thorns ripped at his face, pointed fence posts tore at his legs. Bullets *pinged!* on the sidewalk behind him. He lost his direction. He couldn't remember where he had parked his van. The night was rent by a dozen sirens. Dozens of sirens. All around him. He raced into a park, a place where in the daylight hours old men played bocci, and thudded across the damp grass. Sprinklers suddenly spurted all around him, arcing jets of water glinting in the moonlight. Walker tumbled down a gentle hill and landed against a baseball batting cage. He clawed himself over the chain-link and plopped down on the other side. He crawled to a dark corner and leaned back against the fence, gulping for his breath. His clothes, soaked from the sprinklers and his panicked sweat, were plastered to his body.

Suddenly it was midday.

He was caught in the phosphorous glare of a searchlight shining down from the sky. A helicopter hawked down on him, loudspeakers blaring.

"Don't move! Stay where you are! Don't move!"

Walker pounded across neatly manicured lawns, the spotlight chasing him like a huge, luminous shadow.

"Don't move! Stay where you are! This is the police! Stay where you are!"

There were more little pops behind him. And rapid footsteps. Furious leather on concrete. Several sets. Walker threw himself over a brick wall and a huge German shepherd tore at his heels as he stumbled through a tiny backyard cluttered with plastic lawn furniture. He battered his shoulder against a gate and the wood splintered and gave. The shepherd stood in the street and howled. Walker lost the stabbing probe of the searchlight on a narrow street shadowed by tall palms and avocado and rubber trees. The yellow glare filtered through the leaves as the helicopter hunted for him—*whoomp! Wa-hoomp!*—in frantic little circles.

Walker burst through a thick hedge onto a street and saw it had no rotating red-and-blue lights. His lungs felt on fire and his side ached, but he forced himself to accelerate down the sidewalk.

Footsteps behind him. But only one set. And farther back.

He pumped across the vast, darkened parking lot of a deserted shopping center. The helicopter was searching for him elsewhere now, several blocks away, its pool of light darting over the rooftops. The sirens were far away now, like the distant baying of hounds.

He stopped and tried to quiet his heart, his breathing, so he could hear. No footsteps. No one following behind him.

He found his van where he had left it, parked behind the shopping center's supermarket. He slammed the cargo door open and fell in, too exhausted to close it behind him. His side throbbed. His ragged breath tore at his lungs like a rusty blade. Leaning back against the wall of the van he pulled his knees up to his heaving chest and gulped for oxygen.

Suddenly he went cold and still.

Footsteps! Close and tentative.

Walker slipped his hand into the hollow under the driver's seat and came out with the .357. He laid the weapon in his lap and folded an unsold newspaper over it. He forced himself to breathe slowly, through his nostrils.

The footsteps were very close. Hard rubber heels crunching on pebbles. Walker waited.

A young uniformed cop stepped stealthily into sight through the open cargo door. He saw Walker and tensed, his revolver held stiffly out in front of him.

"Get out of there!" he ordered in a shaky voice.

"What's the matter?" Walker asked.

"Just get the fuck out of there!" the young cop shouted, and Walker shot

him. The bullet crashed through the young cop's forearm and ripped into his heart. The impact threw him back ten feet and his finger jerked reflexively. Walker felt the heat of the cop's bullet as it kissed his cheek on its way through the shell of the van.

Walker stood erect and stared down at the dead cop. He shot the body again, just to be sure.

He slammed the sliding door closed and twisted the van's ignition key. The helicopter was only a few blocks away now, circling like a hungry falcon. Walker drove back streets for several blocks, then slipped into the light late-night traffic on La Cienega. Three police cruisers suddenly appeared in his rearview mirror. Walker drove with his left hand and held the Magnum in his right. The police cars swooshed around him and tore away. Walker breathed again.

A few blocks farther on he entranced onto the freeway and was gone.

5:07 *AM* If before it had been bad, now it was bedlam.

The media were everywhere, stepping on each other's toes, tripping over each other's power lines, babbling in various languages into microphones about the "Delicatessen Massacre." The banks of hot lights gave roped-off Fairfax Avenue an otherworldly illumination, making the block in front of Herschel's Deli appear like nothing so much as a motion picture shoot, and obliterating the smoggy sunrise that glowed in the east.

It *was* like theater, Gold thought. Shakespearean tragedy. Bloody and bloodthirsty and unavoidable. Three dead—four, counting the young cop—two badly wounded, three sustaining superficial injuries and shock. One of the seriously injured was his old friend Herschel Guzman, rushed by ambulance to nearby Cedars-Sinai in critical condition. The other badly wounded victim was one of the New York actors. A random shotgun blast had ripped open his chest, and no one expected him to live. His fellow New Yorker had suffered only the sting of a few stray shotgun pellets, as had the distraught lady screenwriter and the the Scuzz's bassist. The unharmed survivors—the gay couple, the other lady screenwriter, the Scuzz's drummer and guitarist, and the late Scar's old lady–widow, and all the waitresses and busboys who had been in the kitchen when the attack occurred—were currently giving statements and descriptions to members of the task force. Some of them had already been gently guided into the back seats of police cars and driven to Parker to look at mug shots. The mayor and Chief Huntz, looking tousled and hurriedly dressed, had set up a makeshift podium under the lights at one end of the block and were holding an impromptu news conference for the jostling, shouting press. Two reporters from rival Japanese news services got into a fistfight and had to be restrained. Dolly Madison stood just behind the chief, whispering self-importantly into Huntz's ear. Councilman Orenzstein was there, trying to appear pertinent. The reporters kept shouting the mayor down with new questions before he could answer the ones he had already been asked. The mass of journalists kept surging this way and that like some kind of giant amoebic animal. The whole scene had a dangerous anarchic tone and threatened to become a riot at any moment.

The news of the massacre had spread like a fire alarm through the whole Fairfax District, and the residents, mostly elderly and all in robes and bedclothes, had gathered from out of their homes and apartments to crowd twenty and thirty deep behind the yellow police barriers and stare with dead, ancient eyes at the crimson cross scrawled obscenely across the show window of Herschel's Delicatessen.

Gold went into the deli again. Zamora followed. The shattered glass from the deli case crunched beneath their heels. Gold walked through the store silently. The lab people were still there—taking pictures, drawing diagrams, dusting for fingerprints.

Gold stripped the cellophane from a fresh cigar and put the wrapper in his pocket. He lit the cigar.

"What was the rookie's name again?"

Zamora flipped through his notebook. "Estevez."

"How long had he been in harness?"

"Seven months."

Gold shook his head. "If he'd had more experience he wouldn't have gotten separated from his partner like that. Wouldn't have tried to take that motherfucker alone."

Zamora shrugged. "His partner was older, overweight. Couldn't keep up. Estevez is a jogger. *Was.*"

Gold crunched on his cigar. "Probably left a pregnant wife and a houseful of kids."

"Matter of fact, he was a bachelor."

Gold rolled his eyes at the ceiling. "Why doesn't that make me feel any better?"

Gold walked over to where a lab technician was spooning blood from a pool into a test tube. The blood was an inch thick and had jelled into the consistency of custard. Gold puffed his cigar.

"What was that victim's name? The actor from New York? The one who's going to die?"

Zamora studied his notebook again. "O'Connor. David John O'Connor."

"O'Connor," Gold mused. "Birdie Williamson, Catherine 'Qwikie' Acosta, and Milton 'Scar' Scarbrough. And the rookie Estevez. Not a Jew in the bunch. Our boy is slipping. Not as energy-effective. At this rate it'll take him forever to exterminate us."

Zamora gave the older man a puzzled expression.

"Let's get the fuck out of here," Gold growled.

Out in the street the crowd had thickened and tightened, pressing forward for a closer look. The mayor was still addressing the reporters, bathed in the intense white glare of the TV lights.

"What now?" Zamora asked. "Parker, to interview the survivors?"

Gold surveyed the crowd. "I'm going to stop home first. Take a shower. This is going to be a very long day."

"Want me to come with you?"

"No, I'll meet you at Parker."

The two men started to walk in opposite directions. Just then there was a loud disturbance behind one wing of the crowd. The sea of people parted and Jerry Kahn and his JAR recruits jogged forward, angrily chanting, "Never again! Never again! Never again!" Kahn's nose was covered by a wide white bandage. He began shouting over the rhythmic chanting.

"The Jews have long memories, Mr. Mayor!"

He shook his fist at the mayor, who had been interrupted in mid-sentence.

"The Jews have long memories, Mr. Mayor! We will never forget those who use Jewish blood as a lubricant to grease their political wheels."

The reporters turned their backs on the mayor and rushed to stick microphones in Kahn's face. Councilman Orenzstein managed to look distressed and pleased at the same time. Huntz fumed.

"All of you!" Kahn shouted, pointing to the mayor's party. "All of you are guilty of these atrocities! All of you share in this! And this will not go unpunished!"

Dolly Madison rushed forward.

"Those people have weapons," he said to Kahn. "That cannot be tolerated."

"Fuck you, *goy!*" Kahn snarled. "If the police won't protect us, then we'll damn well protect ourselves. We won't tolerate being murdered in the night anymore. The Jews 'go quietly' no longer. Never again! Never again!" He turned to exhort his Resisters. "Never again! Never again!"

They took up the chant.

"Never again! Never again!"

The minicams whirred. Techies raced to beam lights down on the confrontation.

"We can't allow you to carry those weapons," Dolly Madison persisted.

"Then come take them away from us," Kahn challenged, his eyes blazing with messianic zeal. "Before the eyes of the world, show us what the LAPD does to Jews who only want to protect themselves. Show the world how you handle Yids here in Los Angeles."

Dolly Madison was immobilized, confused. He glanced back over his shoulder at the media.

"Wait—wait here!" he sputtered to Kahn, then turned on his heels and trotted over to Chief Huntz, whose face was set and cold.

Kahn gave a signal and his young Resisters fanned out along the perimeter of the crowd behind the yellow police tape. They stood at fifteen-foot intervals, their rifles held at arms inspection across their chests.

"Hey, Uncle Ike!" Kahn had spotted Gold. "That *goy* isn't as ballsy as the token Jew. He needs to talk to his boss. You just bust people up."

Gold shook his head. "You're a *putz,* Kahn. Get the fuck out of here and let us do our job."

"If you cops did your job we wouldn't have to be here. But then why should here, today, be any different? We Jews have always had more to fear from the policemen of the world than to feel safe about. And where does that leave you, Uncle Ike?"

Gold stared pointedly at Kahn's bandaged nose. "You don't look real good now, Commander in Chief. Are you trying for a crutch, too?"

Kahn's smile was more a snarl. "The cameras are rolling, Gold. But then you always do your best work in the black of night. Or is it just in *black*?"

Gold had already started toward Kahn when Dolly Madison ran between them.

"Mr. Kahn," he said, a little out of breath, "due to the extraordinary situation existing in this city at this time, the mayor and the chief have decided that your people may keep their weapons if you give us every assurance they'll be kept unloaded."

"What the fuck good is an empty gun?" Kahn barked.

Dolly Madison blinked rapidly. "That's good enough for the chief," he said, forcing a tight smile. "I hope we can work together on this. I hope the JAR and the LAPD won't be at cross-purposes on this."

Kahn stared at him a second, then burst into laughter. He turned to Gold.

"Hey, Uncle Ike, is this *goyisher shmuck* for real?"

Gold turned and walked away. He could hear Dolly Madison saying, "Maybe, Mr. Kahn, we can give a joint statement to the press, detailing the close cooperation of the police force and the community with regards to this investigation."

Kahn was laughing again.

Gold pushed his way through the crowd. He found his car and started it up. Three blocks from Herschel's Deli the seven o'clock traffic was flowing smoothly, unaware or uncaring of the blood congealing on Herschel's tile floor. Gold was struck, as always, by how small a ripple a pebble thrown into the pond that was Los Angeles seemed to make. L.A. was just too big, too turbulent, too decentralized. The Dodgers in a pennant race united the city. A mass murderer on the Westside seemed to isolate it.

Gold was unlocking the door to his apartment when a rolled newspaper arced through the air and landed with a loud slap at his feet. Genghis, Mrs. Ackermann's Pekinese in the apartment across the courtyard, began barking furiously. The news carrier, well built, thirtyish, in blue jean cut-offs and a long-sleeved sweatshirt, jogged around the narrow walk that squared the courtyard. He hadn't seen Gold yet, so he was startled when Gold said, "Running a little late this morning?"

He stared at Gold and didn't say anything.

Gold stepped forward a few feet. The carrier's face sported several fresh scratches.

"Had a little trouble, did you?" Gold asked.

The carrier looked puzzled. He stared dumbly at Gold.

"You *are* American?" Gold asked. "*¿Habla inglés?* You speak English?"

The carrier nodded slowly.

"Well, you hear that dog barking?" Gold pointed toward the sound of the Pekinese's staccato yapping. "You start that little dog barking every morning because you run through this courtyard a little too carelessly. Mrs. Ackermann, over there, asked me to speak to you because I'm her neighbor and because I'm a police officer. So, do us both a favor and take it a little easier coming through here. Toss your papers with a little less zip, okay?"

The carrier was still silent.

"Okay?" Gold asked again.

The carrier nodded slowly again. "Yes," he finally managed.

"Good." Gold turned his back and stooped to pick up his newspaper. He walked into his apartment and shut the door on the carrier, who stood still staring after him.

Inside, the radio was playing softly. "Miles in Europe," '62 or '63. Seventeen-year-old Tony Williams on drums.

Gold poured himself three ounces of Scotch and belted it back. He poured another half glass and carried it into the bathroom.

2:59 PM By midday the temperature had reached 102 degrees downtown at the Civic Center. And then there was the smog. Third-stage alerts all over the county. "Hazardous to your health" everywhere. The worst episode in seventeen years, the radio proclaimed. Inversion layers. Trapped molecules. Pollutants. Acidics. Visibility was down to half a block. Schools were let out early. Industries shut down. Workers were fined if they didn't carpool. The sidewalks were deserted. Emergency wards were swamped with old people, asthmatics, children who couldn't breathe.

At three o'clock Walker went to his foreman and said he didn't feel good; he wanted the rest of the day off. The foreman, a Mexican, denied him, reminding Walker he had gotten off early the day before. Walker gave him a strange smile, then stalked off the loading dock. He drove his van to the nearest phone booth and ripped out the page of gun shops. The closest was two blocks away. He bought another shotgun, a 12-gauge, to replace the one he'd ditched last night, a hunting knife with a ten-inch blade, and several boxes of shells. At the next location he purchased a 20-gauge pump-action, another heavy-hafted knife, some cartridges for his .357, several canteens, and a pair of heavy-duty hiking boots. From the last shop he got a camping stove, a tent, a sleeping bag, some more canteens, some surplus survival rations, a machete, a fifty-foot length of nylon rope, some gaffer's tape. And a repeating rifle.

He threw the weapons and the paraphernalia into the back of his van and drove over to the small frame house with the tiny screened-in front porch. Terri's place. He double-parked on the quiet, curving street and loaded the new 12-gauge with the double-ought shells. He carried the shotgun with him up the cracked walk. The screen door was unlatched but the front door was locked. He kicked out viciously at the door, but the lock held. He stepped back, brought the shotgun up to waist level, and blasted the lock. The door flew open. He ran through the little house calling softly, "Terri. Terri." Clothes were strewn about. Food was hardening on the cold stove. Walker checked the closets, under the beds, behind the furniture. Finally, he saw the note Scotch-taped to the refrigerator.

Kevin,
Abe and me went to Vegas. Be back Monday morning. You can

stay with André. I talked to Jeanette. Be good and bring your tooth-brush.

Luv ya,
Mom

P.S. Congratulate us!!!!

Walker sat for a while at the dinette table, rereading the note, the shotgun cradled on his lap. Then he trashed the place. Calmly, methodically, he went through the little frame house smashing everything—dishes, furniture, appliances, glasses, dishes, photographs. He used the stock of the shotgun as a club and brought it down again and again. He got a knife from the kitchen cupboard and slashed the mattresses, the pillows, the cushions, Terri and Kevin's clothes, photographs—everything. He took the shotgun into the bathroom and drove the butt through the vanity mirror over the basin. He bludgeoned the fixtures off and water spurted in three-foot geysers. Back in the living room he spray-painted on the walls DEATH TO THE JEW LOVERS and JEW WHORE and ALL JEWS MUST DIE and everywhere the red, slashing crosses.

He walked back out to the van, laid the shotgun on the seat beside him, and drove away slowly. No one had seen him.

He headed east out of the city, toward the desert. In San Bernardino he bought gas and filled all the canteens with water. He turned off the freeway onto a narrow country road leading out into the wilderness. At a ramshackle roadside stand he purchased bread, peanut butter, coffee, and fruit. About three miles beyond the stand the road petered out. Walker pointed the van toward a majestic butte far off in the desert and drove carefully across the sand and chaparral. Several times he had to get out and tear down barbed-wire fences in his way. Once he heard an ATV a few miles away. Walker held the rifle and waited, but the *brrrrr* faded into the distance. When he finally reached the base of the outcropping of rock the sun was setting in a blaze of smoggy reds and oranges. The western sky was a furnace of color. Walker stripped naked except for socks and the hiking boots. He rolled in the desert dust like a dog, laughing and moaning. He squatted on his heels and defecated, bending to watch his excrement plop into the red sand.

He walked toward the setting sun, his arms outstretched. He knelt in the desert and gave thanks to his god, his Christ.

He knew who he was now.

He was the right hand of God.

He was the Avenging Angel.

In his hands rested the fate of the world, he knew that now. He was the Protector of the Christ Child.

No one could harm him. He knew that now. He was invisible. He was immortal. The bullets last night had veered away when they came close to him. He had *seen* that.

He was immortal.

He was the Christkiller. Even the enemy said it now. The Christkiller. The Killer for Christ.

The Killer for Christ.

The Executioner for the Sacred Lamb.

The Christkiller.

The Christkiller.

The Christ.

He *was* the Christ.

He could see that now. That's why they wanted to destroy him, the Jews. That's why he frightened them so. *He was the Christ. He was the Christ.*

"*I am Jeeee-susssss!*" he screamed out to the dying sun. Then in happy celebration he pissed on the desert floor and rolled in the warm mixture of sand and urine.

5:07 PM Clarke Johnson couldn't believe it.

He looked at his watch again, and couldn't believe what the hands told him—5:07!

He was two hours early. How the hell can a man be two hours early? What was wrong with him, to be two hours early?

He was parked in front of Esther Phibbs's house on Crenshaw Boulevard, trying to figure how the hell a fully grown, supposedly mature man could be *two hours early.*

He had left the Probation Center at noon, taking half a day off. What was the point in rushing on what might be a very important day? He had eaten a light lunch—tuna salad croissant and fresh fruit—had gone to his gym for a quick workout, then picked up his blue blazer and gray slacks from the cleaners, gone home to shower, dressed and left, allowing for rush-hour traffic, and here he was, two hours early, like a breathless schoolboy on his first date.

How the hell—

Esther's station wagon pulled into the driveway. Clarke Johnson froze, terrified she would spot him. Esther got out of the station wagon wearing sneakers, jeans, and a floppy T-shirt, took a bag of groceries from the seat beside her, and went into the house.

My God, he thought, I'm two hours early and my date hasn't even started getting ready, yet.

What the hell is wrong with me? What the hell—

The idea suddenly struck him that Esther might be coming out of her house again, and that she might see him sitting here, waiting, like an idiot, *two hours early.*

He burned rubber tearing away from the house, his eyes glued to his rearview mirror, but she didn't come out again. He didn't let out his breath until he was two blocks away.

He drove to Crenshaw Park, a small, green square of gritty, sloping hills around a murky pond. The old-timers told him there used to be ducks in this pond, but the kids caught them and broke their necks. They said this park used to be a place where children played long past dusk. Now it was all graffiti, reeking restrooms, and discarded Thunderbird bottles.

He sat on a crumbling concrete bench at the pond's edge and stared down at a naked, one-armed doll bobbing just below the surface of the dirty water.

He checked his watch—5:32.

My God, he thought, how neurotically boring can one man be?

Very boring. Boring enough to be two hours early. Boring, boring, boring. Boring enough to be eternally punctual, precise, polite, dependable, neat, composed, controlled, loyal, and steadfast. Boring.

Boring enough to drive everyone around him crazy. Especially women.

He had driven his wife crazy; had driven her away from him and into the arms of another man.

"Clarke!" she had cried at the door, her lover waiting in his car. "Go look in your dresser! You arrange your *socks!*"

After Yvonne left he had tried, he really had. He dropped his clothes on the floor; he left dirty dishes in the sink; he didn't set his alarm clock.

And he lay in bed and stared at the ceiling, hearing the egg yolk harden on the good china.

He got up at four in the morning, stood in the bedroom of the daughter Yvonne had taken with her, and cried. Then he had cleaned the whole house.

That had been sixteen years ago.

Since that day he had come to terms with his—his *perfectness.* It wasn't as if he had to live with being a child molester. He was simply too Dudley Do Right, as one of his sisters had phrased it.

A teenage boy carrying schoolbooks walked into Crenshaw Park and sat on another bench across the fifty feet of dirty water from Clarke Johnson. He opened a book and began to read. Johnson felt warm and uncomfortable and he stood up, took off his blazer, sat down again, and carefully folded the blazer across his lap.

After his divorce he had tried to date every woman he met, but that had been a big mistake. He was trying to be someone he wasn't, and the women had sensed it and declined his invitations. Then he went through his "monastic" period, during which he channeled all his sexual energies into jogging and handball, or at least he thought he had, until the Saturday night he found himself in a downtown porno theater with two girls on the screen performing cunnilingus on each other and a Mexican boy across the aisle smiling warmly at him.

By the time he arrived at work Monday morning he had made a decision. He had to meet women, and since he had no social life to speak of, he had to meet them in his workplace, and since the center's five female probation officers and three secretaries were married, that left only the wives, daughters, and sisters of his "clients"—the men in his charge.

Yes, Esther had been dead right on that count, she was not the first wife of a parolee he had asked out. There had been one other, and the sister of another. Both instances had occurred years ago, only a short while after he had joined the Probation Department, and both instances had been disastrous. The wife, whose husband he had just violated and sent back to prison, had threatened to expose their relationship to his superiors if he didn't get her husband out of jail. The other woman, the sister, had simply wanted him to score some dope for her. She promised it would enhance their lovemaking.

He had extricated himself from both affairs with care and dispatch, and had avoided discovery and the end of his career only through the most intricate balance of threats, bribery, and cajoling, and the lesson was burned deep on his psyche. He hadn't made advances toward another of his clients' women until now. Until Esther.

Across the pond another boy joined the other on the cement bench. They laughed and traded soul handshakes.

He had been waiting for someone like Esther for a long time. Someone levelheaded, strong, industrious, loyal. Someone who had been kicked around a little by life. Someone who needed some attention, some loving care. In short, someone who could appreciate someone like Clarke Johnson.

And then, physically, he found her very desirable. She was tall, lean, spare—all the things he liked in a woman, all the things Yvonne, small and pert, had been the opposite of. And her face had character, intelligence, determination, not the soft, flabby blandness he saw in most California girls.

Johnson smiled as he thought about Esther. He was very attracted to her, and the thought of her stirred him, and he began to get an erection under his blazer. He glanced at the boys across the pond and shifted nervously in his seat.

He couldn't believe his good fortune in finding her, and then his further good luck in Bobby Phibbs leaving her. That was Phibbs's bad luck.

On the bench across the pond the first boy handed the second boy a small, foil-wrapped package, and the second boy slipped the first a folded-over bill.

A dope deal! A goddamn dope deal! Right in front of him! It depressed him and intruded on his pleasant thoughts of Esther. He walked quickly across the park and back to his car.

Driving slowly through the heavy traffic, thankful for an opportunity to kill some time, he wondered what Esther thought of him. She probably thought what most women did—that he was a square, a dip, a cube, a nerd, hopelessly out of touch, unhip, uncool, and not with it. But he knew what he had to offer Esther, or any woman who could recognize it—and what none of his "clients" could match—he offered a future. The simple promise of a good future. And he knew, just by talking to her for a moment, that that's what Esther wanted more than anything in the world.

And he could give it to her.

He parked on Esther's street, a full half block from her address, at 6:30. Still half an hour to kill. He turned off the motor and was turning the radio dial, searching for a sports report, when someone rapped on his window. He turned to face Mama Phibbs, with a despondent Little Bobby in tow. She was speaking to him. He rolled the window down.

"Why you waiting out here, Mr. Johnson?" Her smile was warm and wide. "Come on in the house."

"Uh—I'm very early, Mrs. Phibbs." He stupidly pointed to his watch to prove his point.

"Nonsense. Esther'll be upstairs getting dressed. Come on in the house."

"I—I'm not sure, Mrs. Phibbs."

"Of course, you're sure. I was just about to make my grandson here some brownies. He had hisself a rough ol' time at the playground."

Clarke Johnson got out of his car. He turned to the little boy.

"You must be Bobby. I've been anxious to meet you. How are you?"

Little Bobby, exuding deep gloom, wouldn't look up at the adult.

"Little Bobby," Mama Phibbs admonished, "it's polite to speak when you're spoken to."

"Hello," he mumbled.

Mama Phibbs winked at Johnson over the boy's head. "This little man had a very bad day."

"Oh?" Johnson, never a man to leave opportunity tapping at the door, moved in closer to the boy. "What happened, son? At the playground."

Little Bobby refused to speak.

"Go on, child." The old lady touched the boy's shoulder. "Answer the man."

Little Bobby finally looked at Johnson. His voice was desolate. "I didn't make the team. They're going to the playoffs and I got cut."

"Oh?" He looked up at Mama Phibbs.

"Primary school championships."

He looked back at the boy. "Why didn't you make the team?"

"I—I can't hit." He was on the verge of tears.

"Really?"

Little Bobby nodded sadly. He was carrying a ball and bat. "Dwayne said brains can't bat. Dwayne said four-eyes can't see to hit."

"Oh, Dwayne said that, did he?" Johnson said softly.

Mama Phibbs, something of an opportunist herself, said, "Why don't you men hash this over. I'm gonna make us some brownies." She was moving down the sidewalk. "You know which house it is, Mr. Johnson? Come on in a little while."

"Let me see that ball, Bobby," Johnson said. The boy handed it to him. Johnson turned it this way and that, fingering the stitches. "You know, Dwayne's dead wrong. A good batter has got to have a lot of brains."

Little Bobby pouted.

"A good batter," Johnson continued, "has to be thinking all the time. What's the pitcher throwing now? A fast ball or a changeup? Is he going inside or out? What did this guy throw me last time I faced him with this count? You see what I mean, Bobby? Yogi Berra said ninety percent of baseball is half mental. Who's your favorite player?"

"Uh, Darryl Strawberry. He went to Crenshaw."

"There you go, Darryl Strawberry. A great hitter, and you ever hear him talk on TV? Strawberry's a real bright guy. All the best hitters were really smart. Ted Williams, Rod Carew. Mickey Mantle." Mickey Mantle? he thought to himself. "All those guys."

"Really?" the boy said, brightening.

"Sure. And all the players in the majors now have attended college. It takes brains to get through college. It takes brains to play baseball. Brains and a good eye."

"Yeah!" Little Bobby cried bitterly, as if to prove his point. "And I have to wear these!" He pointed to his thick-lensed glasses.

"But don't you see, Bobby? Guys who wear glasses have it *all over* guys who don't."

"What?" He was puzzled.

"Sure. When the optometrist tested our eyes, he made us lenses that allow us to see perfectly. Guys who don't wear glasses, no matter how well they can see, their vision isn't perfect, like ours."

"No kidding?"

"Look. Reggie Jackson—arguably the best slugger who ever played the game. The man hit three home runs in one World Series game. And he's worn glasses his whole career."

"That's true!" Little Bobby exclaimed.

"Of course, it's true. With his glasses on, Reggie can see the ball like a hawk sees a rabbit." They were walking together down the sidewalk together, the man holding the baseball, the boy dragging the bat. "You know, Bobby, baseball is more a science than a sport. And hitting is based on certain principles that can be learned, like mathematics."

"I'm very good at math!" the boy cried happily.

"Keeping your eye on the ball, leaning into the pitch, not committing yourself too early—all these things are lessons that can be mastered. Look, why don't you stand over there and I'll toss a few to you?"

Nearly an hour later Mama Phibbs came out on the little porch just in time to see her grandson hit a line drive that *thunked* off the roof of Mr. Kim's new Toyota. Clarke Johnson scooped up the rolling ball and he and Little Bobby raced up the walk, laughing like pirates.

"Did you see that hit, Grandma? That was at least a double!"

"A triple," Johnson said.

"A triple?" the boy shouted. "You think so?"

"No question."

Mama Phibbs looked from one to the other. "Uh huh," she said slowly. "Uh huh."

"A triple, Grandma!" the boy shouted again.

"Don't holler in the house, child. Brownies ready."

On the coffee table in the living room was a tray containing glasses of milk, a pot of coffee, and a plate of freshly baked brownies.

Little Bobby sat cross-legged on the floor and attacked the brownies.

"Sit down, Mr. Johnson," the old lady invited. "Help yourself. I wish I could offer you something a little stronger, but Esther doesn't have a thing in the house. My late husband, a deacon in his church, mind you, used to say no American home is complete without a bottle of good Kentucky bourbon somewhere on the premises. I'm afraid I've come to agree with him."

She fixed Johnson with a baleful eye.

"You're not a teetotaler, are you, Mr. Johnson?"

Little Bobby was wolfing down a steaming brownie and washing it down with a glass of milk.

"Of course not, Mrs. Phibbs," Johnson said as he took the proffered mug of coffee. "Although I'm afraid I've been made very aware by my occupation of the ravages drink and drugs can wreak on some men—" Clarke Johnson stared suddenly at the old lady. "No offense meant, Mrs. Phibbs."

She waved her hand. "None taken, young man. I'm much too old to be so thin-skinned."

"What do you do?" Little Bobby asked, his mouth stuffed with his third brownie. "Where do you work?"

Johnson smiled at the boy. "I'm a parole and probation officer. I work at the Probation Center."

"I know where that is. My father goes there."

Johnson glanced up at Mama Phibbs. "Yes, I know."

"My father's gone now. Mama says he won't ever come back."

Mama Phibbs and Clarke Johnson looked down at the boy and kept their silence.

"I'm glad," Little Bobby said absently, reaching for his milk. "I hate him."

Then his eyes widened. "Mama!" he exclaimed. "Lookit you!"

Esther came down the stairs and into the living room. She wore a black, high-shouldered, satin jumpsuit with a rope of rhinestones draped over one shoulder. Her hair was done up in tight wet curls. She was trying hard not to look too pleased with herself.

"You look wonderful," breathed Clarke Johnson, standing.

"Oh, *this* old thing?" Esther said, and she and Mama Phibbs burst into laughter.

"Where you going, Mom?"

"We're going to a ballet, son. Isn't that right, Mr. Johnson?"

"Clarke," he said, smiling.

"And then we'll be dining and dancing. I think that's what I heard." She returned Clarke Johnson's smile.

"Just you be sure you stay out of that Westside," Mama Phibbs warned. "That crazy Crosskiller is bound to kill somebody else tonight. And the police sure don't seem to be able to stop him. If it was a black man doing all them things I betcha they'd catch him soon enough. He'd be lynched and buried by now."

"On the basis of the information circulating around the office," Johnson said with a slightly officious air, "I wouldn't exclude the possibility of an imminent arrest."

The other three stared at him.

"Ain't that something else?" Mama Phibbs mumbled, more to herself than to anyone else.

"In any event," Clarke Johnson continued, "we won't be going anywhere near the Beverly-Fairfax area. The dance presentation is in Pasadena, at the Ambassador Auditorium, and the restaurant is downtown. I assure you, Mrs. Phibbs, Esther will be safe."

"It don't matter, anyway," Esther scoffed. "Mama, you know I work all over the Westside every night. And all hours of the night."

"That don't mean I have to like it," Mama Phibbs snapped back.

"Well, I can't be bothered by what one crazy, tripped-out freak is doing. I have to earn a living for myself and my boy. The police sure ain't gonna pay my bills."

A shadow crossed Mama Phibbs's dark face. "I still don't have to like it."

Clarke Johnson was eyeing his wristwatch. "I'm afraid we really have to be going, Esther. Curtain is at eight sharp."

Outside on the steps Mama Phibbs whispered conspiratorially, "I'll take

Little Bobby home with me. You two have a good time." She gave Esther a quick hug. "Don't worry about a thing." Then to Clarke Johnson: "You be careful, Mr. Johnson."

He took Esther's arm and guided her down the sidewalk.

"You have a very close family. A very beautiful family."

Esther chuckled. "Well, they certainly seemed charmed by you."

"Let's hope I am as fortunate with the rest of the family." He beamed.

He led her down the sidewalk to his car, unlocked the door, and held it open for her. She gawked at the red car, then at him, then back at the car.

And shook her head in wonderment.

"Mr. Johnson," she said as she climbed into the late-model Porsche, "you are a man of many surprises."

"Clarke," he said, grinning.

7:31 PM Gold wheeled his old Ford into the cavernous parking structure of the towering Century City office building and drove slowly around and up the spiraling ramps that led to the top floors. He found the Corniche with the DEFENSE license plates on the third level, parked not far from the bank of elevators. He backed into a space two rows away, turned down his radio-receiver, and settled back to wait.

Before a few minutes had passed he caught himself dozing off and, wishing he had brought a container of coffee, slapped himself hard across the face. It was understandable, of course. He couldn't remember the last time he'd been able to rest. It had been a very busy week, to say the least. And it showed no signs of letting up.

Like today.

Chief Huntz had called him and Dolly Madison into his office at seven in the morning and screamed at them till almost eight. *Results,* he kept hammering. Arrests, leads, *anything,* he shouted. Gold, of course, had told him if he thought he could do the job better he could try it himself. It had all gone pretty predictably. Huntz had warned that he, Gold, was skating on thin ice, that he was even losing support among his "coreligionists." To which Gold had replied that *he* wanted to be neither mayor of Los Angeles nor prime minister of Israel, so he, Huntz, could stuff all his threats up his constipated asshole. Dolly Madison, though, seemed to shrivel under his mentor's tirade, and after a while Gold actually began to feel sorry for the little brown-nose. He thought he even spotted a tear or two in Madison's eyes as they left Huntz's office.

Well, at least now they had a description—even if none of the shaken Delicatessen Massacre witnesses could agree on it completely. The perpetrator was a Cauc; aged twenty to forty; height five eight to six three; weight 175 to 225; hair sandy, they all agreed on that; eyes, no one could remember; and that was about it. Oh, yes, two of the survivors were sure they saw tattoos on the killer's arms. The others couldn't recall.

They had immediately computed the description out to the scores of law enforcement agencies in Southern California. The rest of the morning was spent "interviewing" the flotsam that the dragnet was hauling in. Nothing turned up. A lot of likely suspects, but none without alibis. They put stars by the names of the more promising and kicked the others out.

At noon Gold told Zamora to hold down the fort and went alone to lunch. He sneaked his car out Parker Center's back exit, carefully avoiding

the hundreds of reporters camped out on Los Angeles Street, and quickly
made his way to a freeway entrance. He stopped once, to buy a pint of
Scotch and a bag of butter cookies, and he drank and ate on his way down
to Anaheim. There was a different guard at the gate of the miniwarehouse.
He checked Gold's I.D., then waved him through.

Gold ignored the red suitcase this time. He lifted a moldy carpetbag
satchel buried deeper under the old rug. In the satchel were guns—revolv-
ers, automatics, sawed-off shotguns—a cache started sixteen years earlier
with the weapons he and Corliss had taken when they ripped off the drug
house, and added to over the years by the many occasions an illicit weapon
found its way into Gold's hands. A street cop never knows when he might
need a good, untraceable piece. Especially a cop who does a lot of private
business. Gold's attention drifted toward a long, lethal .357, but finally he
selected a silver-plated .22 revolver. It was better for close work. There was
even a box of shells. He buried the satchel under the rolled-up rug and
locked the door.

Back at Parker, Zamora complained that he too was going to take two
hours for lunch. Gold told him he didn't dare. After Zamora left, Gold sat
at his desk and carefully oiled and lubricated the .22. What is more natural
than a policeman cleaning a gun?

Now, sitting in his Ford in the Century City parking structure, smoking
a cigar and watching Natty's Rolls, Gold slipped his hand down the seam
of his trouser leg and touched the .22 stuck in his sock.

By eight o'clock there were only three cars left on the third parking level:
Gold's Ford, the Rolls, and an orange Corvette parked next to the Rolls.

At just after 8:30 the elevator doors rolled open and Natty Saperstein
stepped out. With him was a young boy with spiked, punkish hair dyed
a bright, unnatural yellow. The boy wore a fingerless glove on his right
hand, black leather pants, and a cut-off black T-shirt. Saperstein and the
boy strolled casually over to the side-by-side vehicles. Saperstein had his
arm around the boy's waist and was gently tugging at the short hairs
growing in the small of the boy's back. They talked for a while, laughing,
then kissed lovingly and said good night. Saperstein's Rolls roared out of
the parking structure, followed closely by the punk boy in the orange
Corvette.

Gold stuck the .22 back in his sock, started the Ford, and followed
twenty seconds behind. The Corvette zoomed west toward the lurid sunset.
Gold edged into the traffic three cars behind Natty's Rolls. When Natty
turned off Sunset into Le Parc's parking lot, Gold eased the old Ford to
the curb and watched. Natty tossed his keys to the smiling valet, appraised
his appearance in the blue panel, and entered the restaurant.

Gold relit his dead cigar, checked his rearview, then jerked back into the right lane. He drove east on Sunset to Fairfax, turning south toward the Jewish district around Herschel's Deli. Only a few blocks farther on, the traffic was gridlocked, backed up past Santa Monica Boulevard. He switched on his flasher and siren, jumped the center divider, and roared up the wrong side of the street. Just past Fairfax High the JAR had set up makeshift roadblocks—stacks of old tires, derelict cars maneuvered broadside, orange Traffic Control cones they had appropriated. Resisters in the pale blue T-shirts were checking the drivers' I.D.'s. Those motorists not possessing Jewish names or faces were questioned as to their business in the area. Commuters who complained they were just taking their usual route to the freeway were told to go around, find another way home. Several arguments flared as Gold watched, but the Resisters stood their ground, wearing hard expressions and automatic rifles. Clusters of uniformed LAPD officers observed the scene with blank faces. Gold spotted Dolly Madison speaking into a walkie-talkie. Gold left the Ford in the middle of the street and walked over to him.

"What the fuck is this?"

Madison took the walkie-talkie from his ear.

"Jack. Oh, this? This is SNIPER."

"What?"

"Supplemental Neighborhood Patrol Emergency Reinforcement. The mayor just made a deal with Jerry Kahn and Councilman Orenzstein. The JAR is the law around here now. At least until we catch the Crosskiller."

Gold shook his head. "I can't believe it. What does Huntz say about all this?"

"Oh, the chief is furious, you can be sure of that. But the mayor told him it was out of his hands now. Told him to shut up and do his job. Told him if he couldn't live with this"—Dolly gestured toward the checkpoint—"he could tender his resignation."

Gold was incredulous. "One man is doing all this. One zoned-out wacko is tearing this city apart."

"You really can't blame the mayor," Madison said. "He's just protecting himself against charges of being soft on anti-Semitism and terrorists."

"I don't mean the *mayor,* you asshole," Gold snapped and Dolly Madison looked hurt.

The sunset over the western horizon was steadily darkening. Groups of Jews hurried by on their way to Shabbes services at the many synagogues in the area. Armed JAR troopers walked shotgun alongside them. The Orthodox, in their beards and fur-trimmed hats and heavy black coats, had hired Rent-a-Cops—Shabbes *goys*—to escort them to *shul,* rejecting the JAR's protection. They refused to contribute to Jews breaking the Sabbath. The people congregated on the steps of the various temples, discussing the horrible events that had occurred in the neighborhood since last Friday night's services. The last of the sun's rays fizzled into the western sea. The night closed in, as gentle and lethal as gas. The templegoers filed in. Gold walked the streets, puffing on his cigar. The JAR sentries glared at him. After a while he got back in his car and drove away.

$10{:}45\ PM$ Esther's knife sank easily through the chateaubriand. She had never before in her life tasted beef like this.

"How is your cut?" Clarke Johnson, seated across the white tablecloth, asked solicitously.

Esther chewed a few times, then swallowed. She kept her face a blank page.

"It's okay."

Johnson was instantly concerned. "Is something wrong with it? We can send it back."

Esther looked over at him. "No, it's fine."

"Really," he said, putting down his own fork, "if it's not to your taste we'll send it back to the chef and—"

Esther laughed aloud. The man was a glass pane, completely guileless. A total innocent. How the hell could he be such a hard-assed probation officer?

"Honestly, Clarke, it's fine. Perfect." She quickly chewed and swallowed a second bite to illustrate her pleasure. Johnson beamed.

The ballet performance had been the slowest-moving two hours in Esther's life. She had had to use all of her powers of concentration just to stay awake. It wasn't that the dancers were bad; not at all. In fact, she could recognize immediately that the dancers were extraordinary athletes and wonderful performers. The women were lithe and graceful, and Esther envied their perfect physiques; the men were beautifully muscled, even though Esther suspected the lightness of their steps; and for the first twenty minutes—choreographed to some obscure score by Stravinsky—Esther was fascinated as their supple bodies pivoted and pranced and leapt around the stage with almost superhuman coordination. But though Esther could appreciate intuitively the brilliance of their talent, this was not dance as Esther knew it. This was the act on the television variety show when everyone went to the refrigerator. This was the lead-in to the commercial.

The second half of the program was done to a special piece by the late Duke Ellington, and while Esther found the music more accessible, she suspected that the rhythms and the steps were something Mama Phibbs would be right at home with.

After the concert, as they walked through the leafy Pasadena night streets to the red Porsche, Clarke Johnson had rhapsodized about the program. The choreography was thrilling; the staging a trifle uninventive;

355

the execution of the entire night's performance a little workmanlike, perhaps, but very enjoyable nonetheless.

Esther had smiled to herself as he ran on. He was unquestionably the whitest black man she had ever known or even heard about. In the Deep South of her coming-of-age black men like Clarke Johnson were targets of derision in the black community, as much as those who mirrored the Stephen Fetchit stereotypes. They were called "Oreos" and "Mr. Nigger" and thought to be pretentious and affected and somehow counterfeit. Esther herself had laughed at the jokes about them. Now she was coming to terms with the realization that her own son was going to be this kind of black man, too. And that was the way she wanted it. Little Bobby *was* something special—very special. He was going to be a professional man—a doctor, a lawyer, a news anchorman, a senator—whatever the hell he wanted. She would see to that. He was her everything, now that she had thrown her husband out of her life. But she worried that one day her little boy would outgrow his janitor mother, that someday he would find reason to feel shame for his tin-roof, sharecropper-shack mother. That would kill her, and she prayed never to see that day. Somehow, having a man like Clarke Johnson interested in her, validated those prayers.

Esther dipped a forkful of her chateaubriand into the béarnaise. She smiled across the table at Clarke Johnson.

"—so when I got back from Vietnam," he was saying, "and was mustered out of the Corps—"

"You were in Vietnam?"

"You're surprised." His wine glass was poised halfway to his lips. "Why?"

Esther shrugged. "I don't know. I didn't mean anything. It's just that you're not like any of the other veterans I've known."

"Oh? And how are they?"

Esther felt boxed in. "You know, less—less—"

"Stiff?"

"No," she laughed nervously. "Please. I'm sorry. I'm sorry I interrupted. Please go on." She smiled. "Clarke."

He smiled back. "I almost stayed in the corps. I gave a lot of thought to making it a career. I loved the corps. I was even invited to attend Officer Candidate School. But finally I felt my future lay out in the civilian world."

"And that's when you decided to become a parole officer?"

"It wasn't really a conscious decision." He patted his mouth with his linen napkin. "While I was stationed on Okinawa I had the chance to serve with the Shore Patrol—the Military Police—and I liked it. A lot. After I was discharged I moved to Los Angeles and tried to enlist in the LAPD. At the time there was a manpower freeze imposed on the department and they weren't accepting new recruits, but a sympathetic black officer told me that the Parole and Probation Department was interviewing applicants. He said that people already in place on the municipal government would get priority status when the hiring freeze was finally lifted."

The waiter, gliding by their table, stopped to refill their wine glasses. Clarke Johnson took the carafe from his hands and poured the Beaujolais for Esther. The waiter smiled graciously and floated away.

"So, let me guess," Esther said, arching an eyebrow. "You fell in love with the Probation Department job and stayed put. Right?"

Johnson nodded. "It'll be fourteen years in January. I find working with troubled probationers very gratifying. Much more so than police work, I'm sure. I like to feel I'm helping my people. At least the ones who want to be helped."

Esther kept her gaze steady as she tasted her wine.

"And it gives me the time to pursue my education."

"Oh? You taking college classes?"

Johnson spooned sour cream onto his baked potato. "I'm working on my doctoral thesis."

"Doctoral thesis!" Esther put down her fork. "I *am* impressed! I don't believe I know any *doctorates.* Except maybe to clean up after. What you gonna be—the head of the Probation Department?"

Clarke Johnson shook his head. "No, I'm aiming a little higher than that."

"Well, excuse me!" Esther laughed. "Tell me, Mr. Doctorate. What's your thesis about?"

"Penology."

Esther mugged a frightened face. She was feeling good, warmed by the rich food and heady wine, and by Clarke Johnson's attention.

"Penology! I'm afraid to ask what that means."

He chuckled. "Prisons, Esther. The study of prisons and how they affect the inmates, the guards, the community, the state. Someday I'm going to be a warden of a major American prison."

Esther frowned. "Prisons? They draw up only bad feelings in me. Places where they lock up people and throw away the key. Mostly black people. Why would you want a job like that? You, a black man?"

He pushed his plate away. "I want the job because every day I deal with the graduates of a decadent prison system that brutalizes, dehumanizes, demoralizes, criminalizes, that hardens, angers, perverts, that does everything possible to do to an inmate but what a prison in the late twentieth century is supposed to do—retrieve, rehabilitate, and then reintroduce an inmate into society."

"You feel strongly about this."

"Yes. Yes, I do."

"You think they're gonna give you that kind of job?"

"They're going to have to. Crime is a growth industry. And nowhere more so than in the minority communities. The present prison administrations are failing miserably. With inmate populations averaging sixty to seventy percent black, I think that very soon America is going to realize we need every edge we can acquire in the war against crime. Black administrators will be part of that edge."

"*You* can relate to the modern black criminal?" Esther chided playfully.

"I think so. After fourteen years of dealing with parolees and probationers I'm pretty confident I can. And I don't think I will be subjected to the games and tricks black inmates run on white personnel."

"Such as?"

He leaned forward, his elbows on the table, his fingertips tented, just as he had in his office.

"That whole charade of dealing with black crime as a sociological problem, for one. That it's the result of cultural deprivation."

"You don't buy that?"

"Black criminals are just like white criminals. Or Asian or Hispanic or whatever. They're people who want things without working for them. It's as simple as that."

"You're gonna be a hard-ass."

"The hardest."

"They're gonna love you," Esther laughed.

"I think so," Johnson said, completely serious. "I think they will. Ten percent of the parolees I get assigned are lifelong criminals. They're incorrigible. The most constructive thing we can do is reincarcerate and maintain them, like the animals that they are, for the rest of their lives. The remaining ninety percent want to do the right thing, even if they don't always make it. They want to stay out on the streets; they want to find a decent job and a decent woman and have a family. They want the whole American dream. They just don't know how to go about making that dream a reality. That's why they take solace in narcotics. I consider it my job to take them step by step toward that dream. I care about my clients, and they recognize that concern. My recidivism ratio is the lowest in the department. And when I'm a warden I'll be equally successful."

Esther lit a cigarette. She blew a cloud of smoke to the side.

"I believe you, Clarke. I believe you would be successful at whatever you set out to do."

He smiled again. He was much better-looking when he smiled.

"I don't like to fail," he said simply.

"And you never have?"

"Oh, I have," he said thoughtfully. "Once. Miserably."

"And when was that?"

"My marriage."

It was Esther's turn to lean forward across the table. "Mr. Perfect was married? Do tell me about it."

Clarke Johnson shrugged. "It was during the first year after I enlisted. We were both very young. It should never have happened. The Corps was everything to me, and I guess I neglected Yvonne once too often. I should have realized there was someone else, but when she left it shattered me. She and her—her friend moved all the way to Connecticut. They took Dina with them."

"Dina?"

"My daughter. She's eighteen now. A sophomore at Howard. We're total strangers. It's the bitterest chapter of my life."

Esther didn't know what to say. She studied the red wine in her glass. Finally she looked up at him.

"I only know I would die if someone took Little Bobby away from me."

"Don't ever let that happen, Esther. It's a terrible experience."

"Is that why you never remarried?"

"I—the whole episode made me very cautious, very wary of impulsive behavior. Especially where women are concerned. Made me—well, dull."

Esther reached over and patted his hand.

"You're not dull. Maybe a little nerdy, like the kids say. But not dull. And definitely very nice."

He covered her hand with his and stroked her skin. They gazed at each other through the dim lighting and their eyes shone.

Just then the busboy asked to clear the table. Esther and Clarke sat up quickly and drew their hands back. The waiter came by with a dessert cart. Johnson ordered brandies instead. The band that had been on break started up in the lounge adjoining the dining room. It was a slow, lush ballad.

"Would you like to dance?" He was already getting up.

Esther batted her eyes. "Shouldn't we wait for a waltz?"

Johnson threw back his head and guffawed. "Come on, give me a break. I'm not that square—or am I?" He took her arm and led her into the lounge and onto the dance floor.

"You're pretty square, Clarke." She laughed back. "Pretty damn square."

They stopped talking when they moved into each other's arms. After a stiff moment, Esther relaxed and let her body mold against his. She rested her head on his shoulder and was glad she had worn low heels. They moved around the floor in silence. When the saxophonist started his solo Esther leaned back and looked at him.

"You sure you don't do this all the time?" she asked softly.

"What?"

"Go out with your parolees' wives?"

He shook his head. "First time."

She put her head down on his shoulder again. They swayed to the music.

"Why me?" Esther whispered into his lapel.

"You're special," he whispered back, encircling her waist with both hands.

"Come on," she said. "Why me?"

He kissed her ear. "You mean besides the purely physical?"

She smiled into his shoulder. "Oooo, you so bad. Please tell me."

"Just as I said. You're special."

"I'm a washerwoman. I'm a glorified maid. Maybe not so glorified."

"You are a small businessman—uh, business*person.* You are the backbone of the American economy."

"I'm *what?*" she said, pushing a little away.

"I checked you out thoroughly. I had to when Bobby was being released to your address."

"You checked me out?"

"It's standard procedure. Surreptitiously, of course. We told your employers we were credit checks, prospective clients, that sort of thing. And do you know, every one of your accounts spoke of you in the highest terms. Esther, your future is limitless. You are on the threshold of a very lucrative career. I can visualize the future: Esther Phibbs Enterprises; Esther Phibbs Incorporated; Esther Phibbs International!"

She laughed with him. "You're teasing me! But I *am* expanding. Starting a big new account Sunday night."

"There, you see?"

The band ended the song on a mellow chord. The audience and the other dancers applauded.

"So. You're romancing me for my money?" Esther said over the applause.

He chuckled. "Some of my pimp parolees would be very amused by that statement. They think I'm hopelessly honorable."

The seven-piece band began a funky up-tempo vamp. The smiling bass player slapped his strings and hunched his shoulders to the backbeat. The lead singer—a pretty white girl—made an imitation Madonna move and grabbed her mike with a flourish. Esther started to walk off the dance floor. Johnson grabbed her arm.

"Hey, I thought you wanted to dance?"

Esther's face registered her surprise. "Sure, but I didn't think you know how to—"

He spun away from her, clapping his hands and dipping his shoulders to the beat. Suddenly he froze—stock still. He stayed that way for several seconds, then he swung his neck in a jerky, robotic motion, glided across the parquet in "locker" style, executed a Princely spin, and ended with a flurry of James Brown stutter steps that put him back at Esther's side. The other dancers clapped wildly. The girl singer pointed at him and shimmied her shoulders.

Esther was in shock.

"Why, Mr. *Johnson!*"

Clarke Johnson took her hand and danced her back onto the floor.

11:32 PM The green-and-pink, fake-Egyptian house was in the throes of a lively party. Simply Red, turned up high, thundered through the open French windows.

A half dozen bikinied young men lounged beneath the alabaster statuary arranged around the swimming pool. They trailed their languid hands through the tepid water and their laughter echoed through the hot night and out over the winking lights far below.

Natty Saperstein, in a narrow caftan, strolled through the portico carrying a crystal bowl of cocaine. The young men greeted him warmly and he passed the bowl around. The angelic-faced German boy who had been with Natty at Le Parc came outside bringing Saperstein's drink. Natty took the drink from his hand and threw an arm around his shoulder. The boy smiled. He and Natty went back inside.

Gold carefully picked his way through the shrubbery, down the slope, and back to the street. Seated in the Ford, he lit his cigar, took a swig from his flask, and radioed in. There was nothing happening. The dispatcher requested his location. Gold gave him a phony.

A few minutes later a two-man patrol car cruised the house going very slowly. When the car had passed, Gold started the Ford and drove down the hill.

SATURDAY
August 11

12:02 AM "Where on earth did you learn to dance like that?"

He held the car door open for her.

"I was the only brother in a family of eight children. My sisters tried out all the latest steps on me. I've kept it up ever since. It's great exercise."

Esther shook her head. "You're amazing, Clarke."

He walked her to the door. She put the key in the lock and opened it. Then she turned back to him.

"I had a great time."

"So did I."

"Want to come in for a nightcap?"

"Your mother-in-law said there wasn't any liquor in the house."

Esther smiled. "Let's look anyway."

He was a wonderful lover: slow and gentle and patient. In the beginning she missed Bobby's animal strength, his power and bulk. She hadn't slept with someone else in over ten years, but she quickly relinquished that fantasy and slipped into this man's rhythm. She clung to his hard, dark, compact body and licked at his shoulders and kissed his face. He came quickly, then again, then still ramrod stiff, rocked her gently for the better part of an hour. She cried out when she climaxed and pounded on his back. Then he turned her over and slipped in from behind, whispering, "You're so beautiful, Esther. So beautiful. So beautiful."

She looked back over her shoulder and he was a sweating shadow glistening in the streetlight that crept in the window. She reached back with both hands and pulled him into her. He spurted with a grunt.

Afterward, in the dark, they lay beside each other in the hot, damp bed. Esther lit a cigarette.

"You smoke too much," he said dreamily.

"What do you care?" she purred.

"I care a lot."

She took another deep drag and put the smoke out. He drew her close and she stretched out languidly against him, caressing his testicles in her palm. He shivered faintly and she kissed his chest. A car passed on the street with its radio blaring. They both drifted into an easy sleep.

Bagheera, the kitten, who had been frightened behind the bureau by the noises of serious lovemaking, cautiously crept out of his hiding place with his eyes wide and his whiskers twitching. Reassured by the sounds of somnolent breathing filling the room, the kitten soon grew bold. He arched his back, yawned luxuriously, and strutted around the bed with aristocratic bearing. The worn blue bedspread had spilled down the floor of the bed and across the floor. Bagheera raised up on his hind legs and scratched his claws down the bumpy cloth. Esther stirred in her sleep and rubbed her leg over Clarke Johnson's body. The movement caught Bagheera's attention and he leapt lightly up on the bed. The naked sleeping forms were motionless again. Nothing was happening. Curling and settling down on the sheet, he proceeded to clean himself and was just getting into the erotic rhythm of the act when Johnson's beeper, which in the heat of action had inexplicably found its way out of his coat pocket and under the sheet, just beneath where Bagheera was lying, suddenly went off. The kitten yelped and bolted out of the bed, going airborne for several feet, then slid across the floor and out into the hall and flew down the stairs.

Johnson awoke with a grumble and groped under the bedsheets for the beeper.

"What is it, baby?" Esther mumbled.

"I have to use your phone."

"Um—downstairs." She buried her head under a pillow as he padded naked out the door. A few minutes later he was back. He shook Esther's shoulder.

"Esther, you've got to get up."

"Yes. Yes." She sat up and rubbed her eyes.

"It's Bobby. It's your husband."

"Yes."

"The police just found him."

3:37 AM USC Medical Center's emergency room was in typical weekend panic. Bloody bedlam. The waiting room was packed with pleading, complaining victims of what the Trauma Unit specialists called the Knife and Gun Club. Some of the patients held homemade bandages over still seeping wounds. A grimy old bag lady rocked rapidly back and forth in her chair, singing loudly to herself. A pair of winos argued over who was next in line for treatment. The connecting corridors were jammed with gurneys holding the badly damaged—the gunshot, the overdosed, the hit-and-run-over. And fresh arrivals, heralded by the scream of sirens, coming all the time.

Clarke Johnson spoke to the young Bengali doctor behind a glass partition. The doctor's scrubs were blood-soaked down the front. Esther and Mama Phibbs and Little Bobby watched them through the finger-smudged glass. The doctor looked at Esther and his lips moved. Clarke Johnson nodded. The doctor said something else and Johnson answered, then he came around the partition. His face was ashen.

"He's gone, Esther. I'm sorry."

"Nooooooooo!" Esther wailed and sank to her knees. Mama Phibbs tried to support her, but Esther slipped from her grasp. Johnson grabbed at her, and she snatched her hand away.

"Don't touch me! *Don't ever touch me!*"

"Esther," Mama Phibbs soothed. "Now, now, now." The old lady's face was a study in control, but her eyes were wet and unfocused.

Mama Phibbs turned to Johnson. "What happened?"

"He was badly beaten. They don't know by whom or how many or how long ago. Could have been days ago. They think it took him that long to crawl from under the freeway."

"Oh, sweet Jesus!" Esther moaned.

"The doctor said if he hadn't been so strong he would have died immediately."

"Oh, my poor Bobby! Oh, sweet Jesus, my poor Bobby!"

"Esther, I'm so sorry. I truly am."

Esther raised her head and looked at him. The tears welled in her eyes and streamed down her cheeks. It seemed they would flow forever.

"Let me take you home, Esther."

Esther stared at him in horror.

"My poor Bobby," she groaned softly. "They beat him like a dog while you and I were rutting like pigs."

"Esther!" Mama Phibbs snapped, glancing at Little Bobby.

"While you and I was acting like horny school kids," Esther continued, her voice rising, "my poor Bobby was crawling for his life! *For his goddamn life!*"

"I'm so sorry," Clarke Johnson said and again reached out his hand.

"Get away from me! Don't touch me!" She jerked to her feet. "It's people like you killed Bobby! It's people like you!"

Mama Phibbs grabbed Esther's arm and spun her around.

"Esther! Pull yourself together! We got arrangements to make. Leave this poor man alone."

"Bobby didn't have a chance! They didn't give him a chance!"

"He brought it all on hisself, and you know that," Mama Phibbs said. "This day was gonna come, sooner or later. Bobby turned away from the path of God. He took another way, and it led him to his death. No one did anything to Bobby; he did everything to hisself."

"He was your *son!* How can you talk like that!"

"Because it's the God's honest truth. God rest his troubled soul, but he was a bad son, a bad husband, and a bad father. It's a wonder he didn't try to put you in the street."

"Don't say that! *Don't say that!*" Esther raised her hand as if to strike the old lady.

"You lost your husband tonight," Mama Phibbs said softly, drawing herself up to her full height. "Don't lose a mother, too."

Esther glared at the old woman, then her face collapsed into a mask of grief and shame. "No!" she cried. *"Noooooooooo!"*

Mama Phibbs watched her run from the emergency room. She sighed deeply.

"Little Bobby, go see after your mother. Make sure she's all right."

The little boy hesitated.

"Go on," she nodded. "Go on."

The boy ran out down the corridor where Esther had disappeared.

Mama Phibbs pulled her coat tighter around her and buttoned the top button. She looked at Clarke Johnson.

"It's a sorrowful night, Mr. Johnson."

"Yes, it is, Mrs. Phibbs."

"I'm sorry you had to witness that. Families should grieve and argue in private. I'm sure Esther didn't mean a thing she said."

"It's all right, Mrs. Phibbs. I understand. I just wish I could be of more help."

She shook her head absently. "Will you tell the hospital that we'll make arrangements to pick up Bobby's body as soon as possible?"

"Of course."

"I'll call Coleman Funeral Home as soon as they open."

Johnson nodded but didn't comment.

"I've known Mr. Coleman for almost forty years."

"Oh?"

"Yes." She tucked her purse tightly under her arm. "I should thank the doctors for their efforts."

"It's all right," he said. "Mrs. Phibbs?"

"Yes?"

"I'm truly sorry about your son."

The old lady rubbed a knuckle into the corner of her eye—a single rapid gesture. "Mr. Johnson, my son died a long time ago, the first time he put that needle in his arm. He's been worthless ever since. This is probably the best thing he could have done."

He looked away quickly, then back.

"You're a hard woman, Mrs. Phibbs."

Her eyes flashed. "It's a hard world, Mr. Johnson. And I have the living to look after."

"Yes, ma'am."

"Thank you for your concern."

"Yes."

She turned and walked away.

5:20 AM Cots had been set up in the offices and corridors occupied by the task force. Some cops came in to nap while others cruised the streets. When the dawn broke through the smog a little after 4:30 a shout had gone up and a bottle quickly passed around. The first night in four without a Crosskiller murder. The first in a week without an incident of anti-Jewish vandalism. After the hasty celebration all the cops lay down for a few hours' rest. Zamora dragged a mattress into the tiny office and within seconds he was snoring loudly. Gold sat at his desk and dozed fitfully.

At 5:25 the call came in. Gold answered it.

"Uh huh. Yeah. You're sure? How do you know it's not a celebrity freak? Uh huh. No, hold him there. We'll be right over. I want to talk to him a.s.a.p."

Gold hung up and kicked Zamora's mattress.

"Let's go, Redford. I think we got a break."

On the trip over the hill Gold ran it down for Zamora.

Last night Valley Division in Van Nuys had picked up a guy for assault outside a biker bar. He had attacked another dude with a tire iron. They ran the biker through the computer and he came up with outstanding warrants in Oregon, Washington, and Nevada. Reno police wanted to talk to him about a murder. The arresting cops sat him down and played cat-and-mouse throughout the night. He wasn't coming up with much. Just around five o'clock the dude assaulted with the tire iron expired. When the cops forwarded that information along to the biker, he suddenly became much more open in his demeanor. He had stories to tell, felonies to report. But before he did his civic duty he wanted complete immunity on all counts. The cops laughed and said, Who you got, Hitler? The asshole smiled and said, No, but close—the dude who's been offing all them Jews. That's when they called Gold.

When Gold and Zamora got to Van Nuys the place was already ass-deep in public servants. Dolly Madison, who had gone home to nearby Northridge for a few hours' sleep, was there, as were three high-ranking people from the D.A.'s office. Also there, looking grumpy and freshly awakened, was Irving Tannenbaum, the number-one fast gun from the public defender's office. He and Gold were old adversaries and they eyed each other with cold hostility.

"What's the story?" Gold asked the crowd in the hallway outside the interrogation room.

One of the arresting detectives stepped forward. He was young and obviously awed by the importance of the case he had stumbled onto.

"He says he knows who the Crosskiller is. And I believe him. I think he's telling the truth," the young detective said, a little breathlessly.

"What's he want?"

"Complete immunity," Dolly Madison interjected, moving to wrest control of the situation. "On all counts. That's the sticking point."

"Why? What's the problem?"

"Jack, the victim he assaulted died. Our boy bashed his head in with a tire iron."

Gold turned to the young detective. "Who was the guy who croaked?"

The cop shrugged. "Hell's Angel. We think it was over a burned dope deal."

"Christ!" Gold snorted. "He did a public service." Then to the D.A.: "Give him immunity. I need what he knows."

The senior assistant district attorney sniffed. "We have already conceded to Mr. Tannenbaum total immunity on the manslaughter charge. *If* the information proves helpful."

"Good," Gold said. "Let's talk to him."

"But Mr. Tannenbaum and his client aren't satisfied," the A.D.A. said.

"Oh?" Gold turned to Tannenbaum. "Irving, you're up to your old shit again. What's your problem?"

The lawyer, bald and bearded, smiled acidly. "My client also wants all charges in Oregon and Nevada dropped."

"Mr. Tannenbaum *knows* we can't give what we don't have," the A.D.A. flared angrily. "We can't control the legal apparatuses of other states."

"Barring that," Tannenbaum continued calmly, "my client wants assurances that he won't be extradited to Nevada."

Gold chewed on his cold cigar. "Well?"

Dolly Madison again tried to assert his command. "That would be an empty promise. Mr. Tannenbaum is well aware of that. We cannot supersede a legal extradition order."

"Well, what the hell *can* we promise?"

Dolly Madison looked uncomfortable. "Unofficially?"

"Of course."

"That we would drag our heels on any extradition proceedings. That we wouldn't expedite the process. That—that—"

The A.D.A. picked up the beat. "That papers would be misplaced,

hearing dates continued, that sort of thing. Possibly if the suspect coope-
rated on other cases he could be considered a running informant and
therefore essential to California law enforcement. In which case extradition
to another jurisdiction would be out of the question."

Gold turned to Tannenbaum. "Irving?"

Tannenbaum glowered. "It's not definite enough. It's not what I asked
for. But I'll discuss it with my client."

"You do that, Irving," Gold said, as Tannenbaum disappeared behind
the closed door of the interrogation room.

"Promise this *gonif* anything," Gold hissed when the P.D. was gone.
"We'll hedge our bets later."

Dolly Madison coughed. "That would be extremely unethical,
Jack."

"Fuck that!" Gold snapped. "I've seen Irving Tannenbaum ruin more
good cases than the Supreme Court. Sooner or later he's going to get the
concessions he wants anyway, so we may as well give them to him now.
I need to talk to his man *ahora*. I don't have time to jerk around. Let's
get our priorities straight here."

Just then a uniformed cop came down the hall carrying two large, grease-
stained paper bags with lettering reading Tommy's Fat Boy Burgers.

"What's this?" Gold asked.

"It's for the prisoner," the cop said.

"How many guys you got in there?"

The young detective gave a short laugh. "Wait'll you see this hog."

The cop entered the interrogation room. He came out a few seconds later
followed by Tannenbaum.

"My client finds your terms unacceptable. Nothing short of total immunity from either prosecution or extradition."

The senior assistant district attorney looked at his colleagues and then
at Tannenbaum.

"We're going to have to try and reach the Reno D.A.'s office. I don't
think we could have any kind of answer this weekend. Maybe Monday
after—"

"Are you motherfuckers crazy?" Gold shouted. "I don't have that kind
of time. I got a pass last night, but I don't expect it to last. The asshole
I'm looking for didn't sign a cease-fire, you know."

The other men stared at him.

"Fuck this," Gold said and walked into the interrogation room.

"You can't do that!" Tannenbaum shouted after him.

The suspect was seated at a long table. The two paper bags had been
emptied and the food was arrayed systematically before him. The window-

less room was not small, but it already reeked of onions and fatty fried meat.

"Hi," Gold said, his eyes on the suspect.

The suspect's mouth was full of Fat Boy chilicheeseburger, but he said anyway, "Hey, I know you."

"Don't say a word!" Tannenbaum shouted, running into the room. "You don't have to say a word! Not to him."

The suspect glanced at his lawyer, then looked back to Gold.

"I seen you on TV on the news," the suspect said. He was an enormously fat man with flaming red hair and beard. His huge belly jiggled loosely over his Harley-Davidson belt buckle. His T-shirt exhorted everyone to EAT MORE PUSSY! He took another bite of chilicheeseburger. "I know you," he mumbled behind the food, his eyes on Gold.

The others had followed Tannenbaum into the interrogation room—Sean Zamora and Dolly Madison, the detectives, the D.A.'s—and they lined the back wall, but the suspect paid them no mind. His attention was riveted on Gold.

"You that bad-ass Jew. I seen you on TV on the news."

Gold walked over to the young lieutenant and took the suspect's arrest report from his hand. There was a computer printout stapled to it. The suspect's rap sheet. Gold looked it over.

"Mr. Williamson," Tannenbaum said, staring furiously at Gold, "I am advising you, as your court-appointed attorney, not to speak to this man. You do not have to talk to him in any capacity, and I think it is in your best interests *not* to talk to him. Do you understand me, Mr. Williamson?"

"And I know who you are," Gold said softly, as though he and the suspect were the only two in the room. "Timothy James Williamson," he read, "alias Tiny Tim Williamson, alias Tiny Williams; alias Jumbo Jim, alias Two Ton Tiny Williams, alias Tiny Red Williamson." Gold read on in silence for a moment, then whistled softly. "Tiny! You have been a very, very bad boy. Seven years at San Quentin for armed robbery. Three years in Walla Walla for possession of a machine gun. Membership in the Satans Motorcycle Gang, the Aryan Brotherhood, the Christian Nation, and now the Kalifornia Klan." Gold put the printout down. "Then you went and whacked out that Angel last night. A little too hard, it seems. And you say you don't want to pay a return visit to the great state of Nevada under any circumstances. One would think that right about now you would be doing anything you could to win some friends around here."

"Mr. Williamson," Tannenbaum persisted, "don't talk to this man until we have definite assurances, in writing. We haven't cut a deal yet. Do you understand me, Mr. Williamson?"

Tiny was finishing up his third burger and his second order of fries.

"I ain't going back to Nevada."

"Oh?" Gold said.

"And I ain't gonna do a single fucking day behind offing that punk last night." Tiny belched—a gurgling, unhealthy sound.

"And why is that?"

"Mr. Williamson!" Tannenbaum shouted. "Please do not—"

"You know why."

"Tell me. Tell *me.*"

"Because I got something you want."

"What you got?"

"You know."

"What?"

"Mr. Williamson—"

"I know who's been doing up them Jews. Over there in Jew Town."

Gold watched him closely. "How do you know that?"

Tiny was stuffing a hot dog between his teeth.

"I just know," he said, munching.

"How would you know that, unless maybe it was you doing up them Jews?"

"Mr. Williamson, do you understand me? I strongly advise—"

"It ain't me."

"How do I know that?"

" 'Cause I can tell you who it is."

"Well, if it's not you, then who is it?"

"Mr. Williamson!"

Tiny grinned, showing the room the food in his mouth. "Uh-uh! I ain't stupid, you know. I ain't telling you till I get my deal."

Gold chuckled. Tiny chuckled along with him. Gold fished a book of matches from his pocket, struck a match and put the flame to his cigar. He puffed vigorously until the end glowed red. Tiny, a second hot dog in hand, watched him with fascination. Gold, wreathed in a cloud of white smoke, smiled at him and balanced the cigar on the edge of the table. Gold pointed to the hot dog in Tiny's hand.

"You still hungry, Tiny?"

Tiny shrugged. "I'm taking the edge off. I didn't have no dinner last night. Nothing."

"Awwwww."

Tiny watched him closely. Gold smiled back. Tiny brought the hot dog to his lips and opened his mouth. He closed his eyes and put the dog in his mouth. Gold clamped one hand around the back of Tiny's huge head and with the open palm of the other rammed the entire dog down Tiny's throat. Tiny started choking and tried to get up, but Gold slammed Tiny's face down into the third chili dog.

"*My God! What the hell—*" Tannenbaum sputtered.

"*Jack, what are you doing?*" Dolly Madison cried and moved forward a few feet.

"Partner!" Gold shouted, and Zamora took up position between him and the others. He held his hands up. "Leave him alone!" he said, and the two young detectives nodded and stepped back.

Tiny was choking on the chili he had inhaled. He clutched at his face and fought to catch his breath. Gold stepped up and sank his knee into Tiny's big soft belly. The air whooshed out of the 360 pound man like fetid gas escaping from an opened manhole. Tiny held his middle, leaned over the table, and threw up the two chili dogs, three chilicheeseburgers, and two orders of chili fries. It smelled like raw sewage, all over the table top. Finally, Tiny was dry-heaving, down on all fours, making gurgling noises like a throat-slashed pig. Gold stepped on Tiny's hand and rested his weight on it. Tiny tried to scream but it came out a choked rasp. Gold knelt beside the fat man. He had his cigar in his mouth again. He puffed on it vigorously, then jerked Tiny's head up by his dirty red hair and touched the tip of the cigar against Tiny's cheek. Skin sizzled and Tiny tried to pull his head back.

"*Gold, I'll have your badge for this!*" Tannenbaum screamed.

"*For chrissake, Jack!*" Dolly Madison bellowed.

Gold didn't even look up. "You tell me what you know or I'll put my cigar out in your eye. Do you believe me?"

Tiny nodded, his eyes whitened like a panicked horse.

"You better believe me, because it's true. And you're much too ugly to afford to lose an eye. Don't you agree?"

Tiny nodded again.

"*I'll bring you up on charges! I swear to God I will!*"

Gold ignored Tannenbaum and spoke gently into Tiny's warty ear. "And no matter what anyone in this room says or does, or whatever happens later, you will lose an eye. At the very least. Do you understand me?"

Tiny understood. Perfectly.

"*Don't tell him anything!*"

Tiny glanced over at the public defender, then swiveled his massive neck to look up at Gold.

"Can I wash up first?"

By way of an answer, Gold stoked up his cigar.

"Okay! Okay! It was two days ago. Thursday. At the Klan Headquarters. This dude—"

"Everyone in this room is a party to this!" Tannenbaum screamed. *"Everyone in this room is guilty!"* He slammed out the door.

Tiny watched his P.D. storm out. Then he ran his story down. It only took a few minutes. The interrogation room reeked of sweat and vomit.

"Why did Utter throw the guy out? Why didn't he believe him? Did Utter really have information about an infiltrator?"

Tiny, now reseated and picking the puke out of his beard, shrugged and said, "Jesse's an asshole. Always pretending he's got sympathizers everywhere. He's fulla shit. He likes to shake the boys up from time to time, make 'em think he's got eyes everywhere. He'd been wolfing all that morning 'bout how he knew who the Crosskiller was, how maybe *he* was, you know, secretly giving the dude his orders. Shit like that. So when this dude blows in and starts claiming how *he* was the righteous brother, well, fuck, man, he could of had them fucking Jews' *heads* rolling around in the back of his van, Jesse would still have to say the dude was bogus. Or a snitch. Or something."

"The van was blue, you said?"

"Right."

"Late model?"

"Maybe a seventy-seven or seventy-eight."

"License plate?"

"California. I didn't get the number, but Jesse did."

Gold looked up from his notepad. "How do you know?"

"See, after we pushed the dude around a little, kicked his ass some, and he's driving off, Jesse comes out the headquarters with his binoculars and watches the van go down the mountain. Afterward he tells us he was checking the dude's plates against the number his informant on the FBI give him. See, he's still playing the big man. Trying to impress us. Scare us up a little. Make us think he knows every fucking thing that's going on. Jesse's fulla bullshit. Some of them dudes up in Desert Vista think he's like Jesus Christ, man, but I know he's fulla bullshit. Anyways, we all go back in the headquarters and Jesse, he writes down the license plate number on a little bitty piece of paper and sticks it in his pocket. I seen him do it."

Gold relit his cigar. Tiny watched him with obvious alarm.

"Hey, man, that's all I know. That's all the truth."

Gold smiled at him through the smoke. "You're doing real good, Tiny. Real good. Tell me, Tiny. What makes you think this dude was on the square? About being the Crosskiller?"

Tiny chuckled. "Hey, man, up at 'Q' I used to be part of Charlie Manson's biker bodyguard. This dude had the same fucking eyes, man. *Crazed,* man. Wigged out. Not of this world. He's the dude you looking for, all-fucking-right. No question in my mind."

"And you never caught his name?"

"Never said it."

Gold nodded and closed his notepad. "All right, Tiny. I want you to spend the day looking at mug shots. See if we can find this guy." Gold glanced at the thickening sludge on the table and floor. "We'll get someone in here to clean this mess up. And another breakfast for you. I guess you don't want the same thing."

Tiny thought a moment. "No, Tommy's is fine. I like Tommy's."

Gold motioned to Zamora and the other detectives to follow him from the room.

"Hey," Tiny called, "what about my deal? Didn't I cooperate? What you gonna do for me?"

Gold paused, his hand on the doorknob. "Forget about the thing last night—the Hell's Angel. That was obvious self-defense. About the Nevada matter—I'll do the best I can. If this dude is the right dude, and if that Nevada thing is anything short of first-degree, I'll see you don't have to go."

Tiny's eyes narrowed with suspicion. "How I know you ain't bull-shitting me?"

"You have my word as a gentleman and a Jew."

Tiny started to laugh, then thought better of it.

Out in the hall, Gold spoke softly and rapidly to the two young detectives.

"Sorry, no sleep for you guys today. As of this moment, you are members of the task force. Get some coffee up here and waltz this pig through as many pictures as you can."

"Just right-wing people?" the young cop asked eagerly.

"No," Gold said thoughtfully, "I don't think so. Tiny has obviously run with that bunch's lunatic fringe for a long time. And all over the west. And he'd never run into the perp before. And then the way the guy came in to join the Klan—with his hat in his hand and all. I think it was his first attempt at seeking out compatriots. He went in like a puppy carrying a rabbit, looking for acceptance, a pat on the head. I think we got your classic loner schizo here. And the way the Klan rejected him—I think that pretty much explains the massacre at Herschel's Deli."

"Then you think this is really our guy?" Zamora asked.

"It's the only game in town right now." Gold turned back to the Van Nuys detectives. "Show Tiny pictures of everybody. B and E's, strongarms, sex freaks—everybody. Especially psycho types. If our boy has a jacket at all, it'll probably be as a psycho."

The young detectives nodded.

"But first go get that slob another breakfast. We have to keep his strength up. Get going!"

The two detectives sprang into action, almost trotting down the hall.

"But you don't have to watch him eat it!"

Gold and Zamora walked down the hall in the other direction, toward the parking lot.

"What now?" Zamora asked.

"I got a judge in San Bernardino County owes me a favor. Let's go see if he can get us a quick search warrant."

"Search warrant? For where?"

"Kalifornia Klan Headquarters. I want to rap a little with ol' Jesse Utter."

On the grassy lawn outside the station Dolly Madison and Irving Tannenbaum were having a loud argument. When Tannenbaum spotted Gold he screamed with rage, *"Who the hell do you think you are? Who the hell do you think you are?"*

"Lighten up, Irving. You're gonna have a heart attack."

"You think you're above the law, but you're not! Believe me you're not! I'll see you in court because of this!"

Gold and Zamora were at the Ford. Gold yanked his door open.

"Irving, why don't you go home and tell your little Jewish mother that today, for once in your life, you did the right thing. You walked out of the room when a cop was questioning a witness, and that single act may have saved her life. Go home and tell her that."

"You're a madman! You're worse than the criminals!"

Gold slammed the door and drove away. Tannenbaum was still screaming after him.

11:15 AM Desert Vista choked under a blanket of noxious brown smog that had drifted out from the city. Forty-five minutes before noon, it was already 99 degrees with not a wisp of breeze. The naked hills baked in the sun.

Thirty-seven-year-old Joseph Christopher Cutler, Jr.—the sheriff of the incorporated city of Desert Vista and the pudgy, sandy-haired son of Sergeant Joe Cutler, the veteran cop that the rookie Jack Gold had stood over and defended during the Gunfight at the O.K. Corral nearly thirty years earlier—whipped his speeding patrol car angrily around a mountain curve and up the climbing dirt road, throwing up a shower of pebbles and stones that pelted off the windshields of the two other sheriff's cars that followed close behind, their bubbletops flashing.

"Okay! Okay! You got a warrant! You got a warrant!" Sheriff Cutler fumed, sweat pouring down his fleshy face and staining the starched collar of his khaki uniform shirt. "All I'm asking, all I'm asking is that you go easy, okay? Just go easy, okay?" Sheriff Cutler was a man given to repeating himself.

"What's your story, Junior?" Gold, in the passenger seat, flashed a hard glare at him. "These assholes friends of yours?"

Cutler winced at the sound of his childhood nickname. "Look, Jack, look," Cutler said, both eyes on the road and both hands on the wheel. "The people live up here live up here because it's nice and quiet. Safe. Real safe."

"Safe for who?" Gold interrupted.

Sheriff Cutler gripped the wheel even more tightly. "Safe for the kinda people live up here. The citizens of Desert Vista don't mind these Klan types living up here, long as they don't pull any of their bullshit around here. Fact is, a lot of people in this town think Jesse Utter and his boys keep a lot of the criminal types out of around here. They know the Klan's up here, they keep their asses out, those kinds."

"What kinds?" Gold baited.

"Aw, shit, Jack! What do you want me to say?" Cutler shouted.

"Whatever's on your mind, Junior," Gold shouted back.

"All right! All right! Niggers! Niggers and spicks! Who the hell else robs and rapes, anyway?"

Zamora, in the back seat, snickered and Cutler shot him a hot glare by way of the rearview.

"And Jews?" Gold asked. "Burn a few crosses and keep the Hebes out? Is that the way it is up here? Desert Vista's own special welcome wagon?"

Cutler, obviously uncomfortable, swerved the car and narrowly avoided shearing off a rack of rural mailboxes.

"Gimme a break, Jack! Just gimme a break! I didn't make the fucking world!"

"And you sure the fuck didn't make it any better!"

"Aw, for chrissake! We're serving the warrant, ain't we? Ain't we?"

"But is your heart in it, Junior, is what I want to know."

"Aw, for chrissake, Jack!"

"Did you come up here to your safe little small-town sheriff's office and forget how to be a cop? And what would your old man say if he was still alive?"

Cutler stood on the brakes and in a hail of pebbles the car fishtailed to a screeching halt on the level area just below the Klan World Headquarters. The vehicles following almost plowed into their rear end. Cutler twisted in his seat to face Gold.

"Don't give me that bullshit, Jack! Just don't give me that bullshit! You saved my old man's bacon, and for that he was eternally grateful, and so am I, but he never gave a rat's ass about another Jew his whole fucking life, and you know it. He loved you, but that was you—nobody else. And he was like every other cop I ever knew. So don't break my fucking balls if I ask you not to come up here and cowboy your way around the way I know you love to do. I got to live in this town, and I don't give a rat's ass about what happens on Fairfax Avenue. That's not my lookout. These people pay my salary. They gave me my safe little sheriff's office. They gave me my job."

Gold shoved the warrant under Cutler's nose.

"Then *do* your fucking job, Sheriff. Serve the fucking warrant!"

"All right, I will!" Cutler snatched away the warrant and kicked open his car door.

Four men had come out of the headquarters and stood, looking down at Gold, Cutler, and Zamora as they approached.

"Jesse," Cutler began, "we've got a search war—"

"Hey, kike!" Utter shouted. "I've been expecting you. You and your half-breed Tonto. I've been expecting you for over an hour."

Gold stopped in his tracks and looked over at Cutler, who shook his head. Then they both turned around to glare at the four deputies from the other cars. The deputies stared back without blinking.

"Oh, I've got eyes and ears everywhere, kike. Even on your Zionist controlled police force."

Gold turned back to him. "Then you know what I want."

Utter sneered. "Oh, I know what you want, all right, kike. You want a Communist, anti-Christian takeover of this country, but you won't get it, I promise you."

Gold sighed wearily. "I want that license plate number."

Utter chuckled. "What license plate number?"

"From the guy who came up here on Thursday. The guy with the tattoos. In the blue van."

"I'm sure I don't know what you're talking about, kike."

Gold pointed at the headquarters' open door. "Is it in there?"

Utter smiled. "Stupid kike. I told you, I knew you were on your way up here hours ago. Now what do you think?"

"Do you remember it?"

Utter's smile broadened. "You are one dumb Jew."

"Then we'll have to look for it," Gold said as he moved toward the door.

"Where the hell do you think you're going, Jew?" Utter growled as he stepped into Gold's path. Without breaking stride Gold pushed with both hands against Utter's narrow chest and the smaller man found himself on his back in the red dust. Zamora, who without asking permission had brought the shotgun from Cutler's patrol car, jacked a shell into the chamber and grinned at the other three Klansmen.

"Sheriff, maybe you'd better serve him with the search warrant," Gold said as he stepped over the threshold and into the headquarters.

Utter scrambled to his feet and pointed at Cutler. "You let that dirty Jew defile our sacred headquarters? You let him go in there?"

"Shut up, Jesse." Cutler measured off each word. "Besides, you should give him that plate number."

Utter sputtered like a badly tuned motor. "You better remember who you belong to, Sheriff!"

Cutler glared at him, then followed Gold into the building. Zamora stood in the doorway and kept the shotgun on Utter and the other Klansmen. His smile was as icy as his blue eyes.

In the center of the dim room that constituted the International World Headquarters of the Secret Society of the Kalifornia Klan, Gold stood and turned slowly in a circle, running his gaze over the obscene collection of posters.

Gold's mouth was open. His face darkened with anger. "Utter," he shouted in the direction of the door, "you're one sick motherfucker."

"No!" Utter screamed from outside. "You're the sickness, Jew! You and this mongrel half-breed! You're the cancer in this nation's belly!"

Zamora raised the muzzle of the shotgun to rest against Utter's bony chest.

"*Silencio, culo,*" he grinned. "That's half-breed for shut the fuck up, asshole."

Inside, Gold pointed out to Cutler the vacant gun racks, the hastily emptied file cabinets, the rifled desk drawers left ajar.

"They had hours' notice, like Utter said. Anything incriminating—the arsenal, the ammo, the mailing lists, the slip of paper—is long gone. We could look through this place with a microscope, I don't think we'd find a scrap of anything we could use to bring pressure on the bastard."

Cutler frowned. "I'm sorry, Jack. I hope it wasn't one of my men tipped them off."

Gold said nothing. Cutler started toward the door. "I'm really sorry, Jack," he repeated. He turned back to Gold, who hadn't moved.

"Jack?"

"You holding any dope, Joe? Anything we can drop on this asshole?"

Cutler shook his head. "I don't have a thing."

Gold turned back to stare at the blowups screwed to the wall.

"Let's get out of here, Jack. This place gives me the creeps."

Slowly, Gold shook his head. "We got a search warrant, Joe. Let's search."

"Hey, Jack, c'mon. Let's get—"

Gold's eyes flashed angrily. "If you don't have the stomach for it, Sheriff, then maybe you should wait outside. I wouldn't want you to get in trouble with your friends."

With that Gold strode purposefully to the picture of the stacks of alabaster Jewish corpses being bulldozed like so much garbage. He gripped the edge of the posterboard with his fingertips and pulled. The screws resisted. He pulled harder. One screw popped loose and rattled across the floor. Gold braced his legs and yanked with all his strength and the poster broke away from the wall and crashed to the floor.

"Hey! You can't do that! What the hell are you doing?" Utter yelled through the door.

Gold stepped up and put his foot through the posterboard. It cracked in half. He stomped the remaining pieces into dust and splinters.

"Just looking for that slip of paper, Jesse. Just conducting a legal search," he called out.

Gold went to the next poster—a group of African babies bathing in cow urine. He took a firm grip along the top edge.

"Now, if you wanted to give me that plate number I could terminate this search immediately." Gold paused. "What do you say, Jesse?"

"I say you're a slimy, Christkilling Jew. So don't call me by my *Christian* name."

"I'm sorry you feel that way."

Gold tore the poster from the wall, broke it in two and flung the pieces across the room.

"Nothing behind that one either," he said, almost to himself. He yanked at the next poster. It was recalcitrant. In a closet Gold found a mop handle. He broke it over his knee and using the splintered end as a crowbar, jimmied the other posters from the wall and kicked them into scraps. He overturned desks, tossed typewriters, upended file cabinets. He rammed the broom handle through a computer terminal, a television screen, and the stereo speakers.

Outside, the Klansmen hearing the destruction grew grim and silent. Zamora maintained his smile and his trigger pressure.

"Police work," he said, "can be very strenuous."

Inside, Gold had turned on a floor-to-ceiling bookcase that covered one whole wall of the big room. It held Klan literature, Klan photographs and mementos, framed pictures of Jesse Utter and what was obviously his family. Gold was pushing the bookcase from behind, trying to tip it over. It was too heavy.

"Joe," he grunted, "gimme a hand."

"Jack, for chrissake."

"Gimme a fucking hand!"

Cutler shrugged and threw his beefy frame against one end of the tall bookcase. Together they managed to rock it, then tilt it, then finally throw it over with a resounding crash. Books, cassette tapes, and photographs cascaded down; business machines and typewriters tumbled across the floor. Gold and Cutler looked at each other and giggled. The room was now completely trashed. Gold and Cutler went outside.

"You filthy kike!" Utter screamed.

"That's only the beginning, asshole," Gold said, breathing heavily from the exercise. "Give me that plate number, or I'll never leave you alone."

"Get off my property!"

Cutler quickly moved between Gold and Utter. "Jack, it's not here. Leave it alone."

Gold glared at Cutler, then pointed his finger at Utter. "I don't have time to fuck with you, asshole."

"Get off my property, kike!"

Sheriff Cutler held Gold back. Gold pushed the restraining hands away roughly.

"I'll be back, motherfucker," Gold said to Utter.

"Why don't you come back alone, Jew?" Utter dared. "At night. Without your friends and your badge. We'll have a real Klan party and kick your kike ass all over the mountain."

Just then the thin biker-type Klansman with the wispy blond beard came around the corner of the building, half dragged by a pair of leashed German shepherds. Utter's eyes lit up.

"Hey, kike, have you met our two SS dogs? The big one's named Auschwitz. The white bitch we call Treblinka. Don't you think those are beautiful names?"

Gold nodded to Zamora. "Let's get out of here."

"Wait a minute." Utter's eyes were dancing. "What was it the Gestapo guards at the camps used to say to their dogs when they wanted to sic them on a Jew? Oh, yes, I remember now." Utter snapped his fingers. The dogs' attention riveted on him and he pointed to Gold and ordered the animals, *"Man,* kill that *dog!"*

The dogs leaped to the ends of their leashes, snarling and biting, straining to get at Gold. Utter and the other Klansmen roared with laughter. The wispy-bearded blond giggled as he fought to hold the shepherds back.

"Man," Utter laughed again, "kill that dog! Kill him! Kill him!"

The big gray male lunged forward with renewed ferocity. The smile on the blond biker's lips faded as he felt the leash slipping from his fingers. He jerked back hard, the leather thong wrapped around his fist snapped, and the dog was free and racing toward Gold.

"Auschwitz! *Auschwitz!"* the blond screamed, but the frenzied dog was already bunching his haunches to jump.

Zamora, still standing by the doorway, brought the shotgun around but couldn't get a clear shot.

"Jack!" he shouted. *"Watch out!"*

Gold, who had walked halfway down the hard-beaten path, with one motion turned and ripped his gun from his belt holster. The dog was in midair. The muzzle of the .38 wasn't three feet away when the blast hit the beast in its chest, twisting it and throwing it back on itself.

The dog lay dead in the red dust, still as a rock.

"Auschwitz!" Utter cried in despair.

Treblinka, the white bitch, driven mad by the scent of her dead mate's blood and the roar of the gunshot, emitted a high-pitched scream as she tore at the ground in an effort to get at Gold. The blond knelt behind her and grabbed her collar. The bitch immediately twisted her neck and bit him viciously. Blondie shouted and clutched his bleeding arm, letting the leash fall. The bitch was gone, making for Gold. She got ten yards along before Gold dropped her with a bullet that crushed her right foreleg and shoulder and sent her scuttling head first to the earth. Growling deep in her throat, her eyes dazed with pure hatred, she pulled herself up and limped toward Gold.

"Treblinka!" Utter shouted. *"Stay, girl, stay!"*

It was too late. The dog didn't hear him. She lurched forward. Gold shot her again, again she fell, this time snapping at the ground in her agony. Then she died with an audible passing of fetid air.

"You bastard!" Utter screamed, kneeling over the bitch's body. *"You Jew bastard!"*

Gold held his gun at his side as he backed down to the level parking area. Zamora followed, also backing away from the Klansmen, the shotgun held before him.

"Don't you ever come up here again! *Ever!* We'll *kill* you!"

When they reached Cutler's car Zamora ducked down and looked inside.

"The keys are in it."

"Then let's get the fuck out of here."

"Joe," Gold shouted up the hill, "we'll leave your ride at your station."

"Jack, wait up!"

"See you around, Joe. Thanks for nothing!"

Zamora peeled out, choking the open-mouthed deputies in a wave of dust.

They were almost down the mountain when Cutler, driving alone in another black-and-white, overtook them doing ninety. He gave a short blast on the siren and motioned for them to pull over.

"What are you gonna do? Arrest us?" Gold snarled when Cutler trotted over to the window. "What is it, a felony in Desert Vista not to be Anglo-Saxon? Or are you from the local SPCA?"

"Jack, I'm really sorry about what happened up there."

"Don't lose any fucking sleep."

"Jack, I want to help."

"Why?"

" 'Cause, goddamn it, I *am* a cop! And because I owe you one. For my old man."

Gold's eyes blazed. "So?"

"So—how would you like to catch Jesse Utter on *your* turf? Would that do you any good?"

"Run it down."

"Well, Utter may have sympathizers among my deputies, but I've got a few informants in his organization, too. Guys I've caught being naughty and let walk away. They tell me Utter's every move."

"Hey, maybe you are a cop."

"Look, I keep a close watch on Utter, he's a powder keg. Anyway, I know that Utter's giving a speech tomorrow night at a church in North Hollywood. Very hush-hush, supersecret thing. Special invitation only. He's trying to start a new Klan Klavern right there in the San Fernando Valley. Right in your own backyard."

"Over my dead fucking body."

"I'm telling you, Jack. Tomorrow night. Ten o'clock. In the Bible Study Room of the Blood of the Lamb Christian Church."

Gold stripped the cellophane from a cigar and stuck it in the corner of his mouth.

"What am I gonna roust him for?" he said thoughtfully. "Being a bigot? That gets you Chief Justice."

Sheriff Cutler reached a lighter in the window and lit Gold's cigar with a broad grin.

"I'm sure you'll think of something, Jack. I'm sure you're gonna think of something."

2:26 PM Fairfax Avenue was deserted, its sidewalks devoid of the normal Shabbes crowds. The Israeli felafel stands, the bagel bakeries, the thrift stores—all were closed and battened down like a city waiting for a natural disaster. The tourists who usually flocked to nearby Farmer's Market were staying away in large numbers. Even ultrafashionable Melrose Avenue, which sliced right through the old neighborhood, was empty of its usual weekend crowds of punker poseurs and new-wave shoppers. A show had finally come to L.A. that impressed even the most blasé town in the world. On the streets only a few lategoers, dressed in their Shabbes best, hurried home from temple. At last night's services rabbis had urged their congregations to go home quickly and come back to *shul* in the early morning and stay there all day. Rumors were raging through the Jewish community that a right-wing terrorist organization was going to fire-bomb a synagogue, or dynamite a Hebrew school, or assassinate a rabbi—some kind of bloodbath today, on the Sabbath, to parody Tuesday night's Delicatessen Massacre. The Jewish community was frightened, but angry and united in their fear. Many men were openly armed.

The Jewish Armed Resisters were still at their posts at the roadblocks, ostentatiously shouldering their M-16's and glaring sullenly at passersby.

The Resisters on duty around the perimeter of the armed camp watched closely as Gold and Zamora parked and got out. When they tried to pass a young thin zealot blocked their way.

"He doesn't look Jewish," he accused, pointing his rifle at Zamora.

"He's a cop, for chrissake!" Gold growled. "And get that fucking gun out of my face before someone shoves it up your *tuchis.*"

The kid stepped aside quickly and Gold and Zamora moved into the area.

The streets of the neighborhood appeared strangely wide, and then Gold realized what it was: no cars, no parked cars. People must have been ordered to move their cars. To make defense easier, to provide less cover for snipers, to protect against terrorist car bombs. The place really was an armed camp, Gold thought. Fairfax Avenue had gone to war.

The JAR "Command Center" was upstairs over a candy store a few blocks down from Herschel's Deli. In the empty street before the entrance some Resisters had set up a card table covered with Resistance paraphernalia—pamphlets and softcover books, T-shirts and scarves. Someone had brought a monster cassette player and martial-sounding Israeli music was blaring. Someone else was going around with a mailing list. Young raven-haired girls in the trademark blue T-shirts were serving Sabra-style pita sandwiches and broiling lamb on skewers on portable grills. The guards shared the felafel with the girls and laughter and banter went back and forth. They see themselves as heroes, Gold thought. They're acting out some *cinema verité* French movie they've all seen. Some post-Holocaust racial fantasy. They're children playacting.

Some of the Resisters recognized Gold and bristled. A few of the bolder ones crowded around the two policemen.

"What are you doing here, collaborator?" demanded a smooth-cheeked twenty-year-old. "You're not welcome around here. This is Resistance country."

Gold flashed a cold smile. "Don't play soldier with me, son. You might hurt yourself."

The twenty-year-old stiffened. Gold looked up at the second-floor windows over the candy store.

"Is Jerry Kahn there?"

Gold moved toward the building's entrance and the twenty-year-old barred the door with his carbine. Gold sighed deeply.

"Son," he said wearily, "people have been getting in my face the whole damn day, and one of these times I'm afraid I'm just gonna explode. I hope when I do it's not gonna be all over you. Now, please, stand aside."

The kid hesitated, confused. "Well, *he* can't go up. He's a Gentile."

"He's my partner, son."

The kid shook his head emphatically. "Uh uh! No *goyim* allowed."

Gold turned to Zamora. "Sean—"

"I'll wait down here," Zamora said, staring hard at the twenty-year-old. "If they give you any trouble, just give a holler and I'll walk over this punk and we'll kick ass all over the street!"

Gold went up the narrow stairwell. The steps ended in a second-floor anteroom crowded with Resisters and their supporters. The noise level was just short of painful. An Israeli film crew was shooting a documentary, darting between people with their shoulder-held cameras and shoving microphones in the faces of intense young Resisters in order to capture their grim words.

"My God," Gold mumbled, "it *is* a movie."

The anteroom was stifling hot, even hotter than outside, and smelled of sweating men and gun grease. Several people recognized Gold, but no one made any attempt to speak to him. The twenty-year-old led him through the crowd to another door on the opposite side of the room.

"Wait here," he ordered solemnly and went in.

Gold turned to face the room again. All conversation had ceased; all eyes were on him.

Gold smiled. "How's by you?" he asked. No one answered or smiled back.

The twenty-year-old popped his head out. "Come in. Jerry will see you now."

The room was small and, if possible, hotter than the anteroom. The walls were plastered with travel posters of Israeli vistas: Masada, the Mediterranean, Old Jerusalem. Behind a massive white table that served as a desk sat Jerry Kahn, flanked by the flags of Israel and the United States. There were three other people in the room: a woman in a babushka, a fair young man, and a middle-aged man dressed in heavy black. The adhesive bandage still covered the bridge of Jerry Kahn's nose.

"You've got a lot of *chutzpa,* coming here, Uncle Ike."

Gold smiled. "I've heard that before."

"You broke my nose. And almost my arm."

"You were lucky."

Kahn shot him a hot glare. "Well, what do you want?"

"A glass of tea, maybe."

"What?"

"A glass of tea, served from a samovar. We'll drink it Russian style, through a cube of sugar."

"What are you talking about?"

"Then we'll plot the attack on the English prison. By the way, where's Newman?"

"Newman?"

"Yeah, Paul Newman. This *is* the set for *Exodus,* isn't it? This is a movie, right?"

Everyone glowered at him as he moved about the room.

"I mean, I see all these young *shmucks* swaggering around like little Moshe Dayans, everyone pretending to be tough and acting bad, I figure it's all one big fucking fantasy, right? Saturday-afternoon matinee. Am I right?"

Hostile silence.

"You're all from Central Casting, right? 'Hey, Sol, send over some physical Semitic types in desert fatigues and combat boots. We're doing this bullshit exploitation-adventure flick and we need a bunch of gullible young kids.' Isn't that what's going on here?"

Jerry Kahn's mouth curled into a tiny sneer. "You come in here like Daniel into the lions' den, into a place where you're unwelcome and unwanted, then you insult us. I would be a little more circumspect if I were you."

Gold leaned across the wide white table and spoke into Kahn's face:
"Why don't you let me worry about that one, Jer."

Kahn's patience was being tried. "What the hell do you want anyway?"
he snapped. "We have a charter from the mayor to patrol our neighborhood. Someone's murdering Jews. *Again.* Or haven't you heard? And since
you can't catch 'em, we're gonna stop 'em. If you were doing your job, we
wouldn't be out here. But then Jews have never enjoyed much protection
from America's law enforcement agencies, have they? Even when they put
token figureheads like yourself in high-visibility positions."

Gold dragged over a chair and sat down. He slipped a cigar from his
shirt pocket.

"You know, I just came from somewhere reminds me a lot of this place."

Khan waited a beat, then bit. "Oh? And where was that?"

Gold put a match to his cigar. "Place up in Desert Vista. Kalifornia
Klan Headquarters."

Khan sneered, an actual sneer. A sound and an expression. The other
three people in the room laughed with him.

"We've heard all that *dreck* before," Kahn said. "All you apologist,
assimilationist, secular Jews try to peddle that same old tired line: the JAR
is the other side of the coin, the dark side of the Jewish psyche, right-wing
Jewish terrorists. Well, we don't buy that bullshit. And when the next
depression comes and they blame it on the Jews the way they always do;
when the Arabs cut off the oil again and anti-Jewish hatred is as near as
the next car's bumper sticker; when your beloved, oh-so-wonderful Christian friends come in the night to drag you screaming from your split-level
homes and throw you in the trucks that will take you to the camps and
the ovens—you'll be wetting your pants with happiness the JAR is around
to protect you, to fight for you."

Gold stared at him. "You don't really believe that?" he asked softly.

"Emphatically. We *know* it. Right?"

Everyone answered him with a round of "rights" and "yeses" and
"never agains."

Kahn leveled his gaze at Gold. "Never *never* again."

Gold puffed thoughtfully on his cigar. "I'd like to speak to you alone."

Kahn waved his hand at the others. "These are my unit commanders.
My generals. I have no secrets from them."

Gold shook his head. "Maybe you don't but I do. I've already been
compromised once today. I won't let it happen again. I want to talk to you
alone."

Again Kahn sneered. "Why should I listen to anything you have to say?"

"If you really want to stop these killings, you'll listen. If you really want to save Jewish lives, you'll listen. Or do you just want to blow smoke up everybody's ass?"

Kahn simmered a moment. Finally he said to the others, "Leave me with him."

Immediately cries of protest arose in the room.

"Jerry, he's a madman!"

"Look what he's done already."

"He's dangerous!"

Kahn held up his hand for silence. "We're not ghetto rats, cowering in fear, afraid of our own shadows. We are the descendants of a race of warriors. I will speak to this collaborator alone."

Grumbling, the trio left the room. The babushka'd woman stood in the doorway and said, "We'll be right outside if you need us." Then she shut the door behind her.

Alone together, the two men eyed each other. Kahn shifted his weight in his chair, favoring his right arm. Gold chewed his cigar.

"You're really sitting pretty with all this, ain't you?" Gold said. "A real big shot. This whole sorry mishmash has made you one very important man, hasn't it?"

"I didn't cause this mess," Kahn shot back angrily. "Although none of it surprises me. I've been warning for years that anti-Semitism was on the rise in this country, in this state, in this city. The rich fat-cat Jews, in their stupid complacency, chose to ignore me. So don't lay that guilt on me. If the police force did its job there wouldn't be a need for the JAR."

"There *isn't* a need for the JAR."

"Then why are Jews being exterminated in the streets? And why are you letting the murderers get away?"

"No one's getting away with anything."

"Oh? Arrests you've made?"

"Not yet."

"Well, until you do the JAR protects these people. Forever, if necessary."

Gold chomped furiously on the wet end of his cigar. Kahn leaned back in his chair and grinned. "I heard through the grapevine you told Orenzstein to go to hell. That was beautiful. I'd like to squash that self-serving bastard."

Gold said nothing.

"You know, Gold, in spite of everything, in a way I actually like you. You're the kind of Jew I like to recruit for my Resisters."

"And what kind is that?"

"A Jew with balls, with *chutzpa.* A true descendant of our desert warrior ancestors. Not one of those liberal namby-pambies. Those apologist assimilationists, afraid to call themselves a true Jew. Always trying to be something they're not. Always chasing after *shiksas* and *shvartzehs.*" Kahn smiled evilly. "And not one of those little bookworm stereotypes the Nazis like to draw cartoons of. The Woody Allens. Those bookkeepers and clerks, jewelers and lawyers. Weak and cowardly. Ineffectual, asexual, and filled with self-hatred."

Gold studied Kahn. "Seems to me *self-hatred* is the operative word here."

"I told you," Kahn snarled, "that psychoanalytical tripe doesn't swing much weight around here. We know exactly who we are. Who our friends are. And our enemies."

Gold leaned forward and rested his elbows on Kahn's white desk. "I'll tell you who you are," he began. "What you are. You're bullshit. You're a bunch of overgrown Boy Scouts. Yeshiva Scouts. And you're the fucking den mother. You should be selling cookies! Only somehow you've manipulated the media so well that the politicians can't ignore you, they're afraid of you. Afraid to say what they think. That Jerry Kahn is a big loudmouth asshole. Afraid somebody will accuse them of anti-Semitism. A blow against Jerry Kahn is a blow against all Jews—that's the way you've worked it out, isn't it? You were doing just fine walking old ladies home from the market and marching in nice neat little protest lines for Soviet Jewry, but all of a sudden this golden opportunity got dropped in your lap, and now you're so happy you could shit on yourself. All of a sudden everybody knows who you are, don't they? Your picture's being shown on television all around the world. Jerry Kahn is *somebody,* just like his mother always knew he would be. And all it took was a fucking truckload of corpses—Jewish and Gentile—to get you your recognition. Hey, you should be *paying* the fucking Crosskiller, all the glory he's giving you!"

"That's enough!" Kahn shouted.

"No, that's not nearly enough!" Gold shouted back. "Where do you get off ranking Harvey Orenzstein? Oh, he's a slick piece of shit, all right, but he's a politician, and that's like wearing a sign around your neck saying 'I'm a slick piece of shit.' At least it's right out there, what he is, for everyone to see. You, on the other hand, try to pass yourself off as a hero, a champion of the people. The Lion of Judah. And you don't fool me for a second. What are you looking for out of this? A seat on the City Council? A book deal? State representative? State assemblyman? Hey, maybe you and Jesse Utter could run on the same ticket. The Hate and War Party. Blow away thy neighbor."

"*Get out!*" Kahn thundered, standing to point to the door. The door opened a crack, someone peeked in, then quickly shut it. Gold calmly relit his cigar. He puffed and puffed until he was sitting in a drifting white cloud.

"Kahn," he began slowly, "I'm gonna give you the opportunity of a lifetime. A chance in a million. A chance to finally do what you've always claimed you wanted to do. A chance to save Jewish lives. A chance to—"

"My God!" Kahn interrupted, incredulous. "You came here to ask for a favor. You need my help." A slow smile crawled across his face. "You need my help." He sat down with a plop.

"For once," Gold continued, "you're gonna be useful in the fight against Israel's enemies. For once your actions will have real meaning."

"Such a deal!" Kahn said, grin still in place. "I don't deserve such a *mitzva.*"

Gold eyed him coldly. "This is deadly serious, Kahn. This is no joke."

"What do you want me to do?"

"I can't tell you. You agree first, then I tell you."

Kahn shook his head in disbelief. "And when do I get to perform this godly act?"

"Tomorrow night."

"Sorry," Kahn said, "no can do. Sunday night the JAR is providing security for Jackie Max's Brotherhood Rally at the Bowl."

Gold exploded, standing and waving his arms as he stormed around the room.

"You phony! You two-bit phony! You are *all* bullshit! One hundred percent, twenty-four-karat solid gold bullshit! I'm giving you a shot to help me catch the motherfucker, and all you can think about is kissing ass with a bunch of Bel-Air show biz big shots who are almost as phony as you are! How'd you get the gig, did your fucking press agent get it for you? Have you signed with William Morris yet, you phony bastard? I can't fucking believe this! Do you have a movie deal yet?"

Gold paced the room and shouted up to God.

"Can you believe this Jew, Lord? Big, tough, bad-ass Jew! Warrior of the desert! He's a fucking usherette, now! He's gonna mount a flashlight on the end of his *putz* and show some fat-ass stars to their seats. He's gonn—"

"All right."

Gold halted in the middle of the room. "What?" He turned to Kahn. "What?"

"I said all right. We'll do it. Do we get to bust some Nazi heads?"

Gold leaned over the desk.

"You're gonna love this. I want you to attack a church."

7:57 PM This sunset was even more glorious than yesterday's. From the neon-impressionist school, all awash in smoggy pinks and crimsons, scarlets and orange.

Dolly Madison had slept all day. He came into Parker Center all bright and bouncy and told Gold and Zamora they looked like zombies. He ordered them home to get some sleep. A few hours, at least. For once Gold didn't bristle at being ordered anywhere. He drove Zamora home to East L.A. The hilly streets were the most alive in the city. Babies and small children played on the sidewalks in front of their homes. Their laughter seemed freer and more innocent than Anglo children's laughter. Their dusty laborer fathers gathered in groups on their front porches and drank beer and watched their sons and daughters. The air was redolent with the heady scent of chili peppers and broiling meat. In every vacant corner boys tossed baseballs or kicked around soccer balls. Brown pubescent girls in day-glo eye makeup lounged in front of tiny *bodegas,* sipping diet Pepsi and gossiping and giggling. These people ignored smog warnings. They had seen Mexico City. They had come through T.J. They knew "unhealthful" when they saw it.

When Gold parked in front of Zamora's house, Zamora's head was on the back of his seat and he was snoring loudly.

"Sean. Sean. You're home. Hey, wake up, Redford."

Zamora jerked upright and looked around. Comprehension seeped into his eyes and he smiled.

"Jack, come in and meet my family. Have dinner. *Mi abuela* always makes *menudo* on Saturdays."

Gold grimaced. "Ugh! How can you eat that shit?"

"Hey, *mano,* that's Mexican chicken soup. It'll fix you right up."

Gold laughed. "Another time, Sean."

"You sure? My mother pours a mean glass of Irish whiskey."

"Another time. After all this is over."

Zamora nodded. "Yeah, okay. I can dig it. Then you go home and get some sleep. Like Dolly said. You look about like I feel."

Zamora got out of the car. He turned and opened the rickety wooden gate that led to the modest clapboard house trimmed in Sea of Cortez blue. He waved from the stoop.

Gold drove westward, home.

In his mailbox was a three-day accumulation of bills and junk flyers. But, he was surprised to find, there were no newspapers in front of his door. He had been gone—what?—two, three days, and the paper delivery had obviously stopped. Either that or the kids on the way to school were stealing them. He would have to call the *Times*'s circulation department. The carrier was fucking up. First scaring poor little Genghis, now not coming around at all.

Inside the apartment Gold stripped off his tired, wrinkled clothes and poured himself a drink. He sat at the plastic dinette table and dialed Evelyn and Dr. Stanley Markowitz's number. There was no answer. Then he remembered—they had all gone to Cabo San Lucas. Evelyn had told him they were taking Wendy away. Gold sighed and had another swallow of Scotch.

He took a long, scalding shower, leaning against the tile and letting the spray beat over his back and shoulders until the hot water turned tepid. Drying himself off, he caught a glimpse of his ghost in the steamy mirror. He wiped away the moisture with his hand and looked at himself. With a jolt he realized he was an old man—much nearer the horrors of the grave than the bloom of youth. He looked tired and grim; the shadows under his eyes resembled cheap theatrical makeup; his eyes were sunken, cold and distant, like ice in an empty glass. The Angel of Death, who was himself dying. Gold shuddered and shook off the macabre notion.

He dressed quickly—running shoes, jeans, nondescript shirt left outside his belt to cover his holstered .38. From a crowded drawer in his small desk he took out the .22 and put it in his pants pocket. Then he called Dolly Madison at Parker Center and told him he was going to sleep. Madison congratulated him on his good sense.

Out in the hot streets, night had finally fallen. Another *Shabbes* was over. Traffic was light.

Gold cruised by Le Parc, searching the lot for Saperstein's Rolls. It wasn't there. He drove up to the green-and-pink fake-Egyptian house in the hills. The circular drive was vacant. He coasted slowly down the hill, chewing on an unlit cigar. Three quarters of the way down, he jammed down the accelerator. He made it to Century City in seven minutes. The underground parking structure was closed on weekends to all but monthlies who could punch their cards into the robot sentries and raise the barricades, but there were no safeguards against pedestrians. Gold parked in an alley off the street and walked in—not too briskly, not too slowly. He took the stairs. He met no one. On the third level, almost exactly where he had found it before, was the Corniche with the DEFENSE plates. There were only two other cars on the third level, both of them functional sedans. Gold found a rathole between two fat, circular support pillars. He chewed his cigar and waited. Twenty minutes later a lone woman in a tailored business suit got off the elevator and drove one of the sedans away. Gold waited some more. On another level someone screeched his brakes and the sound reverberated dimly through the structure. The fluorescent lighting seemed to dim periodically, as if a generator somewhere snapped off and on, but he couldn't be sure whether his eyes were playing tricks on him. He spit out a shred of tobacco from between his teeth and was reaching for his matches to light his cigar when the elevator doors slipped open and Natty Saperstein stepped off. He was alone. He was wearing a cotton-candy-pink three-piece suit with matching plumed fedora and carrying a black lizard-skin briefcase. He walked briskly, his tiny feet flashing in their white Gucci loafers. He looked like something from the Court of Louis XVI. When Natty was unlocking the Rolls, Gold stepped out of his hiding place.

"Natty. Natty, wait up."

Saperstein was startled. He peered into the shadows from where the voice had come.

"Who is it? Who's there?"

Gold walked under a light fixture and the greenish glow lit up his features.

"It's me. Jack Gold."

"Jack who? Oh, Jack. It's been years. What the hell are you doing lurking down here in the shadows?"

"Stakeout."

"What? Wait a minute." Saperstein looked around, suddenly afraid. "Are you looking for that Crosskiller suspect? Is he around here?"

Gold shrugged. "You never know. Listen, Natty, since I got you here, I'd like to talk to you about something."

"You're sure that Crosskiller suspect isn't around here?"

"I wouldn't worry about it."

Gold moved a few feet closer. He was across the Rolls's hood from Saperstein.

"I'd really like to talk to you, Natty."

Natty, no longer frightened, turned shrewd lawyer eyes on Gold.

"What about?"

"I've got a problem I'd like to discuss with you."

"You need a lawyer?"

Gold gave him a strange smile. "Not just any lawyer, Natty. It has to be you."

Natty opened the door of the Rolls and tossed his briefcase into the back seat.

"Why don't you call my office, Jack?" he recited. "My girl will give you a date. I'm pretty open the end of next week."

Gold moved closer to the car. He leaned on the roof.

"It's really urgent, Natty. I would really appreciate it. If you could spare a few minutes."

"Jack, for chrissake, it's Saturday night. I just came to the office to look something up. I'm already late for a dinner date. Let's make it next week. Maybe Monday."

Gold persisted. "Just a few minutes, Natty. That's all it'll take. Just a few minutes."

Natty sighed testily. "This can't wait?"

Gold shook his head. Saperstein wagged his finger at him. "This better not take long."

He slipped into the Rolls, leaned his small body across the seat, and unlocked the passenger side. Gold got in. He had never been in a Rolls-Royce before. The seat covers were supple leather, the wood trim burnished to a rich sheen.

"Nice car, Natty. You're doing well by yourself. But then you always have."

Natty inserted the key into the ignition by the door.

"Well? What is it?" he asked impatiently as he eyed the ash dribbling from the dead cigar between Gold's fingers.

"So"—Gold turned in the seat and forced a smile—"long time no see, Natty."

Saperstein grimaced. "Really, Jack, I don't have time right now to go over old times. What's your problem?"

Gold, still smiling, went on as if he hadn't heard him.

"You still working scams with your dope-peddler clients, Natty? Doing dope deals in your penthouse office? You still selling police protection. Working both sides of the street?"

"What is this?" Saperstein's eyes narrowed.

"You still the middleman between the crooks and the cops, Natty? The wholesaler of wholesale corruption?"

Saperstein was furious. "What the hell is this? Is this a setup? Am I being investigated? Are you questioning me? Because if you are, they really sent the wrong man for the wrong job. You made a small fortune off of me, Lieutenant, or have you forgotten? There's no statute of limitations for greedy cops, even for that long ago. So I'll ask you again, is this little tête-à-tête official?"

"I'm not investigating you, Natty."

"Then I'll ask you to leave, get out of my car this instant. Because official or otherwise, I don't see anything positive coming from this conversation. And don't bother calling my secretary, because for the police force I am always out. Out! Just like I want you out of this car. *Now!*"

Gold didn't move. Saperstein turned the key and started the Rolls's engine.

"You're wasting my time, Lieutenant, and *my* time is valuable."

Gold leaned across the wheel and turned the motor off. He pulled the keys and slipped them into his shirt pocket. Saperstein was astounded. *"What—is—the—meaning—of—this?* You do realize you're toying with a false arrest charge? Possibly even kidnapping."

"Shut up," Gold said.

"I eat policemen like you for breakfast," Saperstein threatened. "Every day in court. You'll lose your pension behind this."

"Shut up," Gold said again and reached behind Saperstein's back to lock the driver's door.

"I can't believe you're foolish enough to do this," Saperstein said in astonishment. "I can't believe it."

Gold sat back and stared at Saperstein. His smile was gone.

"You know a lawyer named Howard Gettelman, Natty? You know Howie Gettelman?"

Saperstein blinked, momentarily disconcerted and off balance.

"Yes. Yes, I know Howard, but—"

"Why'd you do it, Natty?" Gold shouted, and the tiny man recoiled as if he had been struck.

"I—I don't under—"

"Don't lie to me, Natty! I want to know the truth! I want to know why! *Why?"*

"Jack, please, I don't know what you're—"

"Dying men don't lie, Natty," Gold said softly.

Natty still didn't understand.

"Bobby Phibbs, Natty. I believe he worked for you. He gave up your name as easy as blowing a kiss. Like a kiss on my ear."

Comprehension, accompanied by fear and horror, suddenly washed over Natty's face.

"It—it was you!" he stammered, his eyes bulging.

"No, Natty, it was *you.* And I want to know why."

Saperstein edged away from Gold and pressed against the far door.

"I can't imagine it was the money. How could you need money? But then it would have to be the money, wouldn't it, Natty? Or was it the coke? Was it the coke?"

Saperstein stared at him. His mouth worked but no sound came out.

"Natty? Talk to me."

Saperstein gulped. "Did—did—did Gettelman hire you? Because—because I can pay you more. Much more."

Gold shook his head. "Tell me *why,* Natty."

Saperstein suddenly bolted and, in panic and confusion, yanked on the Rolls's door latch. It wouldn't open.

"It's locked," Gold said.

"What!" Natty cried as he pushed on the door.

"It's locked. I locked it." Gold reached over and touched the little man's shoulder. Natty jumped. "Here, Natty, look here."

Natty turned back to Gold. Gold was holding the .22, cradling it in his crotch like a lover offering a cock.

"Settle down," Gold said softly. "Relax."

"Jack, for God's sake, let's talk about this." The tiny man was trembling.

"That's what I want to do, Natty. That's just what I want to do."

At that moment the parking level echoed with the sensual ripple of a woman's inviting laughter. A couple—a graying fiftyish businessman escorting a younger woman—had stepped out of the elevator. With his left hand Gold raised the .22 and pressed the muzzle against Natty's temple.

"Shhhhhh—" he whispered.

The couple crossed over to the only other car. The clip-clop of the woman's high heels resounded off the concrete walls. The man said something and the woman laughed again, holding her hand in front of her mouth. The businessman looked pleased with himself. He opened the passenger door and helped the woman in, letting his hand linger on her arm. Then he went around to the other side and got behind the wheel. Framed by the rear window their heads came together and they kissed, their arms around each other's neck. After a long time—three or four minutes—their silhouettes broke apart and the woman laughed again, a rich, throaty, ball-stirring sound. Then the sedan's engine hummed alive and the man backed the car out of its parking slot and whooshed away down the exit ramp.

Gold and Saperstein, frozen in a wax museum tableau, stayed motionless for half a minute. Then Gold, keeping the .22 to Natty's head, said, "I thought they were gonna fuck. I thought they were gonna get it on, right there in the car."

Natty said nothing.

Almost rhetorically, Gold asked, "Did you ever love a woman, Natty?"

Saperstein didn't speak. Gold turned to him and smiled. "No, of course not. Of course not. How could you have ever loved a woman? Well, maybe your mother."

Saperstein uttered something weak, unintelligible.

"I can't hear you," Gold said.

Natty found his voice and the words jumped out, a little too loudly: "I loathed my mother."

In reply, Gold just went on. "I've loved three women. Besides my mother. Three women. And now one of them is dead. Another one hates me." Gold paused for a moment. "And the other one is my daughter, and she's married to Howie Gettelman."

Natty stiffened at the mention of the name. Gold leaned closer and spoke softly and rapidly.

"My daughter adores me. That's what people have always said. Ever since she was a little girl. 'That little girl adores you.' That's what they always say. She's the only one who never judged me. Never. When Angelique died and the whole world blew up, Natty, she never said a word, never asked a question, never passed a judgment. She never stopped loving me. Not for a second. I could feel that, you know what I mean. She loved me more, I think, because she knew I needed it. You wouldn't expect a little seven-year-old girl could be that perceptive, but I could *feel* it. I could feel her reaching out to me. Giving me all her love."

Gold was staring hard at Saperstein's trembling profile.

"She's the only human being in the world gives a rat's ass about me, Natty. And you sent those slimes into her home. You sent that scum into her home to rape her and beat her."

"Jack, Jack, Jack—"

"They beat her like a dog, Natty." Gold's voice was a venomous rattle. "They fucked her in her asshole, Natty. Did *you* tell 'em to do that?"

"Oh, no, J—"

"They made her suck their dicks, Natty. Did you tell 'em to do that?"

"No, Jack, pl—"

"They put a gun to my grandson's head, Natty. They told my Wendy they were gonna blow her baby's brains out, Natty."

"Oh, please, Jack."

"I'm going to kill you, Natty."

"Ohhhhhh—" the little man moaned, trembling violently. The Rolls was filled with the animal stench of fear.

"Why, Natty? The money? The coke? Or were you trying to hurt me?"

"No! No!" Saperstein cried eagerly. "I—I—I didn't know Gettelman was your son-in-law. I didn't know! I swear it! I—I just sent them there to get the cocaine. That's all. I just wanted them to get the coke. I didn't know they were going to do all those things. I didn't know about any of that until—until you just told me. I swear to God it's true!"

"You knew what kind of animals you were sending in there."

"No! No!"

"You know what happens to a woman in that kind of ripoff."

"No, I didn't!"

"Especially a white woman."

"No! Please!"

Natty was sweating profusely. A dark splotch stained his pink suit. He had wet himself.

"Why, Natty?"

"It—it was just the coke, Jack. I needed the coke."

"You can't afford to buy it anymore?"

Natty tried to shake his head, but Gold still had the muzzle of the .22 hard against his skull.

"Not enough! Never enough!" Natty choked out. "It's the young boys. The young boys. The beautiful ones. They're so beautiful. Everybody wants them. They can have anyone they want. And I'm getting so old!" Natty was crying now. "So old! It gets harder and harder. Everyone wants them and they all do coke. So much coke! Oh, *please,* Jack!"

"Even you can't make enough money to support a coke nose?"

"Ohhhh, Jack! I'm in trouble! So much trouble!"

"And why Gettelman?"

"He—he—Howard was just so eager. So stupid. So easy. Oh, please, Jack!"

Neither man moved, neither spoke for several seconds, then Saperstein cried, "Oh, Jack, I'm so sorry! *Please!*"

"Natty, I have nothing else to give her," Gold said and pulled the trigger. Natty Saperstein's face was thrown against the glass of the door on the driver's side. His short legs began to kick convulsively. Gold jammed the .22's muzzle against the base of the little man's skull. There were two quick muffled pops and the Rolls was suddenly filled with the stink of cordite and a delicate, drifting atomized vapor of blood and bone. Natty's legs relaxed and suddenly there was the overwhelming odor of human excrement.

Quickly, Gold snatched up Saperstein's fallen fedora and reached over and wiped the driver's lock with the soft felt hat. Then he got out. He looked at his watch. It was 10:15. From his pocket he took out an aerosol paint cannister. Across the Rolls's windshield he sprayed two big crimson crosses. Then he knelt along the driver's side and painted KILL THE JEWS in crude foot-high letters. He looked up from his work and Natty's dead eyes were staring down at him. Gold sprayed a tiny cross over the little man's face. He went around to the passenger's side and wiped at the door handle, seat back, and roof where he had leaned. From his shirt pocket he extracted Natty's car keys. He carefully wiped each key with the fedora and threw the keys on the seat beside the corpse. Still using the hat as a glove, he carefully closed the big car's passenger door. Then over the passenger side he wrote DEATH TO THE JEWS. The spray can made a hissing sound, like a thousand poisonous snakes crammed into the narrow aluminum tube.

Gold threw the fedora under the car, and without looking back he turned and walked quickly across the empty parking level to the stairs, down the stairs, and out onto the sidewalk. His Ford was still parked in the Japanese restaurant's delivery alley—unticketed and unnoticed. He drove westward on Olympic, slowly for a few miles, then faster after he turned south on Westwood Boulevard. He slipped into the light traffic on the Santa Monica Freeway.

Nine minutes later he was parking the Ford in the parking lot of the Santa Monica Pier. He checked his watch again. It was 10:36. He locked the Ford and walked out onto the pier.

It was Saturday night in August in L.A., and even though just a few miles east a whole section of the city had been put on war-readiness status, out here on the ocean side people were resolutely going about their pleasure. Incredibly hard-bodied, string-bikinied young women glided by, defying the posted signs prohibiting roller-skating. One muscled black youngblood with a massive ghetto-blaster perched on his shoulder did intricate arabesques on the weathered planks to a mechanized music track, his orange wheels clattering with joy. Farther out on the pier, packs of little Mexican kids crowded in front of the pizza-by-the-slice, frozen-banana-on-a-stick cubbyholes, slurping at dripping cones of soft ice cream. At the far end of the pier the serious fishermen huddled—old men measuring out the last of their lives by lengths of ten-pound test line; grim-faced brown-skinned refugee women, some Latin, others Asian, all of them surrounded by hordes of fat children, staring intently at the bobbing corks they used as floaters. A white teenager sat with his back to a barnacled post and played Bach on a silver flute.

Gold leaned on the railing and looked out to sea, the .22 hidden in the palms of his big hands. Within two minutes one of the old men pulled a fish out of the water and dropped it on the pier. A strange, prehistoric-looking fish with blue scales and red gills. Everyone turned to look at the fish. Gold released the .22 and it fell into Santa Monica Bay with a tiny splash. The old man unhooked the ugly fish and dropped it into a plastic bucket full of water. All the others turned back to their lines.

Gold walked back along the pier in the other direction. Up in the hills the lights in the cliffside homes glittered behind a film of night-hidden smog. It was hot.

Gold threw the paper bag containing the aerosol can into a trash receptacle overflowing with greasy popcorn boxes and hot dog wrappers. He strolled up the rest of the pier, almost to where it fed back into the parking lot. He stopped before a fast-food hole-in-the-wall called Jazzbo's Barbecue Roadhouse. Under a caricature of a fat black man in a vest and derby, the sign over the entrance invited the foot traffic to partake of RIBS-AND-RICE,

CHICK-B-Q and HAM-B-Q. Gold went in. The place was tiny, a shed really, containing six oilskin-covered picnic tables and an order counter. All the tables were empty. Gold sat at the one closest to the door. A woman in a white waitress uniform came from behind the counter to take his order. She was small and spare with close-cropped hair and no makeup or jewelry. She was very black and very plain.

"Can I help you, sir?" she said, smiling at the order pad in her hand.

"Hello, Gladys. How are you?"

She looked directly at him and the smile faded.

"What'*chu* want? We ain't done nothing wrong for you to come around here."

"Take it easy, Gladys. I just came by to say hello to Red."

"Well, he ain't here."

"Yes, he is, Gladys. You haven't let him out of your sight for ten years."

"I said he ain't here."

"He's in the kitchen. Go tell him I'm here."

"What'chu want with Red? He don't know nothing 'bout nothing. He don't run with them dope fiends no more. Neither do I."

Gold smiled. "I know that, Gladys," he said gently. "I just want to talk to Red a minute."

The smile didn't charm her. "He ain't here."

Gold got up and walked behind the counter to the hot-slot cut high in the wall.

"Yo, Red!" he shouted through the slot.

"Yeah?" came the answering holler from the kitchen.

"Come on out here. There's a friend wants to see you."

Gold walked back to his table and sat down. He looked up at Gladys.

"I'd like a cup of coffee, please."

She shot him a deadly glare and turned on her heel. "Motherfucking *po*lices think they own the world," she grumbled as she stamped behind the counter. The big door stenciled EMPLOYEES ONLY swung open and a small wiry white man in a cook's apron came through. He had flaming red hair and a deeply lined face aglow with pale freckles. His age was indeterminate—he could have been forty or sixty—but he exuded an aura of world-weariness and pain. He saw Gold and laughed.

"Lieutenant. What's happening? How are you? Baby, why didn't you tell me the lieutenant was out here?"

Gladys, coming around the counter with the coffeepot, didn't even look up as she said, "It's almost closing time."

"Baby! Don't be that way to the lieutenant," Red said as he sat down across the table from Gold. "He's good people."

She grunted and poured Gold's coffee into a Styrofoam container.

"Sorry I can't give you no cup, but it's almost closing time."

"Baby! Don't be that way."

Gladys looked at both men darkly and went back behind the counter.

"I'm going in the kitchen to finish cleaning up," she said, " 'cause it's almost closing time."

When she was gone Red turned to Gold. "Don't mind her, Lieutenant. She means well. She just gets real funny about anybody from my old dope days, cops included. She just sees red. I guess she figures she doesn't even want to be reminded of those days. Man, a coupla years ago this old junko partner of mine showed up at the apartment. I don't know how he got our address. And before I could hip the cat to split Gladys had a poker and was chasing the dude down the stairs. Ironic thing is, I heard the cat had been clean for years. Gladys don't care. She don't want them people around. Guess she's afraid we'll sit around and start talking 'bout our old junkie days. One thing leads to another, she figures. So don't mind Gladys. She means well."

Gold took a sip of coffee. "So how's that going, Red?"

"*That?* That's going just great, Lieutenant. Just great. December nineteenth'll be ten years I'm clean. We're gonna have a party. Cookies and cake and ice cream. Gladys been off the shit for over thirteen."

"That's dynamite, Red. I always knew you could do it."

Red smiled. "Yeah, I guess you did. Even before I did."

Red coughed and pulled his chair closer to the table.

"You know, Lieutenant. I never did really thank you. For coming to speak before the Parole Board like you did."

Gold waved his hand. "It was nothing."

"No," Red said, "it was a lot. A whole helluva lot. It was 'cause of your recommendation they took a chance and cut me loose. Nobody else spoke for me. Only you. That was a wonderful thing you did. A real *mitzva.*"

Gold shrugged. "I had a feeling. About you. That sooner or later you were gonna square up. Straighten up and fly right." Gold took another gulp of coffee. "Besides, I was proud of you."

"Proud?"

Both men laughed.

"Why proud?"

"I don't know. Maybe because you were the best piano player I ever heard. Maybe because you were tough, you held your water. You were a real tough stand-up junkie Jew."

They both laughed again.

"Maybe just because you were a Jew."

They sat a while in a kindly embarrassed silence. Gold picked at the lip of his Styrofoam cup.

Red, scratching absently at his forearm, said, "You know, sometimes I think about all the time I did behind keeping my mouth shut. When I coulda given up some cats and sailed out of court with probably some smack in my kip. I think, Right, I was a real stand-up asshole and altogether, before I was thirty-five, I did nine and a half years in stripes. But, you know, I don't think I'd do a damn thing different. At least I can look at myself when I shave in the morning."

"You did the right thing."

"You think so?"

"No question."

Three black teenagers came in the shed, laughing and cursing. Red went behind the counter and sold them soft drinks and potato chips. On the way out one of the kids spotted Gold.

"Hey, I seen you on TV."

Gold nodded.

"You the *po*lice looking for the bad Crosskiller dude."

"That's right."

"What you gonna do when you ketch him?"

Gold smiled. "I'm gonna blow the motherfucker *away.*"

"Aw-*right!*" the kid said, and traded high-fives with his brothers. "Blow the mutherfucker *away!*" They left laughing.

Red came back to the table. "Lieutenant. I forgot about that. How's the investigation going?"

Gold held up his hands. "Do me a favor, Red. Don't ask."

Red nodded. Then he pointed to Gold's empty Styrofoam cup. "More coffee?"

Gold shook his head and brought out a pint bottle from his back pocket. He poured three fingers of Scotch and then offered the bottle to Red, who said, "No, thanks, Lieutenant. One thing leads to another."

Gold left the bottle on the table. "So, Red, you playing anywhere?"

Red leaned back in his chair. "No, no. I quit that when I put down the heroin. Homeward House discouraged it. Said it was all part of the same thing—playing jazz and shooting smack—all part of my old life-style. Shit, I'd been doing both together since I was sixteen. Homeward House said I had to put it all down, break the syndrome, put it all behind me. Or it would have killed me. You know what? Them cats was right. Completely correct."

Gold poured another shot. "Even still, it's a shame you had to quit playing. I always enjoyed your playing more those few times you were clean."

Red gave him a grim smile. "Yeah, everybody enjoyed my playing more when I was straight. Everybody but me. It left me cold."

Gold grunted with understanding.

"That's the real reason I quit playing. Without heroin none of it felt good, none of it meant anything. You know what I mean?"

"I think I do."

The two men sat in silence for a while, each thinking about the past.

Then Gold said, "You were the best be-bop piano player I ever heard—black or white, junkie or straight-arrow. The best. Red Greenberg was the best."

Red nodded his thanks.

"And I heard 'em all—Garland, Powell, Tyner, all of 'em. You were the best. I heard you play one night up on Sunset when you were with Mint Julep. You played some shit that night that made me feel like when you were a kid in *shul* and the cantor would sing, you remember how you used to feel, like maybe there really *was* more there than just you and the cantor. That's how I felt that night. Like there was somebody else playing. Like you were locked in to something, something more than just you and that banged-up old Steinway. You were the best there was that night. There wasn't any better."

Out on the pier the crowds passing the entrance had thinned. Some of the storefronts were closing, rolling down their grates and dousing their lights. A tiny breeze had sprung up over the bay and the smell of the sea was strong and somehow nostalgic.

"Me and Gladys, we go down to this church in Compton every Sunday. The reverend there keeps getting on my case 'bout playing for the choir, but my heart ain't in it. I keep turning him down."

"You converted?"

"No, not really. Gladys is the one with the spirit. She's a for-real Christian. I just kinda go along for the ride. The reverend *loves* me. He's in hog heaven whenever I walk in. He's got a jazzer, a Jew, and a junkie—all rolled up into one little white man. Makes him feel like the Great Redeemer or something."

Gold puffed on his cigar and stared out the entrance at the darkened pier.

"I used to think that when I got older," he mused, "I'd get serious about religion. Join a synagogue and all. Now I *am* older and I realize I was wrong."

"I can't remember the last time I went to temple. My old man's funeral, I think."

"I went to a bar mitzvah just last week."

"Relative?"

"My ex-wife's kid."

Red glanced at him and then quickly away. "Oh?"

There was a long, subdued moment. Incongruously, someone on the pier was playing a Jerry Vale tape.

"You—you remember," Red began hesitantly, "you remember that chick singer, the one that—that died in that apartment you were in?"

A faint gust of wind swept through the place for a moment, then was gone.

"She wasn't much of a singer," Gold said flatly.

"The other day I was listening to the jazz station—Gladys don't even like me to do *that*—and that Mint Julep track we recorded came on. You know the one? 'Blue Angel.' The one 'Lip wrote for her, you know the one I mean?"

Gold nodded.

"Got me to thinking back. You know, Lieutenant, I don't want to speak out of turn, but years ago when all that shit went down, a lot of the cats thought you did that girl in, but I never went for that story. I knew better. I knew you loved that girl. You could never hurt her."

The breeze withered down to a dead stillness. Somewhere out on the bay a buoy clanged as it rode the tide. The sound seemed to come from the moon.

Gold poured another drink.

"That was one beautiful ballad, that 'Blue Angel,' " Red said.

Gold ran his finger along the rim of the Styrofoam cup. Red scratched his arm habitually.

Gladys came in from the kitchen. Her angry black eyes fastened on Gold's.

"Man, it's *way* past closing. And we could lose our license behind that liquor bottle."

"I'm a cop, Gladys. Don't worry about it."

She cursed under her breath and went back into the kitchen.

"Don't mind her, Lieutenant. She's just watching out for me. That's the way she makes it all work."

"I gotta be going anyway." He stood up. "Say, Red, what time is it?"

Red, puzzled, cast a quick glance at Gold's wristwatch.

"I don't know, Lieutenant."

Gold brought his watch up to his eyes. "It's exactly midnight."

Red said nothing.

"Jesus, Red. We've been sitting here *shmoozing* for over three hours."

Red looked at Gold a long time. Then he nodded. "That's right, Lieutenant. You got here at—"

"Eight forty-five."

"Right—eight forty-five. On the dot."

"How do you know that? You don't wear a watch."

"Gladys does."

"Will she remember what time I came in?"

"I'll remind her."

"Will that be kosher with her?"

Red nodded again. "Sometimes she forgets the things old friends have done for us. I'll remind her. About everything."

"It probably won't ever come up."

"It don't matter. I enjoyed our little three-hour *shmooz.*"

Gold looked at the signs posted around the shed. "Maybe next time I'll have something to eat."

"On the house, Lieutenant. Try the pork ribs. Just like your mammy used to make."

They laughed.

"*Shalom,* Red."

"*Shalom,* Lieutenant. You take care of yourself. That Crosskiller is one evil cat."

Out on the pier the night had become sultry and motionless. The ocean lapped at the pilings like a dog licking a sore. Gold found an open phone booth on the end of the pier and called Parker Center. They put him through to Dolly Madison.

"Anything happening?" Gold asked.

"Everything's quiet so far. Keep your fingers crossed. Are you home?"

"No. I couldn't sleep, can you believe it? My mind kept going around and around like a top. I had to get out. I came out to the beach. Walked around. Saw an old acquaintance of mine on the pier and we shot the shit for hours and hours. I feel a lot better."

"Probably the best thing you could have done," Madison said solicitously, immensely grateful that Gold was being so personal with him. "Clear the cobwebs out."

"Exactly."

"I still think you should try to get some sleep."

"I'm going home right now."

"Because I really have everything under control down here."

"I'm sure you do, Captain," Gold said in an earnest voice. "I have total confidence in you."

Gold could *hear* Dolly beam at the other end of the line. "But, Captain, wake me at home if there's any trouble at all."

Gold drove slowly east on the freeway. There was no hurry now, no pressure. The Ford's airconditioner had finally given up the ghost and was blasting hot air, so Gold rolled down all the windows and let the wind swoosh caressingly through the car.

Back at his apartment Gold stripped the cap from a new fifth of Johnnie Walker Black. Carrying his drink, he sat cross-legged on the worn carpet and flipped through his records stacked on the bottom shelf of the book-case. In only a few minutes he found the side he was looking for: Mint Julep Jackson's fifteen-year-old album entitled *'Lip in Love.* The jacket photo was of a buxom blond model, but Gold knew who the album was dedicated to, who 'Lip was playing for. He laid the record gently on the turntable and dropped the needle on the first cut, "Blue Angel." Instantly Jackson's throaty, painful tenor saxophone filled the apartment—sweet and sexy, masculine and tender, as old and as weary as civilization itself. Older. Gold sat heavily in the old armchair and sipped his Scotch.

Julep played.

And Gold remembered.

The day Angelique died.

The day Angelique died it was raining—a dark, rainy Sunday in December. It had been raining for a week, one of those week-long L.A. deluges that comes once a year. Sometimes once every three years. Million-dollar Malibu retreats were slipping off their mountaintop lots and washing into the Pacific. Maintenance crews stacked sandbags across the entrances of exclusive shops on Wilshire Boulevard.

The first thing Gold awoke to that rainy Sunday morning fourteen years ago was the sensation of being in a warm, hollow drum that someone was lightly tapping with his fingertips. Then he understood—that the rain was pelting against the bedroom window. The second realization he came to, that rainy Sunday in December almost fourteen years ago, was that he had a raging hard-on. And someone was sucking it.

He looked down into Evelyn's twinkling, mischievous eyes. She would have smiled at him, but her mouth was busy, gliding up and down his shining cock. Finally, with agonizing slowness, she dragged her tight, circled lips over the bursting head of his penis and breathed huskily, "Good morning, Jack." Then she laughed a happy, maidenish laugh, grabbed his cock, held it erect, and sat down on it. Her pussy was wet and eager, like an omnivorous wound. She slammed down again and again, undulating her hips and popping her pelvis. He came almost immediately and she laughed again. Keeping him inside her, she lazily stretched out on top of him.

She was heavier than she used to be. Age had widened her, thickened her hips and ass. Laugh lines streamed down from her eyes and lips.

When had they fucked last? A week? A month? Six months? Gold couldn't remember. But he did recall that Evelyn had just recently started attending a new self-actualization/self-realization workshop—another expense!—that had become the rage among all her old realtor friends, real estate agents, of course, being prime targets for any kind of con that nurtured optimism. Obviously, Evelyn had taken upon herself the responsibility for saving their dying marriage. This was to be only the beginning, Gold knew. He knew Evelyn, and the way she went about life.

She lay on him for a long time, her arms around his neck, nuzzling his ear and chuckling with self-satisfaction. "I love you, Jack," she murmured.

After a while they heard seven-year-old Wendy talking to her dolls in her bedroom across the hall, and they got up.

While Gold built a fire and read the comics to Wendy in the living room—*You can trust me, Charlie Brown!*—Evelyn, humming to herself, prepared them her most lavish Sunday breakfast: lox and eggs, toasted bagels with cream cheese, jam, and coffee. They ate in the louvered breakfast room while the rain streamed down the windows and thunder—thunder in L.A.!—rolled over the rooftop. Wendy babbled on about her part in the school Christmas pageant. Every time Gold looked up from his plate Evelyn's glistening eyes were on him, loving and hopeful. Gold swallowed his food and smiled back.

After breakfast Evelyn dressed Wendy to go out in the weather: red jumpsuit, high-snapping galoshes, red rubber raincoat. The child was ecstatic. She was going to visit her Aunt Carol and her new husband—her third, the South African—and his two small daughters.

When Wendy ran down the hall to gather a remembered-at-the-last-minute board game, Evelyn came over to where he was sitting on the overstuffed couch and wrapped her arms around his shoulders.

"I'll drop Wendy off and come right back. We'll have the whole day together."

Gold smiled and patted her arm.

Wendy tromped back into the living room with the game. Evelyn pulled up the hood on her daughter's raincoat, put on her own coat, and the two Golden Girls splashed down the walk to Evelyn's car. Gold watched the Olds back out of the driveway, windshield wipers arcing. Evelyn blew the horn and Wendy waved good-bye, her eager face beaming beneath the red hood.

Gold already had the phone in his hand. As he watched the Olds disappearing down the block he heard Angelique answer. Her voice sounded thick, distant. How was she? Okay. Was she sick? No, not now. She had had her wakeup this morning, but she would need some more soon. He couldn't get away. Why? He just couldn't. But she needed him.

Did she? Very much. She had to see him. Why? Didn't he know? He wanted her to say it. She needed him—to hold her, to fuck her, to ride her and ream her. She needed her daddy, didn't her daddy need her? Yes, he did, he did. Didn't he love her? Oh, so much. So very, very much. Then hurry, hurry. Please hurry.

He left the scribbled note on the refrigerator door, pinned under a magnetic banana:

> Ev,
>
> I'm really sorry. Got a call from the Captain. Big bust coming down. I have to be there. Be home a.s.a.p. I'll make it up to you. I promise.
>
> I love you,
> J.

The rain came down in sliding sheets of water. In Watts the junkies had been driven indoors by the wet and cold. Gold parked in front of a ramshackle white frame house set back from the street behind an overgrown yard littered with brightly colored children's toys. He honked the horn. A few moments later a tall man in an army fatigue jacket ran out to the car and got in the passenger side. Raindrops beaded in his Afro. His skin was tan over chalky white, like soured cream in a cup of old coffee. He smelled bad.

"What you got for me?" Gold asked.

The vet shook his head. "Ain't nothing happening. It be's quiet all over. Too cold for any fucking thing, man."

Gold nodded. He held out a bill folded over so the 50 showed. The vet took the money wordlessly and dropped three small glassine packets into Gold's palm.

"I'll be seeing you," Gold said, and the vet got out and ran back to the house.

Gold drove to the Wilshire District. It rained as if it was never going to stop. Streets and intersections flooded and cars stalled in water up to their fenders. Gold drove around the block three times, finally finding a parking space two streets over from her apartment.

He was unlocking the door when she opened it from the other side. She gave out a small scream and then laughed. He was drenched. He had left home without a coat and his clothes were soaked through, dripping onto the hall floor. Still laughing, she took his hand and led him into the bathroom. She unbuttoned his sopping sweater and draped it over the big claw-legged bathtub. She peeled off his shirt and hung it on the door. Then his shoes and his socks, his pants and his underwear. She took his holstered gun from his waistband and laid it on the back of the toilet, along with his wallet, his change, his keys, and the three glassine packets. With a thick, rough towel that had been warming over a gas heater, she began to dry him, rubbing him gently while she laughed and joked with him. She dried his hair first, then his shoulders and matted chest, then his genitals and between the cheeks of his ass. Then she knelt on the bathroom floor and rubbed his legs and feet. When she stood again, he unknotted her bathrobe and drew her to him. She arched against him and they kissed deeply, her tongue fluttering around in his mouth. He groaned and she pushed him gently away.

"Not yet," she said. "Let me get straight first, Daddy."

From the medicine cabinet she took out a small, black-lacquered Chinese case. She sat on the edge of the ancient bathtub and placed the lacquered case on the vanity table. It contained a plastic syringe, a sleek gold woman's lighter, a fluff of cotton, and a child's antique silver spoon. Angelique laid the slender, evil-looking syringe on the vanity. She looked at Gold and he handed her one of the flat glassine packets. Carefully, she unfolded the edges of the packet, opened it like a flower blooming, and laid the white-powder-filled paper on the vanity. With deft brown fingers she drew the tiny spoon from the Chinese box, held the spoon under the tap, and eased a single pearly droplet of water onto the dull silver. She ignited the gold lighter and held the flame under the spoon's belly. In half a minute the water was heated and she gently tapped in the heroin. It dissolved with the swirling motion of her hand. She set the spoon on the vanity table and picked up the needle.

Outside, on the other side of the small frosted bathroom window, lightning flashed; the rain on the rooftop intensified.

Angelique wadded a tuft of cotton into a tiny hard ball. She impaled the ball on the tip of the needle, then submerged it in the milky liquid and drew out the plunger, sucking up the fix. When the spoon was empty, the syringe filled, she again looked at Gold. He reached over to his hanging pants and with one quick hard motion stripped his belt from the loops. Angelique stood and let her robe slip from her shoulders. Now she was as naked as he was. Only beautiful, so very, very beautiful.

She stepped out of her robe and over to where Gold was seated on the lidded commode, turned and sat down, fitting her ass against his cock, her back arched against his stomach. She turned up the inside of her left arm and Gold reached around her body and wound his belt around her arm. He pulled the belt taut. The leather bit into her flesh and the veins in her forearm jumped up. Angelique giggled and her tongue flashed over her lips. She took up the syringe, turned it on herself, pressed the point of the needle into her arm. The skin dipped and then bounced back as the shaft slipped into her vein. She pulled the plunger back and the bottom of the tube filled with thick red blood. She giggled again and slowly injected the heroin.

"Oooohhhhh, Daddy. Ohhhh, sweet Daddy."

The needle still dangling from her arm, she closed her eyes and leaned back on him. She felt pliable, limp and relaxed, like a cat rubbing against his leg. He felt her breathing slow, her pulse stagger to a junkie's euphoric glide.

He watched her sleep, cradled against his chest, in the makeup mirror over the vanity. Her honey-colored skin seemed to glow with the dope coursing through her body. After a while he reached around and pulled the hypodermic from her arm. She licked her lips in her sleep and her mouth stayed open.

She slept like that for over an hour.

When she awoke, high and happy, she wanted him. They fucked languidly there in the bathroom, watching in the mirror as his pale, scarred body plunged into her sleek brown one.

Later, both of them wrapped in oversized bath towels, Billie Holiday on the stereo, she made dinner—shrimp Creole and rice—while the storm raged outside. They ate in bed, laughing and clowning. Then they put the plates on the floor and made love again.

Afterward Gold watched as Angelique, seated before the big, round antique mirror, brushed her long, raven-black hair with her pink brush. Smiling at his reflection in the smoked glass, she pulled the bristles through her hair with slow, methodical, junkie strokes. Gold watched from the bed, smoking a fresh cigar, sipping a drink and thinking he should at least call Evelyn with more excuses. Instead, with the night closing in outside the rainy windows, he dozed off.

When he again opened his eyes, Angelique was gone from the bedroom. He found her in the bathroom, fixing again.

He was incensed. It was as if he had caught her with another lover. He called her a thief, a black junkie bitch. He accused her of using him for the heroin he brought her. No, no, she slurred, tears in her heavy-lidded eyes, she loved him. She loved him! Only he left her alone so much. She hated being alone. Why did he leave her alone so much? Why didn't he stay here with her? All the time? Her pleas only infuriated him more. He kicked over a table, sent a lamp crashing to the floor. Stupid junkie bitch! He had a family, couldn't she understand that? A wife and a daughter! *A motherfucking family!* That's right! she cried. And all she had was him. No, he shouted back, she had her fucking dope. She would kick, she sobbed. She wanted to. For him. She wanted to just for him. Then he'd stay with her. Every night. Then *she* would be his family. This would be his home. She was a stupid junkie whore. Didn't she understand *anything?* How many times did he have to tell her? He could never leave his wife, his daughter. Not for some junked-out half-white whorey hype who'd been handed around Watts like a cheap bottle of Ripple. She staggered through the apartment screaming, Leave me alone! Leave me alone! All right, if that's what she fucking wanted. He flung the door open; the storm still raged. He stood foolishly naked in the doorway. If that's what she fucking wanted! He was a cruel bastard! she choked. Cruel honkie Jew bastard! Kike cocksucker! He slapped her hard across her face and her head snapped back. She clutched at her cheek and fell backward over a table. Kike! Kike! she screamed up at him. Mr. Whitey! Mr. Iceberg! One of the *frozen* people! Black bitch! He'd kill her! Black bitch! Go ahead! *Go ahead!* That's what she wanted anyway. To die. To *die!* She was killing herself with that shit. *Fuck him!* She raked his arm with her nails. Don't scratch him! Why not? He didn't want his white-cunt Jew wife to know he dipped his dick in nigger shit? He'd kill her! He'd kill her! Then do it! Do it! *Do it!* He wrapped his hands around her throat and started to choke. Do it! *Do it!* she rasped. She didn't want to live without him. She didn't want to live without him. The tears poured down her face and rolled across his hands on her throat as she cried, Oh, Jack, ohJack, ohjackohjackohjack—

He swooped her up into his arms and carried her to the sofa. He lay down beside her and she curled into a fetal position under his arm and sobbed.

It's all right. It's all right, he soothed as he stroked her shoulder. He was sorry. He was so sorry.

Oh, Jack. Oh, Jack, she choked out between sobs. She needed him so much. She was so afraid. So afraid.

Afraid of what?

Afraid of everything. Afraid of getting sick. Afraid of waking up alone in the dark. Afraid he didn't love her—

Of course, he loved her, don't be—

—afraid one day he would leave and never come back. Just walk out the door and—

—would always come back. She knew he couldn't stay a—

—didn't know what she would do if she couldn't have him again.

He kissed the salty tears on her cheeks, her lips.

Oh, baby. Beautiful baby.

Oh, Jack. Fuck me. Fuck me.

He lay atop her and slipped inside and she raised her hips up and moaned and the tears kept coming as she moved under him.

Oh, fuck me, Jack. Just *fuck me.* Don't ever leave me. Stay inside me forever. Forever and ever. Don't leave me, Jack. Forever and ever and ever and ever.

Afterward they fell asleep there on the sofa, their arms and legs entwined. He slept soundly. He slept—for too long.

He dreamed that he was chasing a perp down a long, nightmarish alley, an alley that constantly curved, so that the fleeing suspect was always just out of sight, with only his long shadow visible on the curving wall. And then the curve became a circle and the perp was behind him giving chase, and he was the perp, then the circle became a maze, and the maze was crowded with Clydesdale-sized rats with eyes that glowed red in the dark like a skull ring he wanted when he was a kid, and his father had given him the money to send off for the ring from a tin of change he kept under his sewing machine, and then his father died and the maggots ate him.

Gold was suddenly awake and sitting up, there on the sofa. He was shivering. The room was icy and empty.

Where was Angelique?

He reached for his nearby drink and gulped it down. The fiery liquid burned but didn't warm.

He had to piss. He lurched into the bathroom, his legs wobbly, and realized how drunk he was. Leaning on the wall behind the toilet bowl, he emptied his bladder. Floating in the urine was a piece of crumpled glassine paper. She had done up the rest of the heroin.

He had to get the hell out of here, he thought. He had to go home, get the hell out of here.

Angelique, in the bedroom, suddenly laughed—a distant, unnatural sound—then he could hear her voice drone on in a soft monotone.

She was on the phone. Who the hell was she talking to?

Gold shook himself dry, gathered up his keys, wallet, and revolver from the back of the toilet where Angelique had put them when she undressed him, and maneuvered carefully across the cold floor and into the bedroom.

Angelique was sitting on the edge of the bed, naked, talking intently into her aquamarine Princess phone. Gold set the holstered gun, keys, and wallet on the bed beside her, then went to the closet and searched in the dark for some of the clean clothes he kept there. He stopped and looked back at her. She turned to face him. Her eyes were heavy-lidded and dreamy. She smiled at him.

"I told her," she slurred at him, still holding the phone to her mouth.

"What?" Gold asked.

"I told her," she repeated, grinning. "You don't have to go home. I told her."

Gold walked slowly toward the bed.

"Who?"

"Her!" she insisted, holding the phone out to him. "*Her!* I told her and now you don't have to go home."

There was an explosion of comprehension inside Gold's brain, and he suddenly felt like he was under water, drowning, and his limbs were slow and heavy and his lungs were bursting as he fought his way back to the surface.

"What have you done?" he asked softly, but afraid to know. "What have you done?"

She rose languidly from the bed and stumbled toward him, still holding the phone receiver before her.

"It's okay, Daddy. I told her how much you love me, how much we love each other, how much—"

He struck her with a vicious backhand blow across her face. She fell back on the bed and pressed her hand to her face. There was blood in the corner of her mouth.

"You bastard!" she shouted. "You hurt me! *You hurt me!*"

He wanted to hit her again. He wanted to crush her, to destroy her, make her disappear.

"You bastard!" she screamed, kneeling on the bed now, her mouth bloody.

"What have you done?" he shouted down at her.

"*I told her! I told her!*" she shrieked. "I told her how much you love me. How much you want me. I told her she's a big fat Jew cow with a pussy as big as a bucket!"

"Shut up!" Gold yelled, looming over her. The rage was screaming through his veins like a siren through a quiet night. She edged away from him across the wide bed, and the phone cord, caught up in the twisted sheets, pulled the fallen phone receiver over the floor like a slithering snake. Even through his rage Gold was deathly afraid of it.

"I told her you don't want her anymore, you only want me. I told her her pussy stinks and I wash her stink off of you when you come to me—"

"Shut up!"

"—told her you love me, you don't love her, never loved her, only me, tell her, tell her, Jack, tell her you love me—"

"Shut up!" He stepped closer and raised his hand. He stared at her bloody mouth, her mouth that wouldn't stop, that wouldn't be silent, that was tearing his world apart.

"—tell her you don't need her anymore, only me, me, *me!*" she sobbed angrily as she wrapped the bedsheets around her and the phone bumped across the floor dragged by its cord.

"Shut up!"

"—tell her you don't need anybody but me anymore, not her, big fat Jew cunt, or that fat little brat—"

Wendy?

"—or anybody but—"

"Shut up!"

"—big fat Jew cu—"

"Shut up!" He struck her again, and he hurt his hand on the bones of her cheek. "Shutupshutup*shutup!*"

She came up from the sheets with his gun gripped shakily before her in both hands.

"You bastard, I'll kill you! I'll *kill* you!"

"What have you done to me!" he thundered down at her.

"I'll kill you!"

"You already have!"

"You bastard! You bastard!" She pointed the gun at his heart.

"Do it!" he shouted. *"Do it!"* He wanted *some*one to die.

"Jack, don't you love me?" she suddenly sobbed.

"Do it, you junkie bitch!" he raged.

"I love *you,* Jack!" she cried, then put the muzzle of his .38 Special against her temple and pulled the trigger. The bullet's impact threw her head against her shoulder and she slumped over in a still heap. The sound of the gunshot reverberated through the bedroom like an atomic explosion, destroying his life, his world, his universe.

He saw her blood and brain matter oozing down the wall behind the bed. As if it were alive.

Even if she wasn't.

She was sprawled back across the blue bedspread, and her blood had gushed down her face and rivered down her neck and across her small breasts. Rich red blood, steaming in the icy air.

"Angel," he breathed. "Angel."

He sat on the edge of the bed. Her eyes were dead. Not junkie dead now. Death dead. Animal dead. Glazed and unseeing. Forever and ever. And ever and ever.

"Baby," he said softly, almost a question. "Baby?"

He shook uncontrollably as he took the .38 from her limp fingers and placed it on the bedside table. He took up her hand in his, as if to quiet himself, as if for comfort.

"Baby? Baby?"

Somewhere in his mind a madman screamed from a locked cell, but he pretended not to hear it.

"Angel?"

He slipped a hand under her shoulders and raised her upper torso from the blue bedspread. Angelique's head lolled over, exposing the gaping exit hole the .38 shell had made in the back of her skull. Warm blood and pieces of brain gushed out over Gold's hands and across his naked belly as he cradled her against his chest.

"Of course, I love you," he said. "Of course, I love you. Of course, I love you."

He held her gently and rocked back and forth in the blood-soaked bed. He knew he was doing an insane thing, so therefore *he* was insane, but he didn't care.

"I love you, Angel. I'll always love you. No one but you, baby. No one but you."

He held her to him and rocked her the way he used to rock his daughter when she hurt herself, and he told her how much he needed her, how much he wanted her; he pleaded with her not to leave him, that there would never be anyone he could love the way he loved her and what would he do without her, what could he do without her, without her, without her—

And he heard crying—faint, otherworldly crying—like the sobbing of the voice box in one of Wendy's talking dolls, and then he knew it was coming from the aquamarine Princess telephone coiled like a cobra at the foot of the bed.

And Gold knew nothing would ever be the same.

He couldn't remember many things about the remaining hours of that night.

He couldn't remember calling the department, but he must have at some point—or someone must have—because suddenly they were swarming all over the now tawdry-looking apartment, talking in funereal murmurs and shooting quick glances at him whenever they thought he wasn't looking.

He couldn't recall dressing, but at some time during that hellish night he must have put some clothes on, because everyone else had their clothes on. Maybe his fellow cops dressed him. He couldn't remember.

He couldn't remember what ever happened to Angelique's fit—her syringe kit. He never saw it again, and no one ever mentioned it, but he didn't have a clear picture of where it went, what happened to it.

Or when he had washed Angelique's bloody brains off his hands. He could remember scrubbing his hands almost every hour for weeks after, trying to cleanse away the memory, the *burn,* of her hot blood from his hands, but he couldn't remember the actual deed. It was lost. Gone forever. Like Angelique.

What he could recall—the first thing he saw clearly—was them zipping Angelique into a body bag with a sound like a knife ripping skin, and carrying her out to the coroner's van. When they opened the apartment door the wind blew and rain poured in, so the storm must still have been raging. After they took Angelique's body away—after she was gone—the apartment seemed empty to Gold, even though it was crowded with cops. The center was gone. Suddenly the place seemed small and cheap and sordid. Unfamiliar. Not the kind of place he would like to be at all.

He started to leave, to follow her out, when a detective with a friendly face put his hand on Gold's shoulder and said, gently, "Why don't you sit down, Jack?"

Gold stared at him stupidly, uncomprehending.

"Sit down, Jack. Everything's okay."

Gold sat, staring at his hands. Someone who knew him brought him a cigar, but he let it go out and forgot to light it.

After a long while another cop led him back into the kitchen, and Alan Huntz was there. He was the head of Internal Affairs then. No more chauffeuring the chief around for Alan. He was wet and angry.

"I can't for the life of me figure out how a drunken degenerate like you even got on the force, much less make lieutenant."

Gold blinked at him, trying to zero in on what the man was saying.

"Mr. Hero. Mr. Brave Cowboy Policeman," he was saying. "Mr. Iron Balls. You say it's a suicide, and we're going to say it's a suicide, but you killed that girl and you're going to get away with it. You're going to walk away from murder one, and it makes me want to puke!"

Gold struggled to understand it all. The screaming prisoner still railed inside his brain. All he caught were snatches.

"—your bloody fingerprints all over the weapon . . . neighbors heard you arguing all night long . . . naked and covered with blood, I don't even want to guess what went on in here . . . orders from the top to call it a self-inflicted . . . protect the department . . . like to see you do twenty years, even if she was only a nigger hype—"

Gold knew then that something was wrong, that he wasn't himself, because if he'd been together he would have to kill this bastard, right then and there. His anger would demand it. Only he couldn't muster any anger. Only the dead emptiness, like the wound in the back of Angelique's skull.

He turned away from Huntz and walked out of the kitchen. Huntz followed, shouting after him.

"I'd find myself another line of work, if I were you. You're finished on this force, mister! I don't care how many friends you've got. I'll see you never get another promotion the rest of your life. Never! Mark my words, mister!"

Gold walked through the front door and out into the storm. No one tried to stop him. The rain pelted his face and immediately drenched his clothing. He wandered for half an hour, forgetting where he'd parked his car. When he finally stumbled against it, miraculously he found his keys in his pants pocket.

He drove for hours, totally unaware of his direction. He had lost his watch, so he had no idea what time it was. He knew it was late because the liquor stores were closed. A drink was foremost in his mind. He had the beginnings of an unquenchable thirst. He pulled into a Stop 'n' Go on the Pacific Coast Highway in Malibu, but the clerk refused to sell him a bottle. Farther north the highway was closed because of mudslides and the CHP turned him back. Finally, he parked beneath a grove of palm trees facing out over the ocean. The rain thudded on the car roof and sluiced down the windshield. Gold realized he didn't have a weapon.

Just after dawn the rain stopped. Gold rolled down his fogged-over window. The world outside was wet and gray—a netherworld of clouds and strangers. Out on the sea an oil tanker inched across the horizon like a target in a shooting gallery.

Gold found an old cigar in the glove box. It was stale. He yearned deeply for a hit of Scotch. Finally, when the thickening traffic on the Coast Highway told him it was getting later, he turned the key and drove homeward.

A hundred yards short of his driveway he became aware that there were *things* strewn about his wet front lawn. As he pulled halfway up the drive he recognized the things were his clothes. Or had been his clothes. Now they were rags—soiled, sodden, ripped rags. And his record collection. His jazz records. Some of them irreplaceable; all of them cherished—now shattered or warped by the rain, their jackets a soggy, pulpy ruin.

And he noticed other cherished mementos scattered among the garbage. Little souvenirs and awards, clippings and photographs. Now broken, smashed, torn apart. Wrecked with a vengeance.

Gold started to get out of his car. The front door of the house burst open and Evelyn flew out, her housecoat sailing out behind her.

"You bastard!" she screamed, and when he looked at her face he saw she was snarling like a rabid dog.

"You bastard! I hope she was worth it!"

She raced across the lawn, screaming at him and tripping over the mutilated clothes. In her right hand she clutched a meat cleaver.

"I'll kill you! I'm not afraid of you! I'll kill you! I'll kill you!"

Gold's world tilted. His mind overloaded. He was trapped in an endless nightmare, and all the givens in his life, by which he maintained his reason, were nullified. Canceled. Revoked. If his wife could run at him across an early-morning lawn intent on murdering him with a meat cleaver, then this was surely Judgment Day. Graves could open up; headstones could roll away; and the dead could rise up, grinning foul smiles and farting unspeakable gases; and the ghosts of Adolph Hitler and Golda Meir would fornicate in the gutter.

"I'll kill you, you bastard!"

Gold jumped back in the car and pressed down the lock. Evelyn lunged at his window and hacked at his head through the glass.

"Why did you come home? I heard you! I heard you! You'll never love anyone but her. You've never wanted anyone but her!"

Evelyn swung the axe again and the glass spidered.

"You bastard!"

That's what *she* called me, he thought.

"You bastard, she said you hate it when I touch you she said you told her *you hate it when I touch you! I* want to *kill you!"*

"Please," Gold said softly in the car, but he didn't know who to. "Please."

She swung the cleaver in a wide one-handed arc, and the blade, designed to trim lambchops, broke in two. She hurled herself on the hood and pounded on the windshield with her balled fists. Her eyes were red-rimmed from crying. They glinted with the luster of madness.

"Why did you come here why did you come here I heard you I heard you you said you love her you love her I heard you!"

Gold shifted into reverse and tried to ease out of the driveway, but Evelyn clung to the side of the car.

"Where are you going, back to your *shvartzeh*? Back to your *shvartzeh* whore? What did you do to her? What did you do to her? I heard you! I heard you!" Evelyn howled. "She said she was nineteen!" she screamed, as if that was the greatest crime of all.

"Nineteen, you bastard!"

Gold caught sight of little Wendy, chubby and frightened, in her Pooh Bear jammies, looking out from behind the front door.

Oh, dear God. Dear, dear God.

"Nineteen! Nineteen! *Nineteen! I heard yooouuuuu!"*

It wasn't until days later that Gold finally pieced it all together. Until he finally faced it all. That while he had slept on the sofa, Angelique had gone into the bathroom and shot up the last of the heroin, and then, mumbly and mean with the junk in her veins, sat on the edge of the bed and phoned his home. How she got the number, or how long she had had it, he would never know. Then, while Evelyn listened with horror and fascination, like a defendant hearing his death sentence read, Angelique had told her all about the two of them. Everything about the two of them. Carol told him later, what Evelyn, during a sodden, sobbing, all-night sisterly *shmooz,* told *her.* How Angelique had recounted to Evelyn how they met. How long they had been lovers. How often they fucked. How well they fucked. The various positions. The ones he liked best. How much they loved each other. How he couldn't wait to get away from Evelyn and rush to her. To her arms, to her mouth, her sweet cunt. How they stole away on weekend trips to Santa Barbara, Vegas, Palm Springs, when he was supposed to be working stakeouts, and how they never left the bed, had all their meals sent up. How he loved to lick her sweet, dark pussy, nuzzling his nose in her little pussy hairs. How he always came when, while they fucked, she would reach around and slip her finger up his anus to the knuckle—

Gold lurched up from the armchair. The Johnnie Walker bottle rolled across the floor, spilling a trail of amber beads on the green carpet. Mint Julep Jackson's saxophone wailed on. The automatic turntable replayed the disc over and over. On the other side of the front bay window it was still deep night. Gold didn't make it to the bathroom. Halfway there he vomited down the front of his shirt. Cupping his hands under his mouth, he retched his way to the commode, knelt on the tile, and spewed up a bitter, alcoholic liquid that swirled down the sides of the bowl.

When Gold walked into the bedroom Angelique had been talking to Evelyn for almost an hour—"My God, Jack, an *hour!*" Carol had later teased him. "That must have been quite a torrid love affair! So many things to tell!" Then Evelyn had stayed on the phone and listened to everything that followed. "Tell me, Jack, Ev wouldn't. Were you really in the room when that poor girl killed herself? Were you? What did Ev hear, Jack? What did she *hear?*"

Gold washed his face and rinsed out his mouth. He went back into the living room. The illuminated clock on his desk glowed 4:32. He retrieved the fallen bottle of Scotch, poured himself another drink, sat at the dinette table, and took a sip. Without warning, he found himself crying. He put his hands over his face and sobbed, and the grief washed over him and passed. He wiped his eyes calmly with his fingertips. He took another drink. He noticed his piece lying beside him on the table. Not the .38 that killed Angelique. They destroyed that one, like a killer dog. This was another one. He picked it up and put the barrel in his mouth. It seemed the thing to do. The gun tasted bitter and greasy. He darted the tip of his tongue down the muzzle hole. The way he used to play with Angelique's clitoris. He wondered how much finger pressure was required. He wondered if you heard the report. He wondered—

The phone rang. The sound seemed to come from a long way away. From another world.

It rang again. And then again.

Gold took the gun from his mouth and laid it on the table.
Another ring.
Gold picked up the handset.
"Jack? Jack?"
Gold couldn't find his voice.
"Jack?"
"I—I'm here, Dolly."
"Looks like we got another one, Jack."

SUNDAY
August 12

5:06 AM The press and television had been cordoned off behind police barricades. The reporters pounded on Gold's car when they recognized him, demanding statements, entreating information, snapping film. The cops let him through quickly. Other patrolmen, stationed every fifty feet, waved him up the ramp in the right direction. On the third level over a hundred people were gathered around the Rolls—standing guard, taking pictures, dusting for prints. Actually bumping into each other.

Gold parked the Ford and got out. Madison was approaching.

"Christ, Jack! I sent you home to get some rest. You look *worse,* if that's possible."

Gold managed a weak smile. "You really know how to talk to a girl. Who is it this time?" He nodded toward the Corniche.

Madison looked back at the car. "You're not going to believe this. Natty Saperstein."

Gold whistled and widened his eyes. "No shit. We're gonna have everybody down on us now. The Jews, the gays, and lawyers. And all of 'em prone to running off at the mouth."

They were walking over to the Corniche.

"How long ago did it happen?"

"Coroner's people put the estimated time of death between ten and eleven o'clock last night."

"And nobody found him till now?"

"It's the weekend. Night watchman says on weekends the place—excuse the pun—the place is like a morgue. And he stays in the lobby."

"Then who found the body?"

"Lawyer. He and the wife had been arguing all night and he finally said fuck it he was going to get some sleep on his office couch. He recognized Saperstein's car and came by for a closer look. I'll bet he finds new offices within the month."

They were standing by the car. Natty was still slumped behind the wheel.

"Why haven't they moved him?"

Madison shrugged. "I don't know. Hey, Kazu. When are you guys going to remove the body?"

The coroner's assistant raised his head and looked at Madison.

"I guess we're finished. Just a few more shots."

Snap. *Flash!* Snap. *Flash!*

"Okay, let's do it."

The coroner's people opened the driver's door. Natty's hair was glued to the window by his dried blood. They chiseled him loose and lifted him out of the door. He was stiffening. They zipped him up in a body bag and put him in the van.

"Looks like our boy's extending his territory," Gold said. "He's never killed this far west before."

Madison shook his head. "Tell you the truth, Jack. I don't think this was our boy."

Gold looked straight at him. "What are you getting at, Dolly?"

Madison paused, watched the forensic technicians going over the Rolls.

"I think this is a copycat. I think someone killed Saperstein and wants us to think our boy did it. I think this was an assassination."

Gold brought out a fresh cigar. He shucked its cellophane husk, struck a match, and methodically lit the tip.

"Why do you say that?"

Dolly came closer and spoke in compressed tones.

"Jack, this whole thing has Mafia written all over it. The other stuff, the graffiti and all, that's just coverup."

Gold rolled the cigar between his fingertips, George Burns–style.

"Mafia, you say?"

"It's a hit, Jack. No question in my mind."

"Is that just a hunch?"

Madison glanced around surreptitiously. "First of all, the caliber of gun on this thing is going to come up .22, I'd bet my badge on it. That's pure professional hit man, and unlike any weapon the Crosskiller has used. And—and—look, Jack, working in the chief's office the way I do, I'm privy to a lot of information the average cop on the street would never even come close to."

"Uh huh."

"Saperstein was a high-level informant. For the DEA."

Gold blew out a plume of smoke.

"No shit? For how long?"

"A couple of years. He was working both sides of the street. Selling protection to his dope dealer clients, then turning around and giving names and addresses to the *federales*. I even heard he was doing some dealing himself, with the government's tacit approval and protection."

"No kidding?"

The coroner's van pulled out. They watched it drive off the third level.

"A guy like that, Jack, his days are numbered. People get in line to kill a guy like that. This was a professional hit. I'd stake my badge on it."

Gold picked a flake of tobacco off the tip of his tongue. "I think you might be right."

"You do?" Madison was pleased.

"But I also think we have to sit on your theory. At least for a while. This situation is much too explosive to go throwing around unsubstantiated theories. It's gonna be bad enough just dealing with the heat from another Crosskiller slaying. We start hinting that organized crime is involved, my God, can you imagine the media shit storm?"

Madison looked thoughtful. "You may have something there, Jack."

"And if we come up wrong, after putting out a rumor like that, Huntz will be furious. He'll have our heads on a platter. You know how he hates complications."

That cinched it.

"I don't think we should ignore the possibility of a professional hit, Jack, but probably we should pursue it on our own initiative. Separate from the central investigation."

"You have my complete support, Captain."

"I appreciate that, Jack."

"We'll keep this to ourselves for now."

"Exactly."

One of the task force detectives rushed up. "Captain Madison, some of the press sneaked up a back stair. We've got them contained, but they're demanding to know what's going on."

Madison smiled with confidence. Here was an area he could deal with as well as anyone.

"I'll handle this, Jack, unless you want to speak to them."

"No, thanks. I defer to your expertise in P.R."

Madison's proud smile gleamed. "All right, Detective," he said to the task force cop, "let's go give these press people a statement. Something they can use for the Sunday afternoon newscast."

Dolly Madison strode off purposefully, the detective in tow.

Gold chewed on his cigar and watched as the impound agents hooked the Rolls up to the tow truck. They were having difficulty with the low ceilings, and their curses echoed through the hollow structure.

A red sports convertible screeched up the far ramp and zoomed down the center lane toward Gold. It screamed to a stop a few feet away.

"Hey, what's happening?" Zamora said. His hair was wet and his shirt unbuttoned.

"Another victim. I'll run it down for you." He smiled and pointed to Zamora's damp hair. "Another soap commercial?"

"Nah, I just couldn't wake up. My mother finally had to pour a pot of cold water on me."

"Irish trash. You Christians sell your children for whisky."

"Nah. Tequila, maybe. Never whisky."

Gold got in the other side.

"Gosh! I'm going to breakfast with Robert Redford. In his sexy little car. And *he's* treating."

Zamora rammed the Vette into reverse and spun it around.

"By the way," Gold said, "did you ever land that commercial?"

"Sparkle Scented Soap?" Zamora slammed into gear.

"Yeah."

"Nah, they went with a Jew. Guess they figured he looked dirtier."

The Corvette laid rubber as it fishtailed through the third level.

2:38 PM Clarke Johnson straightened his back, girded himself, and rapped firmly on the screen door frame. Behind him, Sunday traffic droned along on Crenshaw Boulevard.

Through the screen door came the sounds of bereavement conversations, polite laughter choked off at the back of the throat, the strangely ratlike scrapings of people eating from paper plates.

A tall, fat, silver-haired woman in an ankle-length black dress came to the screen. She held the door open with one hand and with the other patted the sweat from her ebony brow with a lace handkerchief.

"Come in, son. Get out of that damn heat." She had a deep, syrupy, operatic voice.

Johnson hesitated on the threshold.

"Well, in or out, boy? You letting the bugs in."

He still held back.

"Is Mrs. Phibbs there?"

"Of course, she is, son. But why make me fetch her? I'm sure if you're a friend of the family you welcome to this wake."

Clarke Johnson gave her a thin smile. "I think perhaps I'd better speak to Mrs. Phibbs."

The big woman frowned and closed the screen. A few moments later Mama Phibbs appeared.

"Mr. Johnson. Please come in."

She, too, held the door open, but still he would not enter.

"Uh, Mrs. Phibbs, I meant Esther. When I asked for Mrs. Phibbs."

"Esther's in the kitchen. Come in."

He put one foot over the threshold and then halted.

"Mrs. Phibbs, perhaps you'd better check with Esther. I'm not sure I'm welcome here."

"Nonsense," she said, gently tugging him in by his sleeve. "Of course you're welcome here."

The smallish living room—its upholstery freshly brushed, furniture and floor newly polished—was crowded with people. Mostly women in their fifties and sixties—thick and stalwart, like the one who had come to the door, wearing dark, somber, rustling dresses. There was a smattering of men, sweating in their Sunday suits. One of them, a bald man with rimless John Lennon glasses, wore a clerical collar. Against a wall, in a straight-backed chair, sat a young Mexican girl. At her knee stood her four-year-old daughter, staring wide-eyed around the room. A buffet had been arranged on a crisply ironed tablecloth joining two card tables. Cold cuts, white bread, cole slaw, barbecued pork and beans, potato salad. For a moment everyone suspended their talking and eating to inspect the new arrival. Then they went about their business.

"Mrs. Phibbs, I want to again offer my sympathies on your son's tragic demise."

Mama Phibbs sighed and clucked her tongue. "Yes, it's a very sad day. I used to worry about outliving my husband, God rest his soul, and now here I've buried my only son. Life's full of bitter surprises, isn't it, Mr. Johnson?"

He said nothing.

She led him through the crowd. Several of the men nodded at him; the women examined him openly.

In the kitchen Esther and Little Bobby were seated at the table, watching Bagheera on the table top eat from a can of Liver-Treat Feline Cuisine. Esther and Clarke Johnson returned each other's stare for a long time, then she looked away and reached for a cigarette.

"You already have one lit, Mama," Little Bobby said.

"Oh," Esther said. She slid the cigarette back into the pack, still avoiding Johnson's eyes. She wore a silly veiled hat pinned to her hair.

"May I sit down?" he asked her.

She didn't reply.

"Wasn't it thoughtful of Mr. Johnson to come and pay his respects?" Mama Phibbs asked from the doorway.

Esther smoked in silence.

"May I sit down?" he asked again.

Esther tapped her ash on the edge of the ashtray.

"Esther—" Mama Phibbs coaxed.

Esther spoke sharply to the older woman. "If the man wants to sit down so damn bad why don't he just *sit down.*"

There was a moment of embarrassed silence, then Johnson pulled a chair out from under the ancient, metal-topped table and sat down. Bagheera looked up from its food, licked its whiskers, and stared wide-eyed at him.

Little Bobby reached out and stroked the kitten's fur. It arched up against the boy's hand.

"There's too many people. He got scared."

Johnson nodded and pulled his chair closer to the table. The kitten stuck its face back into the shallow can.

"You shouldn't make a practice of feeding him on the table, though. He'll jump up here when you're not around and lick the butter."

Little Bobby grimaced. "Yeccch! Would he really do that?"

"Sure, he would."

"I don't believe it. Mama, would Bagheera do that?"

Esther took a final drag on her cigarette and smashed the butt slowly in the ashtray.

"It's not one of the things I spend a lot of time worrying about, baby." She glanced at Johnson. "And neither should you."

Mama Phibbs, still standing in the doorway, cleared her throat.

"I have to see to our guests." She smiled. "They're mostly my church people. Wasn't it thoughtful of them to pay their respects?" She smiled again, not really expecting a reply. "Would you like something to eat, Mr. Johnson? I could fix you a plate."

He turned in his chair to address the old lady. "No, thank you, Mrs. Phibbs. I've already eaten."

"Well, then. Little Bobby, come help me take care of our guests."

"Awww, Mama. Do I have to?"

"Don't talk back to your elders, I told you. If your grandmother tells you to do something, you do it. Without any argument. You're the man of the house now."

Little Bobby slowly rose from his chair. He bowed his head and trudged solemnly toward the door. The little boy looked both impressive and ridiculous in his miniature black suit and tie.

"C'mon, boy," Mama Phibbs urged gently. "Being a man ain't all that bad."

"Bobby," Johnson said, "the Dodgers are starting a home stand this week. With the Mets. Maybe we could take in a game."

The boy's eyes exploded with delight. "The Mets? Wow! Can I, Mama?"

She shrugged, not looking at anyone.

"Maybe we could all go," Johnson suggested.

"You think so?" He looked from one adult to the next.

When Esther didn't answer, he said, "We'll see, Bobby. We'll see."

"That'd be great!"

Mama Phibbs took her beaming grandson's hand. "C'mon, child," the old lady said softly and led him from the kitchen.

"Don't forget!" Little Bobby shouted from the hall.

"I promise."

They sat without talking for several minutes, watching the cat lap up the last of his Liver-Treat. The conversation in the parlor was a steady, sorrowful drone. Finally he looked straight at her.

"I hope you don't object to my presence."

She said nothing.

"I was at the cemetery. I held back. I didn't want to intrude. Where I wasn't welcome."

Esther glanced at him, but didn't speak.

"I'm really sorry about your husband's death. I want you to know that. I'm heartsick."

Silence.

"For heaven's sake, Esther, talk to me. Tell me to get out. Tell me to stay. Tell me anything. But *talk to me.*"

Esther returned his stare. Then she stood and lifted two clean cups from the drainboard.

"Coffee?" she asked, reaching for the pot on the stove.

"Thank you." He smiled.

After pouring the coffee she sat down again and grabbed for another cigarette.

"You smoke too much."

She shook her head as she struck the match and said, "Today's not the day to think about quitting."

"I guess not." He took a quick sip of coffee. The kitten sat back on its haunches and began to clean itself. Esther picked it up with one hand and dropped it gently to the floor. It stared up at her and meowed mournfully.

"What you doing anyway, hanging 'round here?" Esther turned her sullen eyes full on him.

Johnson was momentarily thrown.

"I don't under—"

"You got what you was sniffing after," she bit off angrily. "You got what you came for. Why don't you leave me alone? Leave me alone in my time of grief."

She started to cry quietly.

"Why don't you move on to the next parolee's woman? That's your game, ain't it? Why don't you just get out of here?"

She laid her head down on her hand on the tabletop. Her shoulders shook. Johnson made as if to reach out to her, then stopped and drew back his hand. The kitten leapt on the table and crouched, watching her cry. After a long while, she sighed and raised her head. She wiped her eyes with the back of her hand and reached for a fresh cigarette.

"You still smoke too much," he said and took the Salem Light from her hand.

She wouldn't look at him for a long time.

"I told you," she said finally, taking the smoke back. "Today is not the right time." She smiled wanly. "Give a girl a light, why don'cha."

He found the book of matches, struck one, and held it to her cigarette. She took a deep drag and blew the smoke at the ceiling. Then she put it out.

She got up.

"I'll make some fresh coffee."

7:00 PM Herschel Guzman was in Room 415 at Cedars-Sinai, a private corner room at the end of a long hall and directly across from a nurses' station.

A nurse stepped in their way.

"No smoking, sir," she growled, staring at Gold's cigar as if it were a stool sample. "The designated waiting area only."

She was slim and blond and frosty, with a heavy Scandinavian accent. Gold was about to argue with her, but Zamora stepped between them and flashed her his best Redford. She melted, batting her lashes and giggling.

"Put out the stogie and go on in," Zamora said to Gold from the side of his mouth as he watched her tight, white-uniformed rump glide away. "I'll stake out the nurses' area. Just like Newman in *Fort Apache, the Bronx.*"

The room was cool and dim. Herschel was under an oxygen mask, his wife, Ruth, at his bedside. Around the bed several people stood and sat. Gold recognized Jackie Max. The others were his entourage: a couple of gag writers, a few gofers, and a busty *shiksa* passing as a secretary.

"Jack." Ruth stood up. "Thank you for stopping by."

"Of course. How's he doing? How are you, Herschel?"

Herschel, lying on his side under the oxygen mask, made a shaky thumbs-up sign and winked at Gold. His complexion was chalky, and he looked thirty pounds lighter than when Gold had seen him less than a week ago.

"He's doing very beautifully," Ruth answered for her husband. "They took him out of Intensive Care this morning. He surprised everyone, he's recuperating so fast. Dr. Singh said it's because he's got the constitution of a water buffalo."

"Dr. Singh?" Jackie Max interjected. "Dr. *Singh?* What kinda Jew name is Singh?"

"He's an Indian."

"An Indian?" Jackie Max feigned shock; his sycophants tittered on cue. "You mean a swami Indian? A Gandhi Indian? He's not Jewish?"

"Uh, boss"—one of the gofers suppressed his laughter as he fed his employer the straight lines, "if his name is Singh, that means he's a Sikh."

"Sikh? You mean those diaperheads you see going to all the movies in Westwood? Those people who wear their dirty laundry on their person? Those people? That's what you have for a doctor? A snake charmer? Here,

436

in the biggest Jewish hospital in the world, with the best, most expensive Jew doctors in the world—you, Herschel the Jew, you have a rug merchant for a doctor?"

Everyone was laughing aloud now, even Gold was smiling. Herschel's form shook uncontrollably under the sheets.

"Jackie!" Ruth reprimanded. "You're going to make Herschel lose his tubes!"

"Oy!" Max rolled his eyes heavenward. "God forbid he lose his tubes!" Fresh bursts of laughter around the room.

"Jackie! Please!" Ruth pleaded.

Jackie Max turned to Gold and extended his hand.

"Hello. I'm Jackie Max," he said with a transparent humility, already knowing that Gold had recognized him.

"I'm Jack Gold." Max had one of those painfully earnest handshakes. He wore a beautifully tailored silk tuxedo, patent-leather shoes, and a wafer-thin Patek Phillipe wristwatch. He kept shooting his cuffs, and he smelled of heavy cologne.

"I know who you are, Lieutenant. We're gonna be sharing a stage in just a few hours."

"You mean the Benefit for Brotherhood. At the Bowl. Afraid I'm not gonna be able to make it."

"Oh? I'm disappointed." He looked it. "That's too bad. Everyone is gonna be there. Everyone."

"Everyone," one of the yes-men echoed, in this case a woman writer. A yes-person.

"Frank, Dean, Sammy, Milton, uh," Max recited, "Jerry, Robin, Richard, Warren—"

"Barbra," someone else prompted.

"—Barbra, Liza, Diana, Burt, Clint. Fucking *everybody!* I can't believe you're gonna miss it."

Gold shrugged. "Business is business."

"—Whoopie, Kenny, Eddie, Joan, Johnny—"

Max snapped his fingers to silence the underling.

"You know the mayor's coming? And the chief of police. Probably the governor."

"That's great," Gold said flatly.

Max shook his head. "Whatever you're doing must be pretty damn important to miss this kind of thing."

Gold gave him a cold smile. "I'd like to think so."

Suddenly Max was bored by the whole conversation. He shot his cuffs one more time and eyed his gold watch.

"Well, *bubeleh,* time to go. I'm already late for makeup. NBC is taping tonight. They're gonna use it as a special. Maybe during Sweeps Week."

He leaned over the bed and spoke directly at Herschel, almost shouting into his ear. "It's for you tonight, *bubeleh*. All for you. Understand?"

Herschel nodded weakly.

"I want you to know that, Hersch. I love you. I love you, you old Jew." When Jackie Max straightened his eyes were moist. A gofer raced forward with a Kleenex, but Max waved it away. He put his arm around Ruth Guzman's shoulders, drawing her up from her chair.

"Come walk me to the elevator, sweetheart, and we'll talk about getting the deli open again. You and me."

When everyone else had left the room Gold dragged a chair over to Herschel's bedside and sat down. Herschel had closed his eyes and seemed to be dozing.

"Herschel," Gold said softly.

Herschel opened his eyes. They focused on Gold and smiled.

"Tonight, Herschel. I'm gonna get the motherfucker tonight."

Herschel's eyes turned hard and black.

"I'm gonna stick my gun up his *tuchis* and blow his head off."

Herschel grunted.

"I'm gonna make the motherfucker *hurt,* Herschel."

Herschel stuck out his fist and made a thumbs up sign.

9:16 PM The conductor walked to the podium, held his baton aloft, and captured his musicians' rapt attention. The orchestra—basically the "Tonight Show" band augmented by extra brass and reeds, a string section, and a tympanist—sat poised and expectant. A deep voice boomed over the Hollywood Bowl's state-of-the-art sound system:

"Ladies and gentlemen—"

The conductor pointed to the tympanist and he *whoommmed* a crescendo.

"—taking it to the max . . . Mr. Jackie Max!"

The conductor gave a downbeat and a pulse, and the orchestra wailed out a sultry, bluesy arrangement of "I'll Take Manhattan," Jackie Max's lifelong theme song. The music washed out over the amphitheater carved into the hillside. A single spotlight found Jackie Max at stage left of the shell and the capacity audience leapt to its feet and thundered a welcome. The golden spot followed him as he strode across the stage to the microphone and accepted his applause. The crowd wouldn't stop. Finally, Max held up his hands for quiet, but instead of abating, the roar swelled. Jackie Max stepped back from the mike and seemed genuinely moved. It was seven minutes before the audience allowed him to speak.

"I guess we all know why we're here, don't we!"

Another thunderous roar.

"And I guess we all know who's backstage, don't we!"

An even more tumultuous groundswell.

"Everybody, baby! That's who's backstage! Everybody's backstage!"

An enthusiastic roar, punctuated by hundreds of two-finger whistles and brightened by the lighting of matches and the popping of flashbulbs all over the Bowl.

"And why are they here?"

Jackie Max leaned with the mike stand over the monitors and footlights and worked his audience.

"Love, baby, that's why they're here! Love! And that's why *you're* here!" He stabbed his finger at the crowd, prompting another standing ovation. The acoustics of the Bowl made the eighteen thousand near-hysterical fans sound like a hundred thousand. The roar reverberated through the warm night air and shook the dry earth of the Hollywood Hills.

"That's right, baby! *Love!* Love, love, love, love, *love!* That's what tonight is all about! That's why we're here! That's why you'll see on this

stage tonight the greatest aggregation of talent ever assembled on one stage!
Tonight will truly be a *night of a thousand stars!"*

With a dramatic flourish Jackie Max flung his arms up at the smoggy,
starless L.A. sky, demanding a fresh explosion of applause.

"The Jew has always been a sickness, an infection, poisoning civilization's
bloodstream. An indigestible piece of gristle stuck in Christianity's craw.
Such it has always been; such it will always be. Until we do something
about it."

There were about thirty seated people scattered throughout the folding
metal chairs set up in the dusty, concrete-floored meeting room of the
Blood of the Lamb Church of the Living Christ. Behind the small dais
hung a lurid day-glo-on-black-velvet painting of Jesus suffering the agonies
of the cross.

Jesse Utter cleared his throat and fixed his audience with an angry glare.

"The Jew must leave our midst. He is not fit for the company of Christians. The Jew and all of his mongrelized henchmen must release the
stranglehold they have on this once-great country."

Utter poked the air with his finger and shifted his weight behind the dais.
He and his four Inner Circle security guards who stood sentry before him
were done up in the new, hoodless uniforms of the Klan of the eighties:
white cotton shirt and trousers (purchased from a sympathetic wholesaler
who supplied the staffs of nursing homes); black boots, belt and Sam
Browne, polished to a slick gleam; black tie tucked into the shirt just above
the third button. And on their sleeves their insignia: the silhouette of
California with the KK superimposed, twin lightning bolts, and over their
heart a tiny American flag patch.

"A couple of years ago they went around collecting pennies and nickels
from little white schoolchildren to fix up that hideous Statue of Libertines
over in Jew York City. The Lady in the Harbor they called her. I call her
the Whore of the East. Before she was dumped in Jew York Harbor—the
gift of French Jews, I might add—this country was on the right track. It's
as if, and you must pardon my speaking this way in a house of God, it's
as if the Whore of the East laid down and opened her legs to every dirty
little foreigner who wanted to come in."

There were a few soft gasps and nods of agreement from the mostly
gray-headed crowd.

"This country was created by and intended for," Utter thundered,
"white Christian northern Europeans and their descendants. That's who
discovered it, wrested it away from the savages, conquered it, and carved

it out of the wilderness. And now the Jews and the bureaucrats and the Communist Congress want to give it away. To the yellows and the blacks, the browns and the reds. People who don't believe in our Christ, who don't speak our English, who don't subscribe to our system of government. *Well, we won't let them have it!*"

A smattering of timid applause.

"I'd like to pull down that so-called Statue of Liberty. Just pull it down into that polluted Jew York Harbor and let it sink beneath the foul surface. And in its place erect a huge gate with a big, enormous lock on that huge gate, and then put up an identical gate in Miami, in Seattle, in New Orleans and Chicago, and especially here in Los Angeles Harbor and up in San Francisco Bay. And on those gates I'd carve *'Don't* give us your tired, huddled masses, we have enough already. *Don't* give us your diseased, your criminal, your unemployable, your depraved, your mentally retarded. Keep your foreign gods, your godless isms. Keep your slant-eyed, your greasy, your dirty and unwashed. Your gooks, your spicks, your slopes and coons. Your Hebes, your kikes, your—' "

A brick crashed through one of the painted-over back windows and tumbled end over end across the floor. Everyone in the church leapt to their feet. Some of the older people huddled together. The church door burst open and a white-uniformed Klansman ran in, yelling, "It's the JAR! They're attacking us out on the lawn! About thirty—*Uhh!*"

He was cut down from behind by a baseball bat swung against his rib cage. He writhed in the aisle, clutching his side. Jerry Kahn stood over him, bat in both hands, flanked by several Resisters in their blue logo'd T-shirts.

"Get out of here, Jew!" Utter screamed. "This is a house of Jesus!"

"That sewage you're spouting doesn't sound very Christ-like to me."

"Get out of here or we'll kill you!"

Just then a Resister and a Klansman, locked in combat over an M-16, tumbled through a whitewashed window, sending glass and folding chairs flying.

"Why don't you come move us, Nazi!" Kahn shouted up at the pulpit.

"Kill him! Kill him!" Utter shrieked, and the four Inner Circle security guards lunged forward. Kahn slashed his bat across one Klansman's face, sending blood spurting from the man's mouth. Then the others were upon him and he went over backward. His Resisters waded into the pileup.

Outside on the lawn someone fired a shot. Then another.

Utter jumped from the pulpit and ran to a side exit. An old woman was attempting to flee the battle. Utter pushed her aside, sending her sprawling, and raced through the exit. A paved pathway between the church and the

Bible school led to the tiny rear parking lot. Utter was already behind the wheel of his minipickup when a hand clutched his narrow black necktie and yanked him from the cab.

"*¿Qué pasa, mano?*" Sean Zamora grinned. "How you be, Je*sse?*"

"Leave me alone!" Utter squealed. "Leave me alone!"

A big hand grabbed a fistful of his thinning black hair and dragged him over to another vehicle, a battered green Ford, and threw him face-down across the hood.

"You're under arrest," Gold growled, perfunctorily patting Utter down.

"On what charge?" Utter demanded over his shoulder. The sounds of the battle taking place a hundred yards away drifted loud and strong over the rooftops of the church buildings.

"Incitement to riot. Can't you hear that fight going on?"

"My troops didn't start that." Utter turned to face Gold with a glower.

"Conspiracy to incite to riot, disturbing the peace—"

Another gunshot.

"Fleeing the scene of a crime, destruction of private property, and just being a general all-around asshole."

Utter sneered at him. "Fucking Jew!" he spat out.

Gold smiled. From his breast pocket he withdrew a business card–sized printed rectangle.

"Those Commie kikes over at the ACLU say I have to read this to you. So here goes: 'You have the right to remain silent.' "

Without taking his eyes from the card, Gold threw a short, straight-arm punch into Utter's face that dislodged two incisors and sent Utter crashing back over the Ford's hood.

" 'If you relinquish that right—' "

Gold rammed his elbow into Utter's unprotected groin, and Utter sank slowly to his knees.

" '—anything you say can and will be used against you.' " Gold slipped the card into his pocket, walked around to Utter's side, and leaning on the Ford's fender, lashed out with an ersatz karate kick that landed flat-footed against Utter's cheek, plunging him face-forward to the concrete.

" 'You have the right to an attorney,' " Gold recited as he picked Utter up under his arms and threw him into the rear of the Ford. Zamora got behind the wheel.

" 'And to have an attorney present during any questioning.' "

Gold climbed over Utter into the back seat.

" 'If you cannot afford an attorney—' "

He examined a knuckle he had skinned on Utter's face.

" 'One will be provided for you.' "

* * *

Ten minutes later Gold and Zamora half carried, half dragged Utter down the corridor that led to the booking desk at Van Nuys Station. Utter's white Klan uniform was soaked front and back with the blood that streamed from his nose, mouth, and ears.

"Good God!" the petite Eurasian desk sergeant gasped. "What plane did that dude fall out of?"

They propped Utter up against the booking counter and proceeded to take his fingerprints.

"I want to make a complaint," Utter muttered through his missing teeth.

"Shut up, asshole!" the desk sergeant growled as she filled in Utter's admitting forms. Then, sweetly, she said to Gold, "That's quite a disturbance over at that church. Eighteen units, Riot Control, three shootings, thirty-three arrests. In fifteen minutes this place is going to be ass-deep in assholes."

"Any fatalities?"

"I want to make a complaint!" Utter screamed, cupping his hands under his chin.

"No, just a lot of busted heads. One guy bit off another guy's earlobe." She turned to Zamora. "Say, don't I know you from somewhere?"

Zamora smiled and moved a little closer to the sergeant's desk. "Well, I'm an actor. You may have seen my work on episodic television. I had a part on 'Simon and Simon' last season."

"Let's go, asshole," Gold said.

"I want to call my lawyer!" Utter screamed again, spraying blood all over the booking area.

"You're on TV?" The desk sergeant's black eyes glittered.

"Just some guest shots. But I'm doing a feature this fall. Going down to Mexico to shoot it. Should be a lot of fun."

"Sounds like it."

"I have a right to call a lawyer!"

"Phone's out of order."

"It ishn't! It ishn't!"

Gold went over to the wall phone, lifted the receiver from its cradle, and yanked back with both hands.

"It is now," Gold said and tossed the handset into a wastebasket.

"Jew pig!"

"Let's go," Gold ordered and pushed Utter hard toward the corridor that led back to the holding cells.

"Wait a minute! I know where I saw you. You were in that magazine, oh, what's the name?"

Zamora smiled shyly. *"Playgirl."*

"Right! *Playgirl!* You're the Naked Civil Servant. All the policewomen were talking about you. You looked dynamite!"

Zamora broadened his smile and ran his fingertip along the desk sergeant's blotter. "Thank you, Sergeant."

"Kim. Call me Kim." Her teeth were even and white. "Listen, you've got to tell me something."

"I already know what you're gonna ask me."

"How did you keep your badge on, you know, keep it on where it was. All of the female officers were wondering. Without any clothes like that."

"Zamora!" Gold shouted. "Get over here and bring a nightstick. I'm gonna break this asshole's head!" Utter had wrapped his fingers through the wire mesh covering the steel door and wouldn't let go. Gold was trying to pry him loose.

"Leave me alone! Leave me alone!" Utter shrieked.

Zamora left the pretty desk sergeant's side and came over to the two struggling men.

"They glued it on with this clear theatrical glue. Afterward they peeled it right off." Zamora stood flat-footed and put all of his weight into the roundhouse haymaker that slammed into the area of Utter's unprotected kidney. The Klansman released the door with a grunt and reached back to try to contain the sickening pain that shot through his lower back.

"Oh, that must have really hurt!" the desk sergeant cooed.

"Nah," Zamora said as he turned back to her. "They used alcohol. The glue dissolves when you hit it with alcohol. It only stings a little."

The desk sergeant giggled.

"Let's go, motherfucker." Gold gripped the shiny black Sam Browne belt across Utter's back and dragged him down the short corridor that led back to the cells. Utter kept clutching for handholds on the bars and Gold kept yanking him loose. Zamora, following, kicked him in his behind. At the end of the hall they made a right-angle turn and Gold flung the smaller man to the floor before a long, barred sliding door.

"Here we go, Jesse. The Monkey House."

Utter peered up at him. "What?"

Gold laughed. "Jigaboos, Jesse. Boogie-woogies. Jungle bunnies. Nonwhites. See?"

He pointed into the long, dark cell. In the dimness six or seven black men lounged insolently on the narrow concrete ledge that served as a bench. Some were shirtless, others wore stained, ripped T-shirts and sweatshirts. To Gold the "prisoners" looked like exactly what they were: an unscheduled Sunday night meeting of the Black Peace Officers' Association. In their fishing clothes. But Gold knew that to Utter they were the personification of his dreadest nightmare—violent ghetto criminals.

"Hey! Niggers!" Gold put his face to the bars and shouted into the cell. "You fucking apes better shape up! You know who this dude is, man? He's the grand motherfucking imperial wizard of the Kalifornia Klan, and he's gonna come in there and kick yo' black ass for you, you hear? This is one bad-ass Klansman, you better believe it."

The seven men stared back through the bars with case-hardened faces. Their sullen eyes shone white in the dark.

"You can't put me in there," Utter whispered.

"Sure I can," Gold answered brightly.

"Please don't put me in there."

"You want to make a phone call, don't you? Well, this is the holding pen for assholes who want to make phone calls." He shouted through the bars again. "Ain't all you niggers waiting to use the phone?"

"Fuck you, paddy pig!" Honeywell spat out.

"See?" Gold grinned down at Utter. "Just a bunch of nigger rapists waiting to call their Jew lawyers."

One of the blacks, looking directly at Utter, turned his wrist around to expose the short, wicked-looking blade taped to the underside of his forearm. The black blew Utter a kiss.

"He's got a knife!" Utter yelped. "He's got a knife!"

"You want to call your wife? Sure, okay. If I was you I'd use my one call on my lawyer, but it's your nickel. Sergeant Yamaguchi!" Gold shouted down the corridor. "Holding pen two."

"Deep in the bowels of the jailhouse's walls a giant automatic lever gave a loud *clunk!* and the cell gate jerked open.

"No! No!" Utter yelped and scuttled backward across the floor. "Leave me alone!"

"Let's go, Imperial Wizard." Gold and Zamora caught Utter by either shoulder and yanked him to his feet.

"No! No! Wait!" Utter clutched at his captors in desperation. "I'll give you that license plate number you want."

Gold shook his head. "Too late, *mein Fuehrer.* You went and pissed me off."

Gold nodded at Zamora and they threw Utter into the cell.

"Yamaguchi!" Gold shouted and the gate clanked shut.

Utter jumped up from the piss-puddled floor and threw himself at the bars, groping through for Gold's arm.

"For God's sake, don't leave me in here! *Don't leave me in here!*"

The black men in the cell got up from the cement shelf and started to close in around him. The beaten, frightened little man sank down the bars to the cold floor, sobbing and cringing at their feet.

"Don't. Don't. Don't. Don't," he pleaded softly, over and over.

Gold leaned against the bars, stripped and lighted a cigar. He squatted down to where Utter was weeping and blew a cloud of smoke in his face.

"*Now* you can give me that license plate, Jesse."

11:42 PM Esther fitted the key into the lock and turned it. She pushed the door open with one foot and held it ajar while she lugged in the big, round floor polisher. Lupe followed with an armful of brooms and mops. Florencia brought up the rear with a wooden case containing the cleansers and waxes, the rags and the Windex. From a strap over her shoulder hung a portable radio–cassette player.

"*Mierda!*" Lupe said, surveying the wide central hall. "This place is *big!*"

"Yeah." Esther pushed the polisher against a wall. "We gonna work our asses off."

She sat on the floor polisher's round cannister top and lit a cigarette. Lupe watched her closely. Esther's eyes were red and swollen, her body slumped.

"Es, *hermana,* why don't you go home. Me and Florencia, we clean this big old place."

Esther gave out a short, ironic laugh. "If I had two of *you,* maybe I would think about it. But not with just you—and her." She nodded toward Florencia, who was squatting on the floor, adjusting the ghetto-blaster's rabbit ears, trying to get good reception from a Spanish-language station.

"It's not right, you have to work on the day you bury your husband."

Esther turned her head away quickly as her eyes filled. She fought for a moment for control of herself, then shivered slightly. She stood up and arched her back with a sigh. "Lupe, I leave you here alone with Florencia to clean up this whole building, and I'll have to bury *you* tomorrow. Listen, can't you tell her to find something *fast* on that box—some disco or even some salsa. Something to work by. That stuff'll put us all to sleep."

Florencia's radio station was wailing out a sorrowful Mexican *ranchera.* Lupe spoke to the heavy girl in flashing Spanish and Florencia grunted and twisted the tuner to an R & B station. Heavy, mechanized backbeat jumped from the speakers.

"She's a good girl," Lupe said. "Just a little slow."

"I heard *that.* Anyway, let's take this floor first. *Numero uno,* we'll empty the baskets. *Dos,* mop the floors and dust the—what was that?"

"*¿Como?*"

"What was that? Didn't you hear that?"

"What?"

"I don't know. Tell her to turn that thing off!"

447

"Silencio!" Lupe hissed, pointing at the radio-recorder, and Florencia snapped it off.

In the sudden quiet they could all hear footsteps coming down one of the darkened halls that branched off from the reception area. Heavy-booted male footsteps.

"Who's supposed to be in here?" Lupe asked in a wide-eyed whisper.

"I don't know," Esther whispered back.

"Anybody?"

"I *don't know!*"

Lupe braced her broom out before her like a spear, and Esther picked up a metal waiting-room chair and raised it above her head. The footsteps were closing in, coming around a corner. Esther and Lupe steeled themselves, looked at each other, then back at the corner.

A tall black man came around the corner. He was in a tan uniform and wore a gun on his belt. He spotted the women and jumped back.

"Whoa, ladies! I'm on *your* side."

"You're the night watchman," Esther said accusingly and exhaled.

"Security, I like to call myself."

"They didn't tell me this building had security." Esther set the chair down gently.

"That's *their* oversight. Don't get mad at me, honeybunch." His warm smile revealed a single gold tooth. He looked like he was in his fifties, but Esther thought he was probably older than that.

"Hi, I'm Walter Chappell, but everybody 'round here calls me Chappy. I only allow my *special* friends to address me as Walter."

Esther ignored his flirtation and started wheeling the floor polisher down the hall. Lupe and Florencia had already gone down the corridor about their work, going into various offices, emptying ashtrays and wastebaskets into big green plastic bags.

"Well, *Chappy,* you think you could give us some more lights in this big old barn? We have to have this place spick-'n'-span by eight o'clock."

"Seven," Chappy corrected. "Techno-Cal is on the early schedule, honeybunch. And about these lights." He felt his hand around behind a wall panel and the halls were suddenly bathed in glare. "Mr. Morrison, he don't condone wasting no 'lectricity. Old Abie watches them light bills like a hawk. So when you through cleaning a floor, honeybunch, you make sure you switch everything off, you hear?"

"I hear you," Esther nodded. "You been with the company a while, Chappy?"

"Twenty-three years. Since they first built her. They made transistors and such back then."

"Mr. Morrison likes you?"

"Lemme put it this way, honeybunch. Before old Abie started his austerity program there was three full-time security personnel. Now there's just me. Me and the Rent-a-Cop comes in on my night off."

Esther bent over to plug in her floor polisher.

"He seems like a nice man," she said.

"Nice enough," Chappy said, as he made an expert appraisal of Esther's blue-jeaned rump. Esther straightened and pushed her sleeves up.

"Lookahere, honeybunch. I rigged me up a little office in a storeroom at the end of this hallway. Got me a hot plate and a toaster. A percolator and this old TV." His eyes twinkled. "Got me a cot and a bottle of Ol' Grand-dad, too. You oughta come pay me a visit."

Esther frowned at him.

"I got work to do, man."

"I'm just saying what I got, that's all."

Esther pushed a stray lock of hair back from her face.

"Well, what I got is work to do."

MONDAY
August 13

$2{:}01$ *AM* Gold hit the door low, running with as much speed as he could get on the garage apartment's tiny stair landing. The dime-store lock disintegrated and the door crashed open against a wall. Gold rolled over once and came up in a kneeling position, his weapon outstretched before him. Fourteen feet away, across the floor of the shadowy apartment, someone was kneeling in an identical position, pointing a gun at *him.* Gold fired, and the other gunman shot back. Gold fired rapidly three more times, and the other man exploded in a burst of refracted light.

"*What!*" Gold screamed. Someone was yelling at him. "*What?*"

"It's a mirror! It's a mirror!" Zamora shouted. "It's a motherfucking mirror!"

Gold got up slowly, his .38 still stiff-armed before him. Zamora flicked up the wall switch. Gold blinked his eyes in the sudden light. It reflected off the shards of shattered mirror that now covered the floor. Zamora kicked a dumbbell with his toe and it rolled grittily across the glass.

"It was his workout mirror," he said.

At the first sound of gunfire, dogs all over the block had begun to bark. Now neighbors in their bathrobes gathered at the foot of the garage apartment's stairs and shouted up confused questions. Zamora went out on the landing and held up his badge.

"Everything's under control, folks. We just want to talk to Mr. Walker. Anybody here know where he might happen to be?"

No one did.

"Anybody have any information about where Mr. Walker works, who his friends are, does he have any family, a girl friend? Anything like that?"

Everyone shook their heads and made negative sounds. An old lady in bifocals—obviously the neighborhood busybody—ventured forward, her blue hair done up in pink rollers.

"No one around here knows a thing about that man. Doesn't say a word to anybody, that one. Keeps odd hours, too. I hear him coming and going sometimes. Sometimes it's dawn before he gets home."

"He does own a van, though? A blue one?"

"That's the one. Parks it right here in the driveway. Them things all remind me of hearses."

Back upstairs in the tiny apartment Zamora looked around and shook his head.

"Whew! This guy's a real pig."

The air in the apartment was heavy and stale. Garbage overflowed leaky trash bags under the dish-filled sink. All around the room were stacks of yellowing newspapers and magazines.

"But he's the right pig, Sean," Gold said, a little out of breath. "Look at the newspapers pinned to the wall."

Zamora found the wall Gold was talking about. It was covered with the tacked-up front pages of local newspaper coverage of the recent spate of killings.

"Maybe he's a murder buff. A gore freak," Zamora offered.

Gold was riffling through the closet. "Maybe, but check out the stacks of Kalifornia Klan *Klarions,* the American Nazi Party literature, the anti-Semitic pamphlets. It's all over the place."

Zamora shrugged. "Inconclusive. A lot of people don't like Jews."

Gold came out of the closet and shot him a dark glare. "What is this, stump the band? How about a little help here?"

"What are we looking for?"

"Anything," Gold said as he gripped the cot's threadbare mattress with two fists. "Payroll stubs, address book, letters—" He grunted and turned the cot over.

"—bullets."

Zamora came over and stood by him. Cushioned by a tuft of dust in a corner of the cot's frame were two shiny silver-sided cylinders.

"Three fifty-sevens," Zamora observed.

"Bingo."

"He was loading his piece and he dropped some cartridges. These two he overlooked."

"No shit, Sherlock," Gold grinned. "Someday you'll make chief, I can tell. Look, Sean, we're gonna go over this dump very, very carefully. We have to come up with something that'll help us catch this asshole. I feel something heavy-duty coming down, partner. We have to stop it."

The one-room efficiency with bath was very small. It took only fifteen minutes to go through it. And then once again. Afterward Gold sat on the workout bench and ran his fingers through his hair.

"This motherfucker's a ghost. I've seen men leave more of themselves in the sink after they shave. He has no life. Look at this pigsty. A ghost who lives in a garbage can."

Zamora, leaning against the refrigerator, kept his silence, allowed his boss to rant on.

"William Charles Walker. No prior convictions. No prior arrests. No military service, no phone, no credit rating. This spook doesn't vote, he doesn't buy on time, he doesn't pay taxes, doesn't have insurance on his van. The computer must have gone nuts looking for this asshole. I'm telling you, Sean, this one is our boy. I can feel it."

Gold took a cigar from his pocket, stuck it in his mouth, then put it back into his pocket.

"You know, there's something about these newspapers." He stood and walked to the wall of headlines. "They stop three days ago. There's no Friday or Saturday paper. Or Sunday."

"I would say maybe he rabbited," Zamora suggested. "But if he's the perpetrator, then he had to be around to do up poor little Natty last night."

Gold glanced at Zamora, then quickly looked away. He stared intently at the pushpinned clippings. He zeroed in on the center paper, the one that screamed DELICATESSEN MASSACRE, OFFICER ALSO SLAIN. He ran his fingers over the newsprint. There was something beneath it. Carefully, he pulled the top pushpins and peeled the front page away from the wall. Under the paper, Scotch-taped to the dirty yellow wall, were a score of photographs—color-faded snapshots of a man, a young woman, and a boy-child. The photographs seemed several years old. The hairstyles were longer, the clothes now out of fashion. The girl was blond and busty. Several of the Polaroids were obviously taken during a single day at the beach, and the woman, spilling out of her string bikini like a whipped dessert, showed off her cleavage or her silhouette for the lens. The boy was four or five, with a shock of sandy hair and a nervous smile. The man was heavily muscled. Tattoos ran up and down his arms. He scowled at the camera in every shot.

"I know this motherfucker," Gold said softly.

"What?" Zamora was incredulous. He moved closer. With his fingernail Gold stripped the dried Scotch-tape from a single photograph, freed the print from the wall, and held it up to the light. The man in the picture glared back at him.

"Who is it, Jack?"

Gold handed the photograph to Zamora and he inspected it closely.

"You know who he is? Who is he?"

Gold pointed to the remaining headlines. "No Friday paper. No Saturday, no Sunday. This guy hasn't had a paper in three days. And guess what? Neither have I. And you know why?" He tapped the Polaroid in Zamora's hand. Because he's my fucking paper boy."

"No shit," Zamora breathed. He brought the photo up to his eyes. "So. You think he's skipped town? But that still doesn't explain Natty Saperstein. Did he leave town and then come back to kill Saperstein? Hey, shouldn't we check in with Parker. Maybe Dolly can—"

Zamora heard footsteps clumping down the stairs outside. He looked up from Sonny Walker's glowering face to discover he was alone.

"Jack, wait up! *Wait up!*"

3:02 AM Esther shut off the floor polisher and the motor whirred down to silence. She manhandled the big machine partway down the empty corridor, then stopped, sighed, and leaned her back against the wall. She was exhausted. She slipped slowly down the wall until her buttocks touched the shiny floor, then she made a cradle with her thin arms locked over her knees and rested her head in the cradle. Somewhere, on another floor, she could hear Florencia's *barrio*-blaster thinly pouring out another Mexican wrist-slasher.

"Si quieres verme llorar. Si quieres verme llorar."

Without raising her head, Esther reached into her work shirt pocket and pulled out her pack of smokes. It was empty. She cursed silently, crumpled the pack, and was about to toss the lump of paper away when she realized she'd just have to pick it up again.

It had been a long, tearful night. She was thankful the building was so large, because all night she had worked away from the other two women. Worked and cried. Now she was cried out. Exhausted, mentally and physically. Her mind was as dry as a Santa Ana wind. And just as turbulent. Conflicting emotions kept crashing around inside of her and reverberating like a drummer's cymbal. She had buried her Bobby today. Her husband of twelve years, the father of her son, the man she had dreamed of growing old with. True, he had betrayed and deserted her less than a week ago; still, for the last dozen years he had been the absolute center of her life. Even during the long periods when he was away doing time, her existence had been dominated by his absence. And now he was gone. Forever and finally gone. Burying him had devastated her.

But yet, now, at the moment of her soul's greatest desolation, there came a man bringing with him the promise of hope, of a new tomorrow, of untapped happiness.

Clarke Johnson. An owl of a man. A bureaucrat in gold-rimmed glasses. A three-piece suit. How could anyone so—so—*square,* so straight-arrow, so irrefutably, resolutely *not with it* cause such turmoil in her soul, such delicious tingling in her toes. She thought of the man playing Trivial Pursuit with her son last night after the wake. Two quick minds high-fiving over a gameboard. The image suffused her with warmth. She remembered him surprising her with his killer dance steps and giggled at the memory. She closed her eyes and recalled the night he fucked her. How he had whispered over and over, "You're so beautiful. So very beautiful," as he ground into her. She felt guilt rush through her. How could she have such thoughts, with Bobby not yet cold in his grave? Yet her mind rushed back to thoughts of Clarke Johnson. What did he see in her? Why wouldn't he leave her alone? It wasn't as if she thought herself unworthy. Men were always hitting on her. She had never had problems attracting men. But never one like him—educated, articulate, mainstream. It would not have been more disconcerting had it been a white man who was pursuing her. Or more exciting.

Someone touched her arm, startling her from her doze and sending her crabbing away backward across the polished floor.

"Hey, honeybunch. Don't be ascared." Chappy's gold filling gleamed. "It's only me."

"*Damn,* man!" Esther grunted as she pulled herself up. "You *always* sneaking 'round scaring people?"

"Didn't mean no harm, honeybunch. Just making my rounds. Got to check out the building ev'ry once in a while, you know. Say, girl, you ready for that little taste yet? It'll wake you right up."

Esther shook her head as she wound the power cord around the floor polisher's cannister.

"Don't drink at work."

"How 'bout after work?"

She ignored the question. Chappy cocked his head to one side and inspected her with a discerning eye.

"You got a man, girl?"

The question unleashed a storm of emotions inside Esther. First, anger at Chappy Chappell for asking the question; then a surge of sorrow as she saw the hot, smoggy cemetery where they had just put her Bobby in the cold, cold ground; and finally the sweet, guilt-edged memory of the tender touch of Clarke Johnson's hand upon hers. Maybe she *did* have a man, after all.

"I don't think that's any of your business," she said evenly.

"Ha!" Chappy snorted. "That means you ain't got none."

"Maybe it does, and maybe it doesn't," she countered. "Do you have a woman?"

Chappy's smile glittered. "Several, honeybunch, *several.* I'm a man who lives what you call a full and varied life."

Esther shook her head and smiled at the older man. "Mr. Chappy, you *ba-a-a-d.*"

Chappy laughed along with her. "Damn right. Don't know no other way."

Esther pushed the floor polisher down the hall.

"You sure 'bout that taste?" Chappy called after her.

"I got to find my girls and finish up this job. It's gonna be daylight soon, and I'm dead on my feet."

"Okay, but if you change your mind I'll be around, checking all the doors. In the building or somewhere on the grounds. You think about it."

"Good-*bye,* Mr. Chappy," Esther called over her shoulder as she negotiated the big machine through a set of double doors. She left the polisher in the waiting area by the front entrance and went searching for her girls.

She found them on the second level in the executive washroom, on their hands and knees, scrubbing the commodes. Both girls' sweaty T-shirts clung to their bodies, and the bathroom fixtures sparkled.

"This place looks dynamite!" she marveled.

Lupe beamed proudly as she looked up from the toilet. "Looking good, eh, Esther? Me and Florencia, I had a long talk. I told her you shouldn't even be working tonight, no way, but since you got to, then we got to bust our tails to help you with this new contract."

"I appreciate that, Lupe. I really do."

"But, Es—" Lupe pushed a stray raven tress away from her damp forehead with the back of her hand. "Es, this yob is yust too big for yust the three of us. We're gonna need more *muchachas.*"

"I heard *that!*" Esther slumped down on a lidded toilet seat.

"I mean, *mañana* we got this place *and* all the other contracts."

"We'll make some phone calls today, find some more girls. Maybe I'll go check on buying one of them little vans."

Esther reached for a cigarette, then remembered she was out.

"Loop, let's get out of here before we pass out. The sun'll be up soon. You almost finished?"

Lupe bent back to her work. "Yust a little more. *Poco mas.*"

"Okay," Esther got up. "I think everything else is done."

"The trash bags."

"I'll take them down to the dumpster. Finish up here and let's go home."

At the washroom door Esther turned back to the girls. "Lupe."

"*¿Sí?*"

"Listen. Tonight's a Sunday. I'm gonna pay you guys double-time for tonight."

"You don't have to do that, Es."

"No, you two really busted your humps tonight, and I want you to know I appreciate it. I want you to know working for me won't always be *mucho trabajo, poco dinero.*"

Lupe nodded. "*Gracias,* Es."

Esther smiled. "Now, let's go home."

Esther went back downstairs and found the rear exit that Abe Morrison's secretary, Terri, had showed her. She pushed on the heavy door and it was unlocked. She swung it open and stepped outside. The night was still and warm, the stars overhead dimmed by an umbrella of smog. Esther stretched her long body out to its full length, standing on her toes. She breathed deeply and yawned. She heard a sound behind her and turned around quickly. There was no one there, but the lights in the hall she had just come down had been doused. The hall was in total darkness.

"Chappy?" she said, but there was no answer. She shrugged and turned back to the parking lot. The freight skid was parked by the dumpster, under a bright floodlight. She walked down the ramp, took a firm grip on the skid's iron bar, and pushed the cart up the ramp and into the building. When she reached the end of the dark corridor she found the light switch and flicked the lights back on. She left the skid at the foot of the stairs and went up. Lupe and Florencia had stacked the big green trash bags, stuffed with all the waste from the second-floor offices, at the head of the stairs. Down the hall Florencia's radio played a melancholy ballad that echoed through the empty building. Esther tossed the half dozen bags down the stairwell, then went back down and loaded the bags onto the flat wheeled platform. She pushed the skid through the first-level hallways, piling on the bags that the girls had closed and knotted and left by the office doors. The skid grew heavier and heavier, and Esther struggled to push it through the building. Once, she heard a door slam somewhere, and she braked the skid with her legs and called out, "Chappy?"

Silence was her only answer.

"Chappy, don't you scare me again."

Nothing.

Esther shrugged, then threw her weight against the skid, getting it moving again. Finally she had collected all the bags, and she fought the laden cart back to the rear corridor.

It was dark again.

She pulled back on the skid bar to stop the cart, and it dragged her a few feet before it came to a halt.

Esther peered down the long dark hall. The rear door was open at the other end, showing a rectangle of light blue, and she could smell the night air rushing in.

"Chappy, this ain't funny, man."

Still no answer.

Esther felt along the wall until she found the light switch and flipped it up. She jumped, truly startled, when the lights failed to go on. She flicked the light switch down and up, down and up, several times, to make sure she hadn't made a mistake.

The lights weren't working.

"Shit."

She rubbed her hands over her rump, took a wide, firm grip on the skid's handlebar, and slowly started it down the long, dark hall.

"Chappy," she said loudly, "if you jump out and holler *boo,* I swear to Jesus, man, you and I are gonna go to fist city, you hear me?"

There was no answer, no sound except the creaking of the skid's rusty metal wheels. Halfway down the hall Esther felt someone behind her, a presence, and she whipped her head around. The corridor behind her was vacant. The one thing visible was the square of yellow light at the end, by the reception area, like daylight at the distant exit of a tunnel.

Esther threw all her 115 pounds against the skid and hurried it along to the end of the hallway.

The skid bounced over the back threshold and rumbled out onto the concrete dock and Esther was outside. She breathed in a rush of oxygen and suddenly felt inexplicably joyous and lightheaded. Then the skid was rushing down the ramp and she realized she couldn't stop it, so she let go of the bar and watched as the skid bumped down the ramp and rattled across the parking lot and slammed into the big blue dumpster with a hollow metallic *wank!*

She giggled nervously and then wondered why she had. She looked around guiltily. The executive parking lot was totally empty, the surrounding streets beyond the seven-foot wire fences eerily deserted. She was glad no one had seen her foolishly lose control of the skid. Why had she been so frightened? Just because the lights had gone out? She had never been frightened before, working all hours of the night, all these years. She had to get out of here, go home and get some sleep. Like for a week!

She needed a cigarette.

It really was time to go home. Her back ached, her legs throbbed, her head buzzed, and her eyes were burning from the night-long crying jag. She longed for her bed, her son.

Her lover?

She slouched down the ramp and began tossing the trash bags into the open dumpster. She was about two-thirds of the way through the load when the green bags started backing up and spilling over the dumpster's side. She would have to rearrange them, toss them deeper into the dumpster. She hiked herself up with one hand and with the other shoved the top bags farther back into the dark musty dumpster. When she felt she had made enough space in front for the remaining bags of trash, she jumped down and reached back for another bag.

There was something on her arm. Something wet and sticky.

Ugh, she thought. Now what the hell was that?

She examined it more closely under the floodlight. It was blood. Damn, she must have cut herself on something in that funky old trash bin. Now she would have to stop at a hospital on the way home and get a tetanus shot. She wiped the blood off on her jeans and turned her arm over, searching for the cut. She couldn't find it.

Maybe if whatever she had cut herself on wasn't dirty or rusty, then she wouldn't need the tetanus shot, and she could just go home and go to bed.

She pulled herself back over the lid of the dumpster, both her feet swinging off the ground, reached in and pushed another trash bag out of the way, and there was Chappy's bloody, decapitated head, eyes white and bulging, mouth agape in a silent, gold-toothed scream of horror.

"Oh," Esther said aloud. Her stomach flipflopped and bile rose up in her throat. The icy-cold terror crawled over her body like a giant frozen hand, a rapist's hand, that flashed hungrily over her, ramming freezing fingers up her anus, raking the flesh from her scalp, peeling away the hair and skin with dirty, talon-like nails.

She lost her grip on the dumpster and tumbled backward. Her legs were rubber. They wouldn't support her, and she crumpled, skinning her palms on the pebbled concrete as she fell. Someone was pounding a bass drum in her ears. It was her heartbeat. That same someone had his foot on her chest and was trying to crush her rib cage. She couldn't get enough air. She gasped and wheezed, fighting for her breath.

Run! her terrorized mind screamed. Get away from here! *Get away from here!*

She fought her way to her knees, then clambered to her feet. She stood there, swaying.

Get away from here!

Her vision was telescoping, as if someone in her brain were adjusting a long-range lens. The dumpster seemed to shimmer, a hundred yards away; then it was right there, before her, with its grisly load.

Get away from *here!*

The girls! she thought suddenly. She had to get her girls out of there! She turned shakily to face the building's rear entrance. It was wide open, yawning like a hungry mouth. She could see down the whole black length of the hall to the rectangle of light that was the waiting area. It was like a tunnel to hell.

She found her legs, moved hesitantly up the ramp, and paused at the door, peering down the black funnel. Her pulse still jackhammered through her body; her breath wheezed.

She wanted to scream out Lupe's name, but it came out a husky whisper that died on her lips.

Then she was running as fast as she could—get out of here!—toward the light at the end of the hall. She had to get her girls! Something terrible was going to happen to her girls! She had to get to them! She had almost made it to the square of light when someone—or something—stepped in her way, blocking all the light. She tried to avoid the collision, tried to check her speed, but she tripped and went sprawling, glancing off a man's body in the dark.

She slid, crashing into a wall, and was immediately on her knees, striking out silently at the empty darkness.

It was then that the odor struck her—the stale, musty, animal odor of sweaty, unwashed male. The odor she remembered as a young girl on an Atlanta bus in the late afternoon when the black laborers got on and the white people looked at each other and shook their heads.

But now there was another overlying scent—the coppery, acrid stench of fresh blood.

"Lupe!" she screamed, and then something crashed into the back of her skull and the hall, which was already dark, went black, blacker, blackest.

4:30 AM

"Sonny Walker?" Fat Henry sneered bitterly, his rubbery, liver-colored lips twisting around his plastic cigar holder. "*That* crazy motherfucker. I tell you what, policeman, you tell me where that loony bastard is, and I'll go get the son-of-a-bitch."

They were inside the dusty *Times* circulation office on Pico Boulevard. The two Mexican kids were sitting on the same bench. They watched Gold and Zamora closely. Fat Henry was standing behind his scarred desk. He had rolled in a big fan and it was blowing right at him, molding his flimsy T-shirt over his elephantine stomach.

"Motherfucker disappear! No phone call, no warning, no nothing! Twenty-three years I had this franchise, and nothing like this ever happened before. Man, this is the Westside! I got stockbrokers. I got lawyers. I got business managers, movie producers, television stars. These people, they want to see their newspaper in the driveway when they get up in the morning. They don't, they get real ticked off. That crazy-ass Walker, he just don't show up Friday morning. No phone call. No nothing. Man, he don't even have the courtesy to drop off his route book. I got to *guess* which houses get delivery. I *still* don't have a complete list."

"I haven't had a paper in three days."

"Shit!" Fat Henry sat down and reached for a pencil. "What's your address, Lieutenant?"

"Never mind that. What do you know about Walker? Where can I find him? Does he have any close friends among his coworkers? Does he work anywhere else?"

Fat Henry studied Gold's face for a moment.

"This is about the pills, ain't it?"

"Pills?"

"The speed."

"Walker is a speed freak? He uses amphetamines?"

Fat Henry held his hands up. "Look, I don't wanna get anybody in trouble, but if you wanna find that crazy bastard you talking to the wrong man. You wanna talk to the white man."

"The white man?"

"Fazio. Tommy Fazio."

4:52 AM Esther's eyes popped open and she jerked upright in the same moment. The back of her head ached and she reached up and with her fingertips felt a lump and winced.

The shock of pain cleared her mind, and she remembered Chappy's silent, screaming head in the dumpster.

Getoutofhere!

The girls! The girls! She had to find Lupe and Florencia.

She clawed to her feet and leaned against the wall, struggling to get her bearings. The corridor wasn't so dark now; there was light at both ends. That confused her, until she realized the blue light to her right was the dawn seeping into the building like a luminous gas. She moved to her left, toward the inner offices, inching slowly along the wall.

The reception area was deserted. A chair was overturned. On the wall, in rich red blood, someone had fingerpainted KILL THE JEWZ KILL THE JEWZ KILL THE JEWZ.

Esther stared at the words and her heart pounded.

Get out of here!

She flattened herself against the wall and inched forward, one creeping footstep at a time. She had only gone a few yards when she heard sobbing coming from one of the offices. The door was slightly ajar. She pushed it open a few more inches with her toe. She recognized the swap-meet antique furnishings as Abe Morrison's offices, where she had been interviewed last week. Only this was a different door than the one she had entered through, from Terri's office. This was a side door, opening directly onto the corridor. She shoved open the door a little farther, and there were Lupe and Florencia, tied back to back with nylon rope—TV western style—in two imitation Early American straight-backed chairs. Their wrists and ankles were secured by silver duct tape. Both women had been badly beaten about the face; their eyes were blackened, their noses bloodied. Their T-shirts had been ripped off and their breasts bore bloody fingerprint bruises. There were oval teeth marks in the tender flesh. Lupe, who was facing Esther, had a piece of duct tape over her mouth. Florencia, turned the other way, was sobbing and repeating an act of contrition.

"Oh, mi Dios, yo estoy arrepentido de todos mis pecados, y prometo no volver a pecar, no volver a pecar, no volver a pecar—"

Esther slipped into the office and ran to Lupe. The girl's swollen eyes widened when they saw her.

"Don't worry!" Esther rasped as she tore furiously at the nylon knots. "I'll get you out of here! I'll get you out of here!"

"*Hmmphmm!*" Lupe struggled to say from behind the tape.

"Shhh!" Esther said. The goddamn knots wouldn't give.

"*Hmmghhhmh uuu!*"

"Lupe! Be quiet!" Esther pleaded.

"Hmpf! Hmpf! *Hmpf!*"

"*What?*" Esther angrily tore the tape away from Lupe's lips.

"*He's behind you!*" Lupe screamed.

Esther jumped but it was too late. She saw a blur of movement from the corner of her eye and then a fist slammed into her cheek and sent her crashing over Abe Morrison's tabletop desk. The blow should have rendered her unconscious, but her adrenaline was pumping so hard she was back on her feet immediately. Her jaw felt numb; she thought it was broken. Her hands flailed about, desperately searching for something to use as a weapon. She found a tiny message spike and clutched it in both hands. Holding it before her like a dagger, she turned to meet her assailant.

Her blood ran cold.

Sonny Walker was powdered with dried desert sand and bathed in thick, copper-smelling blood. The blood and sand had caked to form a kind of pinkish-red plaster over most of his body. He looked like a ghost, a zombie from a horror movie. He wore only shorts and heavy boots, and under the pink plaster the tattoos over his upper body were faint pictographs, like messages from a netherworld.

His eyes were the worst. They were bright and expressive and totally insane.

"*Stay away from me!*" Esther screamed. "*Stay away from me!*"

Walker pulled a revolver from his waistband and held it out, pointed straight at her. He moved closer.

"*Leave me alone!*"

Walker came closer.

"*Don't touch me!*"

Esther backed against a bookcase. Walker came closer. He held the gun's muzzle against Esther's ear.

"Please don't kill me," Esther whispered. As she spoke the spike fell from her fingers. "Please don't kill me."

Walker punched her in the face with a hard straight left, and Esther, stunned, sank to her knees, blood streaming from her nose. Walker twisted his fingers in her hair and yanked her across the floor until she was face down on her knees in the middle of the room. He reached around her and ripped her jeans open.

"Nooooo—" she groaned and tried to block his hand with hers. He punched her in the back of the head and she slumped against the carpet. He pulled her jeans off with one vicious motion and stared down at her naked brown buttocks. Then he unzippered his dirt-stiffened cut-offs and stepped out of them. He knelt behind her, clutched her hair again, and yanked her head back until she was kneeling on all fours. Esther moaned, and he plunged into her.

He worked into her viciously, and it felt like a knife in her, ripping and tearing. Esther involuntarily closed up, tried to expel him, but he jammed the gun against the base of her skull and growled, "I'll kill you, you monkey bitch," so she forced herself to relax, to open up; anything to make it end, make it over.

"You love it, don't you, you fucking ape. Bet you never had a white man before."

Sweet Jesus, she prayed. Sweet baby Jesus. Make it be over. Make this all he wants.

Then she remembered Chappy's head in the dumpster and knew it wasn't all.

He was picking up his tempo, driving into her. She was wetter now. With blood? She didn't know.

He grunted with every thrust.

Esther's eyes met Lupe's. She was crying. The two women looked at each other dully, without sympathy. Isolated. Detached. Alone. Like victims everywhere. Like slaves led to the ships. Like Jews to the showers.

Oh, sweet Jesus. Save me. Save me.

"When I come—*uh!*" he groaned, "I'm gonna—*uh!*—blow your nigger brains out—*uh!*"

"No! No! No! No!" Esther wailed and tried to crawl away, but he twisted his hand deeper into her hair and yanked her head down. He was fucking faster.

"Uh!—gonna—uh!—blow—uh!—your—"

"*No! Noooo!*" She tried to claw away from him. Her fingernails scratched catlike at the short-napped carpet. His penis was a carnivorous little rodent inside of her, chewing her up, biting and slashing.

"*Here it comes!*" he shouted, and shoved the gun's barrel hard against the base of her skull.

"*Nooooo!*" she screamed and her arms flailed out, beseeching, helpless. "*Noooo!*"

He shuddered, then spurted inside of her. Then she felt him squeeze the trigger and for a microsecond the universe stood still. Then the hammer fell—*click!*—on an empty chamber.

His cock pulsed again, ejaculating, and then again—*click!*—he fired an unloaded gun.

Click! Click! Click! Click!

He was furious. He pistol-whipped her in an insane frenzy, screaming, *"That stupid nigger! He didn't even load his gun! He didn't even load his gun!"*

He straddled her and beat her. He stood over her and kicked her again and again, over and over. In her buttocks, in her sides, in her head.

Then the world went blessedly black.

5:32 AM It was full gray dawn. Traffic was already buzzing on the Harbor Freeway, half a mile away, but here the neighborhood was quiet. Cemetery quiet.

Sean Zamora placed his feet slowly and carefully over the bungalow's tarred roof as he approached the big skylight that looked down into the bedroom. When he was finally close to the edge, Zamora peeked inside.

Directly below the skylight a young couple were sleeping naked in an oversized waterbed.

Zamora noticed a roll of tar paper forgotten up here by a roofer on some long-ago patch job. He hefted the heavy roll above his head and waited poised, by the skylight.

Thirty seconds later there was a heavy pounding from below, and Gold's angry shout, "Open up! Police! Open up!"

The couple were in action immediately. They jumped from the bed and gathered stuff from their bedside tables. With all his upper-body strength, Zamora flung the roll of tar paper through the skylight. It exploded in a shower of silvery glass, and then Zamora jumped feet first through the opening onto the water bed and trampolined to the floor, his piece already in his hand.

"Fazio! *Fazio!*" he shouted, looking around for the bathroom.

The naked girl, skinny and washed-out-looking, was screaming, "Don't kill him! Don't kill him!"

"Open it up!" Zamora shouted at her and pointed toward the sound of the door Gold was trying to break down.

Zamora heard a toilet flush and raced toward the sound. Down a short hall he kicked open a door and Fazio, acne-faced and stringy-haired, was trying to stuff handfuls of rainbow-colored capsules down an already clogged toilet bowl. Zamora pushed him hard and Fazio fell clattering into the big stained bathtub.

"Don't kill him!" the girl shouted from the hall and then Gold was in the bathroom. He pulled Fazio from the tub, stood him up, and said, "I don't have time to fuck with you. I need some answers and I need them now."

"You got a search warrant?" Fazio demanded.

Without another word Gold and Zamora gripped him on either side, lifted him from his feet, upended him, and dunked his head in the toilet bowl.

"Don't kill him! Don't kill him!"

"It's all right," Zamora smiled at her. "He likes toilets."

They pulled him sputtering from the water, then pushed him in again. When they lifted him the next time he choked out, "All right! All right!"

They spilled him onto the floor and he coughed up pills and water. His longish hair was plastered to his face.

"Sonny Walker," Gold said.

"What—what about him?"

"Tell me everything you know."

Silence.

"Now!"

Fazio looked up at them. "Man, I don't know—"

This time they kept him under until he stopped fighting and when they pulled him out he came up coughing and spitting.

"All I know—all I know, man, is he works at a place off Wilshire called Techno-Cal. Semiconductor place. I delivered some ups to him there once. He works on the loading dock. That's all I know. I swear it on the cross, that's all I know."

$6{:}34\ AM$ Sonny Walker was a happy man. He had found his purpose in life. How many men could say that?

He sat behind Abe Morrison's desk, lining up shotgun shells. He had about forty of them in two neat, even rows. Like little soldiers. Off to do holy war.

Staring at him across Abe Morrison's desk was an antique gilt-framed photograph of Terri and Abe Morrison smiling at the camera from a table in a smoky nightclub. Walker wasn't sure, but he thought the nightclub was somewhere in Mexico. Acapulco maybe. Or Puerto Vallarta.

He wasn't angry at Terri. It wasn't her fault. She had been duped, mystified by the Jewish trickster. Just like the whole world had. In the photograph Terri wore dangling rhinestone earrings. She was smiling and hunching her shoulders forward to accentuate her already abundant cleavage. She always did that when her picture was being taken. She had read about the trick in the *Enquirer*.

Sonny Walker studied Abe Morrison's face. Typical Jew face. Big nose. Rat eyes. Weak chin. He had tricked Sonny's Terri. *Mystified* her. He'd be taken care of soon enough. God don't like ugly. His mother used to tell him that. God don't like ugly. Jews were ugly. That's why God didn't like them. That's why He heaped so much shit on them all through history. Hitler and all. God didn't like the Jews. Didn't like them because they had crucified his Son. So all through history God had sent his punishment down on the Jews. Because they had killed his Son. Like Hitler. God had sent Hitler to punish the Jews. They knew it too, the Jews. Like when you see a nigger acting uppity, acting like he's as good as a white man. If you see a nigger like that and you stare at him real hard, just *stare* at that black bastard, pretty soon he'll just get up and get the hell out of there, just get up and leave, because that nigger understands, he knows that he's been found out, that he's been called on his game. Well, the Jews are like that. They *understand* why there had to be a Hitler. Why Hitler was part of the eternal retribution against the Jews, like it promises in the Scriptures. Retribution for refusing to serve the Son. And now he, Sonny Walker, was here. Was part of that retribution. That was the purpose of his life. He was here to serve the Son. To protect the Body and the Blood.

Walker glanced over at the inert body of the nigger wench he had snuffed. Niggers were abominations before God, therefore unfit to serve the Son. The half-human offspring of Jews mating with she-apes back in Africa, they were an abomination before God, therefore a true Christian's duty was to snuff them whenever you saw them; just step on them whenever you saw them, like a roach or a slug. Because the nigger was dangerous. He had inherited the sneaky cunning of his Jew father, and the brute strength of the she-ape that suckled him. Not as dangerous as that source of all evil—the Jew—but dangerous in a different way. In a vital, brutish way. That's why he had fucked the she-ape. The same way Roman emperors used to fuck tigresses. To capture their strength, their vitality. And that's why he had had to kill her immediately. So that there would be no more half-human offspring. No more abominations before God.

Sonny Walker shifted in Abe Morrison's turn-of-the-century swivel chair, and Florencia Santiago, who had been praying continually for the last two hours, raised her voice and her eyes to supplicate her goddess.

"Ave Maria, llena de gracia. El Señor ésta conpigo. Ave Maria, Ave Maria, Ave Maria—"

Walker studied the girl, and the other one, who had fainted and was slumped forward against the nylon ropes that bound her.

It was simple. Either you were white or you were not. If you were not white, you were a nigger. Therefore all of the nonwhite people in the world were niggers, and abominations, and unfit to serve the Son. All the Mexicans and Japs, Chinks and A-rabs with their ass-a-hole-a ayatollah. Hawaiians and Indians. All of them were abomi—

Someone rattled the locked front door.

Walker stood and gathered up all the toy soldier shotgun shells and put them back in their red box and closed the lid. He picked up his .357 Magnum from the tabletop desk. *His* pistol and fully loaded, not empty like the one he had taken from that stupid nigger security guard, lying headless in the next office. Walker, surprised to find he was still naked, stuck the gun in his high-top hunting sock and grabbed his 12-gauge shotgun. He stepped over Esther's body and went out into the hall, leaving the side door of Abe's office open. He hunkered down in the waiting area and stole a glance around a corner at the translucent-glass-fronted entrance. There were people on the other side—distorted shadows cupping their hands over their eyes to peer into the dark building. They shook the door, tapped their car keys impatiently on the glass. Their angry voices carried muffled through the door.

"Where the hell is Chappy?"

"Probably drunk again."

"Chappy! Chappy! Wake up, man!"

"I *betcha* that nigger's drunk again."

"Watch your mouth, here comes Ernie."

"Ernie. Hey, man, your soul brother's drunk a—"

"Verna, you've got keys. Unlock this goddamn door so we can get to work."

"He didn't even leave the lights on for us."

Walker heard the key slip into the lock and the bolt clunk open. He smiled to himself and caressed the glossy rosewood stock of his shotgun. He was a contented man. He served the Son.

There were about fifteen or twenty employees on the other side of the translucent glass. When Verna, a gray-haired fiftyish marketing executive, pushed the door open they crowded through to hurry to their desks. They had only gone a few yards when the people in front stopped. They had seen the overturned chair, the bloody footprints, the grisly fingerpainting.

KILL THE JEWZ   KILL THE JEWZ

"Oh, my God!" Verna breathed.

"What is it?" the people behind her asked. They jostled for position to see better.

Walker stood up and stepped around the corner. There was a chorus of gasps at the sight of the naked, blood- and dust-caked apparition. They gaped at the shotgun.

"Terri!" Walker screamed. *"It's all right, baby!"*

The workers began to claw at each other in an attempt to get back out of the door. Some of those in the rear still didn't understand what was happening.

"It's all right, Terri! *Terri!*"

Walker opened fire. He sent shell after shell into the crowd, cutting them down where they stood. One young secretary made it back to the sidewalk, but Walker clambered over the bleeding, struggling bodies of the others, stood in the doorway, and blew her out of her shoes. Behind him, two men in bloodied business suits jumped up and ran toward the rear down the long central corridor, but Walker turned and quickly shotgunned them both. A silver-haired woman dashed up the stairs to the second floor and Walker ran after her. The second-floor corridor was empty. Walker went from room to room, searching for her. He ran into one office and could hear her sobs, but couldn't see her. Finally he pinpointed the sounds. She was hiding in a closet. He triggered the 12-gauge and blasted the French doors off their hinges. The woman was curled into a fetal ball on the floor in a corner of the closet. She screamed and screamed. Walker put the barrel to her head and blew her face off.

Downstairs, in the reception area, the dead and dying were sprawled all over each other. The wounded, lying under the corpses, moaned and begged for help. Walker walked among them, listening for voices, and dispatched them with single shots from his .357 to the back of their heads. He had seen the Germans do that on TV in the miniseries "The Holocaust." It was the humane thing to do. The Christian thing. Then he reloaded both weapons and crouched down with his victims. He felt comfortable with them. He belonged with them. He had made them safe, no longer dangerous. That was what he did. That was his purpose.

He served the Son.

He crouched, cradling his shotgun, and watched through the wide front door, now propped open by a body, as people ran about outside, screaming and pointing to the Techno-Cal building. A patrol car screeched up, and the cops jumped out and trained their guns on the entrance, but they didn't come any closer.

The whole scene in the street was distant, dreamlike and detached, like a television with the sound turned off.

Walker rose and went back into Abe Morrison's office. He laid his weapons on the desk and opened the connecting door that led to Terri's adjacent outer office. In here the stench of fresh blood was overpowering. The drying red ooze was inches deep in places. Flies were starting to swarm. The walls were streaked and splattered. It was in here that Walker had decapitated Walter Chappell. The big fire-axe was still imbedded in the headless corpse. Walker put his foot on Chappy's chest and yanked the blade from the neck cavity.

He went back through Abe Morrison's office, picking up his guns as he passed, and back out into the corridor through the side door.

He didn't notice that Esther's body was gone from the floor.

Back in the reception area, Walker propped the shotgun against a wall, stuck the .357 in his sock, and raised the axe high above his head. He brought it down on the closest body, a young white female. He cleaved her head cleanly from her torso with the one stroke. It rolled a few feet. Walker flung the axe away. It clattered down the hallway. He picked up the head, cradled it upside down under his arm, and using it as a paint pot, dipped two fingers into the wound and fingerpainted over and over again on a virgin wall:

KILL THE JEWZ   KILL THE JEWZ
KILL THE JEWZ   KILL THE JEWZ

After a while, as if his head suddenly cleared, he became aware of Florencia Santiago, in Morrison's office, sobbing and praying.

*"Santa Maria! Madre de Dios! Ruega por nosotros pecadores ahora y en
la hora de nuestra muerte! Amen!"*

He put the axe down, picked up the shotgun, and walked to the doorway
that led into Abe Morrison's office. The Latina was crying up to God. Her
eyes were closed tightly. Her heavy breasts shook with every sob.

He watched her for a while. Then he looked down at the bloody goo that
covered his right hand and fingers. He noticed that his penis was stiff.

He began to stroke himself.

It felt good.

6:33 AM Esther had forced herself back up into consciousness when Florencia began screaming hysterically. That had been prompted by the first shotgun blast out in the reception area. It would have been so much easier for Esther to stay where she was—in the dreamy darkness of semiconsciousness—where her body didn't ache; where Bobby was back with her, alive and clearheaded and dope-free; where Little Bobby was grown up and successful and went to work every day in a three-piece suit, like Clarke Johnson. It would have been so much easier to stay in the welcome darkness.

But she forced herself up, up to the surface. She didn't know why she was fighting so hard to come back, only that she felt this overwhelming desire to stop him! *Stop him!*

The first clear awareness, even before she broke through and opened her eyes, was the pain. Searing, pulsing pain that flowed through her like electrical current. Then came the knowledge that she was damaged, that he had inflicted deep injury upon her. She felt the ancient animal instinct to crawl away into a den and lick her wounds.

Then, though her eyes were still sealed, she was suddenly aware that Florencia was shrieking in Spanish.

"*Matale el diablo! Matale el diablo!* Kill the devil!"

And out in the hall the shotgun roared like distant thunder and there was shouting and screaming and something truly horrible was happening out there, in the hall.

Esther wanted to stand up. *Get out of here!* She had to stand up.

She thought the thought, but her body wouldn't respond to the command. She tried to crawl, and then she realized that the left half of her body wasn't working, was numb and unresponsive. Feeling no horror or fright over the situation, she simply reached out and pulled herself along with her right hand and pushed with her right leg. It hurt to breathe and she wondered if she had broken ribs as well. She wormed herself along the carpet and into the next room, grimacing with pain at every movement. Finally, slowly, she dragged herself into Terri's outer office. Here the smell and sense of death was heavy and sweet, and she suddenly found herself crawling in deep, thickening blood. She looked up to see Chappy's headless torso, lying a few feet away in a pool of horrible muck. Her mind registered the scene through a haze of pain, but she felt no fear or horror. It was as if she were looking at a not particularly offensive heap of garbage. The only emotion coursing through her was a strong sense of self-survival. That, and the primordial knowledge that she must *stop him!* She reached out to drag herself a few feet farther—to where?—and her hand touched something. Something hard and lethal. It was Chappy's gun. Her heart skipped like a young girl's at the sight of a new lover. She held the pistol tightly to her breast and cracked a wolfish grin. She had to *stop him!* But wait! Something about the gun. There was something about the gun. Something *wrong* about the gun. What *was* it? She tried to clear the picture, to formulate the idea. It was *empty,* she thought suddenly, and then her elation turned to dread. It was empty. He had held the gun against her head and pulled the trigger—*click!*—six times. It had been empty. That had made him mad. It was Chappy's gun and it had been—*Chappy's gun!* Esther wriggled through the awful sludge to Chappy's gruesome corpse. Tendrils of flesh and gristle dribbled from the open neck. An axe was buried in the hole. *Where? Where?* Where does a man keep bullets? In a box? In his pockets? In—then she saw the row of shells on the hand-tooled leather gunbelt around the dead man's waist. She pulled herself onto the corpse and tried to unbuckle the gunbelt. It was a special trick buckle and she couldn't unfasten it with her one hand. She couldn't figure it out.

Then she jumped at the sound of fresh gunfire out in the reception area. Not the rapid roaring like before, but single sharp reports, like lone firecrackers on the Fourth of July. She ripped at the buckle, but it wouldn't loosen. She ran her fingers over the row of bullets, like beading on a rich woman's gown. She poked at one of the bullets, and it popped loose and rolled down the body and sank into the red ooze. She popped another one loose and caught it. Then another. And another. And then she heard his quick footsteps—*He was looking for her!*—in the next room—*Sweet Jesus, he was looking for her!*—and she scrambled off the body and wiggled through the blood and rolled under Terri's desk. She lay as still as she could, holding her breath with great pain, and from under the desk she watched his heavy-soled, blood-sodden boots tromp through Chappy's muck, saw him brace his feet apart, and saw the axe blade wrenched from Chappy's neck with a sickening sucking sound. Then he turned and walked out.

Hurriedly—*I have to stop him!*—Esther laid the .44 in her lap and examined it. How the hell do you load a gun? Bobby had left a gun lying on the table once, and she had given him hell because the baby had been around. Oh, God! Would she ever see her baby again? Oh, sweet Jesus, how do you load a gun? Wasn't there a catch somewhere? Something to push? Was it this, or was this the safety? What was a safety? She pressed the release and the cylinder popped out and she wedged the gun under her dead hand and found the shells where she had pressed them into the fleshy part of her palm. Her hands, the gun, and the bullets were all covered with a thin sheen of blood, and she dropped the first bullet and it rolled away across the floor. She was more careful with the next and slipped it into the chamber with a tiny *chink* and then she got the next one in and she folded the cylinder back up into the gun's frame and it stayed shut!

She crawled out from under the desk and snailed her way back over the floor, across the threshold, and into Mr. Morrison's office. Lupe was half conscious now, but her flat black eyes stared down at Esther with a madwoman's detachment. Florencia was still mumbling her prayers in Spanish. Esther crawled to a space against the wall between Morrison's nineteenth-century, metal-legged water cooler and his antique walnut filing cabinets. She had to get off the floor; she had to get *up* if she was going to stop him. She hung the pistol on her dead fingers. Then, with her back flush against the wall, she bunched her good leg under her, reached up as high as she could with her right hand, gripped the edge of the file cabinet with her fingertips, and grinding down hard with her teeth, she wrenched herself up into a standing position. The pain from her cracked ribs glowed through her battered body like live current, and she slammed her eyes shut and knitted her forehead until the white heat tamped down to a dull red throb. When she opened her eyes the office swam around for a second before snapping into focus.

Where was he? Where was he?

She took the gun into her good hand and braced herself between the file cabinet and the water cooler. She laid her arm across the top of cabinet and pointed the gun at the side door leading to the hallway to the reception area. Would he come in this way, or through the door from Terri Walker's office? He had gone out through this door when he came for the axe. Would he come back this way? He *had* to come in this way, because if he came in through Terri's office he would see her before she could aim the gun and—

How do you aim a gun? What did they used to say in the TV westerns of her childhood? What did Roy Rogers say? Paladin? Marshal Dillon? Just squeeze the trigger. Don't jerk it. Just aim it at the target and squee—

He was coming! She could hear his footsteps in the hall. *Where was he?* And then she realized the footsteps had halted. She glanced at the door to Terri's office—*where was he?*—and he wasn't there, so she stiffened her arm and pointed the gun at the side door, and then she saw the barrel of the shotgun probing around the door frame—*he's looking for me! he's looking for me!*—and then she saw something else poke through the door, something white and hard and bloody, and then she knew it was his penis, and she suddenly understood: that what he had done to her he was now going to do to her girls. When he climaxed he was going to kill her girls.

She had to stop him!

She couldn't get a good shot at him—*what was a good shot?*—because the door was at a right angle to where she was. If only he would come more into the room. *But then he would see her!* Just a few steps closer. Maybe just a step. She could see just a sliver of him. Should she try to shoot him anyway? *Oh, God! Why was this happening? Why*— He moved! Was he coming into the office? Was he coming? *Coming!* He was leaning in now; he was grunting. She had to do it now, now, *now, now!*

Squee-ee-ee-ee-eeze—

Click.

What had happened what had happened what had she done wrong was the gun loaded? Wasn't the gun loaded?

Click!

No, it wasn't. It wasn't, and now he was going to come and get her, come and get her, *come and get her!*

Walker moaned to himself as he felt the climax begin to rise up from the kernels of his balls. His cock was a machine gun and he was in the TV movie "The Holocaust" and they were lining up naked Jewish women in front of the open pits and he was mowing them down with his machine-cock that was spewing out fire bullets that tore the Jewesses apart when they struck their pale white flesh. Only—some of the women had big black breasts, and some had slanting Asian eyes, and some had curly Afros and some had—oh!—*oh!*—*oh!*

Click.

Walker heard the metallic snap and knew exactly what it was, but couldn't figure out how he could be firing an empty handgun since he was holding the shotgun in his left hand and his machine-cock in his—

Click!

He saw a shadow of movement in the corner of his line of vision and swung the shotgun around toward it. He stepped into Abe Morrison's office, stepped right into the hurtling hunk of fire-hot metal that tore into his chest as the hammer of the late Walter "Chappy" Chappell's .44 finally landed on a live chamber. He was blown backward and the shotgun roared, sending a hail of metal to explode the upturned antique glass water cooler bottle beside Esther.

Florencia screamed, and Esther was thrown against the file cabinets in a geyser of glass shards and water.

Black pain closed over her and she heard Florencia's high-pitched scream fading as she gave herself up to the nothingness.

* * *

It was a hot Sunday in August, and she had gone to live with her mother's Aunt Rowena, in the little green house behind the vegetable stand, down in the easy hills of south Georgia. Aunt Rowena was a good woman, maybe a little too generous with her goodies, but she had never conceived, so what the hell difference did it make, she always said. In any event, Aunt Rowena knew how to treat an eight-year-old girl. She had cut down one of her old white dresses, sewn up some pretty lacy sleeves tied with lavender ribbons, and this morning they were going to the big church picnic. Li'l Esther couldn't pull herself away from the old cracked mirror screwed to the closet door. She kept smiling at her reflection and twisting the pigtails Aunt Rowena had braided for her. Aunt Rowena packed a picnic basket of breaded pork chops, cornbread, black-eyed peas and rice, and a screw-top jar of iced tea. They walked across an open field to the old unpainted church, Aunt Rowena talking all the way. It was hot and humid, and the air was filled with the buzzing and clicking of insects. At the church grounds, Aunt Rowena went off to visit with her girl friends and li'l Esther was left alone to fend for herself in the hard-packed dirt of the churchyard. The little boys, of course, ignored her. The little girls stared and snickered, and then closed in on the stranger. A big, dark girl with cornrows approached.

"What's your name, girl?"

"Esther."

Everyone giggled.

"Where you from?"

" 'Lanta."

"Well, then, what'chu doin' down here? In the country?"

"They sent me to live with my Aunt Rowena."

Snickers again.

"She a 'ho," Cornrows said, and everyone laughed aloud. Esther shrugged. She didn't know what a 'ho was.

"You a 'ho, too?"

Esther didn't answer, sensing that this meeting was getting off on the wrong foot.

"Answer me, bitch!" Cornrow demanded, crowding Esther. Esther stepped back.

"My name's Tanya," Cornrow said proudly. "That's a pretty name. What'chu say your name was?"

"Es—Esther."

"Esther? That's a witch's name. I knew a witch once name Esther. Is that you? Esther the witch."

Laughter all around.

"Esther the witch! Esther the witch!"

Afterward they all ate on long picnic tables in the green, parklike area behind the church. Esther toyed with her food. She had lost her appetite.

"You feelin' all right, baby?" Aunt Rowena asked, her mouth greasy from the breaded pork chops.

After the meal, everyone—adults and children alike—gathered in cliques again, so Esther just kind of drifted away. She walked down by a creek that twisted between some trees at the end of the dirt road that ran in front of the church. It was cooler here. Darker. Li'l Esther pretended she was a fawn, like Bambi, then remembered that Bambi didn't have a mother either, so she pretended she was Robin Hood in Sherwood Forest.

She crouched down by the creek and looked into the water for bugs and crawfish. Finding none, she took off her shoes and trailed her toes in the water. A twig snapped, and she looked up to see a little white boy playing on the other side of the creek. He wasn't twenty feet away, and dressed in full cowboy regalia—chaps and cuffs, double gun belt, vest and hat. He dodged here and there among the trees, making shooting sounds with his mouth. He was beautiful to Esther in an exotic kind of way. His hair and eyebrows were almost white. His eyes were sky blue. His skin was the color of buttermilk.

Esther stood up and shaded her face with her hands. "Hey, you," she called out. "Cowboy."

The white boy stared at her from across the creek.

"What's your name?" Esther asked.

The boy wouldn't speak.

"Cat got'cha tongue?"

The boy twirled his six-shooters on his index fingers. "Orem."

Li'l Esther smiled. "That's a pretty name. You wanna play some?"

He shook his head.

"Why not?"

"Cuz you a nigger. My daddy don't 'low me to play with niggers."

"Why not?"

"He just don't, that's all." The little boy squinted at her.

"I'm gonna come over there," li'l Esther said as she waded out into the creek. "We can play cowboys and Indians. I can be an Indian princess."

"Don't you come over here," he shrilled. "My daddy don't 'low niggers on his property."

Esther kept coming.

"Don't you come over here!" The little boy danced on the balls of his feet. "Don't you come over here!"

He held out his toy six-shooters, long-barreled silvery affairs with ribbons of pink blasting-cap paper hanging from behind the hammers.

"Nigger, nigger, nigger, nigger!"

He pulled the triggers and the guns went pop! pop! pop! pop! *and all the birds stopped singing and the air stank of blasting caps and—*

—and Florencia was still screaming, only it wasn't a human voice anymore, it was a siren wailing somewhere outside the building, and the pain jolted her conscious. She felt the wetness all over her and thought that if the wetness were blood she would have to be dying and then she remembered the water cooler exploding and the water gushing and—

Had she stopped him?

Her eyes were open and her hand flew about until it settled on Chappy's .44 and she grabbed it and pointed it at the door.

He was gone.

Where is he?

"You got him! You got him!" Lupe shouted at her. The Latina's eyes were bright and demented. *"Matale! Matale!* Kill him, Esther! Kill him!"

Where is he?

She grimaced and pulled herself upright again. There were new pinpoints of pain everywhere now—tiny slivers of glass embedded in her naked buttocks and legs. The lower half of her body was covered with blood. She lurched along the wall, limping and dragging her paralyzed left side behind her.

"Matale! Matale!"

She pointed the gun out before her and half fell clumsily through the door and out into the hall. Toward the reception area was carnage. Bloody bodies piled helter-skelter over each other. The floor was a sea of crimson. Down the hall in the other direction was a single thick swath of blood, trailing away and disappearing into another office.

"Matale, Esther! *Matale!* Kill him! *Kill him!"*

Esther limped down the hall, following the trail of blood. It led into a conference room with walls of cloudy tinted glass, like the front entrance. She held the .44 at ready and pushed her shoulder against the door. A bloody hand whipped from behind the door and wrapped its thick fingers around her wrist.

"Nooooo!" Esther screamed. And then she was pulled through the doorway and flung across the room. The .44 went clattering, and Esther went crashing into the neatly arranged rows of metal folding chairs. Shock waves of pain from her many injuries flashed the length and breadth of her body, but she was instantly on her good side scrambling around for her weapon.

"No!" she shouted as she threw the chairs about. *"No! No!"* And then she found the .44. She spun around as quickly as she could, and there he

was, towering over her with the bloody axe above his head. She raised the gun to him and pulled the trigger over and over.

Click! Click!

And then the gun discharged and a fresh geyser of blood spurted from Walker's belly and he tottered and crashed back over a blackboard and lectern.

Esther, breathing like a hounded animal—her sides heaving, her nostrils flaring—watched him.

He pulled himself slowly up the wall, using the axe handle as a crutch.
"No!"

He turned to face her. Blood gushed from the wounds in his chest and abdomen, and streamed down his now limp penis and testicles. His eyes were glazed and dull, but they found her immediately.

"No!"

He picked up the axe, raised it above his head, and lurched toward her. She pointed the .44 at him, even though she knew it was empty.

Click! Click! Click! Click!

"No! No!"

Click! Click! Click!

"No! No!"

6:42 AM Gold's Ford bumped over the curb and came to rest with its bumper in a bed of bird of paradise across the street from Techno-Cal. There were black-and-whites all up and down the block. The secretary who had been shotgunned out of her shoes had been dragged behind a patrol car and covered with someone's sweatshirt.

"What the hell are you doing?" a cop screamed as Gold and Zamora leapt from the Ford. "Oh, it's you, Lieutenant. Better keep your ass down. This dude is serious."

"We're too late!" Zamora shouted at Gold. "We're too fucking late!"

"What's the situation?" Gold calmly asked the street cop.

"We don't know, sir. We think just one shooter. One fatality for certain, but you can bet dozens more. Look, you can see them piled up just inside the entrance. SWAT's on their way. Be here any second. We just sit tight until then. Maybe there's still live hostages in there. We don't—"

There was a single gunshot from somewhere inside the building. All the cops crouched lower behind their vehicles.

"That wasn't directed at us," Gold said. "He's in there killing people right now."

"Inside the building! This is the police!" a cop down the line bullhorned. "We want you to lay down your weapons and come out! Right now! Before anyone else gets hurt!"

"Is there another entrance?"

The cop nodded. "Back and side. We got 'em both covered."

"Let's go," Gold said to Zamora.

"Lieutenant!" the cop called after them. "SWAT's on their way!"

They ignored him and ran, crouched, down the line of vehicles that fronted the building. They rounded the corner and found the two cops guarding the side entrance. Gold pointed at them and motioned for them to follow. When they reached the side entrance Gold whispered, "Stay right here. If you hear any more shooting, come in and get us."

The two uniforms looked at each other and then nodded at Gold.

"You got it, Lieutenant."

The side entrance had been jimmied. Gold pushed it open with his toe, and Zamora slipped in crouched low. Gold went in behind him. This hall wasn't long and straight like all the others; it made quick right-angle turns every ten feet. They proceeded cautiously, slowly, covering every corner thoroughly, not speaking. It had been five minutes since the last gunshot.

They came around a right angle and the shotgunned, mutilated bodies were suddenly there, fresh and bloody, piled all over each other. Zamora gulped, leaned against a wall, and vomited as quietly as he could.

Then they heard the woman's scream. *"No! No!"*

They ran across the shattered bodies, slipping in the blood.

They heard another gunshot and then the woman screaming again, *"No! No! No!"* and then suddenly he was there, a silhouette behind the clouded glass, holding a shadow axe high above a shrieking shadow woman.

"Is that him?" Zamora shouted as he took a firing stance. *"Is that him?"*

"That's him!" Gold shouted back, and then they fired simultaneously at the shadow and the conference room glass shattered and fell away and Walker was thrown against the wall. He sank slowly down, the light in his eyes dimming. When he slumped over on the floor, he was dead.

Gold and Zamora ran into the conference room.

"Kill him!" Esther screamed. They stared down at her. She was naked from the waist down. Beaten, bloody, and bruised.

"Kill him!"

Gold knelt by her. "He's dead," he said gently.

"No! No, he's not!" Esther pounded her fist on the floor. "Kill him! Kill him! *Kill him!*"

Gold reached for her hand, but she whipped away from him. *"Kill him!"* she shrieked directly into his face. She crawled toward Walker's corpse, reached for his axe.

"All right," Gold said. He stepped up and aimed his piece down at Walker's body. He looked over to Zamora.

"Kill him."

They emptied their cylinders into the corpse. The two uniforms, who had just raced up, looked at Esther, then at Gold, then at each other. They said nothing.

"He's dead now," Gold said to her.

Esther looked at the corpse and then up at Gold. She started to cry.

"Is he really?" she whispered, unable to believe it. She looked up at Gold and the tears poured down her face. Her mouth twisted into a rubbery smear.

"Ohhh. Ohhh*hhhh*—," she wailed.

Gold ripped off his shirt, knelt, and tied it around her nakedness. She collapsed against his bare chest. Gold held her lightly while she cried.

He looked up at the two uniforms.

"Bring in the ambulence people. Check out the rest of the building."

The two cops trotted off. Zamora sat in a metal folding chair and ran his fingers through his hair.

"Everthing's all right," Gold whispered into her ear.

MONDAY
Christmas Eve

2:57PM It was raining. It had been raining for a week. Just like the week Angelique died. The Coast Highway was closed. Homes were slipping down into Laurel Canyon. The skies, whenever the rain stopped for a bit, were low and gray and achingly clear. The snow on the mountains was visible from Sunset Boulevard.

It was one of those years when Christmas and Hannukah fell during the same weekend. The glistening streets of Beverly Hills were packed with holiday shoppers. The stores decorated one display window in red and green, another in blue and white.

Gold found the restaurant where he was to meet Wendy for a late lunch. It was one of those chichi places on Beverly Drive, dripping with Boston ferns and graphic art. The waiter's hair was checkerboarded orange and black. Gold ordered a Scotch and the waiter, with a flounce, informed him that they only served beer and wine. Gold asked for a Coors and the waiter rolled his eyes as if to say "naturally" and wiggled away.

Gold stripped the cellophane from a new cigar and lit it. He sipped his beer and watched rivulets of rain course down the restaurant's big front window.

He saw Wendy drive by in her Volvo, looking for a place to park. A few minutes later she was crossing the street toward him. She looked slimmer, older. She spotted him and waved with a warm smile. Gold's heart lightened.

"Hi, Daddy," she said as she slipped out of her coat. "I saw your picture in the paper. That girl's wedding you attended. The one who was hurt by that Nazi." She slid into the booth across from him. She looked wonderful. But different. Very, very different.

"How are you?" Gold asked her.

By way of an answer she waved her hand.

"That was very nice of that girl to invite you to her wedding. Who did she marry, a policeman?"

"A probation officer." Gold inspected his daughter as if he'd never seen her before. She looked *that* different.

"She looked very pretty in the photographs. Is she all healed? From the, uh, beating she took?" For a moment Wendy avoided Gold's eyes when she uttered the word *beating.* Then she consciously fixed on them.

"I think she's still undergoing some therapy. But she's doing fine. Just fine."

"It was very nice of her to invite you."

Gold nodded. "Very nice."

"But appropriate. You did save her life," Wendy said, fiercely proud of her father.

Gold shrugged. "I should have been there sooner. I should have saved the others."

Wendy erased her father's remark with another perfunctory wave of her hand.

"You did as much as anyone could have done. More. You saved her life. Don't be so hard on yourself, Daddy. You're always too hard on yourself."

They sat in silence for a while. Outside, on the other side of the glass, the rain quickened. Shoppers on the street dashed by, their arms laden with packages.

"That other policeman was there, too. At the wedding. That good-looking Mexican boy."

"Mexican-Irish. Only he's not on the force anymore."

"Oh?"

"No, he's an actor now. He's going to be doing a movie down in Mexico right after the holidays."

"I didn't know that."

"He got a lot of offers right after that whole thing happened. He's been working as an actor ever since."

The waiter with the checkerboard hair came back. Wendy ordered the spinach salad and a glass of Chablis. Gold opened his menu and studied it a long time. It was full of quiches and pasta salads, gourmet pizzas and pineapple bran muffins. The waiter fidgeted.

"Hamburger," Gold finally said, and the waiter gave him a superior smile.

"With avocado, sir?"

Gold smiled back. "No, onion. And lots of mayonnaise."

After the waiter left Gold struck a match and relit his dead cigar.

"Hold it, Daddy." Wendy rummaged around in her shoulder bag and came up with a cigarette.

"When did you start *this?*" Gold asked as he held the match for her. Wendy exhaled. "Don't you remember? That night."

For a long while neither of them spoke, then Gold admonished, "It's still not good for you, you know."

Wendy smiled and patted his hand.

"Daddy, you know I've filed for divorce."

Gold nodded. "I think you're doing the right thing." Then his eyes flashed. "Wait a minute. Is that why you asked me to lunch? Howie's not giving you any trouble, is he? He doesn't have the *chutzpa* to fight you for little Joshua, does he?"

"No, no. Nothing like that."

"Because if he tries anything like that, you tell me, and I'll go have a talk with the little *putz.*"

"Daddy," she said, and her eyes flashed, "that's exactly what I don't want you to do. I want you to leave Howie alone. He's scared to death of you, and I don't want you bothering him after the divorce is final. What happened happened. Nothing can change that. But I know how you hold grudges. I want you to promise me you'll leave Howie alone."

Gold chewed his cigar.

"Besides," Wendy continued, "he's suffered enough." Gold snickered, but she went on. "He's lost his wife. He's lost his son. And now I hear he's been asked to leave the firm."

"Couldn't happen to a nicer guy."

"It's killing him, Daddy. He's just a pathetic little man with a drug addiction. I see that now. But whatever you think of him, he's still Joshua's father. He'll always be your grandson's father, even if he won't be my husband anymore. So I want you to promise me you won't hurt him. That you won't try and seek any revenge against him. Promise me."

"Wendy, you don't think your old—"

"Daddy, I know you too well. Now promise me."

Gold squinted over his cigar at her. "*You* should have been the lawyer."

"Promise me!"

Gold waved his hand. "All right already. I'll never speak to the little *gonif* again. I promise."

"The truth?"

"My right hand to God. I swear it. *Emmes.* On my grandson's life."

The waiter brought Wendy's white wine. She tasted it and studied her father.

"There's another reason I wanted to see you. Something else I want to talk to you about."

Gold took a long draught of beer and belched lightly. "Shoot, Pieface." He smiled mischievously, the way he used to when she was a little girl. "That's police talk. *Shoot,* I mean."

"I'm going to Israel."

Gold poured the rest of his Coors down the side of his mug. "That's great, baby. Always wanted to go myself. When are you leaving?"

"Tonight. We're taking the Red-Eye to New York, then El Al from New York to Tel Aviv."

"Who's we? Who's going with you?"

"Just Joshua and I."

"That's a long flight for such a little boy. You sure he'll be all right?"

"If he wasn't such a good baby, I'd worry. But I'm sure we'll be fine."

Gold shrugged and raised his mug to his lips.

"Whatever you think. I'm sure mother knows best. When are you coming back?"

Wendy waited a long heartbeat before speaking.

"That's just it, Daddy. We're not."

Gold put his mug down.

"I don't understand, Wendy."

"I'm moving to Israel. I'm emigrating. I'm exercising my Jewish birthright to Israeli citizenship. Joshua's doing the same. We're going home."

Gold foundered, searched for something to say.

"You—you can't do that."

"Why not?"

"Because—because—you're an American."

"Golda Meir was an American."

"That's different."

"Why is it different?"

"Wasn't she foreign-born, Golda Meir? Of course, she was. She was born in Russia."

"All Jews not born in Israel are foreign-born, Daddy."

"What does your mother have to say about this? What does Evelyn think of all this?"

Wendy lit another cigarette. "She's dead set against it. Whatever argument you're going to throw at me, I've already heard from Mother and Stanley. And nothing's going to change my mind." She exhaled and stared at her father with a determined set to her jaw.

Gold sputtered as he spoke. He couldn't ever remember being so angry with his daughter.

"Wendy, this whole *megillah* is insane. What the hell are you gonna do in Israel? A single woman with a child. No offense, but you're a Beverly Hills brat. We've all pampered you, protected you, because we've always loved you so much. What are you gonna do in Israel? Join a kibbutz? Become a farmer? Clear fields? You'll break your nails. You'll get wrinkles from the sun. What will you do, give Joshua to strangers to raise? Like Communists?"

She laughed and affectionately shook her head.

"Daddy, Daddy, Daddy. I'm not going to join a kibbutz. You remember Lori Frankel? We went to S.C. together. Well, she's got a gift shop in Jerusalem. Caters mostly to Christian pilgrimages. She's opening another shop near Bethlehem, and I'm going to manage it for her. If things go well, I'm going to buy in, become her partner."

"I remember this Lori Frankel," Gold said suspiciously. "Wasn't she a dyke?"

"Daddy! She's married to an Israeli air force captain and has two children. You see, Joshua already has playmates over there waiting for him."

Gold chewed on the wet end of his cigar and stared at her.

"You're doing this because of what happened to you."

Wendy avoided her father's eyes. She stubbed out the fresh cigarette, sipped at her wine. Finally she looked at him.

"It probably has a lot to do with it—"

"That fucking Howie!" Gold cried out, causing gasps at the tables around them. "You can't let what that little *shmuck* did to you ruin your whole life, Wen."

"Let me finish what I have to say, Daddy," she said as she held up her hand.

"What happened that night was certainly horrible. It shattered me. It stripped away, negated, all the sophisticated, protective bullshit all you guys have wrapped me in my whole life. You say you pampered me, coddled me, cocooned me. Well, I say damn right you did, and don't be so proud of it, because I think you and Mother and Stanley did me a total disservice. I couldn't even imagine that animals like that existed, much less that my own husband would lead them into my home, that they were going to beat and rape me and threaten my baby's life. I thought the Six O'clock News was a continuing fiction, like 'Laverne and Shirley.' I now know better. I've seen the reality of this world, and while I'm glad I don't live in a fairy tale anymore, I've had to pay a high price. I don't feel *safe* anymore, Daddy. Not anywhere."

"Those vermin will never—"

"I don't want to hear that, Daddy! That just makes me a part of it all, and I refuse to allow that. I have to get out of here. Out of this city. This country. I need to find out what is really worthwhile and valid in this world. I see my mother caught up in a trap set by America's riches. She has to purchase things just to prove she's alive. Her name's right there on the American Express Gold Card, so she must exist, she must *be* somebody. And then I picked for my husband the worst possible choice. A pitiable man who couldn't even protect his family from himself, much less the world." She tapped her wine glass with her fingernails—a tiny glockenspiel. "And me. What is wrong with me that I should choose such a man?"

He said nothing.

"And my father."

Gold wouldn't look at her.

"The gentlest man I've ever known," she whispered, "who once loved something so much that when it died in his arms, forever after he thought the only way he could express love was by killing things."

Gold started to cry. He covered his face with his hands to hide his shame.

"I'm sorry, Daddy, but I have to leave this place. It's Babylon. I have to get away. And not just because of what happened to me. What about what happened to you? That whole Crosskiller episode disturbed me greatly. All that hate pulsing through this country. It can't be healthy. It's as if the whole nation has a fever that breaks out in a rash from time to time."

She sighed, realigned her silverware absentmindedly.

"Maybe some people weren't meant to be part of the great American melting pot, or salad bowl, or whatever the sociologists choose to call it this week. Maybe some people just weren't meant to assimilate, to become part of the mass."

Out on the street the rain pounded down.

Wendy shook her head slowly. "And maybe it's just me, Daddy. I just don't know who I am anymore." She smiled at him. "I'm going to Israel to look for myself."

The waiter brought their food. He glanced at Gold, then looked away quickly. When he left, Wendy picked up her fork and held it poised over her salad.

"This is my last nonkosher meal. Even the airline is kosher." She took a bite of the spinach leaf salad and chewed thoughtfully. "You know, I honestly don't think I'll miss it."

Gold slipped his hands from his face. He looked dazed, ancient. Wendy reached across the table to touch his arm.

"Come with me. There's nothing to keep you here. Nothing. You could take your retirement, come over to Israel with me. You could start a security agency or something like that. There's got to be a need for your kind of expertise over there. Come with Joshua and me. We could start a whole new life together."

Gold thought a long time before he shook his head.

"I can't, Wendy. I'm an L.A. cop. That's all I've ever known. I go to Riverside, I get itchy because it's too far away from my home turf. I'd be lost over there, Pieface."

"Daddy, you can't police these streets forever."

Gold gave her a weak smile.

"I have to, baby. I have to."

* * *

They said good-bye under the dripping awning in front of the restaurant. She hugged him and whispered, "Wish me luck, Daddy," and then she was gone, hurrying away through the drizzling rain. He watched her until she rounded the corner by the gelato shop. He'd hoped she'd wave one last time, but she didn't. He turned up his collar against the lazy Southern California chill and walked the half block to the next liquor store. He bought two quarts of Johnnie Walker Black. Right inside the liquor store entrance was a pay phone. He dropped in a quarter and dialed.

"Loveline," a breathy female oozed.

Gold was thrown for a second, then he asked, "Is Cookie there?"

"We have three Cookies on line," she said, and every syllable was a promise. "Cookie Johnson, Cookies N. Cream, and Cookie Santos."

"Cookie Santos."

"I'm afraid she's unavailable right now. But if you'll leave your number I'll have her get back to you very shortly. Or maybe you'd be interested in one of our other Cookies."

"What the fuck is this? An answering service for hookers?"

There was the briefest of pauses on the other end of the connection, and then an unperturbed, noncommittal, and still sexy, "This is the Loveline, sir. Would you like to leave your number?"

Gold hung up. He went back outside. It was raining harder again, pounding down over the gas-streaked streets. He walked unhurriedly to his car, double-parked two blocks away. By the time he slid into the front seat, his clothes were soaked. His shoes squished with every step. He set the Scotch beside him on the seat and wiped the wet from his face with his fingertips. Then he started the old Ford and drove home in the rain.